MODERN AMERICAN CLASSICS
An Anthology of Short Fiction

MODERN
AMERICAN

CLASSICS

An Anthology of Short Fiction

Edited by

DAVID R. WEIMER

Rutgers, The State University

RANDOM HOUSE, NEW YORK

For

Jack and Lorraine
Mike and Ruthie
Agnes and Ce
Ruth and Alex
Peg and David
Bob and Joan
Fran

ACKNOWLEDGMENTS

For special aid of various kinds in the preparation of this anthology I want to thank my colleague, Professor Walter E. Bezanson; Mrs. Leonore C. Hauck, Mr. James B. Smith, Mrs. June Fischbein, Mrs. Stefanie Gold, and Miss Carol Green, all of Random House; Mr. Jeremiah M. Bogert and Mr. David A. Dushkin, formerly of Random House; Mrs. Anne McCartney; and the staff of the Rutgers University Library.

The texts of the selections are those of their first publication in book form. Obvious typographical errors in those editions have been silently corrected, but a few other errors or inconsistencies, all minor, have been allowed to stand.

DAVID R. WEIMER

CONTENTS

INTRODUCTION

The stories in this volume have been selected on both artistic and historical grounds. Artistically they are, by common (and uncommon) critical judgment, among the very best short works of fiction written by Americans since World War I. Moreover, each story belongs distinctly to at least one of the principal modes of fiction cultivated in the United States, from terror to the realistic, from the psychological to the naturalistic, from the moral to the fantastic, the comic, or the otherwise extraordinary.

Though restricted to American writers, the anthology is not intended to exhibit any peculiarly 'American' features of their work. I have aimed, instead, to furnish the reader with fiction of the highest quality that illustrates the remarkable diversity of American imaginative expression in an especially fertile literary era. The chronological limits of the collection are necessarily arbitrary to some degree. The *terminus ad quem* is the 1950s, by which time certain innovators like John Barth were reshaping fiction so radically as to require a critical vocabulary beyond that appropriate to the work of Hemingway, Katherine Anne Porter, and other predecessors. The volume opens with a naturalistic Dreiser tale of 1918, partly to suggest the continuation of prewar forms into the postwar years. There were many such continuities, as every mode in this collection attests.

Curiously, apart from a few specialized studies like Richard Chase's *The American Novel and Its Tradition* and Philip Rahv's essay "Notes on the Decline of Naturalism," the historical criticism of American fiction has proved persistently weak in its grasp of connections between the nineteenth and twentieth centuries. A sign of this weakness is the frequency with which the structure of even the best and most recent anthologies goes to pieces once the First World War is passed, the editors taking refuge in such foggy categories for postwar stories as "Fiction in Search of Reality" or, worse yet, "New Consolidations."

But of course the active interplay of creative American minds with experience has continued over the years to the present hour, in a complex dialectic perpetually disrupting established forms, absorbing new perceptions and new experiences, bringing to familiar modes a new vitality. Thus the advent of psychoanalytic ideas early in the century took American fiction rapidly beyond even Henry James' extraordinary sensitivity to the mind, carried it down from the plateau of consciousness, to which James largely confined his attention, into the deep offshore waters of the subconscious, making possible the illuminations of those depths presented here in Conrad Aiken's "Silent Snow, Secret Snow" and Katherine Anne Porter's "Flowering Judas." Or such violent social experiences as American white racism, blazing up in the twentieth century, thrust fresh uses on familiar forms, as seen in Richard Wright's story "Big Boy Leaves Home," which grows out of a naturalistic view of the world as charged with destructive power, a world where individuals are invariably victims of that power. Through its perennial responsiveness to just such emergent ideas and circumstances, American literature has shown how intricately the artist is joined to his own civilization, how he embraces its past in the very act of rejecting that past, asserting his uniqueness and therefore the pluralism of art at the same moment he appeals to the culture he possesses in common with his fellow men.

Behind both the psychological and naturalistic modes—in a way behind all fiction—lies some imitative or representational aim, a desire to translate 'reality' as directly as possible into language. This aim was central to realist movements of the nineteenth century in Europe and Russia and, along with corollary tenets of objectivity and contemporaneity, was imported into the United States after the Civil War, chiefly by James and W. D. Howells. Realism broadly conceived presents experience as both communal and complex, and the individual as working out his particular destiny within the specific historical terms set by his culture. F. Scott Fitzgerald's "The Rich Boy" and Flannery O'Connor's "The River" are varieties of this species. In its simplest, most ingenuous versions, realism has meant the meticulous reporting of talk actually heard, clothes actually worn, meals actually consumed, and so on. While most realism of the last century has been utterly literal and humorless, it lends itself easily to parody and to various other comic and satiric ends. What looks at first like Sinclair Lewis' mechanical transcription of a Congregational Church speech given by Lowell Schmaltz, for instance, proves to be a burlesque of Rotarian Club attitudes. The ordinary language Gertrude Stein employs in her sketch of Miss Furr and Miss Skeene is transformed through relentless repetitions into a kind of mocking incantation, strangely abstract and stylized, pointed less toward some objective reality than toward some more diffuse and inner rhythm of experience. Although Lewis and Miss Stein work toward certain types of verisimilitude, they do so by exploiting a reader's natural tendency to respond to nuance and implication, to the flow of words, and to his own sense of an author's intelligence.

An author's reluctance to allow facts to lie inertly on the page mingles with a reader's pleasure at detecting an author's fictional design. Reader conspires with author to create the work of fiction; both contrive, both fabricate. So it is that patient, toiling mimetics like Howells or James T. Farrell or James Gould Cozzens have always fared poorly in the long run with readers, who respect their sober documentary efforts but sooner or later find them boring. The typical reader is, after all, alert and responsive; he can stand only so much factuality. Usually he prefers authors who let him in on the conspiracy, who stimulate him to react to fiction in imaginative, fanciful, and emotional ways as well as rationally. Surely some such broadly human responsiveness helps explain the recurrent appearance in all literatures of fables, legends, myths, fantasies, allegories, and symbolic narratives.

All those conditions of American life and mind which run to violence and other extremes have also encouraged fictional modes sharply different from the measured restraint of the realist. Indeed the earliest consequential American fiction, that of Charles Brockden Brown, Hawthorne, and Poe, sprang from a perception of experience as inherently terrifying; and this perception, first developed by Brown out of the popular English Gothic romances, proved so congenial to American writers as to find expression in major tales or novels in nearly every literary generation thereafter. The chief representatives of the fiction of terror in the present collection are

Thomas Wolfe's "Death the Proud Brother" and William Faulkner's "A Rose for Emily," although this mode, which focuses strongly on the individual's destructive urges, appears also in the stories of Conrad Aiken, Katherine Anne Porter, and Flannery O'Connor, where irrationalities come frighteningly to possess the mind.

Extraordinary too, though most ungothic, is "The Bear," which belongs to the Yoknapatawpha County of Faulkner's mythic South and to the archetypal myth as well of a boy's passage into manhood through symbolic confrontations with nature. A comparable type of initiation occurs in "The Short Happy Life of Francis Macomber," with its ritualistic killing of great beasts by a man who is set temporarily apart from civilization. But Hemingway's conception of nature and of the ritual through which the unproven male acquires manhood is more limited than Faulkner's, more narrowly mimetic, and allegorical. Sherwood Anderson's tale of the young New England woman is cast in a highly abstract, evocative, nonhistorical mode reminiscent of legend, while Eudora Welty's comic tale of the search for a missing wife, with its improbable events and animal participants, approaches the fable.

The ways in which the linked modes of humor and comedy often incorporate the fantastic may be seen not only in Miss Welty's story but also in Faulkner's yarn of the wild horses that soar like phantoms through time and space, and in Malamud's narrative of the black Jewish angel who appears and disappears even more miraculously than Faulkner's horses. Although each of these three fictions has its own literary identity, all of them share certain tendencies of the humorous and comic modes to reduce individual characters to types, to view them from the outside, as purely social creatures or even as objects. In contrast to these reductive tendencies are those of the fiction of conduct, concerned with the complexities or development of moral relations between individuals. The boy in Sherwood Anderson's story discovers vulgar conceit in the horse trainer he idolizes and wants to know *why*—that is, he wants to understand how conflicting moral qualities can exist side by side in one man, how character can be ambiguous. That question is raised also by Katherine Anne Porter in "Flowering Judas" and, at a lower frequency, by Hemingway in "The Short Happy Life of Francis Macomber."

Other selections in this volume, such as the piece by Gertrude Stein, do not raise specifically moral questions at all. Their imaginative centers lie elsewhere. This multiplicity of perception is what requires a pluralism of judgment on our part. All fiction cannot be analyzed with the same instrument. Thus while some readers demand that every story portray character realistically, or point a moral, or amuse, or be symbolic, or prove the excesses of capitalism, these demands are invariably frustrated by the astonishing variety the world of fiction actually displays. To recognize the existence of this variety frees one to discover the uniqueness of a particular work of art, to appreciate the achievement of art generally, and so to grasp the possibilities of human individuality.

MODERN AMERICAN CLASSICS
An Anthology of Short Fiction

Free

THEODORE DREISER

Dreiser's story beautifully illustrates the ambiguities of literary naturalism. It is paradoxical in its conception of reality and ambivalent toward that reality. Rufus Haymaker, whose views are plainly Dreiser's, sees the forces acting on his passive self in secular, deterministic terms; the forces are essentially physical (body chemistry, temperament, yearnings, fears) and environmental (social conventions). Haymaker also rejects the idea of an afterlife. But he subscribes to comparably unscientific notions of an animate fortune or nature, as well as to the merely superstitious thought that his "dark wishing" might have killed his wife. Along with these conflicting ideas go conflicting attitudes. Haymaker both scorns and accepts conventional social judgments on his family and himself, both despises and embraces the surrender to sentiment; he trusts nature in the shape of human emotions and landscape, but mistrusts it as a universal moving force. Finding life thus "mixed and tangled," with no secure center to it, he vacillates helplessly between allegiances to some speculative Truth and to the truth of the moment, whether of feeling or fact.

The large and rather comfortable apartment of Rufus Haymaker, architect, in Central Park West, was very silent. It was scarcely dawn yet, and at the edge of the park, over the way, looking out from the front windows which graced this abode and gave it its charm, a stately line of poplars was still shrouded in a gray morning mist. From his bedroom at one end of the hall, where, also, a glimpse of the park was to be had, came Mr. Haymaker at this early hour to sit by one of these broader windows and contemplate these trees and a small lake beyond. He was very fond of Nature in its manifold art forms—quite poetic, in fact.

He was a tall and spare man of about sixty, not ungraceful, though slightly stoop-shouldered, with heavy overhanging eyebrows and hair, and a short, professionally cut gray mustache and beard, which gave him a severe and yet agreeable presence. For the present he was clad in a light-blue dressing gown with silver cords, which enveloped him completely. He had thin, pale, long-fingered hands, wrinkled at the back and slightly knotted at the joints, which bespoke the artist, in mood at least, and his eyes had a weary and yet restless look in them.

For only yesterday Doctor Storm, the family physician, who was in attendance on his wife, ill now for these three weeks past with a combination of heart lesion, kidney poisoning and neuritis, had taken him aside and said very softly and affectionately, as though he were trying to spare his feelings: "To-morrow, Mr. Haymaker, if your wife is no better I will call in my friend, Doctor Grainger, whom you know, for a consultation. He is more of an expert in these matters of the heart"—the heart, Mr. Haymaker had time to note ironically—"than I am. Together we will make a thorough examination, and then I hope we will be better able to say what the possibilities of her recovery really are. It's been a very trying case, a very stubborn one, I might say. Still, she has a great deal of vitality and is doing as well as could be expected, all things considered. At the same time, though I don't wish to alarm you unnecessarily—and there is no occasion for great alarm yet—still I feel it my duty to warn you that her condition is very serious indeed. Not that I wish you to feel that she is certain to die. I don't think she is. Not at all. Just the contrary. She may get well, and probably will, and live all of twenty years more." (Mentally Mr. Haymaker sighed a purely spiritual sigh.) "She has fine recuperative powers, so far as I can judge, but she has a bad heart, and this kidney trouble has not helped it any. Just now, when her heart should have the least strain, it has the most.

"She is just at that point where, as I may say, things are in the balance. A day or two, or three or four at the most, ought to show which way things will go. But, as I have said before, I do not wish to alarm you unnecessarily. We are not nearly at the end of our tether. We haven't tried blood transfusion yet, and there are several arrows to that bow. Besides, at any moment she may respond more vigorously to medication than she has heretofore—especially in connection with her kidneys. In that case the situation would be greatly relieved at once.

"However, as I say, I feel it my duty to speak to you in this way in order that you may be mentally prepared for any event, because in such an odd combination as this the worst may happen at any time. We never can tell. As an old friend of yours and Mrs. Haymaker's, and knowing how much you two mean to each other"— Mr. Haymaker merely stared at him vacantly—"I feel it my duty to prepare you in this way. We all of us have to face these things. Only last year I lost my dear Matilda, my youngest child, as you know. Just the same, as I say, I have the feeling that Mrs. Haymaker is not really likely to die soon, and that we—Doctor Grainger and myself—will still be able to pull her through. I really do."

Doctor Storm looked at Mr. Haymaker as though he were very sorry for him—an old man long accustomed to his wife's ways and likely to be made very unhappy by her untimely end; whereas Mr. Haymaker, though staring in an almost sculptural way, was really thinking what a farce it all was, what a dull mixture of error and illusion on the part of all. Here he was, sixty years of age, weary of all this, of life really—a man who had never been really happy in all the time that he had been married; and yet here was his wife, who from conventional reasons believed that he was or should be, and who on account of this was serenely happy herself, or nearly so. And this doctor, who imagined that he was old and weak and therefore in need of this loving woman's care and sympathy and understanding! Unconsciously he raised a deprecating hand.

Also his children, who thought him dependent on her and happy with her; his servants and her and his friends thinking the same thing, and yet he really was not. It was all a lie. He was unhappy. Always he had been unhappy, it seemed, ever since he had been married—for over thirty-one years now. Never in all that time, for even so much as a single day, had he ever done anything but long, long, long, in a pale, constrained way—for what, he scarcely dared think—not to be married any more—to be free—to be as he was before ever he saw Mrs. Haymaker.

And yet being conventional in mood and training and utterly domesticated by time and conditions over which he seemed not to have much control—nature, custom, public opinion, and the like, coming into play as forces—he had drifted, had not taken any drastic action. No, he had merely drifted, wondering if time, accident or something might not interfere and straighten out his life for him, but it never had. Now weary, old, or rapidly becoming so, he condemned himself for his inaction. Why hadn't he done something about it years before? Why hadn't he broken it up before it was too late, and saved his own soul, his longing for life, color? But no, he had not. Why complain so bitterly now?

All the time the doctor had talked this day before he had wanted to smile a wry, dry, cynical smile, for in reality he did not want Mrs. Haymaker to live—or at least at the moment he thought so. He was too miserably tired of it all. And so now, after nearly twenty-four hours of the same unhappy thought, sitting by this window looking at a not distant building which shone faintly in the haze, he ran his fingers through his hair as he gazed, and sighed.

How often in these weary months, and even years, past—ever since he and his wife had been living here, and before—had he come to these or similar windows while she was still asleep, to sit and dream! For some years now they had not even roomed together, so indifferent had the whole state become; though she did not seem to consider that significant, either. Life had become more or less of a practical problem to her, one of position, place, prestige. And yet how often, viewing his life in retrospect, had he wished that his life had been as sweet as his dreams—that his dreams had come true.

After a time on this early morning, for it was still gray, with the faintest touch of pink in the east, he shook his head solemnly and sadly, then rose and returned along the hall to his wife's bedroom, at the door of which he paused to look where she lay seriously ill, and beside her in an armchair, fast asleep, a trained nurse who was supposedly keeping the night vigil ordered by the doctor, but who no doubt was now very weary. His wife was sleeping also— very pale, very thin now, and very weak. He felt sorry for her at times, in spite of his own weariness; now, for instance. Why need he have made so great a mistake so long ago? Perhaps it was his own fault for not having been wiser in his youth. Then he went quietly on to his own room, to lie down and think.

Always these days, now that she was so very ill and the problem of her living was so very acute, the creeping dawn thus roused him —to think. It seemed as though he could not really sleep soundly any more, so stirred and distrait was he. He was not so much tired or physically worn as mentally bored or disappointed. Life had treated him so badly, he kept thinking to himself over and over. He had never had the woman he really wanted, though he had been married so long, had been faithful, respectable and loved by her, in her way. "In her way," he half quoted to himself as he lay there.

Presently he would get up, dress and go down to his office as usual if his wife were not worse. But—but, he asked himself—would she be? Would that slim and yet so durable organism of hers—quite as old as his own, or nearly so—break under the strain of this really severe illness? That would set him free again, and nicely, without blame or comment on him. He could then go where he chose once more, do as he pleased—think of that—without let or hindrance. For she was ill at last, so very ill, the first and really great illness she had endured since their marriage. For weeks now she had been lying so, hovering, as it were, between life and death, one day better, the next day worse, and yet not dying, and with no certainty that she would, and yet not getting better either. Doctor Storm insisted that it was a leak in her heart which had suddenly manifested itself which was causing all the real trouble. He was apparently greatly troubled as to how to control it.

During all this period Mr. Haymaker had been, as usual, most sympathetic. His manner toward her was always soft, kindly, apparently tender. He had never really begrudged her anything— nothing certainly that he could afford. He was always glad to see her and the children humanly happy—though they, too, largely on account of her, he thought, had proved a disappointment to him— because he had always sympathized with her somewhat unhappy youth, narrow and stinted; and yet he had never been happy himself, either, never in all the time that he had been married. If she had endured much, he kept telling himself when he was most unhappy, so had he, only it was harder perhaps for women to endure things than men—he was always willing to admit that—only also she had had his love, or thought she had, an actual spiritual peace, which he had never had. She knew she had a faithful husband. He felt that he had never really had a wife at all, not one that he could love as he knew a wife should be loved. His dreams as to that!

Going to his office later this same day—it was in one of those tall buildings that face Madison Square—he had looked first, in passing, at the trees that line Central Park West, and then at the bright wall of apartment houses facing it, and meditated sadly, heavily. Here the sidewalks were crowded with nursemaids and children at play, and in between them, of course, the occasional citizen loitering or going about his errands. The day was so fine, so youthful, as spring days will seem at times. As he looked, especially at the children, and the young men bustling office-ward, mostly in new spring suits, he sighed and wished that he were young once more. Think how brisk and hopeful they were! Everything was before them. They could still pick and choose—no age or established conditions to stay them. Were any of them, he asked himself for the thousandth time, it seemed to him, as wearily connected as he had been at their age? Did they each have a charming young wife to love—one of whom they were passionately fond—such a one as he had never had; or did they not?

Wondering, he reached his office on one of the topmost floors of one of those highest buildings commanding a wide view of the city, and surveyed it wearily. Here were visible the two great rivers of the city, its towers and spires and far-flung walls. From these sometimes, even yet, he seemed to gain a patience to live, to hope. How in his youth all this had inspired him—or that other city that was then. Even now he was always at peace here, so much more so than in his own home, pleasant as it was. Here he could look out over this great scene and dream or he could lose the memory in his work that his love-life had been a failure. The great city, the buildings he could plan or supervise, the efficient help that always surrounded him—his help, not hers—aided to take his mind off himself and that deep-seated inner ache or loss.

The care of Mr. Haymaker's apartment during his wife's illness and his present absence throughout the day devolved upon a middle-aged woman of great seriousness, Mrs. Elfridge by name, whom Mrs. Haymaker had employed years before; and under her a maid of all work, Hester, who waited on table, opened the door, and the like; and also at present two trained nurses, one for night and one for day service, who were in charge of Mrs. Haymaker. The nurses were both bright, healthy, blue-eyed girls, who attracted Mr. Haymaker and suggested all the youth he had never had—without really disturbing his poise. It would seem as though that could never be any more.

In addition, of course, there was the loving interest of his son Wesley and his daughter Ethelberta—whom his wife had named so in spite of him—both of whom had long since married and had children of their own and were living in different parts of the great city. In this crisis both of them came daily to learn how things were, and occasionally to stay for the entire afternoon or evening, or both. Ethelberta had wanted to come and take charge of the apartment entirely during her mother's illness, only Mrs. Haymaker, who was still able to direct, and fond of doing so, would not hear of it. She was not so ill but that she could still speak, and in this way could inquire and direct. Besides, Mrs. Elfridge was as good as Mrs. Haymaker in all things that related to Mr. Haymaker's physical comfort, or so she thought.

If the truth will come out—as it will in so many pathetic cases—it was never his physical so much as his spiritual or affectional comfort that Mr. Haymaker craved. As said before, he had never loved Mrs. Haymaker, or certainly not since that now long-distant period back in Muskegon, Michigan, where both had been born and where they had lived and met at the ages, she of fifteen, he of seventeen. It had been, strange as it might seem now, a love match at first sight with them. She had seemed so sweet, a girl of his own age or a little younger, the daughter of a local chemist. Later, when he had been forced by poverty to go out into the world to make his own way, he had written her much, and imagined her to be all that she had seemed at fifteen, and more—a dream among fair women. But Fortune, slow in coming to his aid and fickle in fulfilling his dreams, had brought it about that for several years more he had been compelled to stay away nearly all of the time, unable to marry her; during which period, unknown to himself really, his own point of view had altered. How it had happened he could never tell really, but so it was. The great city, larger experiences—while she was still enduring the smaller ones—other faces, dreams of larger things, had all combined to destroy it or her, only he had not quite realized it then. He was always so slow in realizing the full import of the immediate thing, he thought.

That was the time, as he had afterward told himself—how often! —that he should have discovered his mistake and stopped. Later it always seemed to become more and more impossible. Then, in spite of some heartache to her and some distress to himself, no doubt, all would be well for him now. But no; he had been too inexperienced, too ignorant, too bound by all the conventions and punctilio of his simple Western world. He thought an engagement, however unsatisfactory it might come to seem afterward, was an engagement, and binding. An honorable man would not break one—or so his country moralists argued.

Yes, at that time he might have written her, he might have told her, then. But he had been too sensitive and kindly to speak of it. Afterward it was too late. He feared to wound her, to undo her, to undo her life. But now—now—look at his! He had gone back on several occasions before marriage, and might have seen and done and been free if he had had but courage and wisdom—but no; duty, order, the beliefs of the region in which he had been reared, and of America—what it expected and what she expected and was entitled to—had done for him completely. He had not spoken. Instead, he had gone on and married her without speaking of the change in himself, without letting her know how worse than ashes it had all become. God, what a fool he had been! how often since he had told himself over and over.

Well, having made a mistake it was his duty perhaps, at least according to current beliefs, to stick by it and make the best of it— a bargain was a bargain in marriage, if nowhere else—but still that had never prevented him from being unhappy. He could not prevent that himself. During all these long years, therefore, owing to these same conventions—what people would think and say—he had been compelled to live with her, to cherish her, to pretend to be happy with her—"another perfect union," as he sometimes said to himself. In reality he had been unhappy, horribly so. Even her face wearied him at times, and her presence, her mannerisms. Only this other morning Doctor Storm, by his manner indicating that he thought him lonely, in danger of being left all alone and desperately sad and neglected in case she died, had irritated him greatly. Who would take care of him? his eyes had seemed to say—and yet he himself wanted nothing so much as to be alone for a time, at least, in this life, to think for himself, to do for himself, to forget this long, dreary period in which he had pretended to be something that he was not.

Was he never to be rid of the dull round of it, he asked himself now, never before he himself died? And yet shortly afterward he would reproach himself for these very thoughts, as being wrong, hard, unkind—thoughts that would certainly condemn him in the eyes of the general public, that public which made reputations and one's general standing before the world.

During all this time he had never even let her know—no, not once—of the tremendous and soul-crushing sacrifice he had made. Like the Spartan boy, he had concealed the fox gnawing at his vitals. He had not complained. He had been, indeed, the model husband, as such things go in conventional walks. If you doubted it look at his position, or that of his children; or his wife—her mental and physical comfort, even in her illness, her unfailing belief that he was all he should be! Never once apparently, during all these years, had she doubted his love or felt him to be unduly unhappy— or, if not that exactly, if not fully accepting his love as something that was still at a fever heat, the thing it once was—still believing that he found pleasure and happiness in being with her, a part of the home which together they had built up, these children they had reared, comfort in knowing that it would endure to the end! To the end! During all these years she had gone on molding his and her lives—as much as that was possible in his case—and those of their children, to suit herself; and thinking all the time that she was doing what he wanted or at least what was best for him and them.

How she adored convention! What did she not think she knew in regard to how things ought to be—mainly what her old home sur- roundings had taught her, the American idea of this, that and the other. Her theories in regard to friends, education of the children, and so on, had in the main prevailed, even when he did not quite agree with her; her desires for certain types of pleasure and amuse- ment, of companionship, and so on, were conventional types always and had also prevailed. There had been little quarrels, of course, always had been—what happy home is free of them?—but still he had always given in, or nearly always, and had acted as though he were satisfied in so doing.

But why, therefore, should he complain now, or she ever imagine, or ever have imagined, that he was unhappy? She did not, had not. Like all their relatives and friends of the region from which they sprang, and here also—and she had been most careful to regulate that, courting whom she pleased and ignoring all others—she still believed most firmly, more so than ever, that she knew what was best for him, what he really thought and wanted. It made him smile most wearily at times.

For in her eyes—in regard to him, at least, not always so with others, he had found—marriage was a sacrament, sacrosanct, never to be dissolved. One life, one love. Once a man had accepted the yoke or even asked a girl to marry him it was his duty to abide by it. To break an engagement, to be unfaithful to a wife, even unkind to her—what a crime, in her eyes! Such people ought to be drummed out of the world. They were really not fit to live—dogs, brutes!

And yet, look at himself—what of him? What of one who had made a mistake in regard to all this? Where was his compensation to come from, his peace and happiness? Here on earth or only in some mythical heaven—that odd, angelic heaven that she still believed in? What a farce! And all her friends and his would think he would be so miserable now if she died, or at least ought to be. So far had asinine convention and belief in custom carried the world. Think of it!

But even that was not the worst. No; that was not the worst, either. It had been the gradual realization coming along through the years that he had married an essentially small, narrow woman who could never really grasp his point of view—or, rather, the significance of his dreams or emotions—and yet with whom, nevertheless, because of this original promise or mistake, he was compelled to live. Grant her every quality of goodness, energy, industry, intent—as he did freely—still there was this; and it could never be adjusted, never. Essentially, as he had long since discovered, she was narrow, ultraconventional, whereas he was an artist by nature, brooding and dreaming strange dreams and thinking of far-off things which she did not or could not understand or did not sympathize with, save in a general and very remote way. The nuances of his craft, the wonders and subtleties of forms and angles—had she ever realized how significant these were to him, let alone to herself? No, never. She had not the least true appreciation of them—never had had. Architecture? Art? What could they really mean to her, desire as she might to appreciate them? And he could not now go elsewhere to discover that sympathy. No. He had never really wanted to, since the public and she would object, and he thinking it half evil himself.

Still, how was it, he often asked himself, that Nature could thus allow one conditioned or equipped with emotions and seekings such as his, not of an utterly conventional order, to seek out and pursue one like Ernestine, who was not fitted to understand him or to care what his personal moods might be? Was love truly blind, as the old saw insisted, or did Nature really plan, and cleverly, to torture the artist mind—as it did the pearl-bearing oyster with a grain of sand—with something seemingly inimical, in order that it might produce beauty? Sometimes he thought so. Perhaps the many interesting and beautiful buildings he had planned—the world called them so, at least—had been due to the loving care he lavished on them, being shut out from love and beauty elsewhere. Cruel Nature, that cared so little for the dreams of man—the individual man or woman!

At the time he had married Ernestine he was really too young to know exactly what it was he wanted to do or how it was he was going to feel in the years to come; and yet there was no one to guide him, to stop him. The custom of the time was all in favor of this dread disaster. Nature herself seemed to desire it—mere children being the be-all and the end-all of everything everywhere. Think of that as a theory! Later, when it became so clear to him what he had done, and in spite of all the conventional thoughts and conditions that seemed to bind him to this fixed condition, he had grown restless and weary, but never really irritable. No, he had never become that.

Instead he had concealed it all from her, persistently, in all kindness; only this hankering after beauty of mind and body in ways not represented by her had hurt so—grown finally almost too painful to bear. He had dreamed and dreamed of something different until it had become almost an obsession. Was it never to be, that something different, never, anywhere, in all time? What a tragedy! Soon he would be dead and then it would never be anywhere—anymore! Ernestine was charming, he would admit, or had been at first, though time had proved that she was not charming to him either mentally or physically in any compelling way; but how did that help him now? How could it? He had actually found himself bored by her for more than twenty-seven years now, and this other dream growing, growing, growing—until——

But now he was old, and she was dying, or might be, and it could not make so much difference what happened to him or to her; only it could, too, because he wanted to be free for a little while, just for a little while, before he died.

To be free! free!

One of the things that had always irritated him about Mrs. Haymaker was this, that in spite of his determination never to offend the social code in any way—he had felt for so many reasons, emotional

as well as practical, that he could not afford so to do—and also in
spite of the fact that he had been tortured by this show of beauty
in the eyes and bodies of others, his wife, fearing perhaps in some
strange psychic way that he might change, had always tried to make
him feel or believe—premeditatedly and of a purpose, he thought—
that he was not the kind of man who would be attractive to women;
that he lacked some physical fitness, some charm that other men had,
which would cause all young and really charming women to turn
away from him. Think of it! He to whom so many women had turned
with questioning eyes!

Also that she had married him largely because she had felt sorry
for him! He chose to let her believe that, because he was sorry for
her. Because other women had seemed to draw near to him at
times in some appealing or seductive way she had insisted that he
was not even a cavalier, let alone a Lothario; that he was ungainly,
slow, uninteresting—to all women but her!

Persistently, he thought, and without any real need, she had
harped on this, fighting chimeras, a chance danger in the future;
though he had never given her any real reason, and had never even
planned to sin against her in any way—never. She had thus tried to
poison his own mind in regard to himself and his art—and yet—and
yet—— Ah, those eyes of other women, their haunting beauty, the
flitting something they said to him of infinite, inexpressible delight.
Why had his life been so very hard?

One of the disturbing things about all this was the iron truth
which it had driven home, namely, that Nature, unless it were expressed or represented by some fierce determination within, which
drove one to do, be, cared no whit for him or any other man or
woman. Unless one acted for oneself, upon some stern conclusion
nurtured within, one might rot and die spiritually. Nature did not
care. "Blessed be the meek"—yes. Blessed be the strong, rather,
for they made their own happiness. All these years in which he
had dwelt and worked in this knowledge, hoping for something but
not acting, nothing had happened, except to him, and that in an
unsatisfactory way. All along he had seen what was happening to
him; and yet held by convention he had refused to act always,
because somehow he was not hard enough to act. He was not
strong enough, that was the real truth—had not been. Almost like
a bird in a cage, an animal peeping out from behind bars, he had
viewed the world of free thought and freer action. In many a
drawing-room, on the street, or in his own home even, had he not

looked into an eye, the face of someone who seemed to offer understanding, to know, to sympathize, though she might not have, of
course; and yet religiously and moralistically, like an anchorite, because of duty and current belief and what people would say and
think, Ernestine's position and faith in him, her comfort, his career
and that of the children—he had put them all aside, out of his
mind, forgotten them almost, as best he might. It had been hard at
times, and sad, but so it had been.

And look at him now, old, not exactly feeble yet—no, not that
yet, not quite!—but life weary and almost indifferent. All these years
he had wanted, wanted—wanted—an understanding mind, a tender
heart, the some one woman—she must exist somewhere—who
would have sympathized with all the delicate shades and meanings
of his own character, his art, his spiritual as well as his material
dreams—— And yet look at him! Mrs. Haymaker had always been
with him, present in the flesh or the spirit, and—so——

Though he could not ever say that she was disagreeable to him
in a material way—he could not say that she had ever been that
exactly—still she did not correspond to his idea of what he needed,
and so—— Form had meant so much to him, color; the glorious
perfectness of a glorious woman's body, for instance, the color of her
thoughts, moods—exquisite they must be, like his own at times; but
no, he had never had the opportunity to know one intimately. No,
not one, though he had dreamed of her so long. He had never even
dared whisper this to any one, scarcely to himself. It was not wise,
not socially fit. Thoughts like this would tend to social ostracism
in his circle, or rather hers—for had she not made the circle?

And here was the rub with Mr. Haymaker, at least, that he could
not make up his mind whether in his restlessness and private mental
complaints he were not even now guilty of a great moral crime in
so thinking. Was it not true that men and women should be faithful in marriage whether they were happy or not? Was there not
some psychic law governing this matter of union—one life, one
love—which made the thoughts and the pains and the subsequent
sufferings and hardships of the individual, whatever they might
be, seem unimportant? The churches said so. Public opinion and
the law seemed to accept this. There were so many problems, so
much order to be disrupted, so much pain caused, many insoluble
problems where children were concerned—if people did not stick.
Was it not best, more blessed—socially, morally, and in every
other way important—for him to stand by a bad bargain rather

than to cause so much disorder and pain, even though he lost his own soul emotionally? He had thought so—or at least he had acted as though he thought so—and yet—— How often had he wondered over this!

Take, now, some other phases. Granting first that Mrs. Haymaker had, according to the current code, measured up to the requirements of a wife, good and true, and that at first after marriage there had been just enough of physical and social charm about her to keep his state from becoming intolerable, still there was this old ache; and then newer things which came with the birth of the several children: First Elwell—named after a cousin of hers, not his—who had died only two years after he was born; and then Wesley; and then Ethelberta. How he had always disliked that name!—largely because he had hoped to call her Ottilie, a favorite name of his; or Janet, after his mother.

Curiously the arrival of these children and the death of poor little Elwell at two had somehow, in spite of his unrest, bound him to this matrimonial state and filled him with a sense of duty, and pleasure even—almost entirely apart from her, he was sorry to say —in these young lives; though if there had not been children, as he sometimes told himself, he surely would have broken away from her; he could not have stood it. They were so odd in their infancy, those little ones, so troublesome and yet so amusing—little Elwell, for instance, whose nose used to crinkle with delight when he would pretend to bite his neck, and whose gurgle of pleasure was so sweet and heart-filling that it positively thrilled and lured him. In spite of his thoughts concerning Ernestine—and always in those days they were rigidly put down as unmoral and even evil, a certain unsocial streak in him perhaps which was against law and order and social well-being—he came to have a deep and abiding feeling for Elwell. The latter, in some chemic, almost unconscious way, seemed to have arrived as a balm to his misery, a bandage for his growing wound—sent by whom, by what, how? Elwell had seized upon his imagination, and so his heartstrings—had come, indeed, to make him feel understanding and sympathy there in that little child; to supply, or seem to at least, what he lacked in the way of love and affection from one whom he could truly love. Elwell was never so happy apparently as when snuggling in his arms, not Ernestine's, or lying against his neck. And when he went for a walk or elsewhere there was Elwell always ready, arms up, to cling to his neck. He seemed, strangely enough, inordinately fond of his father, rather than his mother, and never happy without him. On his part, Haymaker came to be wildly fond of him—that queer little lump of a face, suggesting a little of himself and of his own mother, not so much of Ernestine, or so he thought, though he would not have objected to that. Not at all. He was not so small as that. Toward the end of the second year, when Elwell was just beginning to be able to utter a word or two, he had taught him that silly old rhyme which ran "There were three kittens," and when it came to "and they shall have no——" he would stop and say to Elwell, "What now?" and the latter would gurgle "puh!"—meaning, of course, pie.

Ah, those happy days with little Elwell, those walks with him over his shoulder or on his arm, those hours in which of an evening he would rock him to sleep in his arms! Always Ernestine was there, and happy in the thought of his love for little Elwell and her, her more than anything else perhaps; but it was an illusion—that latter part. He did not care for her even then as she thought he did. All his fondness was for Elwell, only she took it as evidence of his growing or enduring affection for her—another evidence of the peculiar working of her mind. Women were like that, he supposed—some women.

And then came that dreadful fever, due to some invading microbe which the doctors could not diagnose or isolate, infantile paralysis perhaps; and little Elwell had finally ceased to be as flesh and was eventually carried forth to the lorn, disagreeable graveyard near Woodlawn. How he had groaned internally, indulged in sad, despondent thoughts concerning the futility of all things human, when this had happened! It seemed for the time being as if all color and beauty had really gone out of his life for good.

"Man born of woman is of few days and full of troubles," the preacher whom Mrs. Haymaker had insisted upon having into the house at the time of the funeral had read. "He fleeth also as a shadow and continueth not."

Yes; so little Elwell had fled, as a shadow, and in his own deep sorrow at the time he had come to feel the first and only sad, deep sympathy for Ernestine that he had ever felt since marriage; and that because she had suffered so much—had lain in his arms after the funeral and cried so bitterly. It was terrible, her sorrow. Terrible—a mother grieving for her first-born! Why was it, he had thought at the time, that he had never been able to think or make her all she ought to be to him? Ernestine at this time had seemed better, softer, kinder, wiser, sweeter than she had ever seemed; more worthy, more interesting than ever he had thought her before. She had slaved so during the child's illness, stayed awake night after night, watched over him with such loving care—done everything, in short, that a loving human heart could do to rescue her young from the depths; and yet even then he had not really been able to love her. No, sad and unkind as it might seem, he had not. He had just pitied her and thought her better, worthier! What cursed stars disordered the minds and moods of people so? Why was it that these virtues of people, their good qualities, did not make you love them, did not really bind them to you, as against the things you could not like? Why? He had resolved to do better in his thoughts, but somehow, in spite of himself, he had never been able so to do.

Nevertheless, at that time he seemed to realize more keenly than ever her order, industry, frugality, a sense of beauty within limits, a certain laudable ambition to do something and be somebody—only, only he could not sympathize with her ambitions, could not see that she had anything but a hopelessly common-place and always unimportant point of view. There was never any flare to her, never any true distinction of mind or soul. She seemed always, in spite of anything he might say or do, hopelessly to identify doing and being with money and current opinion—neighborhood public opinion, almost—and local social position, whereas he knew that distinguished doing might as well be connected with poverty and shame and disgrace as with these other things—wealth and station, for instance; a thing which she could never quite understand apparently, though he often tried to tell her, much against her mood always.

Look at the cases of the great artists! Some of the greatest architects right here in the city, or in history, were of peculiar, almost disagreeable, history. But no, Mrs. Haymaker could not understand anything like that, anything connected with history, indeed—she hardly believed in history, its dark, sad pages, and would never read it, or at least did not care to. And as for art and artists—she would never have believed that wisdom and art understanding and true distinction might take their rise out of things necessarily low and evil—never.

Take now, the case of young Zingara. Zingara was an architect like himself, whom he had met more than thirty years before, here in New York, when he had first arrived, a young man struggling to become an architect of significance, only he was very poor and rather unkempt and disreputable-looking. Haymaker had found him several years before his marriage to Ernestine in the dark offices of Pyne & Starboard, Architects, and had been drawn to him definitely; but because he smoked all the time and was shabby as to his clothes and had no money—why, Mrs. Haymaker, after he had married her, and though he had known Zingara nearly four years, would have none of him. To her he was low, and a failure, one who would never succeed. Once she had seen him in some cheap restaurant that she chanced to be passing, in company with a drabby-looking maid, and that was the end.

"I wish you wouldn't bring him here any more, dear," she had insisted; and to have peace he had complied—only, now look. Zingara had since become a great architect, but now of course, owing to Mrs. Haymaker, he was definitely alienated. He was the man who had since designed the Æsculapian Club; and Symphony Hall with its delicate façade; as well as the tower of the Wells Building, sending its sweet lines so high, like a poetic thought or dream. But Zingara was now a dreamy recluse like himself, very exclusive, as Haymaker had long since come to know, and indifferent as to what people thought or said.

But perhaps it was not just obtuseness to certain of the finer shades and meanings of life, but an irritating aggressiveness at times, backed only by her limited understanding, which caused her to seek and wish to be here, there and the other place; wherever, in her mind, the truly successful—which meant nearly always the materially successful of a second or third rate character—were, which irritated him most of all. How often had he tried to point out the difference between true and shoddy distinction—the former rarely connected with great wealth.

But no. So often she seemed to imagine such queer people to be truly successful, when they were really not—usually people with just money, or a very little more.

And in the matter of rearing and educating and marrying their two children, Wesley and Ethelberta, who had come after Elwell —what peculiar pains and feelings had not been involved in all this for him. In infancy both of these had seemed sweet enough, and so close to him, though never quite so wonderful as Elwell. But, as they grew, it seemed somehow as though Ernestine had come between him and them. First, it was the way she had raised them, the very stiff and formal manner in which they were supposed to move and be, copied from the few new-rich whom she had chanced to meet through him—and admired in spite of his warnings. That was the irony of architecture as a profession—it was always bringing such queer people close to one, and for the sake of one's profession, sometimes, particularly in the case of the young architect, one had to be nice to them. Later, it was the kind of school they should attend. He had half imagined at first that it would be the public school, because they both had begun as simple people; but no, since they were prospering it had to be a private school for each, and not one of his selection, either—or hers, really—but one to which the Barlows and the Westervelts, two families of means with whom Ernestine had become intimate, sent their children and therefore thought excellent!

The Barlows! Wealthy, but, to him, gross and mediocre people who had made a great deal of money in the manufacture of patent medicines out West, and who had then come to New York to splurge, and had been attracted to Ernestine—not him particularly, he imagined—because Haymaker had built a town house for them, and also because he was gaining a fine reputation. They were dreadful really, so *gauche*, so truly dull; and yet somehow they seemed to suit Ernestine's sense of fitness and worth at the time, because, as she said, they were good and kind—like her Western home folks; only they were not really. She just imagined so. They were worthy enough people in their way, though with no taste. Young Fred Barlow had been sent to the expensive Gaillard School for Boys, near Morristown, where they were taught manners and airs, and little else, as Haymaker always thought, though Ernestine insisted that they were given a religious training as well. And so Wesley had to go there—for a time, anyhow. It was the best school.

And similarly, because Mercedes Westervelt, senseless, vain little thing, was sent to Briarcliff School, near White Plains, Ethelberta had to go there. Think of it! It was all so silly, so pushing. How well he remembered the long, delicate campaign which preceded this, the logic and tactics employed, the importance of it socially to Ethelberta, the tears and cajolery. Mrs. Haymaker could always cry so easily, or seem to be on the verge of it, when she wanted anything; and somehow, in spite of the fact that he knew her tears were unimportant, or timed and for a purpose, he could never stand out against them, and she knew it. Always he felt moved or weakened in spite of himself. He had no weapon wherewith to fight them, though he resented them as a part of the argument. Positively Mrs. Haymaker could be as sly and as ruthless as Machiavelli himself at times, and yet believe all the while that she was tender, loving, self-sacrificing, generous, moral and a dozen other things, all of which led to the final achievement of her own aims. Perhaps this was admirable from one point of view, but it irritated him always. But if one were unable to see him or herself, their actual disturbing inconsistencies, what were you to do?

And again, he had by then been married so long that it was almost impossible to think of throwing her over, or so it seemed at the time. They had reached the place then where they had supposedly achieved position together, though in reality it was all his —and not such position as he was entitled to, at that. Ernestine— and he was thinking this in all kindness—could never attract the ideal sort. And anyhow, the mere breath of a scandal between them, separation or unfaithfulness, which he never really contemplated, would have led to endless bickering and social and commercial injury, or so he thought. All her strong friends—and his, in a way— those who had originally been his clients, would have deserted him. Their wives, their own social fears, would have compelled them to ostracize him! He would have been a scandal-marked architect, a brute for objecting to so kind and faithful and loving a wife. And perhaps he would have been, at that. He could never quite tell, it was all so mixed and tangled.

Take, again, the marriage of his son Wesley into the De Gaud family—George de Gaud *père* being nothing more than a retired real-estate speculator and promoter who had money, but nothing more; and Irma de Gaud, the daughter, being a gross, coarse, sensuous girl, physically attractive no doubt, and financially reasonably secure, or so she had seemed; but what else? Nothing, literally nothing; and his son had seemed to have at least some spiritual ideals at first. Ernestine had taken up with Mrs. George de Gaud—a miserable, narrow creature, so Haymaker thought—largely for Wesley's sake, he presumed. Anyhow, everything had been done to encourage Wesley in his suit and Irma in her toleration, and now look at them! De Gaud *père* had since failed and left his daughter practically nothing. Irma had been interested in anything but Wesley's career, had followed what she considered the smart among the new-rich— a smarter, wilder, newer new-rich than ever Ernestine had fancied, or could. Today she was without a thought for anything besides teas and country clubs and theaters—and what else?

And long since Wesley had begun to realize it himself. He was an engineer now, in the employ of one of the great construction companies, a moderately successful man. But even Ernestine, who had engineered the match and thought it wonderful, was now down on her. She had begun to see through her some years ago, when Irma had begun to ignore her; only before it was always the De Gauds here, and the De Gauds there. Good gracious, what more could any one want than the De Gauds—Irma de Gaud, for instance? Then came the concealed dissension between Irma and Wesley, and now Mrs. Haymaker insisted that Irma had held, and was holding Wesley back. She was not the right woman for him. Almost—against all her prejudices—she was willing that he should leave her. Only, if Haymaker had broached anything like that in connection with himself!

And yet Mrs. Haymaker had been determined, because of what she considered the position of the De Gauds at that time, that Wesley should marry Irma. Wesley now had to slave at mediocre tasks in order to have enough to allow Irma to run in so-called fast society of a second or third rate. And even at that she was not faithful to him—or so Haymaker believed. There were so many strange evidences. And yet Haymaker felt that he did not care to interfere now. How could he? Irma was tired of Wesley, and that was all there was to it. She was looking elsewhere, he was sure.

Take but one more case, that of Ethelberta. What a name! In spite of all Ernestine's determination to make her so successful and thereby reflect some credit on her had she really succeeded in so doing? To be sure, Ethelberta's marriage was somewhat more successful financially than Wesley's had proved to be, but was she any better placed in other ways? John Kelso—"Jack," as she always called him—with his light ways and lighter mind, was he really any one!—anything more than a waster? His parents stood by him no doubt, but that was all; and so much the worse for him. According to Mrs. Haymaker at the time, he, too, was an ideal boy, admirable, just the man for Ethelberta, because the Kelsos, *père* and *mère*, had money. Horner Kelso had made a kind of fortune in Chicago in the banknote business, and had settled in New York, about the time that Ethelberta was fifteen, to spend it. Ethelberta had met Grace Kelso at school.

And now see! She was not unattractive, and had some pleasant, albeit highly affected, social ways; she had money, and a comfortable apartment in Park Avenue; but what had it all come to? John Kelso had never done anything really, nothing. His parents' money and indulgence and his early training for a better social state had ruined him if he had ever had a mind that amounted to anything. He was idle, pleasure-loving, mentally indolent, like Irma de Gaud. Those two should have met and married, only they could never have endured each other. But how Mrs. Haymaker had courted the Kelsos in her eager and yet diplomatic way, giving teas and receptions and theater parties; and yet he had never been able to exchange ten significant words with either of them, or the younger Kelsos either. Think of it!

And somehow in the process Ethelberta, for all his early affection and tenderness and his still kindly feeling for her, had been weaned away from him and had proved a limited and conventional girl, somewhat like her mother, and more inclined to listen to her than to him—though he had not minded that really. It had been the same with Wesley before her. Perhaps, however, a child was entitled to its likes and dislikes, regardless.

But why had he stood for it all, he now kept asking himself. Why? What grand results, if any, had been achieved? Were their children so wonderful?—their lives? Would he not have been better off without her—his children better, even, by a different woman?— hers by a different man? Wouldn't it have been better if he had destroyed it all, broken away? There would have been pain, of course, terrible consequences, but even so he would have been free to go, to do, to reorganize his life on another basis. Zingara had avoided marriage entirely—wise man. But no, no; always convention, that long list of reasons and terrors he was always reciting to himself. He had allowed himself to be pulled round by the nose, God only knows why, and that was all there was to it. Weakness, if you will, perhaps; fear of convention; fear of what people would think and say.

Always now he found himself brooding over the dire results to him of all this respect on his part for convention, moral order, the duty of keeping society on an even keel, of not bringing disgrace to his children and himself and her, and yet ruining his own life emotionally by so doing. To be respectable had been so important that it had resulted in spiritual failure for him. But now all that was over with him, and Mrs. Haymaker was ill, near to death, and he was expected to wish her to get well, and be happy with her for a long time yet! Be happy! In spite of anything he might wish or think he ought to do, he couldn't. He couldn't even wish her to get well.

It was too much to ask. There was actually a haunting satisfaction in the thought that she might die now. It wouldn't be much, but it would be something—a few years of freedom. That was something. He was not utterly old yet, and he might have a few years of peace and comfort to himself still—and—and—— That dream—that dream—though it might never come true now—it couldn't really —still—still—— He wanted to be free to go his own way once more, to do as he pleased, to walk, to think, to brood over what he had not had—to brood over what he had not had! Only, only, whenever he looked into her pale sick face and felt her damp limp hands he could not quite wish that, either; not quite, not even now. It seemed too hard, too brutal—only—only—— So he wavered.

No; in spite of her long-past struggle over foolish things and in spite of himself and all he had endured or thought he had, he was still willing that she should live; only he couldn't wish it exactly. Yes, let her live if she could. What matter to him now whether she lived or died? Whenever he looked at her he could not help thinking how helpless she would be without him, what a failure at her age, and so on. And all along, as he wryly repeated to himself, she had been thinking and feeling that she was doing the very best for him and her and the children!—that she was really the ideal wife for him, making every dollar go as far as it would, every enjoyment yield the last drop for them all, every move seeming to have been made to their general advantage! Yes, that was true. There was a pathos about it, wasn't there? But as for the actual results——!

The next morning, the second after his talk with Doctor Storm, found him sitting once more beside his front window in the early dawn, and so much of all this, and much more, was coming back to him, as before. For the thousandth or the ten-thousandth time, as it seemed to him, in all the years that had gone, he was concluding again that his life was a failure. If only he were free for a little while just to be alone and think, perhaps to discover what life might bring him yet; only on this occasion his thoughts were colored by a new turn in the situation. Yesterday afternoon, because Mrs. Haymaker's condition had grown worse, the consultation between Grainger and Storm was held, and to-day sometime transfusion was to be tried, that last grim stand taken by physicians in distress over a case; blood taken from a strong ex-cavalryman out of a position, in this case, and the best to be hoped for, but not assured. In this instance his thoughts were as before wavering. Now supposing she really died, in spite of this? What would he think of himself then? He went back after a time and looked in on her where she was still sleeping. Now she was not so strong as before, or so she seemed; her pulse was not so good, the nurse said. And now as before his mood changed in her favor, but only for a little while. For later, waking, she seemed to look and feel better.

Later he came up to the dining room, where the nurse was taking her breakfast, and seating himself beside her, as was his custom these days, asked: "How do you think she is to-day?"

He and the night nurse had thus had their breakfasts together for days. This nurse, Miss Filson, was such a smooth, pink, graceful creature, with light hair and blue eyes, the kind of eyes and color that of late, and in earlier years, had suggested to him the love time or youth that he had missed.

The latter looked grave, as though she really feared the worst but was concealing it.

"No worse, I think, and possibly a little better," she replied, eying him sympathetically. He could see that she too felt that he was old and in danger of being neglected. "Her pulse is a little stronger, nearly normal now, and she is resting easily. Doctor Storm and Doctor Grainger are coming, though, at ten. Then they'll decide what's to be done. I think if she's worse that they are going to try transfusion. The man has been engaged. Doctor Storm said that when she woke to-day she was to be given strong beef tea. Mrs. Elfridge is making it now. The fact that she is not much worse, though, is a good sign in itself, I think."

Haymaker merely stared at her from under his heavy gray eyebrows. He was so tired and gloomy, not only because he had not slept much of late himself but because of this sawing to and fro between his varying moods. Was he never to be able to decide for himself what he really wished? Was he never to be done with this interminable moral or spiritual problem? Why could he not make up his mind on the side of moral order, sympathy, and be at peace? Miss Filson pattered on about other heart cases, how so many people lived years and years after they were supposed to die of heart lesion; and he meditated as to the grayness and strangeness of it all, the worthlessness of his own life, the variability of his own moods. Why was he so? How queer—how almost evil, sinister—he had become at times; how weak at others. Last night as he had looked at Ernestine lying in bed, and this morning before he had seen her, he had thought if she only would die—if he were only really free once more, even at this late date. But then when he had seen her again this morning and now when Miss Filson spoke of transfusion, he felt sorry again. What good would it do him now? Why should he want to kill her? Could such evil ideas go unpunished either in this world or the next? Supposing his children could guess! Supposing she did die now—and he wished it so fervently only this morning—how would he feel? After all, Ernestine had not been so bad. She had tried, hadn't she?—only she had not been able to make a success of things, as he saw it, and he had not been able to love her, that was all. He reproached himself once more now with the hardness and the cruelty of his thoughts.

The opinion of the two physicians was that Mrs. Haymaker was not much better and that this first form of blood transfusion must be resorted to—injected straight via a pump—which should restore her greatly provided her heart did not bleed it out too freely. Before doing so, however, both men once more spoke to Haymaker, who in an excess of self-condemnation insisted that no expense must be spared. If her life was in danger, save it by any means—all. It was precious to her, to him and to her children. So he spoke. Thus he felt that he was lending every force which could be expected of him, aside from fervently wishing for her recovery, which even now, in spite of himself, he could not do. He was too weary of it all, the conventional round of duties and obligations. But if she recovered, as her physicians seemed to think she might if transfusion were tried, if she gained even, it would mean that he would have to take her away for the summer to some quiet mountain resort—to be with her hourly during the long period in which she would be recovering. Well, he would not complain now. That was all right. He would do it. He would be bored of course, as usual, but it would be too bad to have her die when she could be saved. Yes, that was true. And yet——

He went down to his office again and in the meantime this first form of transfusion was tried, and proved a great success, apparently. She was much better, so the day nurse phoned at three; very much better. At five-thirty Mr. Haymaker returned, no unsatisfactory word having come in the interim, and there she was, resting on a raised pillow, if you please, and looking so cheerful, more like her old self than he had seen her in some time.

At once then his mood changed again. They were amazing, these variations in his own thoughts, almost chemic, not volitional, decidedly peculiar for a man who was supposed to know his own mind—only did one, ever? Now she would not die. Now the whole thing would go on as before. He was sure of it. Well, he might as well resign himself to the old sense of failure. He would never be free now. Everything would go on as before, the next and the next day the same. Terrible! Though he seemed glad—really grateful, in a way, seeing her cheerful and hopeful once more—still the obsession of failure and being once more bound forever returned now. In his own bed at midnight he said to himself: "Now she will really get well. All will be as before. I will never be free. I will never have a day—a day! Never!"

But the next morning, to his surprise and fear or comfort, as his moods varied, she was worse again; and then once more he reproached himself for his black thoughts. Was he not really killing her by what he thought? he asked himself—these constant changes in his mood? Did not his dark wishes have power? Was he not as good as a murderer in his way? Think, if he had always to feel from now on that he had killed her by wishing so! Would not that be dreadful—an awful thing really? Why was he this way? Could he not be human, kind?

When Doctor Storm came at nine-thirty, after a telephone call from the nurse, and looked grave and spoke of horses' blood as being better, thicker than human blood—not so easily bled out of the heart when injected as a serum—Haymaker was beside himself with self-reproaches and sad, disturbing fear. His dark, evil thoughts of last night and all these days had done this, he was sure. Was he really a murderer at heart, a dark criminal, plotting her death? —and for what? Why had he wished last night that she would die? Her case must be very desperate.

"You must do your best," he now said to Doctor Storm. "Whatever is needful—she must not die if you can help it."

"No, Mr. Haymaker," returned the latter sympathetically. "All that can be done will be done. You need not fear. I have an idea that we didn't inject enough yesterday, and anyhow human blood is not thick enough in this case. She responded, but not enough. We will see what we can do to-day."

Haymaker, pressed with duties, went away, subdued and sad.

Now once more he decided that he must not tolerate these dark ideas any more, must rid himself of these black wishes, whatever he might feel. It was evil. They would eventually come back to him in some dark way, he might be sure. They might be influencing her. She must be allowed to recover if she could without any opposition on his part. He must now make a further sacrifice of his own life, whatever it cost. It was only decent, only human. Why should he complain now, anyhow, after all these years! What difference would a few more years make? He returned at evening, consoled by his own good thoughts and a telephone message at three to the effect that his wife was much better. This second injection had proved much more effective. Horses' blood was plainly better for her. She was stronger, and sitting up again. He entered at five, and found her lying there pale and weak, but still with a better light in her eye, a touch of color in her cheeks—or so he thought—more force, and a very faint smile for him, so marked had been the change. How great and kind Doctor Storm really was! How resourceful! If she would only get well now! If this dread siege would only abate! Doctor Storm was coming again at eight.

"Well, how are you, dear?" she asked, looking at him sweetly and lovingly, and taking his hand in hers.

He bent and kissed her forehead—a Judas kiss, he had thought up to now, but not so to-night. To-night he was kind, generous—anxious, even, for her to live.

"All right, dearest; very good indeed. And how are you? It's such a fine evening out. You ought to get well soon so as to enjoy these spring days."

"I'm going to," she replied softly. "I feel so much better. And how have you been? Has your work gone all right?"

He nodded and smiled and told her bits of news. Ethelberta had phoned that she was coming, bringing violets. Wesley had said he would be here at six, with Irma! Such-and-such people had asked after her. How could he have been so evil, he now asked himself, as to wish her to die? She was not so bad—really quite charming in her way, an ideal wife for some one, if not him. She was as much entitled to live and enjoy her life as he was to enjoy his; and after all she was the mother of his children, had been with him all these years. Besides, the day had been so fine—it was now—a wondrous May evening. The air and sky were simply delicious. A lavender haze was in the air. The telephone bell now ringing brought still another of a long series of inquiries as to her condition. There had been so many of these during the last few days, the maid said, and especially to-day—and she gave Mr. Haymaker a list of names. See, he thought, she had even more friends than he, being so good, faithful, worthy. Why should he wish her ill?

He sat down to dinner with Ethelberta and Wesley when they arrived, and chatted quite gayly—more hopefully than he had in weeks. His own varying thoughts no longer depressing him, for the moment he was happy. How were they? What were the children all doing? At eight-thirty Doctor Storm came again, and announced that he thought Mrs. Haymaker was doing very well indeed, all things considered.

"Her condition is fairly promising, I must say," he said. "If she gets through another night or two comfortably without falling back I think she'll do very well from now on. Her strength seems to be increasing a fraction. However, we must not be too optimistic. Cases of this kind are very treacherous. To-morrow we'll see how she feels, whether she needs any more blood."

He went away, and at ten Ethelberta and Wesley left for the night, asking to be called if she grew worse, thus leaving him alone once more. He sat and meditated. At eleven, after a few moments at his wife's bedside—absolute quiet had been the doctor's instructions these many days—he himself went to bed. He was very tired. His varying thoughts had afflicted him so much that he was always tired, it seemed—his evil conscience, he called it—but to-night he was sure he would sleep. He felt better about himself, about life. He had done better, to-day. He should never have tolerated such dark thoughts. And yet—and yet—and yet——

He lay on his bed near a window which commanded a view of a small angle of the park, and looked out. There were the spring trees, as usual, silvered now by the light, a bit of lake showing at one end. Here in the city a bit of sylvan scenery such as this was so rare and so expensive. In his youth he had been so fond of water, any small lake or stream or pond. In his youth, also, he had loved the moon, and to walk in the dark. It had all, always, been so suggestive of love and happiness, and he had so craved love and happiness and never had it. Once he had designed a yacht club, the base of which suggested waves. Once, years ago, he had thought of designing a lovely cottage or country house for himself and some new love—that wonderful one—if ever she came and he were free. How wonderful it would all have been. Now—now—the thought at such an hour and especially when it was too late, seemed sacrilegious, hard, cold, unmoral, evil. He turned his face away from the moonlight and sighed, deciding to sleep and shut out these older and darker and sweeter thoughts if he could, and did.

Presently he dreamed, and it was as if some lovely spirit of beauty—that wondrous thing he had always been seeking—came and took him by the hand and led him out, out by dimpling streams and clear rippling lakes and a great, noble highway where were temples and towers and figures in white marble. And it seemed as he walked as if something had been, or were, promised him—a lovely fruition to something which he craved—only the world toward which he walked was still dark or shadowy, with something sad and repressing about it, a haunting sense of a still darker distance. He was going toward beauty apparently, but he was still seeking, seeking, and it was dark there when——

"Mr. Haymaker! Mr. Haymaker!" came a voice—soft, almost mystical at first, and then clearer and more disturbing, as a hand was laid on him. "Will you come at once? It's Mrs. Haymaker!"

On the instant he was on his feet seizing the blue silk dressing gown hanging at his bed's head, and adjusting it as he hurried. Mrs. Elfridge and the nurse were behind him, very pale and distrait, wringing their hands. He could tell by that that the worst was at hand. When he reached the bedroom—her bedroom—there she lay as in life—still, peaceful, already limp, as though she were sleeping. Her thin, and as he sometimes thought, cold, lips were now parted in a faint, gracious smile, or trace of one. He had seen her look that way, too, at times; a really gracious smile, and wise, wiser than she was. The long, thin, graceful hands were open, the fingers spread slightly apart as though she were tired, very tired. The eyelids, too, rested wearily on tired eyes. Her form, spare as always, was outlined clearly under the thin coverlets. Miss Filson, the night nurse, was saying something about having fallen asleep for a moment, and waking only to find her so. She was terribly depressed and disturbed, possibly because of Doctor Storm.

Haymaker paused, greatly shocked and moved by the sight— more so than by anything since the death of little Elwell. After all, she had tried, according to her light. But now she was dead—and they had been together so long! He came forward, tears of sympathy springing to his eyes, then sank down beside the bed on his knees so as not to disturb her right hand where it lay.

"Ernie, dear," he said gently, "Ernie—are you really gone?" His voice was full of sorrow; but to himself it sounded false, traitorous.

He lifted the hand and put it to his lips sadly, then leaned his head against her, thinking of his long, mixed thoughts these many days, while both Mrs. Elfridge and the nurse began wiping their eyes. They were so sorry for him, he was so old now!

After a while he got up—they came forward to persuade him at last—looking tremendously sad and distrait, and asked Mrs. Elfridge and the nurse not to disturb his children. They could not aid her now. Let them rest until morning. Then he went back· to his own room and sat down on the bed for a moment, gazing out on the same silvery scene that had attracted him before. It was dreadful. So then his dark wishing had come true at last? Possibly his black thoughts had killed her after all. Was that possible? Had his voiceless prayers been answered in this grim way? And did she know now what he had really thought? Dark thought. Where was she now? What was she thinking now if she knew? Would she hate him— haunt him? It was not dawn yet, only two or three in the morning, and the moon was still bright. And in the next room she was lying, pale and cool, gone forever now out of his life.

He got up after a time and went forward into that pleasant front room where he had so often loved to sit, then back into her room to view the body again. Now that she was gone, here more than elsewhere, in her dead presence, he seemed better able to collect his scattered thoughts. She might see or she might not—might know or not. It was all over now. Only he could not help but feel a little evil. She had been so faithful, if nothing more, so earnest in behalf of him and of his children. He might have spared her these last dark thoughts of these last few days. His feelings were so jumbled that he could not place them half the time. But at the same time the ethics of the past, of his own irritated feelings and moods in regard to her, had to be adjusted somehow before he could have peace. They must be adjusted, only how—how? He and Mrs. Elfridge had agreed not to disturb Doctor Storm any more to-night. They were all agreed to get what rest they could against the morning.

After a time he came forward once more to the front room to sit and gaze at the park. Here, perhaps, he could solve these mysteries for himself, think them out, find out what he did feel. He was evil for having wished all he had, that he knew and felt. And yet there was his own story, too—his life. The dawn was breaking by now; a faint grayness shaded the east and dimly lightened this room. A tall pier mirror between two windows now revealed him to himself—spare, angular, disheveled, his beard and hair astray and his eyes weary. The figure he made here as against his dreams of a happier life, once he were free, now struck him forcibly. What a farce! What a failure! Why should he, of all people, think of further happiness in love, even if he were free? Look at his reflection here in this mirror. What a picture—old, grizzled, done for! Had he not known that for so long? Was it not too ridiculous? Why should he have tolerated such vain thoughts? What could he of all people hope for now? No thing of beauty would have him now. Of course not. That glorious dream of his youth was gone forever. It was a mirage, an ignis fatuus. His wife might just as well have lived as died, for all the difference it would or could make to him. Only, he was really free just the same, almost as it were in spite of his varying moods. But he was old, weary, done for, a recluse and ungainly.

Now the innate cruelty of life, its blazing ironic indifference to him and so many grew rapidly upon him. What had he had? What all had he not missed? Dismally he stared first at his dark wrinkled skin; the crow's-feet at the sides of his eyes; the wrinkles across his forehead and between the eyes; his long, dark, wrinkled hands— handsome hands they once were, he thought; his angular, stiff body. Once he had been very much of a personage, he thought, striking, forceful, dynamic—but now! He turned and looked out over the park where the young trees were, and the lake, to the pinking dawn—just a trace now—a significant thing in itself at this hour surely—the new dawn, so wondrously new for younger people— then back at himself. What could he wish for now—what hope for?

As he did so his dream came back to him—that strange dream of seeking and being led and promised and yet always being led forward into a dimmer, darker land. What did that mean? Had it any real significance? Was it all to be dimmer, darker still? Was it typical of his life? He pondered.

"Free!" he said after a time. "Free! I know now how that is. I am free now, at last! Free! . . . Free! . . . Yes—free . . . to die!"

So he stood there ruminating and smoothing his hair and his beard.

I Want
to Know Why

SHERWOOD ANDERSON

Although his use of the word "fantods," his vernacular language, and his half-rejection of his own Border State prejudices against Negroes all indicate that the hero of this story is modeled after Huckleberry Finn, Sherwood Anderson's young narrator is decidedly more speculative than Huck and more anxious to know the reasons for an individual's behavior. His conscious concern is, in a word, moral; and although the story fails to answer the question why? that gives rise to the narrative, it skillfully carries out another, more limited aim, which is to present realistically certain circumstances under which a fifteen-year-old boy suddenly finds his youthful judgments of men inadequate.

We got up at four in the morning, that first day in the east. On the evening before we had climbed off a freight train at the edge of town, and with the true instinct of Kentucky boys had found our way across town and to the race track and the stables at once. Then we knew we were all right. Hanley Turner right away found a nigger we knew. It was Bildad Johnson who in the winter works at Ed Becker's livery barn in our home town, Beckersville. Bildad is a good cook as almost all our niggers are and of course he, like everyone in our part of Kentucky who is anyone at all, likes the horses. In the spring Bildad begins to scratch around. A nigger from our country can flatter and wheedle anyone into letting him do most anything he wants. Bildad wheedles the stable men and the trainers from the horse farms in our country around Lexington. The trainers come into town in the evening to stand around and talk and maybe get into a poker game. Bildad gets in with them. He is always doing little favors and telling about things to eat, chicken browned in a pan, and how is the best way to cook sweet potatoes and corn bread. It makes your mouth water to hear him.

When the racing season comes on and the horses go to the races and there is all the talk on the streets in the evenings about the new colts, and everyone says when they are going over to Lexington or to the spring meeting at Churchill Downs or to Latonia, and the horsemen that have been down to New Orleans or maybe at the winter meeting at Havana in Cuba come home to spend a week before they start out again, at such a time when everything talked about in Beckersville is just horses and nothing else and the outfits start out and horse racing is in every breath of air you breathe, Bildad shows up with a job as cook for some outfit. Often when I think about it, his always going all season to the races and working in the livery barn in the winter where horses are and where men like to come and talk about horses, I wish I was a nigger. It's a foolish thing to say, but that's the way I am about being around horses, just crazy. I can't help it.

Well, I must tell you about what we did and let you in on what I'm talking about. Four of us boys from Beckersville, all whites and

sons of men who live in Beckersville regular, made up our minds
we were going to the races, not just to Lexington or Louisville, I
don't mean, but to the big eastern track we were always hearing our
Beckersville men talk about, to Saratoga. We were all pretty young
then. I was just turned fifteen and I was the oldest of the four. It
was my scheme. I admit that and I talked the others into trying it.
There was Hanley Turner and Henry Rieback and Tom Tumberton
and myself. I had thirty-seven dollars I had earned during the
winter working nights and Saturdays in Enoch Myer's grocery.
Henry Rieback had eleven dollars and the others, Hanley and
Tom, had only a dollar or two each. We fixed it all up and laid low
until the Kentucky spring meetings were over and some of our
men, the sportiest ones, the ones we envied the most, had cut out
—then we cut out too.

I won't tell you the trouble we had beating our way on freights
and all. We went through Cleveland and Buffalo and other cities
and saw Niagara Falls. We bought things there, souvenirs and
spoons and cards and shells with pictures of the falls on them for
our sisters and mothers, but thought we had better not send any of
the things home. We didn't want to put the folks on our trail and
maybe be nabbed.

We got into Saratoga as I said at night and went to the track.
Bildad fed us up. He showed us a place to sleep in hay over a shed
and promised to keep still. Niggers are all right about things like
that. They won't squeal on you. Often a white man you might meet,
when you had run away from home like that, might appear to be
all right and give you a quarter or a half dollar or something, and
then go right and give you away. White men will do that, but not a
nigger. You can trust them. They are squarer with kids. I don't
know why.

At the Saratoga meeting that year there were a lot of men from
home. Dave Williams and Arthur Mulford and Jerry Myers and
others. Then there was a lot from Louisville and Lexington Henry
Rieback knew but I didn't. They were professional gamblers and
Henry Rieback's father is one too. He is what is called a sheet writer
and goes away most of the year to tracks. In the winter when he
is home in Beckersville he don't stay there much but goes away to
cities and deals faro. He is a nice man and generous, is always sending Henry presents, a bicycle and a gold watch and a boy scout
suit of clothes and things like that.

My own father is a lawyer. He's all right, but don't make much

money and can't buy me things and anyway I'm getting so old now
I don't expect it. He never said nothing to me against Henry, but
Hanley Turner and Tom Tumberton's fathers did. They said to
their boys that money so come by is no good and they didn't want
their boys brought up to hear gamblers' talk and be thinking about
such things and maybe embrace them.

That's all right and I guess the men know what they are talking
about, but I don't see what it's got to do with Henry or with horses
either. That's what I'm writing this story about. I'm puzzled. I'm
getting to be a man and want to think straight and be O. K., and
there's something I saw at the race meeting at the eastern track I
can't figure out.

I can't help it, I'm crazy about thoroughbred horses. I've always
been that way. When I was ten years old and saw I was growing to
be big and couldn't be a rider I was so sorry I nearly died. Harry
Hellinfinger in Beckersville, whose father is Postmaster, is grown up
and too lazy to work, but likes to stand around in the street and
get up jokes on boys like sending them to a hardware store for a
gimlet to bore square holes and other jokes like that. He played one
on me. He told me that if I would eat a half a cigar I would be
stunted and not grow any more and maybe could be a rider. I did
it. When father wasn't looking I took a cigar out of his pocket and
gagged it down some way. It made me awful sick and the doctor
had to be sent for, and then it did no good. I kept right on growing.
It was a joke. When I told what I had done and why most fathers
would have whipped me but mine didn't.

Well, I didn't get stunted and didn't die. It serves Harry Hellinfinger right. Then I made up my mind I would like to be a stable
boy, but had to give that up too. Mostly niggers do that work and
I knew father wouldn't let me go into it. No use to ask him.

If you've never been crazy about thoroughbreds it's because
you've never been around where they are much and don't know
any better. They're beautiful. There isn't anything so lovely and
clean and full of spunk and honest and everything as some race
horses. On the big horse farms that are all around our town
Beckersville there are tracks and the horses run in the early
morning. More than a thousand times I've got out of bed before
daylight and walked two or three miles to the tracks. Mother
wouldn't of let me go but father always says, "Let him alone."
So I got some bread out of the bread box and some butter and jam,
gobbled it and lit out.

At the tracks you sit on the fence with men, whites and niggers, and they chew tobacco and talk, and then the colts are brought out. It's early and the grass is covered with shiny dew and in another field a man is plowing and they are frying things in a shed where the track niggers sleep, and you know how a nigger can giggle and laugh and say things that make you laugh. A white man can't do it and some niggers can't but a track nigger can every time.

And so the colts are brought out and some are just galloped by stable boys, but almost every morning on a big track owned by a rich man who lives maybe in New York, there are always, nearly every morning, a few colts and some of the old race horses and geldings and mares that are cut loose.

It brings a lump up into my throat when a horse runs. I don't mean all horses but some. I can pick them nearly every time. It's in my blood like in the blood of race track niggers and trainers. Even when they just go slop-jogging along with a little nigger on their backs I can tell a winner. If my throat hurts and it's hard for me to swallow, that's him. He'll run like Sam Hill when you let him out. If he don't win every time it'll be a wonder and because they've got him in a pocket behind another or he was pulled or got off bad at the post or something. If I wanted to be a gambler like Henry Rieback's father I could get rich. I know I could and Henry says so too. All I would have to do is to wait 'til that hurt comes when I see a horse and then bet every cent. That's what I would do if I wanted to be a gambler, but I don't.

When you're at the tracks in the morning—not the race tracks but the training tracks around Beckersville—you don't see a horse, the kind I've been talking about, very often, but it's nice anyway. Any thoroughbred, that is sired right and out of a good mare and trained by a man that knows how, can run. If he couldn't what would he be there for and not pulling a plow?

Well, out of the stables they come and the boys are on their backs and it's lovely to be there. You hunch down on top of the fence and itch inside you. Over in the sheds the niggers giggle and sing. Bacon is being fried and coffee made. Everything smells lovely. Nothing smells better than coffee and manure and horses and niggers and bacon frying and pipes being smoked out of doors on a morning like that. It just gets you, that's what it does.

But about Saratoga. We was there six days and not a soul from home seen us and everything came off just as we wanted it to, fine weather and horses and races and all. We beat our way home and Bildad gave us a basket with fried chicken and bread and other eatables in, and I had eighteen dollars when we got back to Beckersville. Mother jawed and cried but Pop didn't say much. I told everything we done except one thing. I did and saw that alone. That's what I'm writing about. It got me upset. I think about it at night. Here it is.

At Saratoga we laid up nights in the hay in the shed Bildad had showed us and ate with the niggers early and at night when the race people had all gone away. The men from home stayed mostly in the grandstand and betting field, and didn't come out around the places where the horses are kept except to the paddocks just before a race when the horses are saddled. At Saratoga they don't have paddocks under an open shed as at Lexington and Churchill Downs and other tracks down in our country, but saddle the horses right out in an open place under trees on a lawn as smooth and nice as Banker Bohon's front yard here in Beckersville. It's lovely. The horses are sweaty and nervous and shine and the men come out and smoke cigars and look at them and the trainers are there and the owners, and your heart thumps so you can hardly breathe. Then the bugle blows for post and the boys that ride come running out with their silk clothes on and you run to get a place by the fence with the niggers.

I always am wanting to be a trainer or owner, and at the risk of being seen and caught and sent home I went to the paddocks before every race. The other boys didn't but I did.

We got to Saratoga on a Friday and on Wednesday the next week the big Mullford Handicap was to be run. Middlestride was in it and Sunstreak. The weather was fine and the track fast. I couldn't sleep the night before.

What had happened was that both these horses are the kind it makes my throat hurt to see. Middlestride is long and looks awkward and is a gelding. He belongs to Joe Thompson, a little owner from home who only has a half dozen horses. The Mullford Handicap is for a mile and Middlestride can't untrack fast. He goes away slow and is always way back at the half, then he begins to run and if the race is a mile and a quarter he'll just eat up everything and get there.

Sunstreak is different. He is a stallion and nervous and belongs on the biggest farm we've got in our country, the Van Riddle place that belongs to Mr. Van Riddle of New York. Sunstreak is like a girl you think about sometimes but never see. He is hard all over and lovely too. When you look at his head you want to kiss him. He is trained by Jerry Tillford who knows me and has been good to me lots of times, lets me walk into a horse's stall to look at him close and other things. There isn't anything as sweet as that horse. He stands at the post quiet and not letting on, but he is just burning up inside. Then when the barrier goes up he is off like his name, Sunstreak. It makes you ache to see him. It hurts you. He just lays down and runs like a bird dog. There can't anything I ever see run like him except Middlestride when he gets untracked and stretches himself.

Gee! I ached to see that race and those two horses run, ached and dreaded it too. I didn't want to see either of our horses beaten. We had never sent a pair like that to the races before. Old men in Beckersville said so and the niggers said so. It was a fact.

Before the race I went over to the paddocks to see. I looked a last look at Middlestride, who isn't such a much standing in a paddock that way, then I went to see Sunstreak.

It was his day. I knew when I see him. I forgot all about being seen myself and walked right up. All the men from Beckersville were there and no one noticed me except Jerry Tillford. He saw me and something happened. I'll tell you about that.

I was standing looking at that horse and aching. In some way, I can't tell how, I knew just how Sunstreak felt inside. He was quiet and letting the niggers rub his legs and Mr. Van Riddle himself put the saddle on, but he was just a raging torrent inside. He was like the water in the river at Niagara Falls just before it goes plunk down. That horse wasn't thinking about running. He don't have to think about that. He was just thinking about holding himself back 'til the time for the running came. I knew that. I could just in a way see right inside him. He was going to do some awful running and I knew it. He wasn't bragging or letting on much or prancing or making a fuss, but just waiting. I knew it and Jerry Tillford his trainer knew. I looked up and then that man and I looked into each other's eyes. Something happened to me. I guess I loved the man as much as I did the horse because he knew what I knew. Seemed to me there wasn't anything in the world but that man and the horse and me. I cried and Jerry Tillford had a shine in his eyes. Then I came away to the fence to wait for the race. The horse was better than me, more steadier, and now I know better than Jerry. He was the quietest and he had to do the running.

Sunstreak ran first of course and he busted the world's record for a mile. I've seen that if I never see anything more. Everything came out just as I expected. Middlestride got left at the post and was way back and closed up to be second, just as I knew he would. He'll get a world's record too some day. They can't skin the Beckersville country on horses.

I watched the race calm because I knew what would happen. I was sure. Hanley Turner and Henry Rieback and Tom Tumberton were all more excited than me.

A funny thing had happened to me. I was thinking about Jerry Tillford the trainer and how happy he was all through the race. I liked him that afternoon even more than I ever liked my own father. I almost forgot the horses thinking that way about him. It was because of what I had seen in his eyes as he stood in the paddocks beside Sunstreak before the race started. I knew he had been watching and working with Sunstreak since the horse was a baby colt, had taught him to run and be patient and when to let himself out and not to quit, never. I knew that for him it was like a mother seeing her child do something brave or wonderful. It was the first time I ever felt for a man like that.

After the race that night I cut out from Tom and Hanley and Henry. I wanted to be by myself and I wanted to be near Jerry Tillford if I could work it. Here is what happened.

The track in Saratoga is near the edge of town. It is all polished up and trees around, the evergreen kind, and grass and everything painted and nice. If you go past the track you get to a hard road made of asphalt for automobiles, and if you go along this for a few miles there is a road turns off to a little rummy-looking farm house set in a yard.

That night after the race I went along that road because I had seen Jerry and some other men go that way in an automobile. I didn't expect to find them. I walked for a ways and then sat down by a fence to think. It was the direction they went in. I wanted to be as near Jerry as I could. I felt close to him. Pretty soon I went up the side road—I don't know why—and came to the rummy farm house. I was just lonesome to see Jerry, like wanting to see your father at night when you are a young kid. Just then an automobile came along and turned in. Jerry was in it and Henry

Rieback's father, and Arthur Bedford from home, and Dave Williams and two other men I didn't know. They got out of the car and went into the house, all but Henry Rieback's father who quarreled with them and said he wouldn't go. It was only about nine o'clock, but they were all drunk and the rummy looking farm house was a place for bad women to stay in. That's what it was. I crept up along a fence and looked through a window and saw.

It's what give me the fantods. I can't make it out. The women in the house were all ugly mean-looking women, not nice to look at or be near. They were homely too, except one who was tall and looked a little like the gelding Middlestride, but not clean like him, but with a hard ugly mouth. She had red hair. I saw everything plain. I got up by an old rose bush by an open window and looked. The women had on loose dresses and sat around in chairs. The men came in and some sat on the women's laps. The place smelled rotten and there was rotten talk, the kind a kid hears around a livery stable in a town like Beckersville in the winter but don't ever expect to hear talked when there are women around. It was rotten. A nigger wouldn't go into such a place.

I looked at Jerry Tillford. I've told you how I had been feeling about him on account of his knowing what was going on inside of Sunstreak in the minute before he went to the post for the race in which he made a world's record.

Jerry bragged in that bad woman house as I know Sunstreak wouldn't never have bragged. He said that he made that horse, that it was him that won the race and made the record. He lied and bragged like a fool. I never heard such silly talk.

And then, what do you suppose he did! He looked at the woman in there, the one that was lean and hard-mouthed and looked a little like the gelding Middlestride, but not clean like him, and his eyes began to shine just as they did when he looked at me and at Sunstreak in the paddocks at the track in the afternoon. I stood there by the window—gee!—but I wished I hadn't gone away from the tracks, but had stayed with the boys and the niggers and the horses. The tall rotten looking woman was between us just as Sunstreak was in the paddocks in the afternoon.

Then, all of a sudden, I began to hate that man. I wanted to scream and rush in the room and kill him. I never had such a feeling before. I was so mad clean through that I cried and my fists were doubled up so my finger nails cut my hands.

And Jerry's eyes kept shining and he waved back and forth, and then he went and kissed that woman and I crept away and went back to the tracks and to bed and didn't sleep hardly any, and then next day I got the other kids to start home with me and never told them anything I seen.

I been thinking about it ever since. I can't make it out. Spring has come again and I'm nearly sixteen and go to the tracks mornings same as always, and I see Sunstreak and Middlestride and a new colt named Strident I'll bet will lay them all out, but no one thinks so but me and two or three niggers.

But things are different. At the tracks the air don't taste as good or smell as good. It's because a man like Jerry Tillford, who knows what he does, could see a horse like Sunstreak run, and kiss a woman like that the same day. I can't make it out. Darn him, what did he want to do like that for? I keep thinking about it and it spoils looking at horses and smelling things and hearing niggers laugh and everything. Sometimes I'm so mad about it I want to fight someone. It gives me the fantods. What did he do it for? I want to know why.

The
New Englander

SHERWOOD ANDERSON

When, early in the story, the Leanders leave New England in April for the West, the reader will find confirmed what he may only have suspected from the preceding pages—that Elsie's life is to be represented not as realistically complex but as mythically simple. The myth which Elsie reenacts is that of the American who journeys westward toward open experience, fresh beginnings, and renewal in nature. Anderson's chief innovation on this familiar voyage lies in his having transformed it into an erotic awakening for his protagonist, who abandons a Vermont landscape of rocks and infertile soil for an Iowa landscape where men plough their fields and tall corn grows—a landscape crowded with creatures and objects that proclaim her quickening desire for sexual fulfillment.

Her name was Elsie Leander and her girlhood was spent on her father's farm in Vermont. For several generations the Leanders had all lived on the same farm and had all married thin women, and so she was thin. The farm lay in the shadow of a mountain and the soil was not very rich. From the beginning and for several generations there had been a great many sons and few daughters in the family. The sons had gone west or to New York City and the daughters had stayed at home and thought such thoughts as come to New England women who see the sons of their fathers' neighbors slipping away, one by one, into the West.

Her father's house was a small white frame affair and when you went out at the back door, past a small barn and chicken house, you got into a path that ran up the side of a hill and into an orchard. The trees were all old and gnarled. At the back of the orchard the hill dropped away and bare rocks showed.

Inside the fence a large grey rock stuck high up out of the ground. As Elsie sat with her back to the rock, with a mangled hillside at her feet, she could see several large mountains, apparently but a short distance away, and between herself and the mountains lay many tiny fields surrounded by neatly built stone walls. Everywhere rocks appeared. Large ones, too heavy to be moved, stuck out of the ground in the centre of the fields. The fields were like cups filled with a green liquid that turned grey in the fall and white in the winter. The mountains, far off but apparently near at hand, were like giants ready at any moment to reach out their hands and take the cups one by one and drink off the green liquid. The large rocks in the fields were like the thumbs of the giants.

Elsie had three brothers, born before her, but they had all gone away. Two of them had gone to live with her uncle in the West and her oldest brother had gone to New York City where he had married and prospered. All through his youth and manhood her father had worked hard and had lived a hard life, but his son in New York City had begun to send money home, and after that things went better. He still worked every day about the barn or in the fields but he did not worry about the future. Elsie's mother did

From *The Triumph of the Egg* by Sherwood Anderson, published by B. W. Huebsch, Inc., 1921. Copyright 1921 by Eleanor Anderson. Renewed. Reprinted by permission of Harold Ober Associates Inc.

house work in the mornings and in the afternoons sat in a rocking chair in her tiny living room and thought of her sons while she crocheted table covers and tidies for the backs of chairs. She was a silent woman, very thin and with very thin bony hands. She did not ease herself into a rocking chair but sat down and got up suddenly, and when she crocheted her back was as straight as the back of a drill sergeant.

The mother rarely spoke to the daughter. Sometimes in the afternoons as the younger woman went up the hillside to her place by the rock at the back of the orchard, her father came out of the barn and stopped her. He put a hand on her shoulder and asked her where she was going. "To the rock," she said and her father laughed. His laughter was like the creaking of a rusty barn door hinge and the hand he had laid on her shoulders was thin like her own hands and like her mother's hands. The father went into the barn shaking his head. "She's like her mother. She is herself like a rock," he thought. At the head of the path that led from the house to the orchard there was a great cluster of bayberry bushes. The New England farmer came out of his barn to watch his daughter go along the path, but she had disappeared behind the bushes. He looked away past his house to the fields and to the mountains in the distance. He also saw the green cup-like fields and the grim mountains. There was an almost imperceptible tightening of the muscles of his half worn-out old body. For a long time he stood in silence and then, knowing from long experience the danger of having thoughts, he went back into the barn and busied himself with the mending of an agricultural tool that had been mended many times before.

The son of the Leanders who went to live in New York City was the father of one son, a thin sensitive boy who looked like Elsie. The son died when he was twenty-three years old and some years later the father died and left his money to the old people on the New England farm. The two Leanders who had gone west had lived there with their father's brother, a farmer, until they grew into manhood. Then Will, the younger, got a job on a railroad. He was killed one winter morning. It was a cold snowy day and when the freight train he was in charge of as conductor left the city of Des Moines, he started to run over the tops of the cars. His feet slipped and he shot down into space. That was the end of him.

Of the new generation there was only Elsie and her brother

Tom, whom she had never seen, left alive. Her father and mother talked of going west to Tom for two years before they came to a decision. Then it took another year to dispose of the farm and make preparations. During the whole time Elsie did not think much about the change about to take place in her life.

The trip west on the railroad train jolted Elsie out of herself. In spite of her detached attitude toward life she became excited. Her mother sat up very straight and stiff in the seat in the sleeping car and her father walked up and down in the aisle. After a night when the younger of the two women did not sleep but lay awake with red burning cheeks and with her thin fingers incessantly picking at the bed clothes in her berth while the train went through towns and cities, crawled up the sides of hills and fell down into forest-clad valleys, she got up and dressed to sit all day looking at a new kind of land. The train ran for a day and through another sleepless night in a flat land where every field was as large as a farm in her own country. Towns appeared and disappeared in a continual procession. The whole land was so unlike anything she had ever known that she began to feel unlike herself. In the valley where she had been born and where she had lived all her days everything had an air of finality. Nothing could be changed. The tiny fields were chained to the earth. They were fixed in their places and surrounded by aged stone walls. The fields like the mountains that looked down at them were as unchangeable as the passing days. She had a feeling they had always been so, would always be so.

Elsie sat like her mother, upright in the car seat and with a back like the back of a drill sergeant. The train ran swiftly along through Ohio and Indiana. Her thin hands like her mother's hands were crossed and locked. One passing casually through the car might have thought both women prisoners handcuffed and bound to their seats. Night came on and she again got into her berth. Again she lay awake and her thin cheeks became flushed, but she thought new thoughts. Her hands were no longer gripped together and she did not pick at the bed clothes. Twice during the night she stretched herself and yawned, a thing she had never in her life done before. The train stopped at a town on the prairies, and as there was something the matter with one of the wheels of the car in which she lay the trainsmen came with flaming torches to tinker it. There was a great pounding and shouting. When the train went on its way she wanted to get out of her berth and run up and down in the aisle of the car. The fancy had come to her that the men tinkering with the car wheel were new men out of the new land who with strong hammers had broken away the doors of her prison. They had destroyed forever the programme she had made for her life.

Elsie was filled with joy at the thought that the train was still going on into the West. She wanted to go on forever in a straight line into the unknown. She fancied herself no longer on a train and imagined she had become a winged thing flying through space. Her long years of sitting alone by the rock on the New England farm had got her into the habit of expressing her thoughts aloud. Her thin voice broke the silence that lay over the sleeping car and her father and mother, both also lying awake, sat up in their berth to listen.

Tom Leander, the only living male representative of the new generation of Leanders, was a loosely built man of forty inclined to corpulency. At twenty he had married the daughter of a neighboring farmer, and when his wife inherited some money she and Tom moved into the town of Apple Junction in Iowa where Tom opened a grocery. The venture prospered as did Tom's matrimonial venture. When his brother died in New York City and his father, mother, and sister decided to come west Tom was already the father of a daughter and four sons.

On the prairies north of town and in the midst of a vast level stretch of corn fields, there was a partly completed brick house that had belonged to a rich farmer named Russell who had begun to build the house intending to make it the most magnificent place in the county, but when it was almost completed he had found himself without money and heavily in debt. The farm, consisting of several hundred acres of corn land, had been split into three farms and sold. No one had wanted the huge unfinished brick house. For years it had stood vacant, its windows staring out over the fields that had been planted almost up to the door.

In buying the Russell house Tom was moved by two motives. He had a notion that in New England the Leanders had been rather magnificent people. His memory of his father's place in the Vermont valley was shadowy, but in speaking of it to his wife he became very definite. "We had good blood in us, we Leanders," he said, straightening his shoulders. "We lived in a big house. We were important people."

Wanting his father and mother to feel at home in the new place,

Tom had also another motive. He was not a very energetic man and, although he had done well enough as keeper of a grocery, his success was largely due to the boundless energy of his wife. She did not pay much attention to her household and her children, like little animals, had to take care of themselves, but in any matter concerning the store her word was law.

To have his father the owner of the Russell place Tom felt would establish him as a man of consequence in the eyes of his neighbors. "I can tell you what, they're used to a big house," he said to his wife. "I tell you what, my people are used to living in style."

The exaltation that had come over Elsie on the train wore away in the presence of the grey empty Iowa fields, but something of the effect of it remained with her for months. In the big brick house life went on much as it had in the tiny New England house where she had always lived. The Leanders installed themselves in three or four rooms on the ground floor. After a few weeks the furniture that had been shipped by freight arrived and was hauled out from town in one of Tom's grocery wagons. There were three or four acres of ground covered with great piles of boards the unsuccessful farmer had intended to use in the building of stables. Tom sent men to haul the boards away and Elsie's father prepared to plant a garden. They had come west in April and as soon as they were installed in the house ploughing and planting began in the fields nearby. The habit of a lifetime returned to the daughter of the house. In the new place there was no gnarled orchard surrounded by a half-ruined stone fence. All of the fences in all of the fields that stretched away out of sight to the north, south, east, and west were made of wire and looked like spider webs against the blackness of the ground when it had been freshly ploughed.

There was however the house itself. It was like an island rising out of the sea. In an odd way the house, although it was less than ten years old, was very old. Its unnecessary bigness represented an old impulse in men. Elsie felt that. At the east side there was a door leading to a stairway that ran into the upper part of the house that was kept locked. Two or three stone steps led up to it. Elsie could sit on the top step with her back against the door and gaze into the distance without being disturbed. Almost at her feet began the fields that seemed to go on and on forever. The fields were like the waters of a sea. Men came to plough and plant. Giant horses moved in a procession across the prairies. A young man who drove six horses came directly toward her. She was fascinated. The breasts of the horses as they came forward with bowed heads seemed like the breasts of giants. The soft spring air that lay over the fields was also like a sea. The horses were giants walking on the floor of a sea. With their breasts they pushed the waters of the sea before them. They were pushing the waters out of the basin of the sea. The young man who drove them also was a giant.

Elsie pressed her body against the closed door at the top of the steps. In the garden back of the house she could hear her father at work. He was raking dry masses of weeds off the ground preparatory to spading it for a family garden. He had always worked in a tiny confined place and would do the same thing here. In this vast open place he would work with small tools, doing little things with infinite care, raising little vegetables. In the house her mother would crochet little tidies. She herself would be small. She would press her body against the door of the house, try to get herself out of sight. Only the feeling that sometimes took possession of her, and that did not form itself into a thought, would be large.

The six horses turned at the fence and the outside horse got entangled in the traces. The driver swore vigorously. Then he turned and started at the pale New Englander and with another oath pulled the heads of the horses about and drove away into the distance. The field in which he was ploughing contained two hundred acres. Elsie did not wait for him to return but went into the house and sat with folded arms in a room. The house she thought was a ship floating in a sea on the floor of which giants went up and down.

May came and then June. In the great fields work was always going on and Elsie became somewhat used to the sight of the young man in the field that came down to the steps. Sometimes when he drove his horses down to the wire fence he smiled and nodded.

In the month of August, when it is very hot, the corn in Iowa fields grows until the corn stalks resemble young trees. The corn fields become forests. The time for the cultivating of the corn has passed and weeds grow thick between the corn rows. The men with their giant horses have gone away. Over the immense fields silence broods.

When the time of the laying-by of the crop came that first summer after Elsie's arrival in the West her mind, partially awakened by the strangeness of the railroad trip, awakened again. She did not feel like a staid thin woman with a back like the back of a drill sergeant, but like something new and as strange as the new land into which she had come to live. For a time she did not know what was the matter. In the field the corn had grown so high that she could not see into the distance. The corn was like a wall and the little bare spot of land on which her father's house stood was like a house built behind the walls of a prison. For a time she was depressed, thinking that she had come west into a wide open country, only to find herself locked up more closely than ever.

An impulse came to her. She arose and going down three or four steps seated herself almost on a level with the ground.

Immediately she got a sense of release. She could not see over the corn but she could see under it. The corn had long wide leaves that met over the rows. The rows became long tunnels running away into infinity. Out of the black ground grew weeds that made a soft carpet of green. From above light sifted down. The corn rows were mysteriously beautiful. They were warm passageways running out into life. She got up from the steps and, walking timidly to the wire fence that separated her from the field, put her hand between the wires and took hold of one of the corn stalks. For some reason after she had touched the strong young stalk and had held it for a moment firmly in her hand she grew afraid. Running quickly back to the step she sat down and covered her face with her hands. Her body trembled. She tried to imagine herself crawling through the fence and wandering along one of the passageways. The thought of trying the experiment fascinated but at the same time terrified. She got quickly up and went into the house.

One Saturday night in August Elsie found herself unable to sleep. Thoughts, more definite than any she had ever known before, came into her mind. It was a quiet hot night and her bed stood near a window. Her room was the only one the Leanders occupied on the second floor of the house. At midnight a little breeze came up from the south and when she sat up in bed the floor of corn tassels lying below her line of sight looked in the moonlight like the face of a sea just stirred by a gentle breeze.

A murmuring began in the corn and murmuring thoughts and memories awoke in her mind. The long wide succulent leaves had begun to dry in the intense heat of the August days and as the wind stirred the corn they rubbed against each other. A call, far away, as of a thousand voices arose. She imagined the voices were like the voices of children. They were not like her brother Tom's children, noisy boisterous little animals, but something quite different, tiny little things with large eyes and thin sensitive hands. One after another they crept into her arms. She became so excited over the fancy that she sat up in bed and taking a pillow into her arms held it against her breast. The figure of her cousin, the pale sensitive young Leander who had lived with his father in New York City and who had died at the age of twenty-three, came into her mind. It was as though the young man had come suddenly into the room. She dropped the pillow and sat waiting, intense, expectant.

Young Harry Leander had come to visit his cousin on the New England farm during the late summer of the year before he died. He had stayed there for a month and almost every afternoon had gone with Elsie to sit by the rock at the back of the orchard. One afternoon when they had both been for a long time silent he began to talk. "I want to go live in the West," he said. "I want to go live in the West. I want to grow strong and be a man," he repeated. Tears came into his eyes.

They got up to return to the house, Elsie walking in silence beside the young man. The moment marked a high spot in her life. A strange trembling eagerness for something she had not realized in her experience of life had taken possession of her. They went in silence through the orchard but when they came to the bayberry bush her cousin stopped in the path and turned to face her. "I want you to kiss me," he said eagerly, stepping toward her.

A fluttering uncertainty had taken possession of Elsie and had been transmitted to her cousin. After he had made the sudden and unexpected demand and had stepped so close to her that his breath could be felt on her cheek, his own cheeks became scarlet and his hand that had taken her hand trembled. "Well, I wish I were strong. I only wish I were strong," he said hesitatingly and turning walked away along the path toward the house.

And in the strange new house, set like an island in its sea of corn, Harry Leander's voice seemed to arise again above the fancied voices of the children that had been coming out of the fields. Elsie got out of bed and walked up and down in the dim light coming through the window. Her body trembled violently. "I want you to kiss me," the voice said again and to quiet it and to quiet also the answering voice in herself she went to kneel by the bed and taking the pillow again into her arms pressed it against her face.

Tom Leander came with his wife and family to visit his father and mother on Sundays. The family appeared at about ten o'clock in the morning. When the wagon turned out of the road that ran past the Russell place Tom shouted. There was a field between the house and the road and the wagon could not be seen as it came along the narrow way through the corn. After Tom had shouted, his daughter Elizabeth, a tall girl of sixteen, jumped out of the wagon. All five children came tearing toward the house through the corn. A series of wild shouts arose on the still morning air.

The groceryman had brought food from the store. When the horse had been unhitched and put into a shed he and his wife began to carry packages into the house. The four Leander boys, accompanied by their sister, disappeared into the near-by fields. Three dogs that had trotted out from town under the wagon accompanied the children. Two or three children and occasionally a young man from a neighboring farm had come to join in the fun. Elsie's sister-in-law dismissed them all with a wave of her hand. With a wave of her hand she also brushed Elsie aside. Fires were lighted and the house reeked with the smell of cooking. Elsie went to sit on the step at the side of the house. The corn fields that had been so quiet rang with shouts and with the barking of dogs.

Tom Leander's oldest child, Elizabeth, was like her mother, full of energy. She was thin and tall like the women of her father's house but very strong and alive. In secret she wanted to be a lady but when she tried her brothers, led by her father and mother, made fun of her. "Don't put on airs," they said. When she got into the country with no one but her brothers and two or three neighboring farm boys she herself became a boy. With the boys she went tearing through the fields, following the dogs in pursuit of rabbits. Sometimes a young man came with the children from a near-by farm. Then she did not know what to do with herself. She wanted to walk demurely along the rows through the corn but was afraid her brothers would laugh and in desperation outdid the boys in roughness and noisiness. She screamed and shouted and running wildly tore her dress on the wire fences as she scrambled over in pursuit of the dogs. When a rabbit was caught and killed she rushed in and tore it out of the grasp of the dogs. The blood of the little dying animal dripped on her clothes. She swung it over her head and shouted.

The farm hand who had worked all summer in the field within sight of Elsie became enamoured of the young woman from town. When the groceryman's family appeared on Sunday mornings he also appeared but did not come to the house. When the boys and dogs came tearing through the fields he joined them. He also was self-conscious and did not want the boys to know the purpose of his coming and when he and Elizabeth found themselves alone together he became embarrassed. For a moment they walked together in silence. In a wide circle about them, in the forest of the corn, ran the boys and dogs. The young man had something he wanted to say, but when he tried to find words his tongue became thick and his lips felt hot and dry. "Well," he began, "let's you and me——"

Words failed him and Elizabeth turned and ran after her brothers and for the rest of the day he could not manage to get her out of their sight. When he went to join them she became the noisiest member of the party. A frenzy of activity took possession of her. With hair hanging down her back, with clothes torn and with cheeks and hands scratched and bleeding she led her brothers in the endless wild pursuit of the rabbits.

The Sunday in August that followed Elsie Leander's sleepless night was hot and cloudy. In the morning she was half ill and as soon as the visitors from town arrived she crept away to sit on the step at the side of the house. The children ran away into the fields. An almost overpowering desire to run with them, shouting and playing along the corn rows took possession of her. She arose and went to the back of the house. Her father was at work in the garden, pulling weeds from between rows of vegetables. Inside the house she could hear her sister-in-law moving about. On the front porch her brother Tom was asleep with his mother beside him. Elsie went back to the step and then arose and went to where the corn came down to the fence. She climbed awkwardly over and went a little way along one of the rows. Putting out her hand she touched the firm stalks and then, becoming afraid, dropped to her knees on the carpet of weeds that covered the ground. For a long time she stayed thus listening to the voices of the children in the distance.

An hour slipped away. Presently it was time for dinner and her sister-in-law came to the back door and shouted. There was an answering whoop from the distance and the children came running through the fields. They climbed over the fence and ran shouting across her father's garden. Elsie also arose. She was about to attempt to climb back over the fence unobserved when she heard a rustling in the corn. Young Elizabeth Leander appeared. Beside her walked the ploughman who but a few months earlier had planted the corn in the field where Elsie now stood. She could see the two people coming slowly along the rows. An understanding had been established between them. The man reached through between the corn stalks and touched the hand of the girl who laughed awkwardly and running to the fence climbed quickly over. In her hand she held the limp body of a rabbit the dogs had killed.

The farm hand went away and when Elizabeth had gone into the house Elsie climbed over the fence. Her niece stood just within the kitchen door holding the dead rabbit by one leg. The other leg had been torn away by the dogs. At sight of the New England woman, who seemed to look at her with hard unsympathetic eyes, she was ashamed and went quickly into the house. She threw the rabbit upon a table in the parlor and then ran out of the room. Its blood ran out on the delicate flowers of a white crocheted table cover that had been made by Elsie's mother.

The Sunday dinner with all the living Leanders gathered about the table was gone through in a heavy lumbering silence. When the dinner was over and Tom and his wife had washed the dishes they went to sit with the older people on the front porch. Presently they were both asleep. Elsie returned to the step at the side of the house but when the desire to go again into the cornfields came sweeping over her she got up and went indoors.

The woman of thirty-five tip-toed about the big house like a frightened child. The dead rabbit that lay on the table in the parlor had become cold and stiff. Its blood had dried on the white table cover. She went upstairs but did not go to her own room. A spirit of adventure had hold of her. In the upper part of the house there were many rooms and in some of them no glass had been put into the windows. The windows had been boarded up and narrow streaks of light crept in through the cracks between the boards.

Elsie tip-toed up the flight of stairs past the room in which she slept and opening doors went into other rooms. Dust lay thick on the floors. In the silence she could hear her brother snoring as he slept in the chair on the front porch. From what seemed a far away place there came the shrill cries of the children. The cries became soft. They were like the cries of unborn children that had called to her out of the fields on the night before.

Into her mind came the intense silent figure of her mother sitting on the porch beside her son and waiting for the day to wear itself out into night. The thought brought a lump into her throat. She wanted something and did not know what it was. Her own mood frightened her. In a windowless room at the back of the house one of the boards over a window had been broken and a bird had flown in and become imprisoned.

The presence of the woman frightened the bird. It flew wildly about. Its beating wings stirred up dust that danced in the air. Elsie stood perfectly still, also frightened, not by the presence of the bird but by the presence of life. Like the bird she was a prisoner. The thought gripped her. She wanted to go outdoors where her niece Elizabeth walked with the young ploughman through the corn, but was like the bird in the room—a prisoner. She moved restlessly about. The bird flew back and forth across the room. It alighted on the window sill near the place where the board was broken away. She stared into the frightened eyes of the bird that in turn stared into her eyes. Then the bird flew away, out through the window, and Elsie turned and ran nervously downstairs and out into the yard. She climbed over the wire fence and ran with stooped shoulders along one of the tunnels.

Elsie ran into the vastness of the cornfields filled with but one desire. She wanted to get out of her life and into some new and sweeter life she felt must be hidden away somewhere in the fields. After she had run a long way she came to a wire fence and crawled over. Her hair became unloosed and fell down over her shoulders. Her cheeks became flushed and for the moment she looked like a young girl. When she climbed over the fence she tore a great hole in the front of her dress. For a moment her tiny breasts were exposed and then her hand clutched and held nervously the sides of the tear. In the distance she could hear the voices of the boys and the barking of the dogs. A summer storm had been threatening for days and now black clouds had begun to spread themselves over the sky. As she ran nervously forward, stopping to listen and then running on again, the dry corn blades brushed against her shoulders and a fine shower of yellow dust from the corn tassels fell on her hair. A continued crackling noise accompanied her progress. The dust made a golden crown about her head. From the sky overhead a low rumbling sound, like the growling of giant dogs, came to her ears.

The thought that having at last ventured into the corn she would never escape became fixed in the mind of the running woman. Sharp pains shot through her body. Presently she was compelled to stop and sit on the ground. For a long time she sat with closed eyes. Her dress became soiled. Little insects that live in the ground under the corn came out of their holes and crawled over her legs.

Following some obscure impulse the tired woman threw herself on her back and lay still with closed eyes. Her fright passed. It was warm and close in the roomlike tunnels. The pain in her side went away. She opened her eyes and between the wide green corn blades could see patches of a black threatening sky. She did not want to be alarmed and so closed her eyes again. Her thin hand no longer gripped the tear in her dress and her little breasts were exposed. They expanded and contracted in spasmodic jerks. She threw her hands back over her head and lay still.

It seemed to Elsie that hours passed as she lay thus, quiet and passive under the corn. Deep within her there was a feeling that something was about to happen, something that would lift her out of herself, that would tear her away from her past and the past of her people. Her thoughts were not definite. She lay still and waited as she had waited for days and months by the rock at the back of the orchard on the Vermont farm when she was a girl. A deep grumbling noise went on in the sky overhead but the sky and everything she had ever known seemed very far away, no part of herself.

After a long silence, when it seemed to her that she had gone out of herself as in a dream, Elsie heard a man's voice calling. "Aho, aho, aho," shouted the voice and after another period of silence there arose answering voices and then the sound of bodies crashing through the corn and the excited chatter of children. A dog came running along the row where she lay and stood beside her. His cold nose touched her face and she sat up. The dog ran away. The Leander boys passed. She could see their bare legs flashing in and out across one of the tunnels. Her brother had become alarmed by the rapid approach of the thunder storm and wanted to get his family to town. His voice kept calling from the house and the voices of the children answered from the fields.

Elsie sat on the ground with her hands pressed together. An odd feeling of disappointment had possession of her. She arose and walked slowly along in the general direction taken by the children. She came to a fence and crawled over, tearing her dress in a new place. One of her stockings had become unloosed and had slipped down over her shoe top. The long sharp weeds had scratched her leg so that it was criss-crossed with red lines, but she was not conscious of any pain.

The distraught woman followed the children until she came within sight of her father's house and then stopped and again sat on the ground. There was another loud crash of thunder and Tom Leander's voice called again, this time half angrily. The name of the girl Elizabeth was shouted in loud masculine tones that rolled and echoed like the thunder along the aisles under the corn.

And then Elizabeth came into sight accompanied by the young ploughman. They stopped near Elsie and the man took the girl into his arms. At the sound of their approach Elsie had thrown herself face downward on the ground and had twisted herself into a position where she could see without being seen. When their lips met her tense hands grasped one of the corn stalks. Her lips pressed themselves into the dust. When they had gone on their way she raised her head. A dusty powder covered her lips.

What seemed another long period of silence fell over the fields. The murmuring voices of unborn children, her imagination had created in the whispering fields, became a vast shout. The wind blew harder and harder. The corn stalks were twisted and bent. Elizabeth went thoughtfully out of the field and climbing the fence confronted her father. "Where you been? What you been a doing?" he asked. "Don't you think we got to get out of here?"

When Elizabeth went toward the house Elsie followed, creeping on her hands and knees like a little animal, and when she had come within sight of the fence surrounding the house she sat on the ground and put her hands over her face. Something within herself was being twisted and whirled about as the tops of the corn stalks were now being twisted and whirled by the wind. She sat so that she did not look toward the house and when she opened her eyes she could again see along the long mysterious aisles.

Her brother with his wife and children went away. By turning her head Elsie could see them driving at a trot out of the yard back of her father's house. With the going of the younger woman the farm house in the midst of the cornfield rocked by the winds seemed the most desolate place in the world.

Her mother came out at the back door of the house. She ran to the steps where she knew her daughter was in the habit of sitting and then in alarm began to call. It did not occur to Elsie to answer. The voice of the older woman did not seem to have anything to do with herself. It was a thin voice and was quickly lost in the wind and in the crashing sound that arose out of the fields. With her head turned toward the house Elsie stared at her mother who ran wildly around the house and then went indoors. The back door of the house went shut with a bang.

The storm that had been threatening broke with a roar. Broad sheets of water swept over the cornfields. Sheets of water swept over the woman's body. The storm that had for years been gathering in her also broke. Sobs arose out of her throat. She abandoned herself to a storm of grief that was only partially grief. Tears ran out of her eyes and made little furrows through the dust on her face. In the lulls that occasionally came in the storm she raised her head and heard, through the tangled mass of wet hair that covered her ears and above the sound of millions of rain-drops that alighted on the earthen floor inside the house of the corn, the thin voices of her mother and father calling to her out of the Leander house.

Miss Furr and Miss Skeene

GERTRUDE STEIN

Like Czerny exercises for the piano, this work seems designed less for an audience than for the composer, or for performers wanting to develop their technique or get their fingers in shape before going onstage. A virtuoso piece, though, rather than simply an exercise, "Miss Furr and Miss Skeene" demonstrates superbly how inextricable a writer's representation of experience is from the syntactical patterns and other rhythms of language itself, its degrees of precision and flexibility, its modulations of tone, its encrustations over years or centuries of emotional charge and implication, and, finally, the writer's individual and partly arbitrary manipulation of all these resources of language on a given occasion. The piece demonstrates, at the same time, that a writer's use of language can never be wholly arbitrary, that implicit in words to which a reader responds is a recognition of some reality external to the perceiving mind and therefore to language. As demonstrably real things, Miss Furr, Miss Skeene, Miss Furr's voice and home, Mr. Furr, the "little things" they learned, and other "experiences" within this story have only the most tenuous existence. Yet they are in fact assumed to have some discernible status in time and place, to provide an objective world to which the language of the piece is also addressed.

Helen Furr had quite a pleasant home. Mrs. Furr was quite a pleasant woman. Mr. Furr was quite a pleasant man. Helen Furr had quite a pleasant voice a voice quite worth cultivating. She did not mind working. She worked to cultivate her voice. She did not find it gay living in the same place where she had always been living. She went to a place where some were cultivating something, voices and other things needing cultivating. She met Georgine Skeene there who was cultivating her voice which some thought was quite a pleasant one. Helen Furr and Georgine Skeene lived together then. Georgine Skeene liked travelling. Helen Furr did not care about travelling, she liked to stay in one place and be gay there. They were together then and travelled to another place and stayed there and were gay there.

They stayed there and were gay there, not very gay there, just gay there. They were both gay there, they were regularly working there both of them cultivating their voices there, they were both gay there. Georgine Skeene was gay there and she was regular, regular in being gay, regular in not being gay, regular in being a gay one who was one not being gay longer than was needed to be one being quite a gay one. They were both gay then there and both working there then.

They were in a way both gay there where there were many cultivating something. They were both regular in being gay there. Helen Furr was gay there, she was gayer and gayer there and really she was just gay there, she was gayer and gayer there, that is to say she found ways of being gay there that she was using in being gay there. She was gay there, not gayer and gayer, just gay there, that is to say she was not gayer by using the things she found there that were gay things, she was gay there, always she was gay there.

They were quite regularly gay there, Helen Furr and Georgine Skeene, they were regularly gay there where they were gay. They were very regularly gay.

To be regularly gay was to do every day the gay thing that they

From *Selected Writings of Gertrude Stein* edited by Carl Van Vechten. Copyright 1922 by The Four Seasons Company. Reprinted by permission of Random House, Inc.

did every day. To be regularly gay was to end every day at the same time after they had been regularly gay. They were regularly gay. They were gay every day. They ended every day in the same way, at the same time, and they had been every day regularly gay.

The voice Helen Furr was cultivating was quite a pleasant one. The voice Georgine Skeene was cultivating was, some said, a better one. The voice Helen Furr was cultivating she cultivated and it was quite completely a pleasant enough one then, a cultivated enough one then. The voice Georgine Skeene was cultivating she did not cultivate too much. She cultivated it quite some. She cultivated and she would sometime go on cultivating it and it was not then an unpleasant one, it would not be then an unpleasant one, it would be a quite richly enough cultivated one, it would be quite richly enough to be a pleasant enough one.

They were gay where there were many cultivating something. The two were gay there, were regularly gay there. Georgine Skeene would have liked to do more travelling. They did some travelling, not very much travelling, Georgine Skeene would have liked to do more travelling, Helen Furr did not care about doing travelling, she liked to stay in a place and be gay there.

They stayed in a place and were gay there, both of them stayed there, they stayed together there, they were gay there, they were regularly gay there.

They went quite often, not very often, but they did go back to where Helen Furr had a pleasant enough home and then Georgine Skeene went to a place where her brother had quite some distinction. They both went, every few years, went visiting to where Helen Furr had quite a pleasant home. Certainly Helen Furr would not find it gay to stay, she did not find it gay, she said she would not stay, she said she did not find it gay, she said she would not stay where she did not find it gay, she said she found it gay where she did stay and she did stay there where very many were cultivating something. She did stay there. She always did find it gay there.

She went to see them where she had always been living and where she did not find it gay. She had a pleasant home there, Mrs. Furr was a pleasant enough woman, Mr. Furr was a pleasant enough man, Helen told them and they were not worrying, that she did not find it gay living where she had always been living.

Georgine Skeene and Helen Furr were living where they were

both cultivating their voices and they were gay there. They visited where Helen Furr had come from and then they went to where they were living where they were then regularly living.

There were some dark and heavy men there then. There were some who were not so heavy and some who were not so dark. Helen Furr and Georgine Skeene sat regularly with them. They sat regularly with the ones who were dark and heavy. They sat regularly with the ones who were not so dark. They sat regularly with the ones that were not so heavy. They sat with them regularly, sat with some of them. They went with them regularly went with them. They were regular then, they were gay then, they were where they wanted to be then where it was gay to be then, they were regularly gay then. There were men there then who were dark and heavy and they sat with them with Helen Furr and Georgine Skeene and they went with them with Miss Furr and Miss Skeene, and they went with the heavy and dark men Miss Furr and Miss Skeene went with them, and they sat with them, Miss Furr and Miss Skeene sat with them, and there were other men, some were not heavy men and they sat with Miss Furr and Miss Skeene and Miss Furr and Miss Skeene sat with them, and there were other men who were not dark men and they sat with Miss Furr and Miss Skeene and Miss Furr and Miss Skeene sat with them. Miss Furr and Miss Skeene went with them and they went with Miss Furr and Miss Skeene, some who were not heavy men, some who were not dark men. Miss Furr and Miss Skeene sat regularly, they sat with some men. Miss Furr and Miss Skeene went and there were some men with them. There were men and Miss Furr and Miss Skeene went with them, went somewhere with them, went with some of them.

Helen Furr and Georgine Skeene were regularly living where very many were living and cultivating in themselves something. Helen Furr and Georgine Skeene were living very regularly then, being very regular then in being gay then. They did then learn many ways to be gay and they were then being gay being quite regular in being gay, being gay and they were learning little things, little things in ways of being gay, they were very regular then, they were learning very many little things in ways of being gay, they were being gay and using these little things they were learning to have to be gay with regularly gay with then and they were gay the same amount they had been gay. They were quite gay, they were quite regular, they were learning little things, gay little things, they were gay inside them the same amount they had been gay, they were gay the same length of time they had been gay every day.

They were regular in being gay, they learned little things that are things in being gay, they learned many little things that are things in being gay, they were gay every day, they were regular, they were gay, they were gay the same length of time every day, they were gay, they were quite regularly gay.

Georgine Skeene went away to stay two months with her brother. Helen Furr did not go then to stay with her father and her mother. Helen Furr stayed there where they had been regularly living the two of them and she would then certainly not be lonesome, she would go on being gay. She did go on being gay. She was not any more gay but she was gay longer every day than they had been being gay when they were together being gay. She was gay then quite exactly the same way. She learned a few more little ways of being in being gay. She was quite gay and in the same way, the same way she had been gay and she was gay a little longer in the day, more of each day she was gay. She was gay longer every day than when the two of them had been being gay. She was gay quite in the way they had been gay, quite in the same way.

She was not lonesome then, she was not at all feeling any need of having Georgine Skeene. She was not astonished at this thing. She would have been a little astonished by this thing but she knew she was not astonished at anything and so she was not astonished at this thing not astonished at not feeling any need of having Georgine Skeene.

Helen Furr had quite a completely pleasant voice and it was quite well enough cultivated and she could use it and she did use it but then there was not any way of working at cultivating a completely pleasant voice when it has become a quite completely well enough cultivated one, and there was not much use in using it when one was not wanting it to be helping to make one a gay one. Helen Furr was not needing using her voice to be a gay one. She was gay then and sometimes she used her voice and she was not using it very often. It was quite completely enough cultivated and it was quite completely a pleasant one and she did not use it very often. She was then, she was quite exactly as gay as she had been, she was gay a little longer in the day than she had been.

She was gay exactly the same way. She was never tired of being gay that way. She had learned very many little ways to use in being gay. Very many were telling about using other ways in being gay. She was gay enough, she was always gay exactly the same way, she was always learning little things to use in being gay, she was telling about using other ways in being gay, she was telling about learning other ways in being gay, she was learning other ways in being gay, she would be using other ways in being gay, she would always be gay in the same way, when Georgine Skeene was there not so long each day as when Georgine Skeene was away.

She came to using many ways in being gay, she came to use every way in being gay. She went on living where many were cultivating something and she was gay, she had used every way to be gay.

They did not live together then Helen Furr and Georgine Skeene. Helen Furr lived there the longer where they had been living regularly together. Then neither of them were living there any longer. Helen Furr was living somewhere else then and telling some about being gay and she was gay then and she was living quite regularly then. She was regularly gay then. She was quite regular in being gay then. She remembered all the little ways of being gay. She used all the little ways of being gay. She was quite regularly gay. She told many then the way of being gay, she taught very many then little ways they could use in being gay. She was living very well, she was gay then, she went on living then, she was regular in being gay, she always was living very well and was gay very well and was telling about little ways one could be learning to use in being gay, and later was telling them quite often, telling them again and again.

Silent
Snow, Secret Snow

CONRAD AIKEN

To the considerable difficulties of fashioning some recognizable impression of mental activity from words alone Conrad Aiken has added the difficulties of reproducing the mind of a child—a peculiarly sensitive and precocious mind at that—split in its perceptions between ordinary, outer experience and an extraordinary, inner experience that is gradually and delicately unfolding. A part of Aiken's solution to these compositional problems, like Katherine Anne Porter's in "Flowering Judas," is to present thought strongly through imagery, as well as through abstractions. The result is that Paul's mental life becomes for us (as for him) emphatically symbolic. Paul's mind is, at the same time, in the process of developing, under believable circumstances and in believable ways. His illusions are, that is to say, a part of reality. For most readers this reality will prove neither informative nor comforting (as William Dean Howells once thought reality in the United States would invariably be) but—in the chilling remoteness of its preoccupations from the familiar —unbearably moving.

J ust why it should have happened, or why it should have happened just when it did, he could not, of course, possibly have said; nor perhaps would it even have occurred to him to ask. The thing was above all a secret, something to be preciously concealed from Mother and Father; and to that very fact it owed an enormous part of its deliciousness. It was like a peculiarly beautiful trinket to be carried unmentioned in one's trouser pocket— a rare stamp, an old coin, a few tiny gold links found trodden out of shape on the path in the park, a pebble of carnelian, a seashell distinguishable from all others by an unusual spot or stripe— and, as if it were any one of these, he carried around with him everywhere a warm and persistent and increasingly beautiful sense of possession. Nor was it only a sense of possession—it was also a sense of protection. It was as if, in some delightful way, his secret gave him a fortress, a wall behind which he could retreat into heavenly seclusion. This was almost the first thing he had noticed about it—apart from the oddness of the thing itself—and it was this that now again, for the fiftieth time, occurred to him, as he sat in the little schoolroom. It was the half-hour for geography. Miss Buell was revolving with one finger, slowly, a huge terrestrial globe which had been placed on her desk. The green and yellow continents passed and repassed, questions were asked and answered, and now the little girl in front of him, Deirdre, who had a funny little constellation of freckles on the back of her neck, exactly like the Big Dipper, was standing up and telling Miss Buell that the equator was the line that ran round the middle.

Miss Buell's face, which was old and grayish and kindly, with gray stiff curls beside the cheeks, and eyes that swam very brightly, like little minnows, behind thick glasses, wrinkled itself into a complication of amusements.

"Ah! I see. The earth is wearing a belt, or a sash. Or someone drew a line round it!"

"Oh no—not that—I mean——"

In the general laughter, he did not share, or only a very little. He was thinking about the Arctic and Antarctic regions, which of course, on the globe, were white. Miss Buell was now telling them about the tropics, the jungles, the steamy heat of equatorial swamps, where the birds and butterflies, and even the snakes, were like living jewels. As he listened to these things, he was already, with a pleasant sense of half-effort, putting his secret between himself and the words. Was it really an effort at all? For effort implied something voluntary, and perhaps even something one did not especially want; whereas this was distinctly pleasant, and came almost of its own accord. All he needed to do was to think of that morning, the first one, and then of all the others——

But it was all so absurdly simple! It had amounted to so little. It was nothing, just an idea—and just why it should have become so wonderful, so permanent, was a mystery—a very pleasant one, to be sure, but also, in an amusing way, foolish. However, without ceasing to listen to Miss Buell, who had now moved up to the north temperate zones, he deliberately invited his memory of the first morning. It was only a moment or two after he had waked up—or perhaps the moment itself. But was there, to be exact, an exact moment? Was one awake all at once? or was it gradual? Anyway, it was after he had stretched a lazy hand up toward the headrail, and yawned, and then relaxed again among his warm covers, all the more grateful on a December morning, that the thing had happened. Suddenly, for no reason, he had thought of the postman, he remembered the postman. Perhaps there was nothing so odd in that. After all, he heard the postman almost every morning in his life—his heavy boots could be heard clumping round the corner at the top of the little cobbled hill-street, and then, progressively nearer, progressively louder, the double knock at each door, the crossings and re-crossings of the street, till finally the clumsy steps came stumbling across to the very door, and the tremendous knock came which shook the house itself.

(Miss Buell was saying, "Vast wheat-growing areas in North America and Siberia."

Deirdre had for the moment placed her left hand across the back of her neck.)

But on this particular morning, the first morning, as he lay there with his eyes closed, he had for some reason *waited* for the postman. He wanted to hear him come round the corner. And that was precisely the joke—he never did. He never came. He

never had come—*round the corner*—again. For when at last the
steps *were* heard, they had already, he was quite sure, come a
little down the hill, to the first house; and even so, the steps
were curiously different—they were softer, they had a new secrecy about them, they were muffled and indistinct; and while
the rhythm of them was the same, it now said a new thing—it
said peace, it said remoteness, it said cold, it said sleep. And he
had understood the situation at once—nothing could have seemed
simpler—there had been snow in the night, such as all winter
he had been longing for; and it was this which had rendered the
postman's first footsteps inaudible, and the later ones faint. Of
course! How lovely! And even now it must be snowing—it was
going to be a snowy day—the long white ragged lines were drifting
and sifting across the street, across the faces of the old houses,
whispering and hushing, making little triangles of white in the
corners between cobblestones, seething a little when the wind blew
them over the ground to a drifted corner; and so it would be all
day, getting deeper and deeper and silenter and silenter.

(Miss Buell was saying, "Land of perpetual snow.")

All this time, of course (while he lay in bed), he had kept his
eyes closed, listening to the nearer progress of the postman, the
muffled footsteps thumping and slipping on the snow-sheathed
cobbles; and all the other sounds—the double knocks, a frosty
far-off voice or two, a bell ringing thinly and softly as if under
a sheet of ice—had the same slightly abstracted quality, as if
removed by one degree from actuality—as if everything in the
world had been insulated by snow. But when at last, pleased, he
opened his eyes, and turned them toward the window, to see for
himself this long-desired and now so clearly imagined miracle—
what he saw instead was brilliant sunlight on a roof; and when,
astonished, he jumped out of bed and stared down into the
street, expecting to see the cobbles obliterated by the snow, he
saw nothing but the bare bright cobbles themselves.

Queer, the effect this extraordinary surprise had had upon
him—all the following morning he had kept with him a sense as
of snow falling about him, a secret screen of new snow between
himself and the world. If he had not dreamed such a thing—and
how could he have dreamed it while awake?—how else could
one explain it? In any case, the delusion had been so vivid as to
affect his entire behavior. He could not now remember whether
it was on the first or the second morning—or was it even the

third?—that his mother had drawn attention to some oddness in his manner.

"But my darling"—she had said at the breakfast table—"what has come over you? You don't seem to be listening. . . ."

And how often that very thing had happened since!

(Miss Buell was now asking if anyone knew the difference between the North Pole and the Magnetic Pole. Deirdre was holding up her flickering brown hand, and he could see the four white dimples that marked the knuckles.)

Perhaps it hadn't been either the second or third morning—or even the fourth or fifth. How could he be sure? How could he be sure just when the delicious *progress* had become clear? Just when it had really *begun?* The intervals weren't very precise. . . . All he now knew was, that at some point or other—perhaps the second day, perhaps the sixth—he had noticed that the presence of the snow was a little more insistent, the sound of it clearer; and, conversely, the sound of the postman's footsteps more indistinct. Not only could he not hear the steps come round the corner, he could not even hear them at the first house. It was below the first house that he heard them; and then, a few days later, it was below the second house that he heard them; and a few days later again, below the third. Gradually, gradually, the snow was becoming heavier, the sound of its seething louder, the cobblestones more and more muffled. When he found, each morning, on going to the window, after the ritual of listening, that the roofs and cobbles were as bare as ever, it made no difference. This was, after all, only what he had expected. It was even what pleased him, what rewarded him: the thing was his own, belonged to no one else. No one else knew about it, not even his mother and father. There, outside, were the bare cobbles; and here, inside, was the snow. Snow growing heavier each day, muffling the world, hiding the ugly, and deadening increasingly—above all—the steps of the postman.

"But, my darling"—she had said at the luncheon table—"what has come over you? You don't seem to listen when people speak to you. That's the third time I've asked you to pass your plate. . . ."

How was one to explain this to Mother? or to Father? There was, of course, nothing to be done about it: nothing. All one could do was to laugh embarrassedly, pretend to be a little ashamed, apologize, and take a sudden and somewhat disingenuous interest in what was being done or said. The cat had

stayed out all night. He had a curious swelling on his left cheek
—perhaps somebody had kicked him, or a stone had struck him.
Mrs. Kempton was or was not coming to tea. The house was
going to be housecleaned, or "turned out," on Wednesday instead of Friday. A new lamp was provided for his evening work—
perhaps it was eyestrain which accounted for this new and so
peculiar vagueness of his—Mother was looking at him with amusement as she said this, but with something else as well. A new
lamp? A new lamp. Yes, Mother, No, Mother, Yes, Mother. School
is going very well. The geometry is very easy. The history is very
dull. The geography is very interesting—particularly when it takes
one to the North Pole. Why the North Pole? Oh, well, it would
be fun to be an explorer. Another Peary or Scott or Shackleton.
And then abruptly he found his interest in the talk at an end, stared
at the pudding on his plate, listened, waited, and began once
more—ah, how heavenly, too, the first beginnings—to hear or feel—
for could he actually hear it?—the silent snow, the secret snow.

(Miss Buell was telling them about the search for the Northwest Passage, about Hendrik Hudson, the *Half Moon*.)

This had been, indeed, the only distressing feature of the new
experience; the fact that it so increasingly had brought him into
a kind of mute misunderstanding, or even conflict, with his father
and mother. It was as if he were trying to lead a double life.
On the one hand, he had to be Paul Hasleman, and keep up the
appearance of being that person—dress, wash, and answer intel-
ligently when spoken to—; on the other, he had to explore this
new world which had been opened to him. Nor could there be
the slightest doubt—not the slightest—that the new world was
the profounder and more wonderful of the two. It was irresistible.
It was miraculous. Its beauty was simply beyond anything—beyond
speech as beyond thought—utterly incommunicable. But how then,
between the two worlds, of which he was thus constantly aware,
was he to keep a balance? One must get up, one must go to breakfast, one must talk with Mother, go to school, do one's lessons—
and, in all this, try not to appear too much of a fool. But if all
the while one was also trying to extract the full deliciousness of
another and quite separate existence, one which could not easily
(if at all) be spoken of—how was one to manage? How was one
to explain? Would it be safe to explain? Would it be absurd?
Would it merely mean that he would get into some obscure kind
of trouble?

These thoughts came and went, came and went, as softly and secretly as the snow; they were not precisely a disturbance, perhaps they were even a pleasure; he liked to have them; their presence was something almost palpable, something he could stroke with his hand, without closing his eyes, and without ceasing to see Miss Buell and the schoolroom and the globe and the freckles on Deirdre's neck; nevertheless he did in a sense cease to see, or to see the obvious external world, and substituted for this vision the vision of snow, the sound of snow, and the slow, almost soundless, approach of the postman. Yesterday, it had been only at the sixth house that the postman had become audible; the snow was much deeper now, it was falling more swiftly and heavily, the sound of its seething was more distinct, more soothing, more persistent. And this morning, it had been—as nearly as he could figure—just above the seventh house—perhaps only a step or two above; at most, he had heard two or three footsteps before the knock had sounded. . . . And with each such narrowing of the sphere, each nearer approach of the limit at which the postman was first audible, it was odd how sharply was increased the amount of illusion which had to be carried into the ordinary business of daily life. Each day, it was harder to get out of bed, to go to the window, to look out at the—as always—perfectly empty and snowless street. Each day it was more difficult to go through the perfunctory motions of greeting Mother and Father at breakfast, to reply to their questions, to put his books together and go to school. And at school, how extraordinarily hard to conduct with success simultaneously the public life and the life that was secret! There were times when he longed—positively ached—to tell everyone about it—to burst out with it—only to be checked almost at once by a far-off feeling as of some faint absurdity which was inherent in it—but *was* it absurd?—and more importantly by a sense of mysterious power in his very secrecy. Yes; it must be kept secret. That, more and more, became clear. At whatever cost to himself, whatever pain to others——

(Miss Buell looked straight at him, smiling, and said, "Perhaps we'll ask Paul. I'm sure Paul will come out of his daydream long enough to be able to tell us. Won't you, Paul?" He rose slowly from his chair, resting one hand on the brightly varnished desk, and deliberately stared through the snow toward the blackboard. It was an effort, but it was amusing to make it. "Yes," he said slowly, "it was what we now call the Hudson River. This he thought to be the Northwest Passage. He was disappointed." He sat down again, and as he did so Deirdre half turned in her chair and gave him a shy smile, of approval and admiration.)

At whatever pain to others.

This part of it was very puzzling, very puzzling. Mother was very nice, and so was Father. Yes, that was all true enough. He wanted to be nice to them, to tell them everything—and yet, was it really wrong of him to want to have a secret place of his own?

At bed-time, the night before, Mother had said, "If this goes on, my lad, we'll have to see a doctor, we will! We can't have our boy—" But what was it she had said? "Live in another world"? "Live so far away"? The word "far" had been in it, he was sure, and then Mother had taken up a magazine again and laughed a little, but with an expression which wasn't mirthful. He had felt sorry for her. . . .

The bell rang for dismissal. The sound came to him through long curved parallels of falling snow. He saw Deirdre rise, and had himself risen almost as soon—but not quite as soon—as she.

———

II

On the walk homeward, which was timeless, it pleased him to see through the accompaniment, or counterpoint, of snow, the items of mere externality on his way. There were many kinds of brick in the sidewalks, and laid in many kinds of pattern. The garden walls, too, were various, some of wooden palings, some of plaster, some of stone. Twigs of bushes leaned over the walls: the little hard green winter-buds of lilac, on gray stems, sheathed and fat; other branches very thin and fine and black and desiccated. Dirty sparrows huddled in the bushes, as dull in color as dead fruit left in leafless trees. A single starling creaked on a weather vane. In the gutter, beside a drain, was a scrap of torn and dirty newspaper, caught in a little delta of filth; the word ECZEMA appeared in large capitals, and below it was a letter from Mrs. Amelia D. Cravath, 2100 Pine Street, Fort Worth, Texas, to the effect that after being a sufferer for years she had been cured by Caley's Ointment. In the little delta, beside the fan-shaped and deeply runneled continent of brown mud, were lost twigs, descended from their parent trees, dead matches, a rusty horse-chestnut burr, a small concentration of eggshell, a streak of yellow sawdust which had been wet and now was dry and congealed, a brown pebble, and a broken feather. Farther on was a cement sidewalk, ruled into geometrical parallelograms, with a brass inlay at one end commemorating the contractors who had laid it, and, halfway across, an irregular and random series of dog-tracks, immortalized in synthetic stone. He knew these well, and always stepped on them; to cover the little hollows with his own foot had always been a queer pleasure; today he did it once more, but perfunctorily and detachedly, all the while thinking of something else. That was a dog, a long time ago, who had made a mistake and walked on the cement while it was still wet. He had probably wagged his tail, but that hadn't been recorded. Now, Paul Hasleman, aged twelve, on his way home from school, crossed the same river, which in the meantime had frozen into rock. Homeward through the snow, the snow falling in bright sunshine. Homeward?

Then came the gateway with the two posts surmounted by egg-shaped stones which had been cunningly balanced on their ends, as if by Columbus, and mortared in the very act of balance; a source of perpetual wonder. On the brick wall just beyond, the letter H had been stenciled, presumably for some purpose. H? H.

The green hydrant, with a little green-painted chain attached to the brass screw-cap.

The elm tree, with the great gray wound in the bark, kidney-shaped, into which he always put his hand—to feel the cold but living wood. The injury, he had been sure, was due to the gnawings of a tethered horse. But now it deserved only a passing palm, a merely tolerant eye. There were more important things. Miracles. Beyond the thoughts of trees, mere elms. Beyond the thoughts of sidewalks, mere stone, mere brick, mere cement. Beyond the thoughts even of his own shoes, which trod these sidewalks obediently, bearing a burden—far above—of elaborate mystery. He watched them. They were not very well polished; he had neglected them, for a very good reason: they were one of the many parts of the increasing difficulty of the daily return to daily life, the morning struggle. To get up, having at last opened one's eyes, to go to the window, and discover no snow, to wash, to dress, to descend the curving stairs to breakfast——

At whatever pain to others, nevertheless, one must persevere in severance, since the incommunicability of the experience demanded it. It was desirable, of course, to be kind to Mother and Father, especially as they seemed to be worried, but it was also desirable to be resolute. If they should decide—as appeared likely—to consult the doctor, Doctor Howells, and have Paul inspected, his heart listened to through a kind of dictaphone, his lungs, his stomach—well, that was all right. He would go through with it. He would give them answer for question, too—perhaps such answers as they hadn't expected? No. That would never do. For the secret world must, at all costs, be preserved.

The bird-house in the apple tree was empty—it was the wrong time of year for wrens. The little round black door had lost its pleasure. The wrens were enjoying other houses, other nests, remoter trees. But this too was a notion which he only vaguely and grazingly entertained—as if, for the moment, he merely touched an edge of it; there was something further on, which was already assuming a sharper importance; something which already teased at the corners of his eyes, teasing also at the corner of his mind. It was funny to think that he so wanted this, so awaited it—and yet found himself enjoying this momentary dalliance with the bird-house, as if for a quite deliberate postponement and enhancement of the approaching pleasure. He was aware of his delay, of his smiling and detached and now almost uncomprehending gaze at the little bird-house; he knew what he was going to look at next: it was his own little cobbled hill-street, his own house, the little river at the bottom of the hill, the grocer's shop with the cardboard man in the window—and now, thinking of all this, he turned his head, still smiling, and looking quickly right and left through the snow-laden sunlight.

And the mist of snow, as he had foreseen, was still on it—a ghost of snow falling in the bright sunlight, softly and steadily floating and turning and pausing, soundlessly meeting the snow that covered, as with a transparent mirage, the bare bright cobbles. He loved it—he stood still and loved it. Its beauty was paralyzing—beyond all words, all experience, all dream. No fairy story he had ever read could be compared with it—none had ever given him this extraordinary combination of ethereal loveliness with a something else, unnameable, which was just faintly and deliciously terrifying. What was this thing? As he thought of it, he looked upward toward his own bedroom window, which was open—and it was as if he looked straight into the room and saw himself lying half awake in his bed. There he was—at this very instant he was still perhaps actually there—more truly there than standing here at the edge of the cobbled hill-street, with one hand lifted to shade his eyes against the snow-sun. Had he indeed ever left his room, in all this time? since that very first morning? Was the whole progress still being enacted there, was it still the same morning, and himself not yet wholly awake? And even now, had the postman not yet come round the corner? . . .

This idea amused him, and automatically, as he thought of it, he turned his head and looked toward the top of the hill. There was, of course, nothing there—nothing and no one. The street was empty and quiet. And all the more because of its emptiness it occurred to him to count the houses—a thing which, oddly enough, he hadn't before thought of doing. Of course, he had known there weren't many—many, that is, on his own side of the street, which were the ones that figured in the postman's progress—but nevertheless it came as something of a shock to find that there were precisely *six*, above his own house—his own house was the seventh.

Six!

Astonished, he looked at his own house—looked at the door, on which was the number thirteen—and then realized that the whole thing was exactly and logically and absurdly what he ought to have known. Just the same, the realization gave him abruptly, and even a little frighteningly, a sense of hurry. He was being hurried— he was being rushed. For—he knit his brow—he couldn't be mistaken—it was just above the *seventh* house, his *own* house, that the postman had first been audible this very morning. But in that case—in that case—did it mean that tomorrow he would hear nothing? The knock he had heard must have been the knock of their own door. Did it mean—and this was an idea which gave him a really extraordinary feeling of surprise—that he would never hear the postman again?—that tomorrow morning the postman would already have passed the house, in a snow so deep as to render his footsteps completely inaudible? That he would have made his approach down the snow-filled street so soundlessly, so secretly, that he, Paul Hasleman, there lying in bed, would not have waked in time, or waking, would have heard nothing?

But how could that be? Unless even the knocker should be muffled in the snow—frozen tight, perhaps? . . . But in that case——

A vague feeling of disappointment came over him; a vague sadness as if he felt himself deprived of something which he had long looked forward to, something much prized. After all this, all this beautiful progress, the slow delicious advance of the postman through the silent and secret snow, the knock creeping closer each day, and the footsteps nearer, the audible compass of the world thus daily narrowed, narrowed, narrowed, as the snow soothingly and beautifully encroached and deepened, after all this, was he to be defrauded of the one thing he had so wanted—to be able to count, as it were, the last two or three solemn footsteps, as they finally approached his own door? Was it all going to happen, at the end, so suddenly? or indeed, had it already happened? with no slow and subtle gradations of menace, in which he could luxuriate?

He gazed upward again, toward his own window which flashed in the sun; and this time almost with a feeling that it would be better if he *were* still in bed, in that room; for in that case this must still be the first morning, and there would be six more mornings to come—or, for that matter, seven or eight or nine—how could he be sure?—or even more.

III

After supper, the inquisition began. He stood before the doctor, under the lamp, and submitted silently to the usual thumpings and tappings.

"Now will you please say 'Ah!'?"

"Ah!"

"Now again, please, if you don't mind."

"Ah."

"Say it slowly, and hold it if you can——"

"Ah-h-h-h-h-h——"

"Good."

How silly all this was. As if it had anything to do with his throat! Or his heart, or lungs!

Relaxing his mouth, of which the corners, after all this absurd stretching, felt uncomfortable, he avoided the doctor's eyes, and stared toward the fireplace, past his mother's feet (in gray slippers) which projected from the green chair, and his father's feet (in brown slippers) which stood neatly side by side on the hearth rug.

"Hm. There is certainly nothing wrong there . . . ?"

He felt the doctor's eyes fixed upon him, and, as if merely to be polite, returned the look, but with a feeling of justifiable evasiveness.

"Now, young man, tell me—do you feel all right?"

"Yes, sir, quite all right."

"No headaches? no dizziness?"

"No, I don't think so."

"Let me see. Let's get a book, if you don't mind—yes, thank you, that will do splendidly—and now, Paul, if you'll just read it, holding it as you would normally hold it——"

He took the book and read:

"And another praise have I to tell for this the city our mother, the gift of a great god, a glory of the land most high; the might of horses, the might of young horses, the might of the sea. . . . For thou, son of Cronus, our lord Poseidon, hath throned herein this pride, since in these roads first thou didst show forth the curb that cures the rage of steeds. And the shapely oar, apt to men's hands, hath a wondrous speed on the brine, following the hundred-footed Nereids. . . . O land that art praised above all lands, now is it for thee to make those bright praises seen in deeds."

He stopped, tentatively, and lowered the heavy book.

"No—as I thought—there is certainly no superficial sign of eye-strain."

Silence thronged the room, and he was aware of the focused scrutiny of the three people who confronted him. . . .

"We could have his eyes examined—but I believe it is something else."

"What could it be?" That was his father's voice.

"It's only this curious absent-mindedness—" This was his mother's voice.

In the presence of the doctor, they both seemed irritatingly apologetic.

"I believe it is something else. Now Paul—I would like very much to ask you a question or two. You will answer them, won't you—you know I'm an old, old friend of yours, eh? That's right! . . ."

His back was thumped twice by the doctor's fat fist—then the doctor was grinning at him with false amiability, while with one fingernail he was scratching the top button of his waistcoat. Beyond the doctor's shoulder was the fire, the fingers of flame making light prestidigitation against the sooty fireback, the soft sound of their random flutter the only sound.

"I would like to know—is there anything that worries you?"

The doctor was again smiling, his eyelids low against the little black pupils, in each of which was a tiny white bead of light. Why answer him? why answer him at all? "At whatever pain to others"—but it was all a nuisance, this necessity for resistance, this necessity for attention; it was as if one had been stood up on a brilliantly lighted stage, under a great round blaze of spotlight; as if one were merely a trained seal, or a performing dog, or a fish, dipped out of an aquarium and held up by the tail. It would serve them right if he were merely to bark or growl. And meanwhile, to miss these last few precious hours, these hours of which each minute was more beautiful than the last, more menacing—! He still looked, as if from a great distance, at the beads of light in the doctor's eyes, at the fixed false smile, and then, beyond, once more at his mother's slippers, his father's slippers, the soft flutter of the fire. Even here, even amongst these hostile presences, and in this arranged light, he could see the snow, he could hear it—it was in the corners of the room, where the shadow was deepest, under the sofa, behind the half-opened door which led to the dining room. It was gentler here, softer, its seethe the quietest of whispers, as if, in deference to a drawing room, it had quite deliberately put on its "manners"; it kept itself out of sight, obliterated itself, but distinctly with an air of saying, "Ah, but just wait! Wait till we are alone together! Then I will begin to tell you something new! Something white! something cold! something sleepy! something of cease, and peace, and the long bright curve of space! Tell them to go away. Banish them. Refuse to speak. Leave them, go upstairs to your room, turn out the light and get into bed—I will go with you, I will be waiting for you, I will tell you a better story than Little Kay of the Skates, or The Snow Ghost—I will surround your bed, I will close the windows, pile a deep drift against the door, so that none will ever again be able to enter. Speak to them! . . ." It seemed as if the little hissing voice came from a slow white spiral of falling flakes in the corner by the front window—but he could not be sure. He felt himself smiling, then, and said to the doctor, but without looking at him, looking beyond him still——

"Oh no, I think not——"

"But are you sure, my boy?"

His father's voice came softly and coldly then—the familiar voice of silken warning.

"You needn't answer at once, Paul—remember we're trying to help you—think it over and be quite sure, won't you?"

He felt himself smiling again, at the notion of being quite sure. What a joke! As if he weren't so sure that reassurance was no longer necessary, and all this cross-examination a ridiculous farce, a grotesque parody! What could they know about it? these gross intelligences, these humdrum minds so bound to the usual, the ordinary? Impossible to tell them about it! Why, even now, even now, with the proof so abundant, so formidable, so imminent, so appallingly present here in this very room, could they believe it?—could even his mother believe it? No—it was only too plain that if anything were said about it, the merest hint given, they would be incredulous—they would laugh—they would say "Absurd!"—think things about him which weren't true. . . .

"Why no, I'm not worried—why should I be?"

He looked then straight at the doctor's low-lidded eyes, looked from one of them to the other, from one bead of light to the other, and gave a little laugh.

The doctor seemed to be disconcerted by this. He drew back in his chair, resting a fat white hand on either knee. The smile faded slowly from his face.

"Well, Paul!" he said, and paused gravely, "I'm afraid you don't take this quite seriously enough. I think you perhaps don't quite realize—don't quite realize—" He took a deep quick breath, and turned, as if helplessly, at a loss for words, to the others. But Mother and Father were both silent—no help was forthcoming.

"You must surely know, be aware, that you have not been quite yourself, of late? Don't you know that? . . ."

It was amusing to watch the doctor's renewed attempt at a smile, a queer disorganized look, as of confidential embarrassment.

"I feel all right, sir," he said, and again gave the little laugh.

"And we're trying to help you." The doctor's tone sharpened.

"Yes, sir, I know. But why? I'm all right. I'm just *thinking*, that's all."

His mother made a quick movement forward, resting a hand on the back of the doctor's chair.

"Thinking?" she said. "But my dear, about what?"

This was a direct challenge—and would have to be directly met. But before he met it, he looked again into the corner by the door, as if for reassurance. He smiled again at what he saw, at what he heard. The little spiral was still there, still softly whirling, like the ghost of a white kitten chasing the ghost of a white tail, and making as it did so the faintest of whispers. It was all right! If only he could remain firm, everything was going to be all right.

"Oh, about anything, about nothing—*you* know the way you do!"

"You mean—daydreaming?"

"Oh, no—thinking!"

"But thinking about *what?*"

"Anything."

He laughed a third time—but this time, happening to glance upward toward his mother's face, he was appalled at the effect his laughter seemed to have upon her. Her mouth had opened in an expression of horror. . . . This was too bad! Unfortunate! He had known it would cause pain, of course—but he hadn't expected it to be quite so bad as this. Perhaps—perhaps if he just gave them a tiny gleaming hint——?

"About the snow," he said.

"What on earth?" This was his father's voice. The brown slippers came a step nearer on the hearth-rug.

"But my dear, what do you mean?" This was his mother's voice. The doctor merely stared.

"Just *snow*, that's all. I like to think about it."

"Tell us about it, my boy."

"But that's all it is. There's nothing to tell. *You* know what snow is?"

This he said almost angrily, for he felt that they were trying to corner him. He turned sideways so as no longer to face the doctor, and the better to see the inch of blackness between the window-sill and the lowered curtain—the cold inch of beckoning and delicious night. At once he felt better, more assured.

"Mother—can I go to bed, now, please? I've got a headache."

"But I thought you said——"

"It's just come. It's all these questions—! Can I, mother?"

"You can go as soon as the doctor has finished."

"Don't you think this thing ought to be gone into thoroughly, and *now?*" This was Father's voice. The brown slippers again came a step nearer, the voice was the well-known "punishment" voice, resonant and cruel.

"Oh, what's the use, Norman——"

Quite suddenly, everyone was silent. And without precisely facing them, nevertheless he was aware that all three of them

were watching him with an extraordinary intensity—staring hard
at him—as if he had done something monstrous, or was himself
some kind of monster. He could hear the soft irregular flutter
of the flames; the cluck-click-cluck-click of the clock; far and
faint, two sudden spurts of laughter from the kitchen, as quickly
cut off as begun; a murmur of water in the pipes; and then, the
silence seemed to deepen, to spread out, to become world-long
and world-wide, to become timeless and shapeless, and to center
inevitably and rightly, with a slow and sleepy but enormous
concentration of all power, on the beginning of a new sound.
What this new sound was going to be, he knew perfectly well.
It might begin with a hiss, but it would end with a roar—there
was no time to lose—he must escape. It mustn't happen here——
   Without another word, he turned and ran up the stairs.

IV

Not a moment too soon. The darkness was coming in long white
waves. A prolonged sibilance filled the night—a great seamless
seethe of wild influence went abruptly across it—a cold low humming shook the windows. He shut the door and flung off his
clothes in the dark. The bare black floor was like a little raft
tossed in waves of snow, almost overwhelmed, washed under
whitely, up again, smothered in curled billows of feather. The
snow was laughing; it spoke from all sides at once; it pressed
closer to him as he ran and jumped exulting into his bed.
   "Listen to us!" it said. "Listen! We have come to tell you the
story we told you about. You remember? Lie down. Shut your
eyes, now—you will no longer see much—in this white darkness
who could see, or want to see? We will take the place of everything. . . . Listen——"
   A beautiful varying dance of snow began at the front of the
room, came forward and then retreated, flattened out toward
the floor, then rose fountain-like to the ceiling, swayed, recruited
itself from a new stream of flakes which poured laughing in
through the humming window, advanced again, lifted long white
arms. It said peace, it said remoteness, it said cold—it said——
   But then a gash of horrible light fell brutally across the room
from the opening door—the snow drew back hissing—something
alien had come into the room—something hostile. This thing

rushed at him, clutched at him, shook him—and he was not merely horrified, he was filled with such a loathing as he had never known. What was this? this cruel disturbance? this act of anger and hate? It was as if he had to reach up a hand toward another world for any understanding of it—an effort of which he was only barely capable. But of that other world he still remembered just enough to know the exorcising words. They tore themselves from his other life suddenly——

"Mother! Mother! Go away! I hate you!"

And with that effort, everything was solved, everything became all right: the seamless hiss advanced once more, the long white wavering lines rose and fell like enormous whispering sea-waves, the whisper becoming louder, the laughter more numerous.

"Listen!" it said. "We'll tell you the last, the most beautiful and secret story—shut your eyes—it is a very small story—a story that gets smaller and smaller—it comes inward instead of opening like a flower—it is a flower becoming a seed—a little cold seed—do you hear? we are leaning closer to you——"

The hiss was now becoming a roar—the whole world was a vast moving screen of snow—but even now it said peace, it said remoteness, it said cold, it said sleep.

The
Rich Boy

F. SCOTT FITZGERALD

Despite a certain air of posturing in the opening paragraphs, Fitzgerald does point the reader directly toward the two chief modes in which this narrative is cast. His remarks on "queer fish" and "abnormality" and his emphasis on the rich boy's individuality invite a psychological reading of the story, while his interest in "the very rich" is clearly social. The rich as a class and Anson Hunter as a rich individual are noticeably American, and the particularized social conditions of Anson's life in New York and elsewhere give him an unmistakable historical identity. At the same time, Anson has a personal identity that is partially distinct from his social one—an idiosyncratic blend of infantilism or narcissism with a variety of impressionistic qualities like "confident charm" and "solidity." The story comes most startlingly alive in the fragile precision of its insights into behavior, as when Fitzgerald observes of the dialogue between Anson and Paula that "the emotional content that gradually came to fill it grew up not out of the words but out of its enormous seriousness." But "The Rich Boy" finds its artistic strength primarily in the author's secure and subtle sense of those moments when a person's private and social selves are one.

Begin with an individual, and before you know it you find that you have created a type; begin with a type, and you find that you have created—nothing. That is because we are all queer fish, queerer behind our faces and voices than we want any one to know or than we know ourselves. When I hear a man proclaiming himself an "average, honest, open fellow," I feel pretty sure that he has some definite and perhaps terrible abnormality which he has agreed to conceal—and his protestation of being average and honest and open is his way of reminding himself of his misprision.

There are no types, no plurals. There is a rich boy, and this is his and not his brothers' story. All my life I have lived among his brothers but this one has been my friend. Besides, if I wrote about his brothers I should have to begin by attacking all the lies that the poor have told about the rich and the rich have told about themselves—such a wild structure they have erected that when we pick up a book about the rich, some instinct prepares us for unreality. Even the intelligent and impassioned reporters of life have made the country of the rich as unreal as fairy-land.

Let me tell you about the very rich. They are different from you and me. They possess and enjoy early, and it does something to them, makes them soft where we are hard, and cynical where we are trustful, in a way that, unless you were born rich, it is very difficult to understand. They think, deep in their hearts, that they are better than we are because we had to discover the compensations and refuges of life for ourselves. Even when they enter deep into our world or sink below us, they still think that they are better than we are. They are different. The only way I can describe young Anson Hunter is to approach him as if he were a foreigner and cling stubbornly to my point of view. If I accept his for a moment I am lost—I have nothing to show but a preposterous movie.

II

Anson was the eldest of six children who would someday divide a fortune of fifteen million dollars, and he reached the age of reason

—is it seven?—at the beginning of the century when daring young women were already gliding along Fifth Avenue in electric "mobiles." In those days he and his brother had an English governess who spoke the language very clearly and crisply and well, so that the two boys grew to speak as she did—their words and sentences were all crisp and clear and not run together as ours are. They didn't talk exactly like English children but acquired an accent that is peculiar to fashionable people in the city of New York.

In the summer the six children were moved from the house on 71st Street to a big estate in northern Connecticut. It was not a fashionable locality—Anson's father wanted to delay as long as possible his children's knowledge of that side of life. He was a man somewhat superior to his class, which composed New York society, and to his period, which was the snobbish and formalized vulgarity of the Gilded Age, and he wanted his sons to learn habits of concentration and have sound constitutions and grow up into right-living and successful men. He and his wife kept an eye on them as well as they were able until the two older boys went away to school, but in huge establishments this is difficult—it was much simpler in the series of small and medium-sized houses in which my own youth was spent—I was never far out of the reach of my mother's voice, of the sense of her presence, her approval or disapproval.

Anson's first sense of his superiority came to him when he realized the half-grudging American deference that was paid to him in the Connecticut village. The parents of the boys he played with always inquired after his father and mother, and were vaguely excited when their own children were asked to the Hunters' house. He accepted this as the natural state of things, and a sort of impatience with all groups of which he was not the centre—in money, in position, in authority—remained with him for the rest of his life. He disdained to struggle with other boys for precedence—he expected it to be given him freely, and when it wasn't he withdrew into his family. His family was sufficient, for in the East money is still a somewhat feudal thing, a clan-forming thing. In the snobbish West, money separates families to form "sets."

At eighteen, when he went to New Haven, Anson was tall and thick-set, with a clear complexion and a healthy color from the ordered life he had led in school. His hair was yellow and grew in a funny way on his head, his nose was beaked—these two things kept him from being handsome—but he had a confident charm and a certain brusque style, and the upper-class men who passed him on the street knew without being told that he was a rich boy and had gone to one of the best schools. Nevertheless, his very superiority kept him from being a success in college—the independence was mistaken for egotism, and the refusal to accept Yale standards with the proper awe seemed to belittle all those who had. So, long before he graduated, he began to shift the centre of his life to New York.

He was at home in New York—there was his own house with "the kind of servants you can't get any more"—and his own family, of which, because of his good humor and a certain ability to make things go, he was rapidly becoming the centre, and the débutante parties, and the correct manly world of the men's clubs, and the occasional wild spree with the gallant girls whom New Haven only knew from the fifth row. His aspirations were conventional enough—they included even the irreproachable shadow he would some day marry, but they differed from the aspirations of the majority of young men in that there was no mist over them, none of that quality which is variously known as "idealism" or "illusion." Anson accepted without reservation the world of high finance and high extravagance, of divorce and dissipation, of snobbery and of privilege. Most of our lives end as a compromise—it was as a compromise that his life began.

He and I first met in the late summer of 1917 when he was just out of Yale, and, like the rest of us, was swept up into the systematized hysteria of the war. In the blue-green uniform of the naval aviation he came down to Pensacola, where the hotel orchestras played "I'm sorry, dear," and we young officers danced with the girls. Every one liked him, and though he ran with the drinkers and wasn't an especially good pilot, even the instructors treated him with a certain respect. He was always having long talks with them in his confident, logical voice—talks which ended by his getting himself, or, more frequently, another officer, out of some impending trouble. He was convivial, bawdy, robustly avid for pleasure, and we were all surprised when he fell in love with a conservative and rather proper girl.

Her name was Paula Legendre, a dark, serious beauty from somewhere in California. Her family kept a winter residence just outside of town, and in spite of her primness she was enormously popular; there is a large class of men whose egotism can't endure humor in a woman. But Anson wasn't that sort, and I couldn't understand the attraction of her "sincerity"—that was the thing to say about her—for his keen and somewhat sardonic mind.

Nevertheless, they fell in love—and on her terms. He no longer joined the twilight gathering at the DeSoto bar, and whenever they were seen together they were engaged in a long, serious dialogue, which must have gone on several weeks. Long afterward he told me that it was not about anything in particular but was composed on both sides of immature and even meaningless statements—the emotional content that gradually came to fill it grew up not out of the words but out of its enormous seriousness. It was a sort of hypnosis. Often it was interrupted, giving way to that emasculated humor we call fun; when they were alone it was resumed again, solemn, low-keyed, and pitched so as to give each other a sense of unity in feeling and thought. They came to resent any interruptions of it, to be unresponsive to facetiousness about life, even to the mild cynicism of their contemporaries. They were only happy when the dialogue was going on, and its seriousness bathed them like the amber glow of an open fire. Toward the end there came an interruption they did not resent—it began to be interrupted by passion.

Oddly enough, Anson was as engrossed in the dialogue as she was and as profoundly affected by it, yet at the same time aware that on his side much was insincere, and on hers much was merely simple. At first, too, he despised her emotional simplicity as well, but with his love her nature deepened and blossomed, and he could despise it no longer. He felt that if he could enter into Paula's warm safe life he would be happy. The long preparation of the dialogue removed any constraint—he taught her some of what he had learned from more adventurous women, and she responded with a rapt holy intensity. One evening after a dance they agreed to marry, and he wrote a long letter about her to his mother. The next day Paula told him that she was rich, that she had a personal fortune of nearly a million dollars.

III

It was exactly as if they could say "Neither of us has anything: we shall be poor together"—just as delightful that they should be rich instead. It gave them the same communion of adventure. Yet when Anson got leave in April, and Paula and her mother accompanied him North, she was impressed with the standing of his family in New York and with the scale on which they lived. Alone with Anson for the first time in the rooms where he had played as a boy, she was filled with a comfortable emotion, as though she were pre-eminently safe and taken care of. The pictures of Anson in a skull cap at his first school, of Anson on horseback with the sweetheart of a mysterious forgotten summer, of Anson in a gay group of ushers and bridesmaids at a wedding, made her jealous of his life apart from her in the past, and so completely did his authoritative person seem to sum up and typify these possessions of his that she was inspired with the idea of being married immediately and returning to Pensacola as his wife.

But an immediate marriage wasn't discussed—even the engagement was to be secret until after the war. When she realized that only two days of his leave remained, her dissatisfaction crystallized in the intention of making him as unwilling to wait as she was. They were driving to the country for dinner and she determined to force the issue that night.

Now a cousin of Paula's was staying with them at the Ritz, a severe, bitter girl who loved Paula but was somewhat jealous of her impressive engagement, and as Paula was late in dressing, the cousin, who wasn't going to the party, received Anson in the parlor of the suite.

Anson had met friends at five o'clock and drunk freely and indiscreetly with them for an hour. He left the Yale Club at a proper time, and his mother's chauffeur drove him to the Ritz, but his usual capacity was not in evidence, and the impact of the steam-heated sitting-room made him suddenly dizzy. He knew it, and he was both amused and sorry.

Paula's cousin was twenty-five, but she was exceptionally naïve, and at first failed to realize what was up. She had never met Anson before, and she was surprised when he mumbled strange information and nearly fell off his chair, but until Paula appeared it didn't occur to her that what she had taken for the odor of a dry-cleaned uniform was really whiskey. But Paula understood as soon as she appeared; her only thought was to get Anson away before her mother saw him, and at the look in her eyes the cousin understood too.

When Paula and Anson descended to the limousine they found two men inside, both asleep; they were the men with whom he had been drinking at the Yale Club, and they were also going to the party. He had entirely forgotten their presence in the car. On the way to Hempstead they awoke and sang. Some of the songs were rough, and though Paula tried to reconcile herself to the fact that Anson had few verbal inhibitions, her lips tightened with shame and distaste.

Back at the hotel the cousin, confused and agitated, considered the incident, and then walked into Mrs. Legendre's bedroom, saying: "Isn't he funny?"

"Who is funny?"

"Why—Mr. Hunter. He seemed so funny."

Mrs. Legendre looked at her sharply.

"How is he funny?"

"Why, he said he was French. I didn't know he was French."

"That's absurd. You must have misunderstood." She smiled: "It was a joke."

The cousin shook her head stubbornly.

"No. He said he was brought up in France. He said he couldn't speak any English, and that's why he couldn't talk to me. And he couldn't!"

Mr. Legendre looked away with impatience just as the cousin added thoughtfully, "Perhaps it was because he was so drunk," and walked out of the room.

This curious report was true. Anson, finding his voice thick and uncontrollable, had taken the unusual refuge of announcing that he spoke no English. Years afterward he used to tell that part of the story, and he invariably communicated the uproarious laughter which the memory aroused in him.

Five times in the next hour Mrs. Legendre tried to get Hempstead on the phone. When she succeeded, there was a ten-minute delay before she heard Paula's voice on the wire.

"Cousin Jo told me Anson was intoxicated."

"Oh, no . . . ."

"Oh, yes. Cousin Jo says he was intoxicated. He told her he was French, and fell off his chair and behaved as if he was very intoxicated. I don't want you to come home with him."

"Mother, he's all right! Please don't worry about——"

"But I do worry. I think it's dreadful. I want you to promise me not to come home with him."

"I'll take care of it, mother. . . ."

"I don't want you to come home with him."

"All right, mother. Good-by."

"Be sure now, Paula. Ask some one to bring you."

Deliberately Paula took the receiver from her ear and hung it up. Her face was flushed with helpless annoyance. Anson was stretched out asleep in a bedroom up-stairs, while the dinner-party below was proceeding lamely toward conclusion.

The hour's drive had sobered him somewhat—his arrival was merely hilarious—and Paula hoped that the evening was not spoiled, after all, but two imprudent cocktails before dinner completed the disaster. He talked boisterously and somewhat offensively to the party at large for fifteen minutes, and then slid silently under the table, like a man in an old print—but, unlike an old print, it was rather horrible without being at all quaint. None of the young girls present remarked upon the incident—it seemed to merit only silence. His uncle and two other men carried him up-stairs, and it was just after this that Paula was called to the phone.

An hour later Anson awoke in a fog of nervous agony, through which he perceived after a moment the figure of his uncle Robert standing by the door.

" . . . I said are you better?"

"What?"

"Do you feel better, old man?"

"Terrible," said Anson.

"I'm going to try you on another bromo-seltzer. If you can hold it down, it'll do you good to sleep."

With an effort Anson slid his legs from the bed and stood up.

"I'm all right," he said dully.

"Take it easy."

"I thin' if you gave me a glassbrandy I could go down-stairs."

"Oh, no——"

"Yes, that's the only thin'. I'm all right now. . . . I suppose I'm I'm in Dutch dow' there."

"They know you're a little under the weather," said his uncle deprecatingly. "But don't worry about it. Schuyler didn't even get here. He passed away in the locker-room over at the Links."

Indifferent to any opinion, except Paula's, Anson was nevertheless determined to save the débris of the evening, but when after a cold bath he made his appearance most of the party had already left. Paula got up immediately to go home.

In the limousine the old serious dialogue began. She had known that he drank, she admitted, but she had never expected anything like this—it seemed to her that perhaps they were not suited to each other, after all. Their ideas about life were too different, and so forth. When she finished speaking, Anson spoke in turn, very soberly. Then Paula said she'd have to think it over; she wouldn't decide to-night; she was not angry but she was terribly sorry. Nor would she let him come into the hotel with her, but just before she got out of the car she leaned and kissed him unhappily on the cheek.

The next afternoon Anson had a long talk with Mrs. Legendre while Paula sat listening in silence. It was agreed that Paula was to brood over the incident for a proper period and then, if mother and daughter thought it best, they would follow Anson to Pensacola. On his part he apologized with sincerity and dignity—that was all; with every card in her hand Mrs. Legendre was unable to establish any advantage over him. He made no promises, showed no humility, only delivered a few serious comments on life which brought him off with rather a moral superiority at the end. When they came South three weeks later, neither Anson in his satisfaction nor Paula in her relief at the reunion realized that the psychological moment had passed forever.

IV

He dominated and attracted her, and at the same time filled her with anxiety. Confused by his mixture of solidity and self-indulgence, of sentiment and cynicism—incongruities which her gentle mind was unable to resolve—Paula grew to think of him as two alternating personalities. When she saw him alone, or at a formal party, or with his casual inferiors, she felt a tremendous pride in his strong, attractive presence, the paternal, understanding stature of his mind. In other company she became uneasy when what had been a fine imperviousness to mere gentility showed its other face. The other face was gross, humorous, reckless of everything but pleasure. It startled her mind temporarily away from him, even led her into a short covert experiment with an old beau, but it was no use— after four months of Anson's enveloping vitality there was an anemic pallor in all other men.

In July he was ordered abroad, and their tenderness and desire reached a crescendo. Paula considered a last-minute marriage— decided against it only because there were always cocktails on his breath now, but the parting itself made her physically ill with grief.

After his departure she wrote him long letters of regret for the days of love they had missed by waiting. In August Anson's plane slipped down into the North Sea. He was pulled onto a destroyer after a night in the water and sent to hospital with pneumonia; the armistice was signed before he was finally sent home.

Then, with every opportunity given back to them, with no material obstacle to overcome, the secret weavings of their temperaments came between them, drying up their kisses and their tears, making their voices less loud to one another, muffling the intimate chatter of their hearts until the old communication was only possible by letters, from far away. One afternoon a society reporter waited for two hours in the Hunters' house for a confirmation of their engagement. Anson denied it; nevertheless an early issue carried the report as a leading paragraph—they were "constantly seen together at Southampton, Hot Springs, and Tuxedo Park." But the serious dialogue had turned a corner into a long-sustained quarrel, and the affair was almost played out. Anson got drunk flagrantly and missed an engagement with her, whereupon Paula made certain behavioristic demands. His despair was helpless before his pride and his knowledge of himself: the engagement was definitely broken.

"Dearest," said their letters now, "Dearest, Dearest, when I wake up in the middle of the night and realize that after all it was not to be, I feel that I want to die. I can't go on living any more. Perhaps when we meet this summer we may talk things over and decide differently—we were so excited and sad that day, and I don't feel that I can live all my life without you. You speak of other people. Don't you know there are no other people for me, but only you. . . . "

But as Paula drifted here and there around the East she would sometimes mention her gaieties to make him wonder. Anson was too acute to wonder. When he saw a man's name in her letters he felt more sure of her and a little disdainful—he was always superior to such things. But he still hoped that they would some day marry.

Meanwhile he plunged vigorously into all the movement and glitter of post-bellum New York, entering a brokerage house, joining half a dozen clubs, dancing late, and moving in three worlds—his own world, the world of young Yale graduates, and that section of the half-world which rests one end on Broadway. But there was always a thorough and infractible eight hours devoted to his work in Wall Street, where the combination of his influential family connection, his sharp intelligence, and his abundance of sheer physical energy brought him almost immediately forward. He had one of those invaluable minds with partitions in it; sometimes he appeared at his office refreshed by less than an hour's sleep, but such occurrences were rare. So early as 1920 his income in salary and commissions exceeded twelve thousand dollars.

As the Yale tradition slipped into the past he became more and more of a popular figure among his classmates in New York, more popular than he had ever been in college. He lived in a great house, and had the means of introducing young men into other great houses. Moreover, his life already seemed secure, while theirs, for the most part, had arrived again at precarious beginnings. They commenced to turn to him for amusement and escape, and Anson responded readily, taking pleasure in helping people and arranging their affairs.

There were no men in Paula's letters now, but a note of tenderness ran through them that had not been there before. From several sources he heard that she had "a heavy beau," Lowell Thayer, a Bostonian of wealth and position, and though he was sure she still loved him, it made him uneasy to think that he might lose her, after all. Save for one unsatisfactory day she had not been in New York for almost five months, and as the rumors multiplied he became increasingly anxious to see her. In February he took his vacation and went down to Florida.

Palm Beach sprawled plump and opulent between the sparkling sapphire of Lake Worth, flawed here and there by house-boats at anchor, and the great turquoise bar of the Atlantic Ocean. The huge bulks of the Breakers and the Royal Poinciana rose as twin paunches from the bright level of the sand, and around them clustered the Dancing Glade, Bradley's House of Chance, and a dozen modistes and milliners with goods at triple prices from New York. Upon the trellissed veranda of the Breakers two hundred women stepped right, stepped left, wheeled, and slid in that then celebrated calisthenic known as the double-shuffle, while in half-time to the music two thousand bracelets clicked up and down on two hundred arms.

At the Everglades Club after dark Paula and Lowell Thayer and Anson and a casual fourth played bridge with hot cards. It seemed to Anson that her kind, serious face was wan and tired—she had been around now for four, five, years. He had known her for three.

"Two spades."

"Cigarette? . . Oh, I beg your pardon. By me."

"By."

"I'll double three spades."

There were a dozen tables of bridge in the room, which was filling up with smoke. Anson's eyes met Paula's, held them persistently even when Thayer's glance fell between them. . . .

"What was bid?" he asked abstractedly.

"Rose of Washington Square"

sang the young people in the corners:

"I'm withering there
In basement air——"

The smoke banked like fog, and the opening of a door filled the room with blown swirls of ectoplasm. Little Bright Eyes streaked past the tables seeking Mr. Conan Doyle among the Englishmen who were posing as Englishmen about the lobby.

"You could cut it with a knife."

". . . cut it with a knife."

". . . a knife."

At the end of the rubber Paula suddenly got up and spoke to Anson in a tense, low voice. With scarcely a glance at Lowell Thayer, they walked out the door and descended a long flight of stone steps—in a moment they were walking hand in hand along the moonlit beach.

"Darling, darling. . . ." They embraced recklessly, passionately, in a shadow. . . . Then Paula drew back her face to let his lips say what she wanted to hear—she could feel the words forming as they kissed again. . . . Again she broke away, listening, but as he pulled her close once more she realized that he had said nothing —only *"Darling! Darling!"* in that deep, sad whisper that always made her cry. Humbly, obediently, her emotions yielded to him and the tears streamed down her face, but her heart kept on crying: "Ask me—oh, Anson, dearest, ask me!"

"Paula. . . . *Paula!*"

The words wrung her heart like hands, and Anson, feeling her tremble, knew that emotion was enough. He need say no more, commit their destinies to no practical enigma. Why should he, when he might hold her so, biding his own time, for another year—forever? He was considering them both, her more than himself. For a moment, when she said suddenly that she must go back to her hotel, he hesitated, thinking, first, "This is the moment, after all," and then: "No, let it wait—she is mine. . . ."

He had forgotten that Paula too was worn away inside with the strain of three years. Her mood passed forever in the night.

He went back to New York next morning filled with a certain restless dissatisfaction. Late in April, without warning, he received a telegram from Bar Harbor in which Paula told him that she was engaged to Lowell Thayer, and that they would be married immediately in Boston. What he never really believed could happen had happened at last.

Anson filled himself with whiskey that morning, and going to the office, carried on his work without a break—rather with a fear of what would happen if he stopped. In the evening he went out as usual, saying nothing of what had occurred; he was cordial, humorous, unabstracted. But one thing he could not help—for three days, in any place, in any company, he would suddenly bend his head into his hands and cry like a child.

———

V

In 1922 when Anson went abroad with the junior partner to investigate some London loans, the journey intimated that he was to be taken into the firm. He was twenty-seven now, a little heavy without being definitely stout, and with a manner older than his years. Old people and young people liked him and trusted him, and mothers felt safe when their daughters were in his charge, for he had a way, when he came into a room, of putting himself on a footing with the oldest and most conservative people there. "You and I," he seemed to say, "we're solid. We understand."

He had an instinctive and rather charitable knowledge of the weaknesses of men and women, and, like a priest, it made him the more concerned for the maintenance of outward forms. It was typical of him that every Sunday morning he taught in a fashionable Episcopal Sunday-school—even though a cold shower and a quick change into a cutaway coat were all that separated him from the wild night before.

After his father's death he was the practical head of his family, and, in effect, guided the destinies of the younger children. Through a complication his authority did not extend to his father's estate, which was administrated by his Uncle Robert, who was the horsey member of the family, a good-natured, hard-drinking member of that set which centres about Wheatley Hills.

Uncle Robert and his wife, Edna, had been great friends of Anson's youth, and the former was disappointed when his nephew's superiority failed to take a horsey form. He backed him for a city club which was the most difficult in America to enter—one could only join if one's family had "helped to build up New York" (or, in other words, were rich before 1880)—and when Anson, after his election, neglected it for the Yale Club, Uncle Robert gave him a little talk on the subject. But when on top of that Anson declined to enter Robert Hunter's own conservative and somewhat neglected brokerage house, his manner grew cooler. Like a primary teacher who has taught all he knew, he slipped out of Anson's life.

There were so many friends in Anson's life—scarcely one for whom he had not done some unusual kindness and scarcely one whom he did not occasionally embarrass by his bursts of rough conversation or his habit of getting drunk whenever and however he liked. It annoyed him when any one else blundered in that regard— about his own lapses he was always humorous. Odd things happened to him and he told them with infectious laughter.

I was working in New York that spring, and I used to lunch with him at the Yale Club, which my university was sharing until the completion of our own. I had read of Paula's marriage, and one afternoon, when I asked him about her, something moved him to tell me the story. After that he frequently invited me to family dinners at his house and behaved as though there was a special relation between us, as though with his confidence a little of that consuming memory had passed into me.

I found that despite the trusting mothers, his attitude toward girls was not indiscriminately protective. It was up to the girl—if she showed an inclination toward looseness, she must take care of herself, even with him.

"Life," he would explain sometimes, "has made a cynic of me."

By life he meant Paula. Sometimes, especially when he was drinking, it became a little twisted in his mind, and he thought that she had callously thrown him over.

This "cynicism," or rather his realization that naturally fast girls were not worth sparing, led to his affair with Dolly Karger. It wasn't his only affair in those years, but it came nearest to touching him deeply, and it had a profound effect upon his attitude toward life.

Dolly was the daughter of a notorious "publicist" who had married into society. She herself grew up into the Junior League, came out at the Plaza, and went to the Assembly; and only a few old families like the Hunters could question whether or not she "belonged," for her picture was often in the papers, and she had more enviable attention than many girls who undoubtedly did. She was dark-haired, with carmine lips and a high, lovely color, which she concealed under pinkish-gray powder all through the first year out, because high color was unfashionable—Victorian-pale was the thing to be. She wore black, severe suits and stood with her hands in her pockets leaning a little forward, with a humorous restraint on her face. She danced exquisitely—better than anything she liked to dance—better than anything except making love. Since she was ten she had always been in love, and, usually, with some boy who didn't respond to her. Those who did—and there were many—bored her after a brief encounter, but for her failures she reserved the warmest spot in her heart. When she met them she would always try once more—sometimes she succeeded, more often she failed.

It never occurred to this gypsy of the unattainable that there was a certain resemblance in those who refused to love her—they shared a hard intuition that saw through to her weakness, not a weakness of emotion but a weakness of rudder. Anson perceived this when he first met her, less than a month after Paula's marriage. He was drinking rather heavily, and he pretended for a week that he was falling in love with her. Then he dropped her abruptly and forgot—immediately he took up the commanding position in her heart.

Like so many girls of that day Dolly was slackly and indiscreetly wild. The unconventionality of a slightly older generation had been simply one facet of a post-war movement to discredit obsolete manners—Dolly's was both older and shabbier, and she saw in Anson the two extremes which the emotionally shiftless woman seeks, an abandon to indulgence alternating with a protective strength. In his character she felt both the sybarite and the solid rock, and these two satisfied every need of her nature.

She felt that it was going to be difficult, but she mistook the reason—she thought that Anson and his family expected a more spectacular marriage, but she guessed immediately that her advantage lay in his tendency to drink.

They met at the large débutante dances, but as her infatuation increased they managed to be more and more together. Like most mothers, Mrs. Karger believed that Anson was exceptionally reliable, so she allowed Dolly to go with him to distant country clubs and suburban houses without inquiring closely into their activities or questioning her explanations when they came in late. At first these explanations might have been accurate, but Dolly's worldly ideas of capturing Anson were soon engulfed in the rising sweep of her emotion. Kisses in the back of taxis and motor-cars were no longer enough; they did a curious thing:

They dropped out of their world for a while and made another world just beneath it where Anson's tippling and Dolly's irregular hours would be less noticed and commented on. It was composed, this world, of varying elements—several of Anson's Yale friends and their wives, two or three young brokers and bond salesmen and a handful of unattached men, fresh from college, with money and a propensity to dissipation. What this world lacked in spaciousness and scale it made up for by allowing them a liberty that it scarcely permitted itself. Moreover, it centred around them and permitted Dolly the pleasure of a faint condescension—a pleasure which Anson, whose whole life was a condescension from the certitudes of his childhood, was unable to share.

He was not in love with her, and in the long feverish winter of their affair he frequently told her so. In the spring he was weary—he wanted to renew his life at some other source—moreover, he saw that either he must break with her now or accept the responsibility of a definite seduction. Her family's encouraging attitude precipitated his decision—one evening when Mr. Karger knocked discreetly at the library door to announce that he had left a bottle of old brandy in the dining-room, Anson felt that life was hemming him in. That night he wrote her a short letter in which he told her that he was going on his vacation, and that in view of all the circumstances they had better meet no more.

It was June. His family had closed up the house and gone to the country, so he was living temporarily at the Yale Club. I had heard about his affair with Dolly as it developed—accounts salted with humor, for he despised unstable women, and granted them no place in the social edifice in which he believed—and when he told me that night that he was definitely breaking with her I was glad. I had seen Dolly here and there, and each time with a feeling of pity at the hopelessness of her struggle, and of shame at knowing so much about her that I had no right to know. She was what is known as "a pretty little thing," but there was a certain recklessness which rather fascinated me. Her dedication to the goddess of waste would have been less obvious had she been less spirited—she would most certainly throw herself away, but I was glad when I heard that the sacrifice would not be consummated in my sight.

Anson was going to leave the letter of farewell at her house next morning. It was one of the few houses left open in the Fifth Avenue district, and he knew that the Kargers, acting upon erroneous information from Dolly, had foregone a trip abroad to give their daughter her chance. As he stepped out the door of the Yale Club into Madison Avenue the postman passed him, and he followed back inside. The first letter that caught his eye was in Dolly's hand.

He knew what it would be—a lonely and tragic monologue, full of the reproaches he knew, the invoked memories, the "I wonder if's"—all the immemorial intimacies that he had communicated to Paula Legendre in what seemed another age. Thumbing over some bills, he brought it on top again and opened it. To his surprise it was a short, somewhat formal note, which said that Dolly would be unable to go to the country with him for the week-end, because Perry Hull from Chicago had unexpectedly come to town. It added that Anson had brought this on himself: "—if I felt that you loved me as I love you I would go with you at any time, any place, but Perry is *so* nice, and he so much wants me to marry him——"

Anson smiled contemptuously—he had had experience with such decoy epistles. Moreover, he knew how Dolly had labored over this plan, probably sent for the faithful Perry and calculated the time of his arrival—even labored over the note so that it would make him jealous without driving him away. Like most compromises, it had neither force nor vitality but only a timorous despair.

Suddenly he was angry. He sat down in the lobby and read it again. Then he went to the phone, called Dolly and told her in his clear, compelling voice that he had received her note and would call for her at five o'clock as they had previously planned. Scarcely waiting for the pretended uncertainty of her "Perhaps I can see you for an hour," he hung up the receiver and went down to his office. On the way he tore his own letter into bits and dropped it in the street.

He was not jealous—she meant nothing to him—but at her pathetic ruse everything stubborn and self-indulgent in him came to the surface. It was a presumption from a mental inferior and it could not be overlooked. If she wanted to know to whom she belonged she would see.

He was on the door-step at quarter past five. Dolly was dressed for the street, and he listened in silence to the paragraph of "I can only see you for an hour," which she had begun on the phone.

"Put on your hat, Dolly," he said, "we'll take a walk."

They strolled up Madison Avenue and over to Fifth while Anson's shirt dampened upon his portly body in the deep heat. He talked little, scolding her, making no love to her, but before they had walked six blocks she was his again, apologizing for the note, offering not to see Perry at all as an atonement, offering anything. She thought that he had come because he was beginning to love her.

"I'm hot," he said when they reached 71st Street. "This is a winter suit. If I stop by the house and change, would you mind waiting for me down-stairs? I'll only be a minute."

She was happy; the intimacy of his being hot, of any physical fact about him, thrilled her. When they came to the iron-grated door and Anson took out his key she experienced a sort of delight.

Down-stairs it was dark, and after he ascended in the lift Dolly raised a curtain and looked out through opaque lace at the houses over the way. She heard the lift machinery stop, and with the notion of teasing him pressed the button that brought it down. Then on what was more than an impulse she got into it and sent it up to what she guessed was his floor.

"Anson," she called, laughing a little.

"Just a minute," he answered from his bedroom . . . then after a brief delay: "Now you can come in."

He had changed and was buttoning his vest. "This is my room," he said lightly. "How do you like it?"

She caught sight of Paula's picture on the wall and stared at it in fascination, just as Paula had stared at the pictures of Anson's childish sweethearts five years before. She knew something about Paula—sometimes she tortured herself with fragments of the story.

Suddenly she came close to Anson, raising her arms. They embraced. Outside the area window a soft artificial twilight already hovered, though the sun was still bright on a back roof across the way. In half an hour the room would be quite dark. The uncalculated opportunity overwhelmed them, made them both breathless, and they clung more closely. It was imminent, inevitable. Still holding one another, they raised their heads—their eyes fell together upon Paula's picture, staring down at them from the wall.

Suddenly Anson dropped his arms, and sitting down at his desk tried the drawer with a bunch of keys.

"Like a drink?" he asked in a gruff voice.

"No, Anson."

He poured himself half a tumbler of whiskey, swallowed it, and then opened the door into the hall.

"Come on," he said.

Dolly hesitated.

"Anson—I'm going to the country with you to-night, after all. You understand that, don't you?"

"Of course," he answered brusquely.

In Dolly's car they rode on to Long Island, closer in their emotions than they had ever been before. They knew what would happen—not with Paula's face to remind them that something was lacking, but when they were alone in the still, hot Long Island night they did not care.

The estate in Port Washington where they were to spend the week-end belonged to a cousin of Anson's who had married a Montana copper operator. An interminable drive began at the lodge and twisted under imported poplar saplings toward a huge, pink, Spanish house. Anson had often visited there before.

After dinner they danced at the Linx Club. About midnight Anson assured himself that his cousins would not leave before two—then he explained that Dolly was tired; he would take her home and return to the dance later. Trembling a little with excitement, they got into a borrowed car together and drove to Port Washington. As they reached the lodge he stopped and spoke to the night-watchman.

"When are you making a round, Carl?"

"Right away."

"Then you'll be here till everybody's in?"

"Yes, sir."

"All right. Listen: if any automobile, no matter whose it is, turns in at this gate, I want you to phone the house immediately." He put a five-dollar bill into Carl's hand. "Is that clear?"

"Yes, Mr. Anson." Being of the Old World, he neither winked nor smiled. Yet Dolly sat with her face turned slightly away.

Anson had a key. Once inside he poured a drink for both of them—Dolly left hers untouched—then he ascertained definitely the location of the phone, and found that it was within easy hearing distance of their rooms, both of which were on the first floor.

Five minutes later he knocked at the door of Dolly's room.

"Anson?" He went in, closing the door behind him. She was in bed, leaning up anxiously with elbows on the pillow; sitting beside her he took her in his arms.

"Anson, darling."

He didn't answer.

"Anson. . . . Anson! I love you. . . . Say you love me. Say it now—can't you say it now? Even if you don't mean it?"

He did not listen. Over her head he perceived that the picture of Paula was hanging here upon this wall.

He got up and went close to it. The frame gleamed faintly with thrice-reflected moonlight—within was a blurred shadow of a face that he saw he did not know. Almost sobbing, he turned around and stared with abomination at the little figure on the bed.

"This is all foolishness," he said thickly. "I don't know what I was thinking about. I don't love you and you'd better wait for somebody that loves you. I don't love you a bit, can't you understand?"

His voice broke, and he went hurriedly out. Back in the salon he was pouring himself a drink with uneasy fingers, when the front door opened suddenly, and his cousin came in.

"Why, Anson, I hear Dolly's sick," she began solicitously. "I hear she's sick. . . ."

"It was nothing," he interrupted, raising his voice so that it would carry into Dolly's room. "She was a little tired. She went to bed."

For a long time afterward Anson believed that a protective God sometimes interfered in human affairs. But Dolly Karger, lying awake and staring at the ceiling, never again believed in anything at all.

VI

When Dolly married during the following autumn, Anson was in London on business. Like Paula's marriage, it was sudden, but it affected him in a different way. At first he felt that it was funny, and had an inclination to laugh when he thought of it. Later it depressed him—it made him feel old.

There was something repetitive about it—why, Paula and Dolly had belonged to different generations. He had a foretaste of the sensation of a man of forty who hears that the daughter of an old flame has married. He wired congratulations and, as was not the case with Paula, they were sincere—he had never really hoped that Paula would be happy.

When he returned to New York, he was made a partner in the firm, and, as his responsibilities increased, he had less time on his hands. The refusal of a life-insurance company to issue him a policy made such an impression on him that he stopped drinking for a year, and claimed that he felt better physically, though I think he missed the convivial recounting of those Celliniesque adventures which, in his early twenties, had played such a part of his life. But he never abandoned the Yale Club. He was a figure there, a personality, and the tendency of his class, who were now seven years out of college, to drift away to more sober haunts was checked by his presence.

His day was never too full nor his mind too weary to give any sort of aid to any one who asked it. What had been done at first through pride and superiority had become a habit and a passion. And there was always something—a younger brother in trouble at New Haven, a quarrel to be patched up between a friend and his wife, a position to be found for this man, an investment for that. But his specialty was the solving of problems for young married people. Young married people fascinated him and their apartments were almost sacred to him—he knew the story of their love-affair, advised them where to live and how, and remembered their babies' names. Toward young wives his attitude was circumspect: he never abused the trust which their husbands—strangely enough in view of his unconcealed irregularities—invariably reposed in him.

He came to take a vicarious pleasure in happy marriages, and to be inspired to an almost equally pleasant melancholy by those that went astray. Not a season passed that he did not witness the collapse of an affair that perhaps he himself had fathered. When Paula was divorced and almost immediately remarried to another Bostonian, he talked about her to me all one afternoon. He would never love any one as he had loved Paula, but he insisted that he no longer cared.

"I'll never marry," he came to say; "I've seen too much of it, and I know a happy marriage is a very rare thing. Besides, I'm too old."

But he did believe in marriage. Like all men who spring from a happy and successful marriage, he believed in it passionately—nothing he had seen would change his belief, his cynicism dissolved upon it like air. But he did really believe he was too old. At twenty-eight he began to accept with equanimity the prospect of marrying without romantic love; he resolutely chose a New York girl of his own class, pretty, intelligent, congenial, above reproach—and set about falling in love with her. The things he had said to Paula with sincerity, to other girls with grace, he could no longer say at all without smiling, or with the force necessary to convince.

"When I'm forty," he told his friends, "I'll be ripe. I'll fall for some chorus girl like the rest."

Nevertheless, he persisted in his attempt. His mother wanted to see him married, and he could now well afford it—he had a seat on the Stock Exchange, and his earned income came to twenty-five thousand a year. The idea was agreeable: when his friends—he spent most of his time with the set he and Dolly had evolved—closed themselves in behind domestic doors at night, he no longer rejoiced in his freedom. He even wondered if he should have married Dolly. Not even Paula had loved him more, and he was learning the rarity, in a single life, of encountering true emotion.

Just as this mood began to creep over him a disquieting story reached his ear. His aunt Edna, a woman just this side of forty, was carrying on an open intrigue with a dissolute, hard-drinking young man named Cary Sloane. Every one knew of it except Anson's Uncle Robert, who for fifteen years had talked long in clubs and taken his wife for granted.

Anson heard the story again and again with increasing annoyance. Something of his old feeling for his uncle came back to him, a feeling that was more than personal, a reversion toward that family solidarity on which he had based his pride. His intuition singled out the essential point of the affair, which was that his uncle shouldn't be hurt. It was his first experiment in unsolicited meddling, but with his knowledge of Edna's character he felt that he could handle the matter better than a district judge or his uncle.

His uncle was in Hot Springs. Anson traced down the sources of the scandal so that there should be no possibility of mistake and then he called Edna and asked her to lunch with him at the Plaza next day. Something in his tone must have frightened her, for she was reluctant, but he insisted, putting off the date until she had no excuse for refusing.

She met him at the appointed time in the Plaza lobby, a lovely, faded, gray-eyed blonde in a coat of Russian sable. Five great rings, cold with diamonds and emeralds, sparkled on her slender hands.

It occurred to Anson that it was his father's intelligence and not his uncle's that had earned the fur and the stones, the rich brilliance that buoyed up her passing beauty.

Though Edna scented his hostility, she was unprepared for the directness of his approach.

"Edna, I'm astonished at the way you've been acting," he said in a strong, frank voice. "At first I couldn't believe it."

"Believe what?" she demanded sharply.

"You needn't pretend with me, Edna. I'm talking about Cary Sloane. Aside from any other consideration, I didn't think you could treat Uncle Robert——"

"Now look here, Anson——" she began angrily, but his peremptory voice broke through hers:

"——and your children in such a way. You've been married eighteen years, and you're old enough to know better."

"You can't talk to me like that! You——"

"Yes, I can. Uncle Robert has always been my best friend." He was tremendously moved. He felt a real distress about his uncle, about his three young cousins.

Edna stood up, leaving her crab-flake cocktail untasted.

"This is the silliest thing——"

"Very well, if you won't listen to me I'll go to Uncle Robert and tell him the whole story—he's bound to hear it sooner or later. And afterward I'll go to old Moses Sloane."

Edna faltered back into her chair.

"Don't talk so loud," she begged him. Her eyes blurred with tears. "You have no idea how your voice carries. You might have chosen a less public place to make all these crazy accusations."

He didn't answer.

"Oh, you never liked me, I know," she went on. "You're just taking advantage of some silly gossip to try and break up the only interesting friendship I've ever had. What did I ever do to make you hate me so?"

Still Anson waited. There would be the appeal to his chivalry, then to his pity, finally to his superior sophistication—when he had shouldered his way through all these there would be admissions, and he could come to grips with her. By being silent, by being impervious, by returning constantly to his main weapon, which was his own true emotion, he bullied her into frantic despair as the luncheon hour slipped away. At two o'clock she took out a mirror

and a handkerchief, shined away the marks of her tears and pow-
dered the slight hollows where they had lain. She had agreed to
meet him at her own house at five.

When he arrived she was stretched on a *chaise-longue* which was
covered with cretonne for the summer, and the tears he had called
up at luncheon seemed still to be standing in her eyes. Then he was
aware of Cary Sloane's dark anxious presence upon the cold hearth.

"What's this idea of yours?" broke out Sloane immediately. "I
understand you invited Edna to lunch and then threatened her on
the basis of some cheap scandal."

Anson sat down.

"I have no reason to think it's only scandal."

"I hear you're going to take it to Robert Hunter, and to my
father."

Anson nodded.

"Either you break it off—or I will," he said.

"What God damned business is it of yours, Hunter?"

"Don't lose your temper, Cary," said Edna nervously. "It's only
a question of showing him how absurd——"

"For one thing, it's my name that's being handed around," interrupted Anson. "That's all that concerns you, Cary."

"Edna isn't a member of your family."

"She most certainly is!" His anger mounted. "Why—she owes this
house and the rings on her fingers to my father's brains. When Uncle
Robert married her she didn't have a penny."

They all looked at the rings as if they had a significant bearing
on the situation. Edna made a gesture to take them from her hand.

"I guess they're not the only rings in the world," said Sloane.

"Oh, this is absurd," cried Edna. "Anson, will you listen to me?
I've found out how the silly story started. It was a maid I discharged who went right to the Chilicheffs—all these Russians pump
things out of their servants and then put a false meaning on them."
She brought down her fist angrily on the table: "And after Tom
lent them the limousine for a whole month when we were South
last winter——"

"Do you see?" demanded Sloane eagerly. "This maid got hold
of the wrong end of the thing. She knew that Edna and I were
friends, and she carried it to the Chilicheffs. In Russia they assume
that if a man and a woman——"

He enlarged the theme to a disquisition upon social relations in
the Caucasus.

"If that's the case it better be explained to Uncle Robert," said Anson dryly, "so that when the rumors do reach him he'll know they're not true."

Adopting the method he had followed with Edna at luncheon he let them explain it all away. He knew that they were guilty and that presently they would cross the line from explanation into justification and convict themselves more definitely than he could ever do. By seven they had taken the desperate step of telling him the truth —Robert Hunter's neglect, Edna's empty life, the casual dalliance that had flamed up into passion—but like so many true stories it had the misfortune of being old, and its enfeebled body beat helplessly against the armor of Anson's will. The threat to go to Sloane's father sealed their helplessness, for the latter, a retired cotton broker out of Alabama, was a notorious fundamentalist who controlled his son by a rigid allowance and the promise that at his next vagary the allowance would stop forever.

They dined at a small French restaurant, and the discussion continued—at one time Sloane resorted to physical threats, a little later they were both imploring him to give them time. But Anson was obdurate. He saw that Edna was breaking up, and that her spirit must not be refreshed by any renewal of their passion.

At two o'clock in a small night-club on 53rd Street, Edna's nerves suddenly collapsed, and she cried to go home. Sloane had been drinking heavily all evening, and he was faintly maudlin, leaning on the table and weeping a little with his face in his hands. Quickly Anson gave them his terms. Sloane was to leave town for six months, and he must be gone within forty-eight hours. When he returned there was to be no resumption of the affair, but at the end of a year Edna might, if she wished, tell Robert Hunter that she wanted a divorce and go about it in the usual way.

He paused, gaining confidence from their faces for his final word.

"Or there's another thing you can do," he said slowly, "if Edna wants to leave her children, there's nothing I can do to prevent your running off together."

"I want to go home!" cried Edna again. "Oh, haven't you done enough to us for one day?"

Outside it was dark, save for a blurred glow from Sixth Avenue down the street. In that light those two who had been lovers looked for the last time into each other's tragic faces, realizing that between them there was not enough youth and strength to avert their eternal parting. Sloane walked suddenly off down the street and Anson tapped a dozing taxi-driver on the arm.

It was almost four; there was a patient flow of cleaning water along the ghostly pavement of Fifth Avenue, and the shadows of two night women flitted over the dark façade of St. Thomas's church. Then the desolate shrubbery of Central Park where Anson had often played as a child, and the mounting numbers, significant as names, of the marching streets. This was his city, he thought, where his name had flourished through five generations. No change could alter the permanence of its place here, for change itself was the essential substratum by which he and those of his name identified themselves with the spirit of New York. Resourcefulness and a powerful will—for his threats in weaker hands would have been less than nothing—had beaten the gathering dust from his uncle's name, from the name of his family, from even this shivering figure that sat beside him in the car.

Cary Sloane's body was found next morning on the lower shelf of a pillar of Queensboro Bridge. In the darkness and in his excitement he had thought that it was the water flowing black beneath him, but in less than a second it made no possible difference—unless he had planned to think one last thought of Edna, and call out her name as he struggled feebly in the water.

VII

Anson never blamed himself for his part in this affair—the situation which brought it about had not been of his making. But the just suffer with the unjust, and he found that his oldest and somehow his most precious friendship was over. He never knew what distorted story Edna told, but he was welcome in his uncle's house no longer.

Just before Christmas Mrs. Hunter retired to a select Episcopal heaven, and Anson became the responsible head of his family. An unmarried aunt who had lived with them for years ran the house, and attempted with helpless inefficiency to chaperone the younger girls. All the children were less self-reliant than Anson, more conventional both in their virtues and in their shortcomings. Mrs. Hunter's death had postponed the début of one daughter and the wedding of another. Also it had taken something deeply material from all of them, for with her passing the quiet, expensive superiority of the Hunters came to an end.

For one thing, the estate, considerably diminished by two inheritance taxes and soon to be divided among six children, was not a notable fortune any more. Anson saw a tendency in his youngest sisters to speak rather respectfully of families that hadn't "existed" twenty years ago. His own feeling of precedence was not echoed in them—sometimes they were conventionally snobbish, that was all. For another thing, this was the last summer they would spend on the Connecticut estate; the clamor against it was too loud: "Who wants to waste the best months of the year shut up in that dead old town?" Reluctantly he yielded—the house would go into the market in the fall, and next summer they would rent a smaller place in Westchester County. It was a step down from the expensive simplicity of his father's idea, and, while he sympathized with the revolt, it also annoyed him; during his mother's lifetime he had gone up there at least every other week-end—even in the gayest summers.

Yet he himself was part of this change, and his strong instinct for life had turned him in his twenties from the hollow obsequies of that abortive leisure class. He did not see this clearly—he still felt that there was a norm, a standard of society. But there was no norm, it was doubtful if there had ever been a true norm in New York. The few who still paid and fought to enter a particular set succeeded only to find that as a society it scarcely functioned—or, what was more alarming, that the Bohemia from which they fled sat above them at table.

At twenty-nine Anson's chief concern was his own growing loneliness. He was sure now that he would never marry. The number of weddings at which he had officiated as best man or usher was past all counting—there was a drawer at home that bulged with the official neckties of this or that wedding-party, neckties standing for romances that had not endured a year, for couples who had passed completely from his life. Scarf-pins, gold pencils, cuff-buttons, presents from a generation of grooms had passed through his jewel-box and been lost—and with every ceremony he was less and less able to imagine himself in the groom's place. Under his hearty good-will toward all those marriages there was despair about his own.

And as he neared thirty he became not a little depressed at the

inroads that marriage, especially lately, had made upon his friend-
ships. Groups of people had a disconcerting tendency to dissolve and
disappear. The men from his own college—and it was upon them
he had expended the most time and affection—were the most elusive
of all. Most of them were drawn deep into domesticity, two were
dead, one lived abroad, one was in Hollywood writing continuities
for pictures that Anson went faithfully to see.

Most of them, however, were permanent commuters with an
intricate family life centring around some suburban country club,
and it was from these that he felt his estrangement most keenly.

In the early days of their married life they had all needed him;
he gave them advice about their slim finances, he exorcised their
doubts about the advisability of bringing a baby into two rooms
and a bath, especially he stood for the great world outside. But
now their financial troubles were in the past and the fearfully
expected child had evolved into an absorbing family. They were
always glad to see old Anson, but they dressed up for him and
tried to impress him with their present importance, and kept their
troubles to themselves. They needed him no longer.

A few weeks before his thirtieth birthday the last of his early
and intimate friends was married. Anson acted in his usual rôle
of best man, gave his usual silver tea-service, and went down to
the usual *Homeric* to say good-by. It was a hot Friday afternoon
in May, and as he walked from the pier he realized that Saturday
closing had begun and he was free until Monday morning.

"Go where?" he asked himself.

The Yale Club, of course; bridge until dinner, then four or five
raw cocktails in somebody's room and a pleasant confused evening.
He regretted that this afternoon's groom wouldn't be along—they
had always been able to cram so much into such nights: they
knew how to attach women and how to get rid of them, how much
consideration any girl deserved from their intelligent hedonism.
A party was an adjusted thing—you took certain girls to certain
places and spent just so much on their amusement; you drank a
little, not much, more than you ought to drink, and at a certain
time in the morning you stood up and said you were going home.
You avoided college boys, sponges, future engagements, fights,
sentiment, and indiscretions. That was the way it was done. All
the rest was dissipation.

In the morning you were never violently sorry—you made no
resolutions, but if you had overdone it and your heart was slightly

out of order, you went on the wagon for a few days without saying anything about it, and waited until an accumulation of nervous boredom projected you into another party.

The lobby of the Yale Club was unpopulated. In the bar three very young alumni looked up at him, momentarily and without curiosity.

"Hello there, Oscar," he said to the bartender. "Mr. Cahill been around this afternoon?"

"Mr. Cahill's gone to New Haven."

"Oh . . . that so?"

"Gone to the ball game. Lot of men gone up."

Anson looked once again into the lobby, considered for a moment, and then walked out and over to Fifth Avenue. From the broad window of one of his clubs—one that he had scarcely visited in five years—a gray man with watery eyes stared down at him. Anson looked quickly away—that figure sitting in vacant resignation, in supercilious solitude, depressed him. He stopped and, retracing his steps, started over 47th Street toward Teak Warden's apartment. Teak and his wife had once been his most familiar friends—it was a household where he and Dolly Karger had been used to go in the days of their affair. But Teak had taken to drink, and his wife had remarked publicly that Anson was a bad influence on him. The remark reached Anson in an exaggerated form— when it was finally cleared up, the delicate spell of intimacy was broken, never to be renewed.

"Is Mr. Warden at home?" he inquired.

"They've gone to the country."

The fact unexpectedly cut at him. They were gone to the country and he hadn't known. Two years before he would have known the date, the hour, come up at the last moment for a final drink, and planned his first visit to them. Now they had gone without a word.

Anson looked at his watch and considered a week-end with his family, but the only train was a local that would jolt through the aggressive heat for three hours. And to-morrow in the country, and Sunday—he was in no mood for porch-bridge with polite undergraduates, and dancing after dinner at a rural roadhouse, a diminutive of gaiety which his father had estimated too well.

"Oh, no," he said to himself. . . . "No."

He was a dignified, impressive young man, rather stout now, but otherwise unmarked by dissipation. He could have been cast for a pillar of something—at times you were sure it was not society, at others nothing else—for the law, for the church. He stood for a few minutes motionless on the sidewalk in front of a 47th Street apartment-house; for almost the first time in his life he had nothing whatever to do.

Then he began to walk briskly up Fifth Avenue, as if he had just been reminded of an important engagement there. The necessity of dissimulation is one of the few characteristics that we share with dogs, and I think of Anson on that day as some well-bred specimen who had been disappointed at a familiar back door. He was going to see Nick, once a fashionable bartender in demand at all private dances, and now employed in cooling non-alcoholic champagne among the labyrinthine cellars of the Plaza Hotel.

"Nick," he said, "what's happened to everything?"

"Dead," Nick said.

"Make me a whiskey sour." Anson handed a pint bottle over the counter. "Nick, the girls are different; I had a little girl in Brooklyn and she got married last week without letting me know."

"That a fact? Ha-ha-ha," responded Nick diplomatically. "Slipped it over on you."

"Absolutely," said Anson. "And I was out with her the night before."

"Ha-ha-ha," said Nick, "ha-ha-ha!"

"Do you remember the wedding, Nick, in Hot Springs where I had the waiters and the musicians singing 'God save the King'?"

"Now where was that, Mr. Hunter?" Nick concentrated doubtfully. "Seems to me that was——"

"Next time they were back for more, and I began to wonder how much I'd paid them," continued Anson.

"—seems to me that was at Mr. Trenholm's wedding."

"Don't know him," said Anson decisively. He was offended that a strange name should intrude upon his reminiscences; Nick perceived this.

"Naw—aw—" he admitted, "I ought to know that. It was one of *your* crowd—Brakins . . . Baker——"

"Bicker Baker," said Anson responsively. "They put me in a hearse after it was over and covered me up with flowers and drove me away."

"Ha-ha-ha," said Nick. "Ha-ha-ha."

Nick's simulation of the old family servant paled presently and Anson went up-stairs to the lobby. He looked around—his eyes met the glance of an unfamiliar clerk at the desk, then fell upon a flower from the morning's marriage hesitating in the mouth of a brass cuspidor. He went out and walked slowly toward the blood-red sun over Columbus Circle. Suddenly he turned around and, retracing his steps to the Plaza, immured himself in a telephone-booth.

Later he said that he tried to get me three times that afternoon, that he tried every one who might be in New York—men and girls he had not seen for years, an artist's model of his college days whose faded number was still in his address book—Central told him that even the exchange existed no longer. At length his quest roved into the country, and he held brief disappointing conversations with emphatic butlers and maids. So-and-so was out, riding, swimming, playing golf, sailed to Europe last week. Who shall I say phoned?

It was intolerable that he should pass the evening alone—the private reckonings which one plans for a moment of leisure lose every charm when the solitude is enforced. There were always women of a sort, but the ones he knew had temporarily vanished, and to pass a New York evening in the hired company of a stranger never occurred to him—he would have considered that that was something shameful and secret, the diversion of a travelling sales-man in a strange town.

Anson paid the telephone bill—the girl tried unsuccessfully to joke with him about its size—and for the second time that afternoon started to leave the Plaza and go he knew not where. Near the revolving door the figure of a woman, obviously with child, stood sideways to the light—a sheer beige cape fluttered at her shoulders when the door turned and, each time, she looked impatiently toward it as if she were weary of waiting. At the first sight of her a strong nervous thrill of familiarity went over him, but not until he was within five feet of her did he realize that it was Paula.

"Why, Anson Hunter!"

His heart turned over.

"Why, Paula——"

"Why, this is wonderful. I can't believe it, *Anson!*"

She took both his hands, and he saw in the freedom of the gesture that the memory of him had lost poignancy to her. But not to him—he felt that old mood that she evoked in him stealing over his brain, that gentleness with which he had always met her optimism as if afraid to mar its surface.

"We're at Rye for the summer. Pete had to come East on business —you know of course I'm Mrs. Peter Hagerty now—so we brought the children and took a house. You've got to come out and see us."

"Can I?" he asked directly. "When?"

"When you like. Here's Pete." The revolving door functioned, giving up a fine tall man of thirty with a tanned face and a trim mustache. His immaculate fitness made a sharp contrast with Anson's increasing bulk, which was obvious under the faintly tight cut-away coat.

"You oughtn't to be standing," said Hagerty to his wife. "Let's sit down here." He indicated lobby chairs, but Paula hesitated.

"I've got to go right home," she said. "Anson, why don't you— why don't you come out and have dinner with us to-night? We're just getting settled, but if you can stand that——"

Hagerty confirmed the invitation cordially.

"Come out for the night."

Their car waited in front of the hotel, and Paula with a tired gesture sank back against silk cushions in the corner.

"There's so much I want to talk to you about," she said, "it seems hopeless."

"I want to hear about you."

"Well"—she smiled at Hagerty—"that would take a long time too. I have three children—by my first marriage. The oldest is five, then four, then three." She smiled again. "I didn't waste much time having them, did I?"

"Boys?"

"A boy and two girls. Then—oh, a lot of things happened, and I got a divorce in Paris a year ago and married Pete. That's all— except that I'm awfully happy."

In Rye they drove up to a large house near the Beach Club, from which there issued presently three dark, slim children who broke from an English governess and approached them with an esoteric cry. Abstractedly and with difficulty Paula took each one into her arms, a caress which they accepted stiffly, as they had evidently been told not to bump into Mummy. Even against their fresh faces Paula's skin showed scarcely any weariness—for all her physical languor she seemed younger than when he had last seen her at Palm Beach seven years ago.

At dinner she was preoccupied, and afterward, during the homage to the radio, she lay with closed eyes on the sofa, until Anson wondered if his presence at this time were not an intrusion. But at nine o'clock when Hagerty rose and said pleasantly that he was going to leave them by themselves for a while, she began to talk slowly about herself and the past.

"My first baby," she said—"the one we call Darling, the biggest little girl—I wanted to die when I knew I was going to have her, because Lowell was like a stranger to me. It didn't seem as though she could be my own. I wrote you a letter and tore it up. Oh, you were *so* bad to me, Anson."

It was the dialogue again, rising and falling. Anson felt a sudden quickening of memory.

"Weren't you engaged once?" she asked—"a girl named Dolly something?"

"I wasn't ever engaged. I tried to be engaged, but I never loved anybody but you, Paula."

"Oh," she said. Then after a moment: "This baby is the first one I ever really wanted. You see, I'm in love now—at last."

He didn't answer, shocked at the treachery of her remembrance. She must have seen that the "at last" bruised him, for she continued:

"I was infatuated with you, Anson—you could make me do anything you liked. But we wouldn't have been happy. I'm not smart enough for you. I don't like things to be complicated like you do." She paused. "You'll never settle down," she said.

The phrase struck at him from behind—it was an accusation that of all accusations he had never merited.

"I could settle down if women were different," he said. "If I didn't understand so much about them, if women didn't spoil you for other women, if they had only a little pride. If I could go to sleep for a while and wake up into a home that was really mine—why, that's what I'm made for, Paula, that's what women have seen in me and like in me. It's only that I can't get through the preliminaries any more."

Hagerty came in a little before eleven; after a whiskey Paula stood up and announced that she was going to bed. She went over and stood by her husband.

"Where did you go, dearest?" she demanded.

"I had a drink with Ed Saunders."

"I was worried. I thought maybe you'd run away."

She rested her head against his coat.

"He's sweet, isn't he, Anson?" she demanded.

"Absolutely," said Anson, laughing.

She raised her face to her husband.

"Well, I'm ready," she said. She turned to Anson: "Do you want to see our family gymnastic stunt?"

"Yes," he said in an interested voice.

"All right. Here we go!"

Hagerty picked her up easily in his arms.

"This is called the family acrobatic stunt," said Paula. "He carries me up-stairs. Isn't it sweet of him?"

"Yes," said Anson.

Hagerty bent his head slightly until his face touched Paula's.

"And I love him," she said. "I've just been telling you, haven't I, Anson?"

"Yes," he said.

"He's the dearest thing that ever lived in this world, aren't you, darling? . . . Well, good night. Here we go. Isn't he strong?"

"Yes," Anson said.

"You'll find a pair of Pete's pajamas laid out for you. Sweet dreams—see you at breakfast."

"Yes," Anson said.

VIII

The older members of the firm insisted that Anson should go abroad for the summer. He had scarcely had a vacation in seven years, they said. He was stale and needed a change. Anson resisted.

"If I go," he declared, "I won't come back any more."

"That's absurd, old man. You'll be back in three months with all this depression gone. Fit as ever."

"No." He shook his head stubbornly. "If I stop, I won't go back to work. If I stop, that means I've given up—I'm through."

"We'll take a chance on that. Stay six months if you like—we're not afraid you'll leave us. Why, you'd be miserable if you didn't work."

They arranged his passage for him. They liked Anson—every one liked Anson—and the change that had been coming over him cast a sort of pall over the office. The enthusiasm that had invariably signalled up business, the consideration toward his equals and his inferiors, the lift of his vital presence—within the past four months his intense nervousness had melted down these qualities into the fussy pessimism of a man of forty. On every transaction in which he was involved he acted as a drag and a strain.

"If I go I'll never come back," he said.

Three days before he sailed Paula Legendre Hagerty died in childbirth. I was with him a great deal then, for we were crossing together, but for the first time in our friendship he told me not a word of how he felt, nor did I see the slightest sign of emotion. His chief preoccupation was with the fact that he was thirty years old—he would turn the conversation to the point where he could remind you of it and then fall silent, as if he assumed that the statement would start a chain of thought sufficient to itself. Like his partners, I was amazed at the change in him, and I was glad when the *Paris* moved off into the wet space between the worlds, leaving his principality behind.

"How about a drink?" he suggested.

We walked into the bar with that defiant feeling that characterizes the day of departure and ordered four Martinis. After one cocktail a change came over him—he suddenly reached across and slapped my knee with the first joviality I had seen him exhibit for months.

"Did you see that girl in the red tam?" he demanded, "the one with the high color who had the two police dogs down to bid her good-by."

"She's pretty," I agreed.

"I looked her up in the purser's office and found out that she's alone. I'm going down to see the steward in a few minutes. We'll have dinner with her to-night."

After a while he left me, and within an hour he was walking up and down the deck with her, talking to her in his strong, clear voice. Her red tam was a bright spot of color against the steel-green sea, and from time to time she looked up with a flashing bob of her head, and smiled with amusement and interest, and anticipation. At dinner we had champagne, and were very joyous—afterward Anson ran the pool with infectious gusto, and several people who had seen me with him asked me his name. He and the girl were talking and laughing together on a lounge in the bar when I went to bed.

I saw less of him on the trip than I had hoped. He wanted to arrange a foursome, but there was no one available, so I saw him only at meals. Sometimes, though, he would have a cocktail in the bar, and he told me about the girl in the red tam, and his adventures with her, making them all bizarre and amusing, as he had a way of doing, and I was glad that he was himself again, or at least the self that I knew, and with which I felt at home. I don't think he was ever happy unless some one was in love with him, responding to him like filings to a magnet, helping him to explain himself, promising him something. What it was I do not know. Perhaps they promised that there would always be women in the world who would spend their brightest, freshest, rarest hours to nurse and protect that superiority he cherished in his heart.

The Basic and Fundamental Ideals of Christian American Citizenship

SINCLAIR LEWIS

The following excerpt, one of the six chapters that compose The Man Who Knew Coolidge, *suffers little in standing alone. It belongs to a book-length monologue, delivered by Lowell Schmaltz, which has no distinct beginning or end, no firm sequence of thought, no sharp narrative point. Ostensibly reportorial, the speech is actually an ingenious amalgam of formality and folksiness, grammatical correctness and illiteracy, clarity and obfuscation, lightly held together by platitudes, illogicalities, indiscriminacies, and a narrowly commercial ethic. Lewis' ingenuity may be overlooked, and thus his satiric purpose defeated, because the piece lacks a dramatic structure, in which attitudes different from Lowell Schmaltz's could be presented, so that the work depends for its effectiveness much more heavily than most fiction on the reader's agreement with the social and intellectual values taken for granted by the author.*

M r. Chairman, reverend sirs, and friends and brothers of the Men's Club of the Pilgrim Congregational Church:

It is difficult for me to express the pleasure and honor I feel in being thus called on as your speaker. There is no organization in which I have taken a greater pleasure in belonging to. While it is true that, due to the pressure of my Americanization work and other duties, I have not been able to attend the monthly Get-Together Supper and Talk as often as I would like, let me assure you that it has been with a pang that I have missed every supper that I have missed.

I've always been a great believer in what the Great Bard says: "Brevity is the soul of wit," and I could almost express everything I want to say to you in the song in which Bert Hubbard has so dramatically led us:

> *For your friends are my friends*
> *And my friends are your friends,*
> *And the more we get together,*
> *The happier we'll be.*

Let me first of all say that I agree most heartily with our chairman that it is the greatest conceivable pleasure and honor to have with us this evening not only Dr. Edwards, our most honored pastor, but also Dr. Otto Hickenlooper of Central Methodist Church, and Dr. Elmer Gantry, formerly of Wellspring Methodist but now so gloriously located in New York, and I want to most heartily and enthusiastically join our honored chairman and our beloved pastor in welcoming these clerical gentlemen among us.

Whatever slight doctrinal, if I may call them so, differences there may exist between the Methodists and we Congregationalists, there is no difference in our aims, and I'm sure that no Methodist could appreciate and honor Dr. Gantry and Dr. Hickenlooper more than we do.

I doubt if anywheres in the whole length and breadth of the land could be found dominies with more eloquence, more active devotion to institutional Christianity, more exemplary and devotional lives, and more courageous and scholarly devotion to the exact truth than these two gentlemen, and while they come here tonight without any preacher's vests or turned-around collars, yet let us remember that however influential we business men may be in economic affairs, it is thinkers like Dr. Gantry, Dr. Hickenlooper, and Dr. Edwards who finally determine our philosophy, our ideals, our judgment in literary and artistic matters, and our ethics in business—and that they will continue so to control us, thank God, no matter what libelous and lying attacks may be made upon them by disgruntled ignoramuses who try to get a little cheap notoriety by questioning their characters!

I will no further refer to certain filthy books and sheets and publications, that love to wallow in filth and to sell their souls for a few pitiful pennies, and I will answer them by saying that these great ministers of the gospel have—and their detractors can take it or leave it—these renowned pastors have the spiritual sanction and financial support of every man like Lowell Schmaltz!

I've wondered sometimes since I chose the title of this brief and modest talk that I propose to make—"The Basic and Fundamental Ideals of Christian American Citizenship"—if it may not sound a little too highfalutin. It isn't intended to be. I merely want to outline in a simple way the ethics of the New Generation—of the New American Era.

In the old days, preachers were just interested in a lot of confused theories; now they are as practical and as hail-fellow-well-met as any business man. In the old days, business men—the men who produce and sell the conveniences which make life what it is today —were scared of and let themselves be influenced by a lot of kings, lords, generals, journalists, judges, and a lot of impractical people like that.

But now the New Era has come. Now we can breathe a sigh of relief that the old-fashioned aristocratic and leisurely nonsense is over, and that we live in an age dominated by Henry Ford, Woolworth, Marshall Field, Crane, Andrew Mellon, Cyrus H. K. Curtis, Pillsbury, Ward the titanic baker, the founders of the A. & P. groceries, of the United Cigar Stores, and of the Liggett and Owl Drug-Stores, Statler, John D. Rockefeller, William Randolph Hearst, Hart, Schaffner and Marx, Charles Schwab, Heinz of the fifty-seven, Swift and Armour, the McCormick harvester family, and such other rulers of modern industry and commerce—the new princes, the new high priests, the creators and protectors of a new philosophy and a new art.

I yield to no one in my admiration for the America of Abraham Lincoln, Emerson, Poe, Nathaniel Hawthorne. But those gentlemen lived too early to conceive on the one hand of a nation of a hundred and ten million people, imposing its ideals and rule on the whole world, and on the other hand of standards of living in which the radio replaces the parlor organ, an electric lamp with an art shade replaces the old oil light, and a magazine with two million circulation replaces some old dusty calf-bound book.

If they lived today, they would be heart and soul with us of the New Era. I can see Lincoln as the president of United States Steel, of the Paramount Film Company, or the Wrigley Gum Company; I can see Poe as one of the leading writers for the *Red Book*; Emerson as president of Columbia or the University of Illinois, inspiring twenty thousand students with his eloquence; and Hawthorne writing ads for the new model Hupmobile.

But the ethics of this New Era are not yet entirely figured out, and I want, in my tiny and humble way, to contribute what I can to them this evening.

Certain ideals are universal—honesty, chastity, and not boozing too much. But there are two principles almost entirely developed by and peculiar to America of today, and these are *Service* and *Practicalness!* (Or some call it Practicality.)

Now let us take Service. Let me start out by defining what I mean by it.

Service is imagination. Service is that something extra, aside from the mere buying, stocking, and delivery of goods, that so tickles the comfort and self-esteem of a customer that he will feel friendly and come back for more. Service is, in fact, the poetry, the swell manners, the high adventure of business.

And this is the first time in history that a nation has conceived the massive, the daring and glittering idea, that you can do more than just sell the customer the goods he wants—that you can, in fact, tie him to you by that subtle form of friendliness known as Service, so that, without its really costing you much of anything, you can make him feel that he's getting double value for his money.

Service! If the Rotarians and Kiwanians had done nothing else, they would have justified themselves and made their place secure

in history for all time by their insistence on the value and beauty—
the, in fact, if I may without sacrilege say so, *religion* of Service.

Let me give you a few examples of what I have known done or
have fancied might be done in the way of Service.

Take my own profession, office supplies.

Say I sell a fellow an adding-machine. Now there's nothing about
the operation of it that any bright girl couldn't learn in half an
hour, and as to repairs, of course no sensible office ever monkeys
with them, anyway. But when a gentleman buys an adding-machine,
I ask him to send the girl who's going to operate it around for a
course of lessons—of course absolutely free. Then once a week for
a month I send a fellow to the office to look over the adding-
machine, to adjust it, and to give further instruction in its use to
any one who the boss may designate—again all absolutely free.

Now probably the fellow I send around doesn't know any more
about running the ole adding-machine than half the folks in the
office, but that isn't the point. The point is that I thus establish in
the bosses of that office a feeling of coöperation with me, a feeling
of my eagerness to give good measure, pressed down and running
over, as the Good Book says, and then when he wants anything
further in the way of office supplies, he's the more likely to turn
to me. That's Service!

Or take insurance.

In the old days, when a bird—when a solicitor had sold somebody a policy, that ended it, and the solicitor never bothered him
again. But happily a more scientific era has dawned. To the really
enlightened solicitor, the sale of the first policy is merely the beginning. With an air of impersonal friendliness, and with an especial
care to not seem obtrusive, the solicitor makes this customer his
buddy for life.

He keeps a file of newspaper clippings showing every move
of his customer—say like death in the customer's family, his election
to some high position in a lodge, or his wife giving a dinner to
Soroptimist delegates—and on every such occasion he expresses to
the customer his congratulations. Or condolences, as the case
may be.

Of course this has to be done with care. The solicitor must make
sure whether the customer dislikes being bothered or not. If not, he
makes these approaches in a nice, friendly, chatty, gentlemanly
little telephone conversation, working in also some reference to
the weather or the World's Series—but never, you understand,

directly mentioning business, for otherwise it would not be Service. But if the fellow is touchy and irritable, the solicitor contents himself with nice formal little letters, perhaps suggesting that no reply or acknowledgment is needed.

Then finally, when he feels the prospect is ripe, when a really rich feeling of personal friendship has grown up between them, he makes a quick hard touch, and in a surprising number of cases is able to put over a new and larger policy on him.

That's Service—and, like Virtue, it brings its reward.

And so in other businesses. The grocery customer will often prefer a second-rate apple in a handsome wrapper to a first-rate one carelessly bundled in plain tissue paper. A motorist will stand for pretty bad gasoline if the gas-station employees wear handsome uniforms, greet the customer respectfully, and wipe off his windshield free. A man will often put up with small rooms, high prices, and even pretty poor food if both the reception clerk and the manager treat him like a friend, give him a warm handshake, and, this most especially, learn his name thoroughly and greet him by it when he returns a second time.

That's Service!

And remember that only a low and sordid commercialist would look on it as something which merely sells more goods—though it certainly does that, too. But over and above that, it promotes friendliness, good fellowship, brotherhood, and thus makes for the millennial day when all the world shall be one happy Christian fellowship.

And now the second peculiarly modern and American ideal—practicalness.

Europe has always had its art, its beauty, but where we have gone beyond the Old Country is that while we want things beautiful—take like an elegant new gas stove—they must primarily be of *use.* Let me prove my point by going right into the world of professional art and sculpture.

When a European city wants to adorn itself, it puts up, if I may judge from a rather wide reading, and a study of the pictures in the *National Geographic Magazine*—it puts up in its parks a lot of heathen goddesses—which are rather suggestive, to say the least—along with fountains and such things. But we—Well, we want to decorate a park, and we decide on a statue at once handsome and educative. We figure there's a lot of Spaniards in the city that'll be pleased by recognition, so we put up a fine bust of Columbus; or we see there's a bunch of naturalized Italians, with perfectly good votes, and we recognize them by erecting a monument to—to—well, to Dante. Or we please the Germans by a bust of Gerty. And so we kill two birds with one stone.

Or take a more immediate example. Now that Christmas is not long over, I guess there's some of us that feel the gift business is a little overdone. I have heard gentlemen of my own acquaintanceship assert that they felt certain department stores almost commercialize the sacred holiday. But be that as it may, and it is too involved a question for me to go into it on the present occasion, it is an encouraging and outstanding fact that year by year gifts tend to become more *practical.*

I have here a magazine published early in December, and therefore largely devoted to advertisements with the rosy blush of the holidays upon them. And where in the old times there would have been an emphasis on impractical things for Christmas—say like books, etchings, and fancy smoking-jackets—what do we find now?

First of all, of course, there are many suggestions for auto accessories as Christmas gifts, as is suitable in a country where the chief object is to go somewhere quick. Fine! Tire chains, tire locks, radiator shutters, moto-meters, and anti-freeze mixtures done up in handsome holly-decorated cans especially for Christmas.

And then the other practical gifts, suitable to gladden the heart of any recipient: pocket cigar-lighters, sharpeners for safety-razor blades, little scales suitable for the bathroom so that every one, man, lady, or child, can daily check up on his health. And what toys! Real electric trains, just like the real article, so that the fortunate child who gets one for Christmas doesn't have to do a thing but press a lever and the train goes by itself, and the child can just sit there and watch it and enjoy himself. What fun!

And all these gift articles mingled in the advertisements with the customary vast store of such other luxuries as only America produces. Ads of towns in Florida that in less than ten years have come in every way to equal if not surpass Venice, Italy. These wonderful new ladies' overshoes with this business, I forget what it's called, but you just pull a business, and the whole business slides open without buttons or hooks and eyes. Splendid ads of sauerkraut, which thus, nationally advertised, rises from its lowly status and takes its place alongside of candy and the telephone company.

And then this:

Here till just recently both typewriters and fountain pens were always in a dull and I might almost say somber black. But now typewriters are appearing in a variety of lovely colors, suitable to the boudoir as well as the office; and as for your fountain pen, you can have it in opal, lettuce green, dawn pink, elephant-hide gray, La Marquis blue, or any other of a dozen tempting hues and shades.

But in this magazine I found an even greater proof of the way in which America combines beauty with sheer practicalness. One advertisement starts out with a letter—I suppose it is imaginary, the product of some copy-writer's genius, and yet in this New Era it might quite possibly be real—from a young lady who's supposed to be writing to her beau, and she says:

> You are thinking of me, Sweetheart. Even as I am thinking of you. Thinking . . . wondering . . . cherishing each precious hour of anticipation . . . counting the days until . . .
>
> And Christmas is almost here. Perhaps you are thinking of a gift for me. Possibly a jewel! Yet no greater jewel will I ever crave than that of your perfect companionship; nor gift would I ask more royal than the honesty of your own heart.
>
> Let your gift to me be something intimate . . . beautiful . . . reminiscent always of the Dream Days of Now.
>
> And I ask you . . . let it be practical!
>
> Sanctuary for the lovely silks and linens and embroidery I am receiving . . . for the wool blankets . . . downy comforters . . . for those precious possessions which I now hoard away in closet, trunk, or bureau drawer. A place of beauty and fragrance, of convenience and safety, where moth and dust will not corrupt nor inquisitive fingers delve . . . it is of this I whisper, beloved . . .
>
> Something I have always longed for—that every woman has longed for. Something a girl would so gladly have from her sweetheart . . . or her husband. A CEDAR CHEST . . .

Then the advertisement goes on to show pictures of the manufacturer's line of cedar chests. And I want to tell you gentlemen that when we have reached a point in American advertising where we can combine straight selling-talk with not only the joyous spirit of the holiday season, but also the most delicate intimacies of young love, and also a cleverly worked-in quotation from Holy Writ, then by thunder we have reached a point of practicalness never hitherto known in history!

At last has come the glorious era when every noble sentiment, every artistic turn of phrase and elegant wording, every instinct of beauty, is no longer forced to run alone and maverick, but can rejoicingly take its proper place in serving commerce and the merchant kings!

Or one more example, which I take from another magazine of the same festal date, about the practical drink for the Christmas feed. Now Germany may have its beer, France may rejoice in its ruby wine, England may have its—its variety of drinks, but we, thank God, have freed ourselves from the dreadful thralldom of alcohol!

And why? Because we find that for business success, alcohol ain't *practical!* And yet we find ourselves wishing to acknowledge the great feast days with suitable vintages. And so our manufacturers rush in and perfectly fill the gap in an entirely satisfactory manner. Listen to this ad, and note the high-class literary wording:

> A right merrie drink to add new zest to a well-cooked Christmas dinner . . . The majestic turkey has replaced the historic boar's head; the gayly bedecked peacock pie has given way to mince; a fine old ginger ale has taken the place of the flowing Wassail Bowl which once was passed from hand to hand as "the ancient fountain of good feeling where all hearts met together."
>
> In all the world, there is no beverage so appropriate for the Christmas dinner as XXXX Ginger Ale! Served in fragile stemware, it gleams and sparkles like a rare old wine and bids you drink and be merry! Dinner always takes on a new zest, a new distinction when this fine old ginger ale comes to grace your table.

There, gentlemen, is our ringing answer to the opponents of prohibition!

What opportunity in this new and increasingly practical America for any bright fellow today!

Take like Al Smith. Here is a poor boy of the city streets, and a Catholic, and yet we have permitted him to be Governor of New York. Naturally I'm opposed to his being President, but I've been perfectly willing to see him rise as far as he has, and while he's almost certainly never heard of me, if he were here I'd be glad to give him the hand and good wishes of Lowell Schmaltz!

What opportunity today! What coöperation!

You take, for example, the Community Chest. What a colossal and unique American institution that is—all of us combining on every worthy charity, and refusing to support those institutions

which our bankers and other experts consider unworthy. Why, just
this last fall—

There was a young man in the office of a friend of mine who
refused to contribute one red cent to the Community Chest, on
the frivolous and indeed almost flippant grounds that the big men
behind the campaign for funds—the men who were themselves
often the most generous givers!—used their large contributions as a
club with which to keep all radical and wrong-thinking charity-
workers out of jobs with the various institutions.

So my friend very properly fired this sorehead and quietly passed
the word around, and this young man—as you can see, practically
a socialist in disguise—Well, I shall be very much surprised if
he ever finds it possible to get another decent job in this man's
town! I give that just as an example of the way in which, with the
increasingly solid American organization, we can on the one hand
assist the aspiring and right-thinking young crusader, and on the
other hand get rid of all anarchists and hammer-wielders.

For we must never forget that even in the midst of this, the
most luxurious and powerful civilization the world has ever known,
there are always people who, for some insane reason that they
themselves couldn't explain, still criticize and complain and refuse
to climb on the band-wagon.

You take this.

I am reliably informed—though certainly I have not sullied my
self-respect by reading any of them, but I have been informed of
their contents by criticisms given in various sermons—I am informed that during this last year or so there have been published
two books purporting to show that George Washington was not the
great hero we all know him to be but a man that smoked, drank,
used bad language, and flirted. Then there was an alleged biography
claiming that Henry Ward Beecher was not what we all know him
to have been—the greatest preacher and power for righteousness
since Martin Luther, and a man of spotless righteousness and truth
—but instead a man whose word and loving friendliness could not
be relied on. And no less than three disgraceful books, two of them
novels and one a screed by a woman claiming to have known him
too intimately, have dared to hint that our Martyr President,
Harding himself, was a dumb-bell surrounded by crooks.

Well, I've got an answer for all these authorial gentlemen!

And my answer is that it is not worth the while of a serious and
busy man of affairs to pay the slightest attention to notoriety-

hunting hacks, who creep out of their fetid holes to bay the moon, who seek by their filthy and lying accusations to keep a foothold in the public eye!

I see that my allotted time is drawing to a close, but, though it does not strictly belong to my topic, I want to take this opportunity to tell you briefly something of my conversation several months ago with President Coolidge, who was, as many of you may know, a great chum of mine all through our college days.

When I arrived at the White House, the President was just going off on the *Mayflower* with the British ambassador, as I had failed to apprise him of my coming sufficiently in advance. So we had a shorter visit than usual, but he spoke of certain things on which I know you will be glad to get authoritative information.

"Mr. President," I said—he had indicated that he wanted me to call him "Cal," but I didn't feel it to be fitting—"Mr. President," I said, "how do you feel about this question of decreasing our navy?"

"Well, Low," he said, "I think I can put it to you in just a few words. While of course he is thrice armed that is prepared, as the bard says, yet navies cost a deplorable amount of money, and I should be glad to see them reduced—so far as it is safe."

"Well, how do you feel about taxation?" I said.

"In my opinion," he said, "while there should never be such unjust taxes that the burden of taxation shall fall unduly on those that are compelled to carry on great commercial enterprises, which give jobs to all sorts and conditions of men, yet equally there must never be an intolerable assessment against those that for one reason or another are not well off in this world's goods."

"And finally," I said, "if you wouldn't be betraying any state secrets—I should never ask you to do that, even though we are old friends," I said—"what do you think about the situation in China?"

I shall never forget how he straightened up and his eyes flashed fire, as he shot back at me, grimly:

"In my opinion," he said, "there is now arising a situation where it is necessary to do more than merely our obvious duty in safeguarding American rights and properties in China. It is the last desire of myself or of my advisers to involve ourselves in European politics," he said, "but I stand up and say before the world that we do not like the way in which, it is alleged, the Bolsheviks tend to encourage the Chinese to act in an uncivilized manner; and when the proper time comes we shall, if necessary, take whatever action may be necessary."

So there, gentlemen, you have in the President's own words a clear statement of our foreign policy. Yet to me it is no more remarkable, no more worthy of historical recording, than our domestic policy, which I have just tried to outline, in Service and Practicalness.

And I shall be glad if in my small way I have done anything to make clearer to you the New Era of American Civilization; to express modestly to you the motto of Lowell Schmaltz: "Read widely, think scientifically, speak briefly, and sell the goods!"

Flowering Judas

KATHERINE ANNE PORTER

Bearing certain resemblances to the protagonist of a naturalistic tale, Miss Porter's Laura is a victim—but of deeply felt experiences rather than of powerful instincts or environmental forces. As in naturalism, there is considerable violence in the story, but it is either offstage or implied. The revolutionists' activities and Braggioni's lusts appear in "Flowering Judas" primarily as they press in on Laura's mind. That mind, though conscious and analytical, works intensely through memory and feeling, and so concretely as well as abstractly. For Laura, experience is thus markedly symbolic, and her nun's garb, fine lace collars, fears and renunciations all help define her life as one governed by realities that are inner, inseparably psychological and moral.

Braggioni sits heaped upon the edge of a straight-backed chair much too small for him, and sings to Laura in a furry, mournful voice. Laura has begun to find reasons for avoiding her own house until the latest possible moment, for Braggioni is there almost every night. No matter how late she is, he will be sitting there with a surly, waiting expression, pulling at his kinky yellow hair, thumbing the strings of his guitar, snarling a tune under his breath. Lupe the Indian maid meets Laura at the door, and says with a flicker of a glance towards the upper room, "He waits."

Laura wishes to lie down, she is tired of her hairpins and the feel of her long tight sleeves, but she says to him, "Have you a new song for me this evening?" If he says yes, she asks him to sing it. If he says no, she remembers his favorite one, and asks him to sing it again. Lupe brings her a cup of chocolate and a plate of rice, and Laura eats at the small table under the lamp, first inviting Braggioni, whose answer is always the same: "I have eaten, and besides, chocolate thickens the voice."

Laura says, "Sing, then," and Braggioni heaves himself into song. He scratches the guitar familiarly as though it were a pet animal, and sings passionately off key, taking the high notes in a prolonged painful squeal. Laura, who haunts the markets listening to the ballad singers, and stops every day to hear the blind boy playing his reed-flute in Sixteenth of September Street, listens to Braggioni with pitiless courtesy, because she dares not smile at his miserable performance. Nobody dares to smile at him. Braggioni is cruel to everyone, with a kind of specialized insolence, but he is so vain of his talents, and so sensitive to slights, it would require a cruelty and vanity greater than his own to lay a finger on the vast cureless wound of his self-esteem. It would require courage, too, for it is dangerous to offend him, and nobody has this courage.

Braggioni loves himself with such tenderness and amplitude and eternal charity that his followers—for he is a leader of men, a skilled revolutionist, and his skin has been punctured in honorable warfare—warm themselves in the reflected glow, and say to each other: "He has a real nobility, a love of humanity raised above mere personal affections." The excess of this self-love has flowed out, inconveniently for her, over Laura, who, with so many others, owes her comfortable situation and her salary to him. When he is in a very good humor, he tells her, "I am tempted to forgive you for being a *gringa. Gringita!*" and Laura, burning, imagines herself leaning forward suddenly, and with a sound back-handed slap wiping the suety smile from his face. If he notices her eyes at these moments he gives no sign.

She knows what Braggioni would offer her, and she must resist tenaciously without appearing to resist, and if she could avoid it she would not admit even to herself the slow drift of his intention. During these long evenings which have spoiled a long month for her, she sits in her deep chair with an open book on her knees, resting her eyes on the consoling rigidity of the printed page when the sight and sound of Braggioni singing threaten to identify themselves with all her remembered afflictions and to add their weight to her uneasy premonitions of the future. The gluttonous bulk of Braggioni has become a symbol of her many disillusions, for a revolutionist should be lean, animated by heroic faith, a vessel of abstract virtues. This is nonsense, she knows it now and is ashamed of it. Revolution must have leaders, and leadership is a career for energetic men. She is, her comrades tell her, full of romantic error, for what she defines as cynicism in them is merely "a developed sense of reality." She is almost too willing to say, "I am wrong, I suppose I don't really understand the principles," and afterward she makes a secret truce with herself, determined not to surrender her will to such expedient logic. But she cannot help feeling that she has been betrayed irreparably by the disunion between her way of living and her feeling of what life should be, and at times she is almost contented to rest in this sense of grievance as a private store of consolation. Sometimes she wishes to run away, but she stays. Now she longs to fly out of this room, down the narrow stairs, and into the street where the houses lean together like conspirators under a single mottled lamp, and leave Braggioni singing to himself.

Instead she looks at Braggioni, frankly and clearly, like a good child who understands the rules of behavior. Her knees cling together under sound blue serge, and her round white collar is not purposely nun-like. She wears the uniform of an idea, and has renounced vanities. She was born Roman Catholic, and in spite of her fear of being seen by someone who might make a scandal of it, she slips now and again into some crumbling little church, kneels on the chilly stone, and says a Hail Mary on the gold rosary she bought in Tehuantepec. It is no good and she ends by examining the altar with its tinsel flowers and ragged brocades, and feels tender about the battered doll-shape of some male saint whose white, lace-trimmed drawers hang limply around his ankles below the hieratic dignity of his velvet robe. She has encased herself in a set of principles derived from her early training, leaving no detail of gesture or of personal taste untouched, and for this reason she will not wear lace made on machines. This is her private heresy, for in her special group the machine is sacred, and will be the salvation of the workers. She loves fine lace, and there is a tiny edge of fluted cobweb on this collar, which is one of twenty precisely alike, folded in blue tissue paper in the upper drawer of her clothes chest.

Braggioni catches her glance solidly as if he had been waiting for it, leans forward, balancing his paunch between his spread knees, and sings with tremendous emphasis, weighing his words. He has, the song relates, no father and no mother, nor even a friend to console him; lonely as a wave of the sea he comes and goes, lonely as a wave. His mouth opens round and yearns sideways, his balloon cheeks grow oily with the labor of song. He bulges marvelously in his expensive garments. Over his lavender collar, crushed upon a purple necktie, held by a diamond hoop: over his ammunition belt of tooled leather worked in silver, buckled cruelly around his gasping middle: over the tops of his glossy yellow shoes Braggioni swells with ominous ripeness, his mauve silk hose stretched taut, his ankles bound with the stout leather thongs of his shoes.

When he stretches his eyelids at Laura she notes again that his eyes are the true tawny yellow cat's eyes. He is rich, not in money, he tells her, but in power, and this power brings with it the blameless ownership of things, and the right to indulge his love of small luxuries. "I have a taste for the elegant refinements," he said once, flourishing a yellow silk handkerchief before her nose. "Smell that? It is Jockey Club, imported from New York." Nonetheless he is wounded by life. He will say so presently. "It is true everything turns to dust in the hand, to gall on the tongue." He sighs and his leather belt creaks like a saddle girth. "I am disappointed in everything as it comes. Everything." He shakes his head. "You, poor thing, you will be disappointed too. You are born for it. We are more alike than you realize in some things. Wait and see. Some

day you will remember what I have told you, you will know that
Braggioni was your friend."

Laura feels a slow chill, a purely physical sense of danger, a
warning in her blood that violence, mutilation, a shocking death,
wait for her with lessening patience. She has translated this fear
into something homely, immediate, and sometimes hesitates before
crossing the street. "My personal fate is nothing, except as the
testimony of a mental attitude," she reminds herself, quoting from
some forgotten philosophic primer, and is sensible enough to add,
"Anyhow, I shall not be killed by an automobile if I can help it."

"It may be true I am as corrupt, in another way, as Braggioni,"
she thinks in spite of herself, "as callous, as incomplete," and if
this is so, any kind of death seems preferable. Still she sits quietly,
she does not run. Where could she go? Uninvited she has promised
herself to this place; she can no longer imagine herself as living
in another country, and there is no pleasure in remembering her
life before she came here.

Precisely what is the nature of this devotion, its true motives, and
what are its obligations? Laura cannot say. She spends part of her
days in Xochimilco, near by, teaching Indian children to say in
English, "The cat is on the mat." When she appears in the classroom
they crowd about her with smiles on their wise, innocent, clay-
colored faces, crying, "Good morning, my titcher!" in immaculate
voices, and they make of her desk a fresh garden of flowers every
day.

During her leisure she goes to union meetings and listens to busy
important voices quarreling over tactics, methods, internal politics.
She visits the prisoners of her own political faith in their cells,
where they entertain themselves with counting cockroaches, re-
penting of their indiscretions, composing their memoirs, writing out
manifestoes and plans for their comrades who are still walking
about free, hands in pockets, sniffing fresh air. Laura brings them
food and cigarettes and a little money, and she brings messages
disguised in equivocal phrases from the men outside who dare
not set foot in the prison for fear of disappearing into the cells
kept empty for them. If the prisoners confuse night and day, and
complain, "Dear little Laura, time doesn't pass in this infernal
hole, and I won't know when it is time to sleep unless I have
a reminder," she brings them their favorite narcotics, and says in
a tone that does not wound them with pity, "Tonight will really be
night for you," and though her Spanish amuses them, they find her

comforting, useful. If they lose patience and all faith, and curse the slowness of their friends in coming to their rescue with money and influence, they trust her not to repeat everything, and if she inquires, "Where do you think we can find money, or influence?" they are certain to answer, "Well, there is Braggioni, why doesn't he do something?"

She smuggles letters from headquarters to men hiding from firing squads in back streets in mildewed houses, where they sit in tumbled beds and talk bitterly as if all Mexico were at their heels, when Laura knows positively they might appear at the band concert in the Alameda on Sunday morning, and no one would notice them. But Braggioni says, "Let them sweat a little. The next time they may be careful. It is very restful to have them out of the way for a while." She is not afraid to knock on any door in any street after midnight, and enter in the darkness, and say to one of these men who is really in danger: "They will be looking for you—seriously—tomorrow morning after six. Here is some money from Vicente. Go to Vera Cruz and wait."

She borrows money from the Roumanian agitator to give to his bitter enemy the Polish agitator. The favor of Braggioni is their disputed territory, and Braggioni holds the balance nicely, for he can use them both. The Polish agitator talks love to her over café tables, hoping to exploit what he believes is her secret sentimental preference for him, and he gives her misinformation which he begs her to repeat as the solemn truth to certain persons. The Roumanian is more adroit. He is generous with his money in all good causes, and lies to her with an air of ingenuous candor, as if he were her good friend and confidant. She never repeats anything they may say. Braggioni never asks questions. He has other ways to discover all that he wishes to know about them.

Nobody touches her, but all praise her gray eyes, and the soft, round under lip which promises gayety, yet is always grave, nearly always firmly closed: and they cannot understand why she is in Mexico. She walks back and forth on her errands, with puzzled eyebrows, carrying her little folder of drawings and music and school papers. No dancer dances more beautifully than Laura walks, and she inspires some amusing, unexpected ardors, which cause little gossip, because nothing comes of them. A young captain who had been a soldier in Zapata's army attempted, during a horseback ride near Cuernavaca, to express his desire for her with the noble simplicity befitting a rude folk-hero: but gently, because he was gentle. This gentleness was his defeat, for when he alighted, and removed her foot from the stirrup, and essayed to draw her down into his arms, her horse, ordinarily a tame one, shied fiercely, reared and plunged away. The young hero's horse careered blindly after his stable-mate, and the hero did not return to the hotel until rather late that evening. At breakfast he came to her table in full charro dress, gray buckskin jacket and trousers with strings of silver buttons down the leg, and he was in a humorous, careless mood. "May I sit with you?" and "You are a wonderful rider. I was terrified that you might be thrown and dragged. I should never have forgiven myself. But I cannot admire you enough for your riding!"

"I learned to ride in Arizona," said Laura.

"If you will ride with me again this morning, I promise you a horse that will not shy with you," he said. But Laura remembered that she must return to Mexico City at noon.

Next morning the children made a celebration and spent their playtime writing on the blackboard, "We lov ar ticher," and with tinted chalks they drew wreaths of flowers around the words. The young hero wrote her a letter: "I am a very foolish, wasteful, impulsive man. I should have first said I love you, and then you would not have run away. But you shall see me again." Laura thought, "I must send him a box of colored crayons," but she was trying to forgive herself for having spurred her horse at the wrong moment.

A brown, shock-haired youth came and stood in her patio one night and sang like a lost soul for two hours, but Laura could think of nothing to do about it. The moonlight spread a wash of gauzy silver over the clear spaces of the garden, and the shadows were cobalt blue. The scarlet blossoms of the Judas tree were dull purple, and the names of the colors repeated themselves automatically in her mind, while she watched not the boy, but his shadow, fallen like a dark garment across the fountain rim, trailing in the water. Lupe came silently and whispered expert counsel in her ear: "If you will throw him one little flower, he will sing another song or two and go away." Laura threw the flower, and he sang a last song and went away with the flower tucked in the band of his hat. Lupe said, "He is one of the organizers of the Typographers Union, and before that he sold corridos in the Merced market, and before that, he came from Guanajuato, where I was born. I would not trust any man, but I trust least those from Guanajuato."

She did not tell Laura that he would be back again the next night, and the next, nor that he would follow her at a certain fixed distance around the Merced market, through the Zócolo, up Francisco I. Madero Avenue, and so along the Paseo de la Reforma to Chapultepec Park, and into the Philosopher's Footpath, still with that flower withering in his hat, and an indivisible attention in his eyes.

Now Laura is accustomed to him, it means nothing except that he is nineteen years old and is observing a convention with all propriety, as though it were founded on a law of nature, which in the end it might well prove to be. He is beginning to write poems which he prints on a wooden press, and he leaves them stuck like handbills in her door. She is pleasantly disturbed by the abstract, unhurried watchfulness of his black eyes which will in time turn easily towards another object. She tells herself that throwing the flower was a mistake, for she is twenty-two years old and knows better; but she refuses to regret it, and persuades herself that her negation of all external events as they occur is a sign that she is gradually perfecting herself in the stoicism she strives to cultivate against that disaster she fears, though she cannot name it.

She is not at home in the world. Every day she teaches children who remain strangers to her, though she loves their tender round hands and their charming opportunist savagery. She knocks at unfamiliar doors not knowing whether a friend or a stranger shall answer, and even if a known face emerges from the sour gloom of that unknown interior, still it is the face of a stranger. No matter what this stranger says to her, nor what her message to him, the very cells of her flesh reject knowledge and kinship in one monotonous word. No. No. No. She draws her strength from this one holy talismanic word which does not suffer her to be led into evil. Denying everything, she may walk anywhere in safety, she looks at everything without amazement.

No, repeats this firm unchanging voice of her blood; and she looks at Braggioni without amazement. He is a great man, he wishes to impress this simple girl who covers her great round breasts with thick dark cloth, and who hides long, invaluably beautiful legs under a heavy skirt. She is almost thin except for the incomprehensible fullness of her breasts, like a nursing mother's, and Braggioni, who considers himself a judge of women, speculates again on the puzzle of her notorious virginity, and takes the liberty of speech which she permits without a sign of modesty, indeed, without any sort of sign, which is disconcerting.

"You think you are so cold, *gringita!* Wait and see. You will surprise yourself some day! May I be there to advise you!" He stretches his eyelids at her, and his ill-humored cat's eyes waver in a separate glance for the two points of light marking the opposite ends of a smoothly drawn path between the swollen curve of her breasts. He is not put off by that blue serge, nor by her resolutely fixed gaze. There is all the time in the world. His cheeks are bellying with the wind of song. "O girl with the dark eyes," he sings, and reconsiders. "But yours are not dark. I can change all that. O girl with the green eyes, you have stolen my heart away!" then his mind wanders to the song, and Laura feels the weight of his attention being shifted elsewhere. Singing thus, he seems harmless, he is quite harmless, there is nothing to do but sit patiently and say "No," when the moment comes. She draws a full breath, and her mind wanders also, but not far. She dares not wander too far.

Not for nothing has Braggioni taken pains to be a good revolutionist and a professional lover of humanity. He will never die of it. He has the malice, the cleverness, the wickedness, the sharpness of wit, the hardness of heart, stipulated for loving the world profitably. *He will never die of it.* He will live to see himself kicked out from his feeding trough by other hungry world-saviors. Traditionally he must sing in spite of his life which drives him to bloodshed, he tells Laura, for his father was a Tuscany peasant who drifted to Yucatan and married a Maya woman: a woman of race, an aristocrat. They gave him the love and knowledge of music, thus: and under the rip of his thumbnail, the strings of the instrument complain like exposed nerves.

Once he was called Delgadito by all the girls and married women who ran after him; he was so scrawny all his bones showed under his thin cotton clothing, and he could squeeze his emptiness to the very backbone with his two hands. He was a poet and the revolution was only a dream then; too many women loved him and sapped away his youth, and he could never find enough to eat anywhere, anywhere! Now he is a leader of men, crafty men who whisper in his ear, hungry men who wait for hours outside his office for a word with him, emaciated men with wild faces who waylay him at the street gate with a timid, "Comrade, let me tell you . . ." and they blow the foul breath from their empty stomachs in his face.

He is always sympathetic. He gives them handfuls of small coins from his own pocket, he promises them work, there will be demonstrations, they must join the unions and attend the meetings, above all they must be on the watch for spies. They are closer to him than his own brothers, without them he can do nothing—until tomorrow, comrade!

Until tomorrow. "They are stupid, they are lazy, they are treacherous, they would cut my throat for nothing," he says to Laura. He has good food and abundant drink, he hires an automobile and drives in the Paseo on Sunday morning, and enjoys plenty of sleep in a soft bed beside a wife who dares not disturb him; and he sits pampering his bones in easy billows of fat, singing to Laura, who knows and thinks these things about him. When he was fifteen, he tried to drown himself because he loved a girl, his first love, and she laughed at him. "A thousand women have paid for that," and his tight little mouth turns down at the corners. Now he perfumes his hair with Jockey Club, and confides to Laura: "One woman is really as good as another for me, in the dark. I prefer them all."

His wife organizes unions among the girls in the cigarette factories, and walks in picket lines, and even speaks at meetings in the evening. But she cannot be brought to acknowledge the benefits of true liberty. "I tell her I must have my freedom, net. She does not understand my point of view." Laura has heard this many times. Braggioni scratches the guitar and meditates. "She is an instinctively virtuous woman, pure gold, no doubt of that. If she were not, I should lock her up, and she knows it."

His wife, who works so hard for the good of the factory girls, employs part of her leisure lying on the floor weeping because there are so many women in the world, and only one husband for her, and she never knows where nor when to look for him. He told her: "Unless you can learn to cry when I am not here, I must go away for good." That day he went away and took a room at the Hotel Madrid.

It is this month of separation for the sake of higher principles that has been spoiled not only for Mrs. Braggioni, whose sense of reality is beyond criticism, but for Laura, who feels herself bogged in a nightmare. Tonight Laura envies Mrs. Braggioni, who is alone, and free to weep as much as she pleases about a concrete wrong. Laura has just come from a visit to the prison, and she is waiting for tomorrow with a bitter anxiety as if tomorrow may not come, but time may be caught immovably in this hour, with herself transfixed,

Braggioni singing on forever, and Eugenio's body not yet discovered by the guard.

Braggioni says: "Are you going to sleep?" Almost before she can shake her head, he begins telling her about the May-day disturbances coming on in Morelia, for the Catholics hold a festival in honor of the Blessed Virgin, and the Socialists celebrate their martyrs on that day. "There will be two independent processions, starting from either end of town, and they will march until they meet, and the rest depends . . ." He asks her to oil and load his pistols. Standing up, he unbuckles his ammunition belt, and spreads it laden across her knees. Laura sits with the shells slipping through the cleaning cloth dipped in oil, and he says again he cannot understand why she works so hard for the revolutionary idea unless she loves some man who is in it. "Are you not in love with someone?" "No," says Laura. "And no one is in love with you?" "No." "Then it is your own fault. No woman need go begging. Why, what is the matter with you? The legless beggar woman in the Alameda has a perfectly faithful lover. Did you know that?"

Laura peers down the pistol barrel and says nothing, but a long, slow faintness rises and subsides in her; Braggioni curves his swollen fingers around the throat of the guitar and softly smothers the music out of it, and when she hears him again he seems to have forgotten her, and is speaking in the hypnotic voice he uses when talking in small rooms to a listening, close-gathered crowd. Some day this world, now seemingly so composed and eternal, to the edges of every sea shall be merely a tangle of gaping trenches, of crashing walls and broken bodies. Everything must be torn from its accustomed place where it has rotted for centuries, hurled skyward and distributed, cast down again clean as rain, without separate identity. Nothing shall survive that the stiffened hands of poverty have created for the rich and no one shall be left alive except the elect spirits destined to procreate a new world cleansed of cruelty and injustice, ruled by benevolent anarchy: "Pistols are good, I love them, cannon are even better, but in the end I pin my faith to good dynamite," he concludes, and strokes the pistol lying in her hands. "Once I dreamed of destroying this city, in case it offered resistance to General Ortíz, but it fell into his hands like an overripe pear."

He is made restless by his own words, rises and stands waiting. Laura holds up the belt to him: "Put that on, and go kill somebody in Morelia, and you will be happier," she says softly. The presence of death in the room makes her bold. "Today, I found Eugenio going into a stupor. He refused to allow me to call the prison doctor. He had taken all the tablets I brought him yesterday. He said he took them because he was bored."

"He is a fool, and his death is his own business," says Braggioni, fastening his belt carefully.

"I told him if he had waited only a little while longer, you would have got him set free," says Laura. "He said he did not want to wait."

"He is a fool and we are well rid of him," says Braggioni, reaching for his hat.

He goes away. Laura knows his mood has changed, she will not see him any more for a while. He will send word when he needs her to go on errands into strange streets, to speak to the strange faces that will appear, like clay masks with the power of human speech, to mutter their thanks to Braggioni for his help. Now she is free, and she thinks, I must run while there is time. But she does not go.

Braggioni enters his own house where for a month his wife has spent many hours every night weeping and tangling her hair upon her pillow. She is weeping now, and she weeps more at the sight of him, the cause of all her sorrows. He looks about the room. Nothing is changed, the smells are good and familiar, he is well acquainted with the woman who comes toward him with no reproach except grief on her face. He says to her tenderly: "You are so good, please don't cry any more, you dear good creature." She says, "Are you tired, my angel? Sit here and I will wash your feet." She brings a bowl of water, and kneeling, unlaces his shoes, and when from her knees she raises her sad eyes under her blackened lids, he is sorry for everything, and bursts into tears. "Ah, yes, I am hungry, I am tired, let us eat something together," he says, between sobs. His wife leans her head on his arm and says, "Forgive me!" and this time he is refreshed by the solemn, endless rain of her tears.

Laura takes off her serge dress and puts on a white linen nightgown and goes to bed. She turns her head a little to one side, and lying still, reminds herself that it is time to sleep. Numbers tick in her brain like little clocks, soundless doors close of themselves around her. If you would sleep, you must not remember anything, the children will say tomorrow, good morning, my teacher, the poor prisoners who come every day bringing flowers to their jailor. 1-2-3-4-5—it is monstrous to confuse love with revolution, night with day, life with death—ah, Eugenio!

The tolling of the midnight bell is a signal, but what does it mean? Get up, Laura, and follow me: come out of your sleep, out of your bed, out of this strange house. What are you doing in this house? Without a word, without fear she rose and reached for Eugenio's hand, but he eluded her with a sharp, sly smile and drifted away. This is not all, you shall see—Murderer, he said, follow me, I will show you a new country, but it is far away and we must hurry. No, said Laura, not unless you take my hand, no; and she clung first to the stair rail, and then to the topmost branch of the Judas tree that bent down slowly and set her upon the earth, and then to the rocky ledge of a cliff, and then to the jagged wave of a sea that was not water but a desert of crumbling stone. Where are you taking me, she asked in wonder but without fear. To death, and it is a long way off, and we must hurry, said Eugenio. No, said Laura, not unless you take my hand. Then eat these flowers, poor prisoner, said Eugenio in a voice of pity, take and eat: and from the Judas tree he stripped the warm bleeding flowers, and held them to her lips. She saw that his hand was fleshless, a cluster of small white petrified branches, and his eye sockets were without light, but she ate the flowers greedily for they satisfied both hunger and thirst. Murderer! said Eugenio, and Cannibal! This is my body and my blood. Laura cried No! and at the sound of her own voice, she awoke trembling, and was afraid to sleep again.

Death
the Proud Brother

THOMAS WOLFE

The celebration of death so obsessive in Poe's Gothic fiction is here renewed by a more exuberant and more deeply ambivalent imagination. Thomas Wolfe's partly autobiographical narrator tells us that he "had known and loved the figure of proud Death," and his closing paean to Death, Loneliness, and Sleep surely registers the narrator's longing for self-annihilation. But the story as a whole discloses a much more complicated response on the narrator's part to four death scenes that he witnesses. Death moves the narrator to brilliant descriptions of action, as when he portrays the rivet catcher pausing momentarily, crouching, one foot groping into space, before he plunges nine stories to his flaming end. Death also moves the narrator to social comment: on a callous young college couple, the cops, average people, minority groups, and many others. It moves him to hallucinations, in which things and emotions lose their ordinary proportions for him, and in which he glimpses an uncertain and terrifying kind of reality. And death moves him, finally, to moral affirmation, as he rejoices to find life continuing even with death in its midst, and to find even the shabbiest man's dying suggestive of human dignity, power, and grandeur.

The face of the night, the heart of the dark, the tongue of the flame—I had known all things that lived or stirred or worked below her destiny. I was the child of night, a son among her mighty family, and I knew all that moved within the hearts of men who loved the night. I had seen them in a thousand places and nothing that they ever did or said was strange to me. As a child, when I had been a route boy on a morning paper, I had seen them on the streets of a little town—that strange and lonely company of men who prowl the night. Sometimes they were alone, and sometimes they went together in a group of two or three, forever in mid-watches of the night in little towns prowling up and down the empty pavements of bleak streets, passing before the ghastly waxen models in the windows of the clothing stores, passing below hard bulbous clusters of white light, prowling before the façades of a hundred darkened stores, pausing at length in some little lunchroom to drawl and gossip quietly, to thrust snout, lip, and sallow jowl into the stained depths of a coffee mug, or dully to wear the slow gray ash of time away without a word.

The memory of their faces, and their restless prowling of the night, familiar and unquestioned at the time, returned now with the strangeness of a dream. What did they want? What had they hoped to find as they prowled past a thousand doors in those little, bleak, and wintry towns?

Their hope, their wild belief, the dark song that the night awoke in them, this thing that lived in darkness while men slept and knew a secret and exultant triumph, and that was everywhere across the land, were written in my heart. Not in the purity and sweetness of dawn with all the brave and poignant glory of its revelation, nor in the practical and homely lights of morning, nor in the silent stature of the corn at noon, the drowsy hum and stitch of three o'clock across the fields, nor in the strange magic gold and green of its wild lyric wooded earth, nor even in the land that breathed quietly the last heat and violence of day away into the fathomless depth and brooding stillness of the dusk—as brave and glorious as these times and lights had been—had I felt and found the mystery, the grandeur, and the immortal beauty of America.

I had found the dark land at the heart of night, of dark, proud, secret night: the immense and lonely land lived for me in the brain of night. I saw its plains, its rivers, and its mountains spread out before me in all their dark immortal beauty, in all the space and joy of their huge sweep, in all their loneliness, savagery, and terror, and in all their immense and delicate fecundity. And my heart was one with the hearts of all men who had heard the strange wild music that they made, filled with unknown harmonies and a thousand wild and secret tongues crying to men the exultant and terrible music of wild earth, triumph and discovery, singing a strange and bitter prophecy of love and death.

For there was something living on the land at night. There was a dark tide moving in the hearts of men. Wild, strange and jubilant, sweeping on across the immense and sleeping earth, it had spoken to me in a thousand watches of the night, and the language of all its dark and secret tongues was written in my heart. It had passed above me with the rhythmical sustentions of its mighty wing, it had shot away with bullet cries of a demonic ecstasy on the swift howlings of the winter wind, it had come softly, numbly, with a dark impending prescience of wild joy in the dull soft skies of coming snow, and it had brooded, dark and wild and secret, in the night, across the land, and over the tremendous and dynamic silence of the city, stilled in its million cells of sleep, trembling forever in the night with the murmurous, remote and mighty sound of time.

And I was joined in knowledge and in life with an indubitable certitude to the great company of men who lived by night and had known and loved its mystery. I had known all joys and labors and designs that such men know. I had known all things living on the earth by night, and finally, I had known by night the immortal fellowship of those three with whom the best part of my life was passed—proud Death, and his stern brother, Loneliness, and their great sister, Sleep. I had lived and worked and wrought alone with Loneliness, my friend, and in the darkness, in the night, in all the sleeping silence of the earth, I had looked a thousand times into the visages of Sleep, and had heard the sound of her dark horses when they came. And I had watched my brother and my father die in the dark mid-watches of the night, and I had known and loved the figure of proud Death when he had come.

*   *   *

Three times already I had looked upon the visage of death in the city, and now that spring I was to see it once again. One night—on one of those kaleidoscopic nights of madness, drunkenness, and fury that I knew that year, when I prowled the great street of the dark from light to light, from midnight until morning—I saw a man die in the city subway.

He died so quietly that most of us would not admit at first that he was dead, so quietly that his death was only an instant and tranquil cessation of life's movement, so peaceable and natural in its action, that we all stared at it with eyes of fascination and unbelief, recognizing the face of death at once with a terrible sense of recognition which told us we had always known him, and yet, frightened and bewildered as we were, unwilling to admit that he had come.

For although each of the three city deaths that I had seen had come terribly and by violence, there would remain finally in my memory of this one a quality of terror, majesty, and grandeur which the others did not have.

The first of these deaths had occurred four years before in the month of April of my first year in the city. It had happened upon the corner of one of the dingy, swarming streets of the upper East Side, and in the way it had happened there had been a merciless, accidental, and indifferent quality which was far more terrible than any calculated or deliberate cruelty could have been, which spoke terribly and at once through the shining air, the joy and magic of the season, obliterating all the hope and exultancy in the hearts of men who saw it.

I was coming along one of the dingy cross-streets in the upper east-side district—a street still filled with the harsh and angular fronts of old brown-stone houses, which once no doubt had been the homes of prosperous people but were now black with the rust and grime of many years. These streets were seething with the violent and disorderly life of dark-faced, dark-eyed, strange-tongued people, who surged back and forth, innumerably, namelessly, with the tidal, liquid, and swarming fluency that all dark bloods and races have, so that the lean precision, the isolation, and the severe design characteristic of the lives of northern peoples—like something lonely, small, pitifully yet grandly itself—are fractured instantly by this tidal darkness. The numberless and ageless man-swarm of the earth is instantly revealed in all its fathomless horror, and will haunt one later in dreams, even if one sees only a half-dozen of these dark faces in a street.

Upon the corner of this swarming street, where it joined one of the great grimy streets that go up and down the city, and that are darkened forever by the savage violence and noise of the elevated structure, so that not only the light which swarms through the rusty iron webbing, but all the life and movement underneath it seems harsh, driven, beaten, violent, bewildered, and confused—on such a corner the man was killed. He was a little middle-aged Italian who had a kind of flimsy cart which was stationed at the curb, and in which he had a shabby and miscellaneous stock of cigarettes, cheap candies, bottled drinks, a big greasy-looking bottle of orange juice turned neck downward into a battered cylinder of white enamelled tin, and a small oil stove on which several pots of food—sausages and spaghetti—were always cooking.

The accident occurred just as I reached the corner opposite the man's stand. The traffic was roaring north and south beneath the elevated structure. At this moment an enormous covered van—of the kind so powerful and cumbersome that it seems to be as big as a locomotive and to engulf the smaller machines around it, to fill up the street so completely that one wonders at the skill and precision of the driver who can manipulate it—came roaring through beneath the elevated structure. It curved over and around, in an attempt to get ahead of a much smaller truck, and as it did so, swiped the little truck a glancing blow that wrecked it instantly, and sent it crashing across the curb into the vendor's wagon with such terrific force that the cart was smashed to splinters, and the truck turned over it completely and lay beyond it in a stove-in wreckage of shattered glass and twisted steel.

The driver of the truck, by the miracle of chance, was uninjured, but the little Italian vendor was mangled beyond recognition. As the truck smashed over him the bright blood burst out of his head in an instant fountain so that it was incredible so small a man could have such fountains of bright blood in him; and he died there on the sidewalk within a few minutes, and before the ambulance could reach him. A great crowd of shouting, dark-faced people gathered around the dying man at once, police appeared instantly in astonishing numbers, and began to thrust and drive in brutally among the excited people, cursing and mauling them, menacing them with their clubs, and shouting savagely:

"Break it up, deh! Break it up! On your way, now!" . . . "Where yuh goin'?" one snarled suddenly, grabbing a man by the slack of his coat, lifting him and hurling him back into the crowd as if he were a piece of excrement. "Break it up, deh! Break it up! G'wan, youse guys—yuh gotta move!"

Meanwhile the police had carried the dying man across the curb, laid him down on the sidewalk, and made a circle around him from the thrusting mob. Then the ambulance arrived with its furious and dreadful clangor of bells, but by this time the man was dead. The body was taken away, the police drove and lashed the crowds before them, whipping and mauling them along, as if they were surly and stupid animals, until at length the whole space around the wreck was clear of people.

Then two policemen, clearing the street again for its unceasing traffic, half pushed, half carried the twisted wreckage of the vendor's cart to the curb, and began to pick up his strewn stock, boxes, broken cups and saucers, fragments of broken glass, cheap knives and forks, and finally his tin spaghetti pots, and to throw them into the heap of wreckage. The spaghetti, pieces of brain, and fragments of the skull were mixed together on the pavement in a horrible bloody welter. One of the policemen looked at it for a moment, pushed the thick toe of his boot tentatively into it, and then turned away with a grimace of his brutal red face, as he said, "Jesus!"

At this moment, a little gray-faced Jew, with a big nose, screwy and greasy-looking hair that reached backward from his painful and reptilian brow, rushed from the door of a dismal little tailor's shop across the sidewalk, breathing stertorously with excitement, and carrying a bucket full of water in his hand. The Jew ran swiftly out into the street, with a funny bandy-legged movement, dashed the water down upon the bloody welter and then ran back into the shop as fast as he had come. Then a man came out of another shop with a bucket full of sawdust in his hand which he began to strew upon the bloody street until the stain was covered over. Finally, nothing was left except the wreckage of the truck and the vendor's cart, two policemen who conferred quietly together with notebooks in their hands, some people staring with dull fascinated eyes upon the blood-stain on the pavement, and little groups of people on the corners talking to one another in low, excited tones, saying:

"Sure! I seen it! I seen it! Dat's what I'm tellin' yuh! I was talkin' to 'm myself not two minutes before it happened! I saw duh whole

t'ing happen! I was standin' not ten feet away from 'im when it
hit him!"—as they revived the bloody moment, going over it again
and again with an insatiate and feeding hunger.

Such was the first death that I saw in the city. Later, the thing
I would remember most vividly, after the horror of the blood and
brains and the hideous mutilation of man's living flesh were almost
forgotten, was the memory of the bloody and battered tins and
pots in which the vendor had cooked his spaghetti, as they lay
strewn on the pavement, and as the policeman picked them up to
fling them back into the pile of wreckage. For later it seemed
these dingy and lifeless objects were able to evoke, with a huge
pathos, the whole story of the man's life, his kindly warmth and
smiling friendliness—for I had seen him many times—and his
pitiful small enterprise, to eke out shabbily, but with constant hope
and as best he could, beneath an alien sky, in the heart of the
huge indifferent city, some little reward for all his bitter toil and
patient steadfastness—some modest but shining goal of security,
freedom, escape, and repose, for which all men on this earth have
worked and suffered.

And the huge indifference with which the vast and terrible city
had in an instant blotted out this little life, soaking the shining air
and all the glory of the day with blood, the huge and casual irony
of its stroke—for the great van which had wrecked the truck and
killed the man, had thundered ahead and vanished, perhaps without its driver even knowing what had happened—was evoked un-
forgettably, with all its pity, pathos, and immense indifference,
by the memory of a few battered pots and pans. This, then, was
the first time I saw death in the city.

The second time I saw death in the city, it had come by night,
in winter, in a different way.

About mid-night of a night of still bitter cold in February, when
the moon stood cold and blazing in the white-blue radiance of the
frozen skies, a group of people were huddled together upon the
sidewalk of one of those confusing and angular streets which join
Seventh Avenue near Sheridan Square. The people were standing
before a new building which was being put up there, whose front
stood raw and empty in the harsh brown-livid light a few feet
away. Upon the curb, the watchman of the building had made a
fire in a rusty ash-can, and this fire now whipped and blazed in

the frozen air with a crackling flame to which some of the people in the group would go from time to time to warm their hands.

Upon the icy pavement before the building, a man was stretched out on his back and a hospital interne, with the tubes of a stethoscope fastened to his ears, was kneeling beside him moving the instrument from place to place on the man's powerful chest, which was exposed. An ambulance, its motor throbbing with a quiet and reduced power that was somehow ominous, was drawn up at the curb.

The man on the pavement was about forty years old and had the heavy shambling figure, the brutal and powerful visage, of the professional bum. On the scarred and battered surface of that face it seemed that every savage violence of weather, poverty, and physical degradation had left its mark of iron, during the years the vagabond had wandered back and forth across the nation, until now the man's features had a kind of epic brutality in which a legend of lonely skies and terrible distances, of pounding wheel and shining rail, of rust and steel and bloody brawl, and of the wild and savage earth, was plainly written.

The man lay on his back, as still and solid as a rock, eyes closed, his powerful, brutal features upthrust in the rigid and stolid attitude of death. He was still living, but one side of his head, at the temple, had been bashed in—a terrible, gaping wound which he had got when he wandered, drunk and almost blind with the cheap alcohol or "smoke" which he had been drinking, into the building, and had fallen forward across a pile of iron beams, against one of which he had smashed his head. The great black stain of the wound had run down across one side of his face and on the ground, but it had almost ceased to bleed, and in the freezing air the blood was clotting rapidly.

The man's rag of dirty shirt had been torn open and his powerful breast also seemed to swell forward with the same rigid and stolid immobility. No movement of breath was visible: he lay there as if carved out of rock, but a dull, flushed, unwholesome looking red was still burning on his broad and heavy face, and his hands were clenched beside him. His old hat had fallen off and his bald head was exposed. This bald head, with its thin fringe of hair upon each side, gave a final touch of dignity and power to the man's strong and brutal face, that was somehow terrible. It was like the look of strength and stern decorum that one sees on

the faces of those powerful men who do the heavy work in the
trapeze act at the circus, and who are usually bald-headed men.

None of the people who had gathered there about the man
showed any emotion whatever. Instead, they just stood looking
at him quietly with an intent yet indifferent curiosity, as if there
were in the death of this vagabond something casual and pre-
dictable which seemed so natural to them that they felt neither
surprise, pity, nor regret. One man turned to the man next to
him, and said quietly, but with assurance, and a faint grin:

"Well, dat's duh way it happens to dem in duh end. Dey all
go like dat sooner or later. I've neveh known it to fail."

Meanwhile, the young interne quietly and carefully, yet indifferently, moved his stethoscope from place to place, and listened.
A policeman with a dark, heavy face, pitted, seamed, and brutal-
looking, stood over him, surveying the scene calmly as he gently
swung his club, and ruminating slowly on a wad of gum. Several
men, including the night watchman and a news-dealer on the
corner, stood quietly, staring. Finally, a young man and a girl,
both well dressed, and with something insolent, naked, and ugly
in their speech and manner that distinguished them as being a
cut above the others in education, wealth, position—as young college people, young city people, young Village, painting, writing,
art-theatre people, young modern "post-war generation" people—
were looking down at the man, observing him with the curiosity
with which, and with less pity than, one would regard a dying
animal, and laughing, talking, jesting with each other with a con-
temptible and nasty callousness that was horrible, and that made
me want to smash them in the face.

They had been drinking, but they were not drunk: something
hard and ugly was burning nakedly in them—yet, it was not anything forced or deliberate, it was just hard-eyed, schooled in arrogance, dry and false, and fictional, and carried like a style. They
had an astonishing literary reality, as if they might have stepped
out of the pages of a book, as if there really were a new and
desolate race of youth upon the earth that men had never known
before—a race hard, fruitless, and unwholesome, from which man's
ancient bowels of mercy, grief, and wild exultant joy had been
eviscerated as out of date and falsely sentimental to bright arid
creatures who breathed from sullen preference an air of bitterness
and hate, and hugged desolation to the bone with a hard fatality
of arrogance and pride.

Their conversation had in it something secret, sweet, and precious. It was full of swift allusions, little twists and quirks and subtleties of things about which they themselves were in the know, and interspersed with all the trade-marks of the rough-simple speech that at that time was in such favor with this kind of people: the "swell," the "grand," the "fine," the "simply marvellous."

"Where can we go?" the girl was asking him. "Will Louie's still be open? I thought that he closed up at ten o'clock."

The girl was pretty, and had a good figure, but both face and body had no curve or fullness; body and heart and soul, there was no ripeness in her, she was something meager of breast, hard, sterile, and prognathous.

"If he's not," the young man said, "we'll go next door to Steve's. He's open all night long." His face was dark and insolent, the eyes liquid, the mouth soft, weak, pampered, arrogant, and corrupt. When he laughed, his voice had a soft welling burble in it, loose, jeering, evilly assured.

"Oh, swell!" the girl was saying in her naked tone. "I'd love to go there! Let's have another party! Who can we get to go? Do you think Bob and Mary would be in?"

"Bob might be, but I don't think that you'll find Mary," said the young man, adroitly innocent.

"*No!*" the girl exclaimed incredulously. "You don't mean that she's"—and here their voices became low, eager, sly, filled with laughter, and the young man finally could be heard saying with the burble of soft laughter in his voice:

"Oh, I don't know! It's just another of those things! It happens in the best of families, you know."

"No!" the girl cried with a little scream of incredulous laughter. "You *know* she hasn't! After all she said about him, too! . . . I think—that's—simply—priceless!" She then said slowly: "Oh—I—think—that's—simply—*swell!*" She cried: "I'd give anything to see Bob's face when he finds out about it!"—and for a moment they laughed and whispered knowingly together, after which the girl cried once more, with her little shout of incredulous laughter:

"Oh, this is too good to be true! Oh—I think that's *marvellous,* you know!"—then added quickly and impatiently:

"Well, who can we get to go, then? Who *else* can we get?"

"I don't know," the young man said, "it's getting late now. I don't know who we can get unless"—and here his soft dark mouth began to smile, and the burble of laughter appeared in his throat as he nodded towards the man upon the ground "—unless you ask our friend here if he'd like to come along."

"Oh, that would be *grand!*" she cried with a gleeful little laugh. Then for a moment she stared down seriously at the silent figure on the pavement. "I'd *love* it!" the girl said. "Wouldn't it be swell if we could get some one like that to go with us!"

"Well—" the young man said, indefinitely. Then, as he looked down at the man, his soft wet flow of laughter welled up and he spoke softly and slyly to the girl, "I hate to disappoint you, but I don't think we'll get our friend here to go. He looks as if he's going to have a bad head in the morning," and again his dark mouth began to smile, and the burble of soft laughter welled up in his throat.

"Stop!" the girl cried with a little shriek. "Aren't you mean!" she said reproachfully. "I think he's sweet. I think it would be simply marvellous to take some one like that on a party! He looks like a swell person," she continued, looking down at the man curiously. "He really does, you know."

"Well, you know how it is," the young man said. "He was a great guy when he had it!" The burble welled up richly in his soft throat. "Come on," he said. "We'd better go. I think you're trying to make him!"—and laughing and talking together in their naked and arrogant young voices, they went away.

Presently the interne got up, took the ends of the stethoscope from his ears, and spoke a few quiet and matter-of-fact words to the policeman, who scrawled something down in a small book. The interne walked over to the curb, climbed up into the back of the ambulance and sat down on one seat with his feet stetched out upon the other one, meanwhile saying to the driver: "All right, Mike, let's go!" The ambulance moved off smoothly, slid swiftly around the corner with a slow clangor of bells, and was gone.

Then the policeman folded his book, thrust it into his pocket, and, turning on us suddenly, with a weary expression on his heavy, dark, night-time face, stretched out his arms and began to push us all back gently, meanwhile saying in a patient and weary tone of voice: "All right, you guys! On your way, now. Yuh gotta move. It's all oveh."

And obedient to his weary and tolerant command, we moved on and departed. Meanwhile, the dead man lay, as solid as a rock, upon his back, with that great brutal face of power and fortitude, upthrust and rigid, bared with a terrible stillness, an awful dignity, into the face of the cold and blazing moon.

This was the second time that I saw death in the city.

The third time that I saw death in the city, it had come like this:

One morning in May the year before, I had been on my way up-town, along Fifth Avenue. The day was glorious, bright and sparkling, the immense and delicate light of the vast blue-fragile sky was firm and almost palpable. It seemed to breathe, to change, to come and go in a swarming web of iridescent and crystalline magic, and to play and flash upon the spires of the great shining towers, the frontal blaze and sweep of the tremendous buildings, and on the great crowd which swarmed and wove unceasingly on the street, with vivid and multifarious points of light and color, as if the light were shining on a lake of sapphires.

Up and down the great street as far as the eye could reach, the crowd was surging in the slow yet sinuous convolutions of an enormous brilliantly colored reptile. It seemed to slide, to move, to pause, to surge, to writhe here and to be motionless there in a gigantic and undulant rhythm that was infinitely complex and bewildering, but that yet seemed to move to some central and inexorable design and energy. So did the great surge of the man-swarm look from afar, but when one passed it by at close range it all broke up into a million rich, brilliant, and vivid little pictures and histories of life, all of which now seemed so natural and intimate to me that I felt I knew all the people, that I had the warm and palpable substance of their lives in my hands, and knew and owned the street itself as if I had created it.

At one place, a powerful motor with a liveried chauffeur would snake swiftly in toward the curb, and a uniformed door-man of some expensive shop would scramble with obsequious haste across the sidewalk and open the door for some rich beauty of the upper crust. The woman would get out swiftly with a brisk sharp movement of her well-shod little feet and slender ankles, speak a few incisive words of command to her attentive driver, and then walk swiftly across the sidewalk towards the shop with a driving movement of her shapely but rather tailored-looking hips and a cold impatient look on her lovely but hard little face. To her, this great affair of seduction, attraction, and adornment for which she lived—this constant affair of clothing her lovely legs to the best advantage, setting off her solid shapely little buttocks in the most persuasive fashion, getting varnished, plucked, curled, perfumed, and manicured until she smelled like an exotic flower and glittered like a rare and costly jewel—was really as stern a business as her husband's job of getting money, and not to be trifled with or smiled at for a moment.

Again, some lovely and more tender, simple, and good-natured girl would come by on the pavements, jaunty and rich with some glowing spot of color—a scarf of red or blue, or gay hat—her hair fine-spun and blown by light airs, her clear eyes fathomless and luminous with a cat-like potency and health, her delicate loins undulant with a long full stride, and her firm breasts rhythmical with each step she took, her mouth touched by a vague and tender smile as she passed by.

Elsewhere, dark-eyed, dark-faced, gray-faced, driven, meager, harassed and feverish-looking men and women would be swarming along, but the shining light and magic of the day seemed to have touched them all with its sorcery, so that they, too, all seemed filled with hope, gayety, and good nature, and to drink in as from some source of central and exultant energy the glorious intoxication of the day.

Meanwhile in the street the glittering projectiles of machinery were drilling past incredibly in their beetle-bullet flight, the powerful red-faced police stood like towers in the middle of the street stopping, starting, driving them on or halting them with an imperious movement of their mast-like hands.

Finally, even the warm odors of the hot machinery, the smells of oil, gasoline, and worn rubber which rose up from the bluish surface of the furious street, seemed wonderful, mixed as they were with the warm, earthy and delicious fragrance of the trees, grass, and flowers in the Park, which was near by. The whole street burst into life for me immediately as it would on such a day for every young man in the world. Instead of feeling crushed down and smothered beneath its cruel and arrogant blaze of power, wealth, and number, until I seemed to drown in it, a nameless atom, it now seemed to me to be a glorious pageantry and carnival of palpable life, the great and glamorous Fair of all the earth, in which I was moving with certitude as one of the most honored and triumphant figures.

At this moment, with the Park in view, with the sight of the trees, in their young magic green, and all the flash and play of movement, color, and machinery, in the square before the Park, I halted and began to look with a particular interest at the people working on a building which was being erected there across the street. The building was not large, and neither very tall nor wide: it rose up ten flights with its steel girders set against the crystal air with a graceful and almost fragile delicacy, as if already, in this raw skeleton, the future elegance and style of the building were legible.

For I knew that this building was to house the great business which was known as Stein and Rosen and, like the man who once had shaken the hand of John L. Sullivan, I had a feeling of joy, pride, and familiarity when I looked at it. For the sister of a woman that I loved was a director of this mighty shop, its second-in-command, its first in talent and in knowledge, and from that woman's merry lips I had often heard the fabulous stories of what took place daily there. She told of the glittering processions of rich women who came there for their finery; of actresses, dancers, millionaires' wives, moving-picture women, and of all the famous courtesans, who would pay as they bought, and would plank down the ransom of a king in thousand-dollar bills for a coat of chinchilla fur; and of the stupendous things these legendary creatures said.

Through the portals of this temple in the daytime would move the richest women and the greatest harlots in the country. And an exiled princess would be there to sell them underwear, an impoverished duchess would be there to sell perfumery, and Mr. Rosen himself would be there to greet them. He would bend before them from the waist, he would give his large firm hand to them, he would smile and smile with his large pearly teeth, as his eyes went back and forth about his place continually. He would wear striped trousers and he would walk up and down upon rich carpets, he would be splendid and full of power like a well-fed bull, and somehow he would be like that magnificent horse in Job who paweth in the valley and saith among the trumpets, "Ha! Ha!"

And all day long they would be calling all over the place for her sister, who seldom spoke and rarely smiled. They could not get along without her, they would be asking for her everywhere, the rich woman would demand her, and the famous courtesan would say she had to speak to her. And when she came to them, they would say: "I wanted to speak to you, because the rest of them know nothing. You are the only one who understands me. You are the only one I can talk to," and yet they could not talk to her, because she never spoke. But they would want to be near her, to confess to her, to pour their words into her silence: her large still eyes would look at them and make them want to speak. Meanwhile the Rosens smiled.

Thus, while the countless man-swarm of the earth thronged all around me I stood there thinking of these things and people. I thought of Mr. Rosen, and of the woman and her sister, and of a thousand strange and secret moments of our lives. I thought how great Cæsar's dust could patch a wall, and how our lives touch every other life that ever lived, how every obscure moment, every obscure life, every lost voice and forgotten step upon these pavements had somewhere trembled in the air about us. " 'Twere to consider too curiously, to consider so." "No! faith, not a jot!—" the step that passed there in the street rang echoes from the dust of Italy, and still the Rosens smiled.

And it seemed to me that all the crowded and various life of this great earth was like a Fair. Here were the buildings of the Fair, the shops, the booths, the taverns, and the pleasure-places. Here were the places where men bought and sold and traded, ate, drank, hated, loved, and died. Here were the million fashions that they thought eternal, here was the ancient, everlasting Fair, tonight bereft of people, empty and deserted, tomorrow swarming with new crowds and faces in all its million lanes and passages, the people who are born, grow old and weary, and who die here.

They never hear the great dark wing that beats in the air above them, they think their moment lasts forever, they are so intent that they scarcely see themselves falter and grow old. They never lift their eyes up to the deathless stars above the deathless Fair, they never hear the immutable voice of time that lives in the upper air, that never ceases, no matter what men live or die. The voice of time is distant and remote and yet it has all of the voice of million-noted life within its murmur, it feeds on life and yet it lives above it and apart from it, it broods forever like the flowing of a river round the Fair.

Therefore when I looked at the spare webbing of this building on that shining day, and knew that those ingots of lean steel, those flat blocks of fashionable limestone which already sheeted the building's basal front, and which in their slender elegance were somehow like the hips of the women that the building would adorn, had been spun marvellously from the gossamer substance of Parisian frocks, distilled out of the dearest perfumes in the world, shaped from the cunning in man's brain, and from the magic in a woman's hands—it all seemed good and wonderful to me.

For above, beyond, and through that web of steel, and over the whole pulse and surge of life in the great street, over all the sparking surge and shift of the great Fair, I saw suddenly the blazing image of my mistress's jolly, delicate, and rosy face of noble beauty. And the image of that single face seemed to give a tongue to joy, a certitude to all the power and happiness I felt, to resume into its small circle, as into the petals of a flower, all of the glory, radiance, and variousness of life and of the street, until a feeling of such triumph and belief surged up in me that I thought I could eat and drink the city, and possess the earth.

Quite suddenly, as I stood there looking at the little figures of the men who were working on the building, walking along high up against the crystal air with a corky and scuttling move-ment as they swarmed back and forth across the girders, the thing happened with the murderous nonchalance of horror in a dream. Nine floors above the earth, a little figure was deftly catching in a bucket the nails or rivets of red-hot steel which a man with tongs was tossing to him from the forge. For a moment, the feeder had paused in his work, had turned, tongs in hand, for a breather, and had spoken to a man upon another girder. The catcher, meanwhile, grateful for this respite, had put his bucket down and stood erect, a cigarette between his lips, the small flame of a match held in the cave of his brown cupped hands. Then the feeder, his throat still loud with laughter from some scrap of bawdry irrelevant to steel, turned to his forge, gripped with his tongs a glowing rivet, and his throat still trembling with its laughter, tossed deftly, absently, casually, in its accustomed arc, that nail of fire. His scream broke in upon the echoes of his laughter, carrying to the glut of faultless and accurate machinery in the street below him its terrible message of human error.

His scream was "Christ!" and at that word so seldom used for love and mercy the startled eyes of the other man leaped from his match upon the death that whizzed toward him. Even in the six feet of life that still remained to him, his body had its time for several motions. It half turned, the knees bent as if for a spring out into space, the shoulder stooped, the big brown hands groping in a futile, incompleted gesture for the bucket. Then, half crouched and rigid with palms curved out in a kind of grotesque and terrible entreaty, and one foot groping horribly into thin air, he met his death squarely, fronting it. For a moment after the rivet struck him, his body paused, crouched, rigid, like a grotesque image, groping futilely and horribly into space with one clumsy foot, and with a wire of acrid smoke uncoiling at his waist. Then his shabby garments burst into a flame, the man pawed blindly out in sickening vacancy and fell, a blazing torch lit by a single scream.

So that rich cry fell blazing through the radiant and living air. It seemed to me that the cry had filled up life—for a moment I had the sense that all life was absolutely motionless and silent save for that one cry. Perhaps this was true. It is certain that all life in that building had ceased—where but a moment before there had been the slamming racket of the riveting machines, the rattling of the winches, and the hammering of the carpenters, there was now the silence of a cataleptic trance.

Above the street, delicate and spare in the blue weather, two girders swung gently in the clasp of the chain, but all machinery had stopped. The signal-man leaned over bent, staring, his hands still stretched in warning for his mate. The feeder sat astride a girder, gripping it in his curved hands, his face bent forward sightlessly in an oblivion of horror. The body had fallen, like a mass of blazing oil waste, upon the wooden structure that covered the sidewalk, then bounced off into the street.

Then the illusion of frozen silence, which seemed to have touched all the world, was broken. That crowd, which in the city seems to be created on the spot, to spring up from the earth like Gorgon-seed for every calamity, had already grown dense at the spot where the man had fallen. Several policemen were there, mauling, cursing, thrusting back the thickening ring that terribly suggested flesh-flies that work on something dead or sweet. And all the gleaming machinery in the street—which had been halted by the traffic lights—was again in motion.

There had been threat of a longer halt, a disruption of that inevitable flow, because several of the human units in the fore-most squadrons of motors, who had witnessed the accident, refused now, under the strong drug of horror, to "click" as good machinery ought. But they were whipped into action after a moment's pause by a ponderous traffic cop, who stood in the center of the street, swinging his mighty arm back and forth like a flail, sowing the air with rich curses, his accents thickened in the long ape-like upper lip. So, the lights burned green again, the clamors in the street awoke, the hot squadrons of machinery crawled up and down: an army of great beetles driven by an ape. Then the racket of the riveters began anew, high up above the street in the blue air the long arm of the derrick moved, a chain with its balanced weight of steel swung in and down.

Already the body had been carried inside the building, the police were charging like bulls into the persistent crowd, dispersing them. In a closed car, a young woman, bright with the hard enamel of city elegance, stared through the window, her little gloved hand clenched upon the glass, her face full of manicured distress. And as she looked, she kept murmuring sharply and monotonously: "Quick! quick! be quick!" Before her, her driver bent stolidly over his work. He was upset, but he could not show it. Perhaps he was thinking: "Jesus! I've got to get her out of this quick. What'll *he* say if she tells him about it? He can't blame me. I can't help what the *other* guy does! That's *his* lookout. You never know what's gonna happen. A guy's got to think of everything at once."

He took a chance. Smoothly, swiftly, he skirted three cars and slid into the first rank between cursing drivers, just as the lights changed. The lady settled back in her seat with a look of relief. Thank Heaven, that was over! George was so smart. He got in ahead of every one: you never knew how he did it! He had done *that* beautifully.

I leaned against a building. I felt empty and dizzy. It seemed to me suddenly that I had only two dimensions—that everything on earth was like something cut out of stiff paper, with no thickness.

"Brightness falls from the air." Yes, brightness had fallen suddenly from the air, and with it all the marrowy substance of life. The vitality of life and air and people was gone. What remained to me was only a painting of warmth and color that my sick eyes viewed with weariness and disbelief. Everything in that street went up and down. It seemed to me suddenly that everything was thin, two-dimensioned, without body and fullness. The street, the people, the tall thin buildings: these were all plane lines and angles. There were no curves in the street—the only thing that curved had been that one rich cry.

And just as the light of noon had gone out of the day so had the image of that woman's face, struck by the casual horror of this death with all its evocations of a life she knew, now suffered a transforming and sorrowful change.

For where that radiant, good, and lovely face had just the moment before wrought for me its magic certitude and unity of exultant joy, now all this magic world of health and life was shattered by this nameless death, was drowned out in the torrent of this man's nameless blood, and I could see her face no longer as it had looked at noon.

Rather that man's blood and death had awakened the whole black ruin in my heart, the hideous world of death-in-life had instantly returned with all its thousand phantom shapes of madness and despair and, intolerably, unanswerably, like the unsearchable mystery of love and death, the bitter enigma of that face of radiant life was now fixed among these shapes of death to drive me mad with its unsearchable mystery.

For in the image of that face was held all the pity and the wild regret of love that had to die and was undying, of beauty that must molder into age and wither to a handful of dry dust and yet was high as a star, as timeless as a river, undwarfed beneath the whole blind horror of the universe, and taller than man's tallest towers, and more enduring than steel and stone.

And then the shapes of death would wake and move around her, and I could only see her now fixed and secure in an infamous and arrogant power, which could not be opposed or beaten by any man, and against which, like a maddened animal, I could do nothing but batter my life and brains out on the pavements, as this man had done, or madden horribly into a furious death among the other nameless, faceless, man-swarm atoms of the earth.

I saw her, impregnably secure in an immense, complex, and corrupt city-life—a life poisonous, perverse, and sterile that moved smoothly in great chambers of the night ablaze with baleful suavities of vanity and hate, where the word was always fair and courteous, and the eye forever old and evil with the jubilation of a filthy consent. It was a world of the infamous dead so powerful in the entrenchments of its obscene wealth, its corruption that was amorous of death and faithlessness, its insolence of a jaded satiety, and its appalling weight of number and amount that it crushed man's little life beneath its ramified assault and killed and mutilated every living thing it fed upon—not only the heart and spirit of youth, with all the hope and pride and anguish in him, but also the life and body of some obscure worker whose name it did not know, whose death, in its remote impregnability, it would never hear or care about.

I tried to get the fingers of my hate upon that immense and shifting world of shapes and phantoms, but I could not. I could track nothing to its tangible source, trace nothing to some fatal certitude. Words, whispers, laughter, even an ounce of traitorous flesh, all the immense and moving tapestry of that cruel and phantasmal world were all impalpable and hovered above me, the deathless and invincible legend of scorn and defeat.

Then, even as I stood there in the street, the blind horror left me with the magic instancy in which it always came and went; all around me people seemed to live and move, and it was noon, and I could see her face the way it was again, and thought that it was the best face in the world, and knew that there was no one like her.

Two men came rapidly back across the street from the dispersing crowd and one of them was talking in a low earnest tone to the other:

"Jeez!" he said. "Dat gul! Did yuh see her? Sure, sure, he almost fell on top of her! . . . Sure, dat's what I'm tellin' yuh! . . . She fainted! . . . Dey had to carry her into a stoeh! . . . Jeez!" he said. In a moment, and in a quietly confidential tone, he added: "Say— dat makes duh fourt' one on dat building—did yuh know dat?"

Then I saw a man beside me with a proud, shrinking, and sensitive face, set in a blind sightless stare that kept looking through people, feeding on something that could not be seen. As I looked, he moved, turned his head slowly, and presently in the dull voice of some one who has had an opiate he said "What? The fourth? The fourth?"—although no one had spoken to him. Then he moved his thin hand slowly, and with an almost meditative gesture over his forehead and eyes, sighed wearily and slowly like some one waking from a trance or some strong drug, and then began to walk ahead uncertainly.

This was the third time I saw death in the city.

❊   ❊   ❊

Later, the thing I was to remember vividly about these three deaths, in contrast to the fourth one, was this: That, where the first three deaths had come by violence, where almost every circumstance of horror, sudden shock, disgust and terror, was present to convulse the hearts and sicken and wither up the flesh of those who saw death come, the city people, when their first surprise was over, had responded instantly to death, accepting its violence, bloody mutilation, and horror calmly, as one of the natural consequences of daily life. But the fourth time that I saw death come, the city people were stunned, awed, bewildered, and frightened, as they had not been before; and yet the fourth death had come so quietly, easily, and naturally that it seemed as if even a child could have looked at it without terror or surprise.

This is the way it happened:

At the heart and core of the most furious center of the city's life—below Broadway at Times Square—a little after one o'clock in the morning, bewildered, aimless, having no goal or place to which I wished to go, with the old chaos and unrest inside me, I had thrust down the stairs out of the great thronging street, the tidal swarm of atoms who were pressing and hurrying forward in as fierce a haste to be hurled back into their cells again as they had shown when they had rushed out into the streets that evening.

Thus, we streamed down from free night into the tunnel's stale and fetid air again, we swarmed and hurried across the floors of gray cement, we thrust and pushed our way along as furiously as if we ran a race with time, as if some great reward were to be won if only we could save two minutes, or as if we were hastening onward, as fast as we could go, toward some glorious meeting, some happy and fortunate event, some goal of beauty, wealth, or love on whose shining mark our eyes were fastened.

Then, as I put my coin into the slot, and passed on through the wooden turnstile, I saw the man who was about to die. The place was a space of floor, a width of cement which was yet one flight above the level of the trains, and the man was sitting on a wooden bench which had been placed there to the left, as one went down the incline to the tunnel.

The man just sat there quietly at one end of the bench, leaned over slightly to his right with his elbow resting on the arm of the bench, his hat pulled down a little, and his face half lowered. At this moment, there was a slow, tranquil, hardly perceptible movement of his breath—a flutter, a faint sigh—and the man was dead. In a moment, a policeman who had watched him casually from a distance walked over to the bench, bent down, spoke to him, and then shook him by the shoulder. As he did so, the dead man's body slipped a little, his arm slid over the end of the bench and stayed so, one hand hanging over, his shabby hat jammed down, a little to one side, upon his head, his overcoat open, and his short right leg drawn stiffly back. Even as the policeman shook him by the shoulder, the man's face was turning gray. By this time a few people, out of the crowds that swarmed constantly across the floor, had stopped to look, stared curiously and uneasily, started to go on, and then had come back. Now, a few of them were standing here, just looking, saying nothing, casting uneasy and troubled looks at one another from time to time.

And yet I think that we all knew the man was dead. By this time another policeman had arrived, was talking quietly to the other one, and now he, too, began to look curiously at the dead man, went over and shook him by the shoulder as the other one had done, and then after a few quiet words with his comrade, walked off rapidly. In a minute or two he came back again and another policeman was with him. They talked together quietly for a moment. One of them bent over and searched the man's pockets, finding a dirty envelope, a wallet, and a grimy-looking card. After prying into the purse and taking notes upon their findings they just stood beside the dead man, waiting.

The dead man was a shabby-looking fellow of an age hard to determine, but he was scarcely under fifty, and hardly more than fifty-five. And, had one sought long and far for the true portrait of the pavement cipher, the composite photograph of the man-swarm atom, he could have found no better specimen than this man. His only distinction was that there was nothing to distinguish him from a million other men. He had the kind of face that one sees ten thousand times a day upon the city streets, and cannot remember later.

This face, which even when alive, it is true, was of a sallow, sagging, somewhat paunchy and unwholesome hue and texture, was dryly and unmistakably Irish—city-Irish—with the mouth thin, sunken, slightly bowed, and yet touched with something loose and sly, a furtive and corrupt humor. And the face was also surly, hang-dog, petulant, and servile—the face of one of those little men —a door-man at a theatre, a janitor in a shabby warehouse, office

building, or cheap apartment house, the father-in-law of a policeman, the fifth cousin of a desk-sergeant, the uncle of a ward heeler's
wife, a pensioned door-opener, office-guarder, messenger, or ques-
tion-evader for some Irish politician, schooled to vote dutifully for
"the boys" upon election day, and to be flung his little scrap of
patronage for service rendered and silence kept, apt at servility,
fawning, cringing to those sealed with the mark of privilege and
favor, and apt at snarling, snapping, gratuitous and impudent dis-
courtesy to those who had no power, no privilege, no special mark
of favor or advancement to enlarge them in his sight. Such was
indubitably the man who now sat dead upon the subway bench.

And that man's name was legion, his number myriad. On his gray
face, on his dead sunken mouth, the ghost of his still recent life
and speech sat incredibly, until it seemed we heard him speak,
listened to the familiar tones of his voice again, knew every act and
quality of his life, as certainly as if he were yet alive, as he snarled
at one man: "I can't help dat, I don't know nuttin' about dat, misteh.
All I know is dat I got my ordehs, an' my ordehs is to keep every
one out unless dey can prove dey've gotta date wit' Misteh Grogan.
How do *I* know who you are? How can *I* tell what yoeh business is?
What's dat got to do wit' me? No, seh! Unless you can prove you
gotta date wit' Misteh Grogan, I can't let yuh in. . . . Dat may be
true . . . and den again it may not be. . . . Wat t' hell am *I* supposed t' be? A mind-readeh, or somp'n? . . . No, misteh! Yuh can't
come in! . . . I got my ordehs an' dat's all I know."

And yet, the next moment, this same voice could whine, with a
protesting servility, its aggrieved apology to the same man, or to
another one: "W'y didn't yuh say yuh was a friend of Misteh
Grogan's? . . . W'y didn't yuh tell me befoeh you was his brudder-
in-law? . . . If yuh'd told me dat, I'd 'a' let yuh by in a minute.
You know how it is," here the voice would drop to cringing confidence, "so many guys come in here every day an' try to bust
dere way right in to Misteh Grogan's office when dey got no bizness
dere. . . . Dat's duh reason dat I gotta be kehful. . . . But now dat
I know dat you're O.K. wit' Misteh Grogan," it would say fawningly,
"you can go on in any time yuh like. Any one dat's O.K. wit'
Misteh Grogan is *all right*," that voice would say with crawling
courtesy. "*You* know how it is," it whispered, rubbing sly, unwholesome fingers on one's sleeve, "I didn't mean nuttin'—but a guy in
my position has gotta be kehful."

Yes, that was the voice, that was the man, as certainly as if that dead mouth had just moved, that dead tongue stirred and spoken to us its language. There he was, still with the sallow hue of all his life upon his face, as it faded visibly, terribly before us to the gray of death. Poor, shabby, servile, fawning, snarling, and corrupted cipher, poor, meager, cringing, contriving, cunning, drearily hopeful, and dutifully subservient little atom of the million-footed city. Poor, dismal, ugly, sterile, shabby little man—with your little scrabble of harsh oaths, and cries, and stale constricted words, your pitiful little designs and feeble purposes, with your ounce of brain, your thimbleful of courage, the huge cargo of your dull and ugly superstitions. Oh, you wretched little thing of dough and tallow, you eater of poor foods and drinker of vile liquors. Joy, glory, and magnificence were here for you upon this earth, but you scrabbled along the pavements rattling a few stale words like gravel in your throat, and would have none of them, because the smell of the boss, the word of the priest, the little spare approvals of Mike, Mary, Molly, Kate, and Pat were not upon them—and tonight the stars shine, great ships are blowing from the harbor's mouth, and a million more of your own proper kind and quality go stamping on above your head, while you sit here *dead* in your gray tunnel!

We look at your dead face with awe, with pity, and with terror, because we know that you are shaped from our own clay and quality. Something of us all, the high, the low, the base, and the heroic, the rare, the common, and the glorious lies dead here in the heart of the unceasing city, and the destiny of all men living, yes, of the kings of the earth, the princes of the mind, the mightiest lords of language, and the deathless imaginers of verse, all the hope, hunger, and the earth-consuming thirst that can incredibly be held in the small prison of a skull, and that can rack and rend the little tenement in which it is confined, is written here upon this shabby image of corrupted clay.

The dead man was wearing nondescript clothing, and here again, in these dingy garments, the whole quality, the whole station of his life was evident, as if the clothes he wore had had a tongue, a character, and a language of their own. They said that the man had known poverty and a shabby security all his life, that his life had been many degrees above the moment-by-moment desperation of the vagabond and pauper, and many degrees below any real security, substance, or repose. His garments said that he had lived from month to month rather than from day to day, always menaced by the fear of some catastrophe—sickness, the loss of his job, the coming on of age—that would have dealt a ruinous blow to the slender resources which he had built between him and the world, never free from the fear of these calamities, but always just escaping them.

He wore an unpressed baggy gray suit which he filled out pretty well, and which had taken on the whole sagging, paunchy, and unshapely character of his own body. He had a small pot belly, a middling fleshiness and fullness which showed he had known some abundance in his life, and had not suffered much from hunger. He was wearing a dingy old brown felt hat, a shabby gray overcoat, and a ragged red scarf—and in all these garments there was a quality of use and wear and shabbiness that was inimitable and that the greatest costume-artist in the world could never have duplicated by intent.

The lives of millions of people were written in these garments. In their sag and hang and worn dingy textures, the shabby lives of millions of pavement ciphers were revealed, and this character was so strong and legible that as the dead man sat there and his face took on the corpsen gray of death, his body seemed to shrink, to dwindle, to withdraw visibly before our eyes out of its last relationship with life, and the clothes themselves took on a quality and character that were far more living than the shape they covered.

And now the dead man's face had grown ghastly with the strange real-unreality of death that has such terrible irony in it, for, as one looks, the face and figure of the dead seem to have no more of the substance of mortal flesh than a waxen figure in a museum, and to smile, to mock, to stare, to mimic life in the same ghastly and unreal manner that a waxen figure would.

The turnstiles kept clicking with their dull wooden note, the hurrying people kept swarming past over the gray cement floor, the trains kept roaring in and out of the station below with a savage grinding vibrance, and from time to time, out of these swarming throngs, some one would pause, stare curiously for a moment, and stay. By this time, a considerable number of people had gathered in a wide circle about the bench on which the dead man sat, and curiously, although they would not go away, they did not press in, or try to thrust their way up close, as people do when some violent, bloody, or fatal accident has occurred.

Instead, they just stood there in that wide semi-circle, never intruding farther, looking at one another in an uneasy and bewildered manner, asking each other questions in a low voice from time to time which, for the most part, went unanswered since the person asked would squirm, look at his questioner uneasily and with wavering eyes, and then, muttering "I don't know," with a slight gesture of his arms and shoulders, would sidle or shuffle away. And from time to time the policemen, whose number by this time had grown to four, and who just stood around the man's body with a waiting and passive vacancy, would suddenly start, curiously and almost comically, into violent activity, and would come thrusting and shoving at the ring of people, pushing them back and saying in angry and impatient voices: "All right, now! Break it up! Break it up! Break it up! Go on! Go on! Go on! Yuh're blockin' up duh passageway! Go on! Go on! Break it up, now! Break it up!"

And the crowd obediently would give ground, withdraw, shuffle around, and then with the invincible resiliency of a rope of rubber or a ball of mercury would return, coming back once more into their staring, troubled, uneasily whispering circle.

Meanwhile, the wooden stiles kept clicking with their dull, dead, somewhat thunderous note, the people kept thronging past to get their trains, and in their glances, attitudes, and gestures when they saw the ring of staring people and the man upon the bench, there was evident all of the responses which it is possible for men to have when they see death.

Some people would come by, pause, stare at the man, and then begin to whisper to one another in low uneasy tones: "What's wrong with him? Is he sick? Did he faint? Is he drunk—or something?" to which a man might answer, looking intently for a moment at the dead man's face, and then crying out heartily, with a hard derisive movement of his hand, and yet with something troubled and uncertain in his voice: "Nah! He's not sick. Duh guy is drunk! Dat's all it is. Sure! He's just passed out. . . . Look at dem all standin' dere, lookin' at duh guy!" he jeered. "Yuh'd t'ink dey neveh saw a drunk befoeh. Come on!" he cried. "Let's go!" And they would hurry on, while the man mocked at the crowd with hard derisive laughter.

And indeed, the dead man's posture and appearance as he sat there on the bench with his shabby old hat pushed forward over his head, one leg drawn stiffly back, his right hand hanging over the edge of the bench, and his thin, sunken Irish mouth touched by a faint, loose, rather drunken smile, was so much like the appearance of a man in a drunken stupor that many people, as soon as they saw his gray ghastly face, would cry out with a kind of desperate relief in their voices: "Oh! He's only drunk. Come on! Come on! Let's go!"—and would hurry on, knowing in their hearts the man was dead.

Others would come by, see the dead man, start angrily, and then look at the crowd furiously, frowning, shaking their head in a movement of strong deprecation and disgust, and muttering under their breath before they went on, as if somehow the crowd were guilty of some indecent and disorderly act which their own decent and orderly souls abhorred.

Three little Jewesses and a young Jewish boy had come in together, and pressed up in a group into the circle of the crowd. For a moment the girls stood there, staring, frightened, huddled in a group, while the boy looked in a rather stupid and bewildered manner at the dead man, finally saying nervously in a high stunned tone of voice: "What's wrong wit' him? Have dey called duh ambulance yet?"

No one in the ring of silent people answered him, but in a moment a taxi-driver, a man with a brutal heavy night-time face, a swarthy, sallow, pitted skin, black hair and eyes, a cap, a leather jacket, and a shirt of thick black wool—this man turned and, jerking his head contemptuously toward the boy without looking at him, began to address the people around him in a jeering and derisive tone:

"Duh *ambulance!*" he cried. "Duh *ambulance!* Wat t' hell's duh use of duh *ambulance!* Jesus! Duh guy's dead an' he wants t' know if any one has called duh ambulance!" he cried, jerking his head contemptuously toward the boy again, and evidently getting some kind of security and assurance from his own jeering and derisive words. "Jesus!" he snorted. "Duh guy's dead an' he wants to know w'y some one don't call duh ambulance!" And he went off snorting and sneering by himself, saying "Jesus!" and shaking his head, as if the stupidity and folly of people were past his powers of understanding or consent.

The boy kept staring at the dead man on the bench with a fascinated eye of horror and disbelief. Presently he moistened his dry lips wth his tongue, and spoke nervously and dully in a bewildered tone:

"I don't see him breathe or nuttin'," he said. "He don't move or nuttin'."

Then the girl beside him, who had been holding to his arm all this time, and who was a little Jewess with red hair, thin meager features, and an enormous nose that seemed to overshadow her whole face, now plucked nervously and almost frantically at the boy's sleeve, as she whispered:

"Oh! Let's go! Let's get away from heah! . . . Gee! I'm shakin' all oveh! Gee! I'm tremblin'—look!" she whispered, holding up her hand which was trembling visibly. "Let's go!"

"I don't see him breathe or nuttin'," the boy muttered dully, staring.

"Gee! Let's go!" the girl whispered pleadingly again. "Gee! I'm so noivous I'm tremblin' like a leaf—I'm shakin' all oveh! Come on!" she whispered. "Come on! Let's go!" And all four of them, the three frightened girls and the stunned bewildered-looking boy, hurried away in a huddled group, and went down the incline into the tunnel.

And now the other people who up to this time had only stood, looked uneasily at one another, and asked perplexed and troubled questions which no one answered, began to talk quietly and whisper among themselves, and one caught the sound of the word "dead" several times. Having spoken and heard this word, all the people grew very quiet and still, and turned their heads slowly toward the figure of the dead man on the bench, and began to stare at him with a glance full of curiosity, fascination, and a terrible feeding hunger.

At this moment a man's voice was heard speaking quietly, and with an assurance and certainty which seemed to say for every one what they had been unable to say for themselves.

"Sure, he's dead. The man's dead." The quiet and certain voice continued. "I knew all the time that he was dead."

And at the same time a big soldier, who had the seamed and weathered face of a man who has spent years of service in the army, turned and spoke with a quiet and familiar assurance to a little dish-faced Irishman who was standing at his side.

"No matter where they kick off," he said, "they always leave that little black mark behind them, don't they?" His voice was quiet, hard, and casual as he spoke these words, and at the same time he nodded toward a small wet stain upon the cement near the dead man's foot where it had been drawn stiffly back.

The little dish-faced Irishman nodded as soon as the soldier had spoken, and with an air of conviction and agreement, said vigorously:

"You said it!"

At this moment, there was a shuffling commotion, a disturbance in the crowd near the gate beside the turnstiles, the people pressed back respectfully on two sides, and the ambulance doctor entered followed by two attendants, one of whom was bearing a rolled stretcher.

The ambulance surgeon was a young Jew with full lips, a somewhat receding chin, a little silky moustache, and a rather bored, arrogant and indifferent look upon his face. He had on a blue jacket, a flat blue cap with a visor which was pushed back on his head, and even as he entered and came walking slowly and indifferently across the cement floor, he had the tubes of the stethoscope fastened in his ears and was holding the end part in his hand. The two attendants followed him.

About every movement which the ambulance doctor made there was an air of habit, boredom, even weariness, as if he had been summoned too many times on errands such as this to feel any emotion. As he approached the policemen, they separated and opened up a path for him. Without speaking to them he walked over to the dead man, unbuttoned his shirt and pulled it open, bent, and then began to use the stethoscope, listening carefully and intently for some seconds, then moving it to another place upon the dead man's tallowy, hairless, and ghastly-looking breast, and listening carefully again.

During all this time his face showed no emotion whatever of surprise, regret, or discovery. Undoubtedly, the doctor had known the man was dead the moment that he looked at him, and his duties now were only a part of that formality which law and custom demanded. But the people during all this time surged forward a little, with their gaze riveted on the doctor's face with awe, respect, and fascinated interest as if they hoped to read there the confirmation of what they already knew themselves, or as if they expected to see there a look of developing horror, pity, or regret which would put the final stamp of conviction on their own knowledge. But they saw nothing in the doctor's face but deliberation, dutiful intentness, and a look almost of weariness and boredom.

When he had finished with the stethoscope, he got up, took it out of his ears, and then casually opened the half-shut eyelids of the dead man for a moment. The dead eyes stared with a ghastly bluish glitter. The doctor turned and spoke a few words quietly to the police who were standing around him with their note-books open, with the same air of patience, custom, and indifference, and for a moment they wrote dutifully in their little books. One of them asked him a question and wrote down what he said, and then the doctor was on his way out again, walking slowly and indifferently away, followed by his two attendants, neither of whom showed any curiosity or surprise. The dead man, in fact, seemed to be under the control of a régime which worked with a merciless precision, which could not be escaped or altered by a jot, and whose operations all of its servants—doctors, stretcher-bearers, policemen, and even the priests of the church—knew with a weary and unarguable finality.

The police, having written in their books and put the books away, turned and came striding toward the crowd again, thrusting and pushing them back, and shouting, as they had before: "Go on! Go on! Break it up, now! Break it up!"—but even in the way they did this, there was this same movement of régime and custom, a sense of weariness and indifference, and when the people surged back into their former positions with maddening mercurial resiliency, the police said nothing and showed no anger or impatience. They took up their station around the dead man again, and waited stolidly, until the next move in their unalterable program should occur.

And now the people, as if the barriers of silence, restraint, and timidity had been broken, and the confusion and doubt in their own spirits dispersed by a final acknowledgment, and the plain sound of the word "death," which had at last been spoken openly, began to talk to one another easily and naturally as if they had been friends or familiar associates for many years.

A little to one side, and behind the outer ring of the crowd, three sleek creatures of the night and of the great street which roared on above our heads—a young smooth Broadwayite wearing a jaunty gray hat and a light spring overcoat of gray, cut inward toward the waist, an assertive and knowing-looking Jew, with a large nose, an aggressive voice, and a vulturesque smile, and an Italian, smaller, with a vulpine face, a ghastly yellow night-time skin, glittering black eyes and hair—all three smartly dressed and overcoated in the flashy Broadway manner—now gathered together as if they recognized in one another men of substance, worldliness, and knowledge. They began to philosophize in a superbly knowing manner, bestowing on life, death, the brevity of man's days, and the futility of man's hopes and aspirations, the ripe fruit of their experience. The Jew was dominantly the center of this little group, and did most of the talking. In fact, the other two served mainly as a chorus to his harangue, punctuating it whenever he paused to draw breath with vigorous nods of agreement, and such remarks as "You said it!" "And I don't mean maybe!" or "Like I was sayin' to a guy duh otheh day—" an observation which was never completed, as the philosopher would be wound up and on his way again:

"And they ask us, f'r Christ's sake, to save for the future!" he cried, at the same time laughing with jeering and derisive contempt. "For the future!" Here he paused to laugh scornfully again. "When you see a guy like that you ask what for? Am I right?"

"You said it!" said the Italian, nodding his head with energetic assent.

"Like I was sayin' to a guy duh otheh day"—the other younger man began.

"Christ!" cried the Jew. "Save for the *future!* W'y the hell should *I* save for the future?" he demanded in a dominant and aggressive tone, tapping himself on the breast belligerently, glancing around as if someone had just tried to ram this vile proposal down his throat. "What's it goin' to getcha? You may be dead tomorrow! What the hell's the use in saving, f'r Christ's sake! We're only here for a little while. Let's make the most of it, f'r Christ's sake!—Am I right?" he demanded pugnaciously, looking around, and the others dutifully agreed that he was.

"Like I was sayin' to a guy duh otheh day," the young man said, "it only goes to show dat yuh——"

"Insurance!" the Jew cried at this point, with a loud scornful laugh. "The insurance companies, f'r Christ's sake! W'y the hell should any one spend their dough on insurance?" he demanded.

"Nah, nah, nah," the Italian agreed gutturally, with a smile of vulpine scorn, "dat's all a lotta crap."

"A lotta boloney," the young man said, "like I was sayin' to a guy duh otheh——"

"Insurance!" said the Jew. "W'y to listen to *those* bastuds talk you'd think a guy was gonna live forever! Save for the future, f'r Christ's sake," he snarled. "Put something by f'r your old age—your *old* age, f'r Christ's sake," he jeered, "when you may get what this guy got at any minute! Am I right?"

"You said it!"

"Put something by for a rainy day! Leave something for your children when you kick off!" he sneered. "W'y the hell should *I* leave anything for *my* children, f'r Christ's sake?" he snarled, as if the whole pressure of organized society and the demands of fifteen of his progeny had been brought to bear on him at this point. "No, sir!" he said. "Let my children look out for themselves the way·*I* done!" he said. "Nobody ever did anything f'r me!" he said. "W'y the hell should *I* spend *my* life puttin' away jack for a lot of bastuds to spend who wouldn't appreciate it, noway! Am I right?"

"You said it!" said the Italian nodding. "It's all a lotta crap!"

"Like I was sayin' to dis guy—" the young man said.

"No, sir," said the Jew in a hard positive tone, and with a smile of bitter cynicism. "No, sir, misteh! Not for me! When I kick off and they all gatheh around the big cawfin," he continued with a descriptive gesture, "I want them *all* to take a good long look," he said. "I want them all to take a good long look at me and say: 'Well, he didn't bring nothing with him when he came, and he's not taking anything with him when he goes—but *there* was a guy,'" the Jew said loudly, and in an impressive tone, "'there was a guy who spent it when he had it—and *who didn't miss a thing!*'" Here he paused a moment, grasped the lapels of his smart overcoat with both hands, and rocked gently back and forth from heel to toe, as he smiled a bitter and knowing smile.

"Yes, sir!" he said presently in a tone of hard assurance.

"Yes, sir! When I'm out there in that graveyahd pushin' daisies, I don't want no bokays! I want to get what's comin' to me here and now! Am I right?"

"You said it!" the Italian answered.

"Like I was sayin' to a guy duh otheh day," the young man now concluded with an air of triumph, "yuh neveh can tell. No, sir! Yuh neveh can tell what's goin' t' happen. You're here one day an' gone duh next—so wat t' hell!" he said. "Let's make duh most of it."

And they all agreed that he was right, and began to search the dead man's face again with their dark, rapt, fascinated stare.

Elsewhere now, people were gathering into little groups, beginning to talk, to discuss, debate, philosophize, even to smile and laugh, in an earnest and animated way. One man was describing his experience to a little group that pressed around him eagerly, telling again and again, with unwearied repetition, the story of what he had seen, felt, thought and done when he first saw the dead man.

"Sure! Sure!" he cried. "Dat's what I'm tellin' yuh. I seen him when he passed out. I was standin' not ten feet away from 'im! Sure! I watched 'im when he stahted gaspin' t' get his bret'. I was standin' dere. Dat's what I'm sayin'. I tu'ns to duh cop an' says, 'Yuh'd betteh look afteh dat guy,' I says. 'Deh's somet'ing wrong wit' im,' I says. Sure! Dat's when it happened. Dat's what I'm tellin' yuh. I was standin' dere," he cried.

Meanwhile, two men and two women had come in and stopped. They all had the thick clumsy figures, the dull-red smouldering complexions, the thick taffy-colored hair, bleared eyes, and broad, blunted, smeared features of the Slavic races—of Lithuanians or Czechs—and for a while they stared stupidly and brutally at the figure of the dead man, and then began to talk rapidly among themselves in coarse thick tones, and a strange tongue.

And now, some of the people began to drift away, the throng of people swarming homeward across the cement floor had dwindled noticeably, and the circle of people around the dead man had thinned out, leaving only those who would stay like flesh-flies feeding on carrion, until the body was removed.

A young Negro prostitute came through the gate and walked across the floor, glancing about her quickly with every step she took, and smiling a hideous empty smile with her thin encarmined lips. When she saw the circle of men she walked over to it and after one vacant look toward the bench where the dead man sat, she began to glance swiftly about her from right to left, displaying white, shining, fragile-looking teeth.

The thin face of the young Negress, which was originally of a light coppery color, had been smeared over with rouge and powder that it was now a horrible, dusky yellow-and-purplish hue, her black eyelashes were coated with some greasy substance which made them stick out around her large dark eyes in stiff oily spines, and her black hair had been waved and was also coated with this grease.

She was dressed in a purple dress, wore extremely high heels which were colored red, and had the wide hips and the long thin ugly legs of the Negress. There was something at once horrible and seductive in her figure, in her thin stringy lower legs, her wide hips, her mongrel color, her meager empty little whore's face, her thin encarmined lips, and her thin shining frontal teeth, as if the last atom of intelligence in her bird-twitter of brain had been fed into the ravenous maw of a diseased and insatiable sensuality, leaving her with nothing but this thin varnished shell of face, and the idiot and sensual horror of her smile which went brightly and impudently back and forth around the ring of waiting men.

The Italian with the vulpine face, whose former companions, the Jew and the sleek young Broadwayite, had now departed, sidled stealthily over toward the Negress until he stood behind her. Then he eased up on her gently, his glittering eye feeding on her all the time in a reptilian stare, until his body was pressed closely against her buttocks, and his breath was hot upon her neck. The Negress said nothing but looked swiftly around at him with her bright smile of idiot and sensual vacancy, and in a moment started off rapidly, stepping along on her high red heels and long stringy legs, and looking back swiftly toward the Italian, flashing her painted lips and shining teeth at him in a series of seductive invitations to pursuit. The man craned his neck stealthily at the edges of his collar, looked furtively around with glittering eyes and vulpine face, and then started off rapidly after the girl. He caught up with her in the corridor beyond the stiles and they went on together.

The stiles still turned with their blunt, dull, wooden note, belated travellers came by with a lean shuffle of steps upon the cement floors, in the news-stand the dealer sold his wares, giving only an occasional and wearily indifferent glance at the dead man and the people, and in the cleared space round the bench the police were standing, waiting, with a stolid and impassive calm. A man had come in, walked across the space and was now talking to one of the police. The policeman was a young man with a solid strong-necked face that was full of dark color. He talked quietly out of the side of his mouth to the man who questioned him, and who was taking notes in a small black book. The man had a flabby yellowish face, weary eyes, and a flabby roll of flesh beneath his chin.

The people who remained, having greedily sucked the last drop of nourishment from conversation, now stood silent, staring insatiably at the dead man with a quality of vision that had a dark, feeding, glutinous and almost physical property, and that seemed to be stuck upon the thing they watched.

By this time an astonishing thing had happened. Just as the dead man's figure had appeared to shrink and contract visibly within its garments, as if before our eyes the body were withdrawing out of a life with which it had no further relationships, so now did all the other properties of space and light, the dimensions of width, length, and distance that surrounded him undergo an incredible change.

And it seemed to me that this change in the dimensions of space was occurring visibly and momently under my eyes, and that just as the man's body seemed to dwindle and recede so did the gray cement space around him grow tremendously. The space that separated him from the place where the police stood, and the gray space which separated us from the police, together with the distance of the tiled subway wall behind, all grew taller, wider, longer, enlarged themselves terrifically while I looked. It was as if we were all looking at the man across an immense and lonely distance. The dead man looked like a lonely little figure upon an enormous stage, and by his very littleness and loneliness in that immense gray space, he seemed to gain an awful dignity and grandeur.

And now, as it seemed to me, just as the living livid gray-faced dead men of the night were feeding on him with their dark and insatiate stare, so did he return their glance with a deathless and impassive irony, with a terrible mockery and scorn, which were as living as their own dark look, and would endure forever.

Then, as suddenly as it had come, that distorted vision was gone, all shapes and things and distances swam back once more into their proper focus. I could see the dead man sitting there in the gray space, and the people as they looked and were. And the police were driving forward again and thrusting at the people all about me.

But they could not bear to leave that little lonely image of proud death, that sat there stiffly with its grotesque, drunken dignity, its thin smile—as men are loyal to a lifeless shape, and guard and watch and will not leave it till the blind earth takes and covers it again. And they would not leave it now because proud death, dark death, the lonely dignity of proud dark death sat grandly there upon man's shabby image, and because they saw that nothing common, mean, or shabby on earth, nor all the fury, size, and number of the million-footed city could alter for an instant the immortal dignities of death, proud death, even when it rested on the poorest cipher in the streets.

Therefore they would not leave it from a kind of love and loyalty they bore it now; and because proud death was sitting grandly there and had spoken to them, and had stripped them down into their nakedness; and because they had built great towers against proud death, and had hidden from him in gray tunnels, and had tried to still his voice with all the brutal stupefactions of the street, but proud death, dark death, proud brother death, was striding in their city now, and he was taller than their tallest towers, and triumphant even when he touched a shabby atom of base clay, and all their streets were silent when he spoke.

Therefore they looked at him with awe, with terror and humility, and with love, for death, proud death, had come into their common and familiar places, and his face had shone terribly in gray tainted air, and he had matched his tongue, his stride, his dignities against the weary and brutal custom of ten million men, and he had stripped them down at length, and stopped their strident and derisive tongues, and in the image of their poorest fellow had shown them all the way that they must go, the awe and terror that would clothe them—and because of this they stood before him lonely, silent, and afraid.

Then, the last rituals of the law and church were observed, and the dead man was taken from their sight. The dead-wagon of the police had come. Two men in uniform came swiftly down the stairs and entered carrying a rolled stretcher. The stretcher was rolled out upon the cement floor, swiftly the dead man was lifted from the bench and laid down on the stretcher, and at the same moment, a priest stepped from the crowd, and knelt there on the floor beside the body.

He was a young man, plump, well kept, and very white, save for his garments, pork-faced, worldly, and unpriestly, and on his full white jaws was the black shaved smudge of a heavy beard. He wore a fine black overcoat with a velvet collar, and had on a scarf of fine white silk, and a derby hat, which he removed carefully and put aside when he knelt down. His hair was very black, fine-spun as silk, and getting thin on top. He knelt swiftly beside the dead man on the stretcher, raised a white, hairy hand, and as he did so, the five policemen straightened suddenly, whipped off their visored hats with a military movement, and stood rigidly for a moment, with their hats upon their hearts as the priest spoke a few swift words above the body, which no one could hear. In a moment a few of the people in the crowd also took off their hats awkwardly, and presently the priest got up, put on his derby hat carefully, adjusted his coat and scarf, and stepped back into the crowd again. It was all over in a minute, done with the same inhuman and almost weary formality that the ambulance doctor had shown.

Then the two uniformed stretcher-men bent down, took the handles of the stretcher, and, speaking in low voices to each other, lifted it. They started off at a careful step, but as they did so, the dead man's gray-tallow hands flapped out across the edges of the stretcher, and began to jog and jiggle in a grotesque manner with every step the stretcher-bearers took.

One of the men spoke sharply to another, saying, "Wait a minute! Put it down! Some one get his hands!"

The stretcher was laid down upon the floor again, a policeman knelt down beside the body and quickly stripped the dead man's necktie from his collar, which had been opened by the doctor and now gaped wide, showing a brass collar-button in the neck-band of the shirt, and the round greenish discoloration of the brass collar-button in the dead yellowed tissues of the neck. The policeman took the dead man's necktie, which was a soiled, striped, and stringy thing of red and white, and quickly tied it in a knot around the dead man's wrists in order to keep his hands from jerking.

Then the stretcher-bearers lifted him again, and started off, the police striding before them toward the gate-way, thrusting the people back, and crying:

"Get back, there! Get back! Make way! Make way! Make way!"

The dead man's hands were silent now, tied together across his stomach, but his shabby old garments trembled, and his gray-yellow cheek-flanks quivered gently with every step the stretcher-bearers took. The gaping collar ends flapped stiffly as they walked and his soiled white shirt was partially unbuttoned revealing a dead, bony, tallowy-yellow patch of breast beneath, and his battered old brown hat was now pushed down so far over his face that it rested on his nose, and, together with the thin sunken smile of his mouth, intensified the grotesque and horrible appearance of drunkenness.

As for the rest of him—the decaying substance that had been his body—this seemed to have shrunk and dwindled away almost to nothing. One was no longer conscious of its existence. It seemed lost, subsided to nothing and indistinguishable in a pile of shabby old garments—an old gray overcoat, baggy old trousers, an old hat, a pair of scuffed and battered shoes. This in fact was all he now seemed to be: a hat, a thin grotesquely drunken smile, two trembling cheek flanks, two flapping collar-ends, two gray-grimy claws tied with a stringy necktie, and a shabby heap of worn, dingy, and nondescript garments that moved and oscillated gently with every step the stretcher-bearers took.

The stretcher men moved carefully yet swiftly through the gate and up the stairs of an obscure side-opening which was marked "Exit." As they started up the grimy iron steps, the body sloped back a little heavily and the old brown hat fell off, revealing the dead man's thin, disordered, and gray-grimy hair. One of the policemen picked up the hat, saying to one of the stretcher bearers, "O.K., John, I've got it!" then followed him up-stairs.

It was now early morning, about half-past three o'clock, with a sky full of blazing and delicate stars, an immense and lilac darkness, a night still cool, and full of chill, but with all the lonely and jubilant exultancy of spring in it. Far-off, half-heard, immensely mournful, wild with joy and sorrow, there was a ship lowing in the darkness, a great boat blowing at the harbor's mouth.

The street looked dark, tranquil, almost deserted—as quiet as it could ever be, and at that brief hour when all its furious noise and movement of the day seemed stilled for a moment's breathing space, and yet preparing for another day. The taxis drilled past emptily, sparely, and at intervals, like projectiles, the feet of people made a lean and picketing noise upon the pavements, the lights burned green and red and yellow with a small hard lonely radiance that somehow filled the heart with strong joy and victory, and belonged to the wild exultancy of the night, the ships, the springtime, and of April. A few blocks farther up the street where the great shine and glitter of the night had burned immensely like a huge censer steaming always with a dusty, pollenated, immensely brilliant light, that obscene wink had now gone dull, and shone brownly, still livid but subdued.

When the stretcher-men emerged from the subway exit, the green dead-wagon of the police was waiting at the curb, and a few taxi-drivers with dark dingy faces had gathered on the sidewalk near the door. As the stretcher-men moved across the pavement with their burden, one of the taxi-men stepped after them, lifted his cap obsequiously to the dead man, saying eagerly:

"Taxi, sir! Taxi!"

One of the policemen, who was carrying the dead man's hat, stopped suddenly, turned around laughing, and lifted his club with jocular menace, saying to the taxi-man:

"You son-of-a-bitch! Go on!"

Then, still laughing, saying "Jesus!" he tossed the dead man's hat into the green wagon, into which the stretcher-men had already shoved the body. One of the stretcher-men closed the doors, went around to the driver's seat where the other was already sitting, took out a cigarette and lit it between a hard cupped palm and a twisted mouth, climbed up beside the driver saying "O.K., John," and the wagon drove off swiftly. The police looked after it as it drove off. Then they all talked together for a moment more, laughed a little, spoke quietly of the plans, pleasures, and duties of the future, said good-night all around, and walked off, two up the street toward the dull brown-livid smoulder of the lights, and three down the street, where it was darker, quieter, more deserted, and where the lights would shift and burn green, yellow, red.

The jesting taxi-man who had offered his services to the dead man on the stretcher turned briskly to his fellows with an air of something ended, saying sharply and jocosely:

"Well, whattya say, boy! Whattya say!"—at the same time sparring sharply and swiftly at one of the other drivers with his open hands. Then the taxi-drivers walked away toward their lines of shining, silent machines, jesting, debating, denying, laughing in their strident and derisive voices.

And again, I looked and saw the deathless sky, the huge starred visage of the night, and heard the boats then on the river. And instantly an enormous sanity and hope of strong exultant joy surged up in me again; and like a man who knows he is mad with thirst, yet sees real rivers at the desert's edge, I knew I should not die and strangle like a mad dog in the tunnel's dark. I knew I should see light once more and know new coasts and come into strange harbors, and see again, as I had once, new lands and morning.

Therefore, immortal fellowship, proud Death, stern Loneliness, and Sleep, dear friends, in whose communion I shall live forever, out of the passion and the substance of my life, I have made this praise for you:

To you, proud Death, who sit so grandly on the brows of little men—first to you! Proud Death, proud Death, whom I have seen by darkness, at so many times, and always when you came to nameless men, what have you ever touched that you have not touched with love and pity, Death? Proud Death, wherever we have seen your face, you came with mercy, love, and pity, Death, and brought to all of us your compassionate sentences of pardon and release. For have you not retrieved from exile the desperate lives of men who never found their home? Have you not opened your dark door for us who never yet found doors to enter, and given us a room who, roomless, doorless, unassuaged, were driven on forever through the streets of life? Have you not offered us your stern provender, Death, with which to stay the hunger that grew to madness from the food it fed upon, and given all of us the goal for which we sought but never found, the certitude, the peace, for which our over-laden hearts contended, and made for us, in your dark house, an end of all the tortured wandering and unrest that lashed us on forever? Proud Death, proud Death, not for the glory that you added to the glory of the king, proud Death, nor for the honor you imposed upon the dignities of famous men, proud Death, nor for the final magic you have given to the lips of genius, Death, but because you come so gloriously to us who never yet knew glory, so proudly and sublimely to us whose lives were nameless and obscure, because you give to all of us—the nameless, faceless, voiceless atoms of the earth—the awful chrysm of your grandeur, Death, because I have seen and known you so well, and have lived alone so long with Loneliness, your brother, I do not fear you any longer, friend, and I have made this praise for you.

Now, Loneliness forever and the earth again! Dark brother and stern friend, immortal face of darkness and of night, with whom the half part of my life was spent, and with whom I shall abide now till my death forever, what is there for me to fear as long as you are with me? Heroic friend, blood-brother of proud Death, dark face, have we not gone together down a million streets, have we not coursed together the great and furious avenues of night, have we not crossed the stormy seas alone, and known strange lands, and come again to walk the continent of night, and listen to the silence of the earth? Have we not been brave and glorious when we were together, friend, have we not known triumph, joy, and glory on this earth—and will it not be again with me as it was then, if you come back to me? Come to me, brother, in the watches of the night, come to me in the secret and most silent heart of darkness, come to me as you always came, bringing to me once more the old invincible strength, the deathless hope, the triumphant joy and confidence that will storm the ramparts of the earth again.

Come to me through the fields of night, dear friend, come to me with the horses of your sister, Sleep, and we shall listen to the silence of the earth and darkness once again, we shall listen to the heartbeats of the sleeping men, as with soft and rushing thunder of their hooves the strange dark horses of great Sleep come on again.

They come! Ships call! The hooves of night, the horses of great Sleep, are coming on below their manes of darkness. And forever the rivers run. Deep as the tides of Sleep the rivers run. We call!

They come: My great dark horses come! With soft and rushing thunder of their hooves they come, and the horses of Sleep are galloping, galloping over the land.

Oh, softly, softly the great dark horses of Sleep are galloping over the land. The great black bats are flying over us. The tides of Sleep are moving through the nation; beneath the tides of Sleep and time strange fish are moving.

For Sleep has crossed the worn visages of day, and in the night-time, in the dark, in all the sleeping silence of the towns, the faces of ten million men are strange and dark as time. In Sleep we lie all naked and alone, in Sleep we are united at the heart of night and darkness, and we are strange and beautiful asleep; for we are dying in the darkness, and we know no death, there is no death, there is no life, no joy, no sorrow and no glory on the earth but Sleep.

Come, mild and magnificent Sleep, and let your tides flow through the nation. Oh, daughter of unmemoried desire, sister of Death, and my stern comrade, Loneliness, bringer of peace and dark forgetfulness, healer and redeemer, dear enchantress, hear us: come to us through the fields of night, over the plains and rivers of the everlasting earth, bringing to the huge vexed substance of this world and to all the fury, pain, and madness of our lives the merciful anodyne of your redemption. Seal up the porches of our memory, tenderly, gently, steal our lives away from us, blot out the vision of lost love, lost days, and all our ancient hungers; great Transformer, heal us!

Oh, softly, softly, the great dark horses of Sleep are galloping over the land. The tides of Sleep are moving in the hearts of men, they flow like rivers in the night, they flow with glut and fullness of their dark unfathomed strength into a million pockets of the land and over the shores of the whole earth. They flow with the full might of their advancing and inexorable flood across the continent of night, across the breadth and sweep of the immortal earth, until the hearts of all men living are relieved of their harsh weight, the souls of all men who have ever drawn in the breath of anguish and of labor are healed, assuaged, and conquered by the vast enchantments of dark, silent, all-engulfing Sleep.

Sleep falls like silence on the earth, it fills the hearts of ninety million men, it moves like magic in the mountains, and walks like night and darkness across the plains and rivers of the earth, until low upon lowlands, and high upon hills, flows gently sleep, smooth-sliding sleep—oh, sleep—sleep—sleep!

The Short Happy Life of Francis Macomber

ERNEST HEMINGWAY

The distinctiveness of this justly celebrated story may be described to some degree by its departure from a few major patterns of American fiction. Working with the mimetic aim of representing speech, action, and landscape "truly," Hemingway discerns in the objective world a flatness, vividness, spareness, and atomism that bend the imitation of surfaces back acutely toward the subjective and stylized. Seeing his characters as social beings—the Macombers, particularly, as Americans—yet he isolates them from ordinary, complex communities and nearly cuts them loose from their pasts, so that the 'society' they form in the story seems curiously tentative, ephemeral, and ahistorical. Viewing his character relations in decidedly moral terms, he approves courage, self-discipline, hardihood, expertise, and fidelity to a code—a cluster of military or hunting virtues that sits oddly with the moral tradition of inwardness which evolved out of Puritanism through the fiction of Hawthorne and Henry James.

It was now lunch time and they were all sitting under the double green fly of the dining tent pretending that nothing had happened.

"Will you have lime juice or lemon squash?" Macomber asked.

"I'll have a gimlet," Robert Wilson told him.

"I'll have a gimlet too. I need something," Macomber's wife said.

"I suppose it's the thing to do," Macomber agreed. "Tell him to make three gimlets."

The mess boy had started them already, lifting the bottles out of the canvas cooling bags that sweated wet in the wind that blew through the trees that shaded the tents.

"What had I ought to give them?" Macomber asked.

"A quid would be plenty," Wilson told him. "You don't want to spoil them."

"Will the headman distribute it?"

"Absolutely."

Francis Macomber had, half an hour before, been carried to his tent from the edge of the camp in triumph on the arms and shoulders of the cook, the personal boys, the skinner and the porters. The gun-bearers had taken no part in the demonstration. When the native boys put him down at the door of his tent, he had shaken all their hands, received their congratulations, and then gone into the tent and sat on the bed until his wife came in. She did not speak to him when she came in and he left the tent at once to wash his face and hands in the portable wash basin outside and go over to the dining tent to sit in a comfortable canvas chair in the breeze and the shade.

"You've got your lion," Robert Wilson said to him, "and a damned fine one too."

Mrs. Macomber looked at Wilson quickly. She was an extremely handsome and well-kept woman of the beauty and social position which had, five years before, commanded five thousand dollars as the price of endorsing, with photographs, a beauty product which she had never used. She had been married to Francis Macomber for eleven years.

"He is a good lion, isn't he?" Macomber said. His wife looked at him now. She looked at both these men as though she had never seen them before.

One, Wilson, the white hunter, she knew she had never truly seen before. He was about middle height with sandy hair, a stubby mustache, a very red face and extremely cold blue eyes with faint white wrinkles at the corners that grooved merrily when he smiled. He smiled at her now and she looked away from his face at the way his shoulders sloped in the loose tunic he wore with the four big cartridges held in loops where the left breast pocket should have been, at his big brown hands, his old slacks, his very dirty boots and back to his red face again. She noticed where the baked red of his face stopped in a white line that marked the circle left by his Stetson hat that hung now from one of the pegs of the tent pole.

"Well, here's to the lion," Robert Wilson said. He smiled at her again and, not smiling, she looked curiously at her husband.

Francis Macomber was very tall, very well built if you did not mind that length of bone, dark, his hair cropped like an oarsman, rather thin-lipped, and was considered handsome. He was dressed in the same sort of safari clothes that Wilson wore except that his were new, he was thirty-five years old, kept himself very fit, was good at court games, had a number of big-game fishing records, and had just shown himself, very publicly, to be a coward.

"Here's to the lion," he said. "I can't ever thank you for what you did."

Margaret, his wife, looked away from him and back to Wilson.

"Let's not talk about the lion," she said.

Wilson looked over at her without smiling and now she smiled at him.

"It's been a very strange day," she said. "Hadn't you ought to put your hat on even under the canvas at noon? You told me that, you know."

"Might put it on," said Wilson.

"You know you have a very red face, Mr. Wilson," she told him and smiled again.

"Drink," said Wilson.

"I don't think so," she said. "Francis drinks a great deal, but his face is never red."

"It's red today," Macomber tried a joke.

"No," said Margaret. "It's mine that's red today. But Mr. Wilson's is always red."

"Must be racial," said Wilson. "I say, you wouldn't like to drop my beauty as a topic, would you?"

"I've just started on it."

"Let's chuck it," said Wilson.

"Conversation is going to be so difficult," Margaret said.

"Don't be silly, Margot," her husband said.

"No difficulty," Wilson said. "Got a damn fine lion."

Margot looked at them both and they both saw that she was going to cry. Wilson had seen it coming for a long time and he dreaded it. Macomber was past dreading it.

"I wish it hadn't happened. Oh, I wish it hadn't happened," she said and started for her tent. She made no noise of crying but they could see that her shoulders were shaking under the rose-colored, sun-proofed shirt she wore.

"Women upset," said Wilson to the tall man. "Amounts to nothing. Strain on the nerves and one thing'n another."

"No," said Macomber. "I suppose that I rate that for the rest of my life now."

"Nonsense. Let's have a spot of the giant killer," said Wilson. "Forget the whole thing. Nothing to it anyway."

"We might try," said Macomber. "I won't forget what you did for me though."

"Nothing," said Wilson. "All nonsense."

So they sat there in the shade where the camp was pitched under some wide-topped acacia trees with a boulder-strewn cliff behind them, and a stretch of grass that ran to the bank of a boulder-filled stream in front with forest beyond it, and drank their just-cool lime drinks and avoided one another's eyes while the boys set the table for lunch. Wilson could tell that the boys all knew about it now and when he saw Macomber's personal boy looking curiously at his master while he was putting dishes on the table he snapped at him in Swahili. The boy turned away with his face blank.

"What were you telling him?" Macomber asked.

"Nothing. Told him to look alive or I'd see he got about fifteen of the best."

"What's that? Lashes?"

"It's quite illegal," Wilson said. "You're supposed to fine them."

"Do you still have them whipped?"

"Oh, yes. They could raise a row if they chose to complain. But they don't. They prefer it to the fines."

"How strange!" said Macomber.

"Not strange, really," Wilson said. "Which would you rather do? Take a good birching or lose your pay?"

Then he felt embarrassed at asking it and before Macomber could answer he went on, "We all take a beating every day, you know, one way or another."

This was no better. "Good God," he thought. "I am a diplomat, aren't I?"

"Yes, we take a beating," said Macomber, still not looking at him. "I'm awfully sorry about that lion business. It doesn't have to go any further, does it? I mean no one will hear about it, will they?"

"You mean will I tell it at the Mathaiga Club?" Wilson looked at him now coldly. He had not expected this. So he's a bloody four-letter man as well as a bloody coward, he thought. I rather liked him too until today. But how is one to know about an American?

"No," said Wilson. "I'm a professional hunter. We never talk about our clients. You can be quite easy on that. It's supposed to be bad form to ask us not to talk though."

He had decided now that to break would be much easier. He would eat, then, by himself and could read a book with his meals. They would eat by themselves. He would see them through the safari on a very formal basis—what was it the French called it? Distinguished consideration—and it would be a damn sight easier than having to go through this emotional trash. He'd insult him and make a good clean break. Then he could read a book with his meals and he'd still be drinking their whisky. That was the phrase for it when a safari went bad. You ran into another white hunter and you asked, "How is everything going?" and he answered, "Oh, I'm still drinking their whisky," and you knew everything had gone to pot.

"I'm sorry," Macomber said and looked at him with his American face that would stay adolescent until it became middle-aged, and Wilson noted his crew-cropped hair, fine eyes only faintly shifty, good nose, thin lips and handsome jaw. "I'm sorry I didn't realize that. There are lots of things I don't know."

So what could he do, Wilson thought. He was all ready to break it off quickly and neatly and here the beggar was apologizing after he had just insulted him. He made one more attempt. "Don't worry about me talking," he said. "I have a living to make. You know in

Africa no woman ever misses her lion and no white man ever bolts."

"I bolted like a rabbit," Macomber said.

Now what in hell were you going to do about a man who talked like that, Wilson wondered.

Wilson looked at Macomber with his flat, blue, machine-gunner's eyes and the other smiled back at him. He had a pleasant smile if you did not notice how his eyes showed when he was hurt.

"Maybe I can fix it up on buffalo," he said. "We're after them next, aren't we?"

"In the morning if you like," Wilson told him. Perhaps he had been wrong. This was certainly the way to take it. You most certainly could not tell a damned thing about an American. He was all for Macomber again. If you could forget the morning. But, of course, you couldn't. The morning had been about as bad as they come.

"Here comes the Memsahib," he said. She was walking over from her tent looking refreshed and cheerful and quite lovely. She had a very perfect oval face, so perfect that you expected her to be stupid. But she wasn't stupid, Wilson thought, no, not stupid.

"How is the beautiful red-faced Mr. Wilson? Are you feeling better, Francis, my pearl?"

"Oh, much," said Macomber.

"I've dropped the whole thing," she said, sitting down at the table. "What importance is there to whether Francis is any good at killing lions? That's not his trade. That's Mr. Wilson's trade. Mr. Wilson is really very impressive killing anything. You do kill anything, don't you?"

"Oh, anything," said Wilson. "Simply anything." They are, he thought, the hardest in the world; the hardest, the cruelest, the most predatory and the most attractive and their men have softened or gone to pieces nervously as they have hardened. Or is it that they pick men they can handle? They can't know that much at the age they marry, he thought. He was grateful that he had gone through his education on American women before now because this was a very attractive one.

"We're going after buff in the morning," he told her.

"I'm coming," she said.

"No, you're not."

"Oh, yes, I am. Mayn't I, Francis?"

"Why not stay in camp?"

"Not for anything," she said. "I wouldn't miss something like to-day for anything."

When she left, Wilson was thinking, when she went off to cry, she seemed a hell of a fine woman. She seemed to understand, to realize, to be hurt for him and for herself and to know how things really stood. She is away for twenty minutes and now she is back, simply enamelled in that American female cruelty. They are the damnedest women. Really the damnedest.

"We'll put on another show for you tomorrow," Francis Macomber said.

"You're not coming," Wilson said.

"You're very mistaken," she told him. "And I want *so* to see you perform again. You were lovely this morning. That is if blowing things' heads off is lovely."

"Here's the lunch," said Wilson. "You're very merry, aren't you?"

"Why not? I didn't come out here to be dull."

"Well, it hasn't been dull," Wilson said. He could see the boulders in the river and the high bank beyond with the trees and he remembered the morning.

"Oh, no," she said. "It's been charming. And tomorrow. You don't know how I look forward to tomorrow."

"That's eland he's offering you," Wilson said.

"They're the big cowy things that jump like hares, aren't they?"

"I suppose that describes them," Wilson said.

"It's very good meat," Macomber said.

"Did you shoot it, Francis?" she asked.

"Yes."

"They're not dangerous, are they?"

"Only if they fall on you," Wilson told her.

"I'm so glad."

"Why not let up on the bitchery just a little, Margot," Macomber said, cutting the eland steak and putting some mashed potato, gravy and carrot on the down-turned fork that tined through the piece of meat.

"I suppose I could," she said, "since you put it so prettily."

"Tonight we'll have champagne for the lion," Wilson said. "It's a bit too hot at noon."

"Oh, the lion," Margot said. "I'd forgotten the lion!"

So, Robert Wilson thought to himself, she *is* giving him a ride, isn't she? Or do you suppose that's her idea of putting up a good show? How should a woman act when she discovers her husband is a bloody coward? She's damn cruel but they're all cruel. They govern, of course, and to govern one has to be cruel sometimes. Still, I've seen enough of their damn terrorism.

"Have some more eland," he said to her politely.

That afternoon, late, Wilson and Macomber went out in the motor car with the native driver and the two gun-bearers. Mrs. Macomber stayed in the camp. It was too hot to go out, she said, and she was going with them in the early morning. As they drove off Wilson saw her standing under the big tree, looking pretty rather than beautiful in her faintly rosy khaki, her dark hair drawn back off her forehead and gathered in a knot low on her neck, her face as fresh, he thought, as though she were in England. She waved to them as the car went off through the swale of high grass and curved around through the trees into the small hills of orchard bush.

In the orchard bush they found a herd of impala, and leaving the car they stalked one old ram with long, wide-spread horns and Macomber killed it with a very creditable shot that knocked the buck down at a good two hundred yards and sent the herd off bounding wildly and leaping over one another's backs in long, leg-drawn-up leaps as unbelievable and as floating as those one makes sometimes in dreams.

"That was a good shot," Wilson said. "They're a small target."

"Is it a worth-while head?" Macomber asked.

"It's excellent," Wilson told him. "You shoot like that and you'll have no trouble."

"Do you think we'll find buffalo tomorrow?"

"There's a good chance of it. They feed out early in the morning and with luck we may catch them in the open."

"I'd like to clear away that lion business," Macomber said. "It's not very pleasant to have your wife see you do something like that."

I should think it would be even more unpleasant to do it, Wilson thought, wife or no wife, or to talk about having done it. But he said, "I wouldn't think about that any more. Any one could be upset by his first lion. That's all over."

But that night after dinner and a whisky and soda by the fire before going to bed, as Francis Macomber lay on his cot with the mosquito bar over him and listened to the night noises it was not all over. It was neither all over nor was it beginning. It was there exactly as it happened with some parts of it indelibly emphasized and he was miserably ashamed at it. But more than shame he felt cold, hollow fear in him. The fear was still there like a cold slimy hollow in all the emptiness where once his confidence had been and it made him feel sick. It was still there with him now.

It had started the night before when he had wakened and heard the lion roaring somewhere up along the river. It was a deep sound and at the end there were sort of coughing grunts that made him seem just outside the tent, and when Francis Macomber woke in the night to hear it he was afraid. He could hear his wife breathing quietly, asleep. There was no one to tell he was afraid, nor to be afraid with him, and, lying alone, he did not know the Somali proverb that says a brave man is always frightened three times by a lion; when he first sees his track, when he first hears him roar and when he first confronts him. Then while they were eating breakfast by lantern light out in the dining tent, before the sun was up, the lion roared again and Francis thought he was just at the edge of camp.

"Sounds like an old-timer," Robert Wilson said, looking up from his kippers and coffee. "Listen to him cough."

"Is he very close?"

"A mile or so up the stream."

"Will we see him?"

"We'll have a look."

"Does his roaring carry that far? It sounds as though he were right in camp."

"Carries a hell of a long way," said Robert Wilson. "It's strange the way it carries. Hope he's a shootable cat. The boys said there was a very big one about here."

"If I get a shot, where should I hit him," Macomber asked, "to stop him?"

"In the shoulders," Wilson said. "In the neck if you can make it. Shoot for bone. Break him down."

"I hope I can place it properly," Macomber said.

"You shoot very well," Wilson told him. "Take your time. Make sure of him. The first one in is the one that counts."

"What range will it be?"

"Can't tell. Lion has something to say about that. Won't shoot unless it's close enough so you can make sure."

"At under a hundred yards?" Macomber asked.

Wilson looked at him quickly.

"Hundred's about right. Might have to take him a bit under. Shouldn't chance a shot at much over that. A hundred's a decent range. You can hit him wherever you want at that. Here comes the Memsahib."

"Good morning," she said. "Are we going after that lion?"

"As soon as you deal with your breakfast," Wilson said. "How are you feeling?"

"Marvellous," she said. "I'm very excited."

"I'll just go and see that everything is ready," Wilson went off. As he left the lion roared again.

"Noisy beggar," Wilson said. "We'll put a stop to that."

"What's the matter, Francis?" his wife asked him.

"Nothing," Macomber said.

"Yes, there is," she said. "What are you upset about?"

"Nothing," he said.

"Tell me," she looked at him. "Don't you feel well?"

"It's that damned roaring," he said. "It's been going on all night, you know."

"Why didn't you wake me," she said. "I'd love to have heard it."

"I've got to kill the damned thing," Macomber said, miserably.

"Well, that's what you're out here for, isn't it?"

"Yes. But I'm nervous. Hearing the thing roar gets on my nerves."

"Well then, as Wilson said, kill him and stop his roaring."

"Yes, darling," said Francis Macomber. "It sounds easy, doesn't it?"

"You're not afraid, are you?"

"Of course not. But I'm nervous from hearing him roar all night."

"You'll kill him marvellously," she said. "I know you will. I'm awfully anxious to see it."

"Finish your breakfast and we'll be starting."

"It's not light yet," she said. "This is a ridiculous hour."

Just then the lion roared in a deep-chested moaning, suddenly guttural, ascending vibration that seemed to shake the air and ended in a sigh and a heavy, deep-chested grunt.

"He sounds almost here," Macomber's wife said.

"My God," said Macomber. "I hate that damned noise."

"It's very impressive."

"Impressive. It's frightful."

Robert Wilson came up then carrying his short, ugly, shockingly big-bored .505 Gibbs and grinning.

"Come on," he said. "Your gun-bearer has your Springfield and the big gun. Everything's in the car. Have you solids?"

"Yes."

"I'm ready," Mrs. Macomber said.

"Must make him stop that racket," Wilson said. "You get in front. The Memsahib can sit back here with me."

They climbed into the motor car and, in the gray first daylight, moved off up the river through the trees. Macomber opened the breech of his rifle and saw he had metal-cased bullets, shut the bolt and put the rifle on safety. He saw his hand was trembling. He felt in his pocket for more cartridges and moved his fingers over the cartridges in the loops of his tunic front. He turned back to where Wilson sat in the rear seat of the doorless, box-bodied motor car beside his wife, them both grinning with excitement, and Wilson leaned forward and whispered,

"See the birds dropping. Means the old boy has left his kill."

On the far bank of the stream Macomber could see, above the trees, vultures circling and plummeting down.

"Chances are he'll come to drink along here," Wilson whispered. "Before he goes to lay up. Keep an eye out."

They were driving slowly along the high bank of the stream which here cut deeply to its boulder-filled bed, and they wound in and out through big trees as they drove. Macomber was watching the opposite bank when he felt Wilson take hold of his arm. The car stopped.

"There he is," he heard the whisper. "Ahead and to the right. Get out and take him. He's a marvellous lion."

Macomber saw the lion now. He was standing almost broadside, his great head up and turned toward them. The early morning breeze that blew toward them was just stirring his dark mane, and the lion looked huge, silhouetted on the rise of bank in the gray morning light, his shoulders heavy, his barrel of a body bulking smoothly.

"How far is he?" asked Macomber, raising his rifle.

"About seventy-five. Get out and take him."

"Why not shoot from where I am?"

"You don't shoot them from cars," he heard Wilson saying in his ear. "Get out. He's not going to stay there all day."

Macomber stepped out of the curved opening at the side of the front seat, onto the step and down onto the ground. The lion still stood looking majestically and coolly toward this object that his eyes only showed in silhouette, bulking like some super-rhino. There was no man smell carried toward him and he watched the object, moving his great head a little from side to side. Then watching the

object, not afraid, but hesitating before going down the bank to
drink with such a thing opposite him, he saw a man figure detach
itself from it and he turned his heavy head and swung away toward
the cover of the trees as he heard a cracking crash and felt the
slam of a .30–06 220-grain solid bullet that bit his flank and ripped
in sudden hot scalding nausea through his stomach. He trotted,
heavy, big-footed, swinging wounded full-bellied, through the trees
toward the tall grass and cover, and the crash came again to go past
him ripping the air apart. Then it crashed again and he felt the blow
as it hit his lower ribs and ripped on through, blood sudden hot and
frothy in his mouth, and he galloped toward the high grass where
he could crouch and not be seen and make them bring the crashing
thing close enough so he could make a rush and get the man that
held it.

Macomber had not thought how the lion felt as he got out of the
car. He only knew his hands were shaking and as he walked away
from the car it was almost impossible for him to make his legs move.
They were stiff in the thighs, but he could feel the muscles fluttering.
He raised the rifle, sighted on the junction of the lion's head and
shoulders and pulled the trigger. Nothing happened though he
pulled until he thought his finger would break. Then he knew he had
the safety on and as he lowered the rifle to move the safety over
he moved another frozen pace forward, and the lion seeing his
silhouette now clear of the silhouette of the car, turned and started
off at a trot, and, as Macomber fired, he heard a whunk that meant
that the bullet was home; but the lion kept on going. Macomber
shot again and everyone saw the bullet throw a spout of dirt beyond
the trotting lion. He shot again, remembering to lower his aim, and
they all heard the bullet hit, and the lion went into a gallop and was
in the tall grass before he had the bolt pushed forward.

Macomber stood there feeling sick at his stomach, his hands that
held the Springfield still cocked, shaking, and his wife and Robert
Wilson were standing by him. Beside him too were the two gun-
bearers chattering in Wakamba.

"I hit him," Macomber said. "I hit him twice."

"You gut-shot him and you hit him somewhere forward," Wilson
said without enthusiasm. The gun-bearers looked very grave. They
were silent now.

"You may have killed him," Wilson went on. "We'll have to wait
a while before we go in to find out."

"What do you mean?"

"Let him get sick before we follow him up."

"Oh," said Macomber.

"He's a hell of a fine lion," Wilson said cheerfully. "He's gotten into a bad place though."

"Why is it bad?"

"Can't see him until you're on him."

"Oh," said Macomber.

"Come on," said Wilson. "The Memsahib can stay here in the car. We'll go to have a look at the blood spoor."

"Stay here, Margot," Macomber said to his wife. His mouth was very dry and it was hard for him to talk.

"Why?" she asked.

"Wilson says to."

"We're going to have a look," Wilson said. "You stay here. You can see even better from here."

"All right."

Wilson spoke in Swahili to the driver. He nodded and said, "Yes, Bwana."

Then they went down the steep bank and across the stream, climbing over and around the boulders and up the other bank, pulling up by some projecting roots, and along it until they found where the lion had been trotting when Macomber first shot. There was dark blood on the short grass that the gun-bearers pointed out with grass stems, and that ran away behind the river bank trees.

"What do we do?" asked Macomber.

"Not much choice," said Wilson. "We can't bring the car over. Bank's too steep. We'll let him stiffen up a bit and then you and I'll go in and have a look for him."

"Can't we set the grass on fire?" Macomber asked.

"Too green."

"Can't we send beaters?"

Wilson looked at him appraisingly. "Of course we can," he said. "But it's just a touch murderous. You see we know the lion's wounded. You can drive an unwounded lion—he'll move on ahead of a noise—but a wounded lion's going to charge. You can't see him until you're right on him. He'll make himself perfectly flat in cover you wouldn't think would hide a hare. You can't very well send boys in there to that sort of a show. Somebody bound to get mauled."

"What about the gun-bearers?"

"Oh, they'll go with us. It's their *shauri*. You see, they signed on for it. They don't look too happy though, do they?"

"I don't want to go in there," said Macomber. It was out before he knew he'd said it.

"Neither do I," said Wilson very cheerily. "Really no choice though." Then, as an afterthought, he glanced at Macomber and saw suddenly how he was trembling and the pitiful look on his face.

"You don't have to go in, of course," he said. "That's what I'm hired for, you know. That's why I'm so expensive."

"You mean you'd go in by yourself? Why not leave him there?"

Robert Wilson, whose entire occupation had been with the lion and the problem he presented, and who had not been thinking about Macomber except to note that he was rather windy, suddenly felt as though he had opened the wrong door in a hotel and seen something shameful.

"What do you mean?"

"Why not just leave him?"

"You mean pretend to ourselves he hasn't been hit?"

"No. Just drop it."

"It isn't done."

"Why not?"

"For one thing, he's certain to be suffering. For another, some one else might run onto him."

"I see."

"But you don't have to have anything to do with it."

"I'd like to," Macomber said. "I'm just scared, you know."

"I'll go ahead when we go in," Wilson said, "with Kongoni tracking. You keep behind me and a little to one side. Chances are we'll hear him growl. If we see him we'll both shoot. Don't worry about anything. I'll keep you backed up. As a matter of fact, you know, perhaps you'd better not go. It might be much better. Why don't you go over and join the Memsahib while I just get it over with?"

"No, I want to go."

"All right," said Wilson. "But don't go in if you don't want to. This is my *shauri* now, you know."

"I want to go," said Macomber.

They sat under a tree and smoked.

"Want to go back and speak to the Memsahib while we're waiting?" Wilson asked.

"No."

"I'll just step back and tell her to be patient."

"Good," said Macomber. He sat there, sweating under his arms, his mouth dry, his stomach hollow feeling, wanting to find courage to tell Wilson to go on and finish off the lion without him. He could not know that Wilson was furious because he had not noticed the state he was in earlier and sent him back to his wife. While he sat there Wilson came up. "I have your big gun," he said. "Take it. We've given him time, I think. Come on."

Macomber took the big gun and Wilson said:

"Keep behind me and about five yards to the right and do exactly as I tell you." Then he spoke in Swahili to the two gun-bearers who looked the picture of gloom.

"Let's go," he said.

"Could I have a drink of water?" Macomber asked. Wilson spoke to the older gun-bearer, who wore a canteen on his belt, and the man unbuckled it, unscrewed the top and handed it to Macomber, who took it noticing how heavy it seemed and how hairy and shoddy the felt covering was in his hand. He raised it to drink and looked ahead at the high grass with the flat-topped trees behind it. A breeze was blowing toward them and the grass rippled gently in the wind. He looked at the gun-bearer and he could see the gun-bearer was suffering too with fear.

Thirty-five yards into the grass the big lion lay flattened out along the ground. His ears were back and his only movement was a slight twitching up and down of his long, black-tufted tail. He had turned at bay as soon as he had reached this cover and he was sick with the wound through his full belly, and weakening with the wound through his lungs that brought a thin foamy red to his mouth each time he breathed. His flanks were wet and hot and flies were on the little openings the solid bullets had made in his tawny hide, and his big yellow eyes, narrowed with hate, looked straight ahead, only blinking when the pain came as he breathed, and his claws dug in the soft baked earth. All of him, pain, sickness, hatred and all of his remaining strength, was tightening into an absolute concentration for a rush. He could hear the men talking and he waited, gathering all of himself into this preparation for a charge as soon as the men would come into the grass. As he heard their voices his tail stiffened to twitch up and down, and, as they came into the edge of the grass, he made a coughing grunt and charged.

Kongoni, the old gun-bearer, in the lead watching the blood spoor, Wilson watching the grass for any movement, his big gun ready, the second gun-bearer looking ahead and listening, Macomber close to Wilson, his rifle cocked, they had just moved into the grass when Macomber heard the blood-choked coughing grunt, and saw the swishing rush in the grass. The next thing he knew he was running; running wildly, in panic in the open, running toward the stream.

He heard the *ca-ra-wong!* of Wilson's big rifle, and again in a second crashing *carawong!* and turning saw the lion, horrible-looking now, with half his head seeming to be gone, crawling toward Wilson in the edge of the tall grass while the red-faced man worked the bolt on the short ugly rifle and aimed carefully as another blasting *carawong!* came from the muzzle, and the crawling, heavy, yellow bulk of the lion stiffened and the huge, mutilated head slid forward and Macomber, standing by himself in the clearing where he had run, holding a loaded rifle, while two black men and a white man looked back at him in contempt, knew the lion was dead. He came toward Wilson, his tallness all seeming a naked reproach, and Wilson looked at him and said:

"Want to take pictures?"

"No," he said.

That was all any one had said until they reached the motor car. Then Wilson had said:

"Hell of a fine lion. Boys will skin him out. We might as well stay here in the shade."

Macomber's wife had not looked at him nor he at her and he had sat by her in the back seat with Wilson sitting in the front seat. Once he had reached over and taken his wife's hand without looking at her and she had removed her hand from his. Looking across the stream to where the gun-bearers were skinning out the lion he could see that she had been able to see the whole thing. While they sat there his wife had reached forward and put her hand on Wilson's shoulder. He turned and she had leaned forward over the low seat and kissed him on the mouth.

"Oh, I say," said Wilson, going redder than his natural baked color.

"Mr. Robert Wilson," she said. "The beautiful red-faced Mr. Robert Wilson."

Then she sat down beside Macomber again and looked away across the stream to where the lion lay, with uplifted, white-muscled, tendon-marked naked forearms, and white bloating belly, as the black men fleshed away the skin. Finally the gun-bearers brought the skin over, wet and heavy, and climbed in behind with it, rolling it up before they got in, and the motor car started. No one had said anything more until they were back in camp.

That was the story of the lion. Macomber did not know how the lion had felt before he started his rush, nor during it when the unbelievable smash of the .505 with a muzzle velocity of two tons had hit him in the mouth, nor what kept him coming after that, when the second ripping crash had smashed his hind quarters and he had come crawling on toward the crashing, blasting thing that had destroyed him. Wilson knew something about it and only expressed it by saying, "Damned fine lion," but Macomber did not know how Wilson felt about things either. He did not know how his wife felt except that she was through with him.

His wife had been through with him before but it never lasted. He was very wealthy, and would be much wealthier, and he knew she would not leave him ever now. That was one of the few things that he really knew. He knew about that, about motor cycles—that was earliest—about motor cars, about duck-shooting, about fishing, trout, salmon and big-sea, about sex in books, many books, too many books, about all court games, about dogs, not much about horses, about hanging on to his money, about most of the other things his world dealt in, and about his wife not leaving him. His wife had been a great beauty and she was still a great beauty in Africa, but she was not a great enough beauty any more at home to be able to leave him and better herself and she knew it and he knew it. She had missed the chance to leave him and he knew it. If he had been better with women she would probably have started to worry about him getting another new, beautiful wife; but she knew too much about him to worry about him either. Also, he had always had a great tolerance which seemed the nicest thing about him if it were not the most sinister.

All in all they were known as a comparatively happily married couple, one of those whose disruption is often rumored but never occurs, and as the society columnist put it, they were adding more than a spice of *adventure* to their much envied and ever-enduring *Romance* by a *Safari* in what was known as *Darkest Africa* until the Martin Johnsons lighted it on so many silver screens where they were pursuing *Old Simba* the lion, the buffalo, *Tembo* the elephant and as well collecting specimens for the Museum of Natural History. This same columnist had reported them *on the verge* at least three times in the past and they had been. But they always made it up. They had a sound basis of union. Margot was too beautiful for Macomber to divorce her and Macomber had too much money for Margot ever to leave him.

It was now about three o'clock in the morning and Francis Macomber, who had been asleep a little while after he had stopped thinking about the lion, wakened and then slept again, woke suddenly, frightened in a dream of the bloody-headed lion standing over him, and listening while his heart pounded, he realized that his wife was not in the other cot in the tent. He lay awake with that knowledge for two hours.

At the end of that time his wife came into the tent, lifted her mosquito bar and crawled cozily into bed.

"Where have you been?" Macomber asked in the darkness.

"Hello," she said. "Are you awake?"

"Where have you been?"

"I just went out to get a breath of air."

"You did, like hell."

"What do you want me to say, darling?"

"Where have you been?"

"Out to get a breath of air."

"That's a new name for it. You *are* a bitch."

"Well, you're a coward."

"All right," he said. "What of it?"

"Nothing as far as I'm concerned. But please let's not talk, darling, because I'm very sleepy."

"You think that I'll take anything."

"I know you will, sweet."

"Well, I won't."

"Please, darling, let's not talk. I'm so very sleepy."

"There wasn't going to be any of that. You promised there wouldn't be."

"Well, there is now," she said sweetly.

"You said if we made this trip that there would be none of that. You promised."

"Yes, darling. That's the way I meant it to be. But the trip was spoiled yesterday. We don't have to talk about it, do we?"

"You don't wait long when you have an advantage, do you?"

"Please let's not talk. I'm so sleepy, darling."

"I'm going to talk."

"Don't mind me then, because I'm going to sleep." And she did.

At breakfast they were all three at the table before daylight and Francis Macomber found that, of all the many men that he had hated, he had hated Robert Wilson the most.

"Sleep well?" Wilson asked in his throaty voice, filling a pipe.

"Did you?"

"Topping," the white hunter told him.

You bastard, thought Macomber, you insolent bastard.

So she woke him when she came in, Wilson thought, looking at them both with his flat, cold eyes. Well, why doesn't he keep his wife where she belongs? What does he think I am, a bloody plaster saint? Let him keep her where she belongs. It's his own fault.

"Do you think we'll find buffalo?" Margot asked, pushing away a dish of apricots.

"Chance of it," Wilson said and smiled at her. "Why don't you stay in camp?"

"Not for anything," she told him.

"Why not order her to stay in camp?" Wilson said to Macomber.

"You order her," said Macomber coldly.

"Let's not have any ordering, nor," turning to Macomber, "any silliness, Francis," Margot said quite pleasantly.

"Are you ready to start?" Macomber asked.

"Any time," Wilson told him. "Do you want the Memsahib to go?"

"Does it make any difference whether I do or not?"

The hell with it, thought Robert Wilson. The utter complete hell with it. So this is what it's going to be like. Well, this is what it's going to be like, then.

"Makes no difference," he said.

"You're sure you wouldn't like to stay in camp with her yourself and let me go out and hunt the buffalo?" Macomber asked.

"Can't do that," said Wilson. "Wouldn't talk rot if I were you."

"I'm not talking rot. I'm disgusted."

"Bad word, disgusted."

"Francis, will you please try to speak sensibly?" his wife said.

"I speak too damned sensibly," Macomber said. "Did you ever eat such filthy food?"

"Something wrong with the food?" asked Wilson quietly.

"No more than with everything else."

"I'd pull yourself together, laddybuck," Wilson said very quietly. "There's a boy waits at table that understands a little English."

"The hell with him."

Wilson stood up and puffing on his pipe strolled away, speaking a few words in Swahili to one of the gun-bearers who was standing waiting for him. Macomber and his wife sat on at the table. He was staring at his coffee cup.

"If you make a scene I'll leave you, darling," Margot said quietly.

"No, you won't."

"You can try it and see."

"You won't leave me."

"No," she said. "I won't leave you and you'll behave yourself."

"Behave myself? That's a way to talk. Behave myself."

"Yes. Behave yourself."

"Why don't *you* try behaving?"

"I've tried it so long. So very long."

"I hate that red-faced swine," Macomber said. "I loathe the sight of him."

"He's really *very* nice."

"Oh, *shut up*," Macomber almost shouted. Just then the car came up and stopped in front of the dining tent and the driver and the two gun-bearers got out. Wilson walked over and looked at the husband and wife sitting there at the table.

"Going shooting?" he asked.

"Yes," said Macomber, standing up. "Yes."

"Better bring a woolly. It will be cool in the car," Wilson said.

"I'll get my leather jacket," Margot said.

"The boy has it," Wilson told her. He climbed into the front with the driver and Francis Macomber and his wife sat, not speaking, in the back seat.

Hope the silly beggar doesn't take a notion to blow the back of my head off, Wilson thought to himself. Women *are* a nuisance on safari.

The car was grinding down to cross the river at a pebbly ford in the gray daylight and then climbed, angling up the steep bank, where Wilson had ordered a way shovelled out the day before so they could reach the parklike wooded rolling country on the far side.

It was a good morning, Wilson thought. There was a heavy dew and as the wheels went through the grass and low bushes he could smell the odor of the crushed fronds. It was an odor like verbena and he liked this early morning smell of the dew, the crushed bracken and the look of the tree trunks showing black through the early morning mist, as the car made its way through the untracked, parklike country. He had put the two in the back seat out of his mind now and was thinking about buffalo. The buffalo that he was after stayed in the daytime in a thick swamp where it was impossible to get a shot, but in the night they fed out into an open stretch of country and if he could come between them and their swamp with the car, Macomber would have a good chance at them in the open. He did not want to hunt buff with Macomber in thick cover. He did not want to hunt buff or anything else with Macomber at all, but he was a professional hunter and he had hunted with some rare ones in his time. If they got buff today there would only be rhino to come and the poor man would have gone through his dangerous game and things might pick up. He'd have nothing more to do with the woman and Macomber would get over that too. He must have gone through plenty of that before by the look of things. Poor beggar. He must have a way of getting over it. Well, it was the poor sod's own bloody fault.

He, Robert Wilson, carried a double size cot on safari to accommodate any windfalls he might receive. He had hunted for a certain clientele, the international, fast, sporting set, where the women did not feel they were getting their money's worth unless they had shared that cot with the white hunter. He despised them when he was away from them although he liked some of them well enough at the time, but he made his living by them; and their standards were his standards as long as they were hiring him.

They were his standards in all except the shooting. He had his own standards about the killing and they could live up to them or get some one else to hunt them. He knew, too, that they all respected him for this. This Macomber was an odd one though. Damned if he wasn't. Now the wife. Well, the wife. Yes, the wife. Hm, the wife. Well he'd dropped all that. He looked around at them. Macomber sat grim and furious. Margot smiled at him. She looked younger today, more innocent and fresher and not so professionally beautiful. What's in her heart God knows, Wilson thought. She hadn't talked much last night. At that it was a pleasure to see her.

The motor car climbed up a slight rise and went on through the trees and then out into a grassy prairie-like opening and kept in the shelter of the trees along the edge, the driver going slowly and Wilson looking carefully out across the prairie and all along its far side. He stopped the car and studied the opening with his field glasses. Then he motioned to the driver to go on and the car moved slowly along, the driver avoiding wart-hog holes and driving around the mud castles ants had built. Then, looking across the opening, Wilson suddenly turned and said,

"By God, there they are!"

And looking where he pointed, while the car jumped forward and Wilson spoke in rapid Swahili to the driver, Macomber saw three huge, black animals looking almost cylindrical in their long heaviness, like big black tank cars, moving at a gallop across the far edge of the open prairie. They moved at a stiff-necked, stiff-bodied gallop and he could see the upswept wide black horns on their heads as they galloped heads out; the heads not moving.

"They're three old bulls," Wilson said. "We'll cut them off before they get to the swamp."

The car was going a wild forty-five miles an hour across the open and as Macomber watched, the buffalo got bigger and bigger until he could see the gray, hairless, scabby look of one huge bull and how his neck was a part of his shoulders and the shiny black of his horns as he galloped a little behind the others that were strung out in that steady plunging gait; and then, the car swaying as though it had just jumped a road, they drew up close and he could see the plunging hugeness of the bull, and the dust in his sparsely haired hide, the wide boss of horn and his outstretched, wide-nostrilled muzzle, and he was raising his rifle when Wilson shouted, "Not from the car, you fool!" and he had no fear, only hatred of Wilson, while the brakes clamped on and the car skidded, plowing sideways to an almost stop and Wilson was out on one side and he on the other, stumbling as his feet hit the still speeding-by of the earth, and then he was shooting at the bull as he moved away, hearing the bullets whunk into him, emptying his rifle at him as he moved steadily away, finally remembering to get his shots forward into the shoulder, and as he fumbled to re-load, he saw the bull was down. Down on his knees, his big head tossing, and seeing the other two still galloping he shot at the leader and hit him. He shot again and missed and he heard the *carawonging* roar as Wilson shot and saw the leading bull slide forward onto his nose.

"Get that other," Wilson said. "Now you're shooting!"

But the other bull was moving steadily at the same gallop and he missed, throwing a spout of dirt, and Wilson missed and the dust rose in a cloud and Wilson shouted, "Come on. He's too far!" and grabbed his arm and they were in the car again, Macomber and Wilson hanging on the sides and rocketing swayingly over the uneven ground, drawing up on the steady, plunging, heavy-necked, straight-moving gallop of the bull.

They were behind him and Macomber was filling his rifle, dropping shells onto the ground, jamming it, clearing the jam, then they were almost up with the bull when Wilson yelled "Stop," and the car skidded so that it almost swung over and Macomber fell forward onto his feet, slammed his bolt forward and fired as far forward as he could aim into the galloping, rounded black back, aimed and shot again, then again, then again, and the bullets, all of them hitting, had no effect on the buffalo that he could see. Then Wilson shot, the roar deafening him, and he could see the bull stagger. Macomber shot again, aiming carefully, and down he came, onto his knees.

"All right," Wilson said. "Nice work. That's the three."

Macomber felt a drunken elation.

"How many times did you shoot?" he asked.

"Just three," Wilson said. "You killed the first bull. The biggest one. I helped you finish the other two. Afraid they might have got into cover. You had them killed. I was just mopping up a little. You shot damn well."

"Let's go to the car," said Macomber. "I want a drink."

"Got to finish off that buff first," Wilson told him. The buffalo was on his knees and he jerked his head furiously and bellowed in pig-eyed, roaring rage as they came toward him.

"Watch he doesn't get up," Wilson said. Then, "Get a little broadside and take him in the neck just behind the ear."

Macomber aimed carefully at the center of the huge, jerking, rage-driven neck and shot. At the shot the head dropped forward.

"That does it," said Wilson. "Got the spine. They're a hell of a looking thing, aren't they?"

"Let's get the drink," said Macomber. In his life he had never felt so good.

In the car Macomber's wife sat very white faced. "You were marvellous, darling," she said to Macomber. "What a ride."

"Was it rough?" Wilson asked.

"It was frightful. I've never been more frightened in my life."

"Let's all have a drink," Macomber said.

"By all means," said Wilson. "Give it to the Memsahib." She drank the neat whisky from the flask and shuddered a little when she swallowed. She handed the flask to Macomber who handed it to Wilson.

"It was frightfully exciting," she said. "It's given me a dreadful headache. I didn't know you were allowed to shoot them from cars though."

"No one shot from cars," said Wilson coldly.

"I mean chase them from cars."

"Wouldn't ordinarily," Wilson said. "Seemed sporting enough to me though while we were doing it. Taking more chance driving that way across the plain full of holes and one thing and another than hunting on foot. Buffalo could have charged us each time we shot if he liked. Gave him every chance. Wouldn't mention it to any one though. It's illegal if that's what you mean."

"It seemed very unfair to me," Margot said, "chasing those big helpless things in a motor car."

"Did it?" said Wilson.

"What would happen if they heard about it in Nairobi?"

"I'd lose my licence for one thing. Other unpleasantnesses," Wilson said, taking a drink from the flask. "I'd be out of business."

"Really?"

"Yes, really."

"Well," said Macomber, and he smiled for the first time all day. "Now she has something on you."

"You have such a pretty way of putting things, Francis," Margot Macomber said. Wilson looked at them both. If a four-letter man marries a five-letter woman, he was thinking, what number of letters would their children be? What he said was, "We lost a gun-bearer. Did you notice it?"

"My God, no," Macomber said.

"Here he comes," Wilson said. "He's all right. He must have fallen off when we left the first bull."

Approaching them was the middle-aged gun-bearer, limping along in his knitted cap, khaki tunic, shorts and rubber sandals, gloomy-faced and disgusted looking. As he came up he called out to Wilson in Swahili and they all saw the change in the white hunter's face.

"What does he say?" asked Margot.

"He says the first bull got up and went into the bush," Wilson said with no expression in his voice.

"Oh," said Macomber blankly.

"Then it's going to be just like the lion," said Margot, full of anticipation.

"It's not going to be a damned bit like the lion," Wilson told her. "Did you want another drink, Macomber?"

"Thanks, yes," Macomber said. He expected the feeling he had had about the lion to come back but it did not. For the first time in his life he really felt wholly without fear. Instead of fear he had a feeling of definite elation.

"We'll go and have a look at the second bull," Wilson said. "I'll tell the driver to put the car in the shade."

"What are you going to do?" asked Margaret Macomber.

"Take a look at the buff," Wilson said.

"I'll come."

"Come along."

The three of them walked over to where the second buffalo bulked blackly in the open, head forward on the grass, the massive horns swung wide.

"He's a very good head," Wilson said. "That's close to a fifty-inch spread."

Macomber was looking at him with delight.

"He's hateful looking," said Margot. "Can't we go into the shade?"

"Of course," Wilson said. "Look," he said to Macomber, and pointed. "See that patch of bush?"

"Yes."

"That's where the first bull went in. The gun-bearer said when he fell off the bull was down. He was watching us helling along and the other two buff galloping. When he looked up there was the bull up and looking at him. Gun-bearer ran like hell and the bull went off slowly into that bush."

"Can we go in after him now?" asked Macomber eagerly.

Wilson looked at him appraisingly. Damned if this isn't a strange one, he thought. Yesterday he's scared sick and today he's a ruddy fire eater.

"No, we'll give him a while."

"Let's please go into the shade," Margot said. Her face was white and she looked ill.

They made their way to the car where it stood under a single, wide-spreading tree and all climbed in.

"Chances are he's dead in there," Wilson remarked. "After a little we'll have a look."

Macomber felt a wild unreasonable happiness that he had never known before.

"By God, that was a chase," he said. "I've never felt any such feeling. Wasn't it marvellous, Margot?"

"I hated it."

"Why?"

"I hated it," she said bitterly. "I loathed it."

"You know I don't think I'd ever be afraid of anything again,"

Macomber said to Wilson. "Something happened in me after we first saw the buff and started after him. Like a dam bursting. It was pure excitement."

"Cleans out your liver," said Wilson. "Damn funny things happen to people."

Macomber's face was shining. "You know something did happen to me," he said. "I feel absolutely different."

His wife said nothing and eyed him strangely. She was sitting far back in the seat and Macomber was sitting forward talking to Wilson who turned sideways talking over the back of the front seat.

"You know, I'd like to try another lion," Macomber said. "I'm really not afraid of them now. After all, what can they do to you?"

"That's it," said Wilson. "Worst one can do is kill you. How does it go? Shakespeare. Damned good. See if I can remember. Oh, damned good. Used to quote it to myself at one time. Let's see. 'By my troth, I care not; a man can die but once; we owe God a death and let it go which way it will he that dies this year is quit for the next.' Damned fine, eh?"

He was very embarrassed, having brought out this thing he had lived by, but he had seen men come of age before and it always moved him. It was not a matter of their twenty-first birthday.

It had taken a strange chance of hunting, a sudden precipitation into action without opportunity for worrying beforehand, to bring this about with Macomber, but regardless of how it had happened it had most certainly happened. Look at the beggar now, Wilson thought. It's that some of them stay little boys so long, Wilson thought. Sometimes all their lives. Their figures stay boyish when they're fifty. The great American boy-men. Damned strange people. But he liked this Macomber now. Damned strange fellow. Probably meant the end of cuckoldry too. Well, that would be a damned good thing. Damned good thing. Beggar had probably been afraid all his life. Don't know what started it. But over now. Hadn't had time to be afraid with the buff. That and being angry too. Motor car too. Motor cars made it familiar. Be a damn fire eater now. He'd seen it in the war work the same way. More of a change than any loss of virginity. Fear gone like an operation. Something else grew in its place. Main thing a man had. Made him into a man. Women knew it too. No bloody fear.

From the far corner of the seat Margaret Macomber looked at

the two of them. There was no change in Wilson. She saw Wilson as she had seen him the day before when she had first realized what his great talent was. But she saw the change in Francis Macomber now.

"Do you have that feeling of happiness about what's going to happen?" Macomber asked, still exploring his new wealth.

"You're not supposed to mention it," Wilson said, looking in the other's face. "Much more fashionable to say you're scared. Mind you, you'll be scared too, plenty of times."

"But you *have* a feeling of happiness about action to come?"

"Yes," said Wilson. "There's that. Doesn't do to talk too much about all this. Talk the whole thing away. No pleasure in anything if you mouth it up too much."

"You're both talking rot," said Margot. "Just because you've chased some helpless animals in a motor car you talk like heroes."

"Sorry," said Wilson. "I have been gassing too much." She's worried about it already, he thought.

"If you don't know what we're talking about why not keep out of it?" Macomber asked his wife.

"You've gotten awfully brave, awfully suddenly," his wife said contemptuously, but her concept was not secure. She was very afraid of something.

Macomber laughed, a very natural hearty laugh. "You know I *have*," he said. "I really have."

"Isn't it sort of late?" Margot said bitterly. Because she had done the best she could for many years back and the way they were together now was no one person's fault.

"Not for me," said Macomber.

Margot said nothing but sat back in the corner of the seat.

"Do you think we've given him time enough?" Macomber asked Wilson cheerfully.

"We might have a look," Wilson said. "Have you any solids left?"

"The gun-bearer has some."

Wilson called in Swahili and the older gun-bearer, who was skinning out one of the heads, straightened up, pulled a box of solids out of his pocket and brought them over to Macomber, who filled his magazine and put the remaining shells in his pocket.

"You might as well shoot the Springfield," Wilson said. "You're used to it. We'll leave the Mannlicher in the car with the Memsahib. Your gun-bearer can carry your heavy gun. I've this damned cannon. Now let me tell you about them." He had saved this until the last because he did not want to worry Macomber. "When a buff comes he comes with his head high and thrust straight out. The boss of the horns covers any sort of a brain shot. The only shot is straight into the nose. The only other shot is into his chest or, if you're to one side, into the neck or the shoulders. After they've been hit once they take a hell of a lot of killing. Don't try anything fancy. Take the easiest shot there is. They've finished skinning out that head now. Should we get started?"

He called to the gun-bearers, who came up wiping their hands, and the older one got into the back.

"I'll only take Kongoni," Wilson said. "The other can watch to keep the birds away."

As the car moved slowly across the open space toward the island of brushy trees that ran in a tongue of foliage along a dry water course that cut the open swale, Macomber felt his heart pounding and his mouth was dry again, but it was excitement, not fear.

"Here's where he went in," Wilson said. Then to the gun-bearer in Swahili, "Take the blood spoor."

The car was parallel to the patch of bush. Macomber, Wilson and the gun-bearer got down. Macomber, looking back, saw his wife, with the rifle by her side, looking at him. He waved to her and she did not wave back.

The brush was very thick ahead and the ground was dry. The middle-aged gun-bearer was sweating heavily and Wilson had his hat down over his eyes and his red neck showed just ahead of Macomber. Suddenly the gun-bearer said something in Swahili to Wilson and ran forward.

"He's dead in there," Wilson said. "Good work," and he turned to grip Macomber's hand and as they shook hands, grinning at each other, the gun-bearer shouted wildly and they saw him coming out of the bush sideways, fast as a crab, and the bull coming, nose out, mouth tight closed, blood dripping, massive head straight out, coming in a charge, his little pig eyes bloodshot as he looked at them. Wilson, who was ahead was kneeling shooting, and Macomber, as he fired, unhearing his shot in the roaring of Wilson's gun, saw fragments like slate burst from the huge boss of the horns, and the head jerked, he shot again at the wide nostrils and saw the horns jolt again and fragments fly, and he did not see Wilson now and, aiming carefully, shot again with the buffalo's huge bulk almost on him and his rifle almost level with the on-coming head, nose out, and he could see the little wicked eyes and the head started to lower and he felt a sudden white-hot, blinding flash explode inside his head and that was all he ever felt.

Wilson had ducked to one side to get in a shoulder shot. Macomber had stood solid and shot for the nose, shooting a touch high each time and hitting the heavy horns, splintering and chipping them like hitting a slate roof, and Mrs. Macomber, in the car, had shot at the buffalo with the 6.5 Mannlicher as it seemed about to gore Macomber and had hit her husband about two inches up and a little to one side of the base of his skull.

Francis Macomber lay now, face down, not two yards from where the buffalo lay on his side and his wife knelt over him with Wilson beside her.

"I wouldn't turn him over," Wilson said.

The woman was crying hysterically.

"I'd get back in the car," Wilson said. "Where's the rifle?"

She shook her head, her face contorted. The gun-bearer picked up the rifle.

"Leave it as it is," said Wilson. Then, "Go get Abdulla so that he may witness the manner of the accident."

He knelt down, took a handkerchief from his pocket, and spread it over Francis Macomber's crew-cropped head where it lay. The blood sank into the dry, loose earth.

Wilson stood up and saw the buffalo on his side, his legs out, his thinly-haired belly crawling with ticks. "Hell of a good bull," his brain registered automatically. "A good fifty inches, or better. Better." He called to the driver and told him to spread a blanket over the body and stay by it. Then he walked over to the motor car where the woman sat crying in the corner.

"That was a pretty thing to do," he said in a toneless voice. "He *would* have left you too."

"Stop it," she said.

"Of course it's an accident," he said. "I know that."

"Stop it," she said.

"Don't worry," he said. "There will be a certain amount of unpleasantness but I will have some photographs taken that will be very useful at the inquest. There's the testimony of the gun-bearers and the driver too. You're perfectly all right."

"Stop it," she said.

"There's a hell of a lot to be done," he said. "And I'll have to send a truck off to the lake to wireless for a plane to take the three of us into Nairobi. Why didn't you poison him? That's what they do in England."

"Stop it. Stop it. Stop it," the woman cried.

Wilson looked at her with his flat blue eyes.

"I'm through now," he said. "I was a little angry. I'd begun to like your husband."

"Oh, please stop it," she said. "Please, please stop it."

"That's better," Wilson said. "Please is much better. Now I'll stop."

Big Boy
Leaves Home

RICHARD WRIGHT

Evoking the familiar American nostalgia for the old swimming hole, Richard Wright's opening scenes prepare the reader almost at once for the ironies that the folklore of a carefree youth in the American countryside holds for the Negro adolescents of this story. The dominant mood of the tale is not really evocative, though, but grim; its view of experience not shaded but stark, from the shrill black voices rising from the trees at the beginning to the murderous white voices echoing among the trees near the end. While implying the self-destructiveness of a whole society—with a powerless group fated to be destroyed by a powerful one—"Big Boy Leaves Home" is addressed most squarely to a particular historical moment, is thus reportorial and prophetic rather than contemplative and tragic.

Y̶o mama don wear no drawers . . .

Clearly, the voice rose out of the woods, and died away. Like an echo another voice caught it up:

Ah seena when she pulled em off . . .

Another, shrill, cracking, adolescent:

N she washed 'em in alcohol . . .

Then a quartet of voices, blending in harmony, floated high above the tree tops:

N she hung 'em out in the hall . . .

Laughing easily, four black boys came out of the woods into cleared pasture. They walked lollingly in bare feet, beating tangled vines and bushes with long sticks.

"Ah wished Ah knowed some mo lines t tha song."

"Me too."

"Yeah, when yuh gits t where she hangs em out in the hall yuh has t stop."

"Shucks, whut goes wid *hall?*"

"*Call.*"

"*Fall.*"

"*Wall.*"

"*Quall.*"

They threw themselves on the grass, laughing.

"Big Boy?"

"Huh?"

"Yuh know one thing?"

"Whut?"

"Yuh sho is crazy!"

"Crazy?"

"Yeah, yuh crazys a bed-bug!"

"Crazy bout whut?"

"Man, whoever hearda *quall?*"

"Yuh said yuh wanted something to go wid *hall,* didnt yuh?"

"Yeah, but whuts a *quall?*"

"Nigger, a *qualls* a *quall.*"

They laughed easily, catching and pulling long green blades of grass with their toes.

"Waal, ef a *qualls* a *quall,* whut IS a *quall?*"

"Oh, Ah know."

"Whut?"

"Tha ol song goes something like this:

> *Yo mama don wear no drawers,*
> *Ah seena when she pulled em off,*
> *N she washed em in alcohol,*
> *N she hung em out in the hall,*
> *N then she put em back on her QUALL!*"

They laughed again. Their shoulders were flat to the earth, their knees propped up, and their faces square to the sun.

"Big Boy, yuhs CRAZY!"

"Don ax me nothin else."

"Nigger, yuhs CRAZY!"

They fell silent, smiling, drooping the lids of their eyes softly against the sunlight.

"Man, don the groun feel warm?"

"Jus lika bed."

"Jeeesus, Ah could stay here ferever."

"Me too."

"Ah kin feel tha ol sun goin all thu me."

"Feels like mah bones is warm."

In the distance a train whistled mournfully.

"There goes number fo!"

"Hittin on all six!"

"Highballin it down the line!"

"Boun fer up Noth, Lawd, boun fer up Noth!"

They began to chant, pounding bare heels in the grass.

> *Dis train boun fo Glory*
> *Dis train, Oh Hallelujah*
> *Dis train boun fo Glory*
> *Dis train, Oh Hallelujah*
> *Dis train boun fo Glory*
> *Ef yuh ride no need fer fret er worry*
> *Dis train, Oh Hallelujah*
> *Dis train . . .*

Dis train don carry no gambler
Dis train, Oh Hallelujah
Dis train don carry no gambler
Dis train, Oh Hallelujah
Dis train don carry no gambler
No fo day creeper er midnight rambler
Dis train, Oh Hallelujah
Dis train . . .

When the song ended they burst out laughing, thinking of a train bound for Glory.

"Gee, thas a good ol song!"

"Huuuuummmmmmmmman . . ."

"Whut?"

"Geeee whiiiiiiz . . ."

"Whut?"

"Somebody don let win! Das whut!"

Buck, Bobo and Lester jumped up. Big Boy stayed on the ground, feigning sleep.

"Jeeesus, tha sho stinks!"

"Big Boy!"

Big Boy feigned to snore.

"Big Boy!"

Big Boy stirred as though in sleep.

"Big Boy!"

"Hunh?"

"Yuh rotten inside!"

"Rotten?"

"Lawd, cant yuh smell it?"

"Smell whut?"

"Nigger, yuh mus gotta bad col!"

"*Smell whut?*"

"NIGGER, YUH BROKE WIN!"

Big Boy laughed and fell back on the grass, closing his eyes.

"The hen whut cackles is the hen whut laid the egg."

"We ain no hens."

"Yuh cackled, didnt yuh?"

The three moved off with noses turned up.

"C mon!"

"Where yuh-all goin?"

"T the creek fer a swim."

"Yeah, les swim."

"Naw buddy naw!" said Big Boy, slapping the air with a scornful palm.

"Aw, c mon! Don be a heel!"

"N git *lynched?* Hell naw!"

"He ain gonna see us."

"How yuh know?"

"Cause he ain."

"Yuh-all go on. Ahma stay right here," said Big Boy.

"Hell, let im stay! C mon, les go," said Buck.

The three walked off, swishing at grass and bushes with sticks. Big Boy looked lazily at their backs.

"Hey!"

Walking on, they glanced over their shoulders.

"Hey, niggers!"

"C mon!"

Big Boy grunted, picked up his stick, pulled to his feet, and stumbled off.

"Wait!"

"C mon!"

He ran, caught up with them, leaped upon their backs, bearing them to the ground.

"Quit, Big Boy!"

"Gawddam, nigger!"

"Git t hell offa me!"

Big Boy sprawled in the grass beside them, laughing and pounding his heels in the ground.

"Nigger, whut yuh think we is, hosses?"

"How come yuh awways hoppin on us?"

"Lissen, wes gonna double-team on yuh one of these days n beat yo ol ass good."

Big Boy smiled.

"Sho nough?"

"Yeah, don yuh like it?"

"We gonna beat yuh sos yuh cant walk!"

"N dare yuh t do nothin erbout it!"

Big Boy bared his teeth.

"C mon! Try it now!"

The three circled around him.

"Say, Buck, yuh grab his feets!"

"N yuh git his head, Lester!"

"N Bobo, yuh git berhin n grab his arms!"

Keeping more than arm's length, they circled round and round Big Boy.

"C mon!" said Big Boy, feinting at one and then the other.

Round and round they circled, but could not seem to get any closer. Big Boy stopped and braced his hands on his hips.

"Is all three of yuh-all scareda me?"

"Les git im some other time," said Bobo, grinning.

"Yeah, we kin ketch yuh when yuh ain thinkin," said Lester.

"We kin trick yuh," said Buck.

They laughed and walked together.

Big Boy belched.

"Ahm hongry," he said.

"Me too."

"Ah wished Ah hada big hot pota belly-busters!"

"Cooked wid some good ol salty ribs . . ."

"N some good ol egg cornbread . . ."

"N some buttermilk . . ."

"N some hot peach cobbler swimmin in juice . . ."

"Nigger, hush!"

They began to chant, emphasizing the rhythm by cutting at grass with sticks.

> *Bye n bye*
> *Ah wanna piece of pie*
> *Pies too sweet*
> *Ah wanna piece of meat*
> *Meats too red*
> *Ah wanna piece of bread*
> *Breads too brown*
> *Ah wanna go t town*
> *Towns too far*
> *Ah wanna ketch a car*
> *Cars too fas*
> *Ah fall n break mah ass*
> *Ahll understan it better bye n bye . . .*

They climbed over a barbed-wire fence and entered a stretch of thick woods. Big Boy was whistling softly, his eyes half-closed.

"LES GIT IM!"

Buck, Lester, and Bobo whirled, grabbed Big Boy about the

neck, arms, and legs, bearing him to the ground. He grunted and kicked wildly as he went back into weeds.

"Hol im tight!"

"Git his arms! Git his arms!"

"Set on his legs so he cant kick!"

Big Boy puffed heavily, trying to get loose.

"WE GOT YUH NOW, GAWDDAMMIT, WE GOT YUH NOW!"

"Thas a Gawddam lie!" said Big Boy. He kicked, twisted, and clutched for a hold on one and then the other.

"Say, yuh-all hep me hol his arms!" said Bobo.

"Aw, we got this bastard now!" said Lester.

"Thas a Gawddam lie!" said Big Boy again.

"Say, yuh-all hep me hol his arms!" called Bobo.

Big Boy managed to encircle the neck of Bobo with his left arm. He tightened his elbow scissors-like and hissed through his teeth:

"Yuh got me, ain yuh?"

"Hol im!"

"Les beat this bastard's ass!"

"Say, hep me hol his *arms!* Hes got aholda mah *neck!*" cried Bobo.

Big Boy squeezed Bobo's neck and twisted his head to the ground.

"Yuh got me, ain yuh?"

"Quit, Big Boy, yuh chokin me; yuh hurtin mah neck!" cried Bobo.

"Turn me loose!" said Big Boy.

"Ah ain got yuh! Its the others whut got yuh!" pleaded Bobo.

"Tell them others t git t hell offa me or Ahma break yo neck," said Big Boy.

"Ssssay, yyyuh-all gggit ooooffa Bbig Boy. Hhhes got me," gurgled Bobo.

"Cant yuh hol im?"

"Nnaw, hhes ggot mmah nneck . . ."

Big Boy squeezed tighter.

"N Ahma break it too less yuh tell em t git t hell offa me!"

"Ttturn mmmeee lllloose," panted Bobo, tears gushing.

"Cant yuh hol im, Bobo?" asked Buck.

"Nnaw, yuh-all tturn im lloose; hhhes got mah nnneck . . ."

"Grab his neck, Bobo . . ."

"Ah cant; yugurgur . . ."

To save Bobo, Lester and Buck got up and ran to a safe distance. Big Boy released Bobo, who staggered to his feet, slobbering and trying to stretch a crick out of his neck.

"Shucks, nigger, yuh almos broke mah neck," whimpered Bobo.

"Ahm gonna break yo ass nex time," said Big Boy.

"Ef Bobo coulda hel yuh we woulda had yuh," yelled Lester.

"Ah wuznt gonna let im do that," said Big Boy.

They walked together again, swishing sticks.

"Yuh see," began Big Boy, "when a ganga guys jump on yuh, all yuh gotta do is jus put the heat on one of them n make im tell the others t let up, see?"

"Gee, thas a good idee!"

"Yeah, thas a good idee!"

"But yuh almos broke mah neck, man," said Bobo.

"Ahma smart nigger," said Big Boy, thrusting out his chest.

II

They came to the swimming hole.

"Ah ain goin in," said Bobo.

"Done got scared?" asked Big Boy.

"Naw, Ah ain scared . . ."

"How come yuh ain goin in?"

"Yuh know ol man Harvey don erllow no niggers t swim in this hole."

"N just las year he took a shot at Bob fer swimmin in here," said Lester.

"Shucks, ol man Harvey ain studyin bout us niggers," said Big Boy.

"Hes at home thinkin about his jelly-roll," said Buck.

They laughed.

"Buck, yo mins lowern a snakes belly," said Lester.

"Ol man Harveys too doggone ol t think erbout jelly-roll," said Big Boy.

"Hes dried up; all the saps done lef im," said Bobo.

"C mon, les go!" said Big Boy.

Bobo pointed.

"See tha sign over yonder?"

"Yeah."

"Whut it say?"

"NO TRESPASSIN," read Lester.

"Know whut tha mean?"

"Mean ain no dogs n niggers erllowed," said Buck.

"Waal, wes here now," said Big Boy. "Ef he ketched us even like this thered be trouble, so we just as waal go on in . . ."

"Ahm wid the nex one!"

"Ahll go ef anybody else goes!"

Big Boy looked carefully in all directions. Seeing nobody, he began jerking off his overalls.

"LAS ONE INS A OL DEAD DOG!"

"THAS YO MA!"

"THAS YO PA!"

"THAS BOTH YO MA N YO PA!"

They jerked off their clothes and threw them in a pile under a tree. Thirty seconds later they stood, black and naked, on the edge of the hole under a sloping embankment. Gingerly Big Boy touched the water with his foot.

"Man, this waters col," he said.

"Ahm gonna put mah cloes back on," said Bobo, withdrawing his foot.

Big Boy grabbed him about the waist.

"Like hell yuh is!"

"Git outta the way, nigger!" Bobo yelled.

"Thrown im in!" said Lester.

"Duck im!"

Bobo crouched, spread his legs, and braced himself against Big Boy's body. Locked in each other's arms, they tussled on the edge of the hole, neither able to throw the other.

"C mon, les me n yuh push em in."

"O.K."

Laughing, Lester and Buck gave the two locked bodies a running push. Big Boy and Bobo splashed, sending up silver spray in the sunlight. When Big Boy's head came up he yelled:

"Yuh bastard!"

"Tha wuz yo ma yuh pushed!" said Bobo, shaking his head to clear the water from his eyes.

They did a surface dive, came up and struck out across the creek. The muddy water foamed. They swam back, waded into shallow water, breathing heavily and blinking eyes.

"C mon in!"

"Man, the waters fine!"

Lester and Buck hesitated.

"Les wet em," Big Boy whispered to Bobo.

Before Lester and Buck could back away, they were dripping wet from handsful of scooped water.

"Hey, quit!"

"Gawddam, nigger! Tha waters col!"

"C mon in!" called Big Boy.

"We jus as waal go on in now," said Buck.

"Look n see ef anybodys comin."

Kneeling, they squinted among the trees.

"Ain nobody."

"C mon, les go."

They waded in slowly, pausing each few steps to catch their breath. A desperate water battle began. Closing eyes and backing away, they shunted water into one another's faces with the flat palms of hands.

"Hey, cut it out!"

"Yeah, Ahm bout drownin!"

They came together in water up to their navels, blowing and blinking. Big Boy ducked, upsetting Bobo.

"Look out, nigger!"

"Don holler so loud!"

"Yeah, they kin hear yo ol big mouth a mile erway."

"This waters too col fer me."

"Thas cause it rained yistiddy."

They swam across and back again.

"Ah wish we hada bigger place t swim in."

"The white folks got plenty swimmin pools n we ain got none."

"Ah useta swim in the ol Missippi when we lived in Vicksburg."

Big Boy put his head under the water and blew his breath. A sound came like that of a hippopotamus.

"C mon, les be hippos."

Each went to a corner of the creek and put his mouth just below the surface and blew like a hippopotamus. Tiring, they came and sat under the embankment.

"Look like Ah gotta chill."

"Me too."

"Les stay here n dry off."

"Jeeesus, Ahm col!"

They kept still in the sun, suppressing shivers. After some of the water had dried off their bodies they began to talk through clattering teeth.

"Whut would yuh do ef ol man Harveyd come erlong right now?"

"Run like hell!"

"Man, Ahd run so fas hed thinka black streaka lightnin shot pass im."

"But spose he hada gun?"

"Aw, nigger, shut up!"

They were silent. They ran their hands over wet, trembling legs, brushing water away. Then their eyes watched the sun sparkling on the restless creek.

Far away a train whistled.

"There goes number seven!"

"Heading fer up Noth!"

"Blazin it down the line!"

"Lawd, Ahm goin Noth some day."

"Me too, man."

"They say colored folks up Noth is got ekual rights."

They grew pensive. A black winged butterfly hovered at the water's edge. A bee droned. From somewhere came the sweet scent of honeysuckles. Dimly they could hear sparrows twittering in the woods. They rolled from side to side, letting sunshine dry their skins and warm their blood. They plucked blades of grass and chewed them.

"Oh!"

They looked up, their lips parting.

"Oh!"

A white woman, poised on the edge of the opposite embankment, stood directly in front of them, her hat in her hand and her hair lit by the sun.

"Its a woman!" whispered Big Boy in an underbreath. "A *white* woman!"

They stared, their hands instinctively covering their groins. Then they scrambled to their feet. The white woman backed slowly out of sight. They stood for a moment, looking at one another.

"Les git outta here!" Big Boy whispered.

"Wait till she goes erway."

"Les run, theyll ketch us here naked like this!"

"Mabbe theres a man wid her."

"C mon, les git our cloes," said Big Boy.

They waited a moment longer, listening.

"Whut t hell! Ahma git mah cloes," said Big Boy.

Grabbing at short tufts of grass, he climbed the embankment.

"Don run out there now!"

"C mon back, fool!"

Bobo hesitated. He looked at Big Boy, and then at Buck and Lester.

"Ahm goin wid Big Boy n git mah cloes," he said.

"Don run out there naked like tha, fool!" said Buck. "Yuh don know whos out there!"

Big Boy was climbing over the edge of the embankment.

"C mon," he whispered.

Bobo climbed after. Twenty-five feet away the woman stood. She had one hand over her mouth. Hanging by fingers, Buck and Lester peeped over the edge.

"C mon back; that womans scared," said Lester.

Big Boy stopped, puzzled. He looked at the woman. He looked at the bundle of clothes. Then he looked at Buck and Lester.

"C mon, les git our cloes!"

He made a step.

"Jim!" the woman screamed.

Big Boy stopped and looked around. His hands hung loosely at his sides. The woman, her eyes wide, her hand over her mouth, backed away to the tree where their clothes lay in a heap.

"Big Boy, come back n wait till shes gone!"

Bobo ran to Big Boy's side.

"Les go home! Theyll ketch us here," he urged.

Big Boy's throat felt tight.

"Lady, we wanna git our cloes," he said.

Buck and Lester climbed the embankment and stood indecisively. Big Boy ran toward the tree.

"Jim!" the woman screamed. "Jim! Jim!"

Black and naked, Big Boy stopped three feet from her.

"We wanna git our cloes," he said again, his words coming mechanically.

He made a motion.

"You go away! You go away! I tell you, you go away!"

Big Boy stopped again, afraid. Bobo ran and snatched the clothes. Buck and Lester tried to grab theirs out of his hands.

"You go away! You go away! You go away!" the woman screamed.

"Les go!" said Bobo, running toward the woods.

CRACK!

Lester grunted, stiffened, and pitched forward. His forehead struck a toe of the woman's shoes.

Bobo stopped, clutching the clothes. Buck whirled. Big Boy stared at Lester, his lips moving.

"Hes gotta gun; hes gotta gun!" yelled Buck, running wildly. CRACK!

Buck stopped at the edge of the embankment, his head jerked backward, his body arched stiffly to one side; he toppled headlong, sending up a shower of bright spray to the sunlight. The creek bubbled.

Big Boy and Bobo backed away, their eyes fastened fearfully on a white man who was running toward them. He had a rifle and wore an army officer's uniform. He ran to the woman's side and grabbed her hand.

"You hurt, Bertha, you hurt?"

She stared at him and did not answer.

The man turned quickly. His face was red. He raised the rifle and pointed it at Bobo. Bobo ran back, holding the clothes in front of his chest.

"Don shoot me, Mistah, don shoot me . . ."

Big Boy lunged for the rifle, grabbing the barrel.

"You black sonofabitch!"

Big Boy clung desperately.

"Let go, you black bastard!"

The barrel pointed skyward.

CRACK!

The white man, taller and heavier, flung Big Boy to the ground. Bobo dropped the clothes, ran up, and jumped onto the white man's back.

"You black sonsofbitches!"

The white man released the rifle, jerked Bobo to the ground, and began to batter the naked boy with his fists. Then Big Boy swung, striking the man in the mouth with the barrel. His teeth caved in, and he fell, dazed. Bobo was on his feet.

"C mon, Big Boy, les go!"

Breathing hard, the white man got up and faced Big Boy. His lips were trembling, his neck and chin wet with blood. He spoke quietly.

"Give me that gun, boy!"

Big Boy leveled the rifle and backed away.

The white man advanced.

"Boy, I say give me that gun!"

Bobo had the clothes in his arms.

"Run, Big Boy, run!"

The man came at Big Boy.

"Ahll kill yuh; Ahll kill yuh!" said Big Boy.

His fingers fumbled for the trigger.

The man stopped, blinked, spat blood. His eyes were bewildered. His face whitened. Suddenly, he lunged for the rifle, his hands outstretched.

CRACK!

He fell forward on his face.

"Jim!"

Big Boy and Bobo turned in surprise to look at the woman.

"Jim!" she screamed again, and fell weakly at the foot of the tree.

Big Boy dropped the rifle, his eyes wide. He looked around. Bobo was crying and clutching the clothes.

"Big Boy, Big Boy . . ."

Big Boy looked at the rifle, started to pick it up, but didn't. He seemed at a loss. He looked at Lester, then at the white man; his eyes followed a thin stream of blood that seeped to the ground.

"Yuh done killed him," mumbled Bobo.

"Les go home!"

Naked, they turned and ran toward the woods. When they reached the barbed-wire fence they stopped.

"Les git our cloes on," said Big Boy.

They slipped quickly into overalls. Bobo held Lester's and Buck's clothes.

"Whut we gonna do wid these?"

Big Boy stared. His hands twitched.

"Leave em."

They climbed the fence and ran through the woods. Vines and leaves switched their faces. Once Bobo tripped and fell.

"C mon!" said Big Boy.

Bobo started crying, blood streaming from his scratches.

"Ahm scared!"

"C mon! Don cry! We wanna git hom fo they ketches us!"

"Ahm scared!" said Bobo again, his eyes full of tears.

Big Boy grabbed his hand and dragged him along.
"C mon!"

III

They stopped when they got to the end of the woods. They could see the open road leading home, home to ma and pa. But they hung back, afraid. The thick shadows cast from the trees were friendly and sheltering. But the wide glare of sun stretching out over the fields was pitiless. They crouched behind an old log.

"We gotta git home," said Big Boy.

"They's gonna lynch us," said Bobo, half-questioningly.

Big Boy did not answer.

"Theys gonna lynch us," said Bobo again.

Big Boy shuddered.

"Hush!" he said. He did not want to think of it. He could not think of it; there was but one thought, and he clung to that one blindly. He had to get home, home to ma and pa.

Their heads jerked up. Their ears had caught the rhythmic jingle of a wagon. They fell to the ground and clung flat to the side of a log. Over the crest of the hill came the top of a hat. A white face. Then shoulders in a blue shirt. A wagon drawn by two horses pulled into full view.

Big Boy and Bobo held their breath, waiting. Their eyes followed the wagon till it was lost in dust around a bend in the road.

"We gotta git home," said Big Boy.

"Ahm scared," said Bobo.

"C mon! Les keep t the fields."

They ran till they came to the cornfields. Then they went slower, for last year's corn stubbles bruised their feet.

They came in sight of a brickyard.

"Wait a minute," gasped Big Boy.

They stopped.

"Ahm goin on t mah home n yuh better go on t yos."

Bobo's eyes grew round.

"Ahm scared!"

"Yuh better go on!"

"Lemme go wid yuh; they'll ketch me . . ."

"Ef yuh kin git home mabbe yo folks kin hep yuh t git erway."

Big Boy started off. Bobo grabbed him.

"Lemme go wid yuh!"

Big Boy shook free.

"Ef yuh stay here theys gonna lynch yuh!" he yelled, running.

After he had gone about twenty-five yards he turned and looked; Bobo was flying through the woods like the wind.

Big Boy slowed when he came to the railroad. He wondered if he ought to go through the streets or down the track. He decided on the tracks. He could dodge a train better than a mob.

He trotted along the ties, looking ahead and back. His cheek itched, and he felt it. His hand came away smeared with blood. He wiped it nervously on his overalls.

When he came to his back fence he heaved himself over. He landed among a flock of startled chickens. A bantam rooster tried to spur him. He slipped and fell in front of the kitchen steps, grunting heavily. The ground was slick with greasy dishwater.

Panting, he stumbled through the doorway.

"Lawd, Big Boy, whuts wrong wid yuh?"

His mother stood gaping in the middle of the floor. Big Boy flopped wordlessly onto a stool, almost toppling over. Pots simmered on the stove. The kitchen smelled of food cooking.

"Whuts the matter, Big Boy?"

Mutely, he looked at her. Then he burst into tears. She came and felt the scratches on his face.

"Whut happened t yuh, Big Boy? Somebody been botherin yuh?"

"They after me, Ma! They after me . . ."

"Who!"

"Ah . . . Ah . . . We . . ."

"Big Boy, whuts wrong wid yuh?"

"He killed Lester n Buck," he muttered simply.

"Killed!"

"Yessum."

"Lester n Buck!"

"Yessum, Ma!"

"How killed?"

"He shot em, Ma!"

"Lawd Gawd in Heaven, have mercy on us all! This is mo trouble, mo trouble," she moaned, wringing her hands.

"N Ah killed im, Ma . . ."

She stared, trying to understand.

"Whut happened, Big Boy?"

"We tried t git our cloes from the tree . . ."

"Whut tree?"

"We wuz swimmin, Ma. N the white woman . . ."

"*White* woman? . . ."

"Yessum. She wuz at the swimmin hole . . ."

"Lawd have mercy! Ah knowed yuh boys wuz gonna keep on till yuh got into somethin like this!"

She ran into the hall.

"Lucy!"

"Mam?"

"C mere!"

"Mam?"

"C mere, Ah say!"

"Whutcha wan, Ma? Ahm sewin."

"Chile, will yuh c mere like Ah ast yuh?"

Lucy came to the door holding an unfinished apron in her hands. When she saw Big Boy's face she looked wildly at her mother.

"Whuts the matter?"

"Wheres Pa?"

"Hes out front, Ah reckon."

"Git im, quick!"

"Whuts the matter, Ma?"

"Go git yo Pa, Ah say!"

Lucy ran out. The mother sank into a chair, holding a dish rag. Suddenly, she sat up.

"Big Boy, Ah thought yuh wuz at school?"

Big Boy looked at the floor.

"How come yuh didnt go t school?"

"We went t the woods."

She sighed.

"Ah done done all Ah kin fer yuh, Big Boy. Only Gawd kin hep yuh now."

"Ma, don let em git me; don let em git me . . ."

His father came into the doorway. He stared at Big Boy, then at his wife.

"Whuts Big Boy inter now?" he asked sternly.

"Saul, Big Boys done gone n got inter trouble wid the white folks."

The old man's mouth dropped, and he looked from one to the other.

"Saul, we gotta git im erway from here."

"Open yo mouth n talk! Whut yuh been doin?" The old man

gripped Big Boy's shoulders and peered at the scratches on his face.

"Me n Lester n Buck n Bobo wuz out on ol man Harveys place swimmin . . ."

"Saul, its a *white* woman!"

Big Boy winced. The old man compressed his lips and stared at his wife. Lucy gaped at her brother as though she had never seen him before.

"Whut happened? Cant yuh-all talk?" the old man thundered, with a certain helplessness in his voice.

"We wuz swimmin," Big Boy began, "n then a white woman comes up t the hole. We got up right erway t git our cloes sos we could git erway, n she started screamin. Our cloes wuz right by the tree where she wuz standin, n when we started t git em she jus screamed. We tol her we wanted our cloes . . . Yuh see, Pa, she wuz standin right *by* our cloes; n when we went t git em she jus screamed . . . Bobo got the cloes, n then he shot Lester . . ."

"*Who* shot Lester?"

"The white man."

"Whut white man?"

"Ah dunno, Pa. He wuz a soljer, n he had a rifle."

"A soljer?"

"Yessuh."

"A *soljer?*"

"Yessuh, Pa. A soljer."

The old man frowned.

"N then whut yuh-all do?"

"Waal, Buck said, 'Hes gotta gun!' N we started runnin. N then he shot Buck, n he fell in the swimmin hole. We didnt see im no mo . . . He wuz close on us then. He looked at the white woman n then he started t shoot Bobo. Ah grabbed the gun, n we started fightin. Bobo jumped on his back. He started beatin Bobo. Then Ah hit im wid the gun. Then he started at me n Ah shot im. Then we run . . ."

"Who seen?"

"Nobody."

"Wheres Bobo?"

"He went home."

"Anybody run after yuh-all?"

"Nawsuh."

"Yuh see anybody?"

"Nawsuh. Nobody but a white man. But he didnt see us."

"How long fo yuh-all lef the swimmin hole?"

"Little while ergo."

The old man nervously brushed his hand across his eyes and walked to the door. His lips moved, but no words came.

"Saul, whut we gonna do?"

"Lucy," began the old man, "go t Brother Sanders n tell im Ah said c mere; n go t Brother Jenkins n tell im Ah said c mere; n go t Elder Peters n tell im Ah said c mere. N don say nóthin t nobody but whut Ah tol yuh. N when yuh git thu come straight back. Now go!"

Lucy dropped her apron across the back of a chair and ran down the steps. The mother bent over, crying and praying. The old man walked slowly over to Big Boy.

"Big Boy?"

Big Boy swallowed.

"Ahm talkin t yuh!"

"Yessuh."

"How come yuh didnt go t school this mawnin?"

"We went t the woods."

"Didnt yo ma send yuh t school?"

"Yessuh."

"How come yuh didnt go?"

"We went t the woods."

"Don yuh know thas wrong?"

"Yessuh."

"How come yuh go?"

Big Boy looked at his fingers, knotted them, and squirmed in his seat.

"AHM TALKIN T YUH!"

His wife straightened up and said reprovingly:

"Saul!"

The old man desisted, yanking nervously at the shoulder straps of his overalls.

"How long wuz the woman there?"

"Not long."

"Wuz she young?"

"Yessuh. Lika gal."

"Did yuh-all say anythin t her?"

"Nawsuh. We jus said we wanted our cloes."

"N whut she say?"

"Nothin, Pa. She jus backed erway t the tree n screamed."

The old man stared, his lips trying to form a question.

"Big Boy, did yuh-all bother her?"

"Nawsuh, Pa. We didnt *touch* her."

"How long fo the white man come up?"

"Right erway."

"Whut he say?"

"Nothin. He jus cussed us."

Abruptly the old man left the kitchen.

"Ma, cant Ah go fo they ketches me?"

"Sauls doin whut he kin."

"Ma, Ma, Ah don wan em t ketch me . . ."

"Sauls doin whut he kin. Nobody but the good Lawd kin hep us now."

The old man came back with a shotgun and leaned it in a corner. Fascinatedly, Big Boy looked at it.

There was a knock at the front door.

"Liza, see whos there."

She went. They were silent, listening. They could hear her talking.

"Whos there?"

"Me."

"Who?"

"Me, Brother Sanders."

"C mon in. Sauls waitin fer yuh."

Sanders paused in the doorway, smiling.

"Yuh sent fer me, Brother Morrison?"

"Brother Sanders, wes in deep trouble here."

Sanders came all the way into the kitchen.

"Yeah?"

"Big Boy done gone n killed a white man."

Sanders stopped short, then came forward, his face thrust out, his mouth open. His lips moved several times before he could speak.

"A *white* man?"

"They gonna kill me; they gonna kill me!" Big Boy cried, running to the old man.

"Saul, cant we git im erway somewhere?"

"Here now, take it easy; take it easy," said Sanders, holding Big Boy's wrists.

"They gonna kill me; they gonna lynch me!"

Big Boy slipped to the floor. They lifted him to a stool. His mother held him closely, pressing his head to her bosom.

"Whut we gonna do?" asked Sanders.

"Ah done sent fer Brother Jenkins n Elder Peters."

Sanders leaned his shoulders against the wall. Then, as the full meaning of it all came to him, he exclaimed:

"Theys gonna git a mob! . . ." His voice broke off and his eyes fell on the shotgun.

Feet came pounding on the steps. They turned toward the door. Lucy ran in crying. Jenkins followed. The old man met him in the middle of the room, taking his hand.

"Wes in bad trouble here, Brother Jenkins. Big Boy's done gone n killed a white man. Yuh-alls gotta hep me . . ."

Jenkins looked hard at Big Boy.

"Elder Peters says hes comin," said Lucy.

"When all this happen?" asked Jenkins.

"Near bout a hour ergo, now," said the old man.

"Whut we gonna do?" asked Jenkins.

"Ah wanna wait till Elder Peters come," said the old man help-lessly.

"But we gotta work fas ef we gonna do anythin," said Sanders. "Well git in trouble jus standin here like this."

Big Boy pulled away from his mother.

"Pa, lemme go now! Lemme go now!"

"Be still, Big Boy!"

"Where kin yuh go?"

"Ah could ketch a freight!"

"Thas *sho* death!" said Jenkins. "Theyll be watchin em all!"

"Kin yuh-all hep me wid some money?" the old man asked.

They shook their heads.

"Saul, whut kin we do? Big Boy cant stay here."

There was another knock at the door.

The old man backed stealthily to the shotgun.

"Lucy go!"

Lucy looked at him, hesitating.

"Ah better go," said Jenkins.

It was Elder Peters. He came in hurriedly.

"Good evenin, everbody!"

"How yuh, Elder?"

"Good evenin."

"How yuh today?"

Peters looked around the crowded kitchen.

"Whuts the matter?"

"Elder, wes in deep trouble," began the old man. "Big Boy n some mo boys . . ."

". . . Lester n Buck n Bobo . . ."

". . . wuz over on ol man Harveys place swimmin . . ."

"N he don like us niggers *none*," said Peters emphatically. He widened his legs and put his thumbs in the armholes of his vest.

". . . n some white woman . . ."

"Yeah?" said Peters, coming closer.

". . . comes erlong n the boys tries t git their cloes where they don lef em under a tree. Waal, she started screamin n all, see? Reckon she thought the boys wuz after her. Then a white man in a soljers suit shoots two of em . . ."

". . . Lester n Buck . . ."

"Huummm," said Peters. "Tha wuz ol man Harveys son."

"Harveys son?"

"Yuh mean the one tha wuz in the Army?"

"Yuh mean Jim?"

"Yeah," said Peters. "The papers said he wuz here fer a vacation from his regiment. N tha woman the boys saw wuz jus erbout his wife . . ."

They stared at Peters. Now that they knew what white person had been killed, their fears became definite.

"N whut else happened?"

"Big Boy shot the man . . ."

"Harveys *son?*"

"He had t, Elder. He wuz gonna shoot im ef he didnt . . ."

"Lawd!" said Peters. He looked around and put his hat back on.

"How long ergo wuz this?"

"Mighty near an hour, now, Ah reckon."

"Do the white folks know yit?"

"Don know, Elder."

"Yuh-all better git this boy outta here right now," said Peters. "Cause ef yuh don theres gonna be a lynchin . . ."

"Where kin Ah go, Elder?" Big Boy ran up to him.

They crowded around Peters. He stood with his legs wide apart, looking up at the ceiling.

"Mabbe we kin hide im in the church till he kin git erway," said Jenkins.

Peters' lips flexed.

"Naw, Brother, thall never do! Theyll git im there sho. N anyhow, ef they ketch im there itll ruin us all. We gotta git the boy outta town . . ."

Sanders went up to the old man.

"Lissen," he said in a whisper. "Mah son, Will, the one whut drives fer the Magnolia Express Company, is taking a truck o goods t Chicawgo in the mawnin. If we kin hide Big Boy somewhere till then, we kin put im on the truck . . ."

"Pa, please, lemme go wid Will when he goes in the mawnin," Big Boy begged.

The old man stared at Sanders.

"Yuh reckon thas safe?"

"Its the only thing yuh *kin* do," said Peters.

"But where we gonna hide im till then?"

"Whut time yo boy leavin out in the mawnin?"

"At six."

They were quiet, thinking. The water kettle on the stove sang.

"Pa, Ah knows where Will passes erlong wid the truck out on Bullards Road. Ah kin hide in one of them ol kilns . . ."

"Where?"

"In one of them kilns we built . . ."

"But theyll git yuh there," wailed the mother.

"But there ain no place else fer im t go."

"Theres some holes big ernough fer me t git in n stay till Will comes erlong," said Big Boy. "Please, Pa, lemme go fo they ketches me . . ."

"Let im go!"

"Please, Pa . . ."

The old man breathed heavily.

"Lucy, git his things!"

"Saul, theyll git im out there!" wailed the mother, grabbing Big Boy.

Peters pulled her away.

"Sister Morrison, ef yuh don let im go n git erway from here hes gonna be caught shos theres a Gawd in Heaven!"

Lucy came running with Big Boy's shoes and pulled them on his feet. The old man thrust a battered hat on his head. The mother went to the stove and dumped the skillet of corn pone into her apron. She wrapped it, and unbuttoning Big Boy's overalls, pushed it into his bosom.

"Heres somethin fer yuh t eat; n pray, Big Boy, cause thas all anybody kin do now . . ."

Big Boy pulled to the door, his mother clinging to him.

"Let im go, Sister Morrison!"

"Run fas, Big Boy!"

Big Boy raced across the yard, scattering the chickens. He paused at the fence and hollered back:

"Tell Bobo where Ahm hidin n tell im t c mon!"

<hr/>

IV

He made for the railroad, running straight toward the sunset. He held his left hand tightly over his heart, holding the hot pone of corn bread there. At times he stumbled over the ties, for his shoes were tight and hurt his feet. His throat burned from thirst; he had had no water since noon.

He veered off the track and trotted over the crest of a hill, following Bullard's Road. His feet slipped and slid in the dust. He kept his eyes straight ahead, fearing every clump of shrubbery, every tree. He wished it were night. If he could only get to the kilns without meeting anyone. Suddenly a thought came to him like a blow. He recalled hearing the old folks tell tales of bloodhounds, and fear made him run slower. None of them had thought of that. Spose blood-houns wuz put on his trail? Lawd! Spose a whole pack of em, foamin n howlin, tore im t pieces? He went limp and his feet dragged. Yeah, thas whut they wuz gonna send after im, blood-houns! N then thered be no way fer im t dodge! Why hadnt Pa let im take tha shotgun? He stopped. He oughta go back n git tha shotgun. And then when the mob came he would take some with him.

In the distance he heard the approach of a train. It jarred him back to a sharp sense of danger. He ran again, his big shoes sopping up and down in the dust. He was tired and his lungs were bursting from running. He wet his lips, wanting water. As he turned from the road across a plowed field he heard the train roaring at his heels. He ran faster, gripped in terror.

He was nearly there now. He could see the black clay on the sloping hillside. Once inside a kiln he would be safe. For a little while, at least. He thought of the shotgun again. If he only had something! Someone to talk to . . . Thas right! Bobo! Bobod be wid im. Hed almost fergot Bobo. Bobod bringa gun; he knowed he would. N tergether they could kill the whole mob. Then in the mawning theyd git inter Will's truck n go far erway, t Chicawgo . . .

He slowed to a walk, looking back and ahead. A light wind skipped over the grass. A beetle lit on his cheek and he brushed it off. Behind the dark pines hung a red sun. Two bats flapped against that sun. He shivered, for he was growing cold; the sweat on his body was drying.

He stopped at the foot of the hill, trying to choose between two patches of black kilns high above him. He went to the left, for there lay the ones he, Bobo, Lester, and Buck had dug only last week. He looked around again; the landscape was bare. He climbed the embankment and stood before a row of black pits sinking four and five feet deep into the earth. He went to the largest and peered in. He stiffened when his ears caught the sound of a whir. He ran back a few steps and poised on his toes. Six foot of snake slid out of the pit and went into coil. Big Boy looked around wildly for a stick. He ran down the slope, peering into the grass. He stumbled over a tree limb. He picked it up and tested it by striking it against the ground.

Warily, he crept back up the slope, his stick poised. When about seven feet from the snake he stopped and waved the stick. The coil grew tighter, the whir sounded louder, and a flat head reared to strike. He went to the right, and the flat head followed him, the blue-black tongue darting forth; he went to the left, and the flat head followed him there too.

He stopped, teeth clenched. He had to kill this snake. Jus had t kill im! This wuz the safest pit on the hillside. He waved the stick again, looking at the snake before, thinking of a mob behind. The flat head reared higher. With stick over shoulder, he jumped in, swinging. The stick sang through the air, catching the snake on the side of the head, sweeping him out of coil. There was a brown writhing mass. Then Big Boy was upon him, pounding blows home, one on top of the other. He fought viciously, his eyes red, his teeth bared in a snarl. He beat till the snake lay still; then he stomped it with his heel, grinding its head into the dirt.

He stopped, limp, wet. The corners of his lips were white with spittle. He spat and shuddered.

Cautiously, he went to the hole and peered. He longed for a match. He imagined whole nests of them in there waiting. He put the stick into the hole and waved it around. Stooping, he peered again. It mus be awright. He looked over the hillside, his eyes coming back to the dead snake. Then he got to his knees and backed slowly into the hole.

When inside he felt there must be snakes all about him, ready to strike. It seemed he could see and feel them there, waiting tensely in coil. In the dark he imagined long white fangs ready to sink into his neck, his side, his legs. He wanted to come out, but kept still. Shucks, he told himself, ef there wuz any snakes in here they sho woulda done bit me by now. Some of his fear left, and he relaxed.

With elbows on ground and chin on palms, he settled. The clay was cold to his knees and thighs, but his bosom was kept warm by the hot pone of corn bread. His thirst returned and he longed for a drink. He was hungry, too. But he did not want to eat the corn pone. Naw, not now. Mabbe after erwhile, after Bobo came. Then theyd both eat the corn pone.

The view from his hole was fringed by the long tufts of grass. He could see all the way to Bullard's Road, and even beyond. The wind was blowing, and in the east the first touch of dusk was rising. Every now and then a bird floated past, a spot of wheeling black printed against the sky. Big Boy sighed, shifted his weight, and chewed at a blade of grass. A wasp droned. He heard number nine, far away and mournful.

The train made him remember how they had dug these kilns on long hot summer days, how they had made boilers out of big tin cans, filled them with water, fixed stoppers for steam, cemented them in holes with wet clay, and built fires under them. He recalled how they had danced and yelled when a stopper blew out of a boiler, letting out a big spout of steam and a shrill whistle. There were times when they had the whole hillside blazing and smoking. Yeah, yuh see, Big Boy wuz Casey Jones n wuz speedin it down the gleamin rails of the Southern Pacific. Bobo had number two on the Santa Fe. Buck wuz on the Illinoy Central. Lester the Nickel Plate. Lawd, how they shelved the wood in! The boiling water would almost jar the cans loose from the clay. More and more pine-knots and dry leaves would be piled under the cans. Flames would grow so tall they would have to shield their eyes.

Sweat would pour off their faces. Then, suddenly, a peg would shoot high into the air, and

Pssseeeezzzzzzzzzzzzzzzzzzzzz . . .

Big Boy sighed and stretched out his arm, quenching the flames and scattering the smoke. Why didnt Bobo c mon? He looked over the fields; there was nothing but dying sunlight. His mind drifted back to the kilns. He remembered the day when Buck, jealous of his winning, had tried to smash his kiln. Yeah, that ol sonofabitch! Naw, Lawd! He didnt go t say tha! Whut wuz he thinkin erbout? Cussin the dead! Yeah, po ol Buck wuz dead now. N Lester too. Yeah, it wuz awright fer Buck t smash his kiln. Sho. N he wished he hadnt socked ol Buck so hard tha day. He wuz sorry fer Buck now. N he sho wished he hadnt cussed po ol Bucks ma, neither. Tha wuz sinful! Mabbe Gawd would git im fer tha? But he didnt go t do it! Po Buck! Po Lester! Hed never treat anybody like tha ergin, never . . .

Dusk was slowly deepening. Somewhere, he could not tell exactly where, a cricket took up a fitful song. The air was growing soft and heavy. He looked over the fields, longing for Bobo . . .

He shifted his body to ease the cold damp of the ground, and thought back over the day. Yeah, hed been dam right erbout not wantin t go swimmin. N ef hed followed his right min hed neverve gon n got inter all this trouble. At first hed said naw. But shucks, somehow hed just went on wid the res. Yeah, he shoulda went on t school tha mawnin, like Ma told im t do. But, hell, who wouldnt git tireda awways drivin a guy t school! Tha wuz the big trou awways drivin a guy t school. He wouldnt be in all this trouble now ef it wuznt fer that Gawddam school! Impatiently, he took the grass out of his mouth and threw it away, demolishing the little red school house . . .

Yeah, ef they had all kept still n quiet when tha ol white woman showed-up, mabbe shedve went on off. But yuh never kin tell erbout these white folks. Mabbe she wouldntve went. Mabbe tha white man woulda killed all of em! All *fo* of em! Yeah, yuh never kin tell erbout white folks. Then, ergin, mabbe tha white woman woulda went on off n laffed. Yeah, mabbe tha white man woulda said: *Yuh nigger bastards git t hell outta here! Yuh know Gawddam well yuh don berlong here!* N then they woulda grabbed their cloes n run like all hell . . . He blinked the white man away. Where wuz Bobo? Why didnt he hurry up n c mon?

He jerked another blade and chewed. Yeah, ef pa had only let im have tha shotgun! He could stan off a whole mob wid a shotgun. He looked at the ground as he turned a shotgun over in his hands. Then he leveled it at an advancing white man. *Boooom!* The man curled up. Another came. He reloaded quickly, and let him have what the other had got. He too curled up. Then another came. He got the same medicine. Then the whole mob swirled around him, and he blazed away, getting as many as he could. They closed in; but, by Gawd, he had done his part, hadnt he? N the newspapersd say: NIGGER KILLS DOZEN OF MOB BEFO LYNCHED! Er mabbe theyd say: TRAPPED NIGGER SLAYS TWENTY BEFO KILLED! He smiled a little. Tha wouldnt be so bad, would it? Blinking the newspaper away, he looked over the fields. Where wuz Bobo? Why didnt he hurry up n c mon?

He shifted, trying to get a crick out of his legs. Shucks, he wuz gittin tireda this. N it wuz almos dark now. Yeah, there wuz a little bittie star way over yonder in the eas. Mabbe tha white man wuznt dead? Mabbe they wuznt even lookin fer im? Mabbe he could go back home now? Naw, better wait erwhile. Thad be bes. But, Lawd, ef he only had some water! He could hardly swallow, his throat was so dry. Gawddam them white folks! Thas all they wuz good fer, t run a nigger down lika rabbit! Yeah, they git yuh in a corner n then they let yuh have it. A thousan of em! He shivered, for the cold of the clay was chilling his bones. Lawd, spose they foun im here in this hole? N wid nobody t hep im? . . . But ain no use in thinkin erbout tha; wait till trouble come fo yuh start fightin it. But ef tha mob came one by one hed wipe em all out. Clean up the whole bunch. He caught one by the neck and choked him long and hard, choked him till his tongue and eyes popped out. Then he jumped upon his chest and stomped him like he had stomped that snake. When he had finished with one, another came. He choked him too. Choked till he sank slowly to the ground, gasping . . .

"Hoalo!"

Big Boy snatched his fingers from the white man's neck and looked over the fields. He saw nobody. Had someone spied him? He was sure that somebody had hollered. His heart pounded. But, shucks, nobody couldnt see im here in this hole . . . But mabbe theyd seen im when he wuz comin n had laid low n wuz now closin in on im! Praps they wuz signalin fer the others? Yeah, they wuz creepin up on im! Mabbe he oughta git up n run . . . Oh! Mabbe tha wuz Bobo! Yeah, Bobo! He oughta clim out n see ef Bobo wuz lookin fer im . . . He stiffened.

"Hoalo!"

"Hoalo!"

"Wheres yuh?"

"Over here on Bullards Road!"

"C mon over!"

"Awright!"

He heard footsteps. Then voices came again, low and far away this time.

"Seen anybody?"

"Naw. Yuh?"

"Naw."

"Yuh reckon they got erway?"

"Ah dunno. Its hard t tell."

"Gawddam them sonofabitchin niggers!"

"We oughta kill ever black bastard in this country!"

"Waal, Jim got two of em, anyhow."

"But Bertha said there wuz *fo!*"

"Where in hell they hidin?"

"She said one of em wuz named Big Boy, or somethin like tha."

"We went t his shack lookin fer im."

"Yeah?"

"But we didnt fin im."

"These niggers stick together; they don never tell on each other."

"We looked all thu the shack n couldnt fin hide ner hair of im. Then we drove the ol woman n man out n set the shack on fire . . ."

"Jeesus! Ah wished Ah coulda been there!"

"Yuh shoulda heard the ol nigger woman howl . . ."

"Hoalo!"

"C mon over!"

Big Boy eased to the edge and peeped. He saw a white man with a gun slung over his shoulder running down the slope. Wuz they gonna search the hill? Lawd, there wuz no way fer im t git erway now; he wuz caught! He shoulda knowed theyd git im here. N he didnt hava thing, notta thing t fight wid. Yeah, soon as the blood-houns came theyd fin im. Lawd, have mercy! Theyd lynch im right here on the hill . . . Theyd git im n tie im t a stake n burn im erlive! Lawd! Nobody but the good Lawd could hep im now, nobody . . .

He heard more feet running. He nestled deeper. His chest ached. Nobody but the good Lawd could hep now. They wuz crowdin all round im n when they hada big crowd theyd close in on im. Then itd be over . . . The good Lawd would have t hep im, cause nobody could hep im now, nobody . . .

And then he went numb when he remembered Bobo. Spose Bobod come now? Hed be caught sho! Both of em would be caught! They'd make Bobo tell where he wuz! Bobo oughta not try to come now. Somebody oughta tell im . . . But there wuz nobody; there wuz no way . . .

He eased slowly back to the opening. There was a large group of men. More were coming. Many had guns. Some had coils of rope slung over shoulders.

"Ah tell yuh they still here, somewhere . . ."

"But we looked all over!"

"What t hell! Wouldnt do t let em git erway!"

"Naw. Ef they git erway notta woman in this town would be safe."

"Say, whuts tha yuh got?"

"Er pillar."

"Fer whut?"

"Feathers, fool!"

"Chris! Thisll be hot ef we kin ketch them niggers!"

"Ol Anderson said he wuz gonna bringa barrela tar!"

"Ah got some gasoline in mah car ef yuh need it."

Big boy had no feelings now. He was waiting. He did not wonder if they were coming after him. He just waited. He did not wonder about Bobo. He rested his cheek against the cold clay, waiting.

A dog barked. He stiffened. It barked again. He balled himself into a knot at the bottom of the hole, waiting. Then he heard the patter of dog feet.

"Look!"

"Whuts he got?"

"Its a snake!"

"Yeah, the dogs foun a snake!"

"Gee, its a big one!"

"Shucks, Ah wish he could fin one of them sonofabitchin niggers!"

The voices sank to low murmurs. Then he heard number twelve, its bell tolling and whistle crying as it slid along the rails. He flattened himself against the clay. Someone was singing:

"We'll hang ever nigger t a sour apple tree . . ."

When the song ended there was hard laughter. From the other side of the hill he heard the dog barking furiously. He listened. There was more than one dog now. There were many and they were barking their throats out.

"Hush, Ah hear them dogs!"

"When theys barkin like tha theys foun somethin!"

"Here they come over the hill!"

"WE GOT IM! WE GOT IM!"

There came a roar. Tha mus be Bobo; tha mus be Bobo . . . In spite of his fear, Big Boy looked. The road, and half of the hillside across the road, were covered with men. A few were at the top of the hill, stenciled against the sky. He could see dark forms moving up the slopes. They were yelling.

"By Gawd, we got im!"

"C mon!"

"Where is he?"

"Theyre bringin im over the hill!"

"Ah got a rope fer im!"

"Say, somebody go n git the others!"

"Where is he? Cant we see im, Mister?"

"They say Berthas comin, too."

"Jack! Jack! Don leave me! Ah wanna see im!"

"Theyre bringin im over the hill, sweetheart!"

"AH WANNA BE THE FIRS T PUT A ROPE ON THA BLACK BASTARDS NECK!"

"Les start the fire!"

"Heat the tar!"

"Ah got some chains t chain im."

"Bring im over this way!"

"Chris, Ah wished Ah hada drink . . ."

Big Boy saw men moving over the hill. Among them was a long dark spot. Tha mus be Bobo; tha mus be Bobo theys carryin . . . They'll git im here. He oughta git up n run. He clamped his teeth and ran his hand across his forehead, bringing it away wet. He tried to swallow, but could not; his throat was dry.

They had started the song again:

"We'll hang ever nigger t a sour apple tree . . ."

There were women singing now. Their voices made the song round and full. Song waves rolled over the top of pine trees. The sky sagged low, heavy with clouds. Wind was rising. Sometimes cricket cries cut surprisingly across the mob song. A dog had gone to the utmost top of the hill. At each lull of the song his howl floated full into the night.

Big Boy shrank when he saw the first tall flame light the hillside. Would they see im here? Then he remembered you could not see into the dark if you were standing in the light. As flames leaped higher he saw two men rolling a barrel up the slope.

"Say, gimme a han here, will yuh?"

"Awright, heave!"

"C mon! Straight up! Git t the other end!"

"Ah got the feathers here in this pillar!"

"BRING SOME MO WOOD!"

Big Boy could see the barrel surrounded by flames. The mob fell back, forming a dark circle. Theyd fin im here! He had a wild impuse to climb out and fly across the hills. But his legs would not move. He stared hard, trying to find Bobo. His eyes played over a long dark spot near the fire. Fanned by wind, flames leaped higher. He jumped. That dark spot had moved. Lawd, thas Bobo; thas Bobo . . .

He smelt the scent of tar, faint at first, then stronger. The wind brought it full into his face, then blew it away. His eyes burned and he rubbed them with his knuckles. He sneezed.

"LES GIT SOURVINEERS!"

He saw the mob close in around the fire. Their faces were hard and sharp in the light of the flames. More men and women were coming over the hill. The long dark spot was smudged out.

"Everybody git back!"

"Look! Hes gotta finger!"

"C MON! GIT THE GALS BACK FROM THE FIRE!"

"Hes got one of his ears, see?"

"Whuts the matter!"

"A woman fell out! Fainted, Ah reckon . . ."

The stench of tar permeated the hillside. The sky was black and the wind was blowing hard.

"HURRY UP N BURN THE NIGGER FO IT RAINS!"

Big Boy saw the mob fall back, leaving a small knot of men about the fire. Then, for the first time, he had a full glimpse of Bobo. A black body flashed in the light. Bobo was struggling, twisting; they were binding his arms and legs.

When he saw them tilt the barrel he stiffened. A scream quivered. He knew the tar was on Bobo. The mob fell back. He saw a tar-drenched body glistening and turning.

"THE BASTARDS GOT IT!"

There was a sudden quiet. Then he shrank violently as the wind carried, like a flurry of snow, a widening spiral of white feathers into the night. The flames leaped tall as the trees. The scream came again. Big Boy trembled and looked. The mob was running down the slopes, leaving the fire clear. Then he saw a writhing white mass cradled in yellow flame, and heard screams, one on top of the other, each shriller and shorter than the last. The mob was quiet now, standing still, looking up the slopes at the writhing white mass gradually growing black, growing black in a cradle of yellow flame.

"PO ON MO GAS!"

"Gimme a lif, will yuh!"

Two men were struggling, carrying between them a heavy can. They set it down, tilted it, leaving it so that the gas would trickle down to the hollowed earth around the fire.

Big Boy slid back into the hole, his face buried in clay. He had no feelings now, no fears. He was numb, empty, as though all blood had been drawn from him. Then his muscles flexed taut when he heard a faint patter. A tiny stream of cold water seeped to his knees, making him push back to a drier spot. He looked up; rain was beating in the grass.

"Its rainin!"

"C mon, les git t town!"

". . . don worry, when the fire git thu wid im hell be gone . . ."

"Wait, Charles! Don leave me; its slippery here . . ."

"Ahll take some of yuh ladies back in mah car . . ."

Big Boy heard the dogs barking again, this time closer. Running feet pounded past. Cold water chilled his ankles. He could hear raindrops steadily hissing.

Now a dog was barking at the mouth of the hole, barking furiously, sensing a presence there. He balled himself into a knot and clung to the bottom, his knees and shins buried in water. The bark came louder. He heard paws scraping and felt the hot scent of dog breath on his face. Green eyes glowed and drew nearer as the barking, muffled by the closeness of the hole, beat upon his eardrums. Backing till his shoulders pressed against the clay, he held his breath. He pushed out his hands, his fingers stiff. The dog yawped louder, advancing, his bark rising sharp and thin. Big Boy rose to his knees, his hands before him. Then he flattened out still more against the bottom, breathing lungsful of hot dog scent, breathing it slowly, hard, but evenly. The dog came closer, bringing hotter dog scent. Big Boy could go back no more. His knees were slipping and slopping in the water. He braced himself, ready. Then, he never exactly knew how—he never knew whether he had lunged or the dog had lunged—they were together, rolling in the water. The green eyes were beneath him, between his legs. Dognails bit into his arms. His knees slipped backward and he landed full on the dog; the dog's breath left in a heavy gasp. Instinctively, he fumbled for the throat as he felt the dog twisting between his knees. The dog snarled, long and low, as though gathering strength. Big Boy's hands traveled swiftly over the dog's back, groping for the throat. He felt dognails again and saw green eyes, but his fingers had found the throat. He choked, feeling his fingers sink; he choked, throwing back his head and stiffening his arms. He felt the dog's body heave, felt dognails digging into his loins. With strength flowing from fear, he closed his fingers, pushing his full weight on the dog's throat. The dog heaved again, and lay still . . . Big Boy heard the sound of his own breathing filling the hole, and heard shouts and footsteps above him going past.

For a long, long time he held the dog, held it long after the last footstep had died out, long after the rain had stopped.

V

Morning found him still on his knees in a puddle of rainwater, staring at the stiff body of a dog. As the air brightened he came to himself slowly. He held still for a long time, as though waking from a dream, as though trying to remember.

The chug of a truck came over the hill. He tried to crawl to the opening. His knees were stiff and a thousand needle-like pains shot from the bottom of his feet to the calves of his legs. Giddiness made his eyes blur. He pulled up and looked. Through brackish light he saw Will's truck standing some twenty-five yards away, the engine running. Will stood on the runningboard, looking over the slopes of the hill.

Big Boy scuffled out, falling weakly in the wet grass. He tried to call to Will, but his dry throat would make no sound. He tried again.

"Will!"

Will heard, answering:

"Big Boy, c mon!"

He tried to run, and fell. Will came, meeting him in the tall grass.

"C mon," Will said, catching his arm.

They struggled to the truck.

"Hurry up!" said Will, pushing him onto the runningboard.

Will pushed back a square trapdoor which swung above the back of the driver's seat. Big Boy pulled through, landing with a thud on the bottom. On hands and knees he looked around in the semi-darkness.

"Wheres Bobo?"

Big Boy stared.

"Wheres Bobo?"

"They got im."

"When?"

"Las night."

"The mob?"

Big Boy pointed in the direction of a charred sapling on the slope of the opposite hill. Will looked. The trapdoor fell. The engine purred, the gears whined, and the truck lurched forward over the muddy road, sending Big Boy on his side.

For a while he lay as he had fallen, on his side, too weak to move. As he felt the truck swing around a curve he straightened up and rested his back against a stack of wooden boxes. Slowly, he began to make out objects in the darkness. Through two long cracks fell thin blades of daylight. The floor was of smooth steel, and cold to his thighs. Splinters and bits of sawdust danced with the rumble of the truck. Each time they swung around a curve he was pulled over the floor; he grabbed at corners of boxes to steady himself. Once he heard the crow of a rooster. It made him think of home, of ma and pa. He thought he remembered hearing somewhere that the house had burned, but could not remember where . . . It all seemed unreal now.

He was tired. He dozed, swaying with the lurch. Then he jumped awake. The truck was running smoothly, on gravel. Far away he heard two short blasts from the Buckeye Lumber Mill. Unconsciously, the thought sang through his mind: Its six erclock . . .

The trapdoor swung in. Will spoke through a corner of his mouth.

"How yuh comin?"

"Awright."

"How they git Bobo?"

"He wuz comin over the hill."

"Whut they do?"

"They burnt im . . . Will, Ah wan some water; mah throats like fire . . ."

"Well git some when we pass a fillin station."

Big Boy leaned back and dozed. He jerked awake when the truck stopped. He heard Will get out. He wanted to peep through the trapdoor, but was afraid. For a moment, the wild fear he had known in the hole came back. Spose theyd search n fin im? He quieted when he heard Will's footstep on the runningboard. The trapdoor pushed in. Will's hat came through, dripping.

"Take it, quick!"

Big Boy grabbed, spilling water into his face. The truck lurched. He drank. Hard cold lumps of brick rolled into his hot stomach. A dull pain made him bend over. His intestines seemed to be drawing into a tight knot. After a bit it eased, and he sat up, breathing softly.

The truck swerved. He blinked his eyes. The blades of daylight had turned brightly golden. The sun had risen.

The truck sped over the asphalt miles, sped northward, jolting him, shaking out of his bosom the crumbs of corn bread, making them dance with the splinters and sawdust in the golden blades of sunshine.

He turned on his side and slept.

A Rose
for Emily

WILLIAM FAULKNER

A skillful narrative of suspense, this story probably continues to fascinate readers because of the peculiar mixture of Southern and Gothic ends to which Faulkner has turned that suspense. Most fiction of terror has been shaped by the idea of startling disclosures, usually of some horror lurking behind the comfortably familiar surfaces of men's lives. Before the townspeople finally gain access to the secrets of Miss Emily's house, their efforts to do so are shown to involve Southern notions of honorable conduct and also the clash between older and younger generations in the South, as well as a more universal and understandably morbid curiosity. The development of the story lies not so much in the character of Miss Emily as in the progressive revelations by which we see her change from a figure in a tableau or an angel in a church window into a woman.

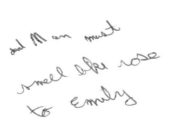

I

When Miss Emily Grierson died, our whole town went to her funeral: the men through a sort of respectful affection for a fallen monument, the women mostly out of curiosity to see the inside of her house, which no one save an old manservant— a combined gardener and cook—had seen in at least ten years.

It was a big, squarish frame house that had once been white, decorated with cupolas and spires and scrolled balconies in the heavily lightsome style of the seventies, set on what had once been our most select street. But garages and cotton gins had encroached and obliterated even the august names of that neighborhood; only Miss Emily's house was left, lifting its stubborn and coquettish decay above the cotton wagons and the gasoline pumps—an eyesore among eyesores. And now Miss Emily had gone to join the representatives of those august names where they lay in the cedar-bemused cemetery among the ranked and anonymous graves of Union and Confederate soldiers who fell at the battle of Jefferson.

Alive, Miss Emily had been a tradition, a duty, and a care; a sort of hereditary obligation upon the town, dating from that day in 1894 when Colonel Sartoris, the mayor—he who fathered the edict that no Negro woman should appear on the streets without an apron—remitted her taxes, the dispensation dating from the death of her father on into perpetuity. Not that Miss Emily would have accepted charity. Colonel Sartoris invented an involved tale to the effect that Miss Emily's father had loaned money to the town, which the town, as a matter of business, preferred this way of repaying. Only a man of Colonel Sartoris' generation and thought could have invented it, and only a woman could have believed it.

When the next generation, with its more modern ideas, became mayors and aldermen, this arrangement created some little dissatisfaction. On the first of the year they mailed her a tax notice. February came, and there was no reply. They wrote her a formal letter, asking her to call at the sheriff's office at her convenience. A week later the mayor wrote her himself, offering to call or to send his car for her, and received in reply a note on paper of an archaic shape, in a thin, flowing calligraphy in faded ink, to the effect that she no longer went out at all. The tax notice was also enclosed, without comment.

They called a special meeting of the Board of Aldermen. A deputation waited upon her, knocked at the door through which no visitor had passed since she ceased giving china-painting lessons eight or ten years earlier. They were admitted by the old Negro into a dim hall from which a stairway mounted into still more shadow. It smelled of dust and disuse—a close, dank smell. The Negro led them into the parlor. It was furnished in heavy, leather-covered furniture. When the Negro opened the blinds of one window, they could see that the leather was cracked; and when they sat down, a faint dust rose sluggishly about their thighs, spinning with slow motes in the single sun-ray. On a tarnished gilt easel before the fireplace stood a crayon portrait of Miss Emily's father.

They rose when she entered—a small, fat woman in black, with a thin gold chain descending to her waist and vanishing into her belt, leaning on an ebony cane with a tarnished gold head. Her skeleton was small and spare; perhaps that was why what would have been merely plumpness in another was obesity in her. She looked bloated, like a body long submerged in motionless water, and of that pallid hue. Her eyes, lost in the fatty ridges of her face, looked like two small pieces of coal pressed into a lump of dough as they moved from one face to another while the visitors stated their errand.

She did not ask them to sit. She just stood in the door and listened quietly until the spokesman came to a stumbling halt. Then they could hear the invisible watch ticking at the end of the gold chain.

Her voice was dry and cold. "I have no taxes in Jefferson. Colonel Sartoris explained it to me. Perhaps one of you can gain access to the city records and satisfy yourselves."

"But we have. We are the city authorities, Miss Emily. Didn't you get a notice from the sheriff, signed by him?"

"I received a paper, yes," Miss Emily said. "Perhaps he considers himself the sheriff . . . I have no taxes in Jefferson."

"But there is nothing on the books to show that, you see. We must go by the—"

"See Colonel Sartoris. I have no taxes in Jefferson."

"But, Miss Emily—"

"See Colonel Sartoris." (Colonel Sartoris had been dead almost ten years.) "I have no taxes in Jefferson. Tobe!" The Negro appeared. "Show these gentlemen out."

II

So she vanquished them, horse and foot, just as she had vanquished their fathers thirty years before about the smell. That was two years after her father's death and a short time after her sweetheart— the one we believed would marry her—had deserted her. After her father's death she went out very little; after her sweetheart went away, people hardly saw her at all. A few of the ladies had the temerity to call, but were not received, and the only sign of life about the place was the Negro man—a young man then—going in and out with a market basket.

"Just as if a man—any man—could keep a kitchen properly," the ladies said; so they were not surprised when the smell developed. It was another link between the gross, teeming world and the high and mighty Griersons.

A neighbor, a woman, complained to the mayor, Judge Stevens, eighty years old.

"But what will you have me do about it, madam?" he said.

"Why, send her word to stop it," the woman said. "Isn't there a law?"

"I'm sure that wont be necessary," Judge Stevens said. "It's probably just a snake or a rat that nigger of hers killed in the yard. I'll speak to him about it."

The next day he received two more complaints, one from a man who came in diffident deprecation. "We really must do something about it, Judge. I'd be the last one in the world to bother Miss Emily, but we've got to do something." That night the Board of Aldermen met—three graybeards and one younger man, a member of the rising generation.

"It's simple enough," he said. "Send her word to have her place cleaned up. Give her a certain time to do it in, and if she dont . . ."

"Dammit, sir," Judge Stevens said, "will you accuse a lady to her face of smelling bad?"

So the next night, after midnight, four men crossed Miss Emily's lawn and slunk about the house like burglars, sniffing along the base of the brickwork and at the cellar openings while one of them performed a regular sowing motion with his hand out of a sack slung from his shoulder. They broke open the cellar door and sprinkled lime there, and in all the outbuildings. As they recrossed the lawn, a window that had been dark was lighted and Miss

Emily sat in it, the light behind her, and her upright torso motionless as that of an idol. They crept quietly across the lawn and into the shadow of the locusts that lined the street. After a week or two the smell went away.

That was when people had begun to feel really sorry for her. People in our town, remembering how old lady Wyatt, her great-aunt, had gone completely crazy at last, believed that the Griersons held themselves a little too high for what they really were. None of the young men were quite good enough to Miss Emily and such. We had long thought of them as a tableau; Miss Emily a slender figure in white in the background, her father a spraddled silhouette in the foreground, his back to her and clutching a horse-whip, the two of them framed by the back-flung front door. So when she got to be thirty and was still single, we were not pleased exactly, but vindicated; even with insanity in the family she wouldn't have turned down all of her chances if they had really materialized.

When her father died, it got about that the house was all that was left to her; and in a way, people were glad. At last they could pity Miss Emily. Being left alone, and a pauper, she had become humanized. Now she too would know the old thrill and the old despair of a penny more or less.

The day after his death all the ladies prepared to call at the house and offer condolence and aid, as is our custom. Miss Emily met them at the door, dressed as usual and with no trace of grief on her face. She told them that her father was not dead. She did that for three days, with the ministers calling on her, and the doctors, trying to persuade her to let them dispose of the body. Just as they were about to resort to law and force, she broke down, and they buried her father quickly.

We did not say she was crazy then. We believed she had to do that. We remembered all the young men her father had driven away, and we knew that with nothing left, she would have to cling to that which had robbed her, as people will.

III

She was sick for a long time. When we saw her again, her hair was cut short, making her look like a girl, with a vague resemblance to those angels in colored church windows—sort of tragic and serene.

The town had just let the contracts for paving the sidewalks, and in the summer after her father's death they began the work. The construction company came with niggers and mules and machinery, and a foreman named Homer Barron, a Yankee—a big, dark, ready man, with a big voice and eyes lighter than his face. The little boys would follow in groups to hear him cuss the niggers, and the niggers singing in time to the rise and fall of picks. Pretty soon he knew everybody in town. Whenever you heard a lot of laughing anywhere about the square, Homer Barron would be in the center of the group. Presently we began to see him and Miss Emily on Sunday afternoons driving in the yellow-wheeled buggy and the matched team of bays from the livery stable.

At first we were glad that Miss Emily would have an interest, because the ladies all said, "Of course a Grierson would not think seriously of a Northerner, a day laborer." But there were still others, older people, who said that even grief could not cause a real lady to forget *noblesse oblige*—without calling it *noblesse oblige*. They just said, "Poor Emily. Her kinsfolk should come to her." She had some kin in Alabama; but years ago her father had fallen out with them over the estate of old lady Wyatt, the crazy woman, and there was no communication between the two families. They had not even been represented at the funeral.

And as soon as the old people said, "Poor Emily," the whispering began. "Do you suppose it's really so?" they said to one another. "Of course it is. What else could . . ." This behind their hands; rustling of craned silk and satin behind jalousies closed upon the sun of Sunday afternoon as the thin, swift clop-clop-clop of the matched team passed: "Poor Emily."

She carried her head high enough—even when we believed that she was fallen. It was as if she demanded more than ever the recognition of her dignity as the last Grierson; as if it had wanted that touch of earthiness to reaffirm her imperviousness. Like when she bought the rat poison, the arsenic. That was over a year after they had begun to say "Poor Emily," and while the two female cousins were visiting her.

"I want some poison," she said to the druggist. She was over thirty then, still a slight woman, though thinner than usual, with cold, haughty black eyes in a face the flesh of which was strained across the temples and about the eye-sockets as you imagine a light-house-keeper's face ought to look. "I want some poison," she said.

"Yes, Miss Emily. What kind? For rats and such? I'd recom—"

"I want the best you have. I dont care what kind."

The druggist named several. "They'll kill anything up to an elephant. But what you want is—"

"Arsenic," Miss Emily said. "Is that a good one?"

"Is . . . arsenic? Yes, ma'am. But what you want—"

"I want arsenic."

The druggist looked down at her. She looked back at him, erect, her face like a strained flag. "Why, of course," the druggist said. "If that's what you want. But the law requires you to tell what you are going to use it for."

Miss Emily just stared at him, her head tilted back in order to look him eye for eye, until he looked away and went and got the arsenic and wrapped it up. The Negro delivery boy brought her the package; the druggist didn't come back. When she opened the package at home there was written on the box, under the skull and bones: "For rats."

IV

So the next day we all said, "She will kill herself"; and we said it would be the best thing. When she had first begun to be seen with Homer Barron, we had said, "She will marry him." Then we said, "She will persuade him yet," because Homer himself had remarked—he liked men, and it was known that he drank with the younger men in the Elks' Club—that he was not a marrying man. Later we said, "Poor Emily" behind the jalousies as they passed on Sunday afternoon in the glittering buggy, Miss Emily with her head high and Homer Barron with his hat cocked and a cigar in his teeth, reins and whip in a yellow glove.

Then some of the ladies began to say that it was a disgrace to the town and a bad example to the young people. The men did not want to interfere, but at last the ladies forced the Baptist minister—Miss Emily's people were Episcopal—to call upon her. He would never divulge what happened during that interview, but he refused to go back again. The next Sunday they again drove about the streets, and the following day the minister's wife wrote to Miss Emily's relations in Alabama.

So she had blood-kin under her roof again and we sat back to watch developments. At first nothing happened. Then we were sure that they were to be married. We learned that Miss Emily had been to the jeweler's and ordered a man's toilet set in silver, with the letters H. B. on each piece. Two days later we learned that she had bought a complete outfit of men's clothing, including a nightshirt, and we said, "They are married." We were really glad. We were glad because the two female cousins were even more Grierson than Miss Emily had ever been.

So we were not surprised when Homer Barron—the streets had been finished some time since—was gone. We were a little disappointed that there was not a public blowing-off, but we believed that he had gone on to prepare for Miss Emily's coming, or to give her a chance to get rid of the cousins. (By that time it was a cabal, and we were all Miss Emily's allies to help circumvent the cousins.) Sure enough, after another week they departed. And, as we had expected all along, within three days Homer Barron was back in town. A neighbor saw the Negro man admit him at the kitchen door at dusk one evening.

And that was the last we saw of Homer Barron. And of Miss Emily for some time. The Negro man went in and out with the market basket, but the front door remained closed. Now and then we would see her at a window for a moment, as the men did that night when they sprinkled the lime, but for almost six months she did not appear on the streets. Then we knew that this was to be expected too; as if that quality of her father which had thwarted her woman's life so many times had been too virulent and too furious to die.

When we next saw Miss Emily, she had grown fat and her hair was turning gray. During the next few years it grew grayer and grayer until it attained an even pepper-and-salt iron-gray, when it ceased turning. Up to the day of her death at seventy-four it was still that vigorous iron-gray, like the hair of an active man.

From that time on her front door remained closed, save for a period of six or seven years, when she was about forty, during which she gave lessons in china-painting. She fitted up a studio in one of the downstairs rooms, where the daughters and grand-daughters of Colonel Sartoris' contemporaries were sent to her with the same regularity and in the same spirit that they were sent to church on Sundays with a twenty-five cent piece for the collection plate. Meanwhile her taxes had been remitted.

Then the newer generation became the backbone and the spirit of the town, and the painting pupils grew up and fell away and did not send their children to her with boxes of color and tedious brushes and pictures cut from the ladies' magazines. The front door closed upon the last one and remained closed for good. When the town got free postal delivery, Miss Emily alone refused to let them fasten the metal numbers above her door and attach a mailbox to it. She would not listen to them.

Daily, monthly, yearly we watched the Negro grow grayer and more stooped, going in and out with the market basket. Each December we sent her a tax notice, which would be returned by the post office a week later, unclaimed. Now and then we would see her in one of the downstairs windows—she had evidently shut up the top floor of the house—like the carven torso of an idol in a niche, looking or not looking at us, we could never tell which. Thus she passed from generation to generation—dear, inescapable, impervious, tranquil, and perverse.

And so she died. Fell ill in the house filled with dust and shadows, with only a doddering Negro man to wait on her. We did not even know she was sick; we had long since given up trying to get any information from the Negro. He talked to no one, probably not even to her, for his voice had grown harsh and rusty, as if from disuse.

She died in one of the downstairs rooms, in a heavy walnut bed with a curtain, her gray head propped on a pillow yellow and moldy with age and lack of sunlight.

V

The Negro met the first of the ladies at the front door and let them in, with their hushed, sibilant voices and their quick, curious glances, and then he disappeared. He walked right through the house and out the back and was not seen again.

The two female cousins came at once. They held the funeral on the second day, with the town coming to look at Miss Emily beneath a mass of bought flowers, with the crayon face of her father musing profoundly above the bier and the ladies sibilant and macabre; and the very old men—some in their brushed Confederate uniforms—on the porch and the lawn, talking of Miss Emily as if she had been a contemporary of theirs, believing that they had danced with her and courted her perhaps, confusing time with its mathematical progression, as the old do, to whom all the past is not a diminishing road but, instead, a huge meadow which no winter ever quite touches, divided from them now by the narrow bottle-neck of the most recent decade of years.

Already we knew that there was one room in that region above stairs which no one had seen in forty years, and which would have to be forced. They waited until Miss Emily was decently in the ground before they opened it.

The violence of breaking down the door seemed to fill this room with pervading dust. A thin, acrid pall as of the tomb ·seemed to lie everywhere upon this room decked and furnished as for a bridal: upon the valence curtains of faded rose color, upon the rose-shaded lights, upon the dressing table, upon the delicate array of crystal and the man's toilet things backed with tarnished silver, silver so tarnished that the monogram was obscured. Among them lay a collar and tie, as if they had just been removed, which, lifted, left upon the surface a pale crescent in the dust. Upon a chair hung the suit, carefully folded; beneath it the two mute shoes and the discarded socks.

The man himself lay in the bed.

For a long while we just stood there, looking down at the profound and fleshless grin. The body had apparently once lain in the attitude of an embrace, but now the long sleep that outlasts love, that conquers even the grimace of love, had cuckolded him. What was left of him, rotted beneath what was left of the nightshirt, had become inextricable from the bed in which he lay; and upon him and upon the pillow beside him lay that even coating of the patient and biding dust.

Then we noticed that in the second pillow was the indentation of a head. One of us lifted something from it, and leaning forward, that faint and invisible dust dry and acrid in the nostrils, we saw a long strand of iron-gray hair.

Spotted Horses

WILLIAM FAULKNER

A humorous yarn in its own right, "Spotted Horses" is also a loosely integral portion of Faulkner's novel, or story cycle, The Hamlet. *That longer work deals with the Snopeses, one of several families whose evolution provides much of the subject matter for the author's fictive Yoknapatawpha County. "Spotted Horses" thus has a dual focus: as a story with its own imaginative center, and as a fragment of a literary myth whose center lies elsewhere. The effect of this duality is sometimes a certain diffuseness, sometimes merely an obscurity of detail, as in the slightly indistinct role played in the story by Ratliff. For the most part, however, the loose-jointedness of this section of* The Hamlet *finds a sufficient rationale in the American tall tale, whose anecdotal, vernacular, hyperbolic, and violent elements are all recognizably here, the wild destructiveness to limb and property sitting grotesquely, as it does in Mark Twain's stretchers, alongside if somewhat in the shadow of the fun.*

A little while before sundown the men lounging about the gallery of the store saw, coming up the road from the south, a covered wagon drawn by mules and followed by a considerable string of obviously alive objects which in the levelling sun resembled vari-sized and -colored tatters torn at random from large billboards —circus posters, say—attached to the rear of the wagon and inherent with its own separate and collective motion, like the tail of a kite.

"What in the hell is that?" one said.

"It's a circus," Quick said. They began to rise, watching the wagon. Now they could see that the animals behind the wagon were horses. Two men rode in the wagon.

"Hell fire," the first man—his name was Freeman—said. "It's Flem Snopes." They were all standing when the wagon came up and stopped and Snopes got down and approached the steps. He might have departed only this morning. He wore the same cloth cap, the minute bow tie against the white shirt, the same gray trousers. He mounted the steps.

"Howdy, Flem," Quick said. The other looked briefly at all of them and none of them, mounting the steps. "Starting you a circus?"

"Gentlemen," he said. He crossed the gallery; they made way for him. Then they descended the steps and approached the wagon, at the tail of which the horses stood in a restive clump, larger than rabbits and gaudy as parrots and shackled to one another and to the wagon itself with sections of barbed wire. Calico-coated, small-bodied, with delicate legs and pink faces in which their mismatched eyes rolled wild and subdued, they huddled, gaudy motionless and alert, wild as deer, deadly as rattlesnakes, quiet as doves. The men stood at a respectful distance, looking at them. At that moment Jody Varner came through the group, shouldering himself to the front of it.

"Watch yourself, doc," a voice said from the rear. But it was already too late. The nearest animal rose on its hind legs with lightning rapidity and struck twice with its forefeet at Varner's face, faster than a boxer, the movement of its surge against the wire which held it travelling backward among the rest of the band in a wave of thuds and lunges. "Hup, you broom-tailed hay-burning side-winders," the same voice said. This was the second man who had arrived in the wagon. He was a stranger. He wore a heavy densely black moustache, a wide pale hat. When he thrust himself through and turned to herd them back from the horses they saw, thrust into the hip pockets of his tight jeans pants, the butt of a heavy pearl-handled pistol and a florid carton such as small cakes come in. "Keep away from them, boys," he said. "They've got kind of skittish, they aint been rode in so long."

"Since when have they been rode?" Quick said. The stranger looked at Quick. He had a broad, quite cold, wind-gnawed face and bleak cold eyes. His belly fitted neat and smooth as a peg into the tight trousers.

"I reckon that was when they were rode on the ferry to get across the Mississippi River," Varner said. The stranger looked at him. "My name's Varner," Jody said.

"Hipps," the other said. "Call me Buck." Across the left side of his head, obliterating the tip of that ear, was a savage and recent gash gummed over with a blackish substance like axle-grease. They looked at the scar. Then they watched him remove the carton from his pocket and tilt a gingersnap into his hand and put the gingersnap into his mouth, beneath the moustache.

"You and Flem have some trouble back yonder?" Quick said. The stranger ceased chewing. When he looked directly at anyone, his eyes became like two pieces of flint turned suddenly up in dug earth.

"Back where?" he said.

"Your nigh ear," Quick said.

"Oh," the other said. "That." He touched his ear. "That was my mistake. I was absent-minded one night when I was staking them out. Studying about something else and forgot how long the wire was." He chewed. They looked at his ear. "Happen to any man careless around a horse. Put a little axle-dope on it and you wont notice it tomorrow though. They're pretty lively now, lazing along all day doing nothing. It'll work out of them in a couple of days." He put another gingersnap into his mouth, chewing, "Dont you be-lieve they'll gentle?" No one answered. They looked at the ponies, grave and noncommittal. Jody turned and went back into the store. "Them's good, gentle ponies," the stranger said. "Watch now." He put the carton back into his pocket and approached the horses, his hand extended. The nearest one was standing on three legs now.

It appeared to be asleep. Its eyelid drooped over the cerulean eye; its head was shaped like an ironingboard. Without even raising the eyelid it flicked its head, the yellow teeth cropped. For an instant it and the man appeared to be inextricable in one violence. Then they became motionless, the stranger's high heels dug into the earth, one hand gripping the animal's nostrils, holding the horse's head wrenched half around while it breathed in hoarse, smothered groans. "See?" the stranger said in a panting voice, the veins standing white and rigid in his neck and along his jaw. "See? All you got to do is handle them a little and work hell out of them for a couple of days. Now look out. Give me room back there." They gave back a little. The stranger gathered himself then sprang away. As he did so, a second horse slashed at his back, severing his vest from collar to hem down the back exactly as the trick swordsman severs a floating veil with one stroke.

"Sho now," Quick said. "But suppose a man dont happen to own a vest."

At that moment Jody Varner, followed by the blacksmith, thrust through them again. "All right, Buck," he said. "Better get them on into the lot. Eck here will help you." The stranger, the several halves of the vest swinging from either shoulder, mounted to the wagon seat, the blacksmith following.

"Get up, you transmogrified hallucinations of Job and Jezebel," the stranger said. The wagon moved on, the tethered ponies coming gaudily into motion behind it, behind which in turn the men followed at a respectful distance, on up the road and into the lane and so to the lot gate behind Mrs Littlejohn's. Eck got down and opened the gate. The wagon passed through but when the ponies saw the fence the herd surged backward against the wire which attached it to the wagon, standing on its collective hind legs and then trying to turn within itself, so that the wagon moved backward for a few feet until the Texan, cursing, managed to saw the mules about and so lock the wheels. The men following had already fallen rapidly back. "Here, Eck," the Texan said. "Get up here and take the reins." The blacksmith got back in the wagon and took the reins. Then they watched the Texan descend, carrying a looped-up blacksnake whip, and go around to the rear of the herd and drive it through the gate, the whip snaking about the harlequin rumps in methodical and pistol-like reports. Then the watchers hurried across Mrs Littlejohn's yard and mounted to the veranda, one end of which overlooked the lot.

"How you reckon he ever got them tied together?" Freeman said.

"I'd a heap rather watch how he aims to turn them loose," Quick said. The Texan had climbed back into the halted wagon. Presently he and Eck both appeared at the rear end of the open hood. The Texan grasped the wire and began to draw the first horse up to the wagon, the animal plunging and surging back against the wire as though trying to hang itself, the contagion passing back through the herd from animal to animal until they were rearing and plunging again against the wire.

"Come on, grab a holt," the Texan said. Eck grasped the wire also. The horses laid back against it, the pink faces tossing above the back-surging mass. "Pull him up, pull him up," the Texan said sharply. "They couldn't get up here in the wagon even if they wanted to." The wagon moved gradually backward until the head of the first horse was snubbed up to the tail-gate. The Texan took a turn of the wire quickly about one of the wagon stakes. "Keep the slack out of it," he said. He vanished and reappeared, almost in the same second, with a pair of heavy wire-cutters. "Hold them like that," he said, and leaped. He vanished, broad hat, flapping vest, wire-cutters and all, into a kaleidoscopic maelstrom of long teeth and wild eyes and slashing feet, from which presently the horses began to burst one by one like partridges flushing, each wearing a necklace of barbed wire. The first one crossed the lot at top speed, on a straight line. It galloped into the fence without any diminution whatever. The wire gave, recovered, and slammed the horse to earth where it lay for a moment, glaring, its legs still galloping in air. It scrambled up without having ceased to gallop and crossed the lot and galloped into the opposite fence and was slammed again to earth. The others were now freed. They whipped and whirled about the lot like dizzy fish in a bowl. It had seemed like a big lot until now, but now the very idea that all that fury and motion should be transpiring inside any one fence was something to be repudiated with contempt, like a mirror trick. From the ultimate dust the stranger, carrying the wire-cutters and his vest completely gone now, emerged. He was not running, he merely moved with a light-poised and watchful celerity, weaving among the calico rushes of the animals, feinting and dodging like a boxer until he reached the gate and crossed the yard and mounted to the veranda. One sleeve of his shirt hung only at one point from his shoulder. He ripped it off and wiped his face with it and threw it away and took out the paper carton and shook a gingersnap into his hand. He was breathing only a little heavily. "Pretty lively now," he said. "But it'll work out of them in a couple of days." The ponies still streaked back and forth through the growing dusk like hysterical fish, but not so violently now.

"What'll you give a man to reduce them odds a little for you?" Quick said. The Texan looked at him, the eyes bleak, pleasant and hard above the chewing jaw, the heavy moustache. "To take one of them off your hands?" Quick said.

At that moment the little periwinkle-eyed boy came along the veranda, saying, "Papa, papa; where's papa?"

"Who you looking for, sonny?" one said.

"It's Eck's boy," Quick said. "He's still out yonder in the wagon. Helping Mr Buck here." The boy went on to the end of the veranda, in diminutive overalls—a miniature replica of the men themselves.

"Papa," he said. "Papa." The blacksmith was still leaning from the rear of the wagon, still holding the end of the severed wire. The ponies, bunched for the moment, now slid past the wagon, flowing, stringing out again so that they appeared to have doubled in number, rushing on; the hard rapid light patter of unshod hooves came out of the dust. "Mamma says to come on to supper," the boy said.

The moon was almost full then. When supper was over and they had gathered again along the veranda, the alteration was hardly one of visibility even. It was merely a translation from the lapidary-dimensional of day to the treacherous and silver receptivity in which the horses huddled in mazy camouflage, or singly or in pairs rushed, fluid, phantom, and unceasing, to huddle again in mirage-like clumps from which came high abrupt squeals and the vicious thudding of hooves.

Ratliff was among them now. He had returned just before supper. He had not dared to take his team into the lot at all. They were now in Bookwright's stable a half mile from the store. "So Flem has come home again," he said. "Well, well, well. Will Varner paid to get him to Texas, so I reckon it aint no more than fair for you fellows to pay the freight on him back." From the lot there came a high thin squeal. One of the animals emerged. It seemed not to gallop but to flow, bodiless, without dimension. Yet there was the rapid light beat of hard hooves on the packed earth.

"He aint said they was his yet," Quick said.

"He aint said they aint neither," Freeman said.

"I see," Ratliff said. "That's what you are holding back on. Until he tells you whether they are his or not. Or maybe you can wait until the auction's over and split up and some can follow Flem and some can follow that Texas fellow and watch to see which one spends the money. But then, when a man's done got trimmed, I dont reckon he cares who's got the money."

"Maybe if Ratliff would leave here tonight, they wouldn't make him buy one of them ponies tomorrow," a third said.

"That's a fact," Ratliff said. "A fellow can dodge a Snopes if he just starts lively enough. In fact, I dont believe he would have to pass more than two folks before he would have another victim intervened betwixt them. You folks aint going to buy them things sho enough, are you?" Nobody answered. They sat on the steps, their backs against the veranda posts, or on the railing itself. Only Ratliff and Quick sat in chairs, so that to them the others were black silhouettes against the dreaming lambence of the moonlight beyond the veranda. The pear tree across the road opposite was now in full and frosty bloom, the twigs and branches springing not outward from the limbs but standing motionless and perpendicular above the horizontal boughs like the separate and upstreaming hair of a drowned woman sleeping upon the uttermost floor of the windless and tideless sea.

"Anse McCallum brought two of them horses back from Texas once," one of the men on the steps said. He did not move to speak. He was not speaking to anyone. "It was a good team. A little light. He worked it for ten years. Light work, it was."

"I mind it," another said. "Anse claimed he traded fourteen rifle cartridges for both of them, didn't he?"

"It was the rifle too, I heard," a third said.

"No, it was just the shells," the first said. "The fellow wanted to swap him four more for the rifle too, but Anse said he never needed them. Cost too much to get six of them back to Mississippi."

"Sho," the second said. "When a man dont have to invest so much into a horse or a team, he dont need to expect so much from it." The three of them were not talking any louder, they were merely talking among themselves, to one another, as if they sat there alone. Ratliff, invisible in the shadow against the wall, made a sound, harsh, sardonic, not loud.

"Ratliff's laughing," a fourth said.

"Dont mind me," Ratliff said. The three speakers had not moved. They did not move now, yet there seemed to gather about the three silhouettes something stubborn, convinced, and passive, like children who have been chidden. A bird, a shadow, fleet and dark and swift, curved across the moonlight, upward into the pear tree and began to sing; a mockingbird.

"First one I've noticed this year," Freeman said.

"You can hear them along Whiteleaf every night," the first man said. "I heard one in February. In that snow. Singing in a gum."

"Gum is the first tree to put out," the third said. "That was why. It made it feel like singing, fixing to put out that way. That was why it taken a gum."

"Gum first to put out?" Quick said. "What about willow?"

"Willow aint a tree," Freeman said. "It's a weed."

"Well, I dont know what it is," the fourth said. "But it aint no weed. Because you can grub up a weed and you are done with it. I been grubbing up a clump of willows outen my spring pasture for fifteen years. They are the same size every year. Only difference is, it's just two or three more trees every time."

"And if I was you," Ratliff said, "that's just exactly where I would be come sunup tomorrow. Which of course you aint going to do. I reckon there aint nothing under the sun or in Frenchman's Bend neither that can keep you folks from giving Flem Snopes and that Texas man your money. But I'd sholy like to know just exactly who I was giving my money to. Seems like Eck here would tell you. Seems like he'd do that for his neighbors, dont it? Besides being Flem's cousin, him and that boy of his, Wallstreet, helped that Texas man tote water for them tonight and Eck's going to help him feed them in the morning too. Why, maybe Eck will be the one that will catch them and lead them up one at a time for you folks to bid on them. Aint that right, Eck?"

The other man sitting on the steps with his back against the post was the blacksmith. "I dont know," he said.

"Boys," Ratliff said, "Eck knows all about them horses. Flem's told him, how much they cost and how much him and that Texas man aim to get for them, make off of them. Come on, Eck. Tell us." The other did not move, sitting on the top step, not quite facing them, sitting there beneath the successive layers of their quiet and intent concentrated listening and waiting.

"I dont know," he said. Ratliff began to laugh. He sat in the chair, laughing while the others sat or lounged upon the steps and the railing, sitting beneath his laughing as Eck had sat beneath their listening and waiting. Ratliff ceased laughing. He rose. He yawned, quite loud.

"All right. You folks can buy them critters if you want to. But me, I'd just as soon buy a tiger or a rattlesnake. And if Flem Snopes offered me either one of them, I would be afraid to touch it for fear it would turn out to be a painted dog or a piece of garden hose when I went up to take possession of it. I bid you one and all goodnight." He entered the house. They did not look after him, though after a while they all shifted a little and looked down into the lot, upon the splotchy, sporadic surge and flow of the horses, from among which from time to time came an abrupt squeal, a thudding blow. In the pear tree the mockingbird's idiot reiteration pulsed and purled.

"Anse McCallum made a good team outen them two of hisn," the first man said. "They was a little light. That was all."

When the sun rose the next morning a wagon and three saddled mules stood in Mrs Littlejohn's lane and six men and Eck Snopes' son were already leaning on the fence, looking at the horses which huddled in a quiet clump before the barn door, watching the men in their turn. A second wagon came up the road and into the lane and stopped, and then there were eight men beside the boy standing at the fence, beyond which the horses stood, their blue-and-brown eyeballs rolling alertly in their gaudy faces. "So this here is the Snopes circus, is it?" one of the newcomers said. He glanced at the faces, then he went to the end of the row and stood beside the blacksmith and the little boy. "Are them Flem's horses?" he said to the blacksmith.

"Eck dont know who them horses belong to anymore than we do," one of the others said. "He knows that Flem come here on the same wagon with them, because he saw him. But that's all."

"And all he will know," a second said. "His own kin will be the last man in the world to find out anything about Flem Snopes's business."

"No," the first said. "He wouldn't even be that. The first man Flem would tell his business to would be the man that was left after the last man died. Flem Snopes dont even tell himself what he is up to. Not if he was laying in bed with himself in a empty house in the dark of the moon."

"That's a fact," a third said. "Flem would trim Eck or any other of his kin quick as he would us. Aint that right, Eck?"

"I dont know," Eck said. They were watching the horses, which at that moment broke into a high-eared, stiff-kneed swirl and flowed in a patchwork wave across the lot and brought up again, facing the men along the fence, so they did not hear the Texan until he was among them. He wore a new shirt and another vest a little too small for him and he was just putting the paper carton back into his hip pocket.

"Morning, morning," he said. "Come to get an early pick, have you? Want to make me an offer for one or two before the bidding starts and runs the prices up?" They had not looked at the stranger long. They were not looking at him now, but at the horses in the lot, which had lowered their heads, snuffing into the dust.

"I reckon we'll look a while first," one said.

"You are in time to look at them eating breakfast, anyhow," the Texan said. "Which is more than they done without they staid up all night." He opened the gate and entered it. At once the horses jerked their heads up, watching him. "Here, Eck," the Texan said over his shoulder, "two or three of you boys help me drive them into the barn." After a moment Eck and two others approached the gate, the little boy at his father's heels, though the other did not see him until he turned to shut the gate.

"You stay out of here," Eck said. "One of them things will snap your head off same as a acorn before you even know it." He shut the gate and went on after the others, whom the Texan had now waved fanwise outward as he approached the horses which now drew into a restive huddle, beginning to mill slightly, watching the men. Mrs Littlejohn came out of the kitchen and crossed the yard to the woodpile, watching the lot. She picked up two or three sticks of wood and paused, watching the lot again. Now there were two more men standing at the fence.

"Come on, come on," the Texan said. "They wont hurt you. They just aint never been in under a roof before."

"I just as lief let them stay out here, if that's what they want to do," Eck said.

"Get yourself a stick—there's a bunch of wagon stakes against the fence yonder—and when one of them tries to rush you, bust him over the head so he will understand what you mean." One of the men went to the fence and got three of the stakes and returned and distributed them. Mrs Littlejohn, her armful of wood complete now, paused again halfway back to the house, looking into the lot. The little boy was directly behind his father again, though this time the father had not discovered him yet. The men advanced toward the horses, the huddle of which began to break into gaudy units turning inward upon themselves. The Texan was cursing them in a loud steady cheerful voice. "Get in there, you banjo-faced jack rabbits. Dont hurry them, now. Let them take their time. Hi! Get in there. What do you think that barn is—a law court maybe? Or maybe a church and somebody is going to take up a collection on you?" The animals fell slowly back. Now and then one feinted to break from the huddle, the Texan driving it back each time with skillfully thrown bits of dirt. Then one at the rear saw the barn door just behind it but before the herd could break the Texan snatched the wagon stake from Eck and, followed by one of the other men, rushed at the horses and began to lay about the heads and shoulders, choosing by unerring instinct the point animal and striking it first square in the face then on the withers as it turned and then on the rump as it turned further, so that when the break came it was reversed and the entire herd rushed into the long open hallway and brought up against the further wall with a hollow, thunderous sound like that of a collapsing mine-shaft. "Seems to have held all right," the Texan said. He and the other man slammed the half-length doors and looked over them into the tunnel of the barn, at the far end of which the ponies were now a splotchy phantom moiling punctuated by crackings of wooden partitions and the dry reports of hooves which gradually died away. "Yep, it held all right," the Texan said. The other two came to the doors and looked over them. The little boy came up beside his father now, trying to see through a crack, and Eck saw him.

"Didn't I tell you to stay out of here?" Eck said. "Dont you know them things will kill you quicker than you can say scat? You go and get outside of that fence and stay there."

"Why dont you get your paw to buy you one of them, Wall?" one of the men said.

"Me buy one of them things?" Eck said. "When I can go to the river anytime and catch me a snapping turtle or a moccasin for nothing? You go on, now. Get out of here and stay out." The Texan had entered the barn. One of the men closed the doors after him and put the bar up again and over the top of the doors they watched the Texan go on down the hallway, toward the ponies which now huddled like gaudy phantoms in the gloom, quiet now and already beginning to snuff experimentally into the long lipworn trough fastened against the rear wall. The little boy had merely gone around behind his father, to the other side, where he stood peering now through a knot-hole in a plank. The Texan opened a smaller door in the wall and entered it, though almost immediately he reappeared.

"I dont see nothing but shelled corn in here," he said. "Snopes said he would send some hay up here last night."

"Wont they eat corn either?" one of the men said.

"I dont know," the Texan said. "They aint never seen any that I know of. We'll find out in a minute though." He disappeared, though they could still hear him in the crib. Then he emerged once more, carrying a big double-ended feed-basket, and retreated into the gloom where the parti-colored rumps of the horses were now ranged quietly along the feeding-trough. Mrs Littlejohn appeared once more, on the veranda this time, carrying a big brass dinner bell. She raised it to make the first stroke. A small commotion set up among the ponies as the Texan approached but he began to speak to them at once, in a brisk loud unemphatic mixture of cursing and cajolery, disappearing among them. The men at the door heard the dry rattling of the corn-pellets into the trough, a sound broken by a single snort of amazed horror. A plank cracked with a loud report; before their eyes the depths of the hallway dissolved in loud fury, and while they stared over the doors, unable yet to begin to move, the entire interior exploded into mad tossing shapes like a downrush of flames.

"Hell fire," one of them said. "Jump!" he shouted. The three turned and ran frantically for the wagon, Eck last. Several voices from the fence were now shouting something but Eck did not even hear them until, in the act of scrambling madly at the tail-gate, he looked behind him and saw the little boy still leaning to the knot-hole in the door which in the next instant vanished into matchwood, the knot-hole itself exploding from his eye and leaving him, motionless in the diminutive overalls and still leaning forward a little until he vanished utterly beneath the towering parti-colored wave full of feet and glaring eyes and wild teeth which, overtopping, burst into scattering units, revealing at last the gaping orifice and the little boy still standing in it, unscratched, his eye still leaned to the vanished knot-hole.

"Wall!" Eck roared. The little boy turned and ran for the wagon. The horses were whipping back and forth across the lot, as if while in the barn they had once more doubled their number; two of them rushed up quartering and galloped all over the boy again without touching him as he ran, earnest and diminutive and seemingly without progress, though he reached the wagon at last, from which Eck, his sunburned skin now a sickly white, reached down and snatched the boy into the wagon by the straps of his overalls and slammed him face down across his knees and caught up a coiled hitching-rope from the bed of the wagon.

"Didn't I tell you to get *out* of here?" Eck said in a shaking voice. "Didn't I tell you?"

"If you're going to whip him, you better whip the rest of us too and then one of us can frail hell out of you," one of the others said.

"Or better still, take the rope and hang that durn fellow yonder," the second said. The Texan was now standing in the wrecked door of the barn, taking the gingersnap carton from his hip pocket. "Before he kills the rest of Frenchman's Bend too."

"You mean Flem Snopes," the first said. The Texan tilted the carton above his other open palm. The horses still rushed and swirled back and forth but they were beginning to slow now, trotting on high, stiff legs, although their eyes were still rolling whitely and various.

"I misdoubted that damned shell corn all along," the Texan said. "But at least they have seen what it looks like. They cant claim they aint got nothing out of this trip." He shook the carton over his open hand. Nothing came out of it. Mrs Littlejohn on the veranda made the first stroke with the dinner bell; at the sound the horses rushed again, the earth of the lot becoming vibrant with the light dry clatter of hooves. The Texan crumpled the carton and threw it aside. "Chuck wagon," he said. There were three more wagons in the lane now and there were twenty or more men at the fence when the Texan, followed by his three assistants and the little boy, passed through the gate. The bright cloudless early sun gleamed upon the pearl butt of the pistol in his hip pocket and upon the bell which Mrs Littlejohn still rang, peremptory, strong, and loud.

When the Texan, picking his teeth with a splintered kitchen match, emerged from the house twenty minutes later, the tethered wagons and riding horses and mules extended from the lot gate to Varner's store, and there were more than fifty men now standing along the fence beside the gate, watching him quietly, a little covertly, as he approached, rolling a little, slightly bowlegged, the high heels of his carved boots printing neatly into the dust. "Morning, gents," he said. "Here, bud," he said to the little boy, who stood slightly behind him, looking at the protruding butt of the pistol. He took a coin from his pocket and gave it to the boy. "Run to the store and get me a box of gingersnaps." He looked about at the quiet faces, protuberant, sucking his teeth. He rolled the match from one side of his mouth to the other without touching it. "You boys done made your picks, have you? Ready to start her off, hah?" They did not answer. They were not looking at him now. That is, he began to have the feeling that each face had stopped looking at him the second before his gaze reached it. After a moment Freeman said:

"Aint you going to wait for Flem?"

"Why?" the Texan said. Then Freeman stopped looking at him too. There was nothing in Freeman's face either. There was nothing, no alteration, in the Texan's voice. "Eck, you done already picked out yours. So we can start her off when you are ready."

"I reckon not," Eck said. "I wouldn't buy nothing I was afraid to walk up and touch."

"Them little ponies?" the Texan said. "You helped water and feed them. I bet that boy of yours could walk up to any one of them."

"He better not let me catch him," Eck said. The Texan looked about at the quiet faces, his gaze at once abstract and alert, with an impenetrable surface quality like flint, as though the surface were impervious or perhaps there was nothing behind it.

"Them ponies is gentle as a dove, boys. The man that buys them will get the best piece of horseflesh he ever forked or druv for the money. Naturally they got spirit; I aint selling crowbait. Besides, who'd want Texas crowbait anyway, with Mississippi full of it?" His stare was still absent and unwinking; there was no mirth or humor in his voice and there was neither mirth nor humor in the single guffaw which came from the rear of the group. Two wagons were now drawing out of the road at the same time, up to the fence. The men got down from them and tied them to the fence and approached. "Come up, boys," the Texan said. "You're just in time to buy a good gentle horse cheap."

"How about that one that cut your vest off last night?" a voice said. This time three or four guffawed. The Texan looked toward the sound, bleak and unwinking.

"What about it?" he said. The laughter, if it had been laughter, ceased. The Texan turned to the nearest gatepost and climbed to the top of it, his alternate thighs deliberate and bulging in the tight trousers, the butt of the pistol catching and losing the sun in pearly gleams. Sitting on the post, he looked down at the faces along the fence which were attentive, grave, reserved and not looking at him. "All right," he said. "Who's going to start her off with a bid?

Step right up; take your pick and make your bid, and when the last one is sold, walk in that lot and put your rope on the best piece of horseflesh you ever forked or druv for the money. There aint a pony there that aint worth fifteen dollars. Young, sound, good for saddle or work stock, guaranteed to outlast four ordinary horses; you couldn't kill one of them with a axle-tree—" There was a small violent commotion at the rear of the group. The little boy appeared, burrowing among the motionless overalls. He approached the post, the new and unbroken paper carton lifted. The Texan leaned down and took it and tore the end from it and shook three or four of the cakes into the boy's hand, a hand as small and almost as black as that of a coon. He held the carton in his hand while he talked, pointing out the horses with it as he indicated them. "Look at that one with the three stocking-feet and the frost-bit ear; watch him now when they pass again. Look at that shoulder-action; that horse is worth twenty dollars of any man's money. Who'll make me a bid on him to start her off?" His voice was harsh, ready, forensic. Along the fence below him the men stood with, buttoned close in their over-alls, the tobacco-sacks and worn purses, the sparse silver and frayed bills hoarded a coin at a time in the cracks of chimneys or chinked into the logs of walls. From time to time the horses broke and rushed with purposeless violence and huddled again, watching the faces along the fence with wild mismatched eyes. The lane was full of wagons now. As the others arrived they would have to stop in the road beyond it and the occupants came up the lane on foot. Mrs Littlejohn came out of her kitchen. She crossed the yard, looking toward the lot gate. There was a blackened wash pot set on four bricks in the corner of the yard. She built a fire beneath the pot and came to the fence and stood there for a time, her hands on her hips and the smoke from the fire drifting blue and slow behind her. Then she turned and went back into the house. "Come on, boys," the Texan said. "Who'll make me a bid?"

"Four bits," a voice said. The Texan did not even glance toward it.

"Or, if he dont suit you, how about that fiddle-head horse without no mane to speak of? For a saddle pony, I'd rather have him than that stocking-foot. I heard somebody say fifty cents just now. I reckon he meant five dollars, didn't he? Do I hear five dollars?"

"Four bits for the lot," the same voice said. This time there were no guffaws. It was the Texan who laughed, harshly, with only his lower face, as if he were reciting a multiplication table.

"Fifty cents for the dried mud offen them, he means," he said. "Who'll give a dollar more for the genuine Texas cockle-burrs?" Mrs Littlejohn came out of the kitchen, carrying the sawn half of a wooden hogshead which she set on a stump beside the smoking pot, and stood with her hands on her hips, looking into the lot for a while without coming to the fence this time. Then she went back into the house. "What's the matter with you boys?" the Texan said. "Here, Eck, you been helping me and you know them horses. How about making me a bid on that wall-eyed one you picked out last night? Here. Wait a minute." He thrust the paper carton into his other hip pocket and swung his feet inward and dropped, cat-light, into the lot. The ponies, huddled, watched him. Then they broke before him and slid stiffly along the fence. He turned them and they whirled and rushed back across the lot; whereupon, as though he had been waiting his chance when they should have turned their backs on him, the Texan began to run too, so that when they reached the opposite side of the lot and turned, slowing to huddle again, he was almost upon them. The earth became thunderous; dust arose, out of which the animals began to burst like flushed quail and into which, with that apparently unflagging faith in his own invulnerability, the Texan rushed. For an instant the watchers could see them in the dust—the pony backed into the angle of the fence and the stable, the man facing it, reaching toward his hip. Then the beast rushed at him in a sort of fatal and hopeless desperation and he struck it between the eyes with the pistol-butt and felled it and leaped onto its prone head. The pony recovered almost at once and pawed itself to its knees and heaved at its prisoned head and fought itself up, dragging the man with it; for an instant in the dust the watchers saw the man free of the earth and in violent lateral motion like a rag attached to the horse's head. Then the Texan's feet came back to earth and the dust blew aside and revealed them, motionless, the Texan's sharp heels braced into the ground, one hand gripping the pony's forelock and the other its nostrils, the long evil muzzle wrung backward over its scarred shoulder while it breathed in labored and hollow groans. Mrs Littlejohn was in the yard again. No one had seen her emerge this time. She carried an armful of clothing and a metal-ridged washboard and she was standing motionless at the kitchen steps, looking into the lot. Then she moved across the yard, still looking into the lot, and dumped the garments into the tub, still looking into the lot. "Look him over, boys," the Texan panted, turning his own suffused face and the protuberant

glare of his eyes toward the fence. "Look him over quick. Them
shoulders and—" He had relaxed for an instant apparently. The animal exploded again; again for an instant the Texan was free of the
earth, though he was still talking: "—and legs you whoa I'll tear your
face right look him over quick boys worth fifteen dollars of let me
get a holt of who'll make me a bid whoa you blare-eyed jack rabbit,
whoa!" They were moving now—a kaleidoscope of inextricable and
incredible violence on the periphery of which the metal clasps of the
Texan's suspenders sun-glinted in ceaseless orbit, with terrific slowness across the lot. Then the broad clay-colored hat soared deliberately outward; an instant later the Texan followed it, though still on
his feet, and the pony shot free in mad, staglike bounds. The Texan
picked up the hat and struck the dust from it against his leg, and
returned to the fence and mounted the post again. He was breathing
heavily. Still the faces did not look at him as he took the carton from
his hip and shook a cake from it and put the cake into his mouth,
chewing, breathing harshly. Mrs Littlejohn turned away and began
to bail water from the pot into the tub, though after each bucketful
she turned her head and looked into the lot again. "Now, boys," the
Texan said. "Who says that pony aint worth fifteen dollars? You
couldn't buy that much dynamite for just fifteen dollars. There aint
one of them cant do a mile in three minutes; turn them into pasture
and they will board themselves; work them like hell all day and
every time you think about it, lay them over the head with a single-
tree and after a couple of days every jack rabbit one of them will be
so tame you will have to put them out of the house at night like a
cat." He shook another cake from the carton and ate it. "Come on,
Eck," he said. "Start her off. How about ten dollars for that horse,
Eck?"

"What need I got for a horse I would need a bear-trap to catch?"
Eck said.

"Didn't you just see me catch him?"

"I seen you," Eck said. "And I don't want nothing as big as a horse
if I got to wrastle with it every time it finds me on the same side of
a fence it's on."

"All right," the Texan said. He was still breathing harshly, but
now there was nothing of fatigue or breathlessness in it. He shook
another cake into his palm and inserted it beneath his moustache.
"All right. I want to get this auction started. I aint come here to live,
no matter how good a country you folks claim you got. I'm going to

give you that horse." For a moment there was no sound, not even that of breathing except the Texan's.

"You going to give it to me?" Eck said.

"Yes. Provided you will start the bidding on the next one." Again there was no sound save the Texan's breathing, and then the clash of Mrs Littlejohn's pail against the rim of the pot.

"I just start the bidding," Eck said. "I dont have to buy it lessen I aint over-topped." Another wagon had come up the lane. It was battered and paintless. One wheel had been repaired by crossed planks bound to the spokes with baling wire and the two underfed mules wore a battered harness patched with bits of cotton rope; the reins were ordinary cotton plow-lines, not new. It contained a woman in a shapeless gray garment and a faded sunbonnet, and a man in faded and patched though clean overalls. There was not room for the wagon to draw out of the lane so the man left it standing where it was and got down and came forward—a thin man, not large, with something about his eyes, something strained and washed-out, at once vague and intense, who shoved into the crowd at the rear, saying,

"What? What's that? Did he give him that horse?"

"All right," the Texan said. "That wall-eyed horse with the scarred neck belongs to you. Now. That one that looks like he's had his head in a flour barrel. What do you say? Ten dollars?"

"Did he give him that horse?" the newcomer said.

"A dollar," Eck said. The Texan's mouth was still open for speech; for an instant his face died so behind the hard eyes.

"A dollar?" he said. "One dollar? Did I actually hear that?"

"Durn it," Eck said. "Two dollars then. But I aint——"

"Wait," the newcomer said. "You, up there on the post." The Texan looked at him. When the others turned, they saw that the woman had left the wagon too, though they had not known she was there since they had not seen the wagon drive up. She came among them behind the man, gaunt in the gray shapeless garment and the sunbonnet, wearing stained canvas gymnasium shoes. She overtook the man but she did not touch him, standing just behind him, her hands rolled before her into the gray dress.

"Henry," she said in a flat voice. The man looked over his shoulder.

"Get back to that wagon," he said.

"Here, missus," the Texan said. "Henry's going to get the bargain of his life in about a minute. Here, boys, let the missus come up close where she can see. Henry's going to pick out that saddle-horse the missus has been wanting. Who says ten——"

"Henry," the woman said. She did not raise her voice. She had not once looked at the Texan. She touched the man's arm. He turned and struck her hand down.

"Get back to that wagon like I told you." The woman stood behind him, her hands rolled again into her dress. She was not looking at anything, speaking to anyone.

"He aint no more despair than to buy one of them things," she said. "And us not but five dollars away from the poorhouse, he aint no more despair." The man turned upon her with that curious air of leashed, of dreamlike fury. The others lounged along the fence in attitudes gravely inattentive, almost oblivious. Mrs Littlejohn had been washing for some time now, pumping rhythmically up and down above the washboard in the sud-foamed tub. She now stood erect again, her soap-raw hands on her hips, looking into the lot.

"Shut your mouth and get back in that wagon," the man said. "Do you want me to take a wagon stake to you?" He turned and looked up at the Texan. "Did you give him that horse?" he said. The Texan was looking at the woman. Then he looked at the man; still watching him, he tilted the paper carton over his open palm. A single cake came out of it.

"Yes," he said.

"Is the fellow that bids in this next horse going to get that first one too?"

"No," the Texan said.

"All right," the other said. "Are you going to give a horse to the man that makes the first bid on the next one?"

"No," the Texan said.

"Then if you were just starting the auction off by giving away a horse, why didn't you wait till we were all here?" The Texan stopped looking at the other. He raised the empty carton and squinted carefully into it, as if it might contain a precious jewel or perhaps a deadly insect. Then he crumbled it and dropped it carefully beside the post on which he sat.

"Eck bids two dollars," he said. "I believe he still thinks he's bidding on them scraps of bob-wire they come here in instead of on one of the horses. But I got to accept it. But are you boys——"

"So Eck's going to get two horses at a dollar a head," the new-comer said. "Three dollars." The woman touched him again. He flung her hand off without turning and she stood again, her hands rolled into her dress across her flat stomach, not looking at anything.

"Misters," she said, "we got chaps in the house that never had shoes last winter. We aint got corn to feed the stock. We got five dollars I earned weaving by firelight after dark. And he aint no more despair."

"Henry bids three dollars," the Texan said. "Raise him a dollar, Eck, and the horse is yours." Beyond the fence the horses rushed suddenly and for no reason and as suddenly stopped, staring at the faces along the fence.

"Henry," the woman said. The man was watching Eck. His stained and broken teeth showed a little beneath his lip. His wrists dangled into fists below the faded sleeves of his shirt too short from many washings.

"Four dollars," Eck said.

"Five dollars!" the husband said, raising one clenched hand. He shouldered himself forward toward the gatepost. The woman did not follow him. She now looked at the Texan for the first time. Her eyes were a washed gray also, as though they had faded too like the dress and the sunbonnet.

"Mister," she said, "if you take that five dollars I earned my chaps a-weaving for one of them things, it'll be a curse on you and yours during all the time of man."

"Five dollars!" the husband shouted. He thrust himself up to the post, his clenched hand on a level with the Texan's knees. He opened it upon a wad of frayed banknotes and silver. "Five dollars! And the man that raises it will have to beat my head off or I'll beat hisn."

"All right," the Texan said. "Five dollars is bid. But dont you shake your hand at me."

At five oclock that afternoon the Texan crumpled the third paper carton and dropped it to the earth beneath him. In the copper slant of the leveling sun which fell also upon the line of limp garments in Mrs Littlejohn's backyard and which cast his shadow and that of the post on which he sat long across the lot where now and then the ponies still rushed in purposeless and tireless surges, the Texan straightened his leg and thrust his hand into his pocket and took out a coin and leaned down to the little boy. His voice was now hoarse, spent. "Here, bud," he said. "Run to the store and get me a box of gingersnaps." The men still stood along the fence, tireless, in their overalls and faded shirts. Flem Snopes was there now, appeared suddenly from nowhere, standing beside the fence with a space the width of three or four men on either side of him, standing there in his small yet definite isolation, chewing tobacco, in the same gray trousers and minute bow tie in which he had departed last summer but in a new cap, gray too like the other, but new, and overlaid with a bright golfer's plaid, looking also at the horses in the lot. All of them save two had been sold for sums ranging from three dollars and a half to eleven and twelve dollars. The purchasers, as they had bid them in, had gathered as though by instinct into a separate group on the other side of the gate, where they stood with their hands lying upon the top strand of the fence, watching with a still more sober intensity the animals which some of them had owned for seven and eight hours now but had not yet laid hands upon. The husband, Henry, stood beside the post on which the Texan sat. The wife had gone back to the wagon, where she sat gray in the gray garment, motionless, looking at nothing still, she might have been something inanimate which he had loaded into the wagon to move it somewhere, waiting now in the wagon until he should be ready to go on again, patient, insensate, timeless.

"I bought a horse and I paid cash for it," he said. His voice was harsh and spent too, the mad look in his eyes had a quality glazed now and even sightless. "And yet you expect me to stand around here till they are all sold before I can get my horse. Well, you can do all the expecting you want. I'm going to take my horse out of there and go home." The Texan looked down at him. The Texan's shirt was blotched with sweat. His big face was cold and still, his voice level.

"Take your horse then." After a moment Henry looked away. He stood with his head bent a little, swallowing from time to time.

"Aint you going to catch him for me?"

"It aint my horse," the Texan said in that flat still voice. After a while Henry raised his head. He did not look at the Texan.

"Who'll help me catch my horse?" he said. Nobody answered. They stood along the fence, looking quietly into the lot where the ponies huddled, already beginning to fade a little where the long shadow of the house lay upon them, deepening. From Mrs Littlejohn's kitchen the smell of frying ham came. A noisy cloud of sparrows swept across the lot and into a chinaberry tree beside the house, and in the high soft vague blue swallows stooped and whirled in erratic indecision, their cries like strings plucked at random. Without looking back, Henry raised his voice: "Bring that ere plowline." After a time the wife moved. She got down from the wagon and took a coil of new cotton rope from it and approached. The

husband took the rope from her and moved toward the gate. The
Texan began to descend from the post, stiffly, as Henry put his hand
on the latch. "Come on here," he said. The wife had stopped when
he took the rope from her. She moved again, obediently, her hands
rolled into the dress across her stomach, passing the Texan without
looking at him.

"Dont go in there, missus," he said. She stopped, not looking at
him, not looking at anything. The husband opened the gate and
entered the lot and turned, holding the gate open but without
raising his eyes.

"Come on here," he said.

"Don't you go in there, missus," the Texan said. The wife stood
motionless between them, her face almost concealed by the sunbonnet, her hands folded across her stomach.

"I reckon I better," she said. The other men did not look at her
at all, at her or Henry either. They stood along the fence, grave and
quiet and inattentive, almost bemused. Then the wife passed through
the gate; the husband shut it behind them and turned and began
to move toward the huddled ponies, the wife following in the gray
and shapeless garment within which she moved without inference
of locomotion, like something on a moving platform, a float. The
horses were watching them. They clotted and blended and shifted
among themselves, on the point of breaking though not breaking
yet. The husband shouted at them. He began to curse them, advancing, the wife following. Then the huddle broke, the animals moving
with high, stiff knees, circling the two people who turned and
followed again as the herd flowed and huddled again at the opposite
side of the lot.

"There he is," the husband said. "Get him into that corner." The
herd divided; the horse which the husband had bought jolted on
stiff legs. The wife shouted at it; it spun and poised, plunging, then
the husband struck it across the face with the coiled rope and it
whirled and slammed into the corner of the fence. "Keep him there
now," the husband said. He shook out the rope, advancing. The
horse watched him with wild, glaring eyes; it rushed again, straight
toward the wife. She shouted at it and waved her arms but it
soared past her in a long bound and rushed again into the huddle
of its fellows. They followed and hemmed it again into another
corner; again the wife failed to stop its rush for freedom and the
husband turned and struck her with the coiled rope. "Why didn't
you head him?" he said. "Why didn't you?" He struck her again;

she did not move, not even to fend the rope with a raised arm. The men along the fence stood quietly, their faces lowered as though brooding upon the earth at their feet. Only Flem Snopes was still watching—if he ever had been looking into the lot at all, standing in his little island of isolation, chewing with his characteristic faint sidewise thrust beneath the new plaid cap.

The Texan said something, not loud, harsh and short. He entered the lot and went to the husband and jerked the uplifted rope from his hand. The husband whirled as though he were about to spring at the Texan, crouched slightly, his knees bent and his arms held slightly away from his sides, though his gaze never mounted higher than the Texan's carved and dusty boots. Then the Texan took the husband by the arm and led him back toward the gate, the wife following, and through the gate which he held open for the woman and then closed. He took a wad of banknotes from his trousers and removed a bill from it and put it into the woman's hand. "Get him into the wagon and get him on home," he said.

"What's that for?" Flem Snopes said. He had approached. He now stood beside the post on which the Texan had been sitting. The Texan did not look at him.

"Thinks he bought one of them ponies," the Texan said. He spoke in a flat still voice, like that of a man after a sharp run. "Get him on away, missus."

"Give him back that money," the husband said, in his lifeless, spent tone. "I bought that horse and I aim to have him if I got to shoot him before I can put a rope on him." The Texan did not even look at him.

"Get him on away from here, missus," he said.

"You take your money and I take my horse," the husband said. He was shaking slowly and steadily now, as though he were cold. His hands open and shut below the frayed cuffs of his shirt. "Give it back to him," he said.

"You dont own no horse of mine," the Texan said. "Get him on home, missus." The husband raised his spent face, his mad glazed eyes. He reached out his hand. The woman held the banknote in her folded hands across her stomach. For a while the husband's shaking hand merely fumbled at it. Then he drew the banknote free.

"It's my horse," he said. "I bought it. These fellows saw me. I paid for it. It's my horse. Here." He turned and extended the banknote toward Snopes. "You got something to do with these horses. I bought one. Here's the money for it. I bought one. Ask him."

Snopes took the banknote. The others stood, gravely inattentive, in relaxed attitudes along the fence. The sun had gone now; there was nothing save violet shadow upon them and upon the lot where once more and for no reason the ponies rushed and flowed. At that moment the little boy came up, tireless and indefatigable still, with the new paper carton. The Texan took it, though he did not open it at once. He had dropped the rope and now the husband stooped for it, fumbling at it for sometime before he lifted it from the ground. Then he stood with his head bent, his knuckles whitening on the rope. The woman had not moved. Twilight was coming fast now; there was a last mazy swirl of swallows against the high and changing azure. Then the Texan tore the end from the carton and tilted one of the cakes into his hand; he seemed to be watching the hand as it shut slowly upon the cake until a fine powder of snuff-colored dust began to rain from his fingers. He rubbed the hand carefully on his thigh and raised his head and glanced about until he saw the little boy and handed the carton back to him.

"Here, bud," he said. Then he looked at the woman, his voice flat, quiet again. "Mr Snopes will have your money for you tomorrow. Better get him in the wagon and get him on home. He dont own no horse. You can get your money tomorrow from Mr Snopes." The wife turned and went back to the wagon and got into it. No one watched her, nor the husband who still stood, his head bent, passing the rope from one hand to the other. They leaned along the fence, grave and quiet, as though the fence were in another land, another time.

"How many you got left?" Snopes said. The Texan roused; they all seemed to rouse then, returning, listening again.

"Got three now," the Texan said. "Swap all three of them for a buggy or a——"

"It's out in the road," Snopes said, a little shortly, a little quickly, turning away. "Get your mules." He went on up the lane. They watched the Texan enter the lot and cross it, the horses flowing before him but without the old irrational violence, as if they too were spent, vitiated with the long day, and enter the barn and then emerge, leading the two harnessed mules. The wagon had been backed under the shed beside the barn. The Texan entered this and came out a moment later, carrying a bedding-roll and his coat, and led the mules back toward the gate, the ponies huddled again and watching him with their various unmatching eyes, quietly now, as if they too realised there was not only an armistice between them at last but that they would never look upon each other again in both their lives. Someone opened the gate. The Texan led the mules through it and they followed in a body, leaving the husband standing beside the closed gate, his head still bent and the coiled rope in his hand. They passed the wagon in which the wife sat, her gray garment fading into the dusk, almost the same color and as still, looking at nothing; they passed the clothesline with its limp and unwinded drying garments, walking through the hot vivid smell of ham from Mrs Littlejohn's kitchen. When they reached the end of the lane they could see the moon, almost full, tremendous and pale and still lightless in the sky from which day had not quite gone. Snopes was standing at the end of the lane beside an empty buggy. It was the one with the glittering wheels and the fringed parasol top in which he and Will Varner had used to drive. The Texan was motionless too, looking at it.

"Well well well," he said. "So this is it."

"If it dont suit you, you can ride one of the mules back to Texas," Snopes said.

"You bet," the Texan said. "Only I ought to have a powder puff or at least a mandolin to ride it with." He backed the mules onto the tongue and lifted the breast-yoke. Two of them came forward and fastened the traces for him. Then they watched him get into the buggy and raise the reins.

"Where you heading for?" one said. "Back to Texas?"

"In this?" the Texan said. "I wouldn't get past the first Texas saloon without starting the vigilance committee. Besides, I aint going to waste all this here lace-trimmed top and these spindle wheels just on Texas. Long as I am this far, I reckon I'll go on a day or two and look-see them Northern towns. Washington and New York and Baltimore. What's the short way to New York from here?" They didn't know. But they told him how to reach Jefferson.

"You're already headed right," Freeman said. "Just keep right on up the road past the schoolhouse."

"All right," the Texan said. "Well, remember about busting them ponies over the head now and then until they get used to you. You wont have any trouble with them then." He lifted the reins again. As he did so Snopes stepped forward and got into the buggy.

"I'll ride as far as Varner's with you," he said.

"I didn't know I was going past Varner's," the Texan said.

"You can go to town that way," Snopes said. "Drive on." The Texan shook the reins. Then he said,

"Whoa." He straightened his leg and put his hand into his pocket. "Here, bud," he said to the little boy, "run to the store and— Never mind. I'll stop and get it myself, long as I am going back that way. Well, boys," he said. "Take care of yourselves." He swung the team around. The buggy went on. They looked after it.

"I reckon he aims to kind of come up on Jefferson from behind," Quick said.

"He'll be lighter when he gets there," Freeman said. "He can come up to it easy from any side he wants."

"Yes," Bookwright said. "His pockets wont rattle." They went back to the lot; they passed on through the narrow way between the two lines of patient and motionless wagons, which at the end was completely closed by the one in which the woman sat. The husband was still standing beside the gate with his coiled rope, and now night had completely come. The light itself had not changed so much; if anything, it was brighter but with that other-worldly quality of moonlight, so that when they stood once more looking into the lot, the splotchy bodies of the ponies had a distinctness, almost a brilliance, but without individual shape and without depth—no longer horses, no longer flesh and bone directed by a principle capable of calculated violence, no longer inherent with the capacity to hurt and harm.

"Well, what are we waiting for?" Freeman said. "For them to go to roost?"

"We better all get our ropes first," Quick said. "Get your ropes everybody." Some of them did not have ropes. When they left home that morning, they had not heard about the horses, the auction. They had merely happened through the village by chance and learned of it and stopped.

"Go to the store and get some then," Freeman said.

"The store will be closed now," Quick said.

"No it wont," Freeman said. "If it was closed, Lump Snopes would a been up here." So while the ones who had come prepared got their ropes from the wagons, the others went down to the store. The clerk was just closing it.

"You all aint started catching them yet, have you?" he said. "Good; I was afraid I wouldn't get there in time." He opened the door again and amid the old strong sunless smells of cheese and leather and molasses he measured and cut off sections of plow-line for them and in a body and the clerk in the center and still talking, voluble and unlistened to, they returned up the road. The pear tree before Mrs Littlejohn's was like drowned silver now in the moon. The mockingbird of last night, or another one, was already singing in it, and they now saw, tied to the fence, Ratliff's buckboard and team.

"I thought something was wrong all day," one said. "Ratliff wasn't there to give nobody advice." When they passed down the lane, Mrs Littlejohn was in her backyard, gathering the garments from the clothesline; they could still smell the ham. The others were waiting at the gate, beyond which the ponies, huddled again, were like phantom fish, suspended apparently without legs now in the brilliant treachery of the moon.

"I reckon the best way will be for us all to take and catch them one at a time," Freeman said.

"One at a time," the husband, Henry, said. Apparently he had not moved since the Texan had led his mules through the gate, save to lift his hands to the top of the gate, one of them still clutching the coiled rope. "One at a time," he said. He began to curse in a harsh, spent monotone. "After I've stood around here all day, waiting for that——" He cursed. He began to jerk at the gate, shaking it with spent violence until one of the others slid the latch back and it swung open and Henry entered it, the others following, the little boy pressing close behind his father until Eck became aware of him and turned.

"Here," he said. "Give me that rope. You stay out of here."

"Aw, paw," the boy said.

"No sir. Them things will kill you. They almost done it this morning. You stay out of here."

"But we got two to catch." For a moment Eck stood looking down at the boy.

"That's right," he said. "We got two. But you stay close to me now. And when I holler run, you run. You hear me?"

"Spread out, boys," Freeman said. "Keep them in front of us." They began to advance across the lot in a ragged crescent-shaped line, each one with his rope. The ponies were now at the far side of the lot. One of them snorted; the mass shifted within itself but without breaking. Freeman, glancing back, saw the little boy. "Get that boy out of here," he said.

"I reckon you better," Eck said to the boy. "You go and get in the wagon yonder. You can see us catch them from there." The little boy turned and trotted toward the shed beneath which the wagon stood. The line of men advanced, Henry a little in front.

"Watch them close now," Freeman said. "Maybe we better try to get them into the barn first——" At that moment the huddle broke. It parted and flowed in both directions along the fence. The men at the ends of the line began to run, waving their arms and shouting. "Head them," Freeman said tensely. "Turn them back." They turned them, driving them back upon themselves again; the animals merged and spun in short, huddling rushes, phantom and inextricable. "Hold them now," Freeman said. "Dont let them get by us." The line advanced again. Eck turned; he did not know why—whether a sound, what. The little boy was just behind him again.

"Didn't I tell you to get in that wagon and stay there?" Eck said.

"Watch out, paw!" the boy said. "There he is! There's ourn!" It was the one the Texan had given Eck. "Catch him, paw!"

"Get out of my way," Eck said. "Get back to that wagon." The line was still advancing. The ponies milled, clotting, forced gradually backward toward the open door of the barn. Henry was still slightly in front, crouched slightly, his thin figure, even in the mazy moonlight, emanating something of that spent fury. The splotchy huddle of animals seemed to be moving before the advancing line of men like a snowball which they might have been pushing before them by some invisible means, gradually nearer and nearer to the black yawn of the barn door. Later it was obvious that the ponies were so intent upon the men that they did not realise the barn was even behind them until they backed into the shadow of it. Then an indescribable sound, a movement desperate and despairing, arose among them; for an instant of static horror men and animals faced one another, then the men whirled and ran before a gaudy vomit of long wild faces and splotched chests which overtook and scattered them and flung them sprawling aside and completely obliterated from sight Henry and the little boy, neither of whom had moved though Henry had flung up both arms, still holding his coiled rope, the herd sweeping on across the lot, to crash through the gate which the last man through it had neglected to close, leaving it slightly ajar, carrying all of the gate save upright to which the hinges were nailed with them, and so among the teams and wagons which choked the lane, the teams springing and lunging too, snapping hitch-reins and tongues. Then the whole inextricable mass crashed among the wagons and eddied and divided about the one in which the woman sat, and rushed on down the lane and into the road, dividing, one half going one way and one half the other.

The men in the lot, except Henry, got to their feet and ran toward the gate. The little boy once more had not been touched, not even thrown off his feet; for a while his father held him clear of the ground in one hand, shaking him like a rag doll. "Didn't I tell you to stay in that wagon?" Eck cried. "Didn't I tell you?"

"Look out, paw!" the boy chattered out of the violent shaking. "There's ourn! There he goes!" It was the horse the Texan had given them again. It was as if they owned no other, the other one did not exist; as if by some absolute and instantaneous rapport of blood they had relegated to oblivion the one for which they had paid money. They ran to the gate and down the lane where the other men had disappeared. They saw the horse the Texan had given them whirl and dash back and rush through the gate into Mrs Littlejohn's yard and run up the front steps and crash once on the wooden veranda and vanish through the front door. Eck and the boy ran up onto the veranda. A lamp sat on a table just inside the door. In its mellow light they saw the horse fill the long hallway like a pinwheel, gaudy, furious and thunderous. A little further down the hall there was a varnished yellow melodeon. The horse crashed into it; it produced a single note, almost a chord, in bass, resonant and grave, of deep and sober astonishment; the horse with its monstrous and antic shadow whirled again and vanished through another door. It was a bedroom; Ratliff, in his underclothes and one sock and with the other sock in his hand and his back to the door, was leaning out the open window facing the lane, the lot. He looked back over his shoulder. For an instant he and the horse glared at one another. Then he sprang through the window as the horse backed out of the room and into the hall again and whirled and saw Eck and the little boy just entering the front door, Eck still carrying his rope. It whirled again and rushed on down the hall and onto the back porch just as Mrs Littlejohn, carrying an armful of clothes from the line and the washboard, mounted the steps.

"Get out of here, you son of a bitch," she said. She struck with the washboard; it divided neatly on the long mad face and the horse whirled and rushed back up the hall, where Eck and the boy now stood.

"Get to hell out of here, Wall!" Eck roared. He dropped to the floor, covering his head with his arms. The boy did not move, and for the third time the horse soared above the unwinking eyes and the unbowed and untouched head and onto the front veranda again just as Ratliff, still carrying the sock, ran around the corner of the house and up the steps. The horse whirled without breaking or pausing. It galloped to the end of the veranda and took the railing and soared outward, hobgoblin and floating, in the moon. It landed in the lot still running and crossed the lot and galloped through the wrecked gate and among the overturned wagons and the still intact one in which Henry's wife still sat, and on down the lane and into the road.

A quarter of a mile further on, the road gashed pallid and moony between the moony shadows of the bordering trees, the horse still galloping, galloping its shadow into the dust, the road descending now toward the creek and the bridge. It was of wood, just wide enough for a single vehicle. When the horse reached it, it was occupied by a wagon coming from the opposite direction and drawn by two mules already asleep in the harness and the soporific motion. On the seat were Tull and his wife, in splint chairs in the wagon behind them sat their four daughters, all returning belated from an all-day visit with some of Mrs Tull's kin. The horse neither checked nor swerved. It crashed once on the wooden bridge and rushed between the two mules which waked lunging in opposite directions in the traces, the horse now apparently scrambling along the wagon-tongue itself like a mad squirrel and scrabbling at the end-gate of the wagon with its forefeet as if it intended to climb into the wagon while Tull shouted at it and struck at its face with his whip. The mules were now trying to turn the wagon around in the middle of the bridge. It slewed and tilted, the bridge-rail cracked with a sharp report above the shrieks of the women; the horse scrambled at last across the back of one of the mules and Tull stood up in the wagon and kicked at its face. Then the front end of the wagon rose, flinging Tull, the reins now wrapped several times about his wrist, backward into the wagon bed among the overturned chairs and the exposed stockings and undergarments of his women. The pony scrambled free and crashed again on the wooden planking, galloping again. The wagon lurched again; the mules had finally turned it on the bridge where there was not room for it to turn and were now kicking themselves free of the traces. When they came free, they snatched Tull bodily out of the wagon. He struck the bridge on his face and was dragged for several feet before the wrist-wrapped reins broke. Far up the road now, distancing the frantic mules, the pony faded on. While the five women still shrieked above Tull's unconscious body, Eck and the little boy came up, trotting, Eck still carrying his rope. He was panting. "Which way'd he go?" he said.

In the now empty and moon-drenched lot, his wife and Mrs Littlejohn and Ratliff and Lump Snopes, the clerk, and three other men raised Henry out of the trampled dust and carried him into Mrs Littlejohn's backyard. His face was blanched and stony, his eyes were closed, the weight of his head tautened his throat across the protruding larynx; his teeth glinted dully beneath his lifted lip. They carried him on toward the house, through the dappled shade of the chinaberry trees. Across the dreaming and silver night a faint sound like remote thunder came and ceased. "There's one of them on the creek bridge," one of the men said.

"It's that one of Eck Snopes's," another said. "The one that was in the house." Mrs Littlejohn had preceded them into the hall. When they entered with Henry, she had already taken the lamp from the table and she stood beside an open door, holding the lamp high.

"Bring him in here," she said. She entered the room first and set the lamp on the dresser. They followed with clumsy scufflings and pantings and laid Henry on the bed and Mrs Littlejohn came to the bed and stood looking down at Henry's peaceful and bloodless face. "I'll declare," she said. "You men." They had drawn back a little, clumped, shifting from one foot to another, not looking at her nor at his wife either, who stood at the foot of the bed, motionless, her hands folded into her dress. "You all get out of here, V. K.," she said to Ratliff. "Go outside. See if you cant find something else to play with that will kill some more of you."

"All right," Ratliff said. "Come on boys. Aint no more horses to catch in here." They followed him toward the door, on tiptoe, their shoes scuffling, their shadows monstrous on the wall.

"Go get Will Varner," Mrs Littlejohn said. "I reckon you can tell him it's still a mule." They went out; they didn't look back. They tiptoed up the hall and crossed the veranda and descended into the moonlight. Now that they could pay attention to it, the silver air seemed to be filled with faint and sourceless sounds—shouts, thin and distant, again a brief thunder of hooves on a wooden bridge, more shouts faint and thin and earnest and clear as bells; once they even distinguished the words: "Whooey. Head him."

"He went through that house quick," Ratliff said. "He must have found another woman at home." Then Henry screamed in the house behind them. They looked back into the dark hall where a square of light fell through the bedroom door, listening while the scream sank into a harsh respiration: "Ah. Ah. Ah" on a rising note about to become screaming again. "Come on," Ratliff said. "We better get Varner." They went up the road in a body, treading the moon-blanched dust in the tremulous April night murmurous with the moving of sap and the wet bursting of burgeoning leaf and bud and constant with the thin and urgent cries and the brief and fading bursts of galloping hooves. Varner's house was dark, blank and without depth in the moonlight. They stood, clumped darkly in the silver yard and called up at the blank windows until suddenly someone was standing in one of them. It was Flem Snopes' wife. She was in a white garment; the heavy braided club of her hair looked almost black against it. She did not lean out, she merely stood there, full in the moon, apparently blank-eyed or certainly not looking downward at them—the heavy gold hair, the mask not tragic and perhaps not even doomed: just damned, the strong faint lift of breasts beneath marblelike fall of the garment; to those below what Brunhilde, what Rhinemaiden on what spurious river-rock of papier-mâché, what Helen returned to what topless and shoddy Argos, waiting for no one. "Evening, Mrs Snopes," Ratliff said. "We want Uncle Will. Henry Armstid is hurt at Mrs Littlejohn's." She vanished from the window. They waited in the moonlight, listening to the faint remote shouts and cries, until Varner emerged, sooner than they had actually expected, hunching into his coat and buttoning his trousers over the tail of his nightshirt, his suspenders still dangling in twin loops below the coat. He was carrying the battered bag which contained the plumber-like tools with which he drenched and wormed and blistered and floated or drew the teeth of horses and mules; he came down the steps, lean and loose-jointed, his shrewd ruthless head cocked a little as he listened also to the faint bell-like cries and shouts with which the silver air was full.

"Are they still trying to catch them rabbits?" he said.

"All of them except Henry Armstid," Ratliff said. "He caught his."

"Hah," Varner said. "That you, V. K.? How many did you buy?"

"I was too late," Ratliff said. "I never got back in time."

"Hah," Varner said. They moved on to the gate and into the road again. "Well, it's a good bright cool night for running them." The moon was now high overhead, a pearled and mazy yawn in the soft sky, the ultimate ends of which rolled onward, whorl on whorl, beyond the pale stars and by pale stars surrounded. They walked in a close clump, tramping their shadows into the road's mild dust, blotting the shadows of the burgeoning trees which soared, trunk branch and twig against the pale sky, delicate and finely thinned. They passed the dark store. Then the pear tree came in sight. It rose in mazed and silver immobility like exploding snow; the mockingbird still sang in it. "Look at that tree," Varner said. "It ought to make this year, sho."

"Corn'll make this year too," one said.

"A moon like this is good for every growing thing outen earth," Varner said. "I mind when me and Mrs Varner was expecting Eula. Already had a mess of children and maybe we ought to quit then. But I wanted some more gals. Others had done married and moved away, and a passel of boys, soon as they get big enough to be worth anything, they aint got time to work. Got to set around store and talk. But a gal will stay home and work until she does get married. So there was a old woman told my mammy once that if a woman showed her belly to the full moon after she had done caught, it would be a gal. So Mrs Varner taken and laid every night with the moon on her nekid belly, until it fulled and after. I could lay my ear to her belly and hear Eula kicking and scrouging like all get-out, feeling the moon."

"You mean it actually worked sho enough, Uncle Will?" the other said.

"Hah," Varner said. "You might try it. You get enough women showing their nekid bellies to the moon or the sun either or even just to your hand fumbling around often enough and more than likely after a while there will be something in it you can lay your ear and listen to, provided something come up and you aint got away by that time. Hah, V. K.?" Someone guffawed.

"Dont ask me," Ratliff said. "I cant even get nowhere in time to buy a cheap horse." Two or three guffawed this time. Then they began to hear Henry's respirations from the house: "Ah. Ah. Ah" and they ceased abruptly, as if they had not been aware of their closeness to it. Varner walked on in front, lean, shambling, yet moving quite rapidly, though his head was still slanted with listening as the faint, urgent, indomitable cries murmured in the silver lambence, sourceless, at times almost musical, like fading bell-notes; again there was a brief rapid thunder of hooves on wooden planking.

"There's another one on the creek bridge," one said.

"They are going to come out even on them things, after all," Varner said. "They'll get the money back in exercise and relaxation.

You take a man that aint got no other relaxation all year except dodging mule-dung up and down a field furrow. And a night like this one, when a man aint old enough yet to lay still and sleep, and yet he aint young enough anymore to be tomcatting in and out of other folks' back windows, something like this is good for him. It'll make him sleep tomorrow night anyhow, provided he gets back home by then. If we had just knowed about this in time, we could have trained up a pack of horse-dogs. Then we could have held one of these field trials."

"That's one way to look at it, I reckon," Ratliff said. "In fact, it might be a considerable comfort to Bookwright and Quick and Freeman and Eck Snopes and them other new horse-owners if that side of it could be brought to their attention, because the chances are aint none of them thought to look at it in that light yet. Probably there aint a one of them that believes now there's any cure a tall for that Texas disease Flem Snopes and that Dead-eye Dick brought here."

"Hah," Varner said. He opened Mrs Littlejohn's gate. The dim light still fell outward across the hall from the bedroom door; beyond it, Armstid was saying "Ah. Ah. Ah" steadily. "There's a pill for every ill but the last one."

"Even if there was always time to take it," Ratliff said.

"Hah," Varner said again. He glanced back at Ratliff for an instant, pausing. But the little hard bright eyes were invisible now; it was only the bushy overhang of the brows which seemed to concentrate downward toward him in writhen immobility, not frowning but with a sort of fierce risibility. "Even if there was time to take it. Breathing is a sight-draft dated yesterday."

At nine oclock on the second morning after that, five men were sitting or squatting along the gallery of the store. The sixth was Ratliff. He was standing up, and talking: "Maybe there wasn't but one of them things in Mrs Littlejohn's house that night, like Eck says. But it was the biggest drove of just one horse I ever seen. It was in my room and it was on the front porch and I could hear Mrs Littlejohn hitting it over the head with that washboard in the backyard all at the same time. And still it was missing everybody everytime. I reckon that's what that Texas man meant by calling them bargains: that a man would need to be powerful unlucky to ever get close enough to one of them to get hurt." They laughed, all except Eck himself. He and the little boy were eating. When they mounted the steps, Eck had gone on into the store and emerged with a paper sack, from which he took a segment of cheese and with his pocket knife divided it carefully into two exact halves and gave one to the boy and took a handful of crackers from the sack and gave them to the boy, and now they squatted against the wall, side by side and, save for the difference in size, identical, eating.

"I wonder what that horse thought Ratliff was," one said. He held a spray of peach bloom between his teeth. It bore four blossoms like miniature ballet skirts of pink tulle. "Jumping out windows and running indoors in his shirt-tail? I wonder how many Ratliffs that horse thought he saw."

"I dont know," Ratliff said. "But if he saw just half as many of me as I saw of him, he was sholy surrounded. Everytime I turned my head, that thing was just running over me or just swirling to run back over that boy again. And that boy there, he stayed right under it one time to my certain knowledge for a full one-and-one-half minutes without ducking his head or even batting his eyes. Yes sir, when I looked around and seen that varmint in the door behind me blaring its eyes at me, I'd a made sho Flem Snopes had brought a tiger back from Texas except I knowed that couldn't no just one tiger completely fill a entire room." They laughed again, quietly. Lump Snopes, the clerk, sitting in the only chair tilted back against the door-facing and partly blocking the entrance, cackled suddenly.

"If Flem had knowed how quick you fellows was going to snap them horses up, he'd a probably brought some tigers," he said. "Monkeys too."

"So they was Flem's horses," Ratliff said. The laughter stopped. The other three had open knives in their hands, with which they had been trimming idly at chips and slivers of wood. Now they sat apparently absorbed in the delicate and almost tedious movements of the knife-blades. The clerk had looked quickly up and found Ratliff watching him. His constant expression of incorrigible and mirthful disbelief had left him now; only the empty wrinkles of it remained about his mouth and eyes.

"Has Flem ever said they was?" he said. "But you town fellows are smarter than us country folks. Likely you done already read Flem's mind." But Ratliff was not looking at him now.

"And I reckon we'd a bought them," he said. He stood above them again, easy, intelligent, perhaps a little sombre but still perfectly impenetrable. "Eck here, for instance. With a wife and family to support. He owns two of them, though to be sho he never had to pay money for but one. I heard folks chasing them things up until midnight last night, but Eck and that boy aint been home a tall in two days." They laughed again, except Eck. He pared off a bit of cheese and speared it on the knife-point and put it into his mouth.

"Eck caught one of hisn," the second man said.

"That so?" Ratliff said. "Which one was it, Eck? The one he give you or the one you bought?"

"The one he give me," Eck said, chewing.

"Well, well," Ratliff said. "I hadn't heard about that. But Eck's still one horse short. And the one he had to pay money for. Which is pure proof enough that them horses wasn't Flem's because wouldn't no man even give his own blood kin something he couldn't even catch." They laughed again, but they stopped when the clerk spoke. There was no mirth in his voice at all.

"Listen," he said. "All right. We done all admitted you are too smart for anybody to get ahead of. You never bought no horse from Flem or nobody else, so maybe it aint none of your business and maybe you better just leave it at that."

"Sholy," Ratliff said. "It's done already been left at that two nights ago. The fellow that forgot to shut that lot gate done that. With the exception of Eck's horse. And we know that wasn't Flem's, because that horse was give to Eck for nothing."

"There's others besides Eck that aint got back home yet," the man with the peach spray said. "Bookwright and Quick are still chasing theirs. They was reported three miles west of Burtsboro Old Town at eight oclock last night. They aint got close enough to it yet to tell which one it belongs to."

"Sholy," Ratliff said. "The only new horse-owner in this country that could a been found without bloodhounds since whoever it was left that gate open two nights ago, is Henry Armstid. He's laying right there in Mrs Littlejohn's bedroom where he can watch the lot so that any time the one he bought happens to run back into it, all he's got to do is to holler at his wife to run out with the rope and catch it—" He ceased, though he said, "Morning, Flem," so immediately afterward and with no change whatever in tone, that the pause was not even discernible. With the exception of the clerk, who sprang up, vacated the chair with a sort of servile alacrity, and Eck and the little boy who continued to eat, they watched above their stilled hands as Snopes in the gray trousers and the minute tie and the new cap with its bright overplaid mounted the steps. He was chewing; he already carried a piece of white pine board; he jerked his head at them, looking at nobody, and took the vacated chair and opened his knife and began to whittle. The clerk now leaned in the opposite side of the door, rubbing his back against the facing. The expression of merry and invincible disbelief had returned to his face, with a quality watchful and secret.

"You're just in time," he said. "Ratliff here seems to be in a considerable sweat about who actually owned them horses." Snopes drew his knife-blade neatly along the board, the neat, surgeon-like sliver curling before it. That others were whittling again, looking carefully at nothing, except Eck and the boy, who were still eating, and the clerk rubbing his back against the door-facing and watching Snopes with that secret and alert intensity. "Maybe you could put his mind at rest." Snopes turned his head slightly and spat, across the gallery and the steps and into the dust beyond them. He drew the knife back and began another curling sliver.

"He was there too," Snopes said. "He knows as much as anybody else." This time the clerk guffawed, chortling, his features gathering toward the center of his face as though plucked there by a hand. He slapped his leg, cackling.

"You might as well to quit," he said. "You cant beat him."

"I reckon not," Ratliff said. He stood above them, not looking at any of them, his gaze fixed apparently on the empty road beyond Mrs Littlejohn's house, impenetrable, brooding even. A hulking, half-grown boy in overalls too small for him, appeared suddenly from nowhere in particular. He stood for a while in the road, just beyond spitting-range of the gallery, with the air of having come from nowhere in particular and of not knowing where he would go next when he should move again and of not being troubled by that fact. He was looking at nothing, certainly not toward the gallery, and no one on the gallery so much as looked at him except the little boy, who now watched the boy in the road, his periwinkle eyes grave and steady above the bitten cracker in his halted hand. The boy in the road moved on, thickly undulant in the tight overalls, and vanished beyond the corner of the store, the round head and the unwinking eyes of the little boy on the gallery turning steadily to watch him out of sight. Then the little boy bit the cracker again, chewing. "Of course there's Mrs Tull," Ratliff said. "But that's Eck she's going to sue for damaging Tull against that bridge. And as for Henry Armstid——"

"If a man aint got gumption enough to protect himself, it's his own look-out," the clerk said.

"Sholy," Ratliff said, still in that dreamy, abstracted tone, actually speaking over his shoulder even. "And Henry Armstid, that's all right because from what I hear of the conversation that taken place, Henry had already stopped owning that horse he thought was his before that Texas man left. And as for that broke leg, that wont put him out none because his wife can make his crop." The clerk had ceased to rub his back against the door. He watched the back of Ratliff's head, unwinking too, sober and intent; he glanced at Snopes who, chewing, was watching another sliver curl away from the advancing knife-blade, then he watched the back of Ratliff's head again.

"It wont be the first time she has made their crop," the man with the peach spray said. Ratliff glanced at him.

"You ought to know. This wont be the first time I ever saw you in their field, doing plowing Henry never got around to. How many days have you already given them this year?" The man with the peach spray removed it and spat carefully and put the spray back between his teeth.

"She can run a furrow straight as I can," the second said.

"They're unlucky," the third said. "When you are unlucky, it dont matter much what you do."

"Sholy," Ratliff said. "I've heard laziness called bad luck so much that maybe it is."

"He aint lazy," the third said. "When their mule died three or four years ago, him and her broke their land working time about in the traces with the other mule. They aint lazy."

"So that's all right," Ratliff said, gazing up the empty road again. "Likely she will begin right away to finish the plowing; that oldest gal is pretty near big enough to work with a mule, aint she? or at least to hold the plow steady while Mrs Armstid helps the mule?" He glanced again toward the man with the peach spray as though for an answer, but he was not looking at the other and he went on talking without any pause. The clerk stood with his rump and back pressed against the door-facing as if he had paused in the act of scratching, watching Ratliff quite hard now, unwinking. If Ratliff had looked at Flem Snopes, he would have seen nothing below the down-slanted peak of the cap save the steady motion of his jaws. Another sliver was curling with neat deliberation before the moving knife. "Plenty of time now because all she's got to do

after she finishes washing Mrs Littlejohn's dishes and sweeping out
the house to pay hers and Henry's board, is to go out home and
milk and cook up enough vittles to last the children until tomorrow
and feed them and get the littlest ones to sleep and wait outside
the door until that biggest gal gets the bar up and gets into bed
herself with the axe——"

"The axe?" the man with the peach spray said.

"She takes it to bed with her. She's just twelve, and what with
this country still more or less full of them uncaught horses that
never belonged to Flem Snopes, likely she feels maybe she cant
swing a mere washboard like Mrs Littlejohn can—and then come
back and wash up the supper dishes. And after that, not nothing to
do until morning except to stay close enough where Henry can
call her until it's light enough to chop the wood to cook breakfast
and then help Mrs Littlejohn wash the dishes and make the beds
and sweep while watching the road. Because likely any time now
Flem Snopes will get back from wherever he has been since the
auction, which of course is to town naturally to see about his
cousin that's got into a little legal trouble, and so get that five
dollars. 'Only maybe he wont give it back to me,' she says, and
maybe that's what Mrs Littlejohn thought too, because she never
said nothing. I could hear her——"

"And where did you happen to be during all this?" the clerk said.

"Listening," Ratliff said. He glanced back at the clerk, then he
was looking away again, almost standing with his back to them.
"—could hear her dumping the dishes into the pan like she was
throwing them at it. 'Do you reckon he will give it back to me?'
Mrs Armstid says. 'That Texas man give it to him and said he
would. All the folks there saw him give Mr Snopes the money
and heard him say I could get it from Mr Snopes tomorrow.' Mrs
Littlejohn was washing the dishes now, washing them like a man
would, like they was made out of iron. 'No,' she says. 'But asking
him wont do no hurt.'—'If he wouldn't give it back, it aint no use to
ask,' Mrs Armstid says. —'Suit yourself,' Mrs Littlejohn says. 'It's
your money.' Then I couldn't hear nothing but the dishes for a
while. 'Do you reckon he might give it back to me?' Mrs Armstid
says. 'That Texas man said he would. They all heard him say it.'—
'Then go and ask him for it,' Mrs Littlejohn says. Then I couldn't
hear nothing but the dishes again. 'He wont give it back to me,'
Mrs Armstid says.—'All right,' Mrs Littlejohn says. 'Dont ask him,
then.' Then I just heard the dishes. They would have two pans,

both washing. 'You dont reckon he would, do you?' Mrs Armstid says. Mrs Littlejohn never said nothing. It sounded like she was throwing the dishes at one another. 'Maybe I better go and talk to Henry,' Mrs Armstid says.—'I would,' Mrs Littlejohn says. And I be dog if it didn't sound exactly like she had two plates in her hands, beating them together like these here brass bucket-lids in a band. 'Then Henry can buy another five-dollar horse with it. Maybe he'll buy one next time that will out and out kill him. If I just thought he would, I'd give him back that money, myself.'—'I reckon I better talk to him first,' Mrs Armstid says. And then it sounded just like Mrs Littlejohn taken up the dishes and pans and all and throwed the whole business at the cookstove—" Ratliff ceased. Behind him the clerk was hissing "Psst! Psst! Flem. Flem!" Then he stopped, and all of them watched Mrs Armstid approach and mount the steps, gaunt in the shapeless gray garment, the stained tennis shoes hissing faintly on the boards. She came among them and stood, facing Snopes but not looking at anyone, her hands rolled into her apron.

"He said that day he wouldn't sell Henry that horse," she said in a flat toneles voice. "He said you had the money and I could get it from you." Snopes raised his head and turned it slightly again and spat neatly past the woman, across the gallery and into the road.

"He took all the money with him when he left," he said. Motionless, the gray garment hanging in rigid, almost formal folds like drapery in bronze, Mrs Armstid appeared to be watching something near Snopes' feet, as though she had not heard him, or as if she had quitted her body as soon as she finished speaking and although her body, hearing, had received the words, they would have no life nor meaning until she returned. The clerk was rubbing his back steadily against the door-facing again, watching her. The little boy was watching her too with his unwinking ineffable gaze, but nobody else was. The man with the peach spray removed it and spat and put the twig back into his mouth.

"He said Henry hadn't bought no horse," she said. "He said I could get the money from you."

"I reckon he forgot it," Snopes said. "He took all the money away with him when he left." He watched her a moment longer, then he trimmed again at the stick. The clerk rubbed his back gently against the door, watching her. After a time Mrs Armstid raised her head and looked up the road where it went on, mild with spring dust, past Mrs Littlejohn's, beginning to rise, on past the not-yet-bloomed (that would be in June) locust grove across the way, on past the schoolhouse, the weathered roof of which, rising beyond an orchard of peach and pear trees, resembled a hive swarmed about by a cloud of pink-and-white bees, ascending, mounting toward the crest of the hill where the church stood among its sparse gleam of marble headstones in the sombre cedar grove where during the long afternoons of summer the constant mourning doves called back and forth. She moved; once more the rubber soles hissed on the gnawed boards.

"I reckon it's about time to get dinner started," she said.

"How's Henry this morning, Mrs Armstid?" Ratliff said. She looked at him, pausing, the blank eyes waking for an instant.

"He's resting, I thank you kindly," she said. Then the eyes died again and she moved again. Snopes rose from the chair, closing his knife with his thumb and brushing a litter of minute shavings from his lap.

"Wait a minute," he said. Mrs Armstid paused again, half-turning, though still not looking at Snopes nor at any of them. Because she cant possibly actually believe it, Ratliff told himself. Anymore than I do. Snopes entered the store, the clerk, motionless again, his back and rump pressed against the door-facing as though waiting to start rubbing again, watched him enter, his head turning as the other passed him like the head of an owl, the little eyes blinking rapidly now. Jody Varner came up the road on his horse. He did not pass but instead turned in beside the store, toward the mulberry tree behind it where he was in the habit of hitching his horse. A wagon came up the road, creaking past. The man driving it lifted his hand; one or two of the men on the gallery lifted theirs in response. The wagon went on. Mrs. Armstid looked after it. Snopes came out of the door carrying a small striped paper bag and approached Mrs Armstid. "Here," he said. Her hand turned just enough to receive it. "A little sweetening for the chaps," he said. His other hand was already in his pocket, and as he turned back to the chair, he drew something from his pocket and handed it to the clerk, who took it. It was a five-cent piece. He sat down in the chair and tilted it back against the door again. He now had the knife in his hand again, already open. He turned his head slightly and spat again, neatly past the gray garment, into the road. The little boy was watching the sack in Mrs. Armstid's hand. Then she seemed to discover it also, rousing.

"You're right kind," she said. She rolled the sack into the apron, the little boy's unwinking gaze fixed upon the lump her hands made beneath the cloth. She moved again. "I reckon I better get on and help with dinner," she said. She descended the steps, though as soon as she reached the level earth and began to retreat, the gray folds of the garment once more lost all inference and intimation of loco-motion, so that she seemed to progress without motion like a figure on a retreating and diminishing float; a gray and blasted tree-trunk moving, somehow intact and upright, upon an unhurried flood. The clerk in the doorway cackled suddenly, explosively, chortling. He slapped his thigh.

"By God," he said, "you cant beat him."

Jody Varner, entering the store from the rear, paused in midstride like a pointing bird-dog. Then, on tiptoe, in complete silence and with astonishing speed, he darted behind the counter and sped up the gloomy tunnel, at the end of which a hulking, bear-shaped figure stooped, its entire head and shoulders wedged into the glass case which contained the needles and thread and snuff and tobacco and the stale gaudy candy. He snatched the boy savagely and viciously out; the boy gave a choked cry and struggled flabbily, cramming a final handful of something into his mouth, chewing. But he ceased to struggle almost at once and became slack and inert save for his jaws. Varner dragged him around the counter as the clerk entered, seemed to bounce suddenly into the store with a sort of alert concern. "You, Saint Elmo!" he said.

"Aint I told you and told you to keep him out of here?" Varner demanded, shaking the boy. "He's damn near eaten that candy-case clean. Stand up!" The boy hung like a half-filled sack from Varner's hand, chewing with a kind of fatalistic desperation, the eyes shut tight in the vast flaccid colorless face, the ears moving steadily and faintly to the chewing. Save for the jaw and the ears, he appeared to have gone to sleep chewing.

"You, Saint Elmo!" the clerk said. "Stand up!" The boy assumed his own weight, though he did not open his eyes yet nor cease to chew. Varner released him. "Git on home," the clerk said. The boy turned obediently to re-enter the store. Varner jerked him about again.

"Not that way," he said. The boy crossed the gallery and de-scended the steps, the tight overalls undulant and reluctant across his flabby thighs. Before he reached the ground, his hand rose from his pocket to his mouth; again his ears moved faintly to the motion of chewing.

"He's worse than a rat, ain't he?" the clerk said.

"Rat, hell," Varner said, breathing harshly. "He's worse than a goat. First thing I know, he'll graze on back and work through that lace leather and them hame-strings and lap-links and ring-bolts and eat me and you and him all three clean out the back door. And then be damned if I wouldn't be afraid to turn my back for fear he would cross the road and start in on the gin and the blacksmith shop. Now you mind what I say. If I catch him hanging around here one more time, I'm going to set a bear-trap for him." He went out onto the gallery, the clerk following. "Morning, gentlemen," he said.

"Who's that one, Jody?" Ratliff said. Save for the clerk in the background, they were the only two standing, and now, in juxta-position, you could see the resemblance between them—a re-semblance intangible, indefinite, not in figure, speech, dress, intelli-gence; certainly not in morals. Yet it was there, but with this bridge-less difference, this hallmark of his fate upon him: he would become an old man; Ratliff, too: but an old man who at about sixty-five would be caught and married by a creature not yet seventeen prob-ably, who would for the rest of his life continue to take revenge upon him for her whole sex; Ratliff, never. The boy was moving without haste up the road. His hand rose again from his pocket to his mouth.

"That boy of I. O.'s," Varner said. "By God, I've done everything but put out poison for him."

"What?" Ratliff said. He glanced quickly about at the faces; for an instant there was in his own not only bewilderment but some-thing almost like terror. "I thought—the other day you fellows told me— You said it was a woman, a young woman with a baby— Here now," he said. "Wait."

"This here's another one," Varner said. "I wish to hell he couldn't walk. Well, Eck, I hear you caught one of your horses."

"That's right," Eck said. He and the little boy had finished the crackers and cheese and he had sat for some time now, holding the empty bag.

"It was the one he give you, wasn't it?" Varner said.

"That's right," Eck said.

"Give the other one to me, paw," the little boy said.

"What happened?" Varner said.

"He broke his neck," Eck said.

"I know," Varner said. "But how?" Eck did not move. Watching him, they could almost see him visibly gathering and arranging words, speech. Varner, looking down at him, began to laugh steadily and harshly, sucking his teeth. "I'll tell you what happened. Eck and that boy finally run it into that blind lane of Freeman's, after a chase of about twenty-four hours. They figured it couldn't possibly climb them eight-foot fences of Freeman's so him and the boy tied their rope across the end of the lane, about three feet off the ground. And sho enough, soon as the horse come to the end of the lane and seen Freeman's barn, it whirled just like Eck figured it would and come helling back up that lane like a scared hen-hawk. It probably never even seen the rope at all. Mrs Freeman was watching from where she had run up onto the porch. She said that when it hit that rope, it looked just like one of these here great big Christmas pinwheels. But the one you bought got clean away, didn't it?"

"That's right," Eck said. "I never had time to see which way the other one went."

"Give him to me, paw," the little boy said.

"You wait till we catch him," Eck said. "We'll see about it then."

That afternoon Ratliff sat in the halted buckboard in front of Bookwright's gate. Bookwright stood in the road beside it. "You were wrong," Bookwright said. "He come back."

"He come back," Ratliff said. "I misjudged his . . . nerve aint the word I want, and sholy lack of it aint. But I wasn't wrong."

"Nonsense," Bookwright said. "He was gone all day yesterday. Nobody saw him going to town or coming back, but that's bound to be where he was at. Aint no man, I dont care if his name is Snopes, going to let his own blood kin rot in jail."

"He wont be in jail long. Court is next month, and after they send him to Parchman, he can stay outdoors again. He will even go back to farming, plowing. Of course it wont be his cotton, but then he never did make enough out of his own cotton to quite pay him for staying alive."

"Nonsense," Bookwright said. "I dont believe it. Flem aint going to let him go to the penitentiary."

"Yes," Ratliff said. "Because Flem Snopes has got to cancel all them loose-flying notes that turns up here and there every now and then. He's going to discharge at least some of the notes for good and all." They looked at one another—Ratliff grave and easy in the blue shirt, Bookwright sober too, black-browed, intent.

"I thought you said you and him burned them notes."

"I said we burned two notes that Mink Snopes gave me. Do you think that any Snopes is going to put all of anything on one piece of paper that can be destroyed by one match? Do you think there is any Snopes that dont know that?"

"Oh," Bookwright said. "Hah," he said, with no mirth. "I reckon you gave Henry Armstid back his five dollars too." Then Ratliff looked away. His face changed—something fleeting, quizzical, but not smiling, his eyes did not smile; it was gone.

"I could have," he said. "But I didn't. I might have if I could just been sho he would buy something this time that would sho enough kill him, like Mrs Littlejohn said. Besides, I wasn't protecting a Snopes from Snopeses; I wasn't even protecting a people from a Snopes. I was protecting something that wasn't even a people, that wasn't nothing but something that dont want nothing but to walk and feel the sun and wouldn't know how to hurt no man even if it would and wouldn't want to even if it could, just like I wouldn't stand by and see you steal a meat-bone from a dog. I never made them Snopeses and I never made the folks that cant wait to bare their backsides to them. I could do more, but I wont. I wont, I tell you!"

"All right," Bookwright said. "Hook your drag up; it aint nothing but a hill. I said it's all right."

———

II

The two actions of Armstid pl. vs. Snopes, and Tull pl. vs. Eckrum Snopes (and anyone else named Snopes or Varner either which Tull's irate wife could contrive to involve, as the village well knew) were accorded a change of venue by mutual agreement and arrangement among the litigants. Three of the parties did, that is, because Flem Snopes flatly refused to recognise the existence of the suit against himself, stating once and without heat and first turning his head slightly aside to spit, "They wasn't none of my horses," then fell to whittling again while the baffled and helpless bailiff stood before the tilted chair with the papers he was trying to serve.

"What a opportunity for that Snopes family lawyer this would a been," Ratliff said when told about it. "What's his name? that quick-fatherer, the Moses with his mouth full of mottoes and his coat-tail full of them already half grown retroactive sons? I dont understand yet how a man that has to spend as much time as I do being constantly reminded of them folks, still cant keep the names straight. I. O. That he never had time to wait. This here would be probably the one tried case in his whole legal existence where he wouldn't be bothered with no narrow-ideaed client trying to make him stop talking, and the squire presiding himself would be the only man in company with authority to tell him to shut up."

So neither did the Varner surrey nor Ratliff's buckboard make one among the wagons, the buggies, and the saddled horses and mules which moved out of the village on that May Saturday morning, to converge upon Whiteleaf store eight miles away, coming not only from Frenchman's Bend but from other directions too since by that time, what Ratliff had called 'that Texas sickness,' that spotted corruption of frantic and uncatchable horses, had spread as far as twenty and thirty miles. So by the time the Frenchman's Bend people began to arrive, there were two dozen wagons, the teams reversed and eased of harness and tied to the rear wheels in order to pass the day, and twice that many saddled animals already standing about the locust grove beside the store and the site of the hearing had already been transferred from the store to an adjacent shed where in the fall cotton would be stored. But by nine oclock it was seen that even the shed would not hold them all, so the palladium was moved again, from the shed to the grove itself. The horses and mules and wagons were cleared from it; the single chair, the gnawed table bearing a thick Bible which had the appearance of loving and constant use of a piece of old and perfectly-kept machinery and an almanac and a copy of Mississippi Reports dated 1881 and bearing along its opening edge a single thread-thin line of soilure as if during all the time of his possession its owner (or user) had opened it at only one page though that quite often, were fetched from the shed to the grove; a wagon and four men were dispatched and returned presently from the church a mile away with four wooden pews for the litigants and their clansmen and witnesses; behind these in turn the spectators stood—the men, the women, the children, sober, attentive, and neat, not in their Sunday clothes to be sure, but in the clean working garments donned that morning for the Saturday's diversion of sitting about the country stores or trips into the county seat, and in which they would return to the field on Monday morning and would wear all that week until Friday night came round again. The Justice of the Peace was a neat, small, plump old man resembling a tender caricature of all grandfathers who ever breathed, in a beautifully laundered though collarless white shirt

with immaculate starch-gleaming cuffs and bosom, and steel-framed
spectacles and neat, faintly curling white hair. He sat behind the
table and looked at them—at the gray woman in the gray sunbonnet
and dress, her clasped and motionless hands on her lap resembling
a gnarl of pallid and drowned roots from a drained swamp; at Tull
in his faded but absolutely clean shirt and the overalls which his
womenfolks not only kept immaculately washed but starched and
ironed also, and not creased through the legs but flat across them
from seam to seam, so that on each Saturday morning they resembled the short pants of a small boy, and the sedate and innocent
blue of his eyes above the month-old corn-silk beard which concealed most of his abraded face and which gave him an air of
incredible and paradoxical dissoluteness, not as though at last and
without warning he had appeared in the sight of his fellowmen in
his true character, but as if an old Italian portrait of a child saint
had been defaced by a vicious and idle boy; at Mrs Tull, a strong,
full-bosomed though slightly dumpy woman with an expression of
grim and seething outrage which the elapsed four weeks had apparently neither increased nor diminished but had merely set, an
outrage which curiously and almost at once began to give the impression of being directed not at any Snopes or at any other man
in particular but at all men, all males, and of which Tull himself was
not at all the victim but the subject, who sat on one side of her
husband while the biggest of the four daughters sat on the other
as if they (or Mrs Tull at least) were not so much convinced that
Tull might leap up and flee, as determined that he would not; and
at Eck and the little boy, identical save for size, and Lump the clerk
in a gray cap which someone actually recognised as being the one
which Flem Snopes had worn when he went to Texas last year, who
between spells of rapid blinking would sit staring at the Justice
with the lidless intensity of a rat—and into the lens-distorted and
irisless old-man's eyes of the Justice there grew an expression not
only of amazement and bewilderment but, as in Ratliff's eyes while
he stood on the store gallery four weeks ago, something very like
terror.

"This—" he said. "I didn't expect—I didn't look to see—. I'm going
to pray," he said. "I aint going to pray aloud. But I hope—" He
looked at them. "I wish . . . Maybe some of you all anyway had
better do the same." He bowed his head. They watched him, quiet
and grave, while he sat motionless behind the table, the light morning wind moving faintly in his thin hair and the shadow-stipple of

windy leaves gliding and flowing across the starched bulge of bosom and the gleaming bone-buttoned cuffs, as rigid and almost as large as sections of six-inch stovepipe, at his joined hands. He raised his head. "Armstid against Snopes," he said. Mrs Armstid spoke. She did not move, she looked at nothing, her hands clasped in her lap, speaking in that flat, toneless and hopeless voice:

"That Texas man said——"

"Wait," the Justice said. He looked about at the faces, the blurred eyes fleeing behind the thick lenses. "Where is the defendant? I dont see him."

"He wouldn't come," the bailiff said.

"Wouldn't come?" the Justice said. "Didn't you serve the papers on him?"

"He wouldn't take them," the bailiff said. "He said——"

"Then he is in contempt!" the Justice cried.

"What for?" Lump Snopes said. "Aint nobody proved yet they was his horses." The Justice looked at him.

"Are you representing the defendant?" he said. Snopes blinked at him for a moment.

"What's that mean?" he said. "That you aim for me to pay whatever fine you think you can clap onto him?"

"So he refuses to defend himself," the Justice said. "Dont he know that I can find against him for that reason, even if pure justice and decency aint enough?"

"It'll be pure something," Snopes said. "It dont take no mind-reader to see how your mind is——"

"Shut up, Snopes," the bailiff said. "If you aint in this case, you keep out of it." He turned back to the Justice. "What you want me to do: go over to the Bend and fetch Snopes here anyway? I reckon I can do it."

"No," the Justice said. "Wait." He looked about at the sober faces again with that bafflement, that dread. "Does anybody here know for sho who them horses belonged to? Anybody?" They looked back at him, sober, attentive—at the neat immaculate old man sitting with his hands locked together on the table before him to still the trembling. "All right, Mrs Armstid," he said. "Tell the court what happened." She told it, unmoving, in the flat, inflectionless voice, looking at nothing, while they listened quietly, coming to the end and ceasing without even any fall of voice, as though the tale mattered nothing and came to nothing. The Justice was looking down at his hands. When she ceased, he looked up at her. "But you haven't showed yet that Snopes owned the horses. The one you want to sue is that Texas man. And he's gone. If you got a judgment against him, you couldn't collect the money. Dont you see?"

"Mr Snopes brought him here," Mrs Armstid said. "Likely that Texas man wouldn't have knowed where Frenchman's Bend was if Mr Snopes hadn't showed him."

"But it was the Texas man that sold the horses and collected the money for them." The Justice looked about again at the faces. "Is that right? You, Bookwright, is that what happened?"

"Yes," Bookwright said. The Justice looked at Mrs Armstid again, with that pity and grief. As the morning increased the wind had risen, so that from time to time gusts of it ran through the branches overhead, bringing a faint snow of petals, prematurely bloomed as the spring itself had condensed with spendthrift speed after the hard winter, and the heavy and drowsing scent of them, about the motionless heads.

"He give Mr Snopes Henry's money. He said Henry hadn't bought no horse. He said I could get the money from Mr Snopes tomorrow."

"And you have witnesses that saw and heard him?"

"Yes, sir. The other men that was there saw him give Mr Snopes the money and say that I could get it——"

"And you asked Snopes for the money?"

"Yes, sir. He said that Texas man taken it away with him when he left. But I would . . ." She ceased again, perhaps looking down at her hands also. Certainly she was not looking at anyone.

"Yes?" the Justice said. "You would what?"

"I would know them five dollars. I earned them myself, weaving at night after Henry and the chaps was asleep. Some of the ladies in Jefferson would save up string and such and give it to me and I would weave things and sell them. I earned that money a little at a time and I would know it when I saw it because I would take the can outen the chimney and count it now and then while it was making up to enough to buy my chaps some shoes for next winter. I would know it if I was to see it again. If Mr Snopes would just let——"

"Suppose there was somebody seen Flem give that money back to that Texas fellow," Lump Snopes said suddenly.

"Did anybody here see that?" the Justice said.

"Yes," Snopes said, harshly and violently. "Eck here did." He looked at Eck. "Go on. Tell him." The Justice looked at Eck; the four Tull girls turned their heads as one head and looked at him, and Mrs Tull leaned forward to look past her husband, her face cold, furious, and contemptuous, and those standing shifted to look past one another's heads at Eck sitting motionless on the bench.

"Did you see Snopes give Armstid's money back to the Texas man, Eck?" the Justice said. Still Eck did not answer nor move, Lump Snopes made a gross violent sound through the side of his mouth.

"By God, I aint afraid to say it if Eck is. I seen him do it."

"Will you swear that as testimony?" Snopes looked at the Justice. He did not blink now.

"So you wont take my word," he said.

"I want the truth," the Justice said. "If I cant find that, I got to have sworn evidence of what I will have to accept as truth." He lifted the Bible from the two other books.

"All right," the bailiff said. "Step up here." Snopes rose from the bench and approached. They watched him, though now there was no shifting nor craning, no movement at all among the faces, the still eyes. Snopes at the table looked back at them once, his gaze traversing swiftly the crescent-shaped rank; he looked at the Justice again. The bailiff grasped the Bible; though the Justice did not release it yet.

"You are ready to swear you saw Snopes give that Texas man back the money he took from Henry Armstid for that horse?" he said.

"I said I was, didn't I?" Snopes said. The Justice released the Bible.

"Swear him," he said.

"Put your left hand on the Book raise your right hand you solemnly swear and affirm——" the bailiff said rapidly. But Snopes had already done so, his left hand clapped onto the extended Bible and the other hand raised and his head turned away as once more his gaze went rapidly along the circle of expressionless and intent faces, saying in that harsh and snarling voice:

"Yes. I saw Flem Snopes give back to that Texas man whatever money Henry Armstid or anybody else thinks Henry Armstid or anybody else paid Flem for any of them horses. Does that suit you?"

"Yes," the Justice said. Then there was no movement, no sound anywhere among them. The bailiff placed the Bible quietly on the table beside the Justice's locked hands, and there was no movement save the flow and recover of the windy shadows and the drift of the locust petals. Then Mrs Armstid rose; she stood once more (or still) looking at nothing, her hands clasped across her middle.

"I reckon I can go now, cant I?" she said.

"Yes," the Justice said, rousing. "Unless you would like——"

"I better get started," she said. "It's a right far piece." She had not come in the wagon, but on one of the gaunt and underfed mules. One of the men followed her across the grove and untied the mule for her and led it up to a wagon, from one hub of which she mounted. Then they looked at the Justice again. He sat behind the table, his hands still joined before him, though his head was not bowed now. Yet he did not move until the bailiff leaned and spoke to him, when he roused, came suddenly awake without starting, as an old man wakes from an old man's light sleep. He removed his hands from the table and, looking down, he spoke exactly as if he were reading from a paper:

"Tull against Snopes. Assault and——"

"Yes!" Mrs Tull said. "I'm going to say a word before you start." She leaned, looking past Tull at Lump Snopes again. "If you think you are going to lie and perjure Flem and Eck Snopes out of——"

"Now, mamma," Tull said. Now she spoke to Tull, without changing her position or her tone or even any break or pause in her speech:

"Dont you say hush to me! You'll let Eck Snopes or Flem Snopes or that whole Varner tribe snatch you out of the wagon and beat you half to death against a wooden bridge. But when it comes to suing them for your just rights and a punishment, oh no. Because that wouldn't be neighborly. What's neighborly got to do with you lying flat on your back in the middle of planting time while we pick splinters out of your face?" By this time the bailiff was shouting.

"Order! Order! This here's a law court!" Mrs Tull ceased. She sat back, breathing hard, staring at the Justice, who sat and spoke again as if he were reading aloud:

"—assault and battery on the person of Vernon Tull, through the agency and instrument of one horse, unnamed, belonging to Eckrum Snopes. Evidence of physical detriment and suffering, defendant himself. Witnesses, Mrs Tull and daughters——"

"Eck Snopes saw it too," Mrs Tull said, though with less violence now. "He was there. He got there in plenty of time to see it. Let him deny it. Let him look me in the face and deny it if he——"

"If you please, ma'am," the Justice said. He said it so quietly that Mrs Tull hushed and became quite calm, almost a rational and composed being. "The injury to your husband aint disputed. And the agency of the horse aint disputed. The law says that when a man owns a creature which he knows to be dangerous and if that creature is restrained and restricted from the public commons by a pen or enclosure capable of restraining and restricting it, if a man enter that pen or enclosure, whether he knows the creature in it is dangerous or not dangerous, then that man has committed trespass and the owner of that creature is not liable. But if that creature known to him to be dangerous ceases to be restrained by that suitable pen or enclosure, either by accident or design and either with or without the owner's knowledge, then that owner is liable. That's the law. All necessary now is to establish first, the ownership of the horse, and second, that the horse was a dangerous creature within the definition of the law as provided."

"Hah," Mrs Tull said. She said it exactly as Bookwright would have. "Dangerous. Ask Vernon Tull. Ask Henry Armstid if them things was pets."

"If you please, ma'am," the Justice said. He was looking at Eck. "What is the defendant's position? Denial of ownership?"

"What?" Eck said.

"Was that your horse that ran over Mr Tull?"

"Yes," Eck said. "It was mine. How much do I have to p——"

"Hah," Mrs Tull said again. "Denial of ownership. When there were at least forty men—fools too, or they wouldn't have been there. But even a fool's word is good about what he saw and heard —at least forty men heard that Texas murderer give that horse to Eck Snopes. Not sell it to him, mind; give it to him."

"What?" the Justice said. "Gave it to him?"

"Yes," Eck said. "He give it to me. I'm sorry Tull happened to be using that bridge too at the same time. How much do I——"

"Wait," the Justice said. "What did you give him? a note? a swap of some kind?"

"No," Eck said. "He just pointed to it in the lot and told me it belonged to me."

"And he didn't give you a bill of sale or a deed or anything in writing?"

"I reckon he never had time," Eck said. "And after Lon Quick forgot and left that gate open, never nobody had time to do no writing even if we had a thought of it."

"What's all this?" Mrs Tull said. "Eck Snopes has just told you he owned that horse. And if you wont take his word, there were forty men standing at that gate all day long doing nothing, that heard that murdering card-playing whiskey-drinking antichrist—" This time the Justice raised one hand, in its enormous pristine cuff, toward her. He did not look at her.

"Wait," he said. "Then what did he do?" he said to Eck. "Just lead the horse up and put the rope in your hand?"

"No," Eck said. "Him nor nobody else never got no ropes on none of them. He just pointed to the horse in the lot and said it was mine and auctioned off the rest of them and got into the buggy and said good-bye and druv off. And we got our ropes and went into the lot, only Lon Quick forgot to shut the gate. I'm sorry it made Tull's mules snatch him outen the wagon. How much do I owe him?" Then he stopped, because the Justice was no longer looking at him and, as he realised a moment later, no longer listening either. Instead, he was sitting back in the chair, actually leaning back in it for the first time, his head bent slightly and his hands resting on the table before him, the fingers lightly overlapped. They watched him quietly for almost a half-minute before anyone realised that he was looking quietly and steadily at Mrs Tull.

"Well, Mrs Tull," he said, "by your own testimony, Eck never owned that horse."

"What?" Mrs Tull said. It was not loud at all. "What did you say?"

"In the law, ownership cant be conferred or invested by word-of-mouth. It must be established either by recorded or authentic document, or by possession or occupation. By your testimony and his both, he never gave that Texan anything in exchange for that horse, and by his testimony the Texas man never gave him any paper to prove he owned it, and by his testimony and by what I know myself from these last four weeks, nobody yet has ever laid hand or rope either on any one of them. So that horse never came into Eck's possession at all. That Texas man could have given that same horse to a dozen other men standing around that gate that day, without even needing to tell Eck he had done it; and Eck himself could have transferred all his title and equity in it to Mr Tull right there while Mr Tull was lying unconscious on that bridge just by thinking it to himself, and Mr Tull's title would be just as legal as Eck's."

"So I get nothing," Mrs Tull said. Her voice was still calm, quiet, though probably no one but Tull realized that it was too calm and quiet. "My team is made to run away by a wild spotted mad dog, my wagon is wrecked; my husband is jerked out of it and knocked unconscious and unable to work for a whole week with less than half of our seed in the ground, and I get nothing."

"Wait," the Justice said. "The law——"

"The law," Mrs Tull said. She stood suddenly up—a short, broad, strong woman, balanced on the balls of her planted feet.

"Now, mamma," Tull said.

"Yes, ma'am," the Justice said. "Your damages are fixed by statute. The law says that when a suit for damages is brought against the owner of an animal which has committed damage or injury, if the owner of the animal either cant or wont assume liability, the injured or damaged party shall find recompense in the body of the animal. And since Eck Snopes never owned that horse at all, and since you just heard a case here this morning that failed to prove that Flem Snopes had any equity in any of them, that horse still belongs to that Texas man. Or did belong. Because now that horse that made your team run away and snatch your husband out of the wagon, belongs to you and Mr Tull."

"Now, mamma!" Tull said. He rose quickly. But Mrs Tull was still quiet, only quite rigid and breathing hard, until Tull spoke. Then she turned on him, not screaming: shouting; presently the bailiff was banging the table-top with his hand-polished hickory cane and roaring "Order! Order!" while the neat old man, thrust backward in his chair as though about to dodge and trembling with an old man's palsy, looked on with amazed unbelief.

"The horse!" Mrs Tull shouted. "We see it for five seconds, while it is climbing into the wagon with us and then out again. Then its gone, God dont know where and thank the Lord He dont! And the mules gone with it and the wagon wrecked and you laying there on the bridge with your face full of kindling-wood and bleeding like a hog and dead for all we knew. And he gives us the horse! Dont hush me! Get on to that wagon, fool that would sit there behind a pair of young mules with the reins tied around his wrist! Get on to that wagon, all of you!"

"I cant stand no more!" the old Justice cried. "I wont! This court's adjourned! Adjourned!"

The
Bear

WILLIAM FAULKNER

Myth, the re-shaping of the historical world through imagina-tion, finds eloquent expression in "The Bear." Embodied in this dense story are indeed various myths, brilliantly fused—the myth of Faulkner's own Yoknapatawpha territory, with its obsessive themes of racial conflict, sexual struggle, social disintegration, and the claims on the living of a glorious and nightmarish past; myths too of the assault by an American technological culture on its wilderness frontier, of the fated shattering of an American pastoral innocence by an insistent modernity, and of the archetypal baptism of the young hero into knowledge and virtuous action. The most inclusive of all modes of fiction, myth commonly embraces several lesser kinds. "The Bear" takes shape particularly through the symbolism of artifacts like the watch, compass, gun, and locomotive; the allegorism of Lion and Old Ben, of the en-counters of the boy Ike McCaslin with Old Ben, and of the hunt itself; the moral conception of the hunt and of an older Ike's pursuit of truth in the cryptic ledgers; and the historical sense of reality, evident particularly in the difficult fourth sec-tion and in the fifth, where Faulkner addresses himself to late-nineteenth-century changes in social relations and on the frontier in Mississippi. Although we can isolate each of these modes to some degree, however, Faulkner's largest achieve-ment in "The Bear" is to have created not a compound of discrete perceptions but a mythopoeic whole.

There was a man and a dog too this time. Two beasts, counting Old Ben, the bear, and two men, counting Boon Hoggan-beck, in whom some of the same blood ran which ran in Sam Fathers, even though Boon's was a plebeian strain of it and only Sam and Old Ben and the mongrel Lion were taintless and incorruptible.

He was sixteen. For six years now he had been a man's hunter. For six years now he had heard the best of all talking. It was of the wilderness, the big woods, bigger and older than any recorded document:—of white man fatuous enough to believe he had bought any fragment of it, of Indian ruthless enough to pretend that any fragment of it had been his to convey; bigger than Major de Spain and the scrap he pretended to, knowing better; older than old Thomas Sutpen of whom Major de Spain had had it and who knew better; older even than old Ikkemotubbe, the Chickasaw chief, of whom old Sutpen had had it and who knew better in his turn. It was of the men, not white nor black nor red but men, hunters, with the will and hardihood to endure and the humility and skill to survive, and the dogs and the bear and deer juxtaposed and reliefed against it, ordered and compelled by and within the wilderness in the ancient and unremitting contest according to the ancient and immitigable rules which voided all regrets and brooked no quarter;—the best game of all, the best of all breathing and forever the best of all listening, the voices quiet and weighty and deliberate for retrospection and recollection and exactitude among the concrete trophies—the racked guns and the heads and skins—in the libraries of town houses or the offices of plantation houses or (and best of all) in the camps themselves where the intact and still-warm meat yet hung, the men who had slain it sitting before the burning logs on hearths when there were houses and hearths or about the smoky blazing of piled wood in front of stretched tarpaulins when there were not. There was always a bottle present, so that it would seem to him that those fine fierce instants of heart and brain and courage and wiliness and speed were concentrated and distilled into that brown liquor which not women, not boys and children, but only hunters drank, drinking not of the blood they spilled but some condensation of the wild immortal spirit, drinking it moderately, humbly even, not with the pagan's base and baseless hope of acquiring thereby the virtues of cunning and strength and speed but in salute to them. Thus it seemed to him on this December morning not only natural but actually fitting that this should have begun with whisky.

He realised later that it had begun long before that. It had already begun on that day when he first wrote his age in two ciphers and his cousin McCaslin brought him for the first time to the camp, the big woods, to earn for himself from the wilderness the name and state of hunter provided he in his turn were humble and enduring enough. He had already inherited then, without ever having seen it, the big old bear with one trap-ruined foot that in an area almost a hundred miles square had earned for himself a name, a definite designation like a living man:—the long legend of corn-cribs broken down and rifled, of shoats and grown pigs and even calves carried bodily into the woods and devoured and traps and deadfalls overthrown and dogs mangled and slain and shotgun and even rifle shots delivered at point-blank range yet with no more effect than so many peas blown through a tube by a child—a corridor of wreckage and destruction beginning back before the boy was born, through which sped, not fast but rather with the ruthless and irresistible deliberation of a locomotive, the shaggy tremendous shape. It ran in his knowledge before he ever saw it. It loomed and towered in his dreams before he even saw the unaxed woods where it left its crooked print, shaggy, tremendous, red-eyed, not malevolent but just big, too big for the dogs which tried to bay it, for the horses which tried to ride it down, for the men and the bullets they fired into it; too big for the very country which was its constricting scope. It was as if the boy had already divined what his senses and intellect had not encompassed yet: that doomed wilderness whose edges were being constantly and punily gnawed at by men with plows and axes who feared it because it was wilderness, men myriad and nameless even to one another in the land where the old bear had earned a name, and through which ran not even a mortal beast but an anachronism indomitable and invincible out of an old dead time, a phantom, epitome and apotheosis of the old wild life which the little puny humans swarmed and hacked at in a fury of abhorrence and fear like pygmies about the ankles of a drowsing elephant;—the old bear, solitary, indomitable, and alone; widowered childless and absolved of mortality—old Priam reft of his old wife and outlived all his sons.

Still a child, with three years then two years then one year yet before he too could make one of them, each November he would watch the wagon containing the dogs and the bedding and food and guns and his cousin McCaslin and Tennie's Jim and Sam Fathers too until Sam moved to the camp to live, depart for the Big Bottom, the big woods. To him, they were going not to hunt bear and deer but to keep yearly rendezvous with the bear which they did not even intend to kill. Two weeks later they would return, with no trophy, no skin. He had not expected it. He had not even feared that it might be in the wagon this time with the other skins and heads. He did not even tell himself that in three years or two years or one year more he would be present and that it might even be his gun. He believed that only after he had served his apprenticeship in the woods which would prove him worthy to be a hunter, would he even be permitted to distinguish the crooked print, and that even then for two November weeks he would merely make another minor one, along with his cousin and Major de Spain and General Compson and Walter Ewell and Boon and the dogs which feared to bay it and the shotguns and rifles which failed even to bleed it, in the yearly pageant-rite of the old bear's furious immortality.

His day came at last. In the surrey with his cousin and Major de Spain and General Compson he saw the wilderness through a slow drizzle of November rain just above the ice point as it seemed to him later he always saw it or at least always remembered it— the tall and endless wall of dense November woods under the dissolving afternoon and the year's death, sombre, impenetrable (he could not even discern yet how, at what point they could possibly hope to enter it even though he knew that Sam Fathers was waiting there with the wagon), the surrey moving through the skeleton stalks of cotton and corn in the last of open country, the last trace of man's puny gnawing at the immemorial flank, until, dwarfed by that perspective into an almost ridiculous diminishment, the surrey itself seemed to have ceased to move (this too to be completed later, years later, after he had grown to a man and had seen the sea) as a solitary small boat hangs in lonely immobility, merely tossing up and down, in the infinite waste of the ocean while the water and then the apparently impenetrable land which it nears without appreciable progress, swings slowly and opens the widening inlet which is the anchorage. He entered it. Sam was waiting, wrapped in a quilt on the wagon seat behind the patient and steaming mules. He entered his novitiate to the true wilderness with Sam beside him as he had begun his apprenticeship in miniature to manhood after the rabbits and such with Sam beside him, the two of them wrapped in the damp, warm, negro-rank quilt while the wilderness closed behind his entrance as it had opened momentarily to accept him, opening before his advancement as it closed behind his progress, no fixed path the wagon followed but a channel nonexistent ten yards ahead of it and ceasing to exist ten yards after it had passed, the wagon progressing not by its own volition but by attrition of their intact yet fluid circumambience, drowsing, earless, almost lightless.

It seemed to him that at the age of ten he was witnessing his own birth. It was not even strange to him. He had experienced it all before, and not merely in dreams. He saw the camp—a paintless six-room bungalow set on piles above the spring high-water—and he knew already how it was going to look. He helped in the rapid orderly disorder of their establishment in it and even his motions were familiar to him, foreknown. Then for two weeks he ate the coarse, rapid food—the shapeless sour bread, the wild strange meat, venison and bear and turkey and coon which he had never tasted before—which men ate, cooked by men who were hunters first and cooks afterward; he slept in harsh sheetless blankets as hunters slept. Each morning the gray of dawn found him and Sam Fathers on the stand, the crossing, which had been allotted him. It was the poorest one, the most barren. He had expected that; he had not dared yet to hope even to himself that he would even hear the running dogs this first time. But he did hear them. It was on the third morning—a murmur, sourceless, almost indistinguishable, yet he knew what it was although he had never before heard that many dogs running at once, the murmur swelling into separate and distinct voices until he could call the five dogs which his cousin owned from among the others. "Now," Sam said, "slant your gun up a little and draw back the hammers and then stand still."

But it was not for him, not yet. The humility was there; he had learned that. And he could learn the patience. He was only ten, only one week. The instant had passed. It seemed to him that he could actually see the deer, the buck, smoke-colored, elongated with speed, vanished, the woods, the gray solitude still ringing even when the voices of the dogs had died away; from far away across the sombre woods and the gray half-liquid morning there came two shots. "Now let your hammers down," Sam said.

He did so. "You knew it too," he said.

"Yes," Sam said. "I want you to learn how to do when you didn't shoot. It's after the chance for the bear or the deer has done already come and gone that men and dogs get killed."

"Anyway, it wasn't him," the boy said. "It wasn't even a bear. It was just a deer."

"Yes," Sam said, "it was just a deer."

Then one morning, it was in the second week, he heard the dogs again. This time before Sam even spoke he readied the too-long, too-heavy, man-size gun as Sam had taught him, even though this time he knew the dogs and the deer were coming less close than ever, hardly within hearing even. They didn't sound like any running dogs he had ever heard before even. Then he found that Sam, who had taught him first of all to cock the gun and take position where he could see best in all directions and then never to move again, had himself moved up beside him. "There," he said. "Listen." The boy listened, to no ringing chorus strong and fast on a free scent but a moiling yapping an octave too high and with something more than indecision and even abjectness in it which he could not yet recognise, reluctant, not even moving very fast, taking a long time to pass out of hearing, leaving even then in the air that echo of thin and almost human hysteria, abject, almost humanly grieving, with this time nothing ahead of it, no sense of a fleeing unseen smoke-colored shape. He could hear Sam breathing at his shoulder. He saw the arched curve of the old man's inhaling nostrils.

"It's Old Ben!" he cried, whispering.

Sam didn't move save for the slow gradual turning of his head as the voices faded on and the faint steady rapid arch and collapse of his nostrils. "Hah," he said. "Not even running. Walking."

"But up here!" the boy cried. "Way up here!"

"He do it every year," Sam said. "Once. Ash and Boon say he comes up here to run the other little bears away. Tell them to get to hell out of here and stay out until the hunters are gone. Maybe." The boy no longer heard anything at all, yet still Sam's head continued to turn gradually and steadily until the back of it was toward him. Then it turned back and looked down at him—the same face, grave, familiar, expressionless until it smiled, the same old man's eyes from which as he watched there faded slowly a quality darkly and fiercely lambent, passionate and proud. "He dont care no more for bears than he does for dogs or men neither. He come to see who's here, who's new in camp this year, whether he can shoot or not, can stay or not. Whether we got the dog yet that can bay and hold him until a man gets there with a gun. Because he's the head bear. He's the man." It faded, was gone; again they were the eyes as he had known them all his life. "He'll let them follow him to the river. Then he'll send them home. We might as well go too; see how they look when they get back to camp."

The dogs were there first, ten of them huddled back under the kitchen, himself and Sam squatting to peer back into the obscurity where they crouched, quiet, the eyes rolling and luminous, vanishing, and no sound, only that effluvium which the boy could not quite place yet, of something more than dog, stronger than dog and not just animal, just beast even. Because there had been nothing in front of the abject and painful yapping except the solitude, the wilderness, so that when the eleventh hound got back about mid-afternoon and he and Tennie's Jim held the passive and still trembling bitch while Sam daubed her tattered ear and raked shoulder with turpentine and axle-grease, it was still no living creature but only the wilderness which, leaning for a moment, had patted lightly once her temerity. "Just like a man," Sam said. "Just like folks. Put off as long as she could having to be brave, knowing all the time that sooner or later she would have to be brave once so she could keep on calling herself a dog, and knowing beforehand what was going to happen when she done it."

He did not know just when Sam left. He only knew that he was gone. For the next three mornings he rose and ate breakfast and Sam was not waiting for him. He went to his stand alone; he found it without help now and stood on it as Sam had taught him. On the third morning he heard the dogs again, running strong and free on a true scent again, and he readied the gun as he had learned to do and heard the hunt sweep past on since he was not ready yet, had not deserved other yet in just one short period of two weeks as compared to all the long life which he had already dedicated to the wilderness with patience and humility; he heard the shot again, one shot, the single clapping report of Walter Ewell's rifle. By now he could not only find his stand and then return to camp without guidance, by using the compass his cousin had given him he reached Walter waiting beside the buck and the moiling of dogs over the cast entrails before any of the others except Major de Spain and Tennie's Jim on the horses, even before Uncle Ash arrived with the one-eyed wagon-mule which did not mind the smell of blood or even, so they said, of bear.

It was not Uncle Ash on the mule. It was Sam, returned. And Sam was waiting when he finished his dinner and, himself on the one-eyed mule and Sam on the other one of the wagon team, they rode for more than three hours through the rapid shortening sunless afternoon, following no path, no trail even that he could discern, into a section of country he had never seen before. Then he understood why Sam had made him ride the one-eyed mule which would not spook at the smell of blood, of wild animals. The other one, the sound one, stopped short and tried to whirl and bolt even as Sam got down, jerking and wrenching at the rein while Sam held it, coaxing it forward with his voice since he did not dare risk hitching it, drawing it forward while the boy dismounted from the marred one which would stand. Then, standing beside Sam in the thick great gloom of ancient woods and the winter's dying afternoon, he looked quietly down at the rotted log scored and gutted with claw-marks and, in the wet earth beside it, the print of the enormous warped two-toed foot. Now he knew what he had heard in the hounds' voices in the woods that morning and what he had smelled when he peered under the kitchen where they huddled. It was in him too, a little different because they were brute beasts and he was not, but only a little different—an eagerness, passive; an abjectness, a sense of his own fragility and impotence against the timeless woods, yet without doubt or dread; a flavor like brass in the sudden run of saliva in his mouth, a hard sharp constriction either in his brain or his stomach, he could not tell which and it did not matter; he knew only that for the first time he realised that the bear which had run in his listening and loomed in his dreams since before he could remember and which therefore must have existed in the listening and the dreams of his cousin and Major de Spain and even old General Compson before they began to remember in their turn, was a mortal animal and that they had departed for the camp each November with no actual intention of slaying it, not because it could not be slain but because so far they had no actual hope of being able to. "It will be tomorrow," he said.

"You mean we will try tomorrow," Sam said. "We aint got the dog yet."

"We've got eleven," he said. "They ran him Monday."

"And you heard them," Sam said. "Saw them too. We aint got the dog yet. It wont take but one. But he aint there. Maybe he

aint nowhere. The only other way will be for him to run by accident over somebody that had a gun and knowed how to shoot it."

"That wouldn't be me," the boy said. "It would be Walter or
Major or——"

"It might," Sam said. "You watch close tomorrow. Because he's
smart. That's how come he has lived this long. If he gets hemmed
up and has got to pick out somebody to run over, he will pick out
you."

"How?" he said. "How will he know. . . ." He ceased. "You
mean he already knows me, that I aint never been to the big bottom
before, aint had time to find out yet whether I . . ." He ceased
again, staring at Sam; he said humbly, not even amazed: "It was
me he was watching. I don't reckon he did need to come but once."

"You watch tomorrow," Sam said. "I reckon we better start back.
It'll be long after dark now before we get to camp."

The next morning they started three hours earlier than they had
ever done. Even Uncle Ash went, the cook, who called himself by
profession a camp cook and who did little else save cook for Major
de Spain's hunting and camping parties, yet who had been marked
by the wilderness from simple juxtaposition to it until he responded
as they all did, even the boy who until two weeks ago had never
even seen the wilderness, to a hound's ripped ear and shoulder and
the print of a crooked foot in a patch of wet earth. They rode. It
was too far to walk: the boy and Sam and Uncle Ash in the wagon
with the dogs, his cousin and Major de Spain and General Compson and Boon and Walter and Tennie's Jim riding double on the
horses; again the first gray light found him, as on that first morning two weeks ago, on the stand where Sam had placed and left
him. With the gun which was too big for him, the breech-loader
which did not even belong to him but to Major de Spain and which
he had fired only once, at a stump on the first day to learn the
recoil and how to reload it with the paper shells, he stood against
a big gum tree beside a little bayou whose black still water crept
without motion out of a cane-brake, across a small clearing and into
the cane again, where, invisible, a bird, the big woodpecker called
Lord-to-God by negroes, clattered at a dead trunk. It was a stand
like any other stand, dissimilar only in incidentals to the one where
he had stood each morning for two weeks; a territory new to him
yet no less familiar than that other one which after two weeks he
had come to believe he knew a little—the same solitude, the same
loneliness through which frail and timorous man had merely passed

without altering it, leaving no mark nor scar, which looked exactly as it must have looked when the first ancestor of Sam Fathers' Chickasaw predecessors crept into it and looked about him, club or stone axe or bone arrow drawn and ready, different only because, squatting at the edge of the kitchen, he had smelled the dogs huddled and cringing beneath it and saw the raked ear and side of the bitch that, as Sam had said, had to be brave once in order to keep on calling herself a dog, and saw yesterday in the earth beside the gutted log, the print of the living foot. He heard no dogs at all. He never did certainly hear them. He only heard the drumming of the woodpecker stop short off, and knew that the bear was looking at him. He never saw it. He did not know whether it was facing him from the cane or behind him. He did not move, holding the useless gun which he knew now he would never fire at it now or ever, tasting in his saliva that taint of brass which he had smelled in the huddled dogs when he peered under the kitchen.

Then it was gone. As abruptly as it had stopped, the woodpecker's dry hammering set up again, and after a while he believed he even heard the dogs—a murmur, scarce a sound even, which he had probably been hearing for a time, perhaps a minute or two, before he remarked it, drifting into hearing and then out again, dying away. They came nowhere near him. If it was dogs he heard, he could not have sworn to it; if it was a bear they ran, it was another bear. It was Sam himself who emerged from the cane and crossed the bayou, the injured bitch following at heel as a bird dog is taught to walk. She came and crouched against his leg, trembling. "I didn't see him," he said. "I didn't, Sam."

"I know it," Sam said. "He done the looking. You didn't hear him neither, did you?"

"No," the boy said. "I——"

"He's smart," Sam said. "Too smart." Again the boy saw in his eyes that quality of dark and brooding lambence as Sam looked down at the bitch trembling faintly and steadily against the boy's leg. From her raked shoulder a few drops of fresh blood clung like bright berries. "Too big. We aint got the dog yet. But maybe some day."

Because there would be a next time, after and after. He was only ten. It seemed to him that he could see them, the two of them, shadowy in the limbo from which time emerged and became time: the old bear absolved of mortality and himself who shared a little of it. Because he recognised now what he had smelled in the huddled dogs and tasted in his own saliva, recognised fear as a boy, a youth, recognises the existence of love and passion and experience which is his heritage but not yet his patrimony, from entering by chance the presence or perhaps even merely the bedroom of a woman who has loved and been loved by many men. *So I will have to see him,* he thought, without dread or even hope. *I will have to look at him.* So it was in June of the next summer. They were at the camp again, celebrating Major de Spain's and General Compson's birthdays. Although the one had been born in September and the other in the depth of winter and almost thirty years earlier, each June the two of them and McCaslin and Boon and Walter Ewell (and the boy too from now on) spent two weeks at the camp, fishing and shooting squirrels and turkey and running coons and wildcats with the dogs at night. That is, Boon and the negroes (and the boy too now) fished and shot squirrels and ran the coons and cats, because the proven hunters, not only Major de Spain and old General Compson (who spent those two weeks sitting in a rocking chair before a tremendous iron pot of Brunswick stew, stirring and tasting, with Uncle Ash to quarrel with about how he was making it and Tennie's Jim to pour whisky into the tin dipper from which he drank it) but even McCaslin and Walter Ewell who were still young enough, scorned such other than shooting the wild gobblers with pistols for wagers or to test their marksmanship.

That is, his cousin McCaslin and the others thought he was hunting squirrels. Until the third evening he believed that Sam Fathers thought so too. Each morning he would leave the camp right after breakfast. He had his own gun now, a new breech-loader, a Christmas gift; he would own and shoot it for almost seventy years, through two new pairs of barrels and locks and one new stock, until all that remained of the original gun was the silver-inlaid triggerguard with his and McCaslin's engraved names and the date in 1878. He found the tree beside the little bayou where he had stood that morning. Using the compass he ranged from that point; he was teaching himself to be better than a fair woodsman without even knowing he was doing it. On the third day he even found the gutted log where he had first seen the print. It was almost completely crumbled now, healing with unbelievable speed, a passionate and almost visible relinquishment, back into the earth from which the tree had grown. He ranged the summer woods now, green with gloom, if anything actually dimmer than they had been in November's gray dissolution, where even at noon the sun fell only in windless dappling upon the earth which never completely dried and which crawled with snakes—moccasins and watersnakes and rattlers, themselves the color of the dappled gloom so that he would not always see them until they moved; returning to camp later and later and later, first day, second day, passing in the twilight of the third evening the little log pen enclosing the log barn where Sam was putting up the stock for the night. "You aint looked right yet," Sam said.

He stopped. For a moment he didn't answer. Then he said peacefully, in a peaceful rushing burst, as when a boy's miniature dam in a little brook gives way: "All right. Yes. But how? I went to the bayou. I even found that log again. I——"

"I reckon that was all right. Likely he's been watching you. You never saw his foot?"

"I . . ." the boy said. "I didn't . . . I never thought . . ."

"It's the gun," Sam said. He stood beside the fence, motionless, the old man, son of a negro slave and a Chickasaw chief, in the battered and faded overalls and the frayed five-cent straw hat which had been the badge of the negro's slavery and was now the regalia of his freedom. The camp—the clearing, the house, the barn and its tiny lot with which Major de Spain in his turn had scratched punily and evanescently at the wilderness—faded in the dusk, back into the immemorial darkness of the woods. *The gun*, the boy thought. *The gun.* "You will have to choose," Sam said.

He left the next morning before light, without breakfast, long before Uncle Ash would wake in his quilts on the kitchen floor and start the fire. He had only the compass and a stick for the snakes. He could go almost a mile before he would need to see the compass. He sat on a log, the invisible compass in his hand, while the secret night-sounds which had ceased at his movements, scurried again and then fell still for good and the owls ceased and gave over to the waking day birds and there was light in the gray wet woods and he could see the compass. He went fast yet still quietly, becoming steadily better and better as a woodsman without yet having time to realise it; he jumped a doe and a fawn, walked them out of the bed, close enough to see them—the crash of undergrowth, the white scut, the fawn scudding along behind her, faster than he had known it could have run. He was hunting right, upwind, as Sam had taught him, but that didn't matter now. He had left the gun; by his own will and relinquishment he had accepted not a gambit, not a choice, but a condition in which not only the bear's heretofore inviolable anonymity but all the ancient rules and balances of hunter and hunted had been abrogated. He would not even be afraid, not even in the moment when the fear would take him completely: blood, skin, bowels, bones, memory from the long time before it even became his memory—all save that thin clear quenchless lucidity which alone differed him from this bear and from all the other bears and bucks he would follow during almost seventy years, to which Sam had said: "Be scared. You cant help that. But dont be afraid. Aint nothing in the woods going to hurt you if you dont corner it or it dont smell that you are afraid. A bear or a deer has got to be scared of a coward the same as a brave man has got to be."

By noon he was far beyond the crossing on the little bayou, farther into the new and alien country than he had ever been, travelling now not only by the compass but by the old, heavy, biscuit-thick silver watch which had been his father's. He had left the camp nine hours ago; nine hours from now, dark would already have been an hour old. He stopped, for the first time since he had risen from the log when he could see the compass face at last, and looked about, mopping his sweating face on his sleeve. He had already relinquished, of his will, because of his need, in humility and peace and without regret, yet apparently that had not been enough, the leaving of the gun was not enough. He stood for a moment—a child, alien and lost in the green and soaring gloom of the markless wilderness. Then he relinquished completely to it. It was the watch and the compass. He was still tainted. He removed the linked chain of the one and the looped thong of the other from his overalls and hung them on a bush and leaned the stick beside them and entered it.

When he realised he was lost, he did as Sam had coached and drilled him: made a cast to cross his backtrack. He had not been going very fast for the last two or three hours, and he had gone even less fast since he left the compass and watch on the bush. So he went slower still now, since the tree could not be very far; in fact, he found it before he really expected to and turned and went to it. But there was no bush beneath it, no compass nor watch, so he did next as Sam had coached and drilled him: made this next circle in the opposite direction and much larger, so that the pattern of the two of them would bisect his track somewhere, but crossing no trace nor mark anywhere of his feet or any feet, and now he was going faster though still not panicked, his heart beating a little more rapidly but strong and steady enough, and this time it was not even the tree because there was a down log beside it which he had never seen before and beyond the log a little swamp, a seepage of moisture somewhere between earth and water, and he did what Sam had coached and drilled him as the next and the last, seeing as he sat down on the log the crooked print, the warped indentation in the wet ground which while he looked at it continued to fill with water until it was level full and the water began to overflow and the sides of the print began to dissolve away. Even as he looked up he saw the next one, and, moving, the one beyond it; moving, not hurrying, running, but merely keeping pace with them as they appeared before him as though they were being shaped out of thin air just one constant pace short of where he would lose them forever and be lost forever himself, tireless, eager, without doubt or dread, panting a little above the strong rapid little hammer of his heart, emerging suddenly into a little glade and the wilderness coalesced. It rushed, soundless, and solidified—the tree, the bush, the compass and the watch glinting where a ray of sunlight touched them. Then he saw the bear. It did not emerge, appear: it was just there, immobile, fixed in the green and windless noon's hot dappling, not as big as he had dreamed it but as big as he had expected, bigger, dimensionless against the dappled obscurity, looking at him. Then it moved. It crossed the glade without haste, walking for an instant into the sun's full glare and out of it, and stopped again and looked back at him across one shoulder. Then it was gone. It didn't walk into the woods. It faded, sank back into the wilderness without motion as he had watched a fish, a huge old bass, sink back into the dark depths of its pool and vanish without even any movement of its fins.

II

So he should have hated and feared Lion. He was thirteen then. He had killed his buck and Sam Fathers had marked his face with the hot blood, and in the next November he killed a bear. But before that accolade he had become as competent in the woods as many grown men with the same experience. By now he was a better woodsman than most grown men with more. There was no territory within twenty-five miles of the camp that he did not know—

bayou, ridge, landmark trees and path; he could have led anyone direct to any spot in it and brought him back. He knew game trails that even Sam Fathers had never seen; in the third fall he found a buck's bedding-place by himself and unbeknown to his cousin he borrowed Walter Ewell's rifle and lay in wait for the buck at dawn and killed it when it walked back to the bed as Sam had told him how the old Chickasaw fathers did.

By now he knew the old bear's footprint better than he did his own, and not only the crooked one. He could see any one of the three sound prints and distinguish it at once from any other, and not only because of its size. There were other bears within that fifty miles which left tracks almost as large, or at least so near that the one would have appeared larger only by juxtaposition. It was more than that. If Sam Fathers had been his mentor and the back-yard rabbits and squirrels his kindergarten, then the wilderness the old bear ran was his college and the old male bear itself, so long unwifed and childless as to have become its own ungendered progenitor, was his alma mater.

He could find the crooked print now whenever he wished, ten miles or five miles or sometimes closer than that, to the camp. Twice while on stand during the next three years he heard the dogs strike its trail and once even jump it by chance, the voices high, abject, almost human in their hysteria. Once, still-hunting with Walter Ewell's rifle, he saw it cross a long corridor of down timber where a tornado had passed. It rushed through rather than across the tangle of trunks and branches as a locomotive would, faster than he had ever believed it could have moved, almost as fast as a deer even because the deer would have spent most of that distance in the air; he realised then why it would take a dog not only of abnormal courage but size and speed too ever to bring it to bay. He had a little dog at home, a mongrel, of the sort called fyce by negroes, a ratter, itself not much bigger than a rat and possessing that sort of courage which had long since stopped being bravery and had become foolhardiness. He brought it with him one June and, timing them as if they were meeting an appointment with another human being, himself carrying the fyce with a sack over its head and Sam Fathers with a brace of the hounds on a rope leash, they lay downwind of the trail and actually ambushed the bear. They were so close that it turned at bay although he realised later this might have been from surprise and amazement at the shrill and frantic uproar of the fyce. It turned at bay against the trunk of a big cypress, on its hind feet; it seemed to the boy that it would never stop rising, taller and taller, and even the two hounds seemed to have taken a kind of desperate and despairing courage from the fyce. Then he realised that the fyce was actually not going to stop. He flung the gun down and ran. When he overtook and grasped the shrill, frantically pinwheeling little dog, it seemed to him that he was directly under the bear. He could smell it, strong and hot and rank. Sprawling, he looked up where it loomed and towered over him like a thunderclap. It was quite familiar, until he remembered: this was the way he had used to dream about it.

Then it was gone. He didn't see it go. He knelt, holding the frantic fyce with both hands, hearing the abased wailing of the two hounds drawing further and further away, until Sam came up, carrying the gun. He laid it quietly down beside the boy and stood looking down at him. "You've done seed him twice now, with a gun in your hands," he said. "This time you couldn't have missed him."

The boy rose. He still held the fyce. Even in his arms it continued to yap frantically, surging and straining toward the fading sound of the hounds like a collection of live-wire springs. The boy was panting a little. "Neither could you," he said. "You had the gun. Why didn't you shoot him?"

Sam didn't seem to have heard. He put out his hand and touched the little dog in the boy's arms which still yapped and strained even though the two hounds were out of hearing now. "He's done gone," Sam said. "You can slack off and rest now, until next time." He stroked the little dog until it began to grow quiet under his hand. "You's almost the one we wants," he said. "You just aint big enough. We aint got that one yet. He will need to be just a little bigger than smart, and a little braver than either." He withdrew his hand from the fyce's head and stood looking into the woods where the bear and the hounds had vanished. "Somebody is going to, some day."

"I know it," the boy said. "That's why it must be one of us. So it wont be until the last day. When even he dont want it to last any longer."

So he should have hated and feared Lion. It was in the fourth summer, the fourth time he had made one in the celebration of Major de Spain's and General Compson's birthday. In the early spring Major de Spain's mare had foaled a horse colt. One evening when Sam brought the horses and mules up to stable them for the night, the colt was missing and it was all he could do to get the frantic mare into the lot. He had thought at first to let the mare lead him back to where she had become separated from the foal. But she would not do it. She would not even feint toward any particular part of the woods or even in any particular direction. She merely ran, as if she couldn't see, still frantic with terror. She whirled and ran at Sam once, as if to attack him in some ultimate desperation, as if she could not for the moment realise that he was a man and a long-familiar one. He got her into the lot at last. It was too dark by that time to back-track her, to unravel the erratic course she had doubtless pursued.

He came to the house and told Major de Spain. It was an animal, of course, a big one, and the colt was dead now, wherever it was. They all knew that. "It's a panther," General Compson said at once. "The same one. That doe and fawn last March." Sam had sent Major de Spain word of it when Boon Hogganbeck came to the camp on a routine visit to see how the stock had wintered—the doe's throat torn out, and the beast had run down the helpless fawn and killed it too.

"Sam never did say that was a panther," Major de Spain said. Sam said nothing now, standing behind Major de Spain where they sat at supper, inscrutable, as if he were just waiting for them to stop talking so he could go home. He didn't even seem to be looking at anything. "A panther might jump a doe, and he wouldn't have much trouble catching the fawn afterward. But no panther would have jumped that colt with the dam right there with it. It was Old Ben," Major de Spain said. "I'm disappointed in him. He has broken the rules. I didn't think he would have done that. He has killed mine and McCaslin's dogs, but that was all right. We gambled the dogs against him; we gave each other warning. But now he has come into my house and destroyed my property, out of season too. He broke the rules. It was Old Ben, Sam." Still Sam said nothing, standing there until Major de Spain should stop talking. "We'll back-track her tomorrow and see," Major de Spain said.

Sam departed. He would not live in the camp; he had built himself a little hut something like Joe Baker's, only stouter, tighter, on the bayou a quarter-mile away, and a stout log crib where he stored a little corn for the shoat he raised each year. The next morning he was waiting when they waked. He had already found the colt. They did not even wait for breakfast. It was not far, not five hundred yards from the stable—the three-months' colt lying on its side, its throat torn out and the entrails and one ham partly eaten. It lay not as if it had been dropped but as if it had been struck and hurled, and no cat-mark, no claw-mark where a panther would have gripped it while finding its throat. They read the tracks where the frantic mare had circled and at last rushed in with that same ultimate desperation with which she had whirled on Sam Fathers yesterday evening, and the long tracks of dead and terrified running and those of the beast which had not even rushed at her when she advanced but had merely walked three or four paces toward her until she broke, and General Compson said, "Good God, what a wolf!"

Still Sam said nothing. The boy watched him while the men knelt, measuring the tracks. There was something in Sam's face now. It was neither exultation nor joy nor hope. Later, a man, the boy realised what it had been, and that Sam had known all the time what had made the tracks and what had torn the throat out of the doe in the spring and killed the fawn. It had been fore-knowledge in Sam's face that morning. *And he was glad,* he told himself. *He was old. He had no children, no people, none of his blood anywhere above earth that he would ever meet again. And even if he were to, he could not have touched it, spoken to it, because for seventy years now he had had to be a negro. It was almost over now and he was glad.*

They returned to camp and had breakfast and came back with guns and the hounds. Afterward the boy realised that they also should have known then what killed the colt as well as Sam Fathers did. But that was neither the first nor the last time he had seen men rationalise from and even act upon their misconceptions. After Boon, standing astride the colt, had whipped the dogs away from it with his belt, they snuffed at the tracks. One of them, a young dog hound without judgment yet, bayed once, and they ran for a few feet on what seemed to be a trail. Then they stopped, looking back at the men, eager enough, not baffled, merely questioning, as if they were asking "Now what?" Then they rushed back to the colt, where Boon, still astride it, slashed at them with the belt.

"I never knew a trail to get cold that quick," General Compson said.

"Maybe a single wolf big enough to kill a colt with the dam right there beside it dont leave scent," Major de Spain said.

"Maybe it was a hant," Walter Ewell said. He looked at Tennie's Jim. "Hah, Jim?"

Because the hounds would not run it, Major de Spain had Sam hunt out and find the tracks a hundred yards farther on and they put the dogs on it again and again the young one bayed and not one of them realised then that the hound was not baying like a dog striking game but was merely bellowing like a country dog whose yard has been invaded. General Compson spoke to the boy and Boon and Tennie's Jim: to the squirrel hunters. "You boys keep the dogs with you this morning. He's probably hanging around somewhere, waiting to get his breakfast off the colt. You might strike him."

But they did not. The boy remembered how Sam stood watching them as they went into the woods with the leashed hounds—the Indian face in which he had never seen anything until it smiled, except that faint arching of the nostrils on that first morning when the hounds had found Old Ben. They took the hounds with them on the next day, though when they reached the place where they hoped to strike a fresh trail, the carcass of the colt was gone. Then on the third morning Sam was waiting again, this time until they had finished breakfast. He said, "Come." He led them to his house, his little hut, to the corn-crib beyond it. He had removed the corn and had made a dead-fall of the door, baiting it with the colt's carcass; peering between the logs, they saw an animal almost the color of a gun or pistol barrel, what little time they had to examine its color or shape. It was not crouched nor even standing. It was in motion, in the air, coming toward them—a heavy body crashing with tremendous force against the door so that the thick door jumped and clattered in its frame, the animal, whatever it was, hurling itself against the door again seemingly before it could have touched the floor and got a new purchase to spring from. "Come away," Sam said, "fore he break his neck." Even when they retreated the heavy and measured crashes continued, the stout door jumping and clattering each time, and still no sound from the beast itself— no snarl, no cry.

"What in hell's name is it?" Major de Spain said.

"It's a dog," Sam said, his nostrils arching and collapsing faintly and steadily and that faint, fierce milkiness in his eyes again as on that first morning when the hounds had struck the old bear. "It's the dog."

"*The* dog?" Major de Spain said.

"That's gonter hold Old Ben."

"Dog the devil," Major de Spain said. "I'd rather have Old Ben himself in my pack than that brute. Shoot him."

"No," Sam said.

"You'll never tame him. How do you ever expect to make an animal like that afraid of you?"

"I dont want him tame," Sam said; again the boy watched his nostrils and the fierce milky light in his eyes. "But I almost rather he be tame than scared, of me or any man or any thing. But he wont be neither, of nothing."

"Then what are you going to do with it?"

"You can watch," Sam said.

Each morning through the second week they would go to Sam's crib. He had removed a few shingles from the roof and had put a rope on the colt's carcass and had drawn it out when the trap fell. Each morning they would watch him lower a pail of water into the crib while the dog hurled itself tirelessly against the door and dropped back and leaped again. It never made any sound and there was nothing frenzied in the act but only a cold and grim indomitable determination. Toward the end of the week it stopped jumping at the door. Yet it had not weakened appreciably and it was not as if it had rationalised the fact that the door was not going to give. It was as if for that time it simply disdained to jump any longer. It was not down. None of them had ever seen it down. It stood, and they could see it now—part mastiff, something of Airedale and something of a dozen other strains probably, better than thirty inches at the shoulders and weighing as they guessed almost ninety pounds, with cold yellow eyes and a tremendous chest and over all that strange color like a blued gun-barrel.

Then the two weeks were up. They prepared to break camp. The boy begged to remain and his cousin let him. He moved into the little hut with Sam Fathers. Each morning he watched Sam lower the pail of water into the crib. By the end of that week the dog was down. It would rise and half stagger, half crawl to the water and drink and collapse again. One morning it could not even reach the water, could not raise its forequarters even from the floor. Sam took a short stick and prepared to enter the crib. "Wait," the boy said. "Let me get the gun——"

"No," Sam said. "He cant move now." Nor could it. It lay on its side while Sam touched it, its head and the gaunted body, the dog lying motionless, the yellow eyes open. They were not fierce and there was nothing of petty malevolence in them, but a cold and almost impersonal malignance like some natural force. It was not even looking at Sam nor at the boy peering at it between the logs.

Sam began to feed it again. The first time he had to raise its head so it could lap the broth. That night he left a bowl of broth containing lumps of meat where the dog could reach it. The next morning the bowl was empty and the dog was lying on its belly, its head up, the cold yellow eyes watching the door as Sam entered, no change whatever in the cold yellow eyes and still no sound from it even when it sprang, its aim and coordination still bad from weakness so that Sam had time to strike it down with the stick and leap from the crib and slam the door as the dog, still without having had time to get its feet under it to jump again seemingly, hurled itself against the door as if the two weeks of starving had never been.

At noon that day someone came whooping through the woods from the direction of the camp. It was Boon. He came and looked for a while between the logs, at the tremendous dog lying again on its belly, its head up, the yellow eyes blinking sleepily at nothing: the indomitable and unbroken spirit. "What we better do," Boon said, "is to let that son of a bitch go and catch Old Ben and run him on the dog." He turned to the boy his weather-reddened and beetling face. "Get your traps together. Cass says for you to come on home. You been in here fooling with that horse-eating varmint long enough."

Boon had a borrowed mule at the camp; the buggy was waiting at the edge of the bottom. He was at home that night. He told McCaslin about it. "Sam's going to starve him again until he can go in and touch him. Then he will feed him again. Then he will starve him again, if he has to."

"But why?" McCaslin said. "What for? Even Sam will never tame that brute."

"We dont want him tame. We want him like he is. We just want him to find out at last that the only way he can get out of that crib and stay out of it is to do what Sam or somebody tells him to do. He's the dog that's going to stop Old Ben and hold him. We've already named him. His name is Lion."

Then November came at last. They returned to the camp. With General Compson and Major de Spain and his cousin and Walter and Boon he stood in the yard among the guns and bedding and boxes of food and watched Sam Fathers and Lion come up the lane from the lot—the Indian, the old man in battered overalls and rubber boots and a worn sheepskin coat and a hat which had belonged to the boy's father; the tremendous dog pacing gravely beside him. The hounds rushed out to meet them and stopped, except the young one which still had but little of judgment. It ran up to Lion, fawning. Lion didn't snap at it. He didn't even pause. He struck it rolling and yelping for five or six feet with a blow of one paw as a bear would have done and came on into the yard and stood, blinking sleepily at nothing, looking at no one, while Boon said, "Jesus. Jesus.—Will he let me touch him?"

"You can touch him," Sam said. "He dont care. He dont care about nothing or nobody."

The boy watched that too. He watched it for the next two years from that moment when Boon touched Lion's head and then knelt beside him, feeling the bones and muscles, the power. It was as if Lion were a woman—or perhaps Boon was the woman. That was more like it—the big, grave, sleepy-seeming dog which, as Sam Fathers said, cared about no man and no thing; and the violent, insensitive, hard-faced man with his touch of remote Indian blood and the mind almost of a child. He watched Boon take over Lion's feeding from Sam and Uncle Ash both. He would see Boon squatting in the cold rain beside the kitchen while Lion ate. Because Lion neither slept nor ate with the other dogs though none of them knew where he did sleep until in the second November, thinking until then that Lion slept in his kennel beside Sam Fathers' hut, when the boy's cousin McCaslin said something about it to Sam by sheer chance and Sam told him. And that night the boy and Major de Spain and McCaslin with a lamp entered the back room where Boon slept—the little, tight, airless room rank with the smell of Boon's unwashed body and his wet hunting-clothes—where Boon, snoring on his back, choked and waked and Lion raised his head beside him and looked back at them from his cold, slumbrous yellow eyes.

"Damn it, Boon," McCaslin said. "Get that dog out of here. He's got to run Old Ben tomorrow morning. How in hell do you expect him to smell anything fainter than a skunk after breathing you all night?"

"The way I smell aint hurt my nose none that I ever noticed," Boon said.

"It wouldn't matter if it had," Major de Spain said. "We're not depending on you to trail a bear. Put him outside. Put him under the house with the other dogs."

Boon began to get up. "He'll kill the first one that happens to yawn or sneeze in his face or touches him."

"I reckon not," Major de Spain said. "None of them are going to risk yawning in his face or touching him either, even asleep. Put him outside. I want his nose right tomorrow. Old Ben fooled him last year. I dont think he will do it again."

Boon put on his shoes without lacing them; in his long soiled underwear, his hair still tousled from sleep, he and Lion went out. The others returned to the front room and the poker game where McCaslin's and Major de Spain's hands waited for them on the table. After a while McCaslin said, "Do you want me to go back and look again?"

"No," Major de Spain said. "I call," he said to Walter Ewell. He spoke to McCaslin again. "If you do, dont tell me. I am beginning to see the first sign of my increasing age: I don't like to know that my orders have been disobeyed, even when I knew when I gave them that they would be.—A small pair," he said to Walter Ewell.

"How small?" Walter said.

"Very small," Major de Spain said.

And the boy, lying beneath his piled quilts and blankets waiting for sleep, knew likewise that Lion was already back in Boon's bed, for the rest of that night and the next one and during all the nights of the next November and the next one. He thought then: *I wonder what Sam thinks. He could have Lion with him, even if Boon is a white man. He could ask Major or McCaslin either. And more than that. It was Sam's hand that touched Lion first and Lion knows it.* Then he became a man and he knew that too. It had been all right. That was the way it should have been. Sam was the chief, the prince; Boon, the plebeian, was his huntsman. Boon should have nursed the dogs.

On the first morning that Lion led the pack after Old Ben, seven strangers appeared in the camp. They were swampers: gaunt, malaria-ridden men appearing from nowhere, who ran trap-lines for coons or perhaps farmed little patches of cotton and corn along the edge of the bottom, in clothes but little better than Sam Fathers' and nowhere near as good as Tennie's Jim's, with worn shotguns and rifles, already squatting patiently in the cold drizzle in the side yard when day broke. They had a spokesman; afterward Sam

Fathers told Major de Spain how all during the past summer and fall they had drifted into the camp singly or in pairs and threes, to look quietly at Lion for a while and then go away: "Mawnin, Major. We heerd you was aimin to put that ere blue dawg on that old two-toed bear this mawnin. We figgered we'd come up and watch, if you dont mind. We wont do no shooting, lessen he runs over us."

"You are welcome," Major de Spain said. "You are welcome to shoot. He's more your bear than ours."

"I reckon that aint no lie. I done fed him enough cawn to have a sheer in him. Not to mention a shoat three years ago."

"I reckon I got a sheer too," another said. "Only it aint in the bear." Major de Spain looked at him. He was chewing tobacco. He spat. "Hit was a heifer calf. Nice un too. Last year. When I finally found her, I reckon she looked about like that colt of yourn looked last June."

"Oh," Major de Spain said. "Be welcome. If you see game in front of my dogs, shoot it."

Nobody shot Old Ben that day. No man saw him. The dogs jumped him within a hundred yards of the glade where the boy had seen him that day in the summer of his eleventh year. The boy was less than a quarter-mile away. He heard the jump but he could distinguish no voice among the dogs that he did not know and therefore would be Lion's, and he thought, believed, that Lion was not among them. Even the fact that they were going much faster than he had ever heard them run behind Old Ben before and that the high thin note of hysteria was missing now from their voices was not enough to disabuse him. He didn't comprehend until that night, when Sam told him that Lion would never cry on a trail. "He gonter growl when he catches Old Ben's throat," Sam said. "But he aint gonter never holler, no more than he ever done when he was jumping at that two-inch door. It's that blue dog in him. What you call it?"

"Airedale," the boy said.

Lion was there; the jump was just too close to the river. When Boon returned with Lion about eleven that night, he swore that Lion had stopped Old Ben once but that the hounds would not go in and Old Ben broke away and took to the river and swam for miles down it and he and Lion went down one bank for about ten miles and crossed and came up the other but it had begun to get dark before they struck any trail where Old Ben had come up out of the water, unless he was still in the water when he passed the ford where they crossed. Then he fell to cursing the hounds and ate the supper Uncle Ash had saved for him and went off to bed and after a while the boy opened the door of the little stale room thunderous with snoring and the great grave dog raised its head from Boon's pillow and blinked at him for a moment and lowered its head again.

When the next November came and the last day, the day on which it was now becoming traditional to save for Old Ben, there were more than a dozen strangers waiting. They were not all swampers this time. Some of them were townsmen, from other county seats like Jefferson, who had heard about Lion and Old Ben and had come to watch the great blue dog keep his yearly rendezvous with the old two-toed bear. Some of them didn't even have guns and the hunting-clothes and boots they wore had been on a store shelf yesterday.

This time Lion jumped Old Ben more than five miles from the river and bayed and held him and this time the hounds went in, in a sort of desperate emulation. The boy heard them; he was that near. He heard Boon whooping; he heard the two shots when General Compson delivered both barrels, one containing five buckshot, the other a single ball, into the bear from as close as he could force his almost unmanageable horse. He heard the dogs when the bear broke free again. He was running now; panting, stumbling, his lungs bursting, he reached the place where General Compson had fired and where Old Ben had killed two of the hounds. He saw the blood from General Compson's shots, but he could go no further. He stopped, leaning against a tree for his breathing to ease and his heart to slow, hearing the sound of the dogs as it faded on and died away.

In camp that night—they had as guests five of the still terrified strangers in new hunting coats and boots who had been lost all day until Sam Fathers went out and got them—he heard the rest of it: how Lion had stopped and held the bear again but only the one-eyed mule which did not mind the smell of wild blood would approach and Boon was riding the mule and Boon had never been known to hit anything. He shot at the bear five times with his pump gun, touching nothing, and Old Ben killed another hound and broke free once more and reached the river and was gone. Again Boon and Lion hunted as far down one bank as they dared. Too far; they crossed in the first of dusk and dark overtook them within a mile. And this time Lion found the broken trail, the blood perhaps, in the darkness where Old Ben had come up out of the water, but Boon had him on a rope, luckily, and he got down from the mule and fought Lion hand-to-hand until he got him back to camp. This time Boon didn't even curse. He stood in the door, muddy, spent, his huge gargoyle's face tragic and still amazed. "I missed him," he said. "I was in twenty-five feet of him and I missed him five times."

"But we have drawn blood," Major de Spain said. "General Compson drew blood. We have never done that before."

"But I missed him," Boon said. "I missed him five times. With Lion looking right at me."

"Never mind," Major de Spain said. "It was a damned fine race. And we drew blood. Next year we'll let General Compson or Walter ride Katie, and we'll get him."

Then McCaslin said, "Where is Lion, Boon?"

"I left him at Sam's," Boon said. He was already turning away. "I aint fit to sleep with him."

So he should have hated and feared Lion. Yet he did not. It seemed to him that there was a fatality in it. It seemed to him that something, he didn't know what, was beginning; had already begun. It was like the last act on a set stage. It was the beginning of the end of something, he didn't know what except that he would not grieve. He would be humble and proud that he had been found worthy to be a part of it too or even just to see it too.

III

It was December. It was the coldest December he had ever remembered. They had been in camp four days over two weeks, waiting for the weather to soften so that Lion and Old Ben could run their yearly race. Then they would break camp and go home. Because of these unforeseen additional days which they had had to pass waiting on the weather, with nothing to do but play poker, the whisky had given out and he and Boon were being sent to Memphis with a suitcase and a note from Major de Spain to Mr Semmes, the distiller, to get more. That is, Major de Spain and McCaslin were sending Boon to get the whisky and sending him to see that Boon got back with it or most of it or at least some of it.

Tennie's Jim waked him at three. He dressed rapidly, shivering, not so much from the cold because a fresh fire already boomed and roared on the hearth, but in that dead winter hour when the blood and the heart are slow and sleep is incomplete. He crossed the gap between house and kitchen, the gap of iron earth beneath the brilliant and rigid night where dawn would not begin for three hours yet, tasting, tongue palate and to the very bottom of his lungs the searing dark, and entered the kitchen, the lamplit warmth where the stove glowed, fogging the windows, and where Boon already sat at the table at breakfast, hunched over his plate, almost in his plate, his working jaws blue with stubble and his face innocent of water and his coarse, horse-mane hair innocent of comb—the quarter Indian, grandson of a Chickasaw squaw, who on occasion resented with his hard and furious fists the intimation of one single drop of alien blood and on others, usually after whisky, affirmed with the same fists and the same fury that his father had been the full-blood Chickasaw and even a chief and that even his mother had been only half white. He was four inches over six feet; he had the mind of a child, the heart of a horse, and little hard shoe-button eyes without depth or meanness or generosity or viciousness or gentleness or anything else, in the ugliest face the boy had ever seen. It looked like somebody had found a walnut a little larger than a football and with a machinist's hammer had shaped features into it and then painted it, mostly red; not Indian red but a fine bright ruddy color which whisky might have had something to do with but which was mostly just happy and violent out-of-doors, the wrinkles in it not the residue of the forty years it had survived but from squinting into the sun or into the gloom of cane-brakes where game had run, baked into it by the camp fires before which he had lain trying to sleep on the cold November or December ground while waiting for daylight so he could rise and hunt again, as though time were merely something he walked through as he did through air, aging him no more than air did. He was brave, faithful, improvident and unreliable; he had neither profession job nor trade and owned one vice and one virtue: whisky, and that absolute and unquestioning fidelity to Major de Spain and the boy's cousin McCaslin. "Sometimes I'd call them both virtues," Major de Spain said once. "Or both vices," McCaslin said.

He ate his breakfast, hearing the dogs under the kitchen, wakened by the smell of frying meat or perhaps by the feet overhead. He heard Lion once, short and peremptory, as the best hunter in any camp has only to speak once to all save the fools, and none other of Major de Spain's and McCaslin's dogs were Lion's equal in size and strength and perhaps even in courage, but they were not fools; Old Ben had killed the last fool among them last year.

Tennie's Jim came in as they finished. The wagon was outside. Ash decided he would drive them over to the log-line where they would flag the outbound log-train and let Tennie's Jim wash the dishes. The boy knew why. It would not be the first time he had listened to old Ash badgering Boon.

It was cold. The wagon wheels banged and clattered on the frozen ground; the sky was fixed and brilliant. He was not shivering, he was shaking, slow and steady and hard, the food he had just eaten still warm and solid inside him while his outside shook slow and steady around it as though his stomach floated loose. "They wont run this morning," he said. "No dog will have any nose today."

"Cep Lion," Ash said. "Lion dont need no nose. All he need is a bear." He had wrapped his feet in towsacks and he had a quilt from his pallet bed on the kitchen floor drawn over his head and wrapped around him until in the thin brilliant starlight he looked like nothing at all that the boy had ever seen before. "He run a bear through a thousand-acre ice-house. Catch him too. Them other dogs dont matter because they aint going to keep up with Lion nohow, long as he got a bear in front of him."

"What's wrong with the other dogs?" Boon said. "What the hell do you know about it anyway? This is the first time you've had your tail out of that kitchen since we got here except to chop a little wood."

"Aint nothing wrong with them," Ash said. "And long as it's left up to them, aint nothing going to be. I just wish I had knowed all my life how to take care of my health good as them hounds knows."

"Well, they aint going to run this morning," Boon said. His voice was harsh and positive. "Major promised they wouldn't until me and Ike get back."

"Weather gonter break today. Gonter soft up. Rain by night." Then Ash laughed, chuckled, somewhere inside the quilt which concealed even his face. "Hum up here, mules!" he said, jerking the reins so that the mules leaped forward and snatched the lurching and banging wagon for several feet before they slowed again into their quick, short-paced, rapid plodding. "Sides, I like to know why Major need to wait on you. It's Lion he aiming to use. I aint never heard tell of you bringing no bear nor no other kind of meat into this camp."

Now Boon's going to curse Ash or maybe even hit him, the boy thought. But Boon never did, never had; the boy knew he never would even though four years ago Boon had shot five times with a borrowed pistol at a negro on the street in Jefferson, with the same result as when he had shot five times at Old Ben last fall. "By God," Boon said, "he aint going to put Lion or no other dog on nothing until I get back tonight. Because he promised me. Whip up them mules and keep them whipped up. Do you want me to freeze to death?"

They reached the log-line and built a fire. After a while the log train came up out of the woods under the paling east and Boon flagged it. Then in the warm caboose the boy slept again while Boon and the conductor and brakeman talked about Lion and Old Ben as people later would talk about Sullivan and Kilrain and, later still, about Dempsey and Tunney. Dozing, swaying as the springless caboose lurched and clattered, he would hear them still talking, about the shoats and calves Old Ben had killed and the cribs he had rifled and the traps and deadfalls he had wrecked and the lead he probably carried under his hide—Old Ben, the two-toed bear in a land where bears with trap-ruined feet had been called Two-Toe or Three-Toe or Cripple-Foot for fifty years, only Old Ben was an extra bear (the head bear, General Compson called him) and so had earned a name such as a human man could have worn and not been sorry.

They reached Hoke's at sunup. They emerged from the warm caboose in their hunting clothes, the muddy boots and stained khaki and Boon's blue unshaven jowls. But that was all right. Hoke's was a sawmill and commissary and two stores and a loading-chute on a sidetrack from the main line, and all the men in it wore boots and khaki too. Presently the Memphis train came. Boon bought three packages of popcorn-and-molasses and a bottle of beer from the news butch and the boy went to sleep again to the sound of his chewing.

But in Memphis it was not all right. It was as if the high buildings and the hard pavements, the fine carriages and the horse cars and the men in starched collars and neckties made their boots and khaki look a little rougher and a little muddier and made Boon's beard look worse and more unshaven and his face look more and more like he should never have brought it out of the woods at all or at least out of reach of Major de Spain or McCaslin or someone who knew it and could have said, "Dont be afraid. He wont hurt you." He walked through the station, on the slick floor, his face moving as he worked the popcorn out of his teeth with his tongue, his legs spraddled and stiff in the hips as if he were walking on buttered glass, and that blue stubble on his face like the filings from a new gun-barrel. They passed the first saloon. Even through the closed doors the boy could seem to smell the sawdust and the reek of old drink. Boon began to cough. He coughed for something less than a minute. "Damn this cold," he said. "I'd sure like to know where I got it."

"Back there in the station," the boy said.

Boon had started to cough again. He stopped. He looked at the boy. "What?" he said.

"You never had it when we left camp nor on the train either." Boon looked at him, blinking. Then he stopped blinking. He didn't cough again. He said quietly:

"Lend me a dollar. Come on. You've got it. If you ever had one, you've still got it. I dont mean you are tight with your money because you aint. You just dont never seem to ever think of nothing you want. When I was sixteen a dollar bill melted off of me before I even had time to read the name of the bank that issued it." He said quietly: "Let me have a dollar, Ike."

"You promised Major. You promised McCaslin. Not till we get back to camp."

"All right," Boon said in that quiet and patient voice. "What can I do on just one dollar? You aint going to lend me another."

"You're damn right I aint," the boy said, his voice quiet too, cold with rage which was not at Boon, remembering: Boon snoring in a hard chair in the kitchen so he could watch the clock and wake him and McCaslin and drive them the seventeen miles in to Jefferson to catch the train to Memphis; the wild, never-bridled Texas paint pony which he had persuaded McCaslin to let him buy and which he and Boon had bought at auction for four dollars and seventy-five cents and fetched home wired between two gentle old mares with pieces of barbed wire and which had never even seen shelled corn before and didn't even know what it was unless the grains were bugs maybe and at last (he was ten and Boon had been ten all his life) Boon said the pony was gentled and with a towsack over its head and four negroes to hold it they backed it into an old two-wheeled cart and hooked up the gear and he and Boon got up and Boon said, "All right, boys. Let him go" and one of the negroes—it was Tennie's Jim—snatched the towsack off and leaped for his life and they lost the first wheel against a post of the open gate only at that moment Boon caught him by the scruff of the neck and flung him into the roadside ditch so he only saw the rest of it in fragments: the other wheel as it slammed through the side gate and crossed the back yard and leaped up onto the gallery and scraps of the cart here and there along the road and Boon vanishing rapidly on his stomach in the leaping and spurting dust and still holding the reins until they broke too and two days later they finally caught the pony seven miles away still wearing the hames and the headstall of the bridle around its neck like a duchess with two necklaces at one time. He gave Boon the dollar.

"All right," Boon said. "Come on in out of the cold."

"I aint cold," he said.

"You can have some lemonade."

"I dont want any lemonade."

The door closed behind him. The sun was well up now. It was a brilliant day, though Ash had said it would rain before night. Already it was warmer; they could run tomorrow. He felt the old lift of the heart, as pristine as ever, as on the first day; he would never lose it, no matter how old in hunting and pursuit: the best, the best of all breathing, the humility and the pride. He must stop thinking about it. Already it seemed to him that he was running, back to the station, to the tracks themselves: the first train going south; he must stop thinking about it. The street was busy. He watched the big Norman draft horses, the Percherons; the trim carriages from which the men in the fine overcoats and the ladies rosy in furs descended and entered the station. (They were still next door to it but one.) Twenty years ago his father had ridden into Memphis as a member of Colonel Sartoris' horse in Forrest's command, up Main street and (the tale told) into the lobby of the Gayoso Hotel where the Yankee officers sat in the leather chairs spitting into the tall bright cuspidors and then out again, scot-free——

The door opened behind him. Boon was wiping his mouth on the back of his hand. "All right," he said. "Let's go tend to it and get the hell out of here."

They went and had the suitcase packed. He never knew where or when Boon got the other bottle. Doubtless Mr Semmes gave it to him. When they reached Hoke's again at sundown, it was empty. They could get a return train to Hoke's in two hours; they went straight back to the station as Major de Spain and then McCaslin

had told Boon to do and then ordered him to do and had sent the
boy along to see that he did. Boon took the first drink from his bottle
in the washroom. A man in a uniform cap came to tell him he
couldn't drink there and looked at Boon's face once and said
nothing. The next time he was pouring into his water glass beneath
the edge of a table in the restaurant when the manager (she was a
woman) did tell him he couldn't drink there and he went back to
the washroom. He had been telling the negro waiter and all the
other people in the restaurant who couldn't help but hear him and
who had never heard of Lion and didn't want to, about Lion and
Old Ben. Then he happened to think of the zoo. He had found out
that there was another train to Hoke's at three oclock and so they
would spend the time at the zoo and take the three oclock train
until he came back from the washroom for the third time. Then
they would take the first train back to camp, get Lion and come
back to the zoo where, he said, the bears were fed on ice cream and
lady fingers and he would match Lion against them all.

So they missed the first train, the one they were supposed to take,
but he got Boon onto the three oclock train and they were all
right again, with Boon not even going to the washroom now but
drinking in the aisle and talking about Lion and the men he but-
tonholed no more daring to tell Boon he couldn't drink there than
the man in the station had dared.

When they reached Hoke's at sundown, Boon was asleep. The
boy waked him at last and got him and the suitcase off the train
and he even persuaded him to eat some supper at the sawmill
commissary. So he was all right when they got in the caboose of
the log-train to go back into the woods, with the sun going down
red and the sky already overcast and the ground would not freeze
tonight. It was the boy who slept now, sitting behind the ruby
stove while the springless caboose jumped and clattered and Boon
and the brakeman and the conductor talked about Lion and Old
Ben because they knew what Boon was talking about because this
was home. "Overcast and already thawing," Boon said. "Lion will
get him tomorrow."

It would have to be Lion, or somebody. It would not be Boon.
He had never hit anything bigger than a squirrel that anybody
ever knew, except the negro woman that day when he was shooting
at the negro man. He was a big negro and not ten feet away but
Boon shot five times with the pistol he had borrowed from Major
de Spain's negro coachman and the negro he was shooting at outed

with a dollar-and-a-half mail-order pistol and would have burned
Boon down with it only it never went off, it just went snicksnick-
snicksnicksnick five times and Boon still blasting away and he
broke a plate-glass window that cost McCaslin forty-five dollars
and hit a negro woman who happened to be passing in the leg
only Major de Spain paid for that; he and McCaslin cut cards, the
plate-glass window against the negro woman's leg. And the first
day on stand this year, the first morning in camp, the buck ran
right over Boon; he heard Boon's old pump gun go whow. whow.
whow. whow. whow. and then his voice: "God damn, here he
comes! Head him! Head him!" and when he got there the buck's
tracks and the five exploded shells were not twenty paces apart.

There were five guests in camp that night, from Jefferson: Mr
Bayard Sartoris and his son and General Compson's son and two
others. And the next morning he looked out the window, into the
gray thin drizzle of daybreak which Ash had predicted, and there
they were, standing and squatting beneath the thin rain, almost
two dozen of them who had fed Old Ben corn and shoats and even
calves for ten years, in their worn hats and hunting coats and
overalls which any town negro would have thrown away or burned
and only the rubber boots strong and sound, and the worn and
blueless guns and some even without guns. While they ate breakfast a dozen more arrived, mounted and on foot: loggers from the
camp thirteen miles below and sawmill men from Hoke's and the
only gun among them that one which the log-train conductor
carried: so that when they went into the woods this morning
Major de Spain led a party almost as strong, excepting that some
of them were not armed, as some he had led in the last darkening
days of '64 and '65. The little yard would not hold them. They
overflowed it, into the lane where Major de Spain sat his mare
while Ash in his dirty apron thrust the greasy cartridges into his
carbine and passed it up to him and the great grave blue dog
stood at his stirrup not as a dog stands but as a horse stands,
blinking his sleepy topaz eyes at nothing, deaf even to the yelling
of the hounds which Boon and Tennie's Jim held on leash.

"We'll put General Compson on Katie this morning," Major de
Spain said. "He drew blood last year; if he'd had a mule then
that would have stood, he would have——"

"No," General Compson said. "I'm too old to go helling through
the woods on a mule or a horse or anything else any more. Besides,

I had my chance last year and missed it. I'm going on a stand this morning. I'm going to let that boy ride Katie."

"No, wait," McCaslin said. "Ike's got the rest of his life to hunt bears in. Let somebody else——"

"No," General Compson said. "I want Ike to ride Katie. He's already a better woodsman than you or me either and in another ten years he'll be as good as Walter."

At first he couldn't believe it, not until Major de Spain spoke to him. Then he was up, on the one-eyed mule which would not spook at wild blood, looking down at the dog motionless at Major de Spain's stirrup, looking in the gray streaming light bigger than a calf, bigger than he knew it actually was—the big head, the chest almost as big as his own, the blue hide beneath which the muscles flinched or quivered to no touch since the heart which drove blood to them loved no man and no thing, standing as a horse stands yet different from a horse which infers only weight and speed while Lion inferred not only courage and all else that went to make up the will and desire to pursue and kill, but endurance, the will and desire to endure beyond all imaginable limits of flesh in order to overtake and slay. Then the dog looked at him. It moved its head and looked at him across the trivial uproar of the hounds, out of the yellow eyes as depthless as Boon's, as free as Boon's of meanness or generosity or gentleness or viciousness. They were just cold and sleepy. Then it blinked, and he knew it was not looking at him and never had been, without even bothering to turn its head away.

That morning he heard the first cry. Lion had already vanished while Sam and Tennie's Jim were putting saddles on the mule and horse which had drawn the wagon and he watched the hounds as they crossed and cast, snuffing and whimpering, until they too disappeared. Then he and Major de Spain and Sam and Tennie's Jim rode after them and heard the first cry out of the wet and thawing woods not two hundred yards ahead, high, with that abject, almost human quality he had come to know, and the other hounds joining in until the gloomed woods rang and clamored. They rode then. It seemed to him that he could actually see the big blue dog boring on, silent, and the bear too: the thick, locomotive-like shape which he had seen that day four years ago crossing the blow-down, crashing on ahead of the dogs faster than he had believed it could have moved, drawing away even from the running mules. He heard a shotgun, once. The woods had opened, they were going fast, the clamor faint and fading on ahead; they passed the man who had fired—a swamper, a pointing arm, a gaunt face, the small black orifice of his yelling studded with rotten teeth.

He heard the changed note in the hounds' uproar and two hundred yards ahead he saw them. The bear had turned. He saw Lion drive in without pausing and saw the bear strike him aside and lunge into the yelling hounds and kill one of them almost in its tracks and whirl and run again. Then they were in a streaming tide of dogs. He heard Major de Spain and Tennie's Jim shouting and the pistol sound of Tennie's Jim's leather thong as he tried to turn them. Then he and Sam Fathers were riding alone. One of the hounds had kept on with Lion though. He recognised its voice. It was the young hound which even a year ago had had no judgment and which, by the lights of the other hounds anyway, still had none. *Maybe that's what courage is,* he thought. "Right," Sam said behind him. "Right. We got to turn him from the river if we can."

Now they were in cane: a brake. He knew the path through it as well as Sam did. They came out of the undergrowth and struck the entrance almost exactly. It would traverse the brake and come out onto a high open ridge above the river. He heard the flat clap of Walter Ewell's rifle, then two more. "No," Sam said. "I can hear the hound. Go on."

They emerged from the narrow roofless tunnel of snapping and hissing cane, still galloping, onto the open ridge below which the thick yellow river, reflectionless in the gray and streaming light, seemed not to move. Now he could hear the hound too. It was not running. The cry was a high frantic yapping and Boon was running along the edge of the bluff, his old gun leaping and jouncing against his back on its sling made of a piece of cotton plow-line. He whirled and ran up to them, wild-faced, and flung himself onto the mule behind the boy. "That damn boat!" he cried. "It's on the other side! He went straight across! Lion was too close to him! That little hound too! Lion was so close I couldn't shoot! Go on!" he cried, beating his heels into the mule's flanks. "Go on!"

They plunged down the bank, slipping and sliding in the thawed earth, crashing through the willows and into the water. He felt no shock, no cold, he on one side of the swimming mule, grasping the pommel with one hand and holding his gun above the water with the other, Boon opposite him. Sam was behind them somewhere, and then the river, the water above them, was full of dogs. They swam faster than the mules; they were scrabbling up the bank before the mules touched bottom. Major de Spain was whooping from the bank they had just left and, looking back, he saw Tennie's Jim and the horse as they went into the water.

Now the woods ahead of them and the rain-heavy air were one uproar. It rang and clamored; it echoed and broke against the bank behind them and reformed and clamored and rang until it seemed to the boy that all the hounds which had ever bayed game in this land were yelling down at him. He got his leg over the mule as it came up out of the water. Boon didn't try to mount again. He grasped one stirrup as they went up the bank and crashed through the undergrowth which fringed the bluff and saw the bear, on its hind feet, its back against a tree while the bellowing hounds swirled around it and once more Lion drove in, leaping clear of the ground.

This time the bear didn't strike him down. It caught the dog in both arms, almost loverlike, and they both went down. He was off the mule now. He drew back both hammers of the gun but he could see nothing but moiling spotted houndbodies until the bear surged up again. Boon was yelling something, he could not tell what; he could see Lion still clinging to the bear's throat and he saw the bear, half erect, strike one of the hounds with one paw and hurl it five or six feet and then, rising and rising as though it would never stop, stand erect again and begin to rake at Lion's belly with its fore-paws. Then Boon was running. The boy saw the gleam of the blade in his hand and watched him leap among the hounds, hurdling them, kicking them aside as he ran, and fling himself astride the bear as he had hurled himself onto the mule, his legs locked around the bear's belly, his left arm under the bear's throat where Lion clung, and the glint of the knife as it rose and fell.

It fell just once. For an instant they almost resembled a piece of statuary: the clinging dog, the bear, the man astride its back, work-ing and probing the buried blade. Then they went down, pulled over backward by Boon's weight, Boon underneath. It was the bear's back which reappeared first but at once Boon was astride it again. He had never released the knife and again the boy saw the almost infinitesimal movement of his arm and shoulder as he probed and sought; then the bear surged erect, raising with it the man and the dog too, and turned and still carrying the man and the dog it took two or three steps toward the woods on its hind feet as a man would have walked and crashed down. It didn't collapse, crumple. It fell all of a piece, as a tree falls, so that all three of them, man dog and bear, seemed to bounce once.

He and Tennie's Jim ran forward. Boon was kneeling at the bear's head. His left ear was shredded, his left coat sleeve was completely gone, his right boot had been ripped from knee to instep; the bright blood thinned in the thin rain down his leg and hand and arm and down the side of his face which was no longer wild but was quite calm. Together they prized Lion's jaws from the bear's throat. "Easy, goddamn it," Boon said. "Cant you see his guts are all out of him?" He began to remove his coat. He spoke to Tennie's Jim in that calm voice: "Bring the boat up. It's about a hundred yards down the bank there. I saw it." Tennie's Jim rose and went away. Then, and he could not remember if it had been a call or an exclamation from Tennie's Jim or if he had glanced up by chance, he saw Tennie's Jim stooping and saw Sam Fathers lying motionless on his face in the trampled mud.

The mule had not thrown him. He remembered that Sam was down too even before Boon began to run. There was no mark on him whatever and when he and Boon turned him over, his eyes were open and he said something in that tongue which he and Joe Baker had used to speak together. But he couldn't move. Tennie's Jim brought the skiff up; they could hear him shouting to Major de Spain across the river. Boon wrapped Lion in his hunting coat and carried him down to the skiff and they carried Sam down and returned and hitched the bear to the one-eyed mule's saddle-bow with Tennie's Jim's leash-thong and dragged him down to the skiff and got him into it and left Tennie's Jim to swim the horse and the two mules back across. Major de Spain caught the bow of the skiff as Boon jumped out and past him before it touched the bank. He looked at Old Ben and said quietly: "Well." Then he walked into the water and leaned down and touched Sam and Sam looked up at him and said something in that old tongue he and Joe Baker spoke. "You dont know what happened?" Major de Spain said.

"No, sir," the boy said. "It wasn't the mule. It wasn't anything. He was off the mule when Boon ran in on the bear. Then we looked up and he was lying on the ground." Boon was shouting at Tennie's Jim, still in the middle of the river.

"Come on, goddamn it!" he said. "Bring me that mule!"

"What do you want with a mule?" Major de Spain said.

Boon didn't even look at him. "I'm going to Hoke's to get the doctor," he said in that calm voice, his face quite calm beneath the steady thinning of the bright blood.

"You need a doctor yourself," Major de Spain said. "Tennie's Jim——"

"Damn that," Boon said. He turned on Major de Spain. His face was still calm, only his voice was a pitch higher. "Cant you see his goddamn guts are all out of him?"

"Boon!" Major de Spain said. They looked at one another. Boon was a good head taller than Major de Spain; even the boy was taller now than Major de Spain.

"I've got to get the doctor," Boon said. "His goddamn guts——"

"All right," Major de Spain said. Tennie's Jim came up out of the water. The horse and the sound mule had already scented Old Ben; they surged and plunged all the way up to the top of the bluff, dragging Tennie's Jim with them, before he could stop them and tie them and come back. Major de Spain unlooped the leather thong of his compass from his buttonhole and gave it to Tennie's Jim. "Go straight to Hoke's," he said. "Bring Doctor Crawford back with you. Tell him there are two men to be looked at. Take my mare. Can you find the road from here?"

"Yes, sir," Tennie's Jim said.

"All right," Major de Spain said. "Go on." He turned to the boy. "Take the mules and the horse and go back and get the wagon. We'll go on down the river in the boat to Coon bridge. Meet us there. Can you find it again?"

"Yes, sir," the boy said.

"All right. Get started."

He went back to the wagon. He realised then how far they had run. It was already afternoon when he put the mules into the traces and tied the horse's lead-rope to the tail-gate. He reached Coon bridge at dusk. The skiff was already there. Before he could see it and almost before he could see the water he had to leap from the tilting wagon, still holding the reins, and work around to where he could grasp the bit and then the ear of the plunging sound mule and dig his heels and hold it until Boon came up the bank. The rope of the lead horse had already snapped and it had already disappeared up the road toward camp. They turned the wagon around and took the mules out and he led the sound mule a hundred yards up the road and tied it. Boon had already brought Lion up to the wagon and Sam was sitting up in the skiff now and when they raised him he tried to walk, up the bank and to the wagon and he tried to climb into the wagon but Boon did not wait; he picked Sam up bodily and set him on the seat. Then they hitched Old Ben to the one-eyed mule's saddle again and dragged him up the bank and set two skid-poles into the open tail-gate and got him into the wagon and he went and got the sound mule and Boon fought it into the traces, striking it across its hard hollow-sounding face until it came into position and stood trembling. Then the rain came down, as though it had held off all day waiting on them.

They returned to camp through it, through the streaming and sightless dark, hearing long before they saw any light the horn and the spaced shots to guide them. When they came to Sam's dark little hut he tried to stand up. He spoke again in the tongue of the old fathers; then he said clearly: "Let me out. Let me out."

"He hasn't got any fire," Major said. "Go on!" he said sharply.

But Sam was struggling now, trying to stand up. "Let me out, Master," he said. "Let me go home."

So he stopped the wagon and Boon got down and lifted Sam out. He did not wait to let Sam try to walk this time. He carried him into the hut and Major de Spain got light on a paper spill from the buried embers on the hearth and lit the lamp and Boon put Sam on his bunk and drew off his boots and Major de Spain covered him and the boy was not there, he was holding the mules, the sound one which was trying again to bolt since when the wagon stopped Old Ben's scent drifted forward again along the streaming blackness of air, but Sam's eyes were probably open again on that profound look which saw further than them or the hut, further than the death of a bear and the dying of a dog. Then they went on, toward the long wailing of the horn and the shots which seemed each to linger intact somewhere in the thick streaming air until the next spaced report joined and blended with it, to the lighted house, the bright streaming windows, the quiet faces as Boon entered, bloody and quite calm, carrying the bundled coat. He laid Lion, blood coat and all, on his stale sheetless pallet bed which not even Ash, as deft in the house as a woman, could ever make smooth.

The sawmill doctor from Hoke's was already there. Boon would not let the doctor touch him until he had seen to Lion. He wouldn't risk giving Lion chloroform. He put the entrails back and sewed him up without it while Major de Spain held his head and Boon his feet. But he never tried to move. He lay there, the yellow eyes open upon nothing while the quiet men in the new hunting clothes and in the old ones crowded into the little airless room rank with the smell of Boon's body and garments, and watched. Then the doctor cleaned and disinfected Boon's face and arm and leg and bandaged them and, the boy in front with a lantern and the doctor and McCaslin and Major de Spain and General Compson following, they went to Sam Fathers' hut. Tennie's Jim had built up the fire; he squatted before it, dozing. Sam had not moved since Boon had put him in the bunk and Major de Spain had covered him with the blankets, yet he opened his eyes and looked from one to another of the faces and when McCaslin touched his shoulder and said, "Sam. The doctor wants to look at you," he even drew his hands out of the blanket and began to fumble at his shirt buttons until McCaslin said, "Wait. We'll do it." They undressed him. He lay there—the copper-brown, almost hairless body, the old man's body, the old man, the wild man not even one generation from the woods, childless, kinless, peopleless—motionless, his eyes open but no longer looking at any of them, while the doctor examined him and drew the blankets up and put the stethoscope back into his bag and snapped the bag and only the boy knew that Sam too was going to die.

"Exhaustion," the doctor said. "Shock maybe. A man his age swimming rivers in December. He'll be all right. Just make him stay in bed for a day or two. Will there be somebody here with him?"

"There will be somebody here," Major de Spain said.

They went back to the house, to the rank little room where Boon still sat on the pallet bed with Lion's head under his hand while the men, the ones who had hunted behind Lion and the ones who had never seen him before today, came quietly in to look at him and went away. Then it was dawn and they all went out into the yard to look at Old Ben, with his eyes open too and his lips snarled back from his worn teeth and his mutilated foot and the little hard lumps under his skin which were the old bullets (there were fifty-two of them, buckshot rifle and ball) and the single almost invisible slit under his left shoulder where Boon's blade had finally found his life. Then Ash began to beat on the bottom of the dishpan with a heavy spoon to call them to breakfast and it was the first time he could remember hearing no sound from the dogs under the kitchen while they were eating. It was as if the old bear, even dead there in the yard, was a more potent terror still than they could face without Lion between them.

The rain had stopped during the night. By midmorning the thin sun appeared, rapidly burning away mist and cloud, warming the air and the earth; it would be one of those windless Mississippi December days which are a sort of Indian summer's Indian summer. They moved Lion out to the front gallery, into the sun. It was Boon's idea. "Goddamn it," he said, "he never did want to stay in the house until I made him. You know that." He took a crowbar and loosened the floor boards under his pallet bed so it could be raised, mattress and all, without disturbing Lion's position, and they carried him out to the gallery and put him down facing the woods.

Then he and the doctor and McCaslin and Major de Spain went to Sam's hut. This time Sam didn't open his eyes and his breathing was so quiet, so peaceful that they could hardly see that he breathed. The doctor didn't even take out his stethoscope nor even touch him. "He's all right," the doctor said. "He didn't even catch cold. He just quit."

"Quit?" McCaslin said.

"Yes. Old people do that sometimes. Then they get a good night's sleep or maybe it's just a drink of whisky, and they change their minds."

They returned to the house. And then they began to arrive—the swamp-dwellers, the gaunt men who ran trap-lines and lived on quinine and coons and river water, the farmers of little corn- and cotton-patches along the bottom's edge whose fields and cribs and pig-pens the old bear had rifled, the loggers from the camp and the sawmill men from Hoke's and the town men from further away than that, whose hounds the old bear had slain and traps and deadfalls he had wrecked and whose lead he carried. They came up mounted and on foot and in wagons, to enter the yard and look at him and then go on to the front where Lion lay, filling the little yard and overflowing it until there were almost a hundred of them squatting and standing in the warm and drowsing sunlight, talking quietly of hunting, of the game and the dogs which ran it, of hounds and bear and deer and men of yesterday vanished from the earth, while from time to time the great blue dog would open his eyes, not as if he were listening to them but as though to look at the woods for a moment before closing his eyes again, to remember the woods or to see that they were still there. He died at sundown.

Major de Spain broke camp that night. They carried Lion into the woods, or Boon carried him that is, wrapped in a quilt from his bed, just as he had refused to let anyone else touch Lion yesterday until the doctor got there; Boon carrying Lion, and the boy and General Compson and Walter and still almost fifty of them following with lanterns and lighted pine-knots—men from Hoke's and even further, who would have to ride out of the bottom in the dark, and swampers and trappers who would have to walk even, scattering toward the little hidden huts where they lived. And Boon would let nobody else dig the grave either and lay Lion in it and cover him and then General Compson stood at the head of it while the blaze and smoke of the pine-knots streamed away among the winter branches and spoke as he would have spoken over a man. Then they returned to camp. Major de Spain and McCaslin and Ash had rolled and tied all the bedding. The mules were hitched to the wagon and pointed out of the bottom and the wagon was already loaded and the stove in the kitchen was cold and the table was set with scraps of cold food and bread and only the coffee was hot when the boy ran into the kitchen where Major de Spain and McCaslin had already eaten. "What?" he cried. "What? I'm not going."

"Yes," McCaslin said, "we're going out tonight. Major wants to get on back home."

"No!" he said. "I'm going to stay."

"You've got to be back in school Monday. You've already missed a week more than I intended. It will take you from now until Monday to catch up. Sam's all right. You heard Doctor Crawford. I'm going to leave Boon and Tennie's Jim both to stay with him until he feels like getting up."

He was panting. The others had come in. He looked rapidly and almost frantically around at the other faces. Boon had a fresh bottle. He upended it and started the cork by striking the bottom of the bottle with the heel of his hand and drew the cork with his teeth and spat it out and drank. "You're damn right you're going back to school," Boon said. "Or I'll burn the tail off of you myself if Cass dont, whether you are sixteen or sixty. Where in hell do you expect to get without education? Where would Cass be? Where in hell would I be if I hadn't never went to school?"

He looked at McCaslin again. He could feel his breath coming shorter and shorter and shallower and shallower, as if there were not enough air in the kitchen for that many to breathe. "This is just Thursday. I'll come home Sunday night on one of the horses. I'll come home Sunday, then. I'll make up the time I lost studying Sunday night, McCaslin," he said, without even despair.

"No, I tell you," McCaslin said. "Sit down here and eat your supper. We're going out to——"

"Hold up, Cass," General Compson said. The boy did not know

General Compson had moved until he put his hand on his shoulder. "What is it, bud?" he said.

"I've got to stay," he said. "I've got to."

"All right," General Compson said. "You can stay. If missing an extra week of school is going to throw you so far behind you'll have to sweat to find out what some hired pedagogue put between the covers of a book, you better quit altogether.—And you shut up, Cass," he said, though McCaslin had not spoken. "You've got one foot straddled into a farm and the other foot straddled into a bank; you aint even got a good hand-hold where this boy was already an old man long before you damned Sartorises and Edmondses invented farms and banks to keep yourselves from having to find out what this boy was born knowing and fearing too maybe but without being afraid, that could go ten miles on a compass because he wanted to look at a bear none of us had ever got near enough to put a bullet in and looked at the bear and came the ten miles back on the compass in the dark; maybe by God that's the why and the wherefore of farms and banks.—I reckon you still aint going to tell what it is?"

But still he could not. "I've got to stay," he said.

"All right," General Compson said. "There's plenty of grub left. And you'll come home Sunday, like you promised McCaslin? Not Sunday night: Sunday."

"Yes, sir," he said.

"All right," General Compson said. "Sit down and eat, boys," he said. "Let's get started. It's going to be cold before we get home."

They ate. The wagon was already loaded and ready to depart; all they had to do was to get into it. Boon would drive them out to the road, to the farmer's stable where the surrey had been left. He stood beside the wagon, in silhouette on the sky, turbaned like a Paythan and taller than any there, the bottle tilted. Then he flung the bottle from his lips without even lowering it, spinning and glinting in the faint starlight, empty. "Them that's going," he said, "get in the goddamn wagon. Them that aint, get out of the goddamn way." The others got in. Boon mounted to the seat beside General Compson and the wagon moved, on into the obscurity until the boy could no longer see it, even the moving density of it amid the greater night. But he could still hear it, for a long while: the slow, deliberate banging of the wooden frame as it lurched from rut to rut. And he could hear Boon even when he could no longer hear the wagon. He was singing, harsh, tuneless, loud.

That was Thursday. On Saturday morning Tennie's Jim left on McCaslin's woods-horse which had not been out of the bottom one time now in six years, and late that afternoon rode through the gate on the spent horse and on to the commissary where McCaslin was rationing the tenants and the wage-hands for the coming week, and this time McCaslin forestalled any necessity or risk of having to wait while Major de Spain's surrey was being horsed and harnessed. He took their own, and with Tennie's Jim already asleep in the back seat he drove in to Jefferson and waited while Major de Spain changed to boots and put on his overcoat, and they drove the thirty miles in the dark of that night and at daybreak on Sunday morning they swapped to the waiting mare and mule and as the sun rose they rode out of the jungle and onto the low ridge where they had buried Lion: the low mound of unannealed earth where Boon's spade-marks still showed and beyond the grave the platform of freshly cut saplings bound between four posts and the blanket-wrapped bundle upon the platform and Boon and the boy squatting between the platform and the grave until Boon, the bandage removed, ripped, from his head so that the long scoriations of Old Ben's claws resembled crusted tar in the sunlight, sprang up and threw down upon them with the old gun with which he had never been known to hit anything although McCaslin was already off the mule, kicked both feet free of the irons and vaulted down before the mule had stopped, walking toward Boon.

"Stand back," Boon said. "By God, you wont touch him. Stand back, McCaslin." Still McCaslin came on, fast yet without haste.

"Cass!" Major de Spain said. Then he said "Boon! You, Boon!" and he was down too and the boy rose too, quickly, and still McCaslin came on not fast but steady and walked up to the grave and reached his hand steadily out, quickly yet still not fast, and took hold the gun by the middle so that he and Boon faced one another across Lion's grave, both holding the gun, Boon's spent indomitable amazed and frantic face almost a head higher than McCaslin's beneath the black scoriations of beast's claws and then Boon's chest began to heave as though there were not enough air in all the woods, in all the wilderness, for all of them, for him and anyone else, even for him alone.

"Turn it loose, Boon," McCaslin said.

"You damn little spindling—" Boon said. "Don't you know I can take it away from you? Dont you know I can tie it around your neck like a damn cravat?"

"Yes," McCaslin said. "Turn it loose, Boon."

"This is the way he wanted it. He told us. He told us exactly how to do it. And by God you aint going to move him. So we did it like he said, and I been sitting here ever since to keep the damn wildcats and varmints away from him and by God—" Then McCaslin had the gun, down-slanted while he pumped the slide, the five shells snicking out of it so fast that the last one was almost out before the first one touched the ground and McCaslin dropped the gun behind him without once having taken his eyes from Boon's.

"Did you kill him, Boon?" he said. Then Boon moved. He turned, he moved like he was still drunk and then for a moment blind too, one hand out as he blundered toward the big tree and seemed to stop walking before he reached the tree so that he plunged, fell toward it, flinging up both hands and catching himself against the tree and turning until his back was against it, backing with the tree's trunk his wild spent scoriated face and the tremendous heave and collapse of his chest, McCaslin following, facing him again, never once having moved his eyes from Boon's eyes. "Did you kill him, Boon?"

"No!" Boon said. "No!"

"Tell the truth," McCaslin said. "I would have done it if he had asked me to." Then the boy moved. He was between them, facing McCaslin; the water felt as if it had burst and sprung not from his eyes alone but from his whole face, like sweat.

"Leave him alone!" he cried. "Goddam it! Leave him alone!"

———

IV

then he was twenty-one. He could say it, himself and his cousin juxtaposed not against the wilderness but against the tamed land which was to have been his heritage, the land which old Carothers McCaslin his grandfather had bought with white man's money from the wild men whose grandfathers without guns hunted it, and tamed and ordered or believed he had tamed and ordered it for the reason that the human beings he held in bondage and in the power of life and death had removed the forest from it and in their sweat scratched the surface of it to a depth of perhaps fourteen inches in order to grow something out of it which had not been there before and which could be translated back into the money he who believed he had bought it had had to pay to get it and hold it and a reasonable profit too: and for which reason old Carothers McCaslin, knowing better, could raise his children, his descendants and heirs, to believe the land was his to hold and bequeath since the strong and ruthless man has a cynical foreknowledge of his own vanity and pride and strength and a contempt for all his get: just as, knowing better, Major de Spain and his fragment of that wilderness which was bigger and older than any recorded deed: just as, knowing better, old Thomas Sutpen, from whom Major de Spain had had his fragment for money: just as Ikkemotubbe, the Chickasaw chief, from whom Thomas Sutpen had had the fragment for money or rum or whatever it was, knew in his turn that not even a fragment of it had been his to relinquish or sell

not against the wilderness but against the land, not in pursuit and lust but in relinquishment, and in the commissary as it should have been, not the heart perhaps but certainly the solar-plexus of the repudiated and relinquished: the square, galleried, wooden building squatting like a portent above the fields whose laborers it still held in thrall '65 or no and placarded over with advertisements for snuff and cures for chills and salves and potions manufactured and sold by white men to bleach the pigment and straighten the hair of negroes that they might resemble the very race which for two hundred years had held them in bondage and from which for another hundred years not even a bloody civil war would have set them completely free

himself and his cousin amid the old smells of cheese and salt meat and kerosene and harness, the ranked shelves of tobacco and overalls and bottled medicine and thread and plow-bolts, the barrels and kegs of flour and meal and molasses and nails, the wall pegs dependant with plowlines and plow-collars and hames and trace-chains, and the desk and the shelf above it on which rested the ledgers in which McCaslin recorded the slow outward trickle of food and supplies and equipment which returned each fall as cotton made and ginned and sold (two threads frail as truth and impalpable as equators yet cable-strong to bind for life them who made the cotton to the land their sweat fell on), and the older ledgers clumsy and archaic in size and shape, on the yellowed pages of which were recorded in the faded hand of his father Theophilus and his uncle Amodeus during the two decades before the Civil War, the manumission in title at least of Carothers McCaslin's slaves:

'Relinquish,' McCaslin said. 'Relinquish. You, the direct male descendant of him who saw the opportunity and took it, bought the land, took the land, got the land no matter how, held it to bequeath, no matter how, out of the old grant, the first patent, when it was a wilderness of wild beasts and wilder men, and cleared it, translated it into something to bequeath to his children, worthy of bequeathment for his descendants' ease and security and pride and to perpetuate his name and accomplishments. Not only the male descendant but the only and last descendant in the male line and in the third generation, while I am not only four generations from old Carothers, I derived through a woman and the very McCaslin in my name is mine only by sufferance and courtesy and my grandmother's pride in what that man accomplished whose legacy and monument you think you can repudiate.' and he

'I cant repudiate it. It was never mine to repudiate. It was never Father's and Uncle Buddy's to bequeath me to repudiate because it was never Grandfather's to bequeath them to bequeath me to repudiate because it was never old Ikkemotubbe's to sell to Grandfather for bequeathment and repudiation. Because it was never Ikkemotubbe's fathers' fathers' to bequeath Ikkemotubbe to sell to Grandfather or any man because on the instant when Ikkemotubbe discovered, realised, that he could sell it for money, on that instant it ceased ever to have been his forever, father to father to father, and the man who bought it bought nothing.'

'Bought nothing?' and he

'Bought nothing. Because He told in the Book how He created the earth, made it and looked at it and said it was all right, and then He made man. He made the earth first and peopled it with dumb creatures, and then He created man to be His overseer on the earth and to hold suzerainty over the earth and the animals on it in His name, not to hold for himself and his descendants inviolable title forever, generation after generation, to the oblongs and squares of the earth, but to hold the earth mutual and intact in the communal anonymity of brotherhood, and all the fee He asked was pity and humility and sufferance and endurance and the sweat of his face for bread. And I know what you are going to say,' he said: 'That nevertheless Grandfather—' and McCaslin

'—did own it. And not the first. Not alone and not the first since, as your Authority states, man was dispossessed of Eden. Nor yet the second and still not alone, on down through the tedious and shabby chronicle of His chosen sprung from Abraham, and of the

sons of them who dispossessed Abraham, and of the five hundred
years during which half the known world and all it contained was
chattel to one city as this plantation and all the life it contained was
chattel and revokeless thrall to this commissary store and those
ledgers yonder during your grandfather's life, and the next thousand
years while men fought over the fragments of that collapse until
at last even the fragments were exhausted and men snarled over
the gnawed bones of the old world's worthless evening until an
accidental egg discovered to them a new hemisphere. So let me
say it: That nevertheless and notwithstanding old Carothers did
own it. Bought it, got it, no matter; kept it, held it, no matter;
bequeathed it: else why do you stand here relinquishing and repudiating? Held it, kept it for fifty years until you could repudiate
it, while He—this Arbiter, this Architect, this Umpire—condoned—
or did He? looked down and saw—or did He? Or at least did
nothing: saw, and could not, or did not see; saw, and would not,
or perhaps He would not see—perverse, impotent, or blind: which?'
and he

'Dispossessed.' and McCaslin

'What?' and he

'Dispossessed. Not impotent: He didn't condone; not blind,
because He watched it. And let me say it. Dispossessed of Eden.
Dispossessed of Canaan, and those who dispossessed him dispossessed him dispossessed, and the five hundred years of absentee
landlords in the Roman bagnios, and the thousand years of wild
men from the northern woods who dispossessed them and devoured
their ravished substance ravished in turn again and then snarled
in what you call the old world's worthless twilight over the old
world's gnawed bones, blasphemous in His name until He used a
simple egg to discover to them a new world where a nation of
people could be founded in humility and pity and sufferance and
pride of one to another. And Grandfather did own the land nevertheless and notwithstanding because He permitted it, not impotent
and not condoning and not blind because He ordered and watched
it. He saw the land already accursed even as Ikkemotubbe and
Ikkemotubbe's father old Issetibbeha and old Issetibbeha's fathers
too held it, already tainted even before any white man owned it
by what Grandfather and his kind, his fathers, had brought into the
new land which He had vouchsafed them out of pity and sufferance,
on condition of pity and humility and sufferance and endurance,
from that old world's corrupt and worthless twilight as though in

the sailfuls of the old world's tainted wind which drove the ships—'
and McCaslin

'Ah.'

'—and no hope for the land anywhere so long as Ikkemotubbe
and Ikkemotubbe's descendants held it in unbroken succession.
Maybe He saw that only by voiding the land for a time of
Ikkemottubbe's blood and substituting for it another blood, could
He accomplish His purpose. Maybe He knew already what that
other blood would be, maybe it was more than justice that only
the white man's blood was available and capable to raise the
white man's curse, more than vengeance when—' and McCaslin

'Ah.'

'—when He used the blood which had brought in the evil to
destroy the evil as doctors use fever to burn up fever, poison to
slay poison. Maybe He chose Grandfather out of all of them He
might have picked. Maybe He knew that Grandfather himself would
not serve His purpose because Grandfather was born too soon too,
but that Grandfather would have descendants, the right descendants;
maybe He had foreseen already the descendants Grandfather would
have, maybe He saw already in Grandfather the seed progenitive of
the three generations He saw it would take to set at least some of
His lowly people free—' and McCaslin

'The sons of Ham. You who quote the Book: the sons of Ham.'
and he

'There are some things He said in the Book, and some things
reported of Him that He did not say. And I know what you will
say now: That if truth is one thing to me and another thing to
you, how will we choose which is truth? You dont need to choose.
The heart already knows. He didn't have His Book written to be
read by what must elect and choose, but by the heart, not by the
wise of the earth because maybe they dont need it or maybe the
wise no longer have any heart, but by the doomed and lowly
of the earth who have nothing else to read with but the heart.
Because the men who wrote his Book for Him were writing about
truth and there is only one truth and it covers all things that touch
the heart.' and McCaslin

'So these men who transcribed His Book for Him were sometimes
liars.' and he

'Yes. Because they were human men. They were trying to write
down the heart's truth out of the heart's driving complexity, for
all the complex and troubled hearts which would beat after them.

What they were trying to tell, what He wanted said, was too simple. Those for whom they transcribed His words could not have believed them. It had to be expounded in the everyday terms which they were familiar with and could comprehend, not only those who listened but those who told it too, because if they who were that near to Him as to have been elected from among all who breathed and spoke language to transcribe and relay His words, could comprehend truth only through the complexity of passion and lust and hate and fear which drives the heart, what distance back to truth must they traverse whom truth could only reach by word-of-mouth?' and McCaslin

'I might answer that, since you have taken to proving your points and disproving mine by the same text, I dont know. But I dont say that, because you have answered yourself: No time at all if, as you say, the heart knows truth, the infallible and unerring heart. And perhaps you are right, since although you admitted three generations from old Carothers to you, there were not three. There were not even completely two. Uncle Buck and Uncle Buddy. And they not the first and not alone. A thousand other Bucks and Buddies in less than two generations and sometimes less than one in this land which so you claim God created and man himself cursed and tainted. Not to mention 1865.' and he

'Yes. More men than Father and Uncle Buddy,' not even glancing toward the shelf above the desk, nor did McCaslin. They did not need to. To him it was as though the ledgers in their scarred cracked leather bindings were being lifted down one by one in their fading sequence and spread open on the desk or perhaps upon some apocryphal Bench or even Altar or perhaps before the Throne Itself for a last perusal and contemplation and refreshment of the All-knowledgeable before the yellowed pages and the brown thin ink in which was recorded the injustice and a little at least of its amelioration and restitution faded back forever into the anonymous communal original dust

the yellowed pages scrawled in fading ink by the hand first of his grandfather and then of his father and uncle, bachelors up to and past fifty and then sixty, the one who ran the plantation and the farming of it and the other who did the housework and the cooking and continued to do it even after his twin married and the boy himself was born

the two brothers who as soon as their father was buried moved out of the tremendously-conceived, the almost barnlike edifice which he had not even completed, into a one-room log cabin which the two of them built themselves and added other rooms to while they lived in it, refusing to allow any slave to touch any timber of it other than the actual raising into place the logs which two men alone could not handle, and domiciled all the slaves in the big house some of the windows of which were still merely boarded up with odds and ends of plank or with the skins of bear and deer nailed over the empty frames: each sundown the brother who superintended the farming would parade the negroes as a first sergeant dismisses a company, and herd them willynilly, man woman and child, without question protest or recourse, into the tremendous abortive edifice scarcely yet out of embryo, as if even old Carothers McCaslin had paused aghast at the concrete indica- tion of his own vanity's boundless conceiving: he would call his mental roll and herd them in and with a hand-wrought nail as long as a flenching-knife and suspended from a short deer-hide thong attached to the door-jamb for that purpose, he would nail to the door of that house which lacked half its windows and had no hinged back door at all, so that presently and for fifty years afterward, when the boy himself was big to hear and remember it, there was in the land a sort of folk-tale: of the countryside all night long full of skulking McCaslin slaves dodging the moonlit roads and the Patrol-riders to visit other plantations, and of the unspoken gentle- men's agreement between the two white men and the two dozen black ones that, after the white man had counted them and driven the home-made nail into the front door at sundown, neither of the white men would go around behind the house and look at the back door, provided that all the negroes were behind the front one when the brother who drove it drew out the nail again at daybreak

the twins who were identical even in their handwriting unless you had specimens side by side to compare, and even when both hands appeared on the same page (as often happened, as if, long since past any oral intercourse, they had used the diurnally ad- vancing pages to conduct the unavoidable business of the com- pulsion which had traversed all the waste wilderness of North Mississippi in 1830 and '40 and singled them out to drive) they both looked as though they had been written by the same perfectly normal ten-year-old boy, even to the spelling, except that the spelling did not improve as one by one the slaves which Carothers McCaslin had inherited and purchased—Roscius and Phoebe and Thucydides and Eunice and their descendants, and Sam Fathers

and his mother for both of whom he had swapped an underbred
trotting gelding to old Ikkemotubbe, the Chickasaw chief from
whom he had likewise bought the land, and Tennie Beauchamp
whom the twin Amodeus had won from a neighbor in a poker-game,
and the anomaly calling itself Percival Brownlee which the twin
Theophilus had purchased, neither he nor his brother ever knew
why apparently, from Bedford Forrest while he was still only a
slave-dealer and not yet a general (It was a single page, not long
and covering less than a year, not seven months in fact, begun in
the hand which the boy had learned to distinguish as that of his
father:

> *Percavil Brownly 26yr Old. cleark @ Bookepper. bought from
> N.B.Forest at Cold Water 3 Mar 1856 $265. dolars*

and beneath that, in the same hand:

> *5 mar 1856 No bookepper any way Cant read. Can write his Name
> but I already put that down My self Says he can Plough but dont
> look like it to Me. sent to Feild to day Mar 5 1856*

and the same hand:

> *6 Mar 1856 Cant plough either Says he aims to be a Precher so may
> be he can lead live stock to Crick to Drink*

and this time it was the other, the hand which he now recognised
as his uncle's when he could see them both on the same page:

> *Mar 23th 1856 Cant do that either Except one at a Time Get shut
> of him*

then the first again:

> *24 Mar 1856 Who in hell would buy him*

then the second:

> *19th of Apr 1856 Nobody You put yourself out of Market at Cold
> Water two months ago I never said sell him Free him*

the first:

> *22 Apr 1856 Ill get it out of him*

the second:

> *Jun 13th 1856 How $1 per yr 265$ 265 yrs Wholl sign his Free
> paper*

then the first again:

> *1 Oct 1856 Mule josephine Broke Leg @ shot Wrong stall wrong niger wrong everything $100. dolars*

and the same:

> *2 Oct 1856 Freed Debit McCaslin @ McCaslin $265. dolars*

then the second again:

> *Oct 3th Debit Theophilus McCaslin Niger 265$ Mule 100$ 365$ He hasnt gone yet Father should be here*

then the first:

> *3 Oct 1856 Son of a bitch wont leave What would father done*

the second:

> *29th of Oct 1856 Renamed him*

the first:

> *31 Oct 1856 Renamed him what*

the second:

> *Chrstms 1856 Spintrius*

) took substance and even a sort of shadowy life with their passions and complexities too as page followed page and year year; all there, not only the general and condoned injustice and its slow amortization but the specific tragedy which had not been condoned and could never be amortized, the new page and the new ledger, the hand which he could now recognise at first glance as his father's:

> *Father dide Lucius Quintus Carothers McCaslin, Callina 1772 Missippy 1837. Dide and burid 27 June 1837*
> *Roskus. rased by Granfather in Callina Dont know how old. Freed 27 June 1837 Dont want to leave. Dide and Burid 12 Jan 1841*
> *Fibby Roskus Wife. bought by granfather in Callina says Fifty Freed 27 June 1837 Dont want to leave. Dide and burd 1 Aug 1849*
> *Thucydus Roskus @ Fibby Son born in Callina 1779. Refused 10acre peace fathers Will 28 Jun 1837 Refused Cash offer $200. dolars from A.@ T. McCaslin 28 Jun 1837 Wants to stay and work it out*

and beneath this and covering the next five pages and almost that many years, the slow, day-by-day accruement of the wages allowed him and the food and clothing—the molasses and meat and meal, the cheap durable shirts and jeans and shoes and now and then a coat against rain and cold—charged against the slowly yet steadily mounting sum of balance (and it would seem to the boy that he could actually see the black man, the slave whom his white owner had forever manumitted by the very act from which the black man could never be free so long as memory lasted, entering the commissary, asking permission perhaps of the white man's son to see the ledger-page which he could not even read, not even asking for the white man's word, which he would have had to accept for the reason that there was absolutely no way under the sun for him to test it, as to how the account stood, how much longer before he could go and never return, even if only as far as Jefferson seventeen miles away) on to the double pen-stroke closing the final entry:

3 Nov 1841 By Cash to Thucydus McCaslin $200. dolars Set Up blaksmith in J. Dec 1841 Dide and burid in J. 17 feb 1854
Eunice Bought by Father in New Orleans 1807 $650. dolars. Marrid to Thucydus 1809 Drownd in Crick Cristmas Day 1832

and then the other hand appeared, the first time he had seen it in the ledger to distinguish it as his uncle's, the cook and housekeeper whom even McCaslin, who had known him and the boy's father for sixteen years before the boy was born, remembered as sitting all day long in the rocking chair from which he cooked the food, before the kitchen fire on which he cooked it:

June 21th 1833 Drownd herself

and the first:

23 Jun 1833 Who in hell ever heard of a niger drownding him self

and the second, unhurried, with a complete finality; the two identical entries might have been made with a rubber stamp save for the date:

Aug 13th 1833 Drownd herself

and he thought *But why? But why?* He was sixteen then. It was neither the first time he had been alone in the commissary nor the first time he had taken down the old ledgers familiar on their shelf above the desk ever since he could remember. As a child and even after nine and ten and eleven, when he had learned to read, he would look up at the scarred and cracked backs and ends but with no particular desire to open them, and though he intended to examine them someday because he realised that they probably contained a chronological and much more comprehensive though doubtless tedious record than he would ever get from any other source, not alone of his own flesh and blood but of all his people, not only the whites but the black ones too, who were as much a part of his ancestry as his white progenitors, and of the land which they had all held and used in common and fed from and on and would continue to use in common without regard to color or titular ownership, it would only be on some idle day when he was old and perhaps even bored a little since what the old books contained would be after all these years fixed immutably, finished, unalterable, harmless. Then he was sixteen. He knew what he was going to find before he found it. He got the commissary key from McCaslin's room after midnight while McCaslin was asleep and with the commissary door shut and locked behind him and the forgotten lantern stinking anew the rank dead icy air, he leaned above the yellowed page and thought not Why drowned herself, but thinking what he believed his father had thought when he found his brother's first comment: Why did Uncle Buddy think she had drowned herself? finding, beginning to find on the next succeeding page what he knew he would find, only this was still not it because he already knew this:

> Tomasina called Tomy Daughter of Thucydus @ Eunice Born 1810 dide in Child bed June 1833 and Burd. Yr stars fell

nor the next:

> Turl Son of Thucydus @ Eunice Tomy born Jun 1833 yr stars fell Fathers will

and nothing more, no tedious recording filling this page of wages day by day and food and clothing charged against them, no entry of his death and burial because he had outlived his white half-brothers and the books which McCaslin kept did not include obituaries: just Fathers will and he had seen that too: old Carothers' bold cramped hand far less legible than his sons' even and not much better in spelling, who while capitalising almost every noun and verb, made no effort to punctuate or construct whatever, just as he made no effort either to explain or obfuscate the thousand-dollar legacy to the son of an unmarried slave-girl, to be paid only at the child's coming-of-age, bearing the consequence of the act of which

there was still no definite incontrovertible proof that he acknowl-
edged, not out of his own substance but penalising his sons with it,
charging them a cash forfeit on the accident of their own paternity;
not even a bribe for silence toward his own fame since his fame
would suffer only after he was no longer present to defend it,
flinging almost contemptuously, as he might a cast-off hat or pair of
shoes, the thousand dollars which could have had no more reality
to him under those conditions than it would have to the negro, the
slave who would not even see it until he came of age, twenty-one
years too late to begin to learn what money was. *So I reckon that
was cheaper than saying My son to a nigger* he thought. *Even if
My son wasn't but just two words. But there must have been love*
he thought. *Some sort of love. Even what he would have called
love: not just an afternoon's or a night's spittoon.* There was the
old man, old, within five years of his life's end, long a widower and,
since his sons were not only bachelors but were approaching
middleage, lonely in the house and doubtless even bored since his
plantation was established now and functioning and there was
enough money now, too much of it probably for a man whose vices
even apparently remained below his means; there was the girl,
husbandless and young, only twenty-three when the child was
born: perhaps he had sent for her at first out of loneliness, to have
a young voice and movement in the house, summoned her, bade
her mother send her each morning to sweep the floors and make
the beds and the mother acquiescing since that was probably already understood, already planned: the only child of a couple who
were not field hands and who held themselves something above
the other slaves not alone for that reason but because the husband
and his father and mother too had been inherited by the white man
from his father, and the white man himself had travelled three
hundred miles and better to New Orleans in a day when men
travelled by horseback or steamboat, and bought the girl's mother
as a wife for

and that was all. The old frail pages seemed to turn of their own
accord even while he thought *His own daughter His own daughter.
No No Not even him* back to that one where the white man (not
even a widower then) who never went anywhere any more than
his sons in their time ever did and who did not need another
slave, had gone all the way to New Orleans and bought one. And
Tomey's Terrel was still alive when the boy was ten years old
and he knew from his own observation and memory that there had

already been some white in Tomey's Terrel's blood before his father gave him the rest of it; and looking down at the yellowed page spread beneath the yellow glow of the lantern smoking and stinking in that rank chill midnight room fifty years later, he seemed to see her actually walking into the icy creek on that Christmas day six months before her daughter's and her lover's (*Her first lover's* he thought. *Her first*) child was born, solitary, inflexible, griefless, ceremonial, in formal and succinct repudiation of grief and despair who had already had to repudiate belief and hope

that was all. He would never need look at the ledgers again nor did he; the yellowed pages in their fading and implacable succession were as much a part of his consciousness and would remain so forever, as the fact of his own nativity:

> *Tennie Beauchamp 21yrs Won by Amodeus McCaslin from Hubert Beauchamp Esqre Posible Strait against three Treys in sigt Not called 1859 Marrid to Tomys Turl 1859*

and no date of freedom because her freedom, as well as that of her first surviving child, derived not from Buck and Buddy McCaslin in the commissary but from a stranger in Washington and no date of death and burial, not only because McCaslin kept no obituaries in his books, but because in this year 1883 she was still alive and would remain so to see a grandson by her last surviving child:

> *Amodeus McCaslin Beauchamp Son of tomys Turl @ Tennie Beauchamp 1859 dide 1859*

then his uncle's hand entire, because his father was now a member of the cavalry command of that man whose name as a slave-dealer he could not even spell: and not even a page and not even a full line:

> *Dauter Tomes Turl and tenny 1862*

and not even a line and not even a sex and no cause given though the boy could guess it because McCaslin was thirteen then and he remembered how there was not always enough to eat in more places than Vicksburg:

> *Child of tomes Turl and Tenny 1863*

and the same hand again and this one lived, as though Tennie's perseverance and the fading and diluted ghost of old Carothers' ruthlessness had at last conquered even starvation: and clearer, fuller, more carefully written and spelled than the boy had yet seen it, as if the old man, who should have been a woman to begin with, trying to run what was left of the plantation in his brother's absence in the intervals of cooking and caring for himself and the fourteen-year-old orphan, had taken as an omen for renewed hope the fact that this nameless inheritor of slaves was at least remaining alive long enough to receive a name:

> *James Thucydus Beauchamp Son of Tomes Turl and Tenny Beauchamp Born 29th december 1864 and both Well Wanted to call him Theophilus but Tride Amodeus McCaslin and Callina McCaslin and both dide so Disswaded Them Born at Two clock A,m, both Well*

but no more, nothing; it would be another two years yet before the boy, almost a man now, would return from the abortive trip into Tennessee with the still-intact third of old Carothers' legacy to his Negro son and his descendants, which as the three surviving children established at last one by one their apparent intention of surviving, their white half-uncles had increased to a thousand dollars each, conditions permitting, as they came of age, and completed the page himself as far as it would even be completed when that day was long passed beyond which a man born in 1864 (or 1867 either, when he himself saw light) could have expected or himself hoped or even wanted to be still alive; his own hand now, queerly enough resembling neither his father's nor his uncle's nor even McCaslin's, but like that of his grandfather's save for the spelling:

> *Vanished sometime on night of his twenty-first birthday Dec 29 1885. Traced by Isaac McCaslin to Jackson Tenn. and there lost. His third of legacy $1000.00 returned to McCaslin Edmonds Trustee this day Jan 12 1886*

but not yet: that would be two years yet, and now his father's again, whose old commander was now quit of soldiering and slave-trading both; once more in the ledger and then not again and more illegible than ever, almost indecipherable at all from the rheumatism which now crippled him and almost completely innocent now even of any sort of spelling as well as punctuation, as if the four years during which he had followed the sword of the only man ever breathing who ever sold him a negro, let alone beat him in a trade, had convinced him not only of the vanity of faith and hope but of orthography too:

Miss sophonsiba b dtr t t @ t 1869

but not of belief and will because it was there, written, as McCaslin had told him, with the left hand, but there in the ledger one time more and then not again, for the boy himself was a year old, and when Lucas was born six years later, his father and uncle had been dead inside the same twelve-months almost five years; his own hand again, who was there and saw it, 1886, she was just seventeen, two years younger than himself, and he was in the commissary when McCaslin entered out of the first of dusk and said, 'He wants to marry Fonsiba,' like that: and he looked past McCaslin and saw the man, the stranger, taller than McCaslin and wearing better clothes than McCaslin and most of the other white men the boy knew habitually wore, who entered the room like a white man and stood in it like a white man, as though he had let McCaslin precede him into it not because McCaslin's skin was white but simply because McCaslin lived there and knew the way, and who talked like a white man too, looking at him past McCaslin's shoulder rapidly and keenly once and then no more, without further interest, as a mature and contained white man not impatient but just pressed for time might have looked. 'Marry Fonsiba?' he cried. 'Marry Fonsiba?' and then no more either, just watching and listening while McCaslin and the Negro talked:

'To live in Arkansas, I believe you said.'
'Yes. I have property there. A farm.'
'Property? A farm? You own it?'
'Yes.'
'You dont say Sir, do you?'
'To my elders, yes.'
'I see. You are from the North.'
'Yes. Since a child.'
'Then your father was a slave.'
'Yes. Once.'
'Then how do you own a farm in Arkansas?'
'I have a grant. It was my father's. From the United States. For military service.'
'I see,' McCaslin said. 'The Yankee army.'
'The United States army,' the stranger said; and then himself again, crying it at McCaslin's back:

'Call aunt Tennie! I'll go get her! I'll—' But McCaslin was not even including him; the stranger did not even glance back toward his voice, the two of them speaking to one another again as if he were not even there:

'Since you seem to have it all settled,' McCaslin said, 'why have you bothered to consult my authority at all?'

'I dont,' the stranger said. 'I acknowledge your authority only so far as you admit your responsibility toward her as a female member of the family of which you are the head. I dont ask your permission. I——'

'That will do!' McCaslin said. But the stranger did not falter. It was neither as if he were ignoring McCaslin nor as if he had failed to hear him. It was as though he were making, not at all an excuse and not exactly a justification, but simply a statement which the situation absolutely required and demanded should be made in McCaslin's hearing whether McCaslin listened to it or not. It was as if he were talking to himself, for himself to hear the words spoken aloud. They faced one another, not close yet at slightly less than foils' distance, erect, their voices not raised, not impactive, just succinct:

'—I inform you, notify you in advance as chief of her family. No man of honor could do less. Besides, you have, in your way, according to your lights and upbringing——'

'That's enough, I said,' McCaslin said. 'Be off this place by full dark. Go.' But for another moment the other did not move, contemplating McCaslin with that detached and heatless look, as if he were watching reflected in McCaslin's pupils the tiny image of the figure he was sustaining.

'Yes,' he said. 'After all, this is your house. And in your fashion you have. . . . But no matter. You are right. This is enough.' He turned back toward the door; he paused again but only for a second, already moving while he spoke: 'Be easy. I will be good to her.' Then he was gone.

'But how did she ever know him?' the boy cried. 'I never even heard of him before! And Fonsiba, that's never been off this place except to go to church since she was born——'

'Ha,' McCaslin said. 'Even their parents dont know until too late how seventeen-year-old girls ever met the men who marry them too, if they are lucky.' And the next morning they were both gone, Fonsiba too. McCaslin never saw her again, nor did he, because the woman he found at last five months later was no one

he had ever known. He carried a third of the three-thousand-dollar
fund in gold in a money-belt, as when he had vainly traced Tennie's
Jim into Tennessee a year ago. They—the man—had left an address
of some sort with Tennie, and three months later a letter came,
written by the man although McCaslin's wife Alice had taught
Fonsiba to read and write too a little. But it bore a different post-
mark from the address the man had left with Tennie, and he
travelled by rail as far as he could and then by contracted stage
and then by a hired livery rig and then by rail again for a distance:
an experienced traveller by now and an experienced bloodhound
too and a successful one this time because he would have to be; as
the slow interminable empty muddy December miles crawled and
crawled and night followed night in hotels, in roadside taverns
of rough logs and containing little else but a bar, and in the cabins of
strangers and the hay of lonely barns, in none of which he dared
undress because of his secret golden girdle like that of a disguised
one of the Magi travelling incognito and not even hope to draw
him but only determination and desperation, he would tell himself:
*I will have to find her. I will have to. We have already lost one
of them. I will have to find her this time.* He did. Hunched in the
slow and icy rain, on a spent hired horse splashed to the chest and
higher, he saw it—a single log edifice with a clay chimney which
seemed in process of being flattened by the rain to a nameless and
valueless rubble of dissolution in that roadless and even pathless
waste of unfenced fallow and wilderness jungle—no barn, no stable,
not so much as a hen-coop: just a log cabin built by hand and no
clever hand either, a meagre pile of clumsily-cut firewood sufficient
for about one day and not even a gaunt hound to come bellowing
out from under the house when he rode up—a farm only in embryo,
perhaps a good farm, maybe even a plantation someday, but not
now, not for years yet and only then with labor, hard and enduring and unflagging work and sacrifice; he shoved open the
crazy kitchen door in its awry frame and entered an icy gloom
where not even a fire for cooking burned and after another moment
saw, crouched into the wall's angle behind a crude table, the
coffee-colored face which he had known all his life but knew no
more, the body which had been born within a hundred yards of
the room that he was born in and in which some of his own blood
ran but which was now completely inheritor of generation after
generation to whom an unannounced white man on a horse was a
white man's hired Patroller wearing a pistol sometimes and a black-

snake whip always; he entered the next room, the only other room
the cabin owned, and found, sitting in a rocking chair before the
hearth, the man himself, reading—sitting there in the only chair
in the house, before that miserable fire for which there was not
wood sufficient to last twenty-four hours, in the same ministerial
clothing in which he had entered the commissary five months ago
and a pair of gold-framed spectacles which, when he looked up
and then rose to his feet, the boy saw did not even contain lenses,
reading a book in the midst of that desolation, that muddy waste
fenceless and even pathless and without even a walled shed for
stock to stand beneath: and over all, permeant, clinging to the man's
very clothing and exuding from his skin itself, that rank stink of
baseless and imbecile delusion, that boundless rapacity and folly,
of the carpet-bagger followers of victorious armies.

'Dont you see?' he cried. 'Dont you see? This whole land, the
whole South, is cursed, and all of us who derive from it, whom
it ever suckled, white and black both, lie under the curse? Granted
that my people brought the curse onto the land: maybe for that
reason their descendants alone can—not resist it, not combat it—
maybe just endure and outlast it until the curse is lifted. Then your
peoples' turn will come because we have forfeited ours. But not
now. Not yet. Dont you see?'

The other stood now, the unfrayed garments still ministerial even
if not quite so fine, the book closed upon one finger to keep the
place, the lenseless spectacles held like a music master's wand
in the other workless hand while the owner of it spoke his measured
and sonorous imbecility of the boundless folly and the baseless
hope: 'You're wrong. The curse you whites brought into this land
has been lifted. It has been voided and discharged. We are seeing
a new era, an era dedicated, as our founders intended it, to freedom,
liberty and equality for all, to which this country will be the new
Canaan——'

'Freedom from what? From work? Canaan?' He jerked his arm,
comprehensive, almost violent: whereupon it all seemed to stand
there about them, intact and complete and visible in the drafty,
damp, heatless, negro-stale negro-rank sorry room—the empty fields
without plow or seed to work them, fenceless against the stock
which did not exist within or without the walled stable which likewise was not there. 'What corner of Canaan is this?'

'You are seeing it at a bad time. This is winter. No man farms
this time of year.'

'I see. And of course her need for food and clothing will stand still while the land lies fallow.'

'I have a pension,' the other said. He said it as a man might say *I have grace* or *I own a gold mine.* 'I have my father's pension too. It will arrive on the first of the month. What day is this?'

'The eleventh,' he said. 'Twenty days more. And until then?'

'I have a few groceries in the house from my credit account with the merchant in Midnight who banks my pension check for me. I have executed to him a power of attorney to handle it for me as a matter of mutual——'

'I see. And if the groceries dont last the twenty days?'

'I still have one more hog.'

'Where?'

'Outside,' the other said. 'It is customary in this country to allow stock to range free during the winter for food. It comes up from time to time. But no matter if it doesn't; I can probably trace its footprints when the need——'

'Yes!' he cried. 'Because no matter: you still have the pension check. And the man in Midnight will cash it and pay himself out of it for what you have already eaten and if there is any left over, it is yours. And the hog will be eaten by then or you still cant catch it, and then what will you do?'

'It will be almost spring then,' the other said. 'I am planning in the spring——'

'It will be January,' he said. 'And then February. And then more than half of March—' and when he stopped again in the kitchen she had not moved, she did not even seem to breathe or to be alive except her eyes watching him; when he took a step toward her it was still not movement because she could have retreated no further: only the tremendous fathomless ink-colored eyes in the narrow, thin, too thin coffee-colored face watching him without alarm, without recognition, without hope. 'Fonsiba,' he said. 'Fonsiba. Are you all right?'

'I'm free,' she said. Midnight was a tavern, a livery stable, a big store (that would be where the pension check banked itself as a matter of mutual elimination of bother and fret, he thought) and a little one, a saloon and a blacksmith shop. But there was a bank there too. The president (the owner, for all practical purposes) of it was a translated Mississippian who had been one of Forrest's men too: and his body lightened of the golden belt for the first time since he left home eight days ago, with pencil and paper he multiplied three dollars by twelve months and divided it into one thousand dollars; it would stretch that way over almost twenty-eight years and for twenty-eight years at least she would not starve, the banker promising to send the three dollars himself by a trusty messenger on the fifteenth of each month and put it into her actual hand, and he returned home and that was all because in 1874 his father and his uncle were both dead and the old ledgers never again came down from the shelf above the desk to which his father had returned them for the last time that day in 1869. But he could have completed it:

> *Lucas Quintus Carothers McCaslin Beauchamp. Last surviving son and child of Tomey's Terrel and Tennie Beauchamp. March 17, 1874*

except that there was no need: not *Lucius Quintus* @c @c @c, but *Lucas Quintus*, not refusing to be called Lucius, because he simply eliminated that word from the name; not denying, declining the name itself, because he used three quarters of it; but simply taking the name and changing, altering it, making it no longer the white man's but his own, by himself composed, himself self-progenitive and nominate, by himself ancestored, as, for all the old ledgers recorded to the contrary, old Carothers himself was

and that was all: 1874 the boy; 1888 the man, repudiated denied and free; 1895 and husband but no father, unwidowered but without a wife, and found long since that no man is ever free and probably could not bear it if he were; married then and living in Jefferson in the little new jerrybuilt bungalow which his wife's father had given them: and one morning Lucas stood suddenly in the doorway of the room where he was reading the Memphis paper and he looked at the paper's dateline and thought *It's his birthday. He's twenty-one today* and Lucas said: 'Whar's the rest of that money old Carothers left? I wants it. All of it.'

that was all: and McCaslin

'More men than that one Buck and Buddy to fumble-heed that truth so mazed for them that spoke it and so confused for them that heard yet still there was 1865:' and he

'But not enough. Not enough of even Father and Uncle Buddy to fumble-heed in even three generations not even three generations fathered by Grandfather not even if there had been nowhere beneath His sight any but Grandfather and so He would not even have needed to elect and choose. But He tried and I know what

you will say. That having Himself created them He could have
known no more of hope than He could have pride and grief but
He didn't hope He just waited because He had made them: not
just because He had set them alive and in motion but because
He had already worried with them so long: worried with them
so long because He had seen how in individual cases they were
capable of anything any height or depth remembered in mazed
incomprehension out of heaven where hell was created too and so
He must admit them or else admit His equal somewhere and so be
no longer God and therefore must accept responsibility for what He
Himself had done in order to live with Himself in His lonely and
paramount heaven. And He probably knew it was vain but He
had created them and knew them capable of all things because
He had shaped them out of the primal Absolute which contained
all and had watched them since in their individual exaltation and
baseness and they themselves not knowing why nor how nor even
when: until at last He saw that they were all Grandfather all of
them and that even from them the elected and chosen the best
the very best He could expect (not hope mind: not hope) would
be Bucks and Buddies and not even enough of them and in the
third generation not even Bucks and Buddies but—' and McCaslin
   'Ah:' and he
   'Yes. If He could see Father and Uncle Buddy in Grandfather
He must have seen me too.—an Isaac born into a later life than
Abraham's and repudiating immolation: fatherless and therefore
safe declining the altar because maybe this time the exasperated
Hand might not supply the kid—' and McCaslin
   'Escape:' and he
   'All right. Escape.—Until one day He said what you told
Fonsiba's husband that afternoon here in this room: *This will do.
This is enough:* not in exasperation or rage or even just sick to
death as you were sick that day: just *This is enough* and looked
about for one last time, for one time more since He had created
them, upon this land this South for which He had done so much
with woods for game and streams for fish and deep rich soil for
seed and lush springs to sprout it and long summers to mature it
and serene falls to harvest it and short mild winters for men
and animals and saw no hope anywhere and looked beyond it
where hope should have been, where to East North and West lay
illimitable that whole hopeful continent dedicated as a refuge and
sanctuary of liberty and freedom from what you called the old

world's worthless evening and saw the rich descendants of slavers, females of both sexes, to whom the black they shrieked of was another specimen another example like the Brazilian macaw brought home in a cage by a traveller, passing resolutions about horror and outrage in warm and air-proof halls: and the thundering cannonade of politicians earning votes and the medicine-shows of pulpiteers earning Chatauqua fees, to whom the outrage and the injustice were as much abstractions as Tariff or Silver or Immortality and who employed the very shackles of its servitude and the sorry rags of its regalia as they did the other beer and banners and mottoes redfire and brimstone and sleight-of-hand and musical handsaws: and the whirling wheels which manufactured for a profit the pristine replacements of the shackles and shoddy garments as they wore out and spun the cotton and made the gins which ginned it and the cars and ships which hauled it, and the men who ran the wheels for that profit and established and collected the taxes it was taxed with and the rates for hauling it and the com-missons for selling it: and He could have repudiated them since they were his creation now and forever more throughout all their generations until not only that old world from which He had res-cued them but this new one too which He had revealed and led them to as a sanctuary and refuge were become the same worth-less tideless rock cooling in the last crimson evening except that out of all that empty sound and bootless fury one silence, among that loud and moiling all of them just one simple enough to believe that horror and outrage were first and last simply horror and out-rage and was crude enough to act upon that, illiterate and had no words for talking or perhaps was just busy and had no time to, one out of them all who did not bother Him with cajolery and adjuration then pleading then threat and had not even bothered to inform Him in advance what he was about so that a lesser than He might have even missed the simple act of lifting the long an-cestral musket down from the deer-horns above the door, where-upon He said *My name is Brown too* and the other *So is mine* and He *Then mine or yours cant be because I am against it* and the other *So am I* and He triumphantly *Then where are you going with that gun?* and the other told him in one sentence one word and He: amazed: Who knew neither hope nor pride nor grief *But your Association, your Committee, your Officers. Where are your Minutes, your Motions, your Parliamentary Procedures?* and the other *I aint against them. They are all right I reckon for them that have the time. I am just against the weak because they are niggers being held in bondage by the strong just because they are white.* So He turned once more to this land which He still intended to save because He had done so much for it—' and McCaslin

'What?' and he

'—to these people He was still committed to because they were his creations—' and McCaslin

'Turned back to us? His face to us?' and he

'—whose wives and daughters at least made soups and jellies for them when they were sick and carried the trays through the mud and the winter too into the stinking cabins and sat in the stinking cabins and kept fires going until crises came and passed but that was not enough: and when they were very sick had them carried into the big house itself into the company room itself maybe and nursed them there which the white man would have done too for any other of his cattle that was sick but at least the man who hired one from a livery wouldn't have and still that was not enough: so that He said and not in grief either Who had made them and so could know no more of grief than He could of pride or hope: *Apparently they can learn nothing save through suffering, remember nothing save when underlined in blood*—' and McCaslin

'Ashby on an afternoon's ride, to call on some remote maiden cousins of his mother or maybe just acquaintances of hers, comes by chance upon a minor engagement of outposts and dismounts and with his crimson-lined cloak for target leads a handful of troops he never saw before against an entrenched position of backwoods-trained riflemen. Lee's battle-order, wrapped maybe about a handful of cigars and doubtless thrown away when the last cigar was smoked, found by a Yankee Intelligence officer on the floor of a saloon behind the Yankee lines after Lee had already divided his forces before Sharpsburg. Jackson on the Plank Road, already rolled up the flank which Hooker believed could not be turned and, waiting only for night to pass to continue the brutal and incessant slogging which would fling that whole wing back into Hooker's lap where he sat on a front gallery in Chancellorsville drinking rum toddies and telegraphing Lincoln that he had defeated Lee, is shot from among a whole covey of minor officers and in the blind night by one of his own patrols, leaving as next by seniority Stuart that gallant man born apparently already horsed and sabred and already knowing all there was to know about war except the slogging and brutal stupidity of it: and that same Stuart

off raiding Pennsylvania hen-roosts when Lee should have known
of all of Meade just where Hancock was on Cemetery Ridge: and
Longstreet too at Gettysburg and that same Longstreet shot out
of saddle by his own men in the dark by mistake just as Jackson
was. His face to us? His face to us?' and he

'How else have made them fight? Who else but Jacksons and
Stuarts and Ashbys and Morgans and Forrests?—the farmers of the
central and middle-west, holding land by the acre instead of the
tens or maybe even the hundreds, farming it themselves and to no
single crop of cotton or tobacco or cane, owning no slaves and needing and wanting none and already looking toward the Pacific
coast, not always as long as two generations there and having
stopped where they did stop only through the fortuitous mischance
that an ox died or a wagon-axle broke. And the New England
mechanics who didn't even own land and measured all things by
the weight of water and the cost of turning wheels and the narrow
fringe of traders and ship-owners still looking backward across the
Atlantic and attached to the continent only by their counting-
houses. And those who should have had the alertness to see: the
wildcat manipulators of mythical wilderness townsites; and the
astuteness to rationalise: the bankers who held the mortgages on
the land which the first were only waiting to abandon and on the
railroads and steamboats to carry them still further west, and on
the factories and the wheels and the rented tenements those who
ran them lived in; and the leisure and scope to comprehend and
fear in time and even anticipate: the Boston-bred (even when not
born in Boston) spinster descendants of long lines of similarly-bred
and likewise spinster aunts and uncles whose hands knew no callus
except that of the indicting pen, to whom the wilderness itself began at the top of tide and who looked, if at anything other than
Beacon Hill, only toward heaven—not to mention all the loud
rabble of the camp-followers of pioneers: the bellowing of politicians, the mellifluous choiring of self-styled men of God, the—' and
McCaslin

'Here, here. Wait a minute:' and he

'Let me talk now. I'm trying to explain to the head of my family
something which I have got to do which I dont quite understand
myself, not in justification of it but to explain it if I can. I could
say I dont know why I must do it but that I do know I have got to
because I have got myself to have to live with for the rest of my
life and all I want is peace to do it in. But you are the head of my

family. More. I knew a long time ago that I would never have
to miss my father, even if you are just finding out that you have
missed your son.—the drawers of bills and the shavers of notes
and the schoolmasters and the self-ordained to teach and lead and
all that horde of the semi-literate with a white shirt but no change
for it, with one eye on themselves and watching each other with
the other one. Who else could have made them fight: could have
struck them so aghast with fear and dread as to turn shoulder
to shoulder and face one way and even stop talking for a while and
even after two years of it keep them still so wrung with terror that
some among them would seriously propose moving their very
capital into a foreign country lest it be ravaged and pillaged by
a people whose entire white male population would have little
more than filled any one of their larger cities: except Jackson in
the Valley and three separate armies trying to catch him and none
of them ever knowing whether they were just retreating from a
battle or just running into one and Stuart riding his whole command
entirely around the biggest single armed force this continent ever
saw in order to see what it looked like from behind and Morgan
leading a cavalry charge against a stranded man-of-war. Who else
could have declared a war against a power with ten times the area
and a hundred times the men and a thousand times the resources,
except men who could believe that all necessary to conduct a
successful war was not acumen nor shrewdness nor politics nor
diplomacy nor money nor even integrity and simple arithmetic
but just love of land and courage——'
    'And an unblemished and gallant ancestry and the ability to ride
a horse,' McCaslin said. 'Dont leave that out.' It was evening now,
the tranquil sunset of October mazy with windless woodsmoke. The
cotton was long since picked and ginned, and all day now the
wagons loaded with gathered corn moved between field and crib,
processional across the enduring land. 'Well, maybe that's what He
wanted. At least, that's what He got.' This time there was no yellowed procession of fading and harmless ledger-pages. This was
chronicled in a harsher book and McCaslin, fourteen and fifteen and
sixteen, had seen it and the boy himself had inherited it as Noah's
grandchildren had inherited the Flood although they had not been
there to see the deluge: that dark corrupt and bloody time while
three separate peoples had tried to adjust not only to one another
but to the new land which they had created and inherited too and
must live in for the reason that those who had lost it were no less

free to quit it than those who had gained it were:—those upon whom freedom and equality had been dumped overnight and without warning or preparation or any training in how to employ it or even just endure it and who misused it not as children would nor yet because they had been so long in bondage and then so suddenly freed, but misused it as human beings always misuse freedom, so that he thought *Apparently there is a wisdom beyond even that learned through suffering necessary for a man to distinguish between liberty and license;* those who had fought for four years and lost to preserve a condition under which that franchisement was anomaly and paradox, not because they were opposed to freedom as freedom but for the old reasons for which man (not the generals and politicians but man) has always fought and died in wars: to preserve a status quo or to establish a better future one to endure for his children; and lastly, as if that were not enough for bitterness and hatred and fear, that third race even more alien to the people whom they resembled in pigment and in whom even the same blood ran, than to the people whom they did not,—that race threefold in one and alien even among themselves save for a single fierce will for rapine and pillage, composed of the sons of middleaged Quartermaster lieutenants and Army sutlers and contractors in military blankets and shoes and transport mules, who followed the battles they themselves had not fought and inherited the conquest they themselves had not helped to gain, sanctioned and protected even if not blessed, and left their bones and in another generation would be engaged in a fierce economic competition of small sloven farms with the black men they were supposed to have freed and the white descendants of fathers who had owned no slaves anyway whom they were supposed to have disinherited and in the third generation would be back once more in the little lost county seats as barbers and garage mechanics and deputy sheriffs and mill- and gin-hands and power-plant firemen, leading, first in mufti then later in an actual formalised regalia of hooded sheets and passwords and fiery christian symbols, lynching mobs against the race their ancestors had come to save: and of all that other nameless horde of speculators in human misery, manipulators of money and politics and land, who follow catastrophe and are their own protection as grasshoppers are and need no blessing and sweat no plow or axe-helve and batten and vanish and leave no bones, just as they derived apparently from no ancestry, no mortal flesh, no act even of passion or even of lust: and the Jew who came without protection too since after two thousand years he had got out of the habit of being or needing it, and solitary, without even the solidarity of the locusts and in this a sort of courage since he had come thinking not in terms of simple pillage but in terms of his great-grandchildren, seeking yet some place to establish them to endure even though forever alien: and unblessed: a pariah about the face of the Western earth which twenty centuries later was still taking revenge on him for the fairy tale with which he had conquered it. McCaslin had actually seen it, and the boy even at almost eighty would never be able to distinguish certainly between what he had seen and what had been told him: a lightless and gutted and empty land where women crouched with the huddled children behind locked doors and men armed in sheets and masks rode the silent roads and the bodies of white and black both, victims not so much of hate as of desperation and despair, swung from lonely limbs: and men shot dead in polling-booths with the still wet pen in one hand and the unblotted ballot in the other: and a United States marshal in Jefferson who signed his official papers with a crude cross, an ex-slave called Sickymo, not at all because his ex-owner was a doctor and apothecary but because, still a slave, he would steal his master's grain alcohol and dilute it with water and peddle it in pint bottles from a cache beneath the roots of a big sycamore tree behind the drug store, who had attained his high office because his half-white sister was the concubine of the Federal A.P.M.: and this time McCaslin did not even say Look but merely lifted one hand, not even pointing, not even specifically toward the shelf of ledgers but toward the desk, toward the corner where it sat beside the scuffed patch on the floor where two decades of heavy shoes had stood while the white man at the desk added and multiplied and subtracted. And again he did not need to look because he had seen this himself and, twenty-three years after the Surrender and twenty-four after the Proclamation, was still watching it: the ledgers, new ones now and filled rapidly, succeeding one another rapidly and containing more names than old Carothers or even his father and Uncle Buddy had ever dreamed of; new names and new faces to go with them, among which the old names and faces that even his father and uncle would have recognised, were lost, vanished—Tomey's Terrel dead, and even the tragic and miscast Percival Brownlee, who couldn't keep books and couldn't farm either, found his true niche at last, reappeared in 1862 during the boy's father's absence and had apparently been living on the plantation for at least a month before his uncle found out about it, conducting impromptu revival meetings among negroes, preaching and leading the singing also in his high sweet true soprano voice and disappeared again on foot and at top speed, not behind but ahead of a body of raiding Federal horse and reappeared for the third and last time in the entourage of a travelling Army paymaster, the two of them passing through Jefferson in a surrey at the exact moment when the boy's father (it was 1866) also happened to be crossing the Square, the surrey and its occupants traversing rapidly that quiet and bucolic scene and even in that fleeting moment and to others beside the boy's father giving an illusion of flight and illicit holiday like a man on an excursion during his wife's absence with his wife's personal maid, until Brownlee glanced up and saw his late co-master and gave him one defiant female glance and then broke again, leaped from the surrey and disappeared this time for good and it was only by chance that McCaslin, twenty years later, heard of him again, an old man now and quite fat, as the well-to-do proprietor of a select New Orleans brothel; and Tennie's Jim gone, nobody knew where, and Fonsiba in Arkansas with her three dollars each month and the scholar-husband with his lenseless spectacles and frock coat and his plans for the spring; and only Lucas was left, the baby, the last save himself of old Carothers' doomed and fatal blood which in the male derivation seemed to destroy all it touched, and even he was repudiating and at least hoping to escape it;—Lucas, the boy of fourteen whose name would not even appear for six years yet among those rapid pages in the bindings new and dustless too since McCaslin lifted them down daily now to write into them the continuation of that record which two hundred years had not been enough to complete and another hundred would not be enough to discharge; that chronicle which was a whole land in miniature, which multiplied and compounded was the entire South, twenty-three years after surrender and twenty-four from emancipation—that slow trickle of molasses and meal and meat, of shoes and straw hats and overalls, of plowlines and collars and heel-bolts and buckheads and clevises, which returned each fall as cotton—the two threads frail as truth and impalpable as equators yet cable-strong to bind for life them who made the cotton to the land their sweat fell on: and he

'Yes. Binding them for a while yet, a little while yet. Through and beyond that life and maybe through and beyond the life of that life's sons and maybe even through and beyond that of the sons of those sons. But not always, because they will endure. They will outlast us because they are—' it was not a pause, barely a falter even, possibly appreciable only to himself, as if he couldn't speak even to McCaslin, even to explain his repudiation, that which to him too, even in the act of escaping (and maybe this was the reality and the truth of his need to escape) was heresy: so that even in escaping he was taking with him more of that evil and unregenerate old man who could summon, because she was his property, a human being because she was old enough and female, to his widower's house and get a child on her and then dismiss her because she was of an inferior race, and then bequeath a thousand dollars to the infant because he would be dead then and wouldn't have to pay it, than even he had feared. 'Yes. He didn't want to. He had to. Because they will endure. They are better than we are. Stronger than we are. Their vices are vices aped from white men or that white men and bondage have taught them: improvidence and intemperance and evasion—not laziness: evasion: of what white men had set them to, not for their aggrandisement or even comfort but his own—' and McCaslin

'All right. Go on: Promiscuity. Violence. Instability and lack of control. Inability to distinguish between mine and thine—' and he

'How distinguish, when for two hundred years mine did not even exist for them?' and McCaslin

'All right. Go on. And their virtues—' and he

'Yes. Their own. Endurance—' and McCaslin

'So have mules:' and he

'—and pity and tolerance and forbearance and fidelity and love of children—' and McCaslin

'So have dogs:' and he

'—whether their own or not or black or not. And more: what they got not only not from white people but not even despite white people because they had it already from the old free fathers a longer time free than us because we have never been free—' and it was in McCaslin's eyes too, he had only to look at McCaslin's eyes and it was there, that summer twilight seven years ago, almost a week after they had returned from the camp before he discovered that Sam Fathers had told McCaslin: an old bear, fierce and ruthless not just to stay alive but ruthless with the fierce pride of liberty and freedom, jealous and proud enough of liberty and freedom to see it threatened not with fear nor even alarm but almost with joy, seem-

ing deliberately to put it into jeopardy in order to savor it and keep
his old strong bones and flesh supple and quick to defend and preserve it; an old man, son of a Negro slave and an Indian king, inheritor on the one hand of the long chronicle of a people who had
learned humility through suffering and learned pride through
the endurance which survived the suffering, and on the other
side the chronicle of a people even longer in the land than the
first, yet who now existed there only in the solitary brotherhood of an old and childless Negro's alien blood and the wild
and invincible spirit of an old bear; a boy who wished to learn
humility and pride in order to become skillful and worthy in
the woods but found himself becoming so skillful so fast that he
feared he would never become worthy because he had not learned
humility and pride though he had tried, until one day an old man
who could not have defined either led him as though by the hand
to where an old bear and a little mongrel dog showed him that, by
possessing one thing other, he would possess them both; and a little
dog, nameless and mongrel and many-fathered, grown yet weighing
less than six pounds, who couldn't be dangerous because there was
nothing anywhere much smaller, not fierce because that would have
been called just noise, not humble because it was already too near
the ground to genuflect, and not proud because it would not have
been close enough for anyone to discern what was casting that
shadow and which didn't even know it was not going to heaven
since they had already decided it had no immortal soul, so that all
it could be was brave even though they would probably call that
too just noise. *'And you didn't shoot,' McCaslin said. 'How close
were you?'*

*'I dont know,' he said. 'There was a big wood tick just inside his
off hind leg. I saw that. But I didn't have the gun then.'*

*'But you didn't shoot when you had the gun,' McCaslin said.
'Why?' But McCaslin didn't wait, rising and crossing the room,
across the pelt of the bear he had killed two years ago and the
bigger one McCaslin had killed before he was born, to the bookcase
beneath the mounted head of his first buck, and returned with the
book and sat down again and opened it. 'Listen,' he said. He read
the five stanzas aloud and closed the book on his finger and looked
up. 'All right,' he said. 'Listen,' and read again, but only one stanza
this time and closed the book and laid it on the table. 'She cannot
fade, though thou hast not thy bliss,' McCaslin said: 'Forever wilt
thou love, and she be fair.'*

'He's talking about a girl,' he said.

'He had to talk about something,' McCaslin said. Then he said, 'He was talking about truth. Truth is one. It doesn't change. It covers all things which touch the heart—honor and pride and pity and justice and courage and love. Do you see now?' He didn't know. Somehow it had seemed simpler than that, simpler than somebody talking in a book about a young man and a girl he would never need to grieve over because he could never approach any nearer and would never have to get any further away. He had heard about an old bear and finally got big enough to hunt it and he hunted it four years and at last met it with a gun in his hands and he didn't shoot. Because a little dog—But he could have shot long before the fyce covered the twenty yards to where the bear waited, and Sam Fathers could have shot at any time during the interminable minute while Old Ben stood on his hind legs over them. . . . He ceased. McCaslin watched him, still speaking, the voice, the words as quiet as the twilight itself was: 'Courage and honor and pride, and pity and love of justice and of liberty. They all touch the heart, and what the heart holds to becomes truth, as far as we know truth. Do you see now?' and he could still hear them, intact in this twilight as in that one seven years ago, no louder still because they did not need to be because they would endure: and he had only to look at McCaslin's eyes beyond the thin and bitter smiling, the faint lip-lift which would have had to be called smiling; —his kinsman, his father almost, who had been born too late into the old time and too soon for the new, the two of them juxtaposed and alien now to each other against their ravaged patrimony, the dark and ravaged fatherland still prone and panting from its etherless operaton:

'Habet then.—So this land is, indubitably, of and by itself cursed:' and he

'Cursed:' and again McCaslin merely lifted one hand, not even speaking and not even toward the ledgers: so that, as the stereopticon condenses into one instantaneous field the myriad minutia of its scope, so did that slight and rapid gesture establish in the small cramped and cluttered twilit room not only the ledgers but the whole plantation in its mazed and intricate entirety—the land, the fields and what they represented in terms of cotton ginned and sold, the men and women whom they fed and clothed and even paid a little cash money at Christmas-time in return for the labor which planted and raised and picked and ginned the cotton, the machinery and mules and gear with which they raised it and their cost and upkeep and replacement—that whole edifice intricate and complex and founded upon injustice and erected by ruthless rapacity and carried on even yet with at times downright savagery not only to the human beings but the valuable animals too, yet solvent and efficient and, more than that: not only still intact but enlarged, increased; brought still intact by McCaslin, himself little more than a child then, through and out of the debacle and chaos of twenty years ago where hardly one in ten survived, and enlarged and increased and would continue so, solvent and efficient and intact and still increasing so long as McCaslin and his McCaslin successors lasted, even though their surnames might not even be Edmonds then: and he: 'Habet too. Because that's it: not the land, but us. Not only the blood, but the name too; not only its color but its designation: Edmonds, white, but, a female line, could have no other but the name his father bore; Beauchamp, the elder line and the male one, but, black, could have had any name he liked and no man would have cared, except the name his father bore who had no name—' and McCaslin

'And since I know too what you know I will say now, once more let me say it: And one other, and in the third generation too, and the male, the eldest, the direct and sole and white and still McCaslin even, father to son to son—' and he

'I am free:' and this time McCaslin did not even gesture, no inference of fading pages, no postulation of the stereoptic whole, but the frail and iron thread strong as truth and impervious as evil and longer than life itself and reaching beyond record and patrimony both to join him with the lusts and passions, the hopes and dreams and griefs, of bones whose names while still fleshed and capable even old Carothers' grandfather had never heard: and he: 'And of that too:' and McCaslin

'Chosen, I suppose (I will concede it) out of all your time by Him as you say Buck and Buddy were from theirs. And it took Him a bear and an old man and four years just for you. And it took you fourteen years to reach that point and about that many, maybe more, for Old Ben, and more than seventy for Sam Fathers. And you are just one. How long then? How long?' and he

'It will be long. I have never said otherwise. But it will be all right because they will endure—' and McCaslin

'And anyway, you will be free.—No, not now nor ever, we from them nor they from us. So I repudiate too. I would deny even if I knew it were true. I would have to. Even you can see that I could do no else. I am what I am; I will be always what I was born and have always been. And more than me. More than me, just as there were more than Buck and Buddy in what you called His first plan which failed:' and he

'And more than me:' and McCaslin

'No. Not even you. Because mark. You said how on that instant when Ikkemotubbe realised that he could sell the land to Grandfather, it ceased forever to have been his. All right; go on: Then it belonged to Sam Fathers, old Ikkemotubbe's son. And who inherited from Sam Fathers, if not you? co-heir perhaps with Boon, if not of his life maybe, at least of his quitting it?' and he

'Yes. Sam Fathers set me free.' And Isaac McCaslin, not yet Uncle Ike, a long time yet before he would be uncle to half a county and still father to none, living in one small cramped fireless rented room in a Jefferson boarding-house where petit juries were domiciled during court terms and itinerant horse- and mule-traders stayed, with his kit of brand-new carpenter's tools and the shotgun McCaslin had given him with his name engraved in silver and old General Compson's compass (and, when the General died, his silver-mounted horn too) and the iron cot and mattress and the blankets which he would take each fall into the woods for more than sixty years and the bright tin coffee-pot

there had been a legacy, from his Uncle Hubert Beauchamp, his godfather, that bluff burly roaring childlike man from whom Uncle Buddy had won Tomey's Terrel's wife Tennie in the poker-game in 1859—'posible strait against three Treys in sigt Not called' —; no pale sentence or paragraph scrawled in cringing fear of death by a weak and trembling hand as a last desperate sop flung backward at retribution, but a Legacy, a Thing, possessing weight to the hand and bulk to the eye and even audible: a silver cup filled with gold pieces and wrapped in burlap and sealed with his godfather's ring in the hot wax, which (intact still) even before his Uncle Hubert's death and long before his own majority, when it would be his, had become not only a legend but one of the family lares. After his father's and his Uncle Hubert's sister's marriage they moved back into the big house, the tremendous cavern which old Carothers had started and never finished, cleared the remaining negroes out of it and with his mother's dowry completed it, at least the rest of the windows and doors and moved into it, all of them save Uncle Buddy who declined to leave the cabin he and his twin had built, the move being the bride's notion and more than just a notion and none ever to know if she really wanted to live in the big house or if she knew before hand that Uncle Buddy would refuse to move: and two weeks after his birth in 1867, the first time he and his mother came down stairs, one night and the silver cup sitting on the cleared dining-room table beneath the bright lamp and while his mother and his father and McCaslin and Tennie (his nurse: carrying him)—all of them again but Uncle Buddy—watched, his Uncle Hubert rang one by one into the cup the bright and glinting mintage and wrapped it into the burlap envelope and heated the wax and sealed it and carried it back home with him where he lived alone now without even his sister either to hold him down as McCaslin said or to try to raise him up as Uncle Buddy said, and (dark times then in Mississippi) Uncle Buddy said most of the niggers gone and the ones that didn't go even Hub Beauchamp could not have wanted: but the dogs remained and Uncle Buddy said Beauchamp fiddled while Nero fox-hunted

they would go and see it there; at last his mother would prevail and they would depart in the surrey, once more all save Uncle Buddy and McCaslin to keep Uncle Buddy company until one winter Uncle Buddy began to fail and from then on it was himself, beginning to remember now, and his mother and Tennie and Tomey's Terrel to drive: the twenty-two miles into the next county, the twin gateposts on one of which McCaslin could remember the half-grown boy blowing a fox-horn at breakfast dinner and supper-time and jumping down to open to any passer who happened to hear it but where there were no gates at all now, the shabby and overgrown entrance to what his mother still insisted that people call Warwick because her brother was if truth but triumphed and justice but prevailed the rightful earl of it, the paintless house which outwardly did not change but which on the inside seemed each time larger because he was too little to realise then that there was less and less in it of the fine furnishings, the rosewood and mahogany and walnut which for him had never existed anywhere anyway save in his mother's tearful lamentations and the occasional piece small enough to be roped somehow onto the rear or the top of the carriage on their return (And he remembered this, he had seen it: an instant, a flash, his mother's soprano 'Even my dress! Even my dress!' loud and outraged in the barren unswept hall; a face young and female and even lighter in color than Tomey's Terrel's for an instant in a closing door; a swirl, a glimpse of the silk gown and the flick and glint of an ear-ring: an apparition rapid and tawdry and illicit yet somehow even to the child, the infant still almost, breathless and exciting and evocative: as though, like two limpid and pellucid streams meeting, the child which he still was had made serene and absolute and perfect rapport and contact through that glimpsed nameless illicit hybrid female flesh with the boy which had existed at that stage of inviolable and immortal adolescence in his uncle for almost sixty years; the dress, the face, the ear-rings gone in that same aghast flash and his uncle's voice: 'She's my cook! She's my new cook! I had to have a cook, didn't I?' then the uncle himself, the face alarmed and aghast too yet still innocently and somehow even indomitably of a boy, they retreating in their turn now, back to the front gallery, and his uncle again, pained and still amazed, in a sort of desperate resurgence if not of courage at least of self-assertion: 'They're free now! They're folks too just like we are!' and his mother: 'That's why! That's why! My mother's house! Defiled! Defiled!' and his uncle: 'Damn it, Sibbey, at least give her time to pack her grip:' then over, finished, the loud uproar and all, himself and Tennie and he remembered Tennie's inscrutable face at the broken shutterless window of the bare room which had once been the parlor while they watched, hurrying down the lane at a stumbling trot, the routed compounder of his uncle's uxory: the back, the nameless face which he had seen only for a moment, the once-hooped dress ballooning and flapping below a man's overcoat, the worn heavy carpet-bag jouncing and banging against her knee, routed and in retreat true enough and in the empty lane solitary young-looking and forlorn yet withal still exciting and evocative and wearing still the silken banner captured inside the very citadel of respectability, and unforgettable.)

the cup, the sealed inscrutable burlap, sitting on the shelf in the locked closet, Uncle Hubert unlocking the door and lifting it down and passing it from hand to hand: his mother, his father, McCaslin and even Tennie, insisting that each take it in turn and heft it for weight and shake it again to prove the sound, Uncle Hubert himself standing spraddled before the cold unswept hearth in which the very bricks themselves were crumbling into a litter of soot and dust and mortar and the droppings of chimney-sweeps, still roaring and still innocent and still indomitable: and for a long time he believed nobody but himself had noticed that his uncle

now put the cup only into his hands, unlocked the door and lifted
it down and put it into his hands and stood over him until he had
shaken it obediently until it sounded then took it from him and
locked it back into the closet before anyone else could have offered
to touch it, and even later, when competent not only to remember
but to rationalise, he could not say what it was or even if it had
been anything because the parcel was still heavy and still rattled,
not even when, Uncle Buddy dead and his father, at last and after
almost seventy-five years in bed after the sun rose, said: 'Go get
that damn cup. Bring that damn Hub Beauchamp too if you have
to:' because it still rattled though his uncle no longer put it even
into his hands now but carried it himself from one to the other, his
mother, McCaslin, Tennie, shaking it before each in turn, saying:
'Hear it? Hear it?' his face still innocent, not quite baffled but only
amazed and not very amazed and still indomitable: and, his father
and Uncle Buddy both gone now, one day without reason or any
warning the almost completely empty house in which his uncle
and Tennie's ancient and quarrelsome great-grandfather (who
claimed to have seen Lafayette and McCaslin said in another ten
years would be remembering God) lived, cooked and slept in one
single room, burst into peaceful conflagration, a tranquil instantaneous sourceless unanimity of combustion, walls floors and roof: at
sunup it stood where his uncle's father had built it sixty years ago,
at sundown the four blackened and smokeless chimneys rose from
a light white powder of ashes and a few charred ends of planks
which did not even appear to have been very hot: and out of the
last of evening, the last one of the twenty-two miles, on the old white
mare which was the last of that stable which McCaslin remembered,
the two old men riding double up to the sister's door, the one
wearing his fox-horn on its braided deerhide thong and the other
carrying the burlap parcel wrapped in a shirt, the tawny wax-
daubed shapeless lump sitting again and on an almost identical
shelf and his uncle holding the half-opened door now, his hand
not only on the knob but one foot against it and the key waiting
in the other hand, the face urgent and still not baffled but still
and even indomitably not very amazed and himself standing in the
half-opened door looking quietly up at the burlap shape become
almost three times its original height and a good half less than its
original thickness and turning away and he would remember not
his mother's look this time nor yet Tennie's inscrutable expression
but McCaslin's dark and aquiline face grave insufferable and be-

mused: then one night they waked him and fetched him still half-
asleep into the lamp light, the smell of medicine which was familiar
by now in that room and the smell of something else which he
had not smelled before and knew at once and would never forget,
the pillow, the worn and ravaged face from which looked out still
the boy innocent and immortal and amazed and urgent, looking
at him and trying to tell him until McCaslin moved and leaned
over the bed and drew from the top of the night shirt the big iron
key on the greasy cord which suspended it, the eyes saying Yes
Yes Yes now, and cut the cord and unlocked the closet and brought
the parcel to the bed, the eyes still trying to tell him even when
he took the parcel so that was still not it, the hands still clinging
to the parcel even while relinquishing it, the eyes more urgent
than ever trying to tell him but they never did; and he was ten
and his mother was dead too and McCaslin said, 'You are almost
halfway now. You might as well open it:' and he: 'No. He said
twenty-one:' and he was twenty-one and McCaslin shifted the
bright lamp to the center of the cleared dining-room table and set
the parcel beside it and laid his open knife beside the parcel and
stood back with that expression of old grave intolerant and repudiating and he lifted it, the burlap lump which fifteen years ago
had changed its shape completely overnight, which shaken gave
forth a thin weightless not-quite-musical curiously muffled clatter,
the bright knife-blade hunting amid the mazed intricacy of string,
the knobby gouts of wax bearing his uncle's Beauchamp seal
rattling onto the table's polished top and, standing amid the collapse
of burlap folds, the unstained tin coffee-pot still brand new, the
handful of copper coins and now he knew what had given them the
muffled sound: a collection of minutely-folded scraps of paper
sufficient almost for a rat's nest, of good linen bond, of the crude
ruled paper such as negroes use, of raggedly-torn ledger-pages and
the margins of newspapers and once the paper label from a new
pair of overalls, all dated and all signed, beginning with the first
one not six months after they had watched him seal the silver
cup into the burlap on this same table in this same room by the
light even of this same lamp almost twenty-one years ago:

I owe my Nephew Isaac Beauchamp McCaslin five (5) pieces Gold
which I,O.U constitues My note of hand with Interest at 5 percent.
                        Hubert Fitz-Hubert Beauchamp
at Warwick 27 Nov 1867

and he: 'Anyway he called it Warwick:' once at least, even if no
more. But there was more:

> *Isaac 24 Dec 1867 I.O.U. 2 pieces Gold H.Fh.B. I.O.U. Isaac 1
> piece Gold 1 Jan 1868 H.Fh.B.*

then five again then three then one then one then a long time and
what dream, what dreamed splendid recoup, not of any injury
or betrayal of trust because it had been merely a loan: nay, a
partnership:

> *I.O.U. Beauchamp McCaslin or his heirs twenty-five (25) pieces
> Gold This & All preceeding constituting My notes of hand at
> twenty (20) percentum compounded annually. This date of 19th
> January 1873*
>
> *Beauchamp*

no location save that in time and signed by the single not name
but word as the old proud earl himself might have scrawled
Nevile: and that made forty-three and he could not remember
himself of course but the legend had it at fifty, which balanced:
one: then one: then one: then one and then the last three and then
the last chit, dated after he came to live in the house with them
and written in the shaky hand not of a beaten old man because
he had never been beaten to know it but of a tired old man maybe
and even at that tired only on the outside and still indomitable,
the simplicity of the last one the simplicity not of resignation but
merely of amazement, like a simple comment or remark, and not
very much of that:

One silver cup. Hubert Beauchamp

and McCaslin: 'So you have plenty of coppers anyway. But they
are still not old enough yet to be either rarities or heirlooms. So
you will have to take the money:' except that he didn't hear Mc-
Caslin, standing quietly beside the table and looking peacefully
at the coffee-pot and the pot sitting one night later on the mantel
above what was not even a fireplace in the little cramped icelike
room in Jefferson as McCaslin tossed the folded banknotes onto
the bed and still standing (there was nowhere to sit save on the
bed) did not even remove his hat and overcoat: and he

'As a loan. From you. This one:' and McCaslin

'You cant. I have no money that I can lend to you. And you will
have to go to the bank and get it next month because I wont bring

it to you:' and he could not hear McCaslin now either, looking peacefully at McCaslin, his kinsman, his father almost yet no kin now as, at the last, even fathers and sons are no kin: and he

'It's seventeen miles, horseback and in the cold. We could both sleep here:' and McCaslin

'Why should I sleep here in my house when you wont sleep yonder in yours?' and gone, and he looking at the bright rustless unstained tin and thinking and not for the first time how much it takes to compound a man (Isaac McCaslin for instance) and of the devious intricate choosing yet unerring path that man's (Isaac McCaslin's for instance) spirit takes among all that mass to make him at last what he is to be, not only to the astonishment of them (the ones who sired the McCaslin who sired his father and Uncle Buddy and their sister, and the ones who sired the Beauchamp who sired his Uncle Hubert and his Uncle Hubert's sister) who believed they had shaped him, but to Isaac McCaslin too

as a loan and used it though he would not have had to: Major de Spain offered him a room in his house as long as he wanted it and asked nor would ever ask any question, and old General Compson more than that, to take him into his own room, to sleep in half of his own bed and more than Major de Spain because he told him baldly why: 'You sleep with me and before this winter is out, I'll know the reason. You'll tell me. Because I dont believe you just quit. It looks like you just quit but I have watched you in the woods too much and I dont believe you just quit even if it does look damn like it:' using it as a loan, paid his board and rent for a month and bought the tools, not simply because he was good with his hands because he had intended to use his hands and it could have been with horses, and not in mere static and hopeful emulation of the Nazarene as the young gambler buys a spotted shirt because the old gambler won in one yesterday, but (without the arrogance of false humility and without the false humbleness of pride, who intended to earn his bread, didn't especially want to earn it but had to earn it and for more than just bread) because if the Nazarene had found carpentering good for the life and ends He had assumed and elected to serve, it would be all right too for Isaac McCaslin even though Isaac McCaslin's ends, although simple enough in their apparent motivation, were and would be always incomprehensible to him, and his life, invincible enough in its needs, if he could have helped himself, not being the Nazarene, he would not have chosen it: and paid it back. He had forgotten the thirty dollars which McCaslin would put into the bank in his name each month, fetched it in to him and flung it onto the bed that first one time but no more; he had a partner now or rather he was the partner: a blasphemous profane clever old dipsomaniac who had built blockade-runners in Charleston in '62 and '3 and had been a ship's carpenter since and appeared in Jefferson two years ago nobody knew from where nor why and spent a good part of his time since recovering from delirium tremens in the jail; they had put a new roof on the stable of the bank's president and (the old man in jail again still celebrating that job) he went to the bank to collect for it and the president said, 'I should borrow from you instead of paying you:' and it had been seven months now and he remembered for the first time, two-hundred-and-ten dollars, and this was the first job of any size and when he left the bank the account stood at two-twenty, two-forty to balance, only twenty dollars more to go, then it did balance though by then the total had increased to three hundred and thirty and he said, 'I will transfer it now:' and the president said, 'I cant do that. McCaslin told me not to. Haven't you got another initial you could use and open another account?' but that was all right, the coins the silver and the bills as they accumulated knotted into a handkerchief and the coffee-pot wrapped in an old shirt as when Tennie's great-grandfather had fetched it from Warwick eighteen years ago, in the bottom of the iron-bound trunk which old Carothers had brought from Carolina and his landlady said, 'Not even a lock! And you dont even lock your door, not even when you leave!' and himself looking at her as peacefully as he had looked at McCaslin that first night in this same room, no kin to him at all yet more than kin as those who serve you even for pay are your kin and those who injure you are more than brother or wife

and had the wife now, got the old man out of jail and fetched him to the rented room and sobered him by superior strength, did not even remove his own shoes for twenty-four hours, got him up and got food into him and they built the barn this time from the ground up and he married her: an only child, a small girl yet curiously bigger than she seemed at first, solider perhaps, with dark eyes and a passionate heart-shaped face, who had time even on that farm to watch most of the day while he sawed timbers to the old man's measurements: and she: 'Papa told me about you. That farm is really yours, isn't it?' and he

'And McCaslin's:' and she

'Was there a will leaving half of it to him?' and he

'There didn't need to be a will. His grandmother was my father's sister. We were the same as brothers:' and she

'You are the same as second cousins and that's all you ever will be. But I dont suppose it matters:' and they were married, they were married and it was the new country, his heritage too as it was the heritage of all, out of the earth, beyond the earth yet of the earth because his too was of the earth's long chronicle, his too because each must share with another in order to come into it and in the sharing they become one: for that while, one: for that little while at least, one: indivisible, that while at least irrevocable and un-recoverable, living in a rented room still but for just a little while and that room wall-less and topless and floorless in glory for him to leave each morning and return to at night; her father already owned the lot in town and furnished the material and he and his partner would build it, her dowry from one: her wedding-present from three, she not to know it until the bungalow was finished and ready to be moved into and he never know who told her, not her father and not his partner and not even in drink though for a while he believed that, himself coming home from work and just time to wash and rest a moment before going down to supper, entering no rented cubicle since it would still partake of glory even after they would have grown old and lost it: and he saw her face then, just before she spoke: 'Sit down:' the two of them sitting on the bed's edge, not even touching yet, her face strained and terrible, her voice a passionate and expiring whisper of immeasurable prom-ise: 'I love you. You know I love you. When are we going to move?' and he

'I didn't—I didn't know—Who told you—' the hot fierce palm clapped over his mouth, crushing his lips into his teeth, the fierce curve of fingers digging into his cheek and only the palm slacked off enough for him to answer:

'The farm. Our farm. Your farm:' and he

'I—' then the hand again, finger and palm, the whole enveloping weight of her although she still was not touching him save the hand, the voice: 'No! No!' and the fingers themselves seeming to follow through the cheek the impulse to speech as it died in his mouth, then the whisper, the breath again, of love and of incredible prom-ise, the palm slackening again to let him answer:

'When?' and he

'I—' then she was gone, the hand too, standing, her back to him and her head bent, the voice so calm now that for an instant it seemed no voice of hers that he ever remembered: 'Stand up and turn your back and shut your eyes:' and repeated before he understood and stood himself with his eyes shut and heard the bell ring for supper below stairs and the calm voice again: 'Lock the door:' and he did so and leaned his forehead against the cold wood, his eyes closed, hearing his heart and the sound he had begun to hear before he moved until it ceased and the bell rang again below stairs and he knew it was for them this time and he heard the bed and turned and he had never seen her naked before, he had asked her to once, and why: that he wanted to see her naked because he loved her and he wanted to see her looking at him naked because he loved her but after that he never mentioned it again, even turning his face when she put the nightgown on over her dress to undress at night and putting the dress on over the gown to remove it in the morning and she would not let him get into bed beside her until the lamp was out and even in the heat of summer she would draw the sheet up over them both before she would let him turn to her: and the landlady came up the stairs up the hall and rapped on the door and then called their names but she didn't move, lying still on the bed outside the covers, her face turned away on the pillow, listening to nothing, thinking of nothing, not of him anyway he thought then the landlady went away and she said, 'Take off your clothes:' her head still turned away, looking at nothing, thinking of nothing, waiting for nothing, not even him, her hand moving as though with volition and vision of its own, catching his wrist at the exact moment when he paused beside the bed so that he never paused but merely changed the direction of moving, downward now, the hand drawing him and she moved at last, shifted, a movement one single complete inherent not practiced and one time older than man, looking at him now, drawing him still downward with the one hand down and down and he neither saw nor felt it shift, palm flat against his chest now and holding him away with the same apparent lack of any effort or any need for strength, and not looking at him now, she didn't need to, the chaste woman, the wife, already looked upon all the men who ever rutted and now her whole body had changed, altered, he had never seen it but once and now it was not even the one he had seen but composite of all woman-flesh since man that ever of its own will reclined on its back and opened, and out of it somewhere, without any movement of lips even, the dying and invincible whisper: 'Promise:' and he

'Promise?'

'The farm.' He moved. He had moved, the hand shifting from his chest once more to his wrist, grasping it, the arm still lax and only the light increasing pressure of the fingers as though arm and hand were a piece of wire cable with one looped end, only the hand tightening as he pulled against it. 'No,' he said. 'No:' and she was not looking at him still but not like the other but still the hand: 'No, I tell you. I wont. I cant. Never:' and still the hand and he said, for the last time, he tried to speak clearly and he knew it was still gently and he thought, *She already knows more than I with all the man-listening in camps where there was nothing to read ever even heard of. They are born already bored with what a boy approaches only at fourteen and fifteen with blundering and aghast trembling:* 'I cant. Not ever. Remember:' and still the steady and invincible hand and he said Yes and he thought, *She is lost. She was born lost. We were all born lost* then he stopped thinking and even saying Yes, it was like nothing he had ever dreamed, let alone heard in mere man-talking until after a no-time he returned and lay spent on the insatiate immemorial beach and again with a movement one time more older than man she turned and freed herself and on their wedding night she had cried and he thought she was crying now at first, into the tossed and wadded pillow, the voice coming from somewhere between the pillow and the cachinnation: 'And that's all. That's all from me. If this dont get you that son you talk about, it wont be mine:' lying on her side, her back to the empty rented room, laughing and laughing

———

V

He went back to the camp one more time before the lumber company moved in and began to cut the timber. Major de Spain himself never saw it again. But he made them welcome to use the house and hunt the land whenever they liked, and in the winter following the last hunt when Sam Fathers and Lion died, General Compson and Walter Ewell invented a plan to corporate themselves, the old group, into a club and lease the camp and the hunting privileges of the woods—an invention doubtless of the somewhat childish old General but actually worthy of Boon Hogganbeck himself. Even the boy, listening, recognised it for the subterfuge it was: to change the leopard's spots when they could not alter the leopard, a baseless and illusory hope to which even McCaslin seemed to subscribe for a while, that once they had persuaded Major de Spain to return to the camp he might revoke himself, which even the boy knew he would not do. And he did not. The boy never knew what occurred when Major de Spain declined. He was not present when the subject was broached and McCaslin never told him. But when June came and the time for the double birthday celebration there was no mention of it and when November came no one spoke of using Major de Spain's house and he never knew whether or not Major de Spain knew they were going on the hunt though without doubt old Ash probably told him: he and McCaslin and General Compson (and that one was the General's last hunt too) and Walter and Boon and Tennie's Jim and old Ash loaded two wagons and drove two days and almost forty miles beyond any country the boy had ever seen before and lived in tents for the two weeks. And the next spring they heard (not from Major de Spain) that he had sold the timber-rights to a Memphis lumber company and in June the boy came to town with McCaslin one Saturday and went to Major de Spain's office—the big, airy, book-lined second-storey room with windows at one end opening upon the shabby hinder purlieus of stores and at the other a door giving onto the railed balcony above the Square, with its curtained alcove where sat a cedar water-bucket and a sugar-bowl and spoon and tumbler and a wicker-covered demijohn of whiskey, and the bamboo-and-paper punkah swinging back and forth above the desk while old Ash in a tilted chair beside the entrance pulled the cord.

"Of course," Major de Spain said. "Ash will probably like to get off in the woods himself for a while, where he wont have to eat Daisy's cooking. Complain about it, anyway. Are you going to take anybody with you?"

"No sir," he said. "I thought that maybe Boon—" For six months now Boon had been town-marshall at Hoke's; Major de Spain had compounded with the lumber company—or perhaps compromised was closer, since it was the lumber company who had decided that Boon might be better as a town-marshall than head of a logging gang.

"Yes," Major de Spain said. "I'll wire him today. He can meet you at Hoke's. I'll send Ash on by the train and they can take some food in and all you will have to do will be to mount your horse and ride over."

"Yes sir," he said. "Thank you." And he heard his voice again. He didn't know he was going to say it yet he did know, he had known it all the time: "Maybe if you . . . ." His voice died. It was stopped, he never knew how because Major de Spain did not speak and it was not until his voice ceased that Major de Spain moved, turned back to the desk and the papers spread on it and even that without moving because he was sitting at the desk with a paper in his hand when the boy entered, the boy standing there looking down at the short plumpish grey-haired man in sober fine broadcloth and an immaculate glazed shirt whom he was used to seeing in boots and muddy corduroy, unshaven, sitting the shaggy powerful long-hocked mare with the worn Winchester carbine across the saddlebow and the great blue dog standing motionless as bronze at the stirrup, the two of them in that last year and to the boy anyway coming to resemble one another somehow as two people competent for love or for business who have been in love or in business together for a long time sometimes do. Major de Spain did not look up again.

"No. I will be too busy. But good luck to you. If you have it, you might bring me a young squirrel."

"Yes sir," he said. "I will."

He rode his mare, the three-year-old filly he had bred and raised and broken himself. He left home a little after midnight and six hours later, without even having sweated her, he rode into Hoke's, the tiny log-line junction which he had always thought of as Major de Spain's property too although Major de Spain had merely sold the company (and that many years ago) the land on which the sidetracks and loading-platforms and the commissary store stood, and looked about in shocked and grieved amazement even though he had had forewarning and had believed himself prepared: a new planing-mill already half completed which would cover two or three acres and what looked like miles and miles of stacked steel rails red with the light bright rust of newness and of piled crossties sharp with creosote, and wire corrals and feeding-troughs for two hundred mules at least and the tents for the men who drove them; so that he arranged for the care and stabling of his mare as rapidly as he could and did not look any more, mounted into the log-train caboose with his gun and climbed into the cupola and looked no more save toward the wall of wilderness ahead within which he would be able to hide himself from it once more anyway.

Then the little locomotive shrieked and began to move: a rapid churning of exhaust, a lethargic deliberate clashing of slack couplings traveling backward along the train, the exhaust changing to

the deep slow clapping bites of power as the caboose too began to
move and from the cupola he watched the train's head complete
the first and only curve in the entire line's length and vanish into
the wilderness, dragging its length of train behind it so that it
resembled a small dingy harmless snake vanishing into weeds, drawing him with it too until soon it ran once more at its maximum
clattering speed between the twin walls of unaxed wilderness as
of old. It had been harmless once. Not five years ago Walter Ewell
had shot a six-point buck from this same moving caboose, and there
was the story of the half-grown bear: the train's first trip in to the
cutting thirty miles away, the bear between the rails, its rear end
elevated like that of a playing puppy while it dug to see what sort
of ants or bugs they might contain or perhaps just to examine the
curious symmetrical squared barkless logs which had appeared
apparently from nowhere in one endless mathematical line overnight, still digging until the driver on the braked engine not fifty
feet away blew the whistle at it, whereupon it broke frantically
and took the first tree it came to: an ash sapling not much bigger
than a man's thigh and climbed as high as it could and clung there,
its head ducked between its arms as a man (a woman perhaps)
might have done while the brakeman threw chunks of ballast at it,
and when the engine returned three hours later with the first load
of outbound logs the bear was halfway down the tree and once
more scrambled back up as high as it could and clung again while
the train passed and was still there when the engine went in again
in the afternoon and still there when it came back out at dusk; and
Boon had been in Hoke's with the wagon after a barrel of flour
that noon when the train-crew told about it and Boon and Ash, both
twenty years younger then, sat under the tree all that night to keep
anybody from shooting it and the next morning Major de Spain
had the log-train held at Hoke's and just before sundown on the
second day, with not only Boon and Ash but Major de Spain and
General Compson and Walter and McCaslin, twelve then, watching, it came down the tree after almost thirty-six hours without even
water and McCaslin told him how for a minute they thought it was
going to stop right there at the barrow-pit where they were standing
and drink, how it looked at the water and paused and looked at
them and at the water again, but did not, gone, running, as bears
run, the two sets of feet, front and back, tracking two separate
though parallel courses.

It had been harmless then. They would hear the passing log-train sometimes from the camp; sometimes, because nobody bothered to listen for it or not. They would hear it going in, running light and fast, the light clatter of the trucks, the exhaust of the diminutive locomotive and its shrill peanut-parcher whistle flung for one petty moment and absorbed by the brooding and inattentive wilderness without even an echo. They would hear it going out, loaded, not quite so fast now yet giving its frantic and toylike illusion of crawling speed, not whistling now to conserve steam, flinging its bitten laboring miniature puffing into the immemorial woodsface with frantic and bootless vainglory, empty and noisy and puerile, carrying to no destination or purpose sticks which left nowhere any scar or stump as the child's toy loads and transports and unloads its dead sand and rushes back for more, tireless and unceasing and rapid yet never quite so fast as the Hand which plays with it moves the toy burden back to load the toy again. But it was different now. It was the same train, engine cars and caboose, even the same enginemen brakeman and conductor to whom Boon, drunk then sober then drunk again then fairly sober once more all in the space of fourteen hours, had bragged that day two years ago about what they were going to do to Old Ben tomorrow, running with its same illusion of frantic rapidity between the same twin walls of impenetrable and impervious woods, passing the old landmarks, the old game crossings over which he had trailed bucks wounded and not wounded and more than once seen them, anything but wounded, bo[l]t out of the woods and up and across the embankment which bore the rails and ties then down and into the woods again as the earth-bound supposedly move but crossing as arrows travel, groundless, elongated, three times its actual length and even paler, different in color, as if there were a point between immobility and absolute motion where even mass chemically altered, changing without pain or agony not only in bulk and shape but in color too, approaching the color of wind, yet this time it was as though the train (and not only the train but himself, not only his vision which had seen it and his memory which remembered it but his clothes too, as garments carry back into the clean edgeless blowing of air the lingering effluvium of a sick-room or of death) had brought with it into the doomed wilderness even before the actual axe the shadow and portent of the new mill not even finished yet and the rails and ties which were not even laid; and he knew now what he had known as soon as he saw Hoke's this morning but had not yet thought into words: why Major de Spain had not come back, and that after this

time he himself, who had had to see it one time other, would return
no more.

Now they were near. He knew it before the engine-driver whistled
to warn him. Then he saw Ash and the wagon, the reins without
doubt wrapped once more about the brake-lever as within the boy's
own memory Major de Spain had been forbidding him for eight
years to do, the train slowing, the slackened couplings jolting and
clashing again from car to car, the caboose slowing past the wagon
as he swung down with his gun, the conductor leaning out above
him to signal the engine, the caboose still slowing, creeping, although the engine's exhaust was already slatting in mounting tempo
against the unechoing wilderness, the crashing of draw-bars once
more travelling backward along the train, the caboose picking up
speed at last. Then it was gone. It had not been. He could no
longer hear it. The wilderness soared, musing, inattentive, myriad,
eternal, green; older than any mill-shed, longer than any spur-line.
"Mr Boon here yet?" he said.

"He beat me in," Ash said. "Had the wagon loaded and ready
for me at Hoke's yistiddy when I got there and setting on the front
steps at camp last night when I got in. He already been in the
woods since fo daylight this morning. Said he gwine up to the
Gum Tree and for you to hunt up that way and meet him." He
knew where that was: a single big sweet-gum just outside the
woods, in an old clearing; if you crept up to it very quietly this time
of year and then ran suddenly into the clearing, sometimes you
caught as many as a dozen squirrels in it, trapped, since there was
no other tree near they could jump to. So he didn't get into the
wagon at all.

"I will," he said.

"I figured you would," Ash said, "I fotch you a box of shells."
He passed the shells down and began to unwrap the lines from the
brake-pole.

"How many times up to now do you reckon Major has told you
not to do that?" the boy said.

"Do which?" Ash said. Then he said: "And tell Boon Hogganbeck dinner gonter be on the table in a hour and if yawl want any
to come on and eat it."

"In an hour?" he said. "It aint nine oclock yet." He drew out his
watch and extended it face-toward Ash. "Look." Ash didn't even
look at the watch.

"That's town time. You aint in town now. You in the woods."

"Look at the sun then."

"Nemmine the sun too," Ash said. "If you and Boon Hogganbeck want any dinner, you better come on in and get it when I tole you. I aim to get done in that kitchen because I got my wood to chop. And watch your feet. They're crawling."

"I will," he said.

Then he was in the woods, not alone but solitary; the solitude closed about him, green with summer. They did not change, and, timeless, would not, anymore than would the green of summer and the fire and rain of fall and the iron cold and sometimes even snow

the day, the morning when he killed the buck and Sam marked his face with its hot blood, they returned to camp and he remembered old Ash's blinking and disgruntled and even outraged disbelief until at last McCaslin had had to affirm the fact that he had really killed it: and that night Ash sat snarling and unapproachable behind the stove so that Tennie's Jim had to serve the supper and waked them with breakfast already on the table the next morning and it was only half-past one oclock and at last out of Major de Spain's angry cursing and Ash's snarling and sullen rejoinders the fact emerged that Ash not only wanted to go into the woods and shoot a deer also but he intended to and Major de Spain said, 'By God, if we dont let him we will probably have to do the cooking from now on.' and Walter Ewell said, 'Or get up at midnight to eat what Ash cooks.' and since he had already killed his buck for this hunt and was not to shoot again unless they needed meat, he offered his gun to Ash until Major de Spain took command and allotted that gun to Boon for the day and gave Boon's unpredictable pump gun to Ash, with two buckshot shells but Ash said, 'I got shells.' and showed them, four: one buck, one of number three shot for rabbits, two of bird-shot and told one by one their history and their origin and he remembered not Ash's face alone but Major de Spain's and Walter's and General Compson's too, and Ash's voice: 'Shoot? In course they'll shoot! Genl Cawmpson guv me this un'—the buckshot—'right outen the same gun he kilt that big buck with eight years ago. And this un'—it was the rabbit shell: triumphantly—'is oldern thisyer boy!' And that morning he loaded the gun himself, reversing the order: the bird-shot, the rabbit, then the buck so that the buckshot would feed first into the chamber, and himself without a gun, he and Ash walked beside Major de Spain's and Tennie's Jim's horses and the dogs (that was the snow) until they cast and struck, the sweet strong cries ringing away into the muffled falling air and gone almost immediately, as if the constant and unmurmuring flakes had already buried even the unformed echoes beneath their myriad and weightless falling, Major de Spain and Tennie's Jim gone too, whooping on into the woods; and then it was all right, he knew as plainly as if Ash had told him that Ash had now hunted his deer and that even his tender years had been forgiven for having killed one, and they turned back toward home through the falling snow—that is, Ash said, 'Now whut?' and he said, 'This way'—himself in front because, although they were less than a mile from camp, he knew that Ash, who had spent two weeks of his life in the camp each year for the last twenty, had no idea whatever where they were, until quite soon the manner in which Ash carried Boon's gun was making him a good deal more than just nervous and he made Ash walk in front, striding on, talk-ing now, an old man's garrulous monologue beginning with where he was at the moment then of the woods and of camping in the woods and of eating in camps then of eating then of cooking it and of his wife's cooking then briefly of his old wife and almost at once and at length of a new light-colored woman who nursed next door to Major de Spain's and if she didn't watch out who she was switching her tail at he would show her how old was an old man or not if his wife just didn't watch him all the time, the two of them in a game trail through a dense brake of cane and brier which would bring them out within a quarter-mile of camp, approaching a big fallen tree-trunk lying athwart the path and just as Ash, still talking, was about to step over it the bear, the yearling, rose sud-denly beyond the log, sitting up, its forearms against its chest and its wrists limply arrested as if it had been surprised in the act of covering its face to pray: and after a certain time Ash's gun yawed jerkily up and he said, 'You haven't got a shell in the barrel yet. Pump it:' but the gun already snicked and he said, 'Pump it. You haven't got a shell in the barrel yet:' and Ash pumped the action and in a certain time the gun steadied again and snicked and he said, 'Pump it:' and watched the buckshot shell jerk, spinning heavily, into the cane. This is the rabbit shot: he thought and the gun snicked and he thought: The next is bird-shot: and he didn't have to say Pump it; he cried, 'Dont shoot! Dont shoot!' but that was already too late too, the light dry vicious snick! before he could speak and the bear turned and dropped to all-fours and then was gone and there was only the log, the cane, the velvet and constant snow and Ash said, 'Now whut?' and he said, 'This way. Come on:'

and began to back away down the path and Ash said, 'I got to find my shells:' and he said, 'Goddamn it, goddamn it, come on:' but Ash leaned the gun against the log and returned and stooped and fumbled among the cane roots until he came back and stooped and found the shells and they rose and at that moment the gun, untouched, leaning against the log six feet away and for that while even forgotten by both of them, roared, bellowed and flamed, and ceased: and he carried it now, pumped out the last mummified shell and gave that one also to Ash and, the action still open, himself carried the gun until he stood it in the corner behind Boon's bed at the camp

—; summer, and fall, and snow, and wet and saprife spring in their ordered immortal sequence, the deathless and immemorial phases of the mother who had shaped him if any had toward the man he almost was, mother and father both to the old man born of a Negro slave and a Chickasaw chief who had been his spirit's father if any had, whom he had revered and harkened to and loved and lost and grieved: and he would marry someday and they too would own for their brief while that brief unsubstanced glory which inherently of itself cannot last and hence why glory: and they would, might, carry even the remembrance of it into the time when flesh no longer talks to flesh because memory at least does last: but still the woods would be his mistress and his wife.

He was not going toward the Gum Tree. Actually he was getting farther from it. Time was and not so long ago either when he would not have been allowed here without someone with him, and a little later, when he had begun to learn how much he did not know, he would not have dared be here without someone with him, and later still, beginning to ascertain, even if only dimly, the limits of what he did not know, he could have attempted and carried it through with a compass, not because of any increased belief in himself but because McCaslin and Major de Spain and Walter and General Compson too had taught him at last to believe the compass regardless of what it seemed to state. Now he did not even use the compass but merely the sun and that only subconsciously, yet he could have taken a scaled map and plotted at any time to within a hundred feet of where he actually was; and sure enough, at almost the exact moment when he expected it, the earth began to rise faintly, he passed one of the four concrete markers set down by the lumber company's surveyor to establish the four corners of the plot which Major de Spain had reserved out of the sale, then he stood on the crest of the knoll itself, the four corner-markers all visible now, blanched still even beneath the winter's weathering, lifeless and shockingly alien in that place where dissolution itself was a seething turmoil of ejaculation tumescence conception and birth, and death did not even exist. After two winters' blanketings of leaves and the flood-waters of two springs, there was no trace of the two graves anymore at all. But those who would have come this far to find them would not need headstones but would have found them as Sam Fathers himself had taught him to find such: by bearings on trees: and did, almost the first thrust of the hunting knife finding (but only to see if it was still there) the round tin box manufactured for axle-grease and containing now Old Ben's dried mutilated paw, resting above Lion's bones.

He didn't disturb it. He didn't even look for the other grave where he and McCaslin and Major de Spain and Boon had laid Sam's body, along with his hunting horn and his knife and his tobacco-pipe, that Sunday morning two years ago; he didn't have to. He had stepped over it, perhaps on it. But that was all right. *He probably knew I was in the woods this morning long before I got here*, he thought, going on to the tree which had supported one end of the platform where Sam lay when McCaslin and Major de Spain found them—the tree, the other axle-grease tin nailed to the trunk, but weathered, rusted, alien too yet healed already into the wilderness' concordant generality, raising no tuneless note, and empty, long since empty of the food and tobacco he had put into it that day, as empty of that as it would presently be of this which he drew from his pocket—the twist of tobacco, the new bandanna handkerchief, the small paper sack of the peppermint candy which Sam had used to love; that gone too, almost before he had turned his back, not vanished but merely translated into the myriad life which printed the dark mold of these secret and sunless places with delicate fairy tracks, which, breathing and biding and immobile, watched him from beyond every twig and leaf until he moved, moving again, walking on; he had not stopped, he had only paused, quitting the knoll which was no abode of the dead because there was no death, not Lion and not Sam: not held fast in earth but free in earth and not in earth but of earth, myriad yet undiffused of every myriad part, leaf and twig and particle, air and sun and rain and dew and night, acorn oak and leaf and acorn again, dark and dawn and dark and dawn again in their immutable progression and, being myriad, one: and Old Ben too, Old Ben too; they would give him his paw back even, certainly they would give him his paw back: then the long challenge and the long chase, no heart to be driven and outraged, no flesh to be mauled and bled— Even as he froze himself, he seemed to hear Ash's parting admonition. He could even hear the voice as he froze, immobile, one foot just taking his weight, the toe of the other just lifted behind him, not breathing, feeling again and as always the sharp shocking inrush from when Isaac McCaslin long yet was not, and so it was fear all right but not fright as he looked down at it. It had not coiled yet and the buzzer had not sounded either, only one thick rapid contraction, one loop cast sideways as though merely for purchase from which the raised head might start slightly backward, not in fright either, not in threat quite yet, more than six feet of it, the head raised higher than his knee and less than his knee's length away, and old, the once-bright markings of its youth dulled now to a monotone concordant too with the wilderness it crawled and lurked: the old one, the ancient and accursed about the earth, fatal and solitary and he could smell it now: the thin sick smell of rotting cucumbers and something else which had no name, evocative of all knowledge and an old weariness and of pariah-hood and of death. At last it moved. Not the head. The elevation of the head did not change as it began to glide away from him, moving erect yet off the perpendicular as if the head and that elevated third were complete and all: an entity walking on two feet and free of all laws of mass and balance and should have been because even now he could not quite believe that all that shift and flow of shadow behind that walking head could have been one snake: going and then gone; he put the other foot down at last and didn't know it, standing with one hand raised as Sam had stood that afternoon six years ago when Sam led him into the wilderness and showed him and he ceased to be a child, speaking the old tongue which Sam had spoken that day without premeditation either: "Chief," he said: "Grandfather."

He couldn't tell when he first began to hear the sound, because when he became aware of it, it seemed to him that he had been already hearing it for several seconds—a sound as though someone were hammering a gun-barrel against a piece of railroad iron, a sound loud and heavy and not rapid yet with something frenzied about it, as the hammerer were not only a strong man and an earnest one but a little hysterical too. Yet it couldn't be on the log-line because, although the track lay in that direction, it was at least two miles from him and this sound was not three hundred yards away. But even as he thought that, he realised where the sound must be coming from: whoever the man was and whatever he was doing, he was somewhere near the edge of the clearing where the Gum Tree was and where he was to meet Boon. So far, he had been hunting as he advanced, moving slowly and quietly and watching the ground and the trees both. Now he went on, his gun unloaded and the barrel slanted up and back to facilitate its passage through brier and undergrowth, approaching as it grew louder and louder that steady savage somehow queerly hysterical beating of metal on metal, emerging from the woods, into the old clearing, with the solitary gum tree directly before him. At first glance the tree seemed to be alive with frantic squirrels. There appeared to be forty or fifty of them leaping and darting from branch to branch until the whole tree had become one green maelstrom of mad leaves, while from time to time, singly or in twos and threes, squirrels would dart down the trunk then whirl without stopping and rush back up again as though sucked violently back by the vacuum of their fellows' frenzied vortex. Then he saw Boon, sitting, his back against the trunk, his head bent, hammering furiously at something on his lap. What he hammered with was the barrel of his dismembered gun, what he hammered at was the breech of it. The rest of the gun lay scattered about him in a half-dozen pieces while he bent over the piece on his lap his scarlet and streaming walnut face, hammering the disjointed barrel against the gun-breech with the frantic abandon of a madman. He didn't even look up to see who it was. Still hammering, he merely shouted back at the boy in a hoarse strangled voice:

"Get out of here! Dont touch them! Dont touch a one of them! They're mine!"

The Wide Net

EUDORA WELTY

*Sharing many qualities of the tall tale with Faulkner's
"Spotted Horses," Miss Welty's story belongs at the same
time to a broader and partly different form of comedy. Like
the American humorous tale, "The Wide Net" is casually
anecdotal and episodic, but it differs in having a coherent
narrative with a well-defined beginning, middle, and end.
The dialogue of "The Wide Net" lies close to the spoken
vernacular, with local idiosyncrasies of syntax and idiom,
but the story also exhibits the selectivity, compression, and
other artifice of a self-conscious, written prose—the latter
characteristics particularly evident in the narrative portions.
Its humor springs from gnomic utterance as well as from
hyperbole; given to farce, it is at least half-serious in its
embrace of folk wisdom, and of the mysteries of dreams and
archetypal rivers, of fish, reptiles, feast and dance, pregnancy
and harvest, and communal celebration. By assimilating the
mode of American humor to that of formal comedy, Miss
Welty brings new life to both.*

William Wallace Jamieson's wife Hazel was going to have a baby. But this was October, and it was six months away, and she acted exactly as though it would be tomorrow. When he came in the room she would not speak to him, but would look as straight at nothing as she could, with her eyes glowing. If he only touched her she stuck out her tongue or ran around the table. So one night he went out with two of the boys down the road and stayed out all night. But that was the worst thing yet, because when he came home in the early morning Hazel had vanished. He went through the house not believing his eyes, balancing with both hands out, his yellow cowlick rising on end, and then he turned the kitchen inside out looking for her, but it did no good. Then when he got back to the front room he saw she had left him a little letter, in an envelope. That was doing something behind someone's back. He took out the letter, pushed it open, held it out at a distance from his eyes. . . . After one look he was scared to read the exact words, and he crushed the whole thing in his hand instantly, but what it had said was that she would not put up with him after that and was going to the river to drown herself.

"Drown herself. . . . But she's in mortal fear of the water!"

He ran out front, his face red like the red of the picked cotton field he ran over, and down in the road he gave a loud shout for Virgil Thomas, who was just going in his own house, to come out again. He could just see the edge of Virgil, he had almost got in, he had one foot inside the door.

They met half-way between the farms, under the shade-tree.

"Haven't you had enough of the night?" asked Virgil. There they were, their pants all covered with dust and dew, and they had had to carry the third man home flat between them.

"I've lost Hazel, she's vanished, she went to drown herself."

"Why, that ain't like Hazel," said Virgil.

William Wallace reached out and shook him. "You heard me. Don't you know we have to drag the river?"

"Right this minute?"

"You ain't got nothing to do till spring."

"Let me go set foot inside the house and speak to my mother and tell her a story, and I'll come back."

"This will take the wide net," said William Wallace. His eyebrows gathered, and he was talking to himself.

"How come Hazel to go and do that way?" asked Virgil as they started out.

William Wallace said, "I reckon she got lonesome."

"That don't argue—drown herself for getting lonesome. My mother gets lonesome."

"Well," said William Wallace. "It argues for Hazel."

"How long is it now since you and her was married?"

"Why, it's been a year."

"It don't seem that long to me. A year!"

"It was this time last year. It seems longer," said William Wallace, breaking a stick off a tree in surprise. They walked along, kicking at the flowers on the road's edge. "I remember the day I seen her first, and that seems a long time ago. She was coming along the road holding a little frying-size chicken from her grandma, under her arm, and she had it real quiet. I spoke to her with nice manners. We knowed each other's names, being bound to, just didn't know each other to speak to. I says, 'Where are you taking the fryer?' and she says, 'Mind your manners,' and I kept on till after while she says, 'If you want to walk me home, take littler steps.' So I didn't lose time. It was just four miles across the field and full of blackberries, and from the top of the hill there was Dover below, looking sizeable-like and clean, spread out between the two churches like that. When we got down, I says to her, 'What kind of water's in this well?' and she says, 'The best water in the world.' So I drew a bucket and took out a dipper and she drank and I drank. I didn't think it was that remarkable, but I didn't tell her."

"What happened that night?" asked Virgil.

"We ate the chicken," said William Wallace, "and it was tender. Of course that wasn't all they had. The night I was trying their table out, it sure had good things to eat from one end to the other. Her mama and papa sat at the head and foot and we was face to face with each other across it, with I remember a pat of butter between. They had real sweet butter, with a tree drawed down it, elegant-like. Her mama eats like a man. I had brought her a whole hat-ful of berries and she didn't even pass them to her husband. Hazel, she would leap up and take a pitcher of new milk and fill up the glasses. I had heard how they couldn't have a singing at the church without a fight over her."

"Oh, she's a pretty girl, all right," said Virgil. "It's a pity for the ones like her to grow old, and get like their mothers."

"Another thing will be that her mother will get wind of this and come after me," said William Wallace.

"Her mother will eat you alive," said Virgil.

"She's just been watching her chance," said William Wallace. "Why did I think I could stay out all night."

"Just something come over you."

"First it was just a carnival at Carthage, and I had to let them guess my weight . . . and after that . . ."

"It was nice to be sitting on your neck in a ditch singing," prompted Virgil, "in the moonlight. And playing on the harmonica like you can play."

"Even if Hazel did sit home knowing I was drunk, that wouldn't kill her," said William Wallace. "What she knows ain't ever killed her yet. . . . She's smart, too, for a girl," he said.

"She's a lot smarter than her cousins in Beula," said Virgil. "And especially Edna Earle, that never did get to be what you'd call a heavy thinker. Edna Earle could sit and ponder all day on how the little tail of the 'C' got through the 'L' in a Coca-Cola sign."

"Hazel *is* smart," said William Wallace. They walked on. "You ought to see her pantry shelf, it looks like a hundred jars when you open the door. I don't see how she could turn around and jump in the river."

"It's a woman's trick."

"I always behaved before. Till the one night—last night."

"Yes, but the one night," said Virgil. "And she was waiting to take advantage."

"She jumped in the river because she was scared to death of the water and that was to make it worse," he said. "She remembered how I used to have to pick her up and carry her over the oak-log bridge, how she'd shut her eyes and make a dead-weight and hold me round the neck, just for a little creek. I don't see how she brought herself to jump."

"Jumped backwards," said Virgil. "Didn't look."

When they turned off, it was still early in the pink and green fields. The fumes of morning, sweet and bitter, sprang up where they walked. The insects ticked softly, their strength in reserve; butterflies chopped the air, going to the east, and the birds flew carelessly and sang by fits and starts, not the way they did in the evening in sustained and drowsy songs.

"It's a pretty *day* for sure," said William Wallace. "It's a pretty *day* for it."

"I don't see a sign of her ever going along here," said Virgil.

"Well," said William Wallace. "She wouldn't have dropped anything. I never saw a girl to leave less signs of where she's been."

"Not even a plum seed," said Virgil, kicking the grass.

In the grove it was so quiet that once William Wallace gave a jump, as if he could almost hear a sound of himself wondering where she had gone. A descent of energy came down on him in the thick of the woods and he ran at a rabbit and caught it in his hands.

"Rabbit . . . Rabbit . . ." He acted as if he wanted to take it off to himself and hold it up and talk to it. He laid a palm against its pushing heart. "Now . . . There now . . ."

"Let her go, William Wallace, let her go." Virgil, chewing on an elderberry whistle he had just made, stood at his shoulder: "What do you want with a live rabbit?"

William Wallace squatted down and set the rabbit on the ground but held it under his hand. It was a little, old, brown rabbit. It did not try to move. "See there?"

"Let her go."

"She can go if she wants to, but she don't want to."

Gently he lifted his hand. The round eye was shining at him sideways in the green gloom.

"Anybody can freeze a rabbit, that wants to," said Virgil. Suddenly he gave a far-reaching blast on the whistle, and the rabbit went in a streak. "Was you out catching cotton-tails, or was you out catching your wife?" he said, taking the turn to the open fields. "I come along to keep you on the track."

"Who'll we get, now?" They stood on top of a hill and William Wallace looked critically over the countryside. "Any of the Malones?"

"I was always scared of the Malones," said Virgil. "Too many *of* them."

"This is my day with the net, and they would have to watch out," said William Wallace. "I reckon some Malones, and the Doyles, will be enough. The six Doyles and their dogs, and you and me, and two little nigger boys is enough, with just a few Malones."

"That ought to be enough," said Virgil, "no matter what."

"I'll bring the Malones, and you bring the Doyles," said William Wallace, and they separated at the spring.

When William Wallace came back, with a string of Malones just showing behind him on the hilltop, he found Virgil with the two little Rippen boys waiting behind him, solemn little towheads. As soon as he walked up, Grady, the one in front, lifted his hand to signal silence and caution to his brother Brucie who began panting merrily and untrustworthily behind him.

Brucie bent readily under William Wallace's hand-pat, and gave him a dreamy look out of the tops of his round eyes, which were pure green-and-white like clover tops. William Wallace gave him a nickel. Grady hung his head; his white hair lay in a little tail in the nape of his neck.

"Let's let them come," said Virgil.

"Well, they can come then, but if we keep letting everybody come it is going to be too many," said William Wallace.

"They'll appreciate it, those little-old boys," said Virgil. Brucie held up at arm's length a long red thread with a bent pin tied on the end; and a look of helpless and intense interest gathered Grady's face like a drawstring—his eyes, one bright with a sty, shone pleadingly under his white bangs, and he snapped his jaw and tried to speak. . . . "Their papa was drowned in the Pearl River," said Virgil.

There was a shout from the gully.

"Here come all the Malones," cried William Wallace. "I asked four of them would they come, but the rest of the family invited themselves."

"Did you ever see a time when they didn't," said Virgil. "And yonder from the other direction comes the Doyles, still with biscuit crumbs on their cheeks, I bet, now it's nothing to do but eat as their mother said."

"If two little niggers would come along now, or one big nigger," said William Wallace. And the words were hardly out of his mouth when two little Negro boys came along, going somewhere, one behind the other, stepping high and gay in their overalls, as though they waded in honeydew to the waist.

"Come here, boys. What's your names?"

"Sam and Robbie Bell."

"Come along with us, we're going to drag the river."

"You hear that, Robbie Bell?" said Sam.

They smiled.

The Doyles came noiselessly, their dogs made all the fuss. The Malones, eight giants with great long black eyelashes, were already stamping the ground and pawing each other, ready to go. Everybody went up together to see Doc.

Old Doc owned the wide net. He had a house on top of the hill and he sat and looked out from a rocker on the front porch.

"Climb the hill and come in!" he began to intone across the valley. "Harvest's over . . . slipped up on everybody . . . cotton's picked, gone to the gin . . . hay cut . . . molasses made around here. . . . Big explosion's over, supervisors elected, some pleased, some not. . . . We're hearing talk of war!"

When they got closer, he was saying, "Many's been saved at revival, twenty-two last Sunday including a Doyle, ought to counted two. Hope they'll be a blessing to Dover community besides a shining star in Heaven. Now what?" he asked, for they had arrived and stood gathered in front of the steps.

"If nobody is using your wide net, could we use it?" asked William Wallace.

"You just used it a month ago," said Doc. "It ain't your turn."

Virgil jogged William Wallace's arm and cleared his throat. "This time is kind of special," he said. "We got reason to think William Wallace's wife Hazel is in the river, drowned."

"What reason have you got to think she's in the river drowned?" asked Doc. He took out his old pipe. "I'm asking the husband."

"Because she's not in the house," said William Wallace.

"Vanished?" and he knocked out the pipe.

"Plum vanished."

"Of course a thousand things could have happened to her," said Doc, and he lighted the pipe.

"Hand him up the letter, William Wallace," said Virgil. "We can't wait around till Doomsday for the net while Doc sits back thinkin'."

"I tore it up, right at the first," said William Wallace. "But I know it by heart. It said she was going to jump straight in the Pearl River and that I'd be sorry."

"Where do you come in, Virgil?" asked Doc.

"I was in the same place William Wallace sat on his neck in, all night, and done as much as he done, and come home the same time."

"You-all were out cuttin' up, so Lady Hazel has to jump in the river, is that it? Cause and effect? Anybody want to argue with me? Where do these others come in, Doyles, Malones, and what not?"

"Doc is the smartest man around," said William Wallace, turning to the solidly waiting Doyles, "but it sure takes time."

"These are the ones that's collected to drag the river for her," said Virgil.

"Of course I am not going on record to say so soon that *I* think she's drowned," Doc said, blowing out blue smoke.

"Do you think . . ." William Wallace mounted a step, and his hands both went into fists. "Do you think she was *carried off?*"

"Now that's the way to argue, see it from all sides," said Doc promptly. "But who by?"

Some Malone whistled, but not so you could tell which one.

"There's no booger around the Dover section that goes around carrying off young girls that's married," stated Doc.

"She was always scared of the Gypsies." William Wallace turned scarlet. "She'd sure turn her ring around on her finger if she passed one, and look in the other direction so they couldn't see she was pretty and carry her off. They come in the end of summer."

"Yes, there are the Gypsies, kidnappers since the world began. But was it to be you that would pay the grand ransom?" asked Doc. He pointed his finger. They all laughed then at how clever old Doc was and clapped William Wallace on the back. But that turned into a scuffle and they fell to the ground.

"Stop it, or you can't have the net," said Doc. "You're scaring my wife's chickens."

"It's time we was gone," said William Wallace.

The big barking dogs jumped to lean their front paws on the men's chests.

"My advice remains, Let well enough alone," said Doc. "Whatever this mysterious event will turn out to be, it has kept one woman from talking a while. However, Lady Hazel is the prettiest girl in Mississippi, you've never seen a prettier one and you never will. A golden-haired girl." He got to his feet with the nimbleness that was always his surprise, and said, "I'll come along with you."

The path they always followed was the Old Natchez Trace. It took them through the deep woods and led them out down below on the Pearl River, where they could begin dragging it upstream to a point near Dover. They walked in silence around William

Wallace, not letting him carry anything, but the net dragged heavily and the buckets were full of clatter in a place so dim and still.

Once they went through a forest of cucumber trees and came up on a high ridge. Grady and Brucie who were running ahead all the way stopped in their tracks; a whistle had blown and far down and far away a long freight train was passing. It seemed like a little festival procession, moving with the slowness of ignorance or a dream, from distance to distance, the tiny pink and gray cars like secret boxes. Grady was counting the cars to himself, as if he could certainly see each one clearly, and Brucie watched his lips, hushed and cautious, the way he would watch a bird drinking. Tears suddenly came to Grady's eyes, but it could only be because a tiny man walked along the top of the train, walking and moving on top of the moving train.

They went down again and soon the smell of the river spread over the woods, cool and secret. Every step they took among the great walls of vines and among the passion-flowers started up a little life, a little flight.

"We're walking along in the changing-time," said Doc. "Any day now the change will come. It's going to turn from hot to cold, and we can kill the hog that's ripe and have fresh meat to eat. Come one of these nights and we can wander down here and tree a nice possum. Old Jack Frost will be pinching things up. Old Mr. Winter will be standing in the door. Hickory tree there will be yellow. Sweet-gum red, hickory yellow, dogwood red, sycamore yellow." He went along rapping the tree trunks with his knuckle. "Magnolia and live-oak never die. Remember that. Persimmons will all get fit to eat, and the nuts will be dropping like rain all through the woods here. And run, little quail, run, for we'll be after you too."

They went on and suddenly the woods opened upon light, and they had reached the river. Everyone stopped, but Doc talked on ahead as though nothing had happened. "Only today," he said, "today, in October sun, it's all gold—sky and tree and water. Everything just before it changes looks to be made of gold."

William Wallace looked down, as though he thought of Hazel with the shining eyes, sitting at home and looking straight before her, like a piece of pure gold, too precious to touch.

Below them the river was glimmering, narrow, soft, and skin-colored, and slowed nearly to stillness. The shining willow trees hung round them. The net that was being drawn out, so old and so long-used, it too looked golden, strung and tied with golden threads.

Standing still on the bank, all of a sudden William Wallace, on whose word they were waiting, spoke up in a voice of surprise. "What is the name of this river?"

They looked at him as if he were crazy not to know the name of the river he had fished in all his life. But a deep frown was on his forehead, as if he were compelled to wonder what people had come to call this river, or to think there was a mystery in the name of a river they all knew so well, the same as if it were some great far torrent of waves that dashed through the mountains somewhere, and almost as if it were a river in some dream, for they could not give him the name of that.

"Everybody knows Pearl River is named the Pearl River," said Doc.

A bird note suddenly bold was like a stone thrown into the water to sound it.

"It's deep here," said Virgil, and jogged William Wallace. "Remember?"

William Wallace stood looking down at the river as if it were still a mystery to him. There under his feet which hung over the bank it was transparent and yellow like an old bottle lying in the sun, filling with light.

Doc clattered all his paraphernalia.

Then all of a sudden all the Malones scattered jumping and tumbling down the bank. They gave their loud shout. Little Brucie started after them, and looked back.

"Do you think she jumped?" Virgil asked William Wallace.

II

Since the net was so wide, when it was all stretched it reached from bank to bank of the Pearl River, and the weights would hold it all the way to the bottom. Jug-like sounds filled the air, splashes lifted in the sun, and the party began to move upstream. The Malones with great groans swam and pulled near the shore, the Doyles swam and pushed from behind with Virgil to tell them how to do it best; Grady and Brucie with his thread and pin trotted along the sandbars hauling buckets and lines. Sam and Robbie Bell, naked and bright, guided the old oarless rowboat that always drifted at the shore, and in it, sitting up tall with his hat on, was Doc—he went along without ever touching water and without ever taking his eyes off the net. William Wallace himself did everything but most of the time he was out of sight, swimming about under water or diving, and he had nothing to say any more.

The dogs chased up and down, in and out of the water, and in and out of the woods.

"Don't let her get too heavy, boys," Doc intoned regularly, every few minutes, "and she won't let nothing through."

"She won't let nothing through, she won't let nothing through," chanted Sam and Robbie Bell, one at his front and one at his back.

The sandbars were pink or violet drifts ahead. Where the light fell on the river, in a wandering from shore to shore, it was leaf-shaped spangles that trembled softly, while the dark of the river was calm. The willow trees leaned overhead under muscadine vines, and their trailing leaves hung like waterfalls in the morning air. The thing that seemed like silence must have been the endless cry of all the crickets and locusts in the world, rising and falling.

Every time William Wallace took hold of a big eel that slipped the net, the Malones all yelled, "Rassle with him, son!"

"Don't let her get too heavy, boys," said Doc.

"This is hard on catfish," William Wallace said once.

There were big and little fishes, dark and bright, that they caught, good ones and bad ones, the same old fish.

"This is more shoes than I ever saw got together in any store," said Virgil when they emptied the net to the bottom. "Get going!" he shouted in the next breath.

The little Rippens who had stayed ahead in the woods stayed ahead on the river. Brucie, leading them all, made small jumps and hops as he went, sometimes on one foot, sometimes on the other.

The winding river looked old sometimes, when it ran wrinkled and deep under high banks where the roots of trees hung down, and sometimes it seemed to be only a young creek, shining with the colors of wildflowers. Sometimes sandbars in the shapes of fishes lay nose to nose across, without the track of even a bird.

"Here comes some alligators," said Virgil. "Let's let them by."

They drew out on the shady side of the water, and three big alligators and four middle-sized ones went by, taking their own time.

"Look at their great big old teeth!" called a shrill voice. It was Grady making his only outcry, and the alligators were not showing their teeth at all.

"The better to eat folks with," said Doc from his boat, looking at him severely.

"Doc, you are bound to declare all you know," said Virgil. "Get going!"

When they started off again the first thing they caught in the net was the baby alligator.

"That's just what we wanted!" cried the Malones.

They set the little alligator down on a sandbar and he squatted perfectly still; they could hardly tell when it was he started to move. They watched with set faces his incredible mechanics, while the dogs after one bark stood off in inquisitive humility, until he winked.

"He's ours!" shouted all the Malones. "We're taking him home with us!"

"He ain't nothing but a little-old baby," said William Wallace.

The Malones only scoffed, as if he might be only a baby but he looked like the oldest and worst lizard.

"What are you going to do with him?" asked Virgil.

"Keep him."

"I'd be more careful what I took out of this net," said Doc.

"Tie him up and throw him in the bucket," the Malones were saying to each other, while Doc was saying, "Don't come running to me and ask me what to do when he gets big."

They kept catching more and more fish, as if there was no end in sight.

"Look, a string of lady's beads," said Virgil. "Here, Sam and Robbie Bell."

Sam wore them around his head, with a knot over his forehead and loops around his ears, and Robbie Bell walked behind and stared at them.

In a shadowy place something white flew up. It was a heron, and it went away over the dark treetops. William Wallace followed it with his eyes and Brucie clapped his hands, but Virgil gave a sigh, as if he knew that when you go looking for what is lost, everything is a sign.

An eel slid out of the net.

"Rassle with him, son!" yelled the Malones. They swam like fiends.

"The Malones are in it for the fish," said Virgil.

It was about noon that there was a little rustle on the bank.

"Who is that yonder?" asked Virgil, and he pointed to a little undersized man with short legs and a little straw hat with a band around it, who was following along on the other side of the river.

"Never saw him and don't know his brother," said Doc.

Nobody had ever seen him before.

"Who invited you?" cried Virgil hotly. "Hi . . . !" and he made signs for the little undersized man to look at him, but he would not.

"Looks like a crazy man, from here," said the Malones.

"Just don't pay any attention to him and maybe he'll go away," advised Doc.

But Virgil had already swum across and was up on the other bank. He and the stranger could be seen exchanging a word apiece and then Virgil put out his hand the way he would pat a child and patted the stranger to the ground. The little man got up again just as quickly, lifted his shoulders, turned around, and walked away with his hat tilted over his eyes.

When Virgil came back he said, "Little-old man claimed he was harmless as a baby. I told him to just try horning in on this river and anything in it."

"What did he look like up close?" asked Doc.

"I wasn't studying how he looked," said Virgil. "But I don't like anybody to come looking at me that I am not familiar with." And he shouted, "Get going!"

"Things are moving in too great a rush," said Doc.

Brucie darted ahead and ran looking into all the bushes, lifting up their branches and looking underneath.

"Not one of the Doyles has spoke a word," said Virgil.

"That's because they're not talkers," said Doc.

All day William Wallace kept diving to the bottom. Once he dived down and down into the dark water, where it was so still that nothing stirred, not even a fish, and so dark that it was no longer the muddy world of the upper river but the dark clear world of deepness, and he must have believed this was the deepest place in the whole Pearl River, and if she was not here she would not be anywhere. He was gone such a long time that the others stared hard at the surface of the water, through which the bubbles came from below. So far down and all alone, had he found Hazel? Had he suspected down there, like some secret, the real, the true trouble that Hazel had fallen into, about which words in a letter could not speak . . . how (who knew?) she had been filled to the brim with that elation that they all remembered, like their own secret, the elation that comes of great hopes and changes, sometimes simply of the harvest time, that comes with a little course of its own like a tune to run in the head, and there was nothing she could do about it—they knew—and so it had turned into this? It could be nothing but the old trouble that William Wallace was finding out, reaching and turning in the gloom of such depths.

"Look down yonder," said Grady softly to Brucie.

He pointed to the surface, where their reflections lay colorless and still side by side. He touched his brother gently as though to impress him.

"That's you and me," he said.

Brucie swayed precariously over the edge, and Grady caught him by the seat of his overalls. Brucie looked, but showed no recognition. Instead, he backed away, and seemed all at once unconcerned and spiritless, and pressed the nickel William Wallace had given him into his palm, rubbing it into his skin. Grady's inflamed eyes rested on the brown water. Without warning he saw something . . . perhaps the image in the river seemed to be his father, the drowned man—with arms open, eyes open, mouth open. . . . Grady stared and blinked, again something wrinkled up his face.

And when William Wallace came up it was in an agony from submersion, which seemed an agony of the blood and of the very heart, so woeful he looked. He was staring and glaring around in astonishment, as if a long time had gone by, away from the pale world where the brown light of the sun and the river and the little party watching him trembled before his eyes.

"What did you bring up?" somebody called—was it Virgil?

One of his hands was holding fast to a little green ribbon of plant, root and all. He was surprised, and let it go.

It was afternoon. The trees spread softly, the clouds hung wet and tinted. A buzzard turned a few slow wheels in the sky, and drifted upwards. The dogs promenaded the banks.

"It's time we ate fish," said Virgil.

On a wide sandbar on which seashells lay they dragged up the haul and built a fire.

Then for a long time among clouds of odors and smoke, all half-naked except Doc, they cooked and ate catfish. They ate until the Malones groaned and all the Doyles stretched out on their faces, though for long after, Sam and Robbie Bell sat up to their own little table on a cypress stump and ate on and on. Then they all were silent and still, and one by one fell asleep.

"There ain't a thing better than fish," muttered William Wallace. He lay stretched on his back in the glimmer and shade of trampled sand. His sunburned forehead and cheeks seemed to glow with fire. His eyelids fell. The shadow of a willow branch dipped and moved over him. "There is nothing in the world as good as . . . fish. The fish of Pearl River." Then slowly he smiled. He was asleep.

But it seemed almost at once that he was leaping up, and one by one up sat the others in their ring and looked at him, for it was impossible to stop and sleep by the river.

"You're feeling as good as you felt last night," said Virgil, setting his head on one side.

"The excursion is the same when you go looking for your sorrow as when you go looking for your joy," said Doc.

But William Wallace answered none of them anything, for he was leaping all over the place and all, over them and the feast and the bones of the feast, trampling the sand, up and down, and doing a dance so crazy that he would die next. He took a big catfish and hooked it to his belt buckle and went up and down so that they all hollered, and the tears of laughter streaming down his cheeks made him put his hand up, and the two days' growth of beard began to jump out, bright red.

But all of a sudden there was an even louder cry, something almost like a cheer, from everybody at once, and all pointed fingers moved from William Wallace to the river. In the center of three light-gold rings across the water was lifted first an old hoary head ("It has whiskers!" a voice cried) and then in an undulation loop after loop and hump after hump of a long dark body, until there were a dozen rings of ripples, one behind the other, stretching all across the river, like a necklace.

"The King of the Snakes!" cried all the Malones at once, in high tenor voices and leaning together.

"The King of the Snakes," intoned old Doc in his profound bass.

"He looked you in the eye."

William Wallace stared back at the King of the Snakes with all his might.

It was Brucie that darted forward, dangling his little thread with the pin tied to it, going toward the water.

"That's the King of the Snakes!" cried Grady, who always looked after him.

Then the snake went down.

The little boy stopped with one leg in the air, spun around on the other, and sank to the ground.

"Git up," Grady whispered. "It was just the King of the Snakes. He went off whistling. Git up. It wasn't a thing but the King of the Snakes."

Brucie's green eyes opened, his tongue darted out, and he sprang up; his feet were heavy, his head light, and he rose like a bubble coming to the surface.

Then thunder like a stone loosened and rolled down the bank.

They all stood unwilling on the sandbar, holding to the net. In the eastern sky were the familiar castles and the round towers to which they were used, gray, pink, and blue, growing darker and filling with thunder. Lightning flickered in the sun along their thick walls. But in the west the sun shone with such a violence that in an illumination like a long-prolonged glare of lightning the heavens looked black and white; all color left the world, the goldenness of everything was like a memory, and only heat, a kind of glamor and oppression, lay on their heads. The thick heavy trees on the other side of the river were brushed with mile-long streaks of silver, and a wind touched each man on the forehead. At the same time there was a long roll of thunder that began behind them, came up and down mountains and valleys of air, passed over their heads, and left them listening still. With a small, near noise a mockingbird followed it, the little white bars of its body flashing over the willow trees.

"We are here for a storm now," Virgil said. "We will have to stay till it's over."

They retreated a little, and hard drops fell in the leathery leaves at their shoulders and about their heads.

"Magnolia's the loudest tree there is in a storm," said Doc.

Then the light changed the water, until all about them the woods in the rising wind seemed to grow taller and blow inward together and suddenly turn dark. The rain struck heavily. A huge tail seemed to lash through the air and the river broke in a wound of silver. In silence the party crouched and stooped beside the trunk of the great tree, which in the push of the storm rose full of a fragrance and unyielding weight. Where they all stared, past their tree, was another tree, and beyond that another and another, all the way down the bank of the river, all towering and darkened in the storm.

"The outside world is full of endurance," said Doc. "Full of endurance."

Robbie Bell and Sam squatted down low and embraced each other from the start.

"Runs in our family to get struck by lightnin'," said Robbie Bell. "Lightnin' drawed a pitchfork right on our grandpappy's cheek, stayed till he died. Pappy got struck by some bolts of lightnin' and was dead three days, dead as that-there axe."

There was a succession of glares and crashes.

"This'n's goin' to be either me or you," said Sam. "Here come a little bug. If he go to the left, be me, and to the right, be you."

But at the next flare a big tree on the hill seemed to turn into fire before their eyes, every branch, twig, and leaf, and a purple cloud hung over it.

"Did you hear that crack?" asked Robbie Bell. "That were its bones."

"Why do you little niggers talk so much!" said Doc. "Nobody's profiting by this information."

"We always talks this much," said Sam, "but now everybody so quiet, they hears us."

The great tree, split and on fire, fell roaring to earth. Just at its moment of falling, a tree like it on the opposite bank split wide open and fell in two parts.

"Hope they ain't goin' to be no balls of fire come rollin' over the water and fry all the fishes with they scales on," said Robbie Bell.

The water in the river had turned purple and was filled with sudden currents and whirlpools. The little willow trees bent almost to its surface, bowing one after another down the bank and almost breaking under the storm. A great curtain of wet leaves was borne along before a blast of wind, and every human being was covered.

"Now us got scales," wailed Sam. "Us is the fishes."

"Hush up, little-old colored children," said Virgil. "This isn't the way to act when somebody takes you out to drag a river."

"Poor lady's-ghost, I bet it is scareder than us," said Sam.

"All I hoping is, us don't find her!" screamed Robbie Bell.

William Wallace bent down and knocked their heads together. After that they clung silently in each other's arms, the two black heads resting, with wind-filled cheeks and tight-closed eyes, one upon the other until the storm was over.

"Right over yonder is Dover," said Virgil. "We've come all the

way. William Wallace, you have walked on a sharp rock and cut
your foot open."

———————

III

In Dover it had rained, and the town looked somehow like new.
The wavy heat of late afternoon came down from the watertank and
fell over everything like shiny mosquito-netting. At the wide place
where the road was paved and patched with tar, it seemed newly
embedded with Coca-Cola tops. The old circus posters on the store
were nearly gone, only bits, the snowflakes of white horses, clinging
to its side. Morning-glory vines started almost visibly to grow over
the roofs and cling round the ties of the railroad track, where bluejays lighted on the rails, and umbrella chinaberry trees hung heavily
over the whole town, dripping intermittently upon the tin roofs.

Each with his counted fish on a string the members of the river-
dragging party walked through the town. They went toward the
town well, and there was Hazel's mother's house, but no sign of her
yet coming out. They all drank a dipper of the water, and still there
was not a soul on the street. Even the bench in front of the store was
empty, except for a little corn-shuck doll.

But something told them somebody had come, for after one
moment people began to look out of the store and out of the post-
office. All the bird dogs woke up to see the Doyle dogs and such a
large number of men and boys materialize suddenly with such a big
catch of fish, and they ran out barking. The Doyle dogs joyously
barked back. The bluejays flashed up and screeched above the
town, whipping through their tunnels in the chinaberry trees. In the
café a nickel clattered inside a music box and a love song began to
play. The whole town of Dover began to throb in its wood and tin,
like an old tired heart, when the men walked through once more,
coming around again and going down the street carrying the fish,
so drenched, exhausted, and muddy that no one could help but admire them.

William Wallace walked through the town as though he did not
see anybody or hear anything. Yet he carried his great string of fish
held high where it could be seen by all. Virgil came next, imitating
William Wallace exactly, then the modest Doyles crowded by the
Malones, who were holding up their alligator, tossing it in the air,

even, like a father tossing his child. Following behind and pointing authoritatively at the ones in front strolled Doc, with Sam and Robbie Bell still chanting in his wake. In and out of the whole little line Grady and Brucie jerked about. Grady, with his head ducked, and stiff as a rod, walked with a springy limp; it made him look forever angry and unapproachable. Under his breath he was whispering, "Sty, sty, git out of my eye, and git on somebody passin' by." He traveled on with narrowed shoulders, and kept his eye unerringly upon his little brother, wary and at the same time proud, as though he held a flying June-bug on a string. Brucie, making a twanging noise with his lips, had shot forth again, and he was darting rapidly everywhere at once, delighted and tantalized, running in circles around William Wallace, pointing to his fish. A frown of pleasure like the print of a bird's foot was stamped between his faint brows, and he trotted in some unknown realm of delight.

"Did you ever see so many fish?" said the people in Dover.

"How much are your fish, mister?"

"Would you sell your fish?"

"Is that all the fish in Pearl River?"

"How much you sell them all for? Everybody's?"

"Three dollars," said William Wallace suddenly, and loud.

The Malones were upon him and shouting, but it was too late.

And just as William Wallace was taking the money in his hand, Hazel's mother walked solidly out of her front door and saw it.

"You can't head her mother off," said Virgil. "Here she comes in full bloom."

But William Wallace turned his back on her, that was all, and on everybody, for that matter, and that was the breaking-up of the party.

Just as the sun went down, Doc climbed his back steps, sat in his chair on the back porch where he sat in the evenings, and lighted his pipe. William Wallace hung out the net and came back and Virgil was waiting for him, so they could say good evening to Doc.

"All in all," said Doc, when they came up, "I've never been on a better river-dragging, or seen better behavior. If it took catching catfish to move the Rock of Gibraltar, I believe this outfit could move it."

"Well, we didn't catch Hazel," said Virgil.

"What did you say?" asked Doc.

"He don't really pay attention," said Virgil. "I said, 'We didn't catch Hazel.'"

"Who says Hazel was to be caught?" asked Doc. "She wasn't in there. Girls don't like the water—remember that. Girls don't just haul off and go jumping in the river to get back at their husbands. They got other ways."

"Didn't you ever think she was in there?" asked William Wallace. "The whole time?"

"Nary once," said Doc.

"He's just smart," said Virgil, putting his hand on William Wallace's arm. "It's only because we didn't find her that he wasn't looking for her."

"I'm beholden to you for the net, anyway," said William Wallace.

"You're welcome to borry it again," said Doc.

On the way home Virgil kept saying, "Calm down, calm down, William Wallace."

"If he wasn't such an old skinny man I'd have wrung his neck for him," said William Wallace. "He had no business coming."

"He's too big for his britches," said Virgil. "Don't nobody know everything. And just because it's his net. Why does it have to be his net?"

"If it wasn't for being polite to old men, I'd have skinned him alive," said William Wallace.

"I guess he don't really know nothing about wives at all, his wife's so deaf," said Virgil.

"He don't know Hazel," said William Wallace. "I'm the only man alive knows Hazel: would she jump in the river or not, and I say she would. She jumped in because I was sitting on the back of my neck in a ditch singing, and that's just what she ought to done. Doc ain't got no right to say one word about it."

"Calm down, calm down, William Wallace," said Virgil.

"If it had been you that talked like that, I'd have broke every bone in your body," said William Wallace. "Just let you talk like that. You're my age and size."

"But I ain't going to talk like that," said Virgil. "What have I done the whole time but keep this river-dragging going straight and running even, without no hitches? You couldn't have drug the river a foot without me."

"What are you talking about! Without who!" cried William Wallace. "This wasn't your river-dragging! It wasn't your wife!" He jumped on Virgil and they began to fight.

"Let me up." Virgil was breathing heavily.

"Say it was my wife. Say it was my river-dragging."

"Yours!" Virgil was on the ground with William Wallace's hand putting dirt in his mouth.

"Say it was my net."

"Your net!"

"Get up then."

They walked along getting their breath, and smelling the honeysuckle in the evening. On a hill William Wallace looked down, and at the same time there went drifting by the sweet sounds of music outdoors. They were having the Sacred Harp Sing on the grounds of an old white church glimmering there at the crossroads, far below. He stared away as if he saw it minutely, as if he could see a lady in white take a flowered cover off the organ, which was set on a little slant in the shade, dust the keys, and start to pump and play. . . . He smiled faintly, as he would at his mother, and at Hazel, and at the singing women in his life, now all one young girl standing up to sing under the trees the oldest and longest ballads there were.

Virgil told him good night and went into his own house and the door shut on him.

When he got to his own house, William Wallace saw to his surprise that it had not rained at all. But there, curved over the roof, was something he had never seen before as long as he could remember, a rainbow at night. In the light of the moon, which had risen again, it looked small and of gauzy material, like a lady's summer dress, a faint veil through which the stars showed.

He went up on the porch and in at the door, and all exhausted he had walked through the front room and through the kitchen when he heard his name called. After a moment, he smiled, as if no matter what he might have hoped for in his wildest heart, it was better than that to hear his name called out in the house. The voice came out of the bedroom.

"What do you want?" he yelled, standing stock-still.

Then she opened the bedroom door with the old complaining creak, and there she stood. She was not changed a bit.

"How do you feel?" he said.

"I feel pretty good. Not too good," Hazel said, looking mysterious.

"I cut my foot," said William Wallace, taking his shoe off so she could see the blood.

"How in the world did you do that?" she cried, with a step back.

"Dragging the river. But it don't hurt any longer."

"You ought to have been more careful," she said. "Supper's ready and I wondered if you would ever come home, or if it would be last night all over again. Go and make yourself fit to be seen," she said, and ran away from him.

After supper they sat on the front steps a while.

"Where were you this morning when I came in?" asked William Wallace when they were ready to go in the house.

"I was hiding," she said. "I was still writing on the letter. And then you tore it up."

"Did you watch me when I was reading it?"

"Yes, and you could have put out your hand and touched me, I was so close."

But he bit his lip, and gave her a little tap and slap, and then turned her up and spanked her.

"Do you think you will do it again?" he asked.

"I'll tell my mother on you for this!"

"Will you do it again?"

"No!" she cried.

"Then pick yourself up off my knee."

It was just as if he had chased her and captured her again. She lay smiling in the crook of his arm. It was the same as any other chase in the end.

"I will do it again if I get ready," she said. "Next time will be different, too."

Then she was ready to go in, and rose up and looked out from the top step, out across their yard where the China tree was and beyond, into the dark fields where the lightning-bugs flickered away. He climbed to his feet too and stood beside her, with the frown on his face, trying to look where she looked. And after a few minutes she took him by the hand and led him into the house, smiling as if she were smiling down on him.

Angel
Levine

BERNARD MALAMUD

As catastrophe piles on catastrophe in the opening paragraph, well beyond the conventional demands of either a somber naturalistic tale or a poignantly amusing Jewish tale of suffering, one suspects parody at work or some comparably covert aim. As it turns out, Malamud has various aims in the story, some of which are slow to appear. If these aims seem imperfectly reconciled, or seem here and there to jostle each other, that impression has its appropriateness: the coherence of "Angel Levine" is threatened by whimsy throughout. Whatever seriousness is promised by Malamud's imitation of urban Negro and Yiddish speech rhythms, by Manischevitz's parabolic revolt against God, or by the mysteries of Fanny's recovery from ill health, is less dissipated than extended into the sphere of comic fantasy by the startling presence of Alexander Levine, the black angel. Angel Levine gives serious point to the social realism of the story and to the religious parable it lightly suggests; but the point on which this particular angel spins changes its location too often for us to inspect it closely.

Manischevitz, a tailor, in his fifty-first year suffered many reverses and indignities. Previously a man of comfortable means, he overnight lost all he had, when his establishment caught fire and, after a metal container of cleaning fluid exploded, burned to the ground. Although Manischevitz was insured against fire, damage suits by two customers who had been hurt in the flames deprived him of every penny he had collected. At almost the same time, his son, of much promise, was killed in the war, and his daughter, without so much as a word of warning, married a lout and disappeared with him as off the face of the earth. Thereafter Manischevitz was victimized by excruciating backaches and found himself unable to work even as a presser—the only kind of work available to him—for more than an hour or two daily, because beyond that the pain from standing became maddening. His Fanny, a good wife and mother, who had taken in washing and sewing, began before his eyes to waste away. Suffering shortness of breath, she at last became seriously ill and took to her bed. The doctor, a former customer of Manischevitz, who out of pity treated them, at first had difficulty diagnosing her ailment but later put it down as hardening of the arteries at an advanced stage. He took Manischevitz aside, prescribed complete rest for her, and in whispers gave him to know there was little hope.

Throughout his trials Manischevitz had remained somewhat stoic, almost unbelieving that all this had descended upon his head, as if it were happening, let us say, to an acquaintance or some distant relative; it was in sheer quantity of woe incomprehensible. It was also ridiculous, unjust, and because he had always been a religious man, it was in a way an affront to God. Manischevitz believed this in all his suffering. When his burden had grown too crushingly heavy to be borne he prayed in his chair with shut hollow eyes: "My dear God, sweetheart, did I deserve that this should happen to me?" Then recognizing the worthlessness of it, he put aside the complaint and prayed humbly for assistance: "Give Fanny back her health, and to me for myself that I shouldn't feel pain in every step.

Help now or tomorrow is too late. This I don't have to tell you." And Manischevitz wept.

Manischevitz's flat, which he had moved into after the disastrous fire, was a meager one, furnished with a few sticks of chairs, a table, and bed, in one of the poorer sections of the city. There were three rooms: a small, poorly-papered living room; an apology for a kitchen, with a wooden icebox; and the comparatively large bedroom where Fanny lay in a sagging secondhand bed, gasping for breath. The bedroom was the warmest room of the house and it was here, after his outburst to God, that Manischevitz, by the light of two small bulbs overhead, sat reading his Jewish newspaper. He was not truly reading, because his thoughts were everywhere; however the print offered a convenient resting place for his eyes, and a word or two, when he permitted himself to comprehend them, had the momentary effect of helping him forget his troubles. After a short while he discovered, to his surprise, that he was actively scanning the news, searching for an item of great interest to him. Exactly what he thought he would read he couldn't say—until he realized, with some astonishment, that he was expecting to discover something about himself. Manischevitz put his paper down and looked up with the distinct impression that someone had entered the apartment, though he could not remember having heard the sound of the door opening. He looked around: the room was very still, Fanny sleeping, for once, quietly. Half-frightened, he watched her until he was satisfied she wasn't dead; then, still disturbed by the thought of an unannounced visitor, he stumbled into the living room and there had the shock of his life, for at the table sat a Negro reading a newspaper he had folded up to fit into one hand.

"What do you want here?" Manischevitz asked in fright.

The Negro put down the paper and glanced up with a gentle expression. "Good evening." He seemed not to be sure of himself, as if he had got into the wrong house. He was a large man, bonily built, with a heavy head covered by a hard derby, which he made no attempt to remove. His eyes seemed sad, but his lips, above which he wore a slight mustache, sought to smile; he was not otherwise prepossessing. The cuffs of his sleeves, Manischevitz noted, were frayed to the lining and the dark suit was badly fitted. He had very large feet. Recovering from his fright, Manischevitz guessed he had left the door open and was being visited by a case worker from the Welfare Department—some came at night—for he had recently applied for relief. Therefore he lowered himself into a chair opposite the Negro, trying, before the man's uncertain smile, to feel comfortable. The former tailor sat stiffly but patiently at the table, waiting for the investigator to take out his pad and pencil and begin asking questions; but before long he became convinced the man intended to do nothing of the sort.

"Who are you?" Manischevitz at last asked uneasily.

"If I may, insofar as one is able to, identify myself, I bear the name of Alexander Levine."

In spite of all his troubles Manischevitz felt a smile growing on his lips. "You said Levine?" he politely inquired.

The Negro nodded. "That is exactly right."

Carrying the jest farther, Manischevitz asked, "You are maybe Jewish?"

"All my life I was, willingly."

The tailor hesitated. He had heard of black Jews but had never met one. It gave an unusual sensation.

Recognizing in afterthought something odd about the tense of Levine's remark, he said doubtfully, "You ain't Jewish anymore?"

Levine at this point removed his hat, revealing a very white part in his black hair, but quickly replaced it. He replied, "I have recently been disincarnated into an angel. As such, I offer you my humble assistance, if to offer is within my province and ability—in the best sense." He lowered his eyes in apology. "Which calls for added explanation: I am what I am granted to be, and at present the completion is in the future."

"What kind of angel is this?" Manischevitz gravely asked.

"A bona fide angel of God, within prescribed limitations," answered Levine, "not to be confused with the members of any particular sect, order, or organization here on earth operating under a similar name."

Manischevitz was thoroughly disturbed. He had been expecting something but not this. What sort of mockery was it—provided Levine was an angel—of a faithful servant who had from childhood lived in the synagogues, always concerned with the word of God?

To test Levine he asked, "Then where are your wings?"

The Negro blushed as well as he was able. Manischevitz understood this from his changed expression. "Under certain circumstances we lose privileges and prerogatives upon returning to earth, no matter for what purpose, or endeavoring to assist whosoever."

"So tell me," Manischevitz said triumphantly, "how did you get here?"

"I was transmitted."

Still troubled, the tailor said, "If you are a Jew, say the blessing for bread."

Levine recited it in sonorous Hebrew.

Although moved by the familiar words Manischevitz still felt doubt that he was dealing with an angel.

"If you are an angel," he demanded somewhat angrily, "give me the proof."

Levine wet his lips. "Frankly, I cannot perform either miracles or near miracles, due to the fact that I am in a condition of probation. How long that will persist or even consist, I admit, depends on the outcome."

Manischevitz racked his brains for some means of causing Levine positively to reveal his true identity, when the Negro spoke again:

"It was given me to understand that both your wife and you require assistance of a salubrious nature?"

The tailor could not rid himself of the feeling that he was the butt of a jokester. Is this what a Jewish angel looks like? he asked himself. This I am not convinced.

He asked a last question. "So if God sends to me an angel, why a black? Why not a white that there are so many of them?"

"It was my turn to go next," Levine explained.

Manischevitz could not be persuaded. "I think you are a faker."

Levine slowly rose. His eyes showed disappointment and worry. "Mr. Manischevitz," he said tonelessly, "if you should desire me to be of assistance to you any time in the near future, or possibly before, I can be found"—he glanced at his fingernails—"in Harlem."

He was by then gone.

The next day Manischevitz felt some relief from his backache and was able to work four hours at pressing. The day after, he put in six hours; and the third day four again. Fanny sat up a little and asked for some halvah to suck. But on the fourth day the stabbing, breaking ache afflicted his back, and Fanny again lay supine, breathing with blue-lipped difficulty.

Manischevitz was profoundly disappointed at the return of his active pain and suffering. He had hoped for a longer interval of easement, long enough to have some thought other than of himself and his troubles. Day by day, hour by hour, minute after minute, he lived in pain, pain his only memory, questioning the necessity of it, inveighing against it, also, though with affection, against God. Why *so much*, Gottenyu? If He wanted to teach His servant a lesson for some reason, some cause—the nature of His nature—to teach him, say, for reasons of his weakness, his pride, perhaps, during his years of prosperity, his frequent neglect of God—to give him a little lesson, why then any of the tragedies that had happened to him, any *one* would have sufficed to chasten him. But *all together*—the loss of both his children, his means of livelihood, Fanny's health and his—that was too much to ask one frail-boned man to endure. Who, after all, was Manischevitz that he had been given so much to suffer? A tailor. Certainly not a man of talent. Upon him suffering was largely wasted. It went nowhere, into nothing: into more suffering. His pain did not earn him bread, nor fill the cracks in the wall, nor lift, in the middle of the night, the kitchen table; only lay upon him, sleepless, so sharply, oppressively, that he could many times have cried out yet not heard himself through this thickness of misery.

In this mood he gave no thought to Mr. Alexander Levine, but at moments when the pain waivered, slightly diminishing, he sometimes wondered if he had been mistaken to dismiss him. A black Jew and angel to boot—very hard to believe, but suppose he *had* been sent to succor him, and he, Manischevitz, was in his blindness too blind to comprehend? It was this thought that put him on the knife-point of agony.

Therefore the tailor, after much self-questioning and continuing doubt, decided he would seek the self-styled angel in Harlem. Of course he had great difficulty, because he had not asked for specific directions, and movement was tedious to him. The subway took him to 116th Street, and from there he wandered in the dark world. It was vast and its lights lit nothing. Everywhere were shadows, often moving. Manischevitz hobbled along with the aid of a cane, and not knowing where to seek in the blackened tenement buildings, looked fruitlessly through store windows. In the stores he saw people and *everybody* was black. It was an amazing thing to observe. When he was too tired, too unhappy to go farther, Manischevitz stopped in front of a tailor's store. Out of familiarity with the appearance of it, with some sadness he entered. The tailor, an old skinny Negro with a mop of woolly gray hair, was sitting cross-legged on his workbench, sewing a pair of full-dress pants that had a razor slit all the way down the seat.

"You'll excuse me, please, gentleman," said Manischevitz, admiring the tailor's deft, thimbled fingerwork, "but you know maybe somebody by the name Alexander Levine?"

The tailor, who Manischevitz thought, seemed a little antagonistic to him, scratched his scalp.

"Cain't say I ever heared dat name."

"Alex-ander Lev-ine," Manischevitz repeated it.

The man shook his head. "Cain't say I heared."

About to depart, Manischevitz remembered to say: "He is an angel, maybe."

"Oh *him*," said the tailor clucking. "He hang out in dat honky tonk down here a ways." He pointed with his skinny finger and returned to the pants.

Manischevitz crossed the street against a red light and was almost run down by a taxi. On the block after the next, the sixth store from the corner was a cabaret, and the name in sparkling lights was Bella's. Ashamed to go in, Manischevitz gazed through the neon-lit window, and when the dancing couples had parted and drifted away, he discovered at a table on the side, towards the rear, Levine.

He was sitting alone, a cigarette butt hanging from the corner of his mouth, playing solitaire with a dirty pack of cards, and Manischevitz felt a touch of pity for him, for Levine had deteriorated in appearance. His derby was dented and had a gray smudge on the side. His ill-fitting suit was shabbier, as if he had been sleeping in it. His shoes and trouser cuffs were muddy, and his face was covered with an impenetrable stubble the color of licorice. Manischevitz, though deeply disappointed, was about to enter, when a big-breasted Negress in a purple evening gown appeared before Levine's table, and with much laughter through many white teeth, broke into a vigorous shimmy. Levine looked straight at Manischevitz with a haunted expression, but the tailor was too paralyzed to move or acknowledge it. As Bella's gyrations continued, Levine rose, his eyes lit in excitement. She embraced him with vigor, both his hands clasped around her big restless buttocks and they tangoed together across the floor, loudly applauded by the noisy customers. She seemed to have lifted Levine off his feet and his large shoes hung limp as they danced. They slid past the windows where Manischevitz, white-faced, stood staring in. Levine winked slyly and the tailor left for home.

. . .

Fanny lay at death's door. Through shrunken lips she muttered concerning her childhood, the sorrows of the marriage bed, the loss of her children, yet wept to live. Manischevitz tried not to listen, but even without ears he would have heard. It was not a gift. The doctor panted up the stairs, a broad but bland, unshaven man (it was Sunday), and soon shook his head. A day at most, or two. He left at once, not without pity, to spare himself Manischevitz's multiplied sorrow; the man who never stopped hurting. He would someday get him into a public home.

Manischevitz visited a synagogue and there spoke to God, but God had absented himself. The tailor searched his heart and found no hope. When she died he would live dead. He considered taking his life although he knew he wouldn't. Yet it was something to consider. Considering, you existed. He railed against God— Can you love a rock, a broom, an emptiness? Baring his chest, he smote the naked bones, cursing himself for having believed.

Asleep in a chair that afternoon, he dreamed of Levine. He was standing before a faded mirror, preening small decaying opalescent wings. "This means," mumbled Manischevitz, as he broke out of sleep, "that it is possible he could be an angel." Begging a neighbor lady to look in on Fanny and occasionally wet her lips with a few drops of water, he drew on his thin coat, gripped his walking stick, exchanged some pennies for a subway token, and rode to Harlem. He knew this act was the last desperate one of his woe: to go without belief, seeking a black magician to restore his wife to invalidism. Yet if there was no choice, he did at least what was chosen.

He hobbled to Bella's but the place had changed hands. It was now, as he breathed, a synagogue in a store. In the front, towards him, were several rows of empty wooden benches. In the rear stood the Ark, its portals of rough wood covered with rainbows of sequins; under it a long table on which lay the sacred scroll unrolled, illuminated by the dim light from a bulb on a chain overhead. Around the table, as if frozen to it and the scroll, which they all touched with their fingers, sat four Negroes wearing skullcaps. Now as they read the Holy Word, Manischevitz could, through the plate glass window, hear the singsong chant of their voices. One of them was old, with a gray beard. One was bubble-eyed. One was humpbacked. The fourth was a boy, no older than thirteen. Their heads moved in rhythmic swaying. Touched by this sight from his childhood and youth, Manischevitz entered and stood silent in the rear.

"Neshoma," said bubble eyes, pointing to the word with a stubby finger. "Now what dat mean?"

"That's the word that means soul," said the boy. He wore glasses.

"Let's git on wid de commentary," said the old man.

"Ain't necessary," said the humpback. "Souls is immaterial substance. That's all. The soul is derived in that manner. The immateriality is derived from the substance, and they both, causally an' otherwise, derived from the soul. There can be no higher."

"That's the highest."

"Over de top."

"Wait a minute," said bubble eyes. "I don't see what is dat immaterial substance. How come de one gits hitched up to de odder?" He addressed the humpback.

"Ask me something hard. Because it is substanceless immateriality. It couldn't be closer together, like all the parts of the body under one skin—closer."

"Hear now," said the old man.

"All you done is switched de words."

"It's the primum mobile, the substanceless substance from which comes all things that were incepted in the idea—you, me and everything and body else."

"Now how did all dat happen? Make it sound simple."

"It de speerit," said the old man. "On de face of de water moved de speerit. An' dat was good. It say so in de Book. From de speerit ariz de man."

"But now listen here. How come it become substance if it all de time a spirit?"

"God alone done dat."

"Holy! Holy! Praise His Name."

"But has dis spirit got some kind of a shade or color?" asked bubble eyes, deadpan.

"Man of course not. A spirit is a spirit."

"Then how come we is colored?" he said with a triumphant glare.

"Ain't got nothing to do wid dat."

"I still like to know."

"God put the spirit in all things," answered the boy. "He put it in the green leaves and the yellow flowers. He put it with the gold in the fishes and the blue in the sky. That's how come it came to us."

"Amen."

"Praise Lawd and utter loud His speechless name."

"Blow de bugle till it bust the sky."

They fell silent, intent upon the next word. Manischevitz approached them.

"You'll excuse me," he said. "I am looking for Alexander Levine. You know him maybe?"

"That's the angel," said the boy.

"Oh, *him*," snuffed bubble eyes.

"You'll find him at Bella's. It's the establishment right across the street," the humpback said.

Manischevitz said he was sorry that he could not stay, thanked them, and limped across the street. It was already night. The city was dark and he could barely find his way.

But Bella's was bursting with the blues. Through the window Manischevitz recognized the dancing crowd and among them sought Levine. He was sitting loose-lipped at Bella's side table. They were tippling from an almost empty whiskey fifth. Levine had shed his old clothes, wore a shiny new checkered suit, pearl-gray derby, cigar, and big, two-tone button shoes. To the tailor's dismay, a drunken look had settled upon his formerly dignified face. He leaned toward Bella, tickled her ear lobe with his pinky, while whispering words that sent her into gales of raucous laughter. She fondled his knee.

Manischevitz, girding himself, pushed open the door and was not welcomed.

"This place reserved."

"Beat it, pale puss."

"Exit, Yankel, Semitic trash."

But he moved towards the table where Levine sat, the crowd breaking before him as he hobbled forward.

"Mr. Levine," he spoke in a trembly voice. "Is here Manischevitz."

Levine glared blearily. "Speak yo' piece, son."

Manischevitz shuddered. His back plagued him. Cold tremors tormented his crooked legs. He looked around, everybody was all ears.

"You'll excuse me. I would like to talk to you in a private place."

"Speak, Ah is a private pusson."

Bella laughed piercingly. "Stop it, boy, you killin' me."

Manischevitz, no end disturbed, considered fleeing but Levine addressed him:

"Kindly state the pu'pose of yo' communication with yo's truly."

The tailor wet cracked lips. "You are Jewish. This I am sure."

Levine rose, nostrils flaring. "Anythin' else yo' got to say?"

Manischevitz's tongue lay like stone.

"Speak now or fo'ever hold off."

Tears blinded the tailor's eyes. Was ever man so tried? Should he say he believed a half-drunken Negro to be an angel?

The silence slowly petrified.

Manischevitz was recalling scenes of his youth as a wheel in his mind whirred: believe, do not, yes, no, yes, no. The pointer pointed to yes, to between yes and no, to no, no it was yes. He sighed. It moved but one had still to make a choice.

"I think you are an angel from God." He said it in a broken voice, thinking, If you said it it was said. If you believed it you must say it. If you believed, you believed.

The hush broke. Everybody talked but the music began and they went on dancing. Bella, grown bored, picked up the cards and dealt herself a hand.

Levine burst into tears. "How you have humiliated me."

Manischevitz apologized.

"Wait'll I freshen up." Levine went to the men's room and returned in his old clothes.

No one said goodbye as they left.

They rode to the flat via subway. As they walked up the stairs Manischevitz pointed with his cane at his door.

"That's all been taken care of," Levine said. "You best go in while I take off."

Disappointed that it was so soon over but torn by curiosity, Manischevitz followed the angel up three flights to the roof. When he got there the door was already padlocked.

Luckily he could see through a small broken window. He heard an odd noise, as though of a whirring of wings, and when he strained for a wider view, could have sworn he saw a dark figure borne aloft on a pair of magnificent black wings.

A feather drifted down. Manischevitz gasped as it turned white, but it was only snowing.

He rushed downstairs. In the flat Fanny wielded a dust mop under the bed and then upon the cobwebs on the wall.

"A wonderful thing, Fanny," Manischevitz said. "Believe me, there are Jews everywhere."

The River

FLANNERY O'CONNOR

As the child Harry first stands by the river, the topography of this story is given in a succession of striking images: "Across the river there was a low red and gold grove of sassafras with hills of dark blue trees behind it and an occasional pine jutting over the skyline. Behind, in the distance, the city rose like a cluster of warts on the side of the mountain." This landscape is social as well as physical, moral as well as very nearly religious. The story moves and descends complexly from the middle-class Ashfield apartment high in the city to the Connin shack in the low-lying countryside near the river. The two poles of this movement are fixed graphically in the watercolor abstraction hanging in the Ashfield apartment and the contrasting pictures of human individuals and of Jesus on the walls of Mrs. Connin's shack. Young Harry's descent is from the loveless Ashfield family to the Connin family, in which, despite its vulgarity and witlessness, human beings are at least valued and cared for. The boy goes from a self-indulgent and irreverent middle class, where everything is a joke, to a gaunt and credulous lower class, where nothing is fundamentally laughable. If the comedy of this unusual story turns at last into its opposite, Harry's downward path takes him also toward other, less terrifying conversions.

The child stood glum and limp in the middle of the dark living room while his father pulled him into a plaid coat. His right arm was hung in the sleeve but the father buttoned the coat anyway and pushed him forward toward a pale spotted hand that stuck through the half-open door.

"He ain't fixed right," a loud voice said from the hall.

"Well then for Christ's sake fix him," the father muttered. "It's six o'clock in the morning." He was in his bathrobe and barefooted. When he got the child to the door and tried to shut it, he found her looming in it, a speckled skeleton in a long pea-green coat and felt helmet.

"And his and my carfare," she said. "It'll be twicet we have to ride the car."

He went in the bedroom again to get the money and when he came back, she and the boy were both standing in the middle of the room. She was taking stock. "I couldn't smell those dead cigarette butts long if I was ever to come sit with you," she said, shaking him down in his coat.

"Here's the change," the father said. He went to the door and opened it wide and waited.

After she had counted the money she slipped it somewhere inside her coat and walked over to a watercolor hanging near the phonograph. "I know what time it is," she said, peering closely at the black lines crossing into broken planes of violent color. "I ought to. My shift goes on at 10 P.M. and don't get off till 5 and it takes me one hour to ride the Vine Street car."

"Oh, I see," he said; "well, we'll expect him back tonight, about eight or nine?"

"Maybe later," she said. "We're going to the river to a healing. This particular preacher don't get around this way often. I wouldn't have paid for that," she said, nodding at the painting, "I would have drew it myself."

"All right, Mrs. Connin, we'll see you then," he said, drumming on the door.

A toneless voice called from the bedroom, "Bring me an icepack."

"Too bad his mamma's sick," Mrs. Connin said. "What's her trouble?"

"We don't know," he muttered.

"We'll ask the preacher to pray for her. He's healed a lot of folks. The Reverend Bevel Summers. Maybe she ought to see him sometime."

"Maybe so," he said. "We'll see you tonight," and he disappeared into the bedroom and left them to go.

The little boy stared at her silently, his nose and eyes running. He was four or five. He had a long face and bulging chin and half-shut eyes set far apart. He seemed mute and patient, like an old sheep waiting to be let out.

"You'll like this preacher," she said. "The Reverend Bevel Summers. You ought to hear him sing."

The bedroom door opened suddenly and the father stuck his head out and said, "Good-by, old man. Have a good time."

"Good-by," the little boy said and jumped as if he had been shot.

Mrs. Connin gave the watercolor another look. Then they went out into the hall and rang for the elevator. "I wouldn't have drew it," she said.

Outside the gray morning was blocked off on either side by the unlit empty buildings. "It's going to fair up later," she said, "but this is the last time we'll be able to have any preaching at the river this year. Wipe your nose, Sugar Boy."

He began rubbing his sleeve across it but she stopped him. "That ain't nice," she said. "Where's your handkerchief?"

He put his hands in his pockets and pretended to look for it while she waited. "Some people don't care how they send one off," she murmured to her reflection in the coffee shop window. "You pervide." She took a red and blue flowered handkerchief out of her pocket and stooped down and began to work on his nose. "Now blow," she said and he blew. "You can borry it. Put it in your pocket."

He folded it up and put it in his pocket carefully and they walked on to the corner and leaned against the side of a closed drugstore to wait for the car. Mrs. Connin turned up her coat collar so that it met her hat in the back. Her eyelids began to droop and she looked as if she might go to sleep against the wall. The little boy put a slight pressure on her hand.

"What's your name?" she asked in a drowsy voice. "I don't know but only your last name. I should have found out your first name."

His name was Harry Ashfield and he had never thought at any time before of changing it. "Bevel," he said.

Mrs. Connin raised herself from the wall. "Why ain't that a coincident!" she said. "I told you that's the name of this preacher!"

"Bevel," he repeated.

She stood looking down at him as if he had become a marvel to her. "I'll have to see you meet him today," she said. "He's no ordinary preacher. He's a healer. He couldn't do nothing for Mr. Connin though. Mr. Connin didn't have the faith but he said he would try anything once. He had this griping in his gut."

The trolley appeared as a yellow spot at the end of the deserted street.

"He's gone to the government hospital now," she said, "and they taken one-third of his stomach. I tell him he better thank Jesus for what he's got left but he says he ain't thanking nobody. Well I declare," she murmured, "Bevel!"

They walked out to the tracks to wait. "Will he heal me?" Bevel asked.

"What you got?"

"I'm hungry," he decided finally.

"Didn't you have your breakfast?"

"I didn't have time to be hungry yet then," he said.

"Well when we get home we'll both have us something," she said. "I'm ready myself."

They got on the car and sat down a few seats behind the driver and Mrs. Connin took Bevel on her knees. "Now you be a good boy," she said, "and let me get some sleep. Just don't get off my lap." She lay her head back and as he watched, gradually her eyes closed and her mouth fell open to show a few long scattered teeth, some gold and some darker than her face; she began to whistle and blow like a musical skeleton. There was no one in the car but themselves and the driver and when he saw she was asleep, he took out the flowered handkerchief and unfolded it and examined it carefully. Then he folded it up again and unzipped a place in the innerlining of his coat and hid it in there and shortly he went to sleep himself.

Her house was a half-mile from the end of the car line, set back a little from the road. It was tan paper brick with a porch across the front of it and a tin top. On the porch there were three little boys of different sizes with identical speckled faces and one tall girl who had her hair up in so many aluminum curlers that it glared like the roof. The three boys followed them inside and closed in on Bevel. They looked at him silently, not smiling.

"That's Bevel," Mrs. Connin said, taking off her coat. "It's a coincident he's named the same as the preacher. These boys are J. C., Spivey, and Sinclair, and that's Sarah Mildred on the porch. Take off that coat and hang it on the bed post, Bevel."

The three boys watched him while he unbuttoned the coat and took it off. Then they watched him hang it on the bed post and then they stood, watching the coat. They turned abruptly and went out the door and had a conference on the porch.

Bevel stood looking around him at the room. It was part kitchen and part bedroom. The entire house was two rooms and two porches. Close to his foot the tail of a light-colored dog moved up and down between two floor boards as he scratched his back on the underside of the house. Bevel jumped on it but the hound was experienced and had already withdrawn when his feet hit the spot.

The walls were filled with pictures and calendars. There were two round photographs of an old man and woman with collapsed mouths and another picture of a man whose eyebrows dashed out of two bushes of hair and clashed in a heap on the bridge of his nose; the rest of his face stuck out like a bare cliff to fall from. "That's Mr. Connin," Mrs. Connin said, standing back from the stove for a second to admire the face with him, "but it don't favor him any more." Bevel turned from Mr. Connin to a colored picture over the bed of a man wearing a white sheet. He had long hair and a gold circle around his head and he was sawing on a board while some children stood watching him. He was going to ask who that was when the three boys came in again and motioned for him to follow them. He thought of crawling under the bed and hanging onto one of the legs but the three boys only stood there, speckled and silent, waiting, and after a second he followed them at a little distance out on the porch and around the corner of the house. They started off through a field of rough yellow weeds to the hog pen, a five-foot boarded square full of shoats, which they intended to ease him over into. When they reached it, they turned and waited silently, leaning against the side.

He was coming very slowly, deliberately bumping his feet together as if he had trouble walking. Once he had been beaten up in the park by some strange boys when his sitter forgot him, but he hadn't known anything was going to happen that time until it was over. He began to smell a strong odor of garbage and to hear the noises of a wild animal. He stopped a few feet from the pen and waited, pale but dogged.

The three boys didn't move. Something seemed to have happened to them. They stared over his head as if they saw something coming behind him but he was afraid to turn his own head and look. Their speckles were pale and their eyes were still and gray as glass. Only their ears twitched slightly. Nothing happened. Finally, the one in the middle said, "She'd kill us," and turned, dejected and hacked, and climbed up on the pen and hung over, staring in.

Bevel sat down on the ground, dazed with relief, and grinned up at them.

The one sitting on the pen glanced at him severely. "Hey you," he said after a second, "if you can't climb up and see these pigs you can lift that bottom board off and look in thataway." He appeared to offer this as a kindness.

Bevel had never seen a real pig but he had seen a pig in a book and knew that they were small fat pink animals with curly tails and round grinning faces and bow ties. He leaned forward and pulled eagerly at the board.

"Pull harder," the littlest boy said. "It's nice and rotten. Just lift out thet nail."

He eased a long reddish nail out of the soft wood.

"Now you can lift up the board and put your face to the . . ." a quiet voice began.

He had already done it and another face, gray, wet and sour, was pushing into his, knocking him down and back as it scraped out under the plank. Something snorted over him and charged back again, rolling him over and pushing him up from behind and then sending him forward, screaming through the yellow field, while it bounded behind.

The three Connins watched from where they were. The one sitting on the pen held the loose board back with his dangling foot. Their stern faces didn't brighten any but they seemed to become less taut, as if some great need had been partly satisfied. "Maw ain't going to like him lettin out thet hawg," the smallest one said.

Mrs. Connin was on the back porch and caught Bevel up as he reached the steps. The hog ran under the house and subsided, panting, but the child screamed for five minutes. When she had finally calmed him down, she gave him his breakfast and let him sit on her lap while he ate it. The shoat climbed the two steps onto the back porch and stood outside the screen door, looking in with his head lowered sullenly. He was long-legged and humpbacked and part of one of his ears had been bitten off.

"Git away!" Mrs. Connin shouted. "That one yonder favors Mr. Paradise that has the gas station," she said. "You'll see him today at the healing. He's got the cancer over his ear. He always comes to show he ain't been healed."

The shoat stood squinting a few seconds longer and then moved off slowly. "I don't want to see him," Bevel said.

They walked to the river, Mrs. Connin in front with him and the three boys strung out behind and Sarah Mildred, the tall girl, at the end to holler if one of them ran out on the road. They looked like the skeleton of an old boat with two pointed ends, sailing slowly on the edge of the highway. The white Sunday sun followed at a little distance, climbing fast through a scum of gray cloud as if it meant to overtake them. Bevel walked on the outside edge, holding Mrs. Connin's hand and looking down into the orange and purple gulley that dropped off from the concrete.

It occurred to him that he was lucky this time that they had found Mrs. Connin who would take you away for the day instead of an ordinary sitter who only sat where you lived or went to the park. You found out more when you left where you lived. He had found out already this morning that he had been made by a carpenter named Jesus Christ. Before he had thought it had been a doctor named Sladewall, a fat man with a yellow mustache who gave him shots and thought his name was Herbert, but this must have been a joke. They joked a lot where he lived. If he had thought about it before, he would have thought Jesus Christ was a word like "oh" or "damm" or "God," or maybe somebody who had cheated them out of something sometime. When he had asked Mrs. Connin who the man in the sheet in the picture over her bed was, she had looked at him a while with her mouth open. Then she had said, "That's Jesus," and she had kept on looking at him.

In a few minutes she had got up and got a book out of the other room. "See here," she said, turning over the cover, "this belonged to my great grandmamma. I wouldn't part with it for nothing on earth." She ran her finger under some brown writing on a spotted page. "Emma Stevens Oakley, 1832," she said. "Ain't that something to have? And every word of it the gospel truth." She turned the next page and read him the name: "The Life of Jesus Christ for Readers Under Twelve." Then she read him the book.

It was a small book, pale brown on the outside with gold edges and a smell like old putty. It was full of pictures, one of the carpenter driving a crowd of pigs out of a man. They were real pigs, gray and sour-looking, and Mrs. Connin said Jesus had driven them all out of this one man. When she finished reading, she let him sit on the floor and look at the pictures again.

Just before they left for the healing, he had managed to get the book inside his innerlining without her seeing him. Now it made his coat hang down a little farther on one side than the other. His mind was dreamy and serene as they walked along and when they turned off the highway onto a long red clay road winding between banks of honeysuckle, he began to make wild leaps and pull forward on her hand as if he wanted to dash off and snatch the sun which was rolling away ahead of them now.

They walked on the dirt road for a while and then they crossed a field stippled with purple weeds and entered the shadows of a wood where the ground was covered with thick pine needles. He had never been in woods before and he walked carefully, looking from side to side as if he were entering a strange country. They moved along a bridle path that twisted downhill through crackling red leaves, and once, catching at a branch to keep himself from slipping, he looked into two frozen green-gold eyes enclosed in the darkness of a tree hole. At the bottom of the hill, the woods opened suddenly onto a pasture dotted here and there with black and white cows and sloping down, tier after tier, to a broad orange stream where the reflection of the sun was set like a diamond.

There were people standing on the near bank in a group, singing. Long tables were set up behind them and a few cars and trucks were parked in a road that came up by the river. They crossed the pasture, hurrying, because Mrs. Connin, using her hand for a shed over her eyes, saw the preacher already standing out in the water. She dropped her basket on one of the tables and pushed the three boys in front of her into the knot of people so that they wouldn't linger by the food. She kept Bevel by the hand and eased her way up to the front.

The preacher was standing about ten feet out in the stream where the water came up to his knees. He was a tall youth in khaki trousers that he had rolled up higher than the water. He had on a blue shirt and a red scarf around his neck but no hat and his light-colored hair was cut in sideburns that curved into the hollows of his cheeks. His face was all bone and red light reflected from the river. He looked as if he might have been nineteen years old. He was singing in a high twangy voice, above the singing on the bank, and he kept his hands behind him and his head tilted back.

He ended the hymn on a high note and stood silent, looking down at the water and shifting his feet in it. Then he looked up at the people on the bank. They stood close together, waiting; their faces were solemn but expectant and every eye was on him. He shifted his feet again.

"Maybe I know why you come," he said in the twangy voice, "maybe I don't.

"If you ain't come for Jesus, you ain't come for me. If you just come to see can you leave your pain in the river, you ain't come for Jesus. You can't leave your pain in the river," he said. "I never told nobody that." He stopped and looked down at his knees.

"I seen you cure a woman oncet!" a sudden high voice shouted from the hump of people. "Seen that woman git up and walk out straight where she had limped in!"

The preacher lifted one foot and then the other. He seemed almost but not quite to smile. "You might as well go home if that's what you come for," he said.

Then he lifted his head and arms and shouted, "Listen to what I got to say, you people! There ain't but one river and that's the River of Life, made out of Jesus' Blood. That's the river you have to lay your pain in, in the River of Faith, in the River of Life, in the River of Love, in the rich red river of Jesus' Blood, you people!"

His voice grew soft and musical. "All the rivers come from that one River and go back to it like it was the ocean sea and if you believe, you can lay your pain in that River and get rid of it because that's the River that was made to carry sin. It's a River full of pain itself, pain itself, moving toward the Kingdom of Christ, to be washed away, slow, you people, slow as this here old red water river round my feet.

"Listen," he sang, "I read in Mark about an unclean man, I read in Luke about a blind man, I read in John about a dead man! Oh you people hear! The same blood that makes this River red, made the leper clean, made that blind man stare, made that dead man leap! You people with trouble," he cried, "lay it in that River of Blood, lay it in that River of Pain, and watch it move away toward the Kingdom of Christ."

While he preached, Bevel's eyes followed drowsily the slow circles of two silent birds revolving high in the air. Across the river there was a low red and gold grove of sassafras with hills of dark blue trees behind it and an occasional pine jutting over the skyline. Behind, in the distance, the city rose like a cluster of warts on the side of the mountain. The birds revolved downward and dropped lightly in the top of the highest pine and sat hunch-shouldered as if they were supporting the sky.

"If it's this River of Life you want to lay your pain in, then come up," the preacher said, "and lay your sorrow here. But don't be thinking this is the last of it because this old red river don't end here. This old red suffering stream goes on, you people, slow to the Kingdom of Christ. This old red river is good to Baptize in, good to lay your faith in, good to lay your pain in, but it ain't this muddy water here that saves you. I been all up and down this river this week," he said. "Tuesday I was in Fortune Lake, next day in Ideal, Friday me and my wife drove to Lulawillow to see a sick man there. Them people didn't see no healing," he said and his face burned redder for a second. "I never said they would."

While he was talking a fluttering figure had begun to move forward with a kind of butterfly movement—an old woman with flapping arms whose head wobbled as if it might fall off any second. She managed to lower herself at the edge of the bank and let her arms churn in the water. Then she bent farther and pushed her face down in it and raised herself up finally, streaming wet; and still flapping, she turned a time or two in a blind circle until someone reached out and pulled her back into the group.

"She's been that way for thirteen years," a rough voice shouted. "Pass the hat and give this kid his money. That's what he's here for." The shout, directed out to the boy in the river, came from a huge old man who sat like a humped stone on the bumper of a long ancient gray automobile. He had on a gray hat that was turned down over one ear and up over the other to expose a purple bulge on his left temple. He sat bent forward with his hands hanging between his knees and his small eyes half closed.

Bevel stared at him once and then moved into the folds of Mrs. Connin's coat and hid himself.

The boy in the river glanced at the old man quickly and raised his fist. "Believe Jesus or the devil!" he cried. "Testify to one or the other!"

"I know from my own self-experience," a woman's mysterious

voice called from the knot of people, "I know from it that this preacher can heal. My eyes have been opened! I testify to Jesus!"

The preacher lifted his arms quickly and began to repeat all that he had said before about the River and the Kingdom of Christ and the old man sat on the bumper, fixing him with a narrow squint. From time to time Bevel stared at him again from around Mrs. Connin.

A man in overalls and a brown coat leaned forward and dipped his hand in the water quickly and shook it and leaned back, and a woman held a baby over the edge of the bank and splashed its feet with water. One man moved a little distance away and sat down on the bank and took off his shoes and waded out into the stream; he stood there for a few minutes with his face tilted as far back as it would go, then he waded back and put on his shoes. All this time, the preacher sang and did not appear to watch what went on.

As soon as he stopped singing, Mrs. Connin lifted Bevel up and said, "Listen here, preacher, I got a boy from town today that I'm keeping. His mamma's sick and he wants you to pray for her. And this is a coincident—his name is Bevel! Bevel," she said, turning to look at the people behind her, "same as his. Ain't that a coincident, though?"

There were some murmurs and Bevel turned and grinned over her shoulder at the faces looking at him. "Bevel," he said in a loud jaunty voice.

"Listen," Mrs. Connin said, "have you ever been Baptized, Bevel?"

He only grinned.

"I suspect he ain't ever been Baptized," Mrs. Connin said, raising her eyebrows at the preacher.

"Swang him over here," the preacher said and took a stride forward and caught him.

He held him in the crook of his arm and looked at the grinning face. Bevel rolled his eyes in a comical way and thrust his face forward, close to the preacher's. "My name is Bevvvuuuuul," he said in a loud deep voice and let the tip of his tongue slide across his mouth.

The preacher didn't smile. His bony face was rigid and his narrow gray eyes reflected the almost colorless sky. There was a loud laugh from the old man sitting on the car bumper and Bevel grasped the back of the preacher's collar and held it tightly. The grin had already disappeared from his face. He had the sudden feeling that this was not a joke. Where he lived everything was a joke. From the preacher's face, he knew immediately that nothing the preacher said or did was a joke. "My mother named me that," he said quickly.

"Have you ever been Baptized?" the preacher asked.

"What's that?" he murmured.

"If I Baptize you," the preacher said, "you'll be able to go to the Kingdom of Christ. You'll be washed in the river of suffering, son, and you'll go by the deep river of life. Do you want that?"

"Yes," the child said, and thought, I won't go back to the apartment then, I'll go under the river.

"You won't be the same again," the preacher said. "You'll count." Then he turned his face to the people and began to preach and Bevel looked over his shoulder at the pieces of the white sun scattered in the river. Suddenly the preacher said, "All right, I'm going to Baptize you now," and without more warning, he tightened his hold and swung him upside down and plunged his head into the water. He held him under while he said the words of Baptism and then he jerked him up again and looked sternly at the gasping child. Bevel's eyes were dark and dilated. "You count now," the preacher said. "You didn't even count before."

The little boy was too shocked to cry. He spit out the muddy water and rubbed his wet sleeve into his eyes and over his face.

"Don't forget his mamma," Mrs. Connin called. "He wants you to pray for his mamma. She's sick."

"Lord," the preacher said, "we pray for somebody in affliction who isn't here to testify. Is your mother sick in the hospital?" he asked. "Is she in pain?"

The child stared at him. "She hasn't got up yet," he said in a high dazed voice. "She has a hangover." The air was so quiet he could hear the broken pieces of the sun knocking in the water.

The preacher looked angry and startled. The red drained out of his face and the sky appeared to darken in his eyes. There was a loud guffaw from the bank and Mr. Paradise shouted, "Haw! Cure the afflicted woman with the hangover!" and began to beat his knee with his fist.

"He's had a long day," Mrs. Connin said, standing with him in the door of the apartment and looking sharply into the room where the party was going on. "I reckon it's past his regular bedtime." One of Bevel's eyes was closed and the other half closed; his nose was running and he kept his mouth open and breathed through it. The damp plaid coat dragged down on one side.

That would be her, Mrs. Connin decided, in the black britches— long black satin britches and barefoot sandals and red toenails. She was lying on half the sofa, with her knees crossed in the air and her head propped on the arm. She didn't get up.

"Hello Harry," she said. "Did you have a big day?" She had a long pale face, smooth and blank, and straight sweet-potato-colored hair, pulled back.

The father went off to get the money. There were two other couples. One of the men, blond with little violet-blue eyes, leaned out of his chair and said, "Well Harry, old man, have a big day?"

"His name ain't Harry. It's Bevel," Mrs. Connin said.

"His name is Harry," *she* said from the sofa. "Whoever heard of anybody named Bevel?"

The little boy had seemed to be going to sleep on his feet, his head drooping farther and farther forward; he pulled it back suddenly and opened one eye; the other was stuck.

"He told me this morning his name was Bevel," Mrs. Connin said in a shocked voice. "The same as our preacher. We been all day at a preaching and healing at the river. He said his name was Bevel, the same as the preacher's. That's what he told me."

"Bevel!" his mother said. "My God! what a name."

"This preacher is named Bevel and there's no better preacher around," Mrs. Connin said. "And furthermore," she added in a defiant tone, "he Baptized this child this morning!"

His mother sat straight up. "Well the nerve!" she muttered.

"Furthermore," Mrs. Connin said, "he's a healer and he prayed for you to be healed."

"Healed!" she almost shouted. "Healed of what for Christ's sake?"

"Of your affliction," Mrs. Connin said icily.

The father had returned with the money and was standing near Mrs. Connin waiting to give it to her. His eyes were lined with red threads. "Go on, go on," he said, "I want to hear more about her affliction. The exact nature of it has escaped . . ." He waved the bill and his voice trailed off. "Healing by prayer is mighty inexpensive," he murmured.

Mrs. Connin stood a second, staring into the room, with a skeleton's appearance of seeing everything. Then, without taking the money, she turned and shut the door behind her. The father swung around, smiling vaguely, and shrugged. The rest of them were looking at Harry. The little boy began to shamble toward the bedroom.

"Come here, Harry," his mother said. He automatically shifted his direction toward her without opening his eye any farther. "Tell me what happened today," she said when he reached her. She began to pull off his coat.

"I don't know," he muttered.

"Yes you do know," she said, feeling the coat heavier on one side. She unzipped the innerlining and caught the book and a dirty handkerchief as they fell out. "Where did you get these?"

"I don't know," he said and grabbed for them. "They're mine. She gave them to me."

She threw the handkerchief down and held the book too high for him to reach and began to read it, her face after a second assuming an exaggerated comical expression. The others moved around and looked at it over her shoulder. "My God," somebody said.

One of the men peered at it sharply from behind a thick pair of glasses. "That's valuable," he said. "That's a collector's item," and he took it away from the rest of them and retired to another chair.

"Don't let George go off with that," his girl said.

"I tell you it's valuable," George said. "1832."

Bevel shifted his direction again toward the room where he slept. He shut the door behind him and moved slowly in the darkness to the bed and sat down and took off his shoes and got under the cover. After a minute a shaft of light let in the tall silhouette of his mother. She tiptoed lightly across the room and sat down on the edge of his bed. "What did that dolt of a preacher say about me?" she whispered. "What lies have you been telling today, honey?"

He shut his eye and heard her voice from a long way away, as if he were under the river and she on top of it. She shook his shoulder. "Harry," she said, leaning down and putting her mouth to his ear, "tell me what he said." She pulled him into a sitting position and he felt as if he had been drawn up from under the river. "Tell me," she whispered and her bitter breath covered his face.

He saw the pale oval close to him in the dark. "He said I'm not the same now," he muttered. "I count."

After a second, she lowered him by his shirt front onto the pillow. She hung over him an instant and brushed her lips against his forehead. Then she got up and moved away, swaying her hips lightly through the shaft of light.

He didn't wake up early but the apartment was still dark and close when he did. For a while he lay there, picking his nose and eyes. Then he sat up in bed and looked out the window. The sun came in palely, stained gray by the glass. Across the street at the Empire Hotel, a colored cleaning woman was looking down from an upper window, resting her face on her folded arms. He got up and put on his shoes and went to the bathroom and then into the front room. He ate two crackers spread with anchovy paste, that he found on the coffee table, and drank some ginger ale left in a bottle and looked around for his book but it was not there.

The apartment was silent except for the faint humming of the refrigerator. He went into the kitchen and found some raisin bread heels and spread a half jar of peanut butter between them and climbed up on the tall kitchen stool and sat chewing the sandwich slowly, wiping his nose every now and then on his shoulder. When he finished he found some chocolate milk and drank that. He would rather have had the ginger ale he saw but they left the bottle openers where he couldn't reach them. He studied what was left in the refrigerator for a while—some shriveled vegetables that she had forgot were there and a lot of brown oranges that she bought and didn't squeeze; there were three or four kinds of cheese and something fishy in a paper bag; the rest was a pork bone. He left the refrigerator door open and wandered back into the dark living room and sat down on the sofa.

He decided they would be out cold until one o'clock and that they would all have to go to a restaurant for lunch. He wasn't high enough for the table yet and the waiter would bring a highchair and he was too big for a highchair. He sat in the middle of the sofa, kicking it with his heels. Then he got up and wandered around the room, looking into the ashtrays at the butts as if this might be a habit. In his own room he had picture books and blocks but they were for the most part torn up; he found the way to get new ones was to tear up the ones he had. There was very little to do at any time but eat; however, he was not a fat boy.

He decided he would empty a few of the ashtrays on the floor. If he only emptied a few, she would think they had fallen. He emptied two, rubbing the ashes carefully into the rug with his finger. Then he lay on the floor for a while, studying his feet which he held up in the air. His shoes were still damp and he began to think about the river.

Very slowly, his expression changed as if he were gradually seeing appear what he didn't know he'd been looking for. Then all of a sudden he knew what he wanted to do.

He got up and tiptoed into their bedroom and stood in the dim light there, looking for her pocketbook. His glance passed her long pale arm hanging off the edge of the bed down to the floor, and across the white mound his father made, and past the crowded bureau, until it rested on the pocketbook hung on the back of a chair. He took a car-token out of it and half a package of Life Savers. Then he left the apartment and caught the car at the corner. He hadn't taken a suitcase because there was nothing from there he wanted to keep.

He got off the car at the end of the line and started down the road he and Mrs. Connin had taken the day before. He knew there wouldn't be anybody at her house because the three boys and the girl went to school and Mrs. Connin had told him she went out to clean. He passed her yard and walked on the way they had gone to the river. The paper brick houses were far apart and after a while the dirt place to walk on ended and he had to walk on the edge of the highway. The sun was pale yellow and high and hot.

He passed a shack with an orange gas pump in front of it but he didn't see the old man looking out at nothing in particular from the doorway. Mr. Paradise was having an orange drink. He finished it slowly, squinting over the bottle at the small plaid-coated figure disappearing down the road. Then he set the empty bottle on a bench and, still squinting, wiped his sleeve over his mouth. He went in the shack and picked out a peppermint stick, a foot long and two inches thick, from the candy shelf, and stuck it in his hip pocket. Then he got in his car and drove slowly down the highway after the boy.

By the time Bevel came to the field speckled with purple weeds, he was dusty and sweating and he crossed it at a trot to get into the woods as fast as he could. Once inside, he wandered from tree to tree, trying to find the path they had taken yesterday. Finally he found a line worn in the pine needles and followed it until he saw the steep trail twisting down through the trees.

Mr. Paradise had left his automobile back some way on the road and had walked to the place where he was accustomed to sit almost every day, holding an unbaited fishline in the water while he stared at the river passing in front of him. Anyone looking at him from a distance would have seen an old boulder half hidden in the bushes.

Bevel didn't see him at all. He only saw the river, shimmering reddish yellow, and bounded into it with his shoes and his coat on and took a gulp. He swallowed some and spit the rest out and then he stood there in water up to his chest and looked around him. The sky was a clear pale blue, all in one piece—except for the hole the sun made—and fringed around the bottom with treetops. His coat floated to the surface and surrounded him like a strange gay lily pad and he stood grinning in the sun. He intended not to fool with preachers any more but to Baptize himself and to keep on going this time until he found the Kingdom of Christ in the river. He didn't mean to waste any more time. He put his head under the water at once and pushed forward.

In a second he began to gasp and sputter and his head reappeared on the surface; he started under again and the same thing happened. The river wouldn't have him. He tried again and came up, choking. This was the way it had been when the preacher held him under— he had had to fight with something that pushed him back in the face. He stopped and thought suddenly: it's another joke, it's just another joke! He thought how far he had come for nothing and he began to hit and splash and kick the filthy river. His feet were already treading on nothing. He gave one low cry of pain and indignation. Then he heard a shout and turned his head and saw something like a giant pig bounding after him, shaking a red and white club and shouting. He plunged under once and this time, the waiting current caught him like a long gentle hand and pulled him swiftly forward and down. For an instant he was overcome with surprise; then since he was moving quickly and knew that he was getting somewhere, all his fury and his fear left him.

Mr. Paradise's head appeared from time to time on the surface of the water. Finally, far downstream, the old man rose like some ancient water monster and stood empty-handed, staring with his dull eyes as far down the river line as he could see.